DESTROYING EDEN

BY ERIC BERGMAN

If you enjoy this book,
please recommend it to your friends.
Tweet it
Facebook it
e-mail it
MySpace it
Gift it

HydrOzone Publishing
Copyright © 2010 Eric J. Bergman
All rights reserved.
ISBN: 1480215651
ISBN-13: 978-1480215658

Library of Congress Control Number: 2012904308

Also available as an e-book
10062012

Cover Art By Erin Recht Ferguson
Contact: erinrecht@gmail.com

DEDICATION

To Mom and Dad,
for making me work and helping me dream.

To Rita,
for changing my world.

And especially
to my wonderful wife,
The Lady Anita Dalene Bergman,
without whose encouragement, love and determination
this book might never have taken form.
You make me complete.

Prologue		1
Chapter 1	Death and Life	4
Chapter 2	Lost and Found	13
Chapter 3	The Long Night	26
Chapter 4	Resurrection	43
Chapter 5	Outsider	57
Chapter 6	Education	69
Chapter 7	To Business	98
Chapter 8	Corrupting Influences	110
Chapter 9	The Horse	124
Chapter 10	Elam's Evaluation	129
Chapter 11	The Council	145
Chapter 12	Escape and Pursuit	157
Chapter 13	The Anakims	176
Chapter 14	Plots and Plans	187
Chapter 15	Return to Aidon	197
Chapter 16	Evaluation	218
Chapter 17	Trial	244
Chapter 18	History Lessons	259
Chapter 19	The Library	271
Chapter 20	Cavalry	297
Chapter 21	Invitations	331
Chapter 22	The Serpent	343
Chapter 23	The Tree of Life	347
Chapter 24	Attack	357
Chapter 25	The Messenger	371

Chapter 26	*Repercussions*	*380*
Chapter 27	*Retribution*	*390*
Chapter 28	*Resistance*	*400*
Chapter 29	*Reckoning*	*414*
Chapter 30	*Life and Death*	*438*
Epilogue		*451*

Prologue

It was unfortunate that the delicate ballet of light was invisible to the spectators surrounding it. The two brilliant spheres of light circled and darted, trailing subtle tendrils as they each sought dominion over the other in the dance of the Evaluation. These glowing orbs, the life-force and true-self of the contestants had been locked in the contest for over two hours. The battle was long for an Evaluation, but this contest would decide which would ascend as Regent of Aidon.

Beatrice Tregard's gaze never wavered from the two men facing each other in the interlocking geometric pattern of hexagons, eyes closed and immobile since The Evaluation had begun. No one outside the Boxes of Aidon could see the struggle between the contestants, but each of them had experienced the contest, though never for such high stakes. Beatrice felt that her heart must surely hammer right out of her chest. She desperately willed her husband to succeed. It was she who had convinced him that he must try, for Lucian Krainik could not be permitted to rule. She couldn't even say why, but she sensed an evil about him that made her skin crawl. She was certain that he would rule Aidon with the same contempt he displayed towards his son. He must not become Regent. She recalled her last conversation with Gareth earlier this morning.

"Beatrice, are you sure I'm doing the right thing? There must be someone better suited to be Regent than me."

She shook her head. "Who? I'm not saying you're wrong. I know you don't want this, but who is going to challenge Lucian? You've seen what he's like on the High Council. Can you support him as Regent?"

Gareth sighed, "No. If it were anyone else………." His voice trailed off. "But have you thought about Dalene? What if I succeed? Can we really do this to her?"

Tears sprang to Beatrice's eyes at the mention of their young daughter. "Of course I've thought of Dalene! But what choice do we have? Give me a name! Who is going to challenge him? Who has a chance of defeating him?"

Gareth had made no answer and now each passing minute increased her fear. The Great Hall of the Praetorium was almost silent, with only the occasional whisper or rustling as tired muscles shifted in their seats. Beatrice heard none of it. Her attention suddenly sharpened, accompanied by a buzz of muted exclamations. The two men were twitching subtly. The movements were slight, but this was most unusual. Someone forgot himself so far as to shout, "Look!" It was completely unnecessary, as every eye was glued on the two figures. While both still jerked with muscle spasms, it was clear that one was inexorably bowing to the other until his torso was almost parallel to the ground. At this acquiescence, the bond of the Evaluation was broken and Lucian Krainick's eyes flared open in undisguised malevolence as he jerked erect. With complete disregard for protocol he whirled and stormed from The Great Hall as cheers erupted for the new Regent of Aidon.

Gareth Tregard's pain filled eyes locked on his wife for a brief second before he forced a smile and turned to accept the congratulations being offered to him. Beatrice was filled with conflicting waves of relief and grief as she whispered, "Oh, Dalene, will you ever forgive us?"

*** *Nine Years Later* ***

Beatrice hesitated at the doorway of the dimly lit chamber which smelled softly of death. Not of disease or decay nor even of age, but of an enveloping warmth that would not be denied. The healer at her side was speaking, but she only half heard. "I don't know what's wrong with her. She's not that old. I think the prophecy has come to claim her."

Beatrice started at the mention of prophecy and glared at her companion who averted her eyes and bit her lip. "I'm sorry. You'd best go in. I'll leave you." She bowed and backed away, fearful at having offended one of the 12th File.

Entering the room, Beatrice approached the still form lying on the bed. The healer had been right. She looked well enough. Few lines marred the gracefully aging face and an aura of serenity seemed to emanate from her. "Lady Larissa." She spoke the name softly. Eyes opened, and a faint smile played at her lips as she attempted an almost imperceptible nod of her head in deference to the wife of the Regent.

"I wondered if you would come." Her voice was soft and low, but not weak.

"I'm sorry. I should have come sooner. I need your help."

Shaking her head slightly, The Lady Larissa replied, "My help? I know of nothing that I can do for you."

"For Dalene then. Please. Help me. Help her. We need you to teach her."

"You ask what cannot be. My time is finished. Now it is her time. I'm sorry. What you ask is not mine to give."

"You have to try! I'm begging you. Help me break this prophecy! It has claimed too many lives already. Help me save my daughter!"

Tears collected in the corner of eyes which could no longer see. "If I could do what you ask, that alone might bring to pass what I have fought to prevent. I will not be the fulfillment of that prophecy. Your daughter, my successor, she must embrace our sisters of Duty and Death. Duty will give her the strength to bear what she must. Death will release her when she is finished. Only they can save her. I cannot."

Anger evaporated in a cloud of despair. Beatrice grasped a hand now almost limp. "I am so sorry, Larissa. I wish I had been stronger. I wish I had trusted and gotten to know you."

Somehow Larissa found the strength to squeeze her hand in understanding and forgiveness. "Thank you for using my name. Even now, that means a great deal to me." Her voice dropped to a whisper. "Tell The Lady Dalene that I love her. Never yield. Protect Aidon. Defeat the prophecy. The title is now hers."

It was over that quickly, and she was gone. Beatrice bowed over the still form as she silently wept and could not say if the tears were for Larissa or for Dalene. In the emptiness of her aching heart she felt the last ember of hope die. She was almost right.

Chapter 1   Death and Life

Up until the moment he died, Colin Ericsson thought he would welcome death. The pounding weight of the waterfall had him pinned against the bottom of the Flathead River. Though his eyes were open, all he could see was a swirling mass of bubbles. As an engineer, the incongruity of drowning while surrounded by so much air almost offended him. There wasn't enough air to breathe, but too much for his life-jacket to provide the buoyancy necessary to bring him to the surface. While his body desperately wanted to breathe, the detached part of his mind whispered, "Don't fight. Just let it end."

Two days ago he'd agreed to come on this rafting trip with the Boy Scouts. He didn't want to. He didn't want to do much of anything, but Mike had insisted. "Come on, Colin. I need you. I promised the boys I'd take them on the Middle Fork, and I have to have a second adult. I can't get anyone else. Help me out."

"Mike, you know I'm a lousy swimmer. I really don't want to go. There has to be someone else you can get."

Mike shook his head, "I've tried. Look, we're not going swimming. It's just a rafting trip. You won't even get wet." He paused before continuing gently, "Colin, it's been three years. It's time to start living again. You know Rita wouldn't want you going on like this." Mike almost regretted his words when he saw the flash of pain on his friend's face at the mention of Rita's name, but he pressed on. "I know you're still hurting. I'm sorry. I miss her too, but you can't keep grieving like this. You're not healing. You've got to get involved. I'd want you to come regardless, but I really do need your help and you need this."

Colin sighed and shook his head, "I appreciate what you're trying to do. Maybe you're even right. When Rita got sick………." His voice trailed off, but then he continued, "It was just so fast. The doctor said she'd be fine. He was sure they could diagnosis what was causing the seizures and control it but two days later she was gone. The autopsy couldn't even say why. I was pretty shattered. You know that. You and Vivian were great. I thought I was handling it OK, but when Mom and Dad were killed in the car accident three months later………….I don't know. Something inside broke. I kept thinking the numbness would wear off……but it's like a part of me is just gone. I don't feel like I belong anywhere." He attempted a smile, but it never reached his eyes. "Look, if you're stuck, I'll come. I owe you, but just don't expect me to make it a habit, OK?"

Mike shook his head, "No promises. You're too good a friend. You just need to start doing things like before. You'll be OK."

Two day later Colin was unenthusiastic as he helped load gear on the raft. Spring had been late and the snowpack had been high. The result was that the normally benign Flathead River was still a growling torrent well past the usual spring run-off. They attacked the rapids aggressively – Bone Crusher, Widowmaker – names made up to make tourists and locals feel tough and fearless as they shot them and came through unscathed. They were nearing the midpoint of their trip when they came to a small stretch of white water not even granted the dignity of a name.

They watched the professional river guide in the raft ahead as he executed a neat trick for his clients. The current cut to the right, washing up on a large, flat slab of rock angled sharply into the water. By hanging hard right, the current washed the raft up on the slab, holding it briefly before spinning it around to the left, finally pulling it off the rock and back into the main stream over a drop of about four feet into a swirling pool below the fall which whirled the boat out of the eddy back into the current to drift peacefully downstream. Colin watched with marginal interest, then dug hard with his paddle at Mike's command in order to duplicate the stunt. Unfortunately, their raft was overloaded with a dozen people onboard. It handled like the bloated corpse of a drowned hippopotamus. Still, they managed to hit the current perfectly, the boys whooped as they were swept up onto the rock, but due to the heavily loaded condition, instead of spinning off the slab and back into the current, there they stuck. The whooping and laughter abruptly stopped. Colin was perched right in the middle of the stern, putting him about half way up the raft canted at something north of a 45 degree angle. The guys straddling the tube on the high side of the raft were starting to slip, with a real risk of severe impact as they fell onto the boys sitting on the lower pontoon. The current was now pushing water over the float and into the bottom of their sorely canted raft, increasing the weight even more. Colin noted all of this in a very few seconds, which seemed to drag on forever. Mike was shouting instructions for people to shift weight in order to try and dislodge the raft, but the addition of a ton of water in the few seconds they had been lodged there took matters out of their hands. The entire lower pontoon was suddenly dragged under, causing the upper side of the raft to whip straight off the rock and launch everyone through the air and into the water where they were swept over the falls.

Colin was carried over along with everyone and everything else. He couldn't see anything in the boiling cauldron under the falls. Tossed and tumbled, he had no idea where the surface lay, but he figured he ought to at least pretend to swim while he was busy drowning. His lungs were bursting. The white, foaming froth began to go dark. He knew he was losing the battle. As his vision finally went black, Colin realized, "I'm not going to make it. I am drowning." And then he wasn't.

******

Consciousness returned gradually. The first impression Colin had was of profound silence. He hadn't felt so at peace since............Rita. But even that thought did not disturb the calm warmth he felt permeating his being. His eyes slowly opened, almost against his will. Everything he saw was white, but it wasn't foamy. He was lying on a floor of hard, white marble. But it wasn't cold, and it didn't feel like he had lain there long – at least not long enough to feel any aches, and that too seemed very strange. He rolled over and sat up, suddenly very confused. There was no river. No forest. No raft and no people. He found himself on the steps of what looked like the pictures he had seen of ancient Greek temples – right down to the fluted columns. He distinctly recalled being in the river – of drowning. Being an engineer, Colin considered himself to be rational and reasonably intelligent. He was not prone to letting his imagination run away with him, but he could come up with no explanation for what he was experiencing. Taking inventory of himself, he realized there was no residual burning in his lungs. In fact, he felt no pain or discomfort at all and he was completely dry. The life jacket, tee shirt and nylon athletic pants that he had worn on the river were gone, replaced by a pair of comfortable, white trousers and a loose fitting jacket of the same white, material. Taking stock of his surroundings and present condition, he began to entertain the idea that he might, in fact, be dead.

The thought of being dead intrigued rather than alarmed him. He'd been raised in a religious home and had a quiet belief in God and a divine plan for individuals in mortality and beyond. Admittedly, with the death of his young wife followed by the death of his parents, he had become mentally and emotionally very detached from personal relationships, but in some ways, that had only served to strengthen his religious convictions, so the idea of being dead was one which he entertained with a certain degree of anticipation. He had only contemplated this possibility for a moment when he became aware of someone approaching, walking briskly from between two of the columns. Recognition came in a flash. "Dad? Dad!"

He jumped to his feet and ran to embrace his father. But this was not the man who had died almost three years ago. He was too young. This was the father he remembered from his childhood. Tall, strong, erect and invincible. That was how Colin remembered him. They embraced warmly, Colin felt hot tears sting his eyes as he buried his face in his Dad's shoulder. Finally, his father pushed him back, holding him by the shoulders and inspected him intently, "How are you feeling, Colin?"

"OK. Mom? Rita? Are they here, too?"

His Dad nodded, "They're here, and they're fine. Come sit down. We need to talk."

"So, is it over? I thought I was drowning."

A hint of a smile accompanied another nod, but his response left Colin perplexed. "You are. Come. Sit."

They sat on the steps in front of the columns. "Dad? What is all this? Where am I?"

His father looked at him with some interest before replying, "That is a good question. I suppose the simplest answer would be that you are currently in a temporal vacuole."

That definitely was not on Colin's short list of speculation and his eyes widened just a bit. He asked, "What do you mean?"

"Come on, Colin, You've read enough science fiction to have a grasp of a temporal vacuole. That is most descriptive of where you are. Outside of both time and space as you normally think of it."

Colin finally managed to get his mind around a thought enough to articulate it, albeit stupidly, and said, "So I'm dead?"

His Dad shook his head and said, "You're always trying to rush things. No, you're not dead. I've been asked to offer you an assignment."

Colin's mind was in a whirl, "But what about the Scouts? They were all in the river and I'm worried............"

"Take it easy, son. They'll have a great story to tell, and it will become more exciting with the telling, but they're all fine. Ignore the novelty of what's around you. Accept what you are experiencing, because we don't have a lot of time here – where time doesn't exist.

His father paused, eyeing him critically yet not unkindly before continuing, "You're not doing well, are you Colin?"

Tears came unbidden as he shrugged and averted his eyes, "No." It was almost a whisper. "After Rita..........and then you and Mom..........I don't know." His shoulders slumped. "I'm just glad it's over."

As his Dad rested a hand on his shoulder, he felt a comforting warmth flood through his entire body. "It's not over, son. You are still needed."

Colin jerked away, flaring with the memory of his pain, "I needed you! I needed all of you. But you weren't there. I tried.........you have no idea how I tried, but I couldn't do it! I'm done! I can't go back there!"

His Dad nodded calmly, "You're wrong, son. You wanted me – us, to be there. But we had to leave so that you could become what you must. However, you're also right. You can't go back there."

Colin drew a deep breath, struggling to control his emotions. "I don't understand. I just want to be with you."

His Dad nodded in understanding, "I know. But you're stagnating, and I've been assigned to offer you an opportunity to get back on track. I need to give you a bit of background, so bear with me while I explain. We, all the family of man on the face of the Earth are children of a Heavenly Father – of God. In a sense, He created us, yet in another sense, we have always existed. You, the real you, your essence or intelligence, what your friend Scott Card called your 'aiua' or life-force has always existed. As our Father, God prepared a housing for that intelligence, in what we call our spirit. He provided a means for our intelligence to progress and grow by placing it into this housing - your spirit-self, which allows you to have experiences which would have been unavailable to you as long as you were only an intelligence. We had no ability as an intelligence to manipulate our surroundings. We knew no joy or happiness because we knew no sorrow nor misery. We existed, but had no capability of advancement in that state. We became His children when we accepted the spirit bodies which He prepared. We lived with him and were able to grow in knowledge and ability. Eventually, we were ready for the next stage of existence. One day the memory of that prior state will be restored. We needed physical bodies which permit a greater degree of power – power to choose and power to manipulate our surroundings. Some chose not to accept this next stage of progression, at least not on the required terms. Their progression was stopped. Others, yourself included, accepted the contract and were, through the procreative process, provided with physical bodies and went on to the next stage of existence and progression. That is where you are today. Not all of us possess the same talents and abilities. Consequently, we don't all benefit from the same experiences in what you think of as mortality. Some have mastered various laws to a much greater degree than others. Referring to your own experience, just as it would not be exceptionally beneficial to place high school seniors in the same learning environment as children in kindergarten, so it would not do for all of us to be schooled together on the same planet, having abilities which differ so broadly. And, continuing the scholastic simile, just as not all choose to become engineers or auto mechanics, so too do some of our spirit siblings tend to specialize in certain areas, at least for a time."

At this Colin could stand it no longer and he broke in, "Do you mean to say that there really are other inhabited planets?"

"Oh, that would be far too limiting. Not just other inhabited planets, but worlds without end. And not worlds only, but universes as well. There really is no end to His creations."

Colin sat silent for a long moment. "Other universes?" he finally asked.

"Yes, but not the way you're thinking. Despite what you learned in mathematics, all infinities are not equal. You struggled with that concept yourself. It's obvious that the infinite set of integers, for example is very different from the infinite fractions between zero and one. Both are infinite, but neither is all inclusive. So despite the infinite number of universes, they are not all equal. Every decision point in your life - whether you chose sausage versus bacon this morning, for example, did not create a branch point and an alternate universe. Even potentially life-altering choices, such as whether you went into work this morning or went rafting and wound up drowning at the bottom of a waterfall don't cause branch points. There is only one you. There was only one Abraham Lincoln, and John Wilkes

Booth chose to shoot and kill him. There is no universe in which Abraham Lincoln survived."

At length Colin said, "So there really are aliens and all of that?"

His Dad didn't quite laugh, but looked as if he might, as he said, "Well, yes and no. While there are certainly alien life forms, meaning plant and animal life beyond anything you can imagine at this point, our Father never created physical bodies for His children other than that they have been created in His own likeness. Don't tell me you have forgotten Genesis. 'In His own image, male and female, created He them."

"So," Colin said, "are all the other worlds the same as Earth?"

"Each of them is similar, but not the same as Earth. Each world thinks of itself as 'Earth.' However, there are some rather marked differences as well. Recall my analogy of having high school seniors attend kindergarten. Imagine, if you will, with your background in chemistry, the response you might get from a group of kindergarten children suddenly placed in a high school chemistry lab. Remember the uproar you caused your Senior year of high school when you demonstrated welding without electricity? The tremendous shower of sparks when you lit the magnesium fuse and ignited the mixture of thermite and iron oxide? It not only welded the steel plates under the stone crucible, but also broke the crucible and melted the sand underneath the steel plates and turned it into glass. Now, what do you suppose the response of our kindergarten children would be to that particular demonstration?"

"At best they would think it was cool and at worst they would think it was terrifying."

His Dad nodded, "Exactly. They would find it magical even though, to you, no magic is involved. You mastered certain laws of chemistry and physics which, when applied, would be beyond the comprehension of those children. In a similar manner, there are worlds where the inhabitants have mastered various laws to a degree that would seem magical to you – transmutation of elemental substances or walking on water for example. This is simply a matter of changing the composition or make-up of what you refer to as the alternate universe. In many cases, the law itself doesn't have to be understood in order to be applied. People flip on electrical switches every day with no concept of the physical laws which are brought into play in order to operate their appliances."

"I don't understand."

"No, and you won't fully for a very long time. Look at it this way. Graphite, diamond and charcoal are all simply different forms of carbon. In a similar manner, by altering proportions and structures, the properties of the universe can be changed - yet always operate within the bounds of laws which are natural and eternal. Consequently, what would be truly magical on our Earth is entirely common on another, and is permitted for the welfare and growth of those who are prepared to live and learn under such laws.

Simply a different course of study if you will, compared to that which those of us on Earth selected."

Again Colin interrupted, "But couldn't such powers be used for tremendous destruction and evil? Look at the terrible things that happen even from a limited application of science."

"The potential is there. But the law dictates that mastery of such abilities requires strict adherence to specific principles even if the principles are not fully understood. Those who would use such power for evil rarely have the discipline necessary to master the principles which would release the power. Within their sphere of choice, many exercise their power, whether to hurt or to heal. The ability to choose is granted to them. Those within their sphere have embarked on their own program for learning and progression. While they might benefit greatly from the kindness of others, how they respond to the unkind acts of others is also part of their curriculum. It will help to shape them as they <u>choose</u> how they will respond to the circumstances in which they find themselves, and those choices will define what they become. There is no part of their existence that isn't designed to offer them the opportunity for growth. However, if they respond in a negative manner to the actions of others, whether those actions were kind or not is of little consequence to them personally, but how they choose to respond is of the utmost importance in their progression."

Colin was intrigued by what he was hearing, "But why doesn't God just teach everyone these principles? Show them how they can be used for good. Why not use this power to eliminate the suffering in the world?"

His Dad shook his head. "They have been taught. What God will not do, cannot do, is force them to learn. The evidence is there. What He teaches and encourages brings only happiness. Rejection of those principles brings misery and destruction. God <u>cannot</u> do just anything. He can only do what's right. In order for us to progress, we must embrace the law, subject ourselves to it. Only in that manner can we master it. And the key to mastering the law is to exercise faith. Faith is a principle of power which governs all other laws, because faith only operates within the law – within truth. Faith is inseparably bound to truth – to things as they truly are. That is the great challenge – to see things as they truly are and develop faith even when we don't understand what we are seeing. All will be as it should be if we willingly subject ourselves to the law."

Colin sat quietly, thinking. Finally, he spoke. "I'm sorry for all the questions. I can't claim that I fully understand everything you've said, but what do you want me to do?"

His Dad grinned, "The questions aren't a problem, it's accepting the answers that's important. Now, as for what I need from you, the real issue is what <u>you</u> need for yourself."

I don't understand what you mean," Colin replied.

"You are on your own quest for progression. You have developed to an admirable degree in some aspects, but are yet lacking in others. Colin, I know that death - this separation from Rita and your Mom and I, has been incredibly difficult for you. You've become increasingly disconnected from those around you. It's time for you to again become engaged in your own progression and in the progression of others. You have the opportunity to use your talents to help some of your more distant siblings in a manner and setting which will give you the chance to grow and develop much more rapidly than you could in the environment from which you were becoming increasingly detached. It won't be easy, but it will be possible. Will you do it?"

Reluctantly, Colin replied, "I don't know. The past couple of years........." His voice trailed off. "I'll try. I don't know what you want me to do, but I'll try."

His Dad smiled slightly, "Thank you, son. I know you'll try. You always have. It may not be as bad as you think. It's not like you're being assigned to be prophet – not with your temper and temperament." He laughed quietly as he shook his head. "No, I think you're better suited to the role of 'monkey wrench.'"

Again he paused, and with a slight raise of one eyebrow and a hint of a smile, he continued. "You have developed what you like to refer to as an 'engineering intellect.' You weigh things. Analyze them. Try to break them down to their simplest form. And, you don't tend to reject things just because you don't understand them. As you have been prone to summarize, 'The first law of engineering is whatever works.' And yet, with that analysis, you are willing to accept what you don't fully understand simply on faith. There is power in that." He paused briefly and then continued, "I knew that you would accept. But the important thing is that you needed to know it. This is and must be your choice to make." Once again, there was a pause, as his Dad gave Colin an appraising inspection. He then said, "Colin, permit me to ask you a question. Do you believe that God would cause, not permit, but cause His children to disobey His instructions?"

Colin immediately responded, "No, I don't see how He possibly could."

"Then what would have happened if Eve had not disobeyed by partaking of the fruit in the Garden of Eden?"

This time, Colin hesitated before replying, "I'm not sure. I've heard the idea put forward that Adam and Eve would have remained forever in the Garden in a state of innocence. I've heard others promote the idea that we, that is, all of their descendants would have been born into that state of innocence in the Garden."

"But you don't believe that." It was a statement, not a question, and Colin remained silent. "These things are not necessarily vital to your education, but they are of some value to contemplate, so that you may understand God's purposes and know that He wants what is for our best good. Son, I know that you don't fully understand. You won't for a very long time. But you understand enough, and you have chosen to help. That is what is important. Unfortunately, for the duration of this task, you will remember very little of this conversation, and that only vaguely - as feelings and impressions rather than as a memory. What is important is that you know _now_ and the choice you make, you have made freely."

Distressed, Colin asked, "Why? Why won't I remember? I don't want to forget this. I _need_ to remember."

Gently, and with a kind smile his Dad replied, "Colin, you _want_ to remember. That isn't the same as need. As I already explained, you are still on your own journey of progression. You also need to develop faith so that you can master the power that comes from being wholly subject to law – sometimes a higher law than you now understand. Having this memory, or at least too clear of a memory of this time we've had to visit would weaken the faith that you will need to succeed. This experience will remain with you as a subtle impression, but not as a distinct memory. What you will remember is that Rita, your mother and I love you. You will be helped so far as you will allow, and so far as it will be for your best good – to help you become what you truly want to be."

Sensing that the interview was about to conclude, Colin rushed his last questions, "All of this, is it real? Is this really you, Dad? Will I get to come back here?"

His Dad paused for a moment and then said, "Yes, this is real, but reality is a somewhat subjective commodity, as you are about to learn to a greater degree. This is indeed 'me,' but in a context and setting that you are comfortable with, so that we can touch and communicate. What you are experiencing here is 'real,' but not necessarily complete – so that you can get your mind around it more easily. I _am_ real, physical and here. Whether or not you return here, and by 'here' I take you to mean where I am, well, that will largely depend on you. I know that leaves you unsatisfied, but for now it will have to suffice. Are you ready?"

"Ready for what?" Colin asked.

His Dad smiled slightly, and, Colin thought, a little bit sadly, "Remember, son? You're drowning." And so he was.

Chapter 2   Lost and Found

Colin's lungs were bursting. He could still see nothing but the white froth of a boiling cauldron of water, but his vision was beginning to go dark. He had no choice but to kick and stroke, still not knowing which direction was up. Just as he was certain he could hold his breath no longer and was about to suck in a great lungful of water, he suddenly broke the surface. He gasped in the wonderful, deliciously cool air. Whipping his head around to clear the water from his eyes, he looked desperately for the boys who'd been thrown from the raft. It seemed ages ago that he'd been swept over the falls, but it could have only been a couple of minutes at most. He couldn't have held his breath any longer than that. Treading water, he sucked in great gulps of air when it seemed as if his hammering heart suddenly skipped several beats. He had no idea where he was, but he was certain it couldn't be on the Flathead River. Sharp, volcanic walls rose steeply out of the water on either side of him. He bobbed in swells that were rising and falling by at least four feet. He rotated slowly, still treading water. As he rose on the next swell he could see the expanse extending away to disappear at the horizon. He was in the ocean, the taste of salt confirming his suspicions and adding to his confusion. His frantic thoughts raced, "What happened? Where am I?" He was rapidly tiring, the added buoyancy of the salt water negated by the disappearance of his lifejacket. The tide was washing him deeper into a volcanic cleft. Colin remembered standing up on top of just such a cleft on the Oregon coast and seeing how the waves churned and boomed against the jagged basalt. He knew that if he got pushed onto those rocks, he would be cut to shreds in short order. The overhanging rock left little chance of climbing out, even if he could get a toehold. Nothing short of a starfish could cling in those pounding waves. The current was too strong. There was no chance to swim out. All he could do was try to stay in the middle of the channel as he was washed further in, the swells rising and falling more as the chasm narrowed. Colin had drifted about 40 yards when he briefly touched bottom as he dipped into a trough. The next swell lifted him, but the cut in the rock was shoaling steeply. He thought the tide must be at low ebb, just starting to come in, as there was exposed rock and sand at the end of the cleft. But the rock wall had become no less steep. It was only about 15 or 20 feet to the top, but he doubted he could climb the jagged face.

Suddenly he touched firm ground and before the next wave could snatch him back, he threw himself forward, floundering up onto the sand and rock. He was exhausted and lay panting on the rugged beach for several minutes, letting the burning exhaustion drain from his tired arms and legs. He didn't know how long he lay there, but he was roused by the thought that if he was right and the tide was starting to come in, he might have very little time to escape this rock prison. He sat up and took stock of his surroundings.

The spit of sand and rock extended only about six feet from the lapping water, ending in a steep wall which climbed vertically for perhaps 40 feet. To either side, the walls were not so high, but were deeply undercut, leaving no chance to escape, the overhanging wall a good three feet above his outstretched fingers. The cleft was about 30 feet wide, with large boulders littering the bottom, but none close enough to the wall to aide in climbing out. Colin contemplated his situation. He needed to get out of this volcanic prison, for it was indeed a death trap. The tide was definitely coming in, as the sand spit was now half the size it had been when he had lunged ashore. The starfish and seaweed clinging to the walls above his head gave some indication as to how deep the water was soon likely to be. With growing desperation, Colin explored the narrow confines once again. Behind a litter of boulders to his left he saw a hole. It was small, and rapidly filling with water, but it appeared to be deep. Perhaps deep enough to connect to the other side of this wall, and provide a way out. He had seen such tunnels, forming natural bridges between jagged channels in Oregon. There was no assurance that entering the dark hole would improve his situation, and he was reluctant to get into the water again with the memory of his near drowning still vivid. The water was rising rapidly, and given his limited options, Colin shook his head grimly remembering how often he had said, "If you are going to get into trouble, get into trouble for doing something rather than doing nothing." He dove into the hole and scrambled through the rock, scraping hands and knees and whacking his head painfully on a sharp corner. He could feel water flowing in from ahead, but he could see no exit. Almost frantic, he thrashed his way forward. The roof was dropping toward the water. Desperately he ducked under and pulled himself along, heedless of the sharp rock biting at his hands. The swirling sand made it impossible to open his eyes. He kept clawing forward blindly until he sensed, rather than felt, open air above. He thrust his hand up, and felt the rock, cautiously allowing his head to follow into the few inches of air space. Gratefully he breathed and coughed. He was really getting tired of drowning. Wiping the sand and water from his face, he made his way the short distance out of the tunnel. As he looked around, his heart sank. He was in another cleft, wider than the other, but still rapidly filling with water. Then he saw it. There on his right was a faint trail leading up a gentle slope. There was a way out.

Staggering with exhaustion, Colin climbed the path. He came out in the shadow of the rock wall that had formed the head of his first prison. He was starting to shake uncontrollably from cold and shock. His head hurt, and when he touched it, his hand came away bloody. He remembered striking it as he had scrambled through the escape hole. He knew that head wounds tend to bleed profusely, and so had no idea just how badly he might be injured. Reaction was setting in, and he could stand no longer. He closed his eyes, just for a moment, he thought, and wondered if he would freeze in his wet clothes. The blackness claimed him.

Colin was having such a wonderful dream. He was someplace white. It was so peaceful. He was talking to someone. The face was indistinct, but he was being told something important. He was told......what? The cold began to intrude. Colin hurt all over. He squinted, trying to force his eyes open. He found his face pressed in the sand staring at a blurry image of a sand crab – purple shell glinting in the morning sun, with claws raised threateningly – at least as threatening as a two inch crab can be. The sound of the surf and calling of the seagulls seemed strangely calming. Colin felt a mess. His head was throbbing, and he remembered the cut on his scalp. Carefully, his fingers explored the wound. The hair was matted, but at least it had stopped bleeding. There was a painful lump. It didn't seem to be serious, but he didn't know how to tell. Memory returned in a sudden flood – the raft trip, the scouts, finding himself bobbing in the ocean, - and finding himself .... here, wherever here was. And that was the problem. He had no idea where he was or how he had arrived.

Colin sat up, and his head swam. He took stock of his physical situation. His injured head was throbbing, and his hands were badly lacerated from the sharp rocks and coral he had crawled over. He rolled up the legs of his trousers. Thankfully they were now dried, so he must have slept for several hours. While his knees were painful, he was surprised to find they were only bruised. He didn't like the inflammation of his hands, and thought he had heard of infections from coral cuts. He shrugged. There was nothing to be gained by worrying about it for the moment. Other than being extremely thirsty and very hungry he decided that he felt OK, all things considered. Sitting quietly, he was suddenly perplexed by his attire. Distracted as he had been, he hadn't really taken note of his apparel. He was wearing a pair of loose fitting white trousers and a light, loose fitting jacket of similar material. It was soft, but felt amazingly tough. It had certainly withstood the abrasion of his escape better than his hands had. It reminded him of one of those outfits he saw in martial arts movies. He'd noted the disappearance of his life jacket previously. His feet were encased in a pair of white, lightweight boots, laced to mid shin, and unlike anything he had ever owned. For a moment, Colin evaluated his mental state. Working backwards, he attempted to recall every detail he possibly could – first of the river trip, then of his home, job, acquaintances, education and finally his childhood. His mind seemed intact. "Am I crazy? Or just dreaming?"

He spoke aloud but his voice sounded strange in his ears. He stood slowly. His vision blurred momentarily as he winced with pain. Looking around, he took notice of what he could see. He was still by the large headwall that dropped down into the narrow cleft which had been his initial landing the previous day. The rock appeared to be volcanic in nature, very porous and jagged. The shelf on which he stood extended as far as he could see in either direction along the coast. The tide appeared to be going out, but both the narrow gorges into which he could see were filled with water, the surf booming and pounding against the rock. A full moon was just rising over the horizon formed by the headland rising above him. With the horizon so close, the moon appeared to be supernaturally large. The rock shelf on which he stood extended inland for 30 or 40 yards, and then transitioned to yellow-brown dirt, rising sharply for a hundred feet or so before disappearing into a carpet of vegetation and a scattering of trees. He was entirely alone and saw no indication of human activity.

Colin knew that he was occupying himself with the mundane so as to not have to confront his fear, and he was afraid. Nothing seemed to make sense. His surroundings. His clothing. Nothing. Having discarded, temporarily at least, the idea that he just might be insane, he needed a plan. Lacking anything better, he turned his back to the sea and started walking. He felt his weakened state keenly, but thought that his best chance of getting help would be to climb up off this rock shelf in the hopes of finding a house or at least a road to give him some idea where he was. He knew he needed water, and sitting by an ocean of salt wasn't going to help. Reaching the slope, he climbed, but he had no stamina and paused, panting every few feet before he could continue. At last he clawed his way on hands and knees over the lip of the slope onto a grassy plain with small, shrub-like trees forming the occasional clump or thicket. He was sweating heavily, and his head throbbed terribly. The exertion made him nauseous, but he had nothing in his stomach. After resting for several minutes, he stood, gazing inland at the distant hills. He suddenly staggered back, falling as he did so, catching himself painfully on his swollen hands. Where he had before watched the moon, now high overhead, clear the horizon he now saw a second moon beginning its ascent into the sky over the distant hills. His glance shifted rapidly between the two orbs, assuring himself of their presence. Unexpectedly, he smiled, as a wave of relief washed through him. Aloud he said, "I'm not crazy!"

He was surprised at his reaction to the dual moons shining faintly in the sky. He took a moment to quietly whisper one of his favorite mantras, "That which cannot happen does not happen. That which has happened, is possible." Recognizing that what he was seeing was real, and knowing there was nothing to be gained by questioning his sanity, he decided to deal with the tangibles, and began to catalog them aloud, a habit he had gotten into over the past few years living alone, "OK, for the moment we accept the fact that I'm not on Earth. Two moons equals 'not Earth.' That means I'm on another planet. Or maybe I'm on earth, but just not in 2012. Is time travel less feasible than inter-planetary travel? Probably. I don't think time travel is allowed under Einstein's theory of relativity. Maybe. Probably not. I guess if I don't see the Big Dipper or Orion's belt tonight, maybe that will support the idea, but I don't know if those are visible from the southern hemisphere, so even if I don't see them, maybe I could still be on Earth."

With that, he fell silent and continued to admire the two moons. They were an anchor to his reality for the moment, despite their very alien appearance.

He shook his head, finding comfort in the sound of his own voice, "Rob would have a fit."

Rob was his older brother, and had always been a big science fiction fan. It would be nice if he were here right now. Rob always knew a lot more about astronomy, the stars and stuff like that. He'd think this was the coolest thing ever, and would probably be able to look at the stars and give confirmation that he really wasn't on Earth.

"So, how did I get here?"

After a moment, he asked himself, "Does your faith reside only within the confines of your own world? If you <u>really</u> believe in God, doesn't that mean that He continues to watch over you wherever you are? Wherever 'here' is? Occam's razor: In a complex problem with many possible solutions, the simplest answer is most likely to be the correct one. Therefore, you are here because God sent you here, or at least allowed you to be sent here. <u>How</u> may not matter, but <u>why</u> probably does."

Surprisingly, he still felt more intrigued than alarmed, but he knew that he was going to have to get moving. He needed water, and was pretty sure that he was running a fever. But before he went anyplace, he decided that he ought to pray, especially in light of his limited options.

After praying he continued to kneel quietly for a minute, then with a sigh of resignation, got to his feet muttering, "Then pick up your handcart and head west - or maybe east in this case."

Colin took note of the position of the sun, rapidly dropping toward the ocean behind him so he decided to think of this as the west coast of wherever he was. Since one direction was about as likely to yield a stream, food or shelter as another, he started to walk, heading towards what he thought of now as "southeast," angling inland in the hopes of intersecting a road at some point. He was feeling weak and light headed, but was afraid to rest without finding a water to relieve his thirst in the limited daylight he had left. In good shape, he could hike at about three miles per hour. In his current condition and no means of telling time, he figured it didn't matter.

He hiked inland, angling away from the sea. The terrain was basically flat grassland with a few rolling hills. The trees were scattered for the most part, with small thickets nestled in the folds of the low hills. In the distance, he thought he could see mountains, but the coastal haze and approaching darkness obscured his vision. He was feeling worse with each passing hour. At last, unable to see, he collapsed curled up against a scrubby tree.

He was moving again at first light. His hands were swollen, with streaks of black, purple and yellow radiating up from his fingers, raising his concerns of infection. The afternoon was beginning to give way to evening when he saw a ribbon of trees meandering across the plain perhaps a mile away. This was the most promising sign of water he had seen, and hope quickened his pace so that in a short time, he entered the thin belt of forest and was grateful to hear the sound of a stream as it flowed gently over the rocky bed. Colin hesitated for only a moment, as thoughts of giardia flashed briefly through his mind, but he noted wryly that he was short on water filters - and equally short on patience, so he simply found a large, flat rock to lie down on and dip his face into the cool, clear stream. He drank cautiously, not wanting to overdo it. The delicious coolness seeped through his whole body, and for the moment, he was content just to lie still and re-hydrate. The salt water in his clothing had been irritating him for most of the day, but with night now fast approaching, he was reluctant to wash out his clothing and spend another cold, wet night. Instead, he contented himself with washing his hair, face and arms as much as he could without getting his clothes wet. Afterwards he drank deeply before retreating to the trees to find shelter as best he could for the night.

The next day was torment. While he had access to water, his hands were exceptionally painful. The swelling and discoloration continued to worsen as did his fever. The day passed in a haze of pain. Toward midday, he stopped and stripped off his clothing to wash it in the stream, removing the salt of the ocean and his own sweat. He spread his clothing on some bushes to dry. He slept only briefly, awakened by his shivering. His clothing was still damp but he knew he had to get moving. Every hour of delay sapped his strength, and without help, or at least food, he was unlikely to survive. He dressed and started on. He continued his steady, plodding pace until he finally realized he could no longer see. Night had fallen without his realizing it. He collapsed where he was and slept.

Dawn was breaking when Colin began to regain consciousness, and he knew he was in real trouble. Pain was radiating up and down his arms. The swelling had become severe. It was now difficult to bend the joints in his fingers, and he didn't seem to be able to focus his eyes. The dull throbbing in his head had been replaced by a constant lancing pain, and he wished for nothing so much as a couple of aspirin, or better yet, codeine. He muttered to himself, "If you're going to wish, don't waste your wishes on small things. Add a bottle of antibiotics and throw in some sausage and eggs for breakfast." He knew he couldn't survive without water, and doubted he had the strength to make it to another stream. Since he didn't know where he was going, there was little point in altering his course.

Despite his weakness, he rarely stopped. He had no way of keeping track of the time. He had no plan and no real thought at this point, only the drive to keep moving upstream like some mindless salmon returning to its spawning ground. Toward late afternoon, it finally registered with him that his surroundings had changed. Gradually he had entered a forested region. It was fairly open with hardly any deadfall and very little underbrush cluttering the floor, so the walking was relatively easy. He also realized that he had been climbing over the course of the day, and that he was now in a series of low hills. For the first time in hours, he was really aware of his surroundings, and inspected the trees and bushes, hopeful to find some edible seeds, nuts or berries, but there was nothing. The sun was just beginning to set when he stumbled out of the forest into a clearing. Exhaustion and illness hit him, forcing him to his knees, and for the first time in many hours, a very distinct thought formed itself in his mind. It was such a unique thought, he felt like he ought to give it voice, and so he said, or at least tried to say, "I'm not going to make it." It came out as an unintelligible croak, and that too intrigued him. That thought was the catalyst which finally forced his eyes to focus as he knelt there in the dirt, and the realization that it <u>was</u> dirt gradually dawned on him. He cocked his head, and stared as he looked at his hands, painfully swollen, but somehow comforted, buried in the warm, loose soil of a cultivated field. Lifting his head in amazement, he was further surprised to see the figure of a man, not 50 yards away, staring at him in open mouthed amazement. Flooded with relief, he lifted one hand to wave. He tried to call out, but as he lifted his hand, he pitched forward, burying his face in the tilled soil. He thought maybe he could lie there for just a moment, and then he would ask for help. Just for a moment he would enjoy the soft earth, and then the darkness closed in.

******

Elam was unhappy. Tomorrow was his 15th birthday and he should have been home. His mother would be cooking something special and he ought to be home sampling whatever she was making instead of chasing the goats. His father would be coming in from work and would compliment him on how much he had accomplished. Elam's job was to follow after his father as he plowed the field. Elam would have to haul the rock from the field to the forest boundary. Every year their field produced rock. Elam couldn't understand how so much rock could keep appearing in their field. But he knew that they were fortunate, as he had seen the fields of many of his friends, and he wouldn't want to trade with them. The day had been warm, and he had worked hard. His father had told him to go home a few minutes early so he could milk their two goats, Betty and Bonnie, before the evening meal. But when he got home, the gate hung limp and the goats were gone, having again chewed through the rope used to tie the gate shut.

The goats were Elam's responsibility and he knew that he had better find them before the evening gave way to night. If there was any good news, at least this early in the spring there were no crops to be eaten or he would have been scolded about that. Tomorrow would be work again. There was always work, but tonight there would be food and quiet celebration. His parents would make much of him and how big he had grown this past year. But none of that would happen if he didn't find the goats.

Elam knew his goats. Most of the time he liked them. They had almost grown up together. But tonight he was angry, and muttering what he would do to them when he found them, though he didn't really mean it. He headed toward the hay meadow. He'd been taking the goats there frequently to graze during the cooler months. The meadow didn't grow enough to cut during those months, and so they used it to pasture their limited livestock, there being too many rocks to bring it under cultivation. Elam's back was tired from his exertions of the day and he was grateful that his father didn't want the meadow planted as well. He hoped the goats would be there. If they weren't, he didn't know where to start looking and it would be dark soon.

The sun was just beginning to set so he was almost blinded when he looked west. He wasn't really looking at anything, just trudging across the tilled field and enjoying the feel of the soft earth under his feet. Startled, he noticed the figure of a man kneeling in the dirt some distance away. Elam stopped, unsure of what to do. The man looked up and saw him. He started as if to rise but suddenly pitched forward on his face and was still. Elam's heart was pounding. He didn't know if he should run for home or see if the man needed help. But he would be 15 tomorrow, that's practically a man, isn't it? He briefly thought of just going on, pretending that he didn't see the man. But the thought shamed him, and so he approached the still figure and spoke to him, "Sir, are you alright? Are you in need of help?"

There was no response. Reaching the fallen figure, Elam froze when he saw the hands - swollen, bloated, black and yellow stripes shooting up the arms, disappearing under the sleeves of his shirt. He was about to touch him, to try and roll him over, but he froze once again. The man's shirt was white. No other color at all. And his shirt, more of a jacket really, had a hood! With that, all thought of being almost a man evaporated, and Elam took to his heels and ran for home.

Elam could run! He had always been fast, but never had he run as he did this night. He broke through the trees and saw the small cottage, smoke rising lazily from the chimney in the darkening sky. Without slowing, he burst through the door, slamming it back on its hinges, startling his mother, cooking at the open fireplace, drawing a surprised exclamation from her and a stern look of disapproval from his father who had come in just before him. "Elam!" His father rebuked him, "Do <u>not</u> race into this house, destroying my door and scaring your mother! I don't care if tomorrow is your birthday! You will conduct yourself properly!"

Panting, Elam accepted the rebuke and breathlessly blurted, "I'm sorry father. But a man! In our field. I think he's wounded! Father, he wears only white, and he has a mantle!"

Jorge regarded his son silently for a moment. He knew Elam well and both loved and respected the boy, but he couldn't help questioning, "A mantle? Elam, are you certain?"

Elam was still too out of breath to speak clearly, so he only nodded. Jorge looked to his wife, Miran, frozen by the cooking fire. Her eyes were wide, whether in fear or amazement, he could not tell. But they had lived together long enough, he knew that she was waiting for his decision. His head sank down on his chest as he considered. At last, he looked up and said, "Elam, you will have to run. You must go to Salem and notify the 5th File. There may be trouble in this, but we haven't time to waste with Councilor Linape. This must be brought to the attention of the 2nd Order right away. I'm sorry. I know it's your birthday tomorrow. We'll try to make it up to you, but right now we haven't a choice. I will go to Baylor's. He can help me. Miran, would you prepare food and drink? Bandages as well, I think."

Miran smiled wistfully, and said, "Do you think it possible? Can there be one who wears the mantle among us again?"

Jorge shrugged, "I don't know. If he wears it not by right, his death will be upon his own head. But we will do what we can, that his death be not upon ours. Go, Elam, hurry."

Miran told Elam to wait while she quickly prepared a pouch with bread and a small flask of water for his journey. She hugged him and said, "Swiftly my son, but not faster than you have strength." As Elam trotted out onto the path, he found Betty and Bonnie feeding quietly in their pen. This was indeed a night of surprises.

Elam ran. The night was pleasantly cool, and the twin moons gave sufficient light for him to see the worn path along the edge of the field, breaking on occasion through dark patches of forest separating the cultivated fields. He liked to run, but on this night, the exhilaration was subdued by the sense of worry that he felt, wondering if he had done the right thing in telling his parents about the man he had found in the field. This path would take him to the village, his village, Tyber, where he had lived his entire life. From there the going would be easier, as he could follow the road to Salem. He had been there many times with his parents. His family was of the 3rd File, placing them in the 1st Order which is why they lived in Tyber. Salem was the capitol, the city of the 12th File, yet the head of their File, along with those of the 1st Order who performed the menial labor in the city also lived there. Since there was always a need for gardeners, stable hands and unskilled labor, those of the 1st Order were to be found everywhere. Elam had never been to Salem on his own, and never at night even with his parents. From his father's farm to Tyber was about two miles, but they would be the slowest part of his journey. There was no real road, just the wagon path along the edges of the fields, cutting through the woods on occasion. The path through the woods was shorter, but slower in the dark.

From Tyber to Salem would be another nine miles. Elam estimated that it would be nearly the fourth hour of the night before he would arrive.

Periodically, he would stop to rest his legs, catch his breath and sip from the water flask his mother had provided. In the bottom of the pouch, he found a small packet tied with string. Curious, he opened it and found two honey cookies. Elam smiled, grateful to his mother for her kindness in providing the special birthday treat she had been preparing. Knowing that he would not be home that night, she had sent this with him. Quickly, he ate one of the cookies, and immediately regretted his haste with such a rare treat. But he had far to go. Sighing, he shouldered his pouch and set off down the road once again, knowing there was nothing he could do about it now.

Jorge quickly gathered the blankets, food and the water flask which Miran had prepared. Setting off along the same path his son had used just minutes before, he strode swiftly along the edge of the field until the path intersected another coming through a copse of trees. It was no more than a quarter of an hour before he arrived at the home of his nearest neighbor. Baylor was older than Jorge by several years, and had a size and manner which intimidated many. However, the two had been neighbors for as long as Jorge could remember, and shared an easy friendship. As he approached the house, Jorge called out, "Baylor! Are you about?" It was Baylor's wife, Kath, who opened the door. Kath was a heavyset woman of pleasant countenance and manner.

Wiping her hands on her apron, she answered, "Jorge! Whatever is the matter? Is it Miran? Is she all right?"

Jorge waved a deprecating hand, "Aye Kath, the family is well. I have need of Baylor. Is he about?" Just then Baylor came from around the corner of the house, having finished his chores for the evening.

He called gruffly, "Jorge, is it? And what might you be doing calling in the middle of the night like this?" Jorge knew his neighbor was prodding him a bit, as it was not yet the second hour, but he had no time for banter this evening.

"Sorry to get you up so well past your bedtime, Baylor," he replied dryly, "But I've a need for your help." Briefly he explained about the man his son, Elam, had found in the field that evening.

Baylor said, "Fair enough. Sure and I'll lend a hand and we'll bring the fellow in. Let me grab a cloak and staves. We'll make a litter for him if need be."

Jorge replied, "I'm grateful." Hesitating a moment, but uncomfortable without disclosing the whole story, he said, "There's a mite more to it, however. The lad says the man is all in white. And he wears a hooded cloak."

Involuntarily, Kath started. Baylor raised an eyebrow, "A mantle? Sure of it was he?"

Jorge shrugged and said, "I've no more information than that. But I'd not have you help without knowing."

Baylor responded with a shrug of his own. "Matters not. If he's hurt, we'll be offering help. 'Tis the proper thing to be doing. I'll grab the staves."

Kath still stood in wide eyed silence. Then her eyes dropped, and with a trembling voice she said, "It cannot be. That I should live to see the day when one wearing the mantle should come. Oh, can it possibly be true?"

Jorge cocked his head and said, "Kath, don't be reading too much into it just yet. It was coming on dark when Elam found him. It may be nothing. Or it may be another pretender. Not for the likes of us to concern ourselves with anyway."

Kath nodded, but her eyes were moist as she said, "Aye Jorge. Not for the likes of us. But just think. If he really is........." and her voice trailed off as Baylor came from the shed carrying two stout staves, each about nine feet in length and a heavy cloak tossed over one arm. Kath handed a lantern to Jorge and said, "You may be needing this. Take care of my man." Jorge nodded, and Baylor gave his wife an affectionate glance as they took to the path back towards Jorge's field.

The two men walked swiftly through the darkness. Jorge held the lantern high as they began crossing his freshly tilled field. He thought they must have missed the stranger in the darkness when he caught a glimmer of white, just inside the boundary of trees. "There!" He said, indicating with a nod of his head where the still figure lay. Baylor only grunted, but they quickened their pace and soon reached the fallen man, still lying with his face pressed into the soft earth. Baylor was about to turn him over, when Jorge said, "Wait!" Using the lantern to better view the scene, Jorge noted the terrible swelling and discoloration on the arms as Elam had described. Lastly, he turned his attention to the clothing the man was wearing. All white. Dirty, perhaps, but white. No color adorned any hem of his clothing. Focusing on the collar at the back of the coat, he verified a hood. It wasn't just a wide collar, as he had been hoping. It was a full hood - a mantle. He had never seen one, but he knew it for what it was. As far as he knew, no one in his lifetime had dared to wear a mantle. In the lifetime of his father, and his father's father, there had been only two or perhaps three, and they hadn't survived the Evaluation. For just a moment, Jorge wished that Elam had never seen this man. He would be sitting happily in his home with Miran and Elam right now, celebrating his son's birthday. Sighing, he glanced at Baylor. His neighbor was staring at the hood, chewing on a corner of the mustache that flowed from his upper lip into the coarse, heavy beard which covered his face.

At length, Baylor felt his gaze and glanced up, seemingly embarrassed. Gruffly he said, "Best be getting on with it. Those hands look bad. Maybe he's another impostor, and God be sparin' the Council the task."

Jorge simply said, "Perhaps, but he seems to be breathing still. We'll do for him what's to be done. Beyond that, it's up to God or the Council."

Baylor's teeth actually showed in a momentary smile, "You figure they mayn't be the same, eh?"

The two men fashioned a litter using the heavy staves and rolled the unconscious man onto it. Hefting the dead weight, Jorge grunted with the effort. "Big 'un, hey?" said Baylor.

Jorge made a non-committal sound, but mentally agreed. Both he and Baylor were farmers, and considered strong men. While the man they carried was not the biggest he had ever seen, it was true that he was certainly bigger, or at least taller, than the average. Jorge figured him to be at least four inches taller than he, and Jorge was considered to be tall. By the time they had carried their load back to Jorge's home, they were both sweating and panting. Miran was waiting at the door, and held it open for them, but Jorge shook his head. "The shed," he said. "We'll lay him in there."

Miran objected, but Jorge stubbornly said, "There's nothing to be done for him in the house that cannot be done as well in the shed. I've naught against him, but we know not the nature of his illness. I'll not be taking him under my roof. At least not yet."

Miran clenched her jaw and her hands toyed with her apron. Finally she nodded and said, "Light a lamp. Whatever can be done, we'll see to it."

Baylor and Jorge carried their burden into the shed, where the two goats eyed them sleepily and let out a plaintive bleat. They deposited him onto a bed of hay carelessly scraped together. Jorge thanked Baylor, saying, "Appreciate your coming. I'd have had a time doing the job by myself."

Baylor nodded, and stood quietly, looking at the face of the man he had helped to bring in. "Something's not right here. Did you note his hair? It's light, fine it is, too, like a child's. And his face. Fair. Very fair. It isn't that he's not been in the sun. You can see the tan of it. But his face is lighter than most any I've seen"

Jorge looked. He had to admit that he hadn't taken note before, but now with a moment to catch his breath, he realized his friend was right. The man just <u>looked</u> different. Nothing drastic, but the features were sharper - the nose especially. But Baylor was right. The hair <u>was</u> different. It was fine, but it was such a light brown, almost the color of canvas on top, as though lit by some unseen illumination. He had never seen anything quite like it. It was unsettling. Aloud he said, "Perhaps he's from over at Neims," naming the governing village of the Second Order.

Baylor snorted, "I've never been that far myself. But I'd think to have heard."

Just then Miran came in, carrying a pan of warm water and a soft bundle of cloths. "Oh!" she exclaimed, "He's so different! And his hair! How strange it looks!" Jorge agreed, and was beginning to feel more uneasy by the moment, having this peculiar stranger in his shed. He was glad that he hadn't taken him into the house.

Miran's practical nature took over, and she knelt by the unconscious man, setting her pan of water near his head. Wetting a cloth, she began to tenderly wipe the dirt from his face. "His head is injured," she said, noting the residual blood still matting his hair. "Perhaps two or three days since, I would judge." The swollen hands caught her attention. She momentarily faltered. They were ugly things. The fingers were swollen to the point where the joints had no distinction, and there could be no movement. The angry, vivid streaks of mottled red, yellow and blue running to black ranged up his arms, disappearing under the sleeves of his shirt. She swallowed, and spoke slowly, "I cannot be certain, but I think he must have been in the sea. I've never seen it, but I've heard of the ocean sickness. There's only one place where the rocks are poisoned so. If he has been to the forbidden place, if he has been cut on the rocks there. Then nothing can be done. He will die."

Jorge was shamed by his momentary relief. If the stranger died, that would be the end of it. "But you cannot be sure?"

Miran shook her head and said, "No. Tales I've heard, that's all. They say it is a most cruel way to die. But if this be the cause, it looks like his suffering may be nearly at an end. Remove his shirt. We'll see if other wounds he has."

Jorge shook his head in turn and said, "No, Miran. Elam saw correctly. It is a mantle he wears. Right or wrong, it would be worth our lives to remove it. That is not for such as us."

Miran glared at him for just a moment, before her gaze softened and her eyes dropped again to the still figure, "Aye. Not for the likes of us. So we'll do what we can. Take the poor man's shoes off, Jorge. We can at least go that far to make him comfortable." and she continued her ministrations.

Jorge knelt down and unlaced the boots. He was puzzled, as they were unlike anything he had seen. Unlike the cloth and canvas shoes he wore, these were of some unfamiliar material. They were thin and light. The soles were hard, but seemed very flexible. He had no idea what they were, but he liked the feel of them. Jorge looked at the inert form, wondering what he had brought into his shed.

Chapter 3 The Long Night

The walls of Salem came into view, dimly illuminated by the single moon hovering at the horizon. Elam slowed to a trot, still panting. Two guards stood watch at the gate, eyeing him with bored disinterest.

"Please, I must speak to one of the 5th File. It is urgent!" Belatedly, Elam remembered to bow, and he did so now, more deeply than was customary, by way of apology for his discourtesy.

The watchmen were too bored to be offended. One responded gruffly, "It's late. Come back in the morning and pursue your business then."

Elam was uncertain in the face of authority. "Please, I know it's late. I ran all the way from Tyber. My father sent me!"

The guard was unimpressed, "Be off boy. I'll not be rousing anyone for your sick goat!"

The other guard smirked. Elam flushed. He hung his head and turned as if to leave while the guards shared some comment at his expense. Seeing his opportunity, he spun and sprinted through the gate, ignoring the guard's shouts. He raced through the courtyard and into a broad avenue lit by lanterns. He'd been to the capitol before, but had to slow briefly to orient himself. He had to reach the Praetorium! His hesitation allowed the pursuing guard to close the distance. He feared that the other guard was already alerting the city watch. He had his bearings now, and was in full sprint. The guard continued to yell at Elam to stop, and now faces were appearing in doorways and windows as he raced past, roused by the commotion. As he took the next corner, he was gratified by the sound of a crash and cursing behind him, indicating that the guard had failed to negotiate the turn. There! The Praetorium! He launched himself up the broad stairway and into the huge, lighted entry just as two guards hurtled toward him from the adjoining alcove.

Desperately, Elam dodged them and shot up the stairway, sparing some of his precious wind now to yell as loudly as he could, "5th File! I crave audience with the 5th File!"

He reached the top of the stairs and was racing along the balcony when a jarring collision brought him to the ground. Dazed, he lay there in a tangle with a liveried steward who had exited a room to his right. The pursuing guards were upon him immediately, grasping him roughly by the arms and hauling him to his feet. One of them gave him a vicious clout behind the ear, making his head swim. Other guards were running up as well and a crowd was gathering in the great hall below. Elam was too winded and hurt to speak. The city watch had caught up, flushed and angry, he forced his way through the crowd to confront Elam. Grabbing him by the hair he snarled, "You young pup! It's 5th File you want, is it? Well, it's a cell you'll be having! Lock him up!"

Elam was being dragged by angry hands. He was too cowed and exhausted to struggle. At the head of the stairs, his captors halted and their angry clamor suddenly dropped to hushed mutterings. A young woman stood there, framed in the doorway. She wore a long, simple dress, all the color of ripened wheat except for a thin band of purple adorning the hem and neckline, and a narrow sash of the same color gathering the waist. Her dark hair hung to her shoulders in a graceful cascade. She was taller than Elam, though not by much. Her dark, brown eyes regarded him coolly, but not unkindly, and at that moment, Elam thought she was the most beautiful woman he'd ever seen.

She spoke, to no one in particular, "Is this the source of so much commotion in the Praetorium this night?"

The guard, shamed by his failure to prevent Elam's entrance to the city, jerked his head in angry acknowledgment, "It is, Lady Dalene. Some lad from the countryside off on a lark. We wasn't expecting it. But he'll not be troubling us more! Take him!" he snarled.

Elam's heart pounded in his chest. The Lady Dalene! He had heard of her. Everyone had heard of her! He was mortified that, held as he was, he was unable to bow properly, so he did the best he could by dropping his chin to his chest, and his knees practically buckled at the same time.

The Lady Dalene noticed this, and a faint smile touched her mouth. "Hold, captain," she said, "Let us see what trouble arouses the city this night." The guard hesitated, but saw no option. He jerked Elam forward angrily, his vice-like grip on Elam's arm a clear warning.

"Why do you violate the peace of all those around this night? Should you not be at home?" She questioned.

Elam tried to swallow, but his mouth was suddenly very dry, and he stammered, without raising his eyes, "I was sent by my father. I must speak with one of the 5th File, for I am but of the 3rd File."

"Of the 3rd File? Have you then been Examined?" She asked.

He shook his head, "No, Lady. I misspoke. It is my parents who are of the 3rd File. I am due to be examined at the next moon."

The Lady Dalene cocked her head to one side and said, "Well, captain, before you haul this criminal off to the dungeon, let us grant his final request. An audience with the 5th File should not be difficult. Bring him."

The guard began to object, but a piercing glance from The Lady Dalene caused his protest to die in his throat. They followed her into the assembly room. "Councilor Lev!" she called. "A young man of the 3rd File craves audience!"

Elam's heart had sunk at the mention of the dungeon. It sank further with the call for Councilor Lev. He'd not expected to be seeing the High Councilor of the 5th File.

Councilor Lev was older than his grandfather, thought Elam. His hair still retained much of its dark luster, but was now fringed with gray, and his beard was entirely gray. He wore an ornate robe, white, but with a yellow vesture and broad, rich yellow border. He looked at Elam quite severely and his voice was sharp, as he spoke, "For what purpose do you seek audience?"

Elam was held so tightly by the guards that he still couldn't bow properly. He tried to mitigate his fault by bobbing his head deferentially, and replied, "Sir, I am most sorry to disturb you at this hour. I am Elam, son of Jorge, from Tyber. I was sent by my father and instructed to seek audience."

Elam paused to swallow, and Councilor Lev said dryly, "So we have gathered. Speak, boy! What is this urgent matter?"

Elam swallowed again, "One wearing a mantle has come to Tyber!"

His voice was drowned out in the uproar that followed. The Lady Dalene felt the blood drain from her face as she stood frozen, showing no emotion. The reaction of Councilor Lev was quite the opposite, his face was flushed and angry as he shouted, "Silence! You will all be silent or I'll have the guards clear the hall!" Fixing Elam with a ferocious glare, he said, "A mantle! If this be a joke, boy........"

Elam blanched but shook his head vigorously, "No! I speak truly!"

The Lady Dalene stepped forward, "Peace, Councilor. Let us hear the boy out and then we shall perhaps know how to proceed." Turning to the guards, she said, "Release him. I think there shall be no more running tonight."

The guards protested, but only weakly as they released him. Without their support, Elam's knees almost buckled, as he stood uncertainly and rubbed the circulation back into his arms. The Lady Dalene drew him to a chair, indicating he should sit. Turning to Councilor Lev, she said, "Call representatives of all the Files. Immediately. We will hear what the boy has to say." As Councilor Lev turned to arrange for summoning the members of the other Files, she spoke kindly to Elam, "Are you in need of food or drink? The meeting may be long."

Elam could only shake his head as he dumbly indicated the pouch, which held the crumbled remnants of his scant provisions. At this, The Lady Dalene smiled and said, "Perhaps we can find you a little something more."

Beckoning one of the ladies nearby, she asked them to bring refreshment and soon a platter of meat, cheese and bread was brought, along with a beautiful glass cup and a pitcher of wine. Elam had never drunk from glass before. At home, all of their cups and plates were of stone or clay. He was afraid to touch it, but when The Lady Dalene offered him the glass, he gingerly accepted it and thought it tasted wonderful.

He had little enough time to refresh himself, as the room was rapidly filling with men and women. Their robes were finer than any he had seen, with vibrant borders on each of them, including vivid blue or lavender as well as red and orange. He saw the simple brown of his own File, and felt a grateful kinship that one of Tyber would be here. There were borders of black and gray present, the colors of the 1st and 2nd Files as well. Elam was uncomfortable, recognizing the colors of all twelve Files now present in the room. The Lady Dalene was studying him, and he flushed at the attention. She smiled encouragingly, calming him, and then turned to address the assembly.

"I know the hour is late. Elam, the son of Jorge from the 3rd File has come from Tyber this night bearing news of one wearing a mantle."

At her words, the audience erupted in a sea of comment and exclamation, but she paused only a moment.

"We will hear of this and then decide what is to be done." With that, she turned to him and said, "Elam, do not be alarmed. Tell the errand upon which you were sent. Tell us all you know, quickly."

Nervous and awkward, he said, "Sirs, Ladies......" he paused and bowed to the assembly, "I am Elam, of Tyber. Tonight at dusk, as we were preparing to retire the day, I went to find our goats. As I was crossing the field where my father and I had worked all day, I saw a man on the opposite side. He was down on his hands and knees, as though he had fallen. I thought to help him, but before I could offer assistance, he fell to the earth with his face in the dirt. I was afraid, because I didn't know what was wrong, but I went over to him. He did not move nor speak. I saw his hands first. They were badly injured. I was going to try and roll him over, but when I went to do so, I saw his coat. He wore the colors of no file and his cloak had a hood. I ran for home then and told my parents what I had seen. The stranger wore a mantle."

At that, the crowd again erupted in a buzz of conversation, but a stern look from The Lady Dalene silenced them, and Elam continued, "My father said he might be a pretender, but it was not for us to decide. He sent me to Salem to seek audience with one of the 5th File. I ran all the way," he said proudly, but then hung his head, "I'm sorry I created a disturbance. I know I must be punished for that. But I didn't know what to do when I was refused entrance to the city." At that he sat down, and The Lady Dalene placed a comforting hand on his shoulder.

"There will be no punishment for young Elam," she said sternly. "Our law is clear. Any citizen may request audience with a higher File, or Order. There is no restriction regarding age or the timing of the request. The city watch will be reminded of this." Elam felt a wave of relief wash through him, and stared in grateful amazement at The Lady Dalene who continued, "But that is not of greatest importance just now. You have heard that one wearing a mantle has arrived in Tyber. Whether he wears it by right or not, we do not know, but he is injured. We do not know how severely. I propose we send a delegation immediately......this night....to further examine the matter."

Once again the room dissolved into a cacophony of questions and conversation before The Lady Dalene silenced them. "Assistant Councilor Belak, I see you are here in place of Councilor Linape. Is she absent?"

Councilor Belak was a middle-aged, reedy looking man, wearing the brown cloak of the 3rd File. "Arlena is not present, Lady Dalene. She was taken ill, and has gone to be administered to by a Healer."

"Very well," she nodded, "then the choice is yours. Do you wish to lead the delegation, or, in the absence of Councilor Linape, would you prefer to defer to the head of your Order?"

Belak cleared his throat and looked about nervously, "Ah....I'm really not sure what Councilor Linape would like to have me do. I suppose that in her absence, perhaps it would be wise to defer the honor to the 4th File."

"As you wish. Councilor Rabin, as head of the 4th File, the responsibility will be yours. You will lead the delegation. Councilor Lev, you will select a representative of the 2nd Order." He still looked angry, but agreed with a curt nod.

She spoke again, more softly this time, "And I shall accompany you, as representative of the 3rd Order." She cut off the weak objections. "The man is injured. I am qualified as Healer. I shall go. We will depart within the hour."

The Lady Dalene turned to Elam and said, "Elam, I am sorry. I know that you must be tired, but we will need you to guide us to your home as quickly as possible. Will you be able?"

The look of compassion she gave him swept the exhaustion from Elam in a wave. At that moment, he thought, he would have gladly died for her had she but asked it. Stammering, he said, "Yes, Lady. I am strong. I will take you to my home," and impetuously he added, "And you will be made welcome there."

She smiled, and he blushed furiously. "Thank you, Elam," she replied, "That is a kindness I am often not extended. Now, you must excuse me, as I have things to prepare. Rest and eat. I'll be back soon." With that, she was gone.

Elam ate quickly, realizing how tired he was. He was not looking forward to the trip back to Tyber. He pulled out the remains of his last honey cookie, and said softly, "Happy Birthday." Before he could feel too sorry for himself, several people started gathering. Councilor Rabin had returned, and acknowledged Elam with a curt nod in his direction. Elam jumped to his feet and returned the nod with a deep bow. A younger man, wearing the uniform of the City Guard of Salem smiled. Remembering his earlier encounter with the guards, Elam bowed nervously.

The younger man spoke, "Councilor Rabin, I am Veret Lev. My father, Councilor Lev has excused himself from the journey due to his age and health. He assigned me to accompany you in his stead, and to represent the 5th File."

Councilor Rabin bowed, "It's an honor to travel with you. I've known your father for many years. I'm sure that you'll represent the 5th File admirably."

Elam eyed the guard. Over his uniform he wore a simple traveling tunic of light brown material, but fringed with the yellow designating his File. Heavily padded shoes covered his feet and his leggings were dark brown. A heavy canvas belt held a simple metal scabbard, showing the hilt of a functional looking sword. A dagger and two soft cloth pouches weighed down the other side of the belt. Elam glanced enviously at the sword.

The Lady Dalene soon returned, accompanied by a couple in their late 20's or early 30's. Both wore simple traveling attire, trimmed with red, indicating that they were of the 8th File. Both Councilor Rabin and Veret bowed deeply when The Lady Dalene entered, and bowed again to her two companions, though neither looked to be very happy about it.

The Lady Dalene said, "Marcus and Alicia Verlach will accompany us and assist me."

Elam thought both Councilor Rabin and Veret looked even more unhappy at this news, though Elam couldn't understand why. Marcus and Alicia appeared quite cheerful. They were both large boned and round of face. The Lady Dalene continued, "The carts should be loaded by the time we reach the stable. If you have everything you need, we should be going."

Councilor Rabin and Veret picked up their belongings, and the group descended the stairs and exited out the rear of the Praetorium. It was a short walk to the stables. Servants accompanied them with lanterns. The twin moons had set and the night was very dark. Two carts were waiting, harnessed to a pair of horses. The Lady Dalene indicated that Elam should climb up in the back of one of the carts where he was joined by Alicia. Marcus was seated up on the box and took the reins. Elam had to push and arrange the baggage, but soon had a reasonably comfortable niche carved out, as had Alicia. In the other cart, The Lady Dalene was seated beside Veret on the box, while Councilor Rabin was unhappily moving items to make space in the wagon bed and was having a difficult time.

It was nearing the sixth hour of the night, about midnight, when they departed. Night travel was unusual unless there was considerable urgency, for the roads were rough. Elam was delighted to be traveling by cart. And drawn by horses even! On the farm, horses were considered a great luxury, as oxen could work harder and longer, plus their food was more coarse, making them better suited for the farm. His father had two oxen. Mostly they were used for plowing, but at harvest time, they were hitched to the heavy wagon to haul hay and grain from the fields to market. But Elam soon grew to regret their haste. The horses trotted, eating up the miles, but the jarring ride in the back of the cart beat Elam against the side and floorboards unmercifully. The load kept shifting, falling on him or against him, making him altogether quite uncomfortable. After a half hour of being jostled and tossed, he sighed and gave up. Finding a couple of large bags, he arranged an uncomfortable seat with his feet against the floorboard, enabling him to absorb the jolting ride better. He glanced enviously at Alicia, who, amazingly, was sound asleep.

The silence was broken only by the steady clop of hooves, accompanied by the creaking of the cart wheels, with the occasional crashing jolt as they hit a particularly nasty bump. Despite his discomfort, Elam managed to doze, and awakened only when Marcus pulled up to rest and water the horses. Shyly, he asked if he might join him up on the driver's seat. Marcus responded with a ready smile, "Certainly, lad, and I'd be pleased for the company."

Elam bowed his thanks. After all, he was speaking to one of the 8th File! But his chest swelled a little in pride. After all, none of his friends had ever had association with one of such high rank! He glanced at the other cart, seen only dimly. He could just make out the ghostly shape of The Lady Dalene, her light cloak forming a vague outline drifting about the darker shadow of the other cart, and he could hear murmured conversation, but the words were indistinct.

The Lady Dalene's mind was busy with too many thoughts. Outwardly, she presented a picture of perfect calm and deliberation. She had been schooled her entire life in hiding her emotions. Emotion, after all, was a tool which her enemies could use to attack her. And she did have enemies. Enemies of her own, and enemies of her father, for her father was Councilor Tregard. They were not the type to offer an overt threat or attempt to harm her. They would be satisfied to discredit her, and by association, her father, thereby reducing his power and influence in the hopes of increasing their own. Gareth Tregard headed the 12th File, making him Regent of Aidon and the defacto head of the government. While the High Council of Aidon governed, the Regent presided over the Council. For the present, that meant Councilor Tregard, for he had risen in every Evaluation, subjecting all challengers in the test of Compliance, to emerge as the preeminent mind in Aidon, and thus most fit to rule. Not that Gareth Tregard sought to force his will unjustly on the people or the other eleven Councilors. He was a fair man, if stern. Some said he was lacking in humor or kindness. The Lady Dalene knew this was not true. But her father had taught her the danger of becoming too familiar with people, particularly those of her Order. While some sought only an elevation of their own status, others sought personal power either through usurping the government of Aidon, or by betraying

Aidon to her neighboring country of Kernsidon. The grandfather of The Lady Dalene had been a young man when Kernsidon had last invaded her country. Kernsidon had at last been pushed back, at the cost of much blood, but they had finally withdrawn to their own borders. Her father was worried, she knew. There was a sense that Kernsidon was about to become a threat once more. The usual maneuverings for advantage within the government was bad enough, but if war were to come, it could prove fatal.

It was easy to become melancholy, sitting in the dark stillness of the night. Clouds now obscured the stars which had accompanied the first portion of their journey. She was anxious to be on their way, but she knew the horses had to be rested. She sighed. Her father kept telling her to be patient, to observe and to think before acting. He was a good teacher. She was not sure that he would have approved her being on this journey this night. But that one wearing a mantle had appeared! She had to see him! She had to know if he wore the mantle by right or if he were another impostor. Her smile faded, replaced by a grim set to her jaw. Impostors were rare - almost as rare as those who wore the mantle by right. For if this were an impostor, there would be much more than an Evaluation of Compliance. No, for the crime of impersonating one who wore the mantle by right, the entire weight of the Council would be brought to bear in a trial of Compulsion. He would be destroyed. She experienced an involuntary shiver, and wrapped her cloak more tightly about her.

Veret approached her and said, "Lady Dalene, we can be going now. The horses are ready."

She nodded, unseen in the darkness, and climbed back up onto the cart. Once more, the horses began trotting down the road, and once more, she was lost in her thoughts.

Alicia was asleep almost as soon as the cart started moving. Marcus gave her an affectionate glance over his shoulder and commented to Elam, "I swear, that woman could sleep through an earthquake."

Elam asked, "She is your wife?" Marcus replied, "Aye, going on six years now. A good six years it has been." and he nodded as he spoke. With a glance at Elam, he said, "And you, you'd look to be about 15, I'd say. Have you had your first Evaluation then?"

"Not yet," Elam replied, "I'll not be 15 until tomorrow........I guess I mean today."

Marcus laughed softly and said, "Well then let me be the first to wish you a Happy Birthday. Not quite the way you expected to celebrate though, is it?"

Elam smiled, "No, but it surely won't be a day I'll soon forget!"

He blushed suddenly, realizing how familiar he was while speaking to one of the 8th File.

While Marcus couldn't see the color rise in Elam's face, he sensed a sudden reserve and asked, "Are you alright, Elam?"

"Yes, sir." Elam said, "I meant no disrespect, sir, in speaking so informally."

"Elam, I took no offense. We may be of different Files – different Orders, to be sure, but we're both men. Just men. You owe me no more courtesy than you do to any man. Oh, there's some that set too much store by their File and their rank within the File, but I be not one of them!" He sounded angry as he spoke the last.

Elam was a little embarrassed, but at the same time, he was proud to have been acknowledged as a man! And despite Marcus' words, the fact that such praise came from one of the 8th File meant a great deal to him. After several minutes of silence, Marcus said, "So at the next moon, you'll be taking the Evaluation?"

Elam said, "Yes. I'm excited, but a little bit nervous about it as well. I'd not like to shame my parents."

Marcus said, "Yes, there's that. We all teach and talk that it matters not what File you are of. But in the end, it does matter. The rewards of society seem to place a premium on the Evaluation as well. Take me, for example. I am what I am. I can claim no special credit for being of the 8th File. I am fortunate – blessed if you will – but no credit to me. When I took my Evaluation, I was 8th File, even though my parents were both 6th File! No reason. I've not advanced even a single File since then. I simply am what I am."

Elam hesitated, but had to ask, "But, if your parents are of the 6th File, what happened after your Evaluation?"

Marcus spoke into the darkness, bitterly, "They took me. As 8th File, I wasn't permitted to live in Riverton. I was placed with a family in Sarepta, as befits one of the 8th File!" He was silent for a minute, and then continued, "The family that took me in – an older couple – they were good folks. I could go home for the odd visit, but it was all different. My old friends……" his voice trailed off and he shook his head. Brightening a bit, he said, "Ah, it wasn't all bad, you know. I was happy enough. And then I met Alicia. Now, well, I can't imagine life without her, and I'd never have even met her had my Evaluation not placed me in the 8th File."

The two rode on in silence for some time, content to listen to the sounds of the horses and cart as they moved on through the night. Changing the subject, Marcus asked, "And you, what do you hope to be?"

Elam was surprised. He'd never really thought about it, but replied, "A farmer like my father, I suppose. It's a good enough life."

"Oh, to be sure. Farming is a wonderful life, I guess. But have you never longed for something more? Promotion to the Second Order would open up options. No interest at all?" asked Marcus.

Elam shrugged, "Maybe. But I'd miss my folks, and I like living in Tyber. If I weren't in the 1st Order, I'd have to move."

Marcus said, "But sooner or later, you'll move anyway. You're not going to live with your folks too much longer no matter what. Just don't sell yourself short, Elam. You are what you are."

Alicia's voice from the back of the cart made it evident that she had been listening for some time. "Marcus, he's still just a lad. Don't be growing him up and moving him out too soon!"

Marcus laughed, "I didn't know you were awake! But you're right! No point worrying away today over what the morrow might bring, but while we're on the subject of today, you might be kind enough to wish young Elam here a Happy Birthday! Elam will be doing his Evaluation at the next moon."

"Well then, Elam, I hope you'll accept my wishes for your happiness this day, and success to you in your Evaluation. Not the best way to start your birthday, bumping along in this cart with the likes of us."

Elam was shocked, both at the kindness of the words and that any of the 8th File should refer to themselves so casually. He stammered his thanks, and they lapsed once again into silence.

The town of Tyber was indistinct in the darkness. It was now just past the ninth hour of the night. Soon, light would begin to paint the distant horizon to the east. Elam directed that they should drive on through the town. Marcus turned his attention again to Elam and asked, "How do we reach your father's farm?"

Elam said, "It's not far now – perhaps a couple of miles. I always take the woods path. It's the fastest way if you're on foot. The road doesn't go to my father's farm. Mostly we use the path, but at harvest time we can take the wagon along the edge of the fields. If we take the carts, we'll have to go that way."

The Lady Dalene considered. It was obvious that the others would defer to her. At last she spoke, "Councilor Rabin, do you know Tyber at all? Do you think you can find Elam's farm?"

Councilor Rabin shook his head, "No. Especially not in the dark. Come day, I'm sure I can find someone to direct me, but in the dark I'd be lost."

The Lady Dalene nodded, appreciating his candor, "Very well. We can't wait. We'll take what things we need. Veret, Marcus, would you prepare packs? Elam, you'll lead us on the woods path. We'll follow. Councilor Rabin, I'd like you to stay with the carts. In the morning, come along as quickly as you can. Find someone to drive the second cart if possible – a guide who can be discrete"

Councilor Rabin nodded, but he looked none too happy about it. Veret and Marcus had already begun to make up packs for each of them.

The Lady Dalene halted him, saying, "Marcus, I'll need the Healer's box. It's heavy."

Marcus shrugged and said, "I'll manage." He made to set the pack he had been preparing for himself aside, but Elam stepped forward and said, "I'll carry it."

Marcus hesitated, but with an appraising glance at Elam, said, "I'd be obliged."

With ropes and spare harness, Marcus attached shoulder straps to the Healer's box and hoisted it onto his back, making Elam reconsider his first impression of Marcus being soft. Elam's pack was heavy, but no worse than many of the rocks he had hauled from the fields. He led out, with The Lady Dalene following closely, while Veret, Alicia and Marcus trailed behind.

It was cooler now, in the waning hours of the night, but their pace was swift and the weight of the packs had them sweating lightly. Elam was growing more anxious as he approached his home. He could smell wood smoke before he saw the thin gleam of light around the shuttered windows. His pace quickened, as he hurried to the door and burst in. "Mother, father! I'm home. We have guests!" He called.

There was no answer. Perplexed, he stepped further into the house, followed by his companions who gratefully set down their loads. Just then his father's voice called from outside, "Elam! Is it you?"

A wave of relief swept through Elam, as he leapt to the door, "Father! Yes, I'm back. We have guests."

Elam's father entered, looking distrustfully at the group which now seemed to fill his small cottage. Noting the colors on the hems of their jackets and cloaks, he bowed deeply and said, "Jorge of Tyber, at your service. I bid you welcome to my home."

The others acknowledged this greeting with brief nods of their own. Veret stepped forward, saying, "I am Veret Lev of Ramah. May I present Marcus and Alicia, formerly of Sarepta, and presently of Salem," he continued. "And may I also present, The Lady Dalene of Salem," he added dryly.

At this last, Jorge paled, and bowed more deeply than Elam had ever seen. The Lady Dalene stepped towards Jorge, nodding courteously and extending her hand, "Thank you, Jorge of Tyber, for your welcome to your home. And thank you as well, for sending your son, Elam, to inform us of the arrival of ……….. your injured guest. May we see him, please?"

Jorge swallowed. He accepted the proffered hand gingerly, unused to any such courtesy from those of the higher Orders. After clasping her hand briefly, he said, "Of course, Lady Dalene. We have tried to make him comfortable in the shed. My wife is tending to him even now."

Jorge led the way holding a lantern. Ducking through the low doorway, they saw a woman bending over an unconscious figure, wiping his fevered brow with a damp cloth. Miran looked up when she heard them come in. She jumped quickly to her feet when she saw the colors of yellow, red and purple on the various cloaks. Jorge cleared his throat, and said, "My wife, Miran. Miran, this is The Lady Dalene and her companions."

At the name, Miran looked stunned and bowed deeply, saying, "We are honored by your visit."

The Lady Dalene acknowledged her with a brief nod, but her eyes were on the still figure. She stared at him with a strange intensity, concern furrowing her brow. But then, as if suddenly remembering that she was not alone, she turned to Miran and smiled, "Thank you for the care you have given this man, and for your kindness in allowing this intrusion. May I examine him?"

Miran's eyes widened at the kind words, as well as at the request. Who was she to deny any in the 12th File what they wished? Especially one such as The Lady Dalene? She simply nodded. The Lady Dalene approached and knelt by the stranger. As she looked at his hands, her heart skipped a beat. They were ugly things, now swollen almost beyond recognition as belonging to anything human. Beads of sweat were collecting on his face, a face so still that she feared he no longer lived. But she could detect his shallow breathing. Turning to Miran she asked, "Has he been like this the entire time?"

Miran answered, "Yes. The swelling in his hands has been getting worse and I think his fever has been increasing as well." Hesitating, she said, "I think he may have the ocean sickness. I've never seen it, but the swelling and the discoloration of the hands…….you can see the palms, where they've been scraped. I think he's dying."

The Lady Dalene's eyes widened at the mention of the ocean sickness, but she asked, "The forbidden place, you know of it?" Miran nodded. "How far is it from here?"

Miran looked to her husband, who shrugged, "Perhaps 60 miles. Less maybe. No one knows."

The Lady Dalene nodded, "It's possible then. He could have walked that far – if he were strong. The sickness kills quickly. I think you're right. The hands look like what I was taught." Businesslike now, she spoke in a tone of command, "We have no time to lose. I will want everyone out. Marcus, will you bring the Healer's box? We will need the fire built up. We must heat salt. I don't think I have enough. Do you have salt?" She asked, looking at Miran.

"Yes, we have a small supply."

"Good. We'll replace what we use, but get all you have. Softening for a moment she said, "You must be tired. When you get the salt, go and rest. Alicia will be able to help me."

Miran smiled her thanks at the concern, but said, "I'm grateful. But might I be able to help? I feel a responsibility for him now."

The Lady Dalene smiled and touched Miran lightly on the arm, "I would appreciate your help, if you're not too tired. It's not for me to tell you what to do in your own home. Thank you."

Miran was puzzled by this show of courtesy, but quickly went to work.

Marcus brought in the Healer's box and set it near the unconscious man. The Lady Dalene said, "Help Miran. We need a large kettle to heat salt in. Build up the fire, and heat the salt as hot as you can stand to hold your hand in. It mustn't burn, but it must be hot. Use what's here and whatever Miran has."

Marcus hurried away. Elam had been standing quietly by the goats nibbling at his fingers. Shyly he asked, "May I help?"

The Lady Dalene looked up from rummaging in her box, startled. "Elam! I'm sorry, I didn't notice you. If you would help Marcus get the fire going. Then I think you should go to bed. You made twice the journey as the rest of us. You must be exhausted!"

Elam nodded and left, while The Lady Dalene knelt once again by her patient. She was, she admitted, frightened, for she believed that he did indeed have the ocean sickness……and there was no known cure. There had been so few cases, there had been no real chance to find a cure, at least not in the past several hundred years. The legends claimed that there was a lonely stretch of volcanic rock jutting out into the ocean. Any who found themselves in the water there would soon die of fever and horrible swelling which would discolor the limbs. The place was said to be where the great Serpent had been banished shortly after the creation, and that it was the poison of the Serpent which infected the region and caused death. From the look of this man's hands, the stories could be true. The bloating and discoloration looked like it could be from a poison. Hot salt packs had been successful at drawing poison from limbs, but what to do next, she didn't know.

Kneeling by the still form, she brushed back his damp hair. It was very fine – at least for an adult. The color fascinated her. While her hair was a deep, rich brown, it was, if anything, considered light by the standards of her people. She had never seen hair of such a light color, and the color varied! Even though damp, she could see lighter streaks that caught the lamplight and seemed almost as light as honey. His skin was also strangely light, more like a child's skin than the adults of her people. The beard stubble showing on his face and neck gave him a certain coarseness. For a time, she forgot her main interest in this man as one who had appeared wearing a mantle. In fact, she had made no effort to inspect the hooded coat which he wore. For the moment, he was simply an ill and injured man, and she very much wanted him to live.

She pushed the sleeves up his arms as far as she could, exposing them above the elbow, noting that the swelling diminished rapidly above this point. She thought this was a good sign. The poison hadn't spread too drastically through his body. Gently, she lifted each arm in turn, placing a large, soft towel under them. Her Healer's box had such limited stores! But even if she had all the apothecary supplies of Salem at her disposal, she had to admit that she still wouldn't know what to use. Taking two bottles from her box, she dipped water from the bucket. She had dried willow bark. She would make an infusion and try to get him to drink some for the fever. It should help with the swelling as well. She had corydalis and curcumin as well as aloe vera. She hesitated, but knew that if she did nothing, he would die, so she began mixing all three together in a single bottle. Just then Miran came in. "We have the salt heating in my largest kettle. Alicia is stirring it so it will heat evenly," she said.

"Good. Would you set these two bottles near the fire? They mustn't boil, and I don't like heating them, but it will speed the infusion, and I fear that we haven't as much time as I would like," said The Lady Dalene.

Miran nodded, and took the two bottles back to the house. The Lady Dalene remained kneeling, looking at the still form beside her, "Dear Father," she said, "Please help me. Without your help, this man will die, and I don't know what to do. Please show me how to preserve his life." She continued to kneel there, feeling no inspiration, just a rising sense of desperation, but she refused to give in to it.

Marcus carried the large cast iron kettle filled with salt. He set it gently beside her and looked a question at her. She simply shook her head, and he left quietly. Miran had followed Marcus in and came to kneel opposite her, with their patient lying between them. The Lady Dalene said, "Lift his arm. Careful now. I'll place salt under his arm. As soon as it's layered, set his arm down and cover it with more salt. When it's covered, wrap the towel around it to hold the heat."

They quickly did the first arm and then the second. Miran asked, "Will he recover, do you think?"

The Lady Dalene didn't look at her, "I don't know. I don't know what to do." Pausing, she continued, "Could you get some rocks warming by the fire. If we set them by the towels it will help hold the heat better and I'm afraid we haven't enough salt to warm and wrap his arms again."

Miran nodded and left. The Lady Dalene maintained her vigil. Suddenly, the patient's eyes flared open, and he groaned. She was shocked! His eyes! They were green! Well, not quite green, not like the grass or trees, but they were green! Never had she seen eyes of such color. All eyes were brown, some bordering on black, but his were colored! What was he? She placed her cool hand on his forehead. He looked directly at her, but his eyes didn't seem to focus. They rolled back in their sockets, and his eyelids closed. Her heart was hammering. She thought he had died, but no, she could see he was still breathing. She felt so helpless! What could she possibly do? Salt. Where could she get more salt? Muttering to herself, she recited, "But if the salt has lost its flavor, it is good for nothing." Salt – the preservative. The symbol of Messias. The One who would preserve all people who would come to Him. It was Messias who had cast out the Serpent – banished him into the ocean after he attacked their first parents. But He had not acted alone. The Father and The Spirit had supported Messias! The symbols? Could the answer possibly lie with the symbols of the Eternals? With hope borne of desperation, she yelled, "Miran! Miran! Quickly!"

Miran came rushing in, followed by Marcus and Alicia.

"I need maize! Ground as finely as possible! Do you have any?" demanded The Lady Dalene.

"Yes, it's coarse, but we can grind it again. We have a small mill here."

The Lady Dalene said, "Quickly then! But the first meal must be thrown away. It will have wheat or other grain with it. This must be <u>only</u> maize. Do you understand?"

Miran nodded, and immediately left to see to it. The Lady Dalene turned quickly to her Healer's box. "Oil! There must be oil! Ah! Here it is," speaking to herself. Glancing now at Marcus and Alicia, she said, "Miran was getting some stones heated by the fire. We will need quite a lot – enough to line the sides of each arm, and to bridge over the top of the arm as well. Oh, and set this jar of oil in by the fire – as close as you can. I want it warm as well."

Marcus needed no further instruction and left. Alicia came and knelt beside The Lady Dalene, "Is there anything I can do to help?" she asked.

The Lady Dalene gave her a wan smile and said, "I don't know. I don't even know what <u>I'm</u> doing."

Alicia looked puzzled, "But you must know! I mean, the salt, the maize..........you can heal him, can't you?"

The Lady Dalene shook her head, "I don't know. If it's the ocean sickness, none ever recovered from it. The records don't say what was tried, only that none lived. I just feel so helpless!"

Alicia placed a comforting hand on her arm and said, "It is in God's hands. You can only do so much." The Lady Dalene dropped her eyes and nodded. It was only a few minutes wait before Miran hurried in, carrying a large, earthenware bowl half filled with the finely ground maize. "It's ready," she said, "Is it enough?"

The Lady Dalene nodded and said, "Quickly then. We must hurry. He is far gone already. Now, Alicia, Miran, if you will help me. We must unwrap his arms – gently – he is unconscious, but they will still be causing him pain. I want to conserve the heat left in the salt as much as possible."

Sighing, she spoke again, "I guess we are as ready as we can be, so let's begin. Alicia, if you would fetch the oil. Ask Marcus to start bringing in the heated stones and set them near to hand. Once we begin, please don't speak unless it is truly necessary." She smiled faintly and said, "I really don't know what I'm doing, and I have to concentrate."

Alicia returned with the heated oil, followed by Marcus, Jorge and Veret, all bringing in large heated stones wrapped in coarse cloth. The Lady Dalene spoke again, "I would like all of you to unite in a Compliance. One of you must touch him at all times. Marcus, if you would maintain the contact, I would be grateful. The rest of you can maintain contact through Marcus. Stay as close as you can without getting in the way. Reach into his mind and urge him to open to us. Get him to release the poison and to speed it to his arms where I hope to extract it. You mustn't force him. If he feels you using a Compulsion, weak as he is, he may still fight it, and he hasn't the strength for that. Calm him, if you can. Get him to help us. It's his only chance."

Drawing a breath, she said, "We begin."

The three women quickly unwrapped each arm. There was still some salt left in the cauldron, and this was added to the layer already on each arm. The Lady Dalene was speaking softly to herself, so softly that Alicia and Miran could barely hear her. She almost seemed to be reciting, perhaps something she had learned when being trained as a Healer. She was almost unaware of what she said, as if recalling some all-but-forgotten memory. "As Messias may draw from us our infirmity, so does the salt draw forth the poison. As Messias preserves us from destruction, so will the salt preserve things temporal from corruption." When she finished packing salt around each arm, she next took the earthen bowl filled with the finely ground maize while Alicia and Miran each supported an arm. Jorge rested one hand lightly on the back of Miran's neck while Marcus and Veret touched his other arm, eyes closed, trying to reach into the mind of the unconscious man. The Lady Dalene layered the maize on top of the salt under each arm, and indicated that Miran and Alicia should set the arms down. She piled the spilled salt back up on his arms and sprinkled the maize in a thick layer over top of each salt encrusted limb, muttering softly to herself, "As the maize comes as a gift from the sun, and as the sun represents the Father, from whom all good things flow and whose glory is in His children, so the maize shall consume that which is destructive in the body, which comes as a gift from God. The gift of God shall heal God's gift."

She then grabbed the vessel filled with the warm oil, and continued, "The Spirit fills all things and carries forth the love of Messias and the Father into the hearts of His children, so does the oil represent the Spirit, and carries the healing power of the salt and the maize into wounded flesh, to draw forth that which would destroy and to give comfort and relief to that which is injured."

The oil infused the ground corn and salt, spreading warmth and carrying their compounds, speeding them to the swollen limbs. The Lady Dalene finished by wrapping the towels snugly around each arm, and having Alicia and Miran lay his arms down, well away from his sides. She then began placing the stones along his body, filling the gap between arm and body with their warmth. Finally, she placed additional stones along the outside of each arm and a bridge over the top, the weight resting upon the supporting stones at his side rather than on his arms.

At length, she was finished, and slumped exhausted by his side. It was not until then that she noticed light coming through the door from outside. The long night was over and the sun would soon be rising. Dazed, she gathered her faculties to give instructions, "He must be kept warm. Bring the two infusions from by the fire. We need to get some of the liquid from each into him – just a spoonful or two now, and then again every hour. It will help with his fever and the swelling as well. Any liquid we can get into him at all will help at this stage".

Miran placed a hand on her shoulder, "We'll see to it. Now, you must rest. Come in the house, you can sleep there."

The Lady Dalene shook her head, "No. You've been up all night as well. We have blankets. I'll be fine here. There's plenty of hay, and I really don't want to leave him just yet."

Jorge and Miran exchanged a glance – the very idea of having one of the 12th File sleeping in their shed! And no less than The Lady Dalene herself! Unaccustomed to arguing with any of the upper Files, however, they simply nodded. Jorge released the goats, from their pen and led them out. The others turned to leave as well, but Marcus lagged behind. He hesitated, "Lady Dalene, I tried to reach him while you were tending him. I couldn't find him. I couldn't feel him at all."

Lady Dalene looked perplexed, "What do you mean?" she asked.

Marcus shrugged, "I don't know. In the Compliance………there was nothing. It was like he didn't exist. It was so strange, I had to open my eyes to make sure he was really there, but when I reached out, when all of us reached for him to extend a Compliance, I couldn't see or feel anything."

The Lady Dalene's chin sank down on her chest in defeat, "Thank you for telling me this, Marcus. Maybe he is already too far gone. Maybe his 'self' is gone, and the body will soon follow. I just don't know."

At last, Marcus turned and left to follow the others, whether to eat or to sleep, she didn't know and for the moment at least, she didn't care. She scraped together a pile of loose hay, spread a blanket over it and gratefully lay down, pulling another blanket over herself. "Just for a minute," she thought as she closed her eyes, "I'll rest just for a minute." Then she was asleep.

Chapter 4   Resurrection

It is said that there is no pillow like exhaustion, and The Lady Dalene was exhausted. Physically and emotionally she was worn out, and so she slept. The others ate and rested. Yes, they were tired, but they had been spared the strain from the effort of healing. Even the Healer's did not fully recognize how much their craft cost them, but in order to fully heal, a part of them was invested in the patient, and that took a toll. Occasionally, Marcus or Alicia would peek in the door of the shed, and each time the scene was the same. Faithfully, each hour either Alicia or Miran would tiptoe in quietly and spoon a little of the medications which The Lady Dalene had prepared into the mouth of their unconscious patient. They weren't sure how much they got into him. Too much dribbled from his mouth. He appeared unchanged.

About the fourth hour of the day, Councilor Rabin arrived with the carts. He had prevailed upon one of the townsmen in Tyber to act as guide and drive the other cart and walk back to town – for a fee large enough to ensure his silence without being quite large enough to stimulate his curiosity. Everyone spoke in hushed tones and mounting concern as the day wore on, yet The Lady Dalene did not rise. Finally, about the eighth hour, she emerged from the shed, still looking very tired and somewhat disheveled. Miran took her by the arm, escorting her to the back of the house where she could bathe from a basin of warm water. Composing herself, she rejoined her hosts and companions in the cramped living quarters. Alicia ladled a bowl full of soup to set before her, as The Lady Dalene sat at the table. She smiled her thanks and picked up a spoon, hesitating a moment, then asking, "Has he awakened at all while I was asleep?"

Both Alicia and Miran shook their heads, "No, he hasn't stirred. We've been giving him the medicines, but he swallows only a little." said Alicia. She paused and then continued, "Marcus and I have talked. He told me what he said last night – this morning, I guess – about not being able to find him when they attempted to do the Compliance. I spoke with the others, and they experienced the same thing. None of them could feel his true-self. It's as though he doesn't exist." Again she hesitated, before admitting, "I tried myself – when I took him the medicine. I was right there, touching him even, at the face. But when I closed my eyes and felt for him, I couldn't find him."

The Lady Dalene looked down at her bowl, her appetite suddenly gone, and absently set the spoon down. For several moments she did not speak, but at last she sighed and said, "Then I have failed. Perhaps I was just too late, or maybe what I did wasn't enough. But if his true-self is gone………" Her voice trailed off. She picked up her spoon, and began to eat, woodenly, and without pleasure.

In spite of herself, she felt refreshed, having been washed and fed. Until just now, she had quite forgotten the reason this stranger was of so much concern, was the fact that he wore the hooded cloak. Remembering this, she flushed. How could she have forgotten? She was the daughter of the Regent. She knew there were things more important than individuals, and yet she had become so caught up in the life of this one man, she had forgotten her purpose for making that journey in the night. She must examine his garment more closely. No sooner had she thought this, than she arose to do so.

Colin was someplace very white. It was calm and peaceful here, unlike the boiling cauldron under water where he had so nearly drowned. He remembered drowning. It had hurt. He remembered how his lungs had burned, and he knew that he had to draw in that breath – not of air, but of water –that lungful of water that would kill him. But it hadn't happened. He remembered that. Just as he was about to suck in that liquid death, he was someplace else white. But he remembered something. Wasn't that before he found himself in the ocean? But how could that be? He remembered being there, but it was after he almost drowned, wasn't it? It was calm and peaceful, like the place he was now. He remembered that white place. It was calm, and there was someone there with him. Someone who had told him something very important. Why couldn't he remember what it was? Colin didn't know how long he had been here. He wasn't sure where 'here' was, and he really didn't care. He was just floating anchored to the earth only by the weight of his hands, and he was at peace. He thought maybe he could just stay here and float forever, and that would be OK.

But then something began to intrude. Colin didn't like the intrusion. It began pushing at the edges of his consciousness. It brought color into his white, peaceful place. It was pushing him out of that place, into a place where there was color, and there were areas of darkness and with the darkness came pain. His hands were still anchors, holding him to ....life? But they hurt. He wanted to go back to the white place, where nothing hurt, where he felt nothing, where he could just float. But he was being driven away from there. He tried to fight it, to push back, but the more he pushed, the more rapidly he was drawn into the place of color and pain and darkness. Suddenly, his eyes flared open, and he didn't know where he was. He hurt. A soft groan escaped his clenched jaw. And with a flash of fear, he realized he couldn't move. He was paralyzed.

The Lady Dalene entered the shed. The lantern had long since been extinguished, and it took a moment for her eyes to adjust to the dim light. As they did so, she quickly stepped over to the side of the unconscious stranger. She knelt immediately to inspect his cloak. She fingered it softly at the open neckline. Just as she did so, his eyes opened and he gave a low groan of pain. She jumped a little, her heart suddenly pounding, and she let go of his cloak. Recovering, she leaned over him and stared into eyes filled with pain. His jaw was quivering with effort to control it. Stupidly, all she could manage was, "You're awake! We thought you were dead!"

His eyes focused on her face, and despite his clenched teeth he managed a faint smile and replied, "I think I was, and I liked it there – except the scenery here is better."

The Lady Dalene blushed at that. It was unheard of for anyone to assume such a manner with the daughter of the Regent. But she decided to overlook his indiscretion. He was obviously in pain and probably delirious. She said, "You were badly hurt. I tried to heal your injuries. You've been unconscious. Now that you are awake, I'll get you some medicine. If you can keep it down it should help with the pain. I'll be right back."

His nod was almost imperceptible but he didn't attempt to speak. Reaction was setting in and he was beginning to shake more by the minute. He tried to relax and pace his breathing. He tried to not think too much about his unresponsive arms. One thing at a time.

The Lady Dalene rushed into the house and yelled, almost triumphantly, "He's awake! He spoke to me!" Then remembering her station, she calmed almost immediately, but couldn't help smiling as she addressed the stunned faces in the room, "Our patient is awake, but he's in a great deal of pain. I need the infusions we prepared. Now that he's awake, he should be able to take a strong dose to control the pain."

Alicia rushed to grab the two bottles from the hearth, and everyone turned to follow her out to the shed, but she halted them at the doorway, "He's still very ill. We can't all go rushing in there. I'd like no more than two people with him at a time, but I also want at least one person there all the time. Alicia, would you come with me for now? Marcus, we will be removing the stones, and I'd like to have them heated again. There is still the risk of shock, and we must keep him warm."

Marcus nodded that he understood.

Re-entering the shed, The Lady Dalene paused to smooth her dress. Composing herself, she moved to kneel by the patient again, and saw that he was having a difficult time controlling his shaking. Quickly, she administered the two medications to him, and sat to wipe his face with a cool cloth, waiting and hoping for the medicine to take effect. She could tell it was beginning to work when she saw the tightness gradually leave his jaw. At last she said, "Are you feeling better?"

He closed his eyes, and nodded. The relief was beginning to spread throughout his body. He said, "I can't move my arms."

The Lady Dalene said, "I'm sorry. We covered you with warm rocks. They're cooled now, and we're going to remove them, but they may need to be replaced. You must be kept warm."

The two women began to remove the rocks, depositing them near the door. Colin felt tremendous relief as he found he could move his arms.

Stiffly, painfully, but they moved. The Lady Dalene said, "We'll leave them off for a little bit, while they're warming, but we may need to put them back if you begin to chill again."

Colin just nodded his thanks, conserving his strength.

"Now that you're awake, let me make introductions. This is Alicia. She has been assisting me with your care." Alicia nodded to him, and he returned the gesture as best he could. Hesitating, The Lady Dalene continued, "And I……..am Dalene."

Alicia shot her a sharp look, which she pretended not to notice. For the life of her, she could not explain why she had introduced herself without the title that was hers by right. She tried to tell herself that she didn't want to upset the patient in his weakened state. But even as she told herself that, she knew that she lied. For some reason, just for today, she didn't want to be The Lady Dalene, known throughout all Aidon. Today, she wanted to be simply, Dalene.

Colin spoke, in a hoarse, weak voice, "Thank you Alicia, and thank you Dalene. I feel like I'm returned from the dead."

Alicia involuntarily started when Colin had addressed her mistress as "Dalene," but she smiled kindly, and said, "You were badly hurt. Do you remember how it happened?"

His brow furrowed with the effort to recall, "Not sure. I was in the water………the ocean I think. I hit my head coming ashore. I walked. I didn't think my hands were too bad, but they must have gotten infected. Beyond that, I don't remember."

Dalene thought for a minute. What he said seemed to confirm her suspicions. He had been in the ocean, and it very well could have been at the forbidden place, but how had he gotten there? What he was doing there? She asked, "What's your name?"

"Colin Ericsson." He replied.

"What city are you from?"

He hesitated before answering, remembering the twin moons, "The city is called Kalispell."

Dalene's face froze, and she looked at him with a neutral expression. "There is no such city in Aidon."

He shook his head, "No. I'm not from Aidon. Kalispell is far from here. I don't know how far. I remember being in the water, but I have no memory of the journey or how I came to be here. I'm sorry."

She was not satisfied, but softened for a moment, "Your pain, it is better? Are you hungry?"

"The pain is better – manageable at least. And yes, I'm starved. Haven't eaten in days."

She nodded and said, "We'll change the dressing on your arms, and then get you something to eat. Miran made soup, but I think we will only let you have the broth to begin with."

The Lady Dalene was perplexed. Colin was asleep. He had eaten a little and they had changed the dressing on his arms. The swelling was noticeably improved. The angry discoloration would take time to fade, but even that was looking better. He would be weak for some time, but she felt sure he would recover. That was not what bothered her. "Kalispell," she murmured to herself. The name felt strange on her tongue. She had never heard of this place. He was an outlander, but that was impossible unless he was from their enemies, Kernsidon. She had not asked him about his mantle. She told herself it was because he was still too weak. Yes, he was weak, but for a matter of such importance, she knew she should have raised the issue, yet she could find no sense of urgency within herself. And then she thought of his eyes, and was disturbed once again. Before, when his eyes had opened for that brief moment, she was sure that they were a pale green. But today they had looked blue. How could his eyes change color like that? And why were they colored at all? Thinking about it made her very uneasy, but they were so……pretty. There was something almost hypnotic about them.

His appearance was strange. While she had never seen the Kernsidonians, she had never heard them described thus. She was sure they could not be so different. After all, did not both nations come from common parents? Despite his tan, she could see that his skin was fair. But his hair! How could it be so light? And impossibly, it had different shades – almost completely different colors! Underneath it was light brown, lighter than any of her people, but on top, it was lighter still, but not uniform. It ran in streaks of light. Where could he be from? And why was he <u>here</u>? She released a drawn out sigh. She had gone over these questions a hundred times, and there were no answers. She must question him further.

Alicia was out sitting with Colin in the shed, simply watching him as he slept. She had been instructed to come and fetch The Lady Dalene if he should awaken. Miran was tidying up her kitchen. She was flushed, genuinely pleased with all the activity in her home, while Jorge seemed to hover in the background, uncomfortable with so many strangers of high station about. Veret was talking with Elam, and it was obvious the boy was completely taken by this dashing figure from the 5th File, who was willing to share so much of his attention and seemed to accept him as an equal. The Lady Dalene smiled at the two young men, and then suddenly remembered. Alicia had told her that today was Elam's birthday. The Lady Dalene quietly excused herself, and went out to rummage in her belongings. She found what she was looking for, and went back into the house, calling, "Elam, may I speak with you please?"

Elam immediately left his conversation with Veret, and approached, bowing as he did so. "Yes, Lady, may I be of assistance?" Miran and Jorge watched with some apprehension. They still couldn't get used to the idea of one of the 12th File in their house – and speaking to their son.

"Elam, I understand that today is your 15th birthday, is it not?" Elam only nodded. "Then please accept this gift, not only for your birthday, but as a token of my thanks for making the journey to Salem last night. It was important, and you did well." With that she handed Elam a fine knife in a heavy canvas sheathe. This was not an ornate decoration for court, but a functional blade of fine steel.

Elam accepted it, and stood staring at the blade. He glanced at his parents, who stared in wide-eyed amazement of their own. His eyes dropped and he extended the gift back to her. "I cannot accept. I did nothing, and it is too fine a gift."

"Elam," she said softly, "The gift is given because I wish to do so, as a token of my esteem and my appreciation."

Elam again glanced at his parents, and received an encouraging smile from his mother and a nod from his father. "Then I thank you Lady. I shall cherish it always." And he knew that this birthday, above all others, he would remember for his entire life.

Colin slept through the late afternoon, and all through the night. At daybreak, he awoke, feeling weak, but surprisingly well rested. His fever had broken and though his arms were wrapped they were unrestrained by the heavy rocks. He rolled over quietly, and managed to get unsteadily to his feet. "Head rush!" he whispered to himself. Not until his head cleared did he notice the blanketed form lying in the hay close by. The Lady Dalene had not stirred as he had arisen, and he was reluctant to wake her. He picked up his boots with difficulty, his fingers stiff and awkward. Quietly he slipped out the door of the shed. He was unsteady on his feet, and felt grimy. His mouth was dry, and he knew that he looked a mess. Bands of yellow and pink showed the silhouettes of distant hills. The morning was cool and calm, and birds were chirping in the surrounding woods. Behind the shed, over towards the house he found a small spring lined with rocks trickling past a corner of the livestock pen. There was a basin and a towel set on a wooden bench at the side of the spring. He knelt and drank deeply before filling the basin with water, removing his shirt and washing his hair, face and upper body. The hands were still discolored with pale red and blue streaks fading to yellow. But these only extended to below the elbow. His head hurt, and he gingerly explored the wound as he washed it, but it too seemed to be healing nicely. He refilled the basin with fresh water, and washed his shirt as best he could before hanging it on a nail behind the shed to dry. He then sat heavily on the bench by the spring, having exhausted his meager strength in the simple act of washing, but he felt better. The cool air felt good on his arms and chest.

The sun had just peeked above the hills, and he was enjoying its warmth. He was hungry, but didn't know if anyone was awake in the house, and was reluctant to disturb these people who had already done so much for him. He knew they had probably saved his life. And that brought his attention back to a major problem. Where was he? The woman, Dalene, had said he was in Aidon. That meant nothing to him. But he had noticed a sudden chill when he had said he was not from there. Looking around, at what he could see of the farm, he was puzzled further. The house and shed were made of square-cut logs, very sturdy, and finely crafted. Growing up in Montana, he had worked at a log home business for awhile – peeling logs. This craftsmanship was far better than anything he had seen. There was very little caulking. He remembered the lantern in the shed, and noticed that there was no evidence of electricity on the premises. He could see two wooden carts and a fairly large wagon. The wheels were rimmed with iron, but there was no sign of a motorized vehicle of any kind. Again he wondered, "Where am I? Or is 'when am I?' a better question?"

His thoughts turned to the people he had met or seen. Without exception, all had been of a darker complexion, similar to the people he had worked with on the island of Sicily. He nodded at the thought, and realized that they did all have a very "Mediterranean" appearance. Their hair had ranged from dark brown to black. He didn't know about the others, but Dalene's eyes had also been a beautiful shade of brown. Her skin was tan, with a hint of the olive complexion that the Sicilians were noted for. They were shorter than he was, though the men were sturdily built. His engineering perspective told him to not draw conclusions until he had a larger sample size, and he grinned at the analytical thought concerning his strange predicament. But all told, he felt good. He was grateful to be alive – a feeling, he noted, that he hadn't had in some time. He thought that maybe he should get his shirt back on, but he was content for the moment to let it dry further while he enjoyed the morning sun on his skin.

Just then, a figure rushing around the edge of the shed drew his attention. With the sun just over the distant hills silhouetting her perfectly, Colin thought he had never seen anyone look so much like an angel before. His breath caught, and for just a moment the face of his deceased wife filled his mind, but for the life of him he couldn't say why, as Rita and Dalene looked nothing alike. Dalene skidded to a sudden stop, looking a little disheveled and very confused. Colin thought she looked very pretty with her hair still tangled from the night and bits of hay decorating it in a haphazard manner. The look of alarm left her face immediately, replaced by a cool sort of detachment as she regarded him. She saw him sitting there, face on to the sun, and was amazed at how pale his skin was with his shirt removed. She felt foolish, running around the corner that way, and knew that she must look a mess, but she erased all expression from her face and simply said, "You shouldn't be up. I was worried that something had happened to you."

"I'm sorry. You were resting so peacefully, I didn't have the heart to disturb you. You've already lost more sleep over me than you should. I was awake, and just couldn't lay there any longer. It was a beautiful morning to watch the sunrise, and I needed to clean up. It felt like something had crawled in my mouth and died."

Dalene was confused at the reference. "You are not well? There is something in your mouth? Quickly, let me see!"

Colin smiled, "No. I'm sorry. It's just an expression. After being ill for so long I just needed to clean up and rinse out my mouth. I feel much better now."

Relieved, she replied, "Your speech is strange. I can understand you, but it is different. I'm glad to see you are doing better. Are you in pain? Do you feel like you could eat?"

Colin nodded, "I'm starved. The pain is better, but if something were offered for it, I'd not turn it down." He arose and went to retrieve his shirt or sweatshirt.....whatever it was. He grabbed it by the hood and shook it out, and slipped it on over his head. It lacked buttons, but had a lacing through a series of holes to gather it and tie it across his chest. It was still slightly damp, but not uncomfortably so. The hood had wound up on his head as he pulled it on. He slipped it off as he turned to face Dalene. She looked at him strangely, and had paled noticeably. "Are you OK?" he asked.

"OK? I am Dalene. Have you forgotten?"

Realizing his error, Colin said, "No. I'm sorry. Again, it is just an expression from my......land." He finished lamely. "It just means, 'good' or 'all right.'"

Dalene cocked her head prettily to the side, and tried the unfamiliar phrase. "OK. Good. Yes, I am, as you say, I am OK."

Colin laughed, for the first time since he had arrived here, he noted, and said, "Yes. I think you are."

Dalene smiled with him and said, "You are hungry. I'm sure the others are awake. We will go in the house and fix you something to eat."

Colin followed her into the house. Alicia was helping Miran prepare breakfast. Jorge and Elam were sitting at the table planning their work for the day. Both jumped to their feet when The Lady Dalene entered, and their eyes widened when they saw Colin. All of them bowed in their direction, and Colin assumed they were bowing to Dalene, but he bowed deeply in their direction as well. He had spent several months working at various semiconductor companies in Japan, so the custom of bowing was not foreign to him. Eyes in the room widened at his return bow, but nobody said anything. Dalene seemed puzzled by his gesture, and was about to speak, but then thought better of it and made introductions. "Colin, you have already met Alicia," who nodded and smiled at him. "This home and the farm belong to Miran and Jorge. They have been most kind in providing assistance." They both nodded to him as well. Then she turned to Elam, "This is Elam, son of Jorge and Miran. It was he who found you the other evening when you collapsed in their field."

Colin stepped forward and extended his hand to Elam, who looked at it strangely, and then took it hesitantly, unaccustomed to shaking hands with any of a higher File. "Elam, thank you for helping me. I remember seeing you there in the field. I'm sure I surprised you, but I think you saved my life."

Embarrassed, Elam said, "No. All I did was run for help."

"If you hadn't run for help, I would have died. Thank you. I appreciate what you did."

Colin was suddenly self-conscious, realizing everyone was staring at him. Miran relieved the tension, saying, "Please. We have forgotten our manners. Be seated. You are still not well."

Colin sat gratefully, as he was still feeling a bit unsteady on his feet. The food smelled wonderful. Soon, plates were set and the six of them crowded at a table that would obviously have been more comfortable for four. The food was good, and there was lots of it. Colin ate slowly, knowing the dangers of taking in too much after having had so little to eat for so many days. Eggs, he recognized. There was some kind of fried meat, and a large bowl of mush, similar to oatmeal. It was flavorless, but everyone else was eating it, so he hoped it was nourishing. He was so focused on breakfast, that he was quite unaware he was being stared at. The Lady Dalene, however, was very aware of the attention directed at him, and finally cleared her throat loudly to get the others to stop staring, but that was precisely what made Colin note that he was the focus of five sets of eyes. He paused with his spoon halfway to his mouth. "What? Am I doing something wrong?"

Elam blurted, "His eyes are blue!"

"Green," his mother corrected him.

Colin looked around the table. Everyone was still staring at him, but as he looked at each set of eyes, he realized that they were all brown and very dark. This didn't surprise him, as he had already noted the similarity to the Sicilians. But it was obvious that his eye color was shocking to his hosts. He smiled, and his face was quite transformed. Colin rarely showed much emotion, except with family and close friends. He had a certain air of detachment. Over the years, his lack of emotional display and the intensity with which he tended to analyze problems, both in his profession and in regards to life in general, had created a crease between his eyes, giving him a slightly angry, intimidating appearance to those who didn't know him. But when he smiled, that crease suddenly disappeared and his face lit up. He smiled now, and looked full on at each face in turn. "It's OK. I mean, that's alright. I don't mind. In my land, we call this color of eyes 'hazel.' Depending on the light and the angle you view them from, they appear to be kind of a light green ranging to a light blue, or so I've been told."

Embarrassed now, they muttered apologies, except for Alicia, who continued to stare. Willing to accommodate her, Colin stared back. Finally she said enviously, "They're so pretty! I wish I had eyes that color!"

Teasing, Miran said, "You should wish Marcus had eyes that color. If you had them, you couldn't see them and wouldn't enjoy them nearly as much as you would if Marcus had them!" Everyone laughed, and the moment's tension was broken.

Colin felt much better after breakfast. He was still tired and weak, but he definitely felt like he was on the road to recovery. He attempted to help with the breakfast clean-up, but none of the women would hear of it. Jorge and Elam headed off to the fields. Colin went outside to sit in the sun, on the bench by the spring. He still wanted the chance to bathe more thoroughly, but for now he was content to just sit. Soon, Dalene came and joined him. He scooted over and invited her to sit. She seemed uncertain, but accepted. The bench was small, so their legs almost, but not quite, touched.

Dalene began, "Colin, we need to talk. There are important matters to discuss." Colin simply looked at her expectantly, willing to let her continue.

"Your appearance here has created a great deal of excitement. By your own admission, you are not of Aidon, and you don't know how you got here. That is going to create suspicion among some people. Your physical appearance is unusual. There will be no hiding that you are a stranger. Strangers are uncommon, and none like you has ever been seen. That too, will be cause for suspicion."

Colin still said nothing. She seemed to be building up to something, but he had no idea what. Hesitating, she then continued. "Your clothing is also strange. It is all white. You do not wear any color on the hem or border to identify the File to which you belong. That is not lawful and we must correct that immediately. What File are you part of?"

"I don't know what you mean by 'File.' I told you, I'm not from this land. I don't belong to a File that I know of."

"All people belong to a File. Even the Kernsidonians are organized and ruled by Files. There are four Files in each Order. There are three Orders. Each file is ruled by twelve Councilors. The Chief Councilor from each File has a seat on the High Council in Salem. All people are represented so no File may dominate any other File, so all are equal. You must belong to a File!"

Colin realized that he could be in serious trouble, if he fell outside of the established order. But at the same time, it was hard to not be a little bit amused by the frustration, almost desperation that Dalene was displaying as she lectured him on the government of Aidon. Trying not to smile, he said, "I'm sorry. I've told you the truth. I'm unfamiliar with your customs and government. I don't belong to a File. But you're also upset because my clothing is white. Why is that?"

Dalene stamped her foot in frustration, then caught herself. Such emotional displays were not befitting her. She tried to calm herself, but her eyes were angry as she continued. "Each File is assigned a color. The clothing of that File must conform to the assigned color. The 1st File is black. The 8th File is red. The 12th is purple. Not that the entire garment must be of the assigned color, but it must be displayed. That is how we know one's station, and we know to offer honor to those of the higher Files. You wear no color!"

Colin shrugged and said, "Then that supports what I told you. I belong to no File. I have no color on my clothing. I've worn colors in the past, in my country, but that was a matter of personal preference. It had no meaning in regards to social status."

Stubbornly, Dalene said, "It is not permitted!"

"Can't help you there. If it will make you feel better, maybe I can get some clothing here that conforms to your dress code."

"You cannot just wear clothing because it suits you!"

Colin couldn't help it. It just slipped out, "Well, I can't just not wear clothing because it suits *you* either!"

She was shocked. How could he joke about not wearing clothing? And with one who was not his mate! Especially with one who was the daughter of the Regent! And then, in spite of herself, she laughed at his look of wide-eyed innocence, and his eyes crinkled up in a smile. She was perplexed. Why was he being so difficult?

"Colin, you must understand. Aidon has been ruled in this manner for thousands of years. Have you never been through your Evaluation? None has ever tested you to see what File you belong to?"

"I have no idea what you mean by an 'Evaluation.' I'm familiar with the term. I've been involved in a great many 'evaluations,' but not with the intent of assigning me to a File. I'm sorry."

She decided to let this go for now. "There is still a matter of greater concern." Now she hesitated, but finally asked, "By what right do you wear the mantle?"

"I have no idea what you are referring to."

Her anger, which she thought she had suppressed, immediately boiled back to life, "You cannot pretend! You wear the mantle! Right here!" And she impulsively reached over his shoulder and grabbed the hood and shoved it right in his face!

"A hood? You're mad at me because my jacket has a hood on it? Are you nuts?"

Momentarily put off by the unfamiliar expression, she said, "Nuts?"

"Sorry, I mean, that's crazy. What taboo am I violating by having a hood on my jacket?"

She clenched her teeth and closed her eyes, trying to steady her breathing and get her anger under control once again. Finally, in a calm tone one might use to lecture a small child caught in mischief, she said, "The mantle is a symbol of the messenger of the Most High. None but the messenger of Messias may wear the mantle. All who wear the mantle must appear before the High Council in Salem for Evaluation. If it is found that the one wearing the mantle wears it not by right, then he is a pretender, a deceiver and not the messenger of God and the High Council will exercise a Compulsion to destroy him!"

"Dalene," he said softly, "I'm not a messenger from God. It's just a jacket or cloak or shirt. Whatever you want to call it. It's what I was wearing when I washed up from the ocean. I'm not from here. Please understand, I do believe in God. I'm not sure if I believe in quite the same way that you do. I don't know anything about your belief system. But I believe that He is real and that He has a plan and a purpose for each of us, but I am not His messenger, not the way you mean. I'm sorry if I am not wearing the right thing. Tell me what you want me to do."

She just stared at him. Believing him. But that didn't make it any easier. Tears of frustration collected in her eyes, and she clenched them tightly shut to keep them from falling down her cheeks. The disappointment was bitter. She had hoped that he was indeed a messenger. It had been so long! To be alive when the Highest once more gave direction to his people! Colin's appearance was different enough, it would have been easy to believe. If he were an impostor, she would have the anger to give her strength to do what must be done. But he was neither. By his own admission, he was no messenger, but in admitting it so freely, casually even, it was obvious that he was no deceiver. Was it so easy for him to set aside the mantle, if she were but to request it? But it didn't matter.

"It's too late for that. You were seen. You have been reported to the Council in Salem. I came here to learn who and what you are and to summon you to the Evaluation by the Council. If you do not wear the mantle by right, you will be destroyed."

Colin was silent. "They will kill me?"

She shook her head, "No. They do not kill. Our history says that long ago, perhaps then they used the Compulsion to kill. Maybe what they do now is worse. The combined power of each of the Twelve Files will be brought to bear............on you. They will probe your mind, they must find your true-self, your core, where the real you, your essence, exists. There they will see if you are a messenger from the Most High. If they find any fault, any weakness, they will know you are an impostor. They will focus all their will on your true-self, and you will simply cease to be. Your body will go on living, breathing, but you have no will. You will have no thought. You will do what you are commanded to do by whomever commands you. Those who are destroyed in the Compulsion are not..........that is, by our law they do not exist. Usually they are completely and totally ignored. With no one to tell them when to eat, when to rest, when to take shelter, they simply waste away, and their body dies. Sometimes, someone will take them as a slave. They will order them because the lost one will always obey. It used to be that those who took charge of one who was destroyed would order them to do things so terrible or dangerous that the body soon died. Our law does not permit this, but in the long ago, the writings say that this was done. Before the Compliance, criminals would be treated thus and used as weapons in war. They were fearsome, because they knew no fear. They had no life, but they had to be killed. This is no longer done, but it was once. Now, if one is destroyed, perhaps the family will still care for them, in memory of who they once were. Usually, however, the shame is so great that the family will also reject them and they are left to perish."

Colin sat quietly, trying to absorb what he'd been told. He knew he was in serious trouble. He didn't pretend to understand all of this, but he had traveled the world – his world – enough to know that the local customs didn't have to make sense, and an outsider who came up on the wrong side of the local customs didn't stand a whole lot of chance changing them by claiming the rule didn't apply to him. "So, if I understand correctly: First, I'm in trouble because I'm an outsider. I'm too tall, too light and my hair and eyes are the wrong color."

Dalene only nodded.

"Second, I should have had some color on the edge of my coat, and because I don't, I don't fit in anywhere in Aidon.

"Third, I made a big mistake when I wore a jacket with a hood – a mantle as you call it – instead of just bringing a hat with me! Does that pretty much cover it?"

Dalene nodded again and said, "I can't think of anything to do. Believe me, if I could, I would." And she placed her hand on his as she said it.

Colin just stared at her hand. It had been a long time since anyone had shown that level of personal concern for him, and it sent a jolt through him. With no solution to his dilemma coming readily to mind, he just shrugged and said, "Alright. So when am I supposed to go to my Evaluation?"

She brightened somewhat at the question, and said, "That is one thing I can help with. The Evaluation can only be held at the full moon. That is just past. I can delay your Evaluation for three moons. That gives us 85 days. Maybe we can think of something before then. Is there anything I can do for you now, anything you need?"

"Yes. Is there someplace I can go to have a bath?"

At that, Dalene laughed out loud.

The bath, it turned out, consisted of several buckets of cold water and no soap. Still, he was able to clean both himself and his clothes more thoroughly than his brief wash at the spring that morning. Afterwards, he asked if he might borrow a razor, as his beard stubble was beginning to bother him. Miran had scissors with which she trimmed Jorge's hair and beard, but the idea of a razor for fully removing facial hair seemed novel to them, and explaining that it was the custom for most of the men in his country made it no less strange to them. Veret Lev, in particular seemed especially amused at the concept, but in the end, it was he who donated an especially fine stiletto blade for that purpose. Colin asked for shaving soap, but even the concept of 'soap' seemed unheard of. In the end, Colin had to shave with great care, and considerable discomfort, using a piece of polished metal for a mirror. He only nicked himself twice, which caused Veret to laugh and comment, "An interesting ritual in your land, my friend, where a man must cut his own throat on a daily basis to be accepted by his peers!"

Dalene eyed him critically, and then pronounced her approval. She thought it suited his fair skin and light hair nicely. For some reason, Colin was pleased.

Chapter 5   Outsider

For the next two days, Colin rested and began to recover his strength. He was fascinated by everything, no matter how insignificant. Each day brought new experiences and new surprises. He had largely given up trying to figure out the "How" and "Why" of his situation, and instead just immersed himself in it and tried to learn all he could. Marcus and Alicia shared a tent while Councilor Rabin returned to Salem. Jorge and Miran were over the initial shock of having The Lady Dalene in their house, but were still adjusting to finding her to be so approachable and considerate. Indeed, they had grown increasingly fond of her, and a close friendship was springing up between the two women. For his part, Colin was content sleeping in the shed. It was quiet and gave him a certain degree of privacy. The barn was located about 30 yards away. There was a poultry shed for chickens and ducks. Two oxen had their own sturdy corral and three-sided shelter in a small clearing. Colin was amazed at the massive size of the beasts. He had heard once that the true American Ox, the one famed for plowing up the sod of the mid-west and hauling wagons across the plains, was extinct. But these were about what he had always imagined them to be like. They were huge, but very docile. The horses, however, amazed him the most. They were unlike any "horses" he had ever seen. True, they had some equine features, especially through the head and face. But from the neck on back, if anything they seemed much more like the elk which he was familiar with in Montana, though significantly larger. They were lighter boned than most horses he had worked with back home. But they were tall and had powerful hindquarters. They were big enough to ride comfortably, he thought, but the way they moved was again more like elk, and he figured it would be a challenge to adjust to their gait.

By the second day, Colin was spending time in the garden despite Miran and Dalene's objections that he wasn't strong enough. Miran was planting a variety of crops. He recognized many of the seeds, or at least he thought that he did. There was also an orchard, but the blossoms had fallen and the fruit too immature to tell for sure what differences or similarities they might have to what he was familiar with. He thought that he recognized cherry, apple, plum and pear trees. He had always loved trees, and the forest fascinated him. The forest surrounding the small house and accompanying fields seemed largely to consist of deciduous hardwoods. There were a few evergreens scattered about, but they were a definite minority. He recognized oaks, beech, maple, ash and chestnut. Others he recognized, but couldn't name. While the familiar or similar things were comforting, the unfamiliar was puzzling. He couldn't quite come to think of anything as "alien." The word just didn't fit. He had traveled enough back on earth to be fairly comfortable with new experiences, and that is how he thought of this, simply accepting it. The whole thing fascinated him. Of course he hadn't forgotten about the Evaluation. Never a day went by that Elam didn't express some excitement about his Evaluation. He was counting the days – 22 to be precise. Colin's excitement certainly didn't match Elam's, but then the outcome was expected to be considerably different as well. The idea of running, as soon as he regained his strength, had crossed his mind, but he just couldn't seem to get serious about the thought. Maybe later, but right now there was just too much new to see and learn.

Late in the afternoon, they had a visitor. He came walking up the forest path as Colin was sitting by the spring. It was his favorite spot to rest. The gurgling of the water was peaceful and he enjoyed watching it flow over rocks and through the corner of the pen by the shed. He was unaware that anyone was near until a voice called out, "Greetings! Have I come to the farm of Jorge and Miran of Tyber?"

Colin arose from the wooden bench and turned to see a young man, probably in his mid to early 20's, clothed in rather coarse attire. His cloak was open, and Colin could see that both the cloak and heavy shirt he wore underneath were edged in a lavender trim, as was the light pack which he carried. Like all of the others he had met, Colin noted that his hair was dark as was his complexion. The beard and moustache were full, though close cropped. He was a striking young man, exuding confidence and an air of command. Colin said, "Yes. I believe Jorge is working his fields with his son. Miran was out back in her garden the last I saw her."

The young man approached, giving Colin an indifferent bow, which Colin returned more deeply, causing the younger man to raise an eyebrow questioningly. "You are the stranger. The one who wears the mantle."

Statements, not questions, Colin noted. He smiled faintly and replied, "I am, I fear, guilty as charged."

This in turn brought a grim smile to the face of the young man, but he appeared to relax. "Forgive me. I am Halvor, Arbor Guard of Aidon."

"Colin Ericsson, lately of Kalispell." He heard the door to the house bang open, and just then Dalene came around the corner of the house. She froze momentarily, staring at the two men facing each other. Then with a squeal of delight she ran forward, "Halvor!" she cried, throwing her arms around him.

"Dalene! It's good to see you! Are you well?" And he lifted her completely off her feet and swung her around. Suddenly embarrassed, they both became aware of Colin standing there, and hastily released each other, backing away a pace. Dalene said, "Colin, may I present Halvor, Arbor Guard of Aidon."

"Thank you, we've just met, replied Colin, a little surprised by the affection exhibited between these two.

Turning back to Halvor, Dalene asked, "What are you doing here? I thought you were on station for at least another six moons."

Halvor shrugged and said, "We'll discuss that – privately," giving a meaningful glance in Colin's direction.

Colin smiled politely and said, "I've probably spent too much time here being lazy already. I'll go see if Miran needs any help in the garden." Dalene started to say something, but abruptly closed her mouth and took Halvor by the arm and led him toward the orchard.

Colin found Miran and coaxed her into assigning him a few chores to do. He recognized the strawberry plants, and spent a quiet couple of hours pinching off the runners until he was called for the evening meal, which seemed subdued. Nobody did much talking. After the dishes were cleared and the cleaning done, Dalene asked Colin to sit while she and Halvor joined him. She was obviously uncomfortable, as she began, "Colin, As you know Halvor has come from Salem today. He has been assigned by the High Council to assist you during your period of recovery."

She looked at him guiltily, but then continued, "Messengers were dispatched from Tyber to Salem both yesterday and today. The Council felt it would be best to have someone assigned to……..help, if you should need it. As an indication of the……concern felt by the Council, Halvor has been released from his other responsibilities for the time being."

Colin considered this. He suspected that Halvor was assigned to be something more than an "assistant," but as there was nothing to be done about it he simply said, "I'm grateful for the Council's concern and appreciate any help Halvor can give."

Halvor simply nodded slightly, and gave Colin a tight smile, conveying neither warmth nor humor. The conversation died, so Colin excused himself and retired to the shed for the night.

At breakfast the third day Dalene announced that she would be returning to Salem that afternoon, accompanied by all of her party. She said, "Colin, Jorge and Miran have agreed to have you to stay here while you recover. The Council has arranged to take care of any expenses they incur, so you will not have to work and you can focus on regaining your strength. Halvor will be here, and he will see to such matters. If there is anything else you need, don't hesitate to ask him. He will, I am sure, be most helpful." She shot Halvor a hard look while she said this, and Halvor responded with a smile akin to a smirk.

"That is very kind of you." Turning to Jorge and Miran, he said, "And I thank you for your hospitality. You've already done too much. But I'm afraid I can't stay…." Immediately voices were raised in objection, but he raised a hand to silence them. "I can't stay at the expense of the Council and without working. I need to work. I know I'm unfamiliar with much of your labor, but there must be something I can do. Perhaps I can help Elam, but I want to work."

Miran looked skeptical, while Jorge looked pleased. Elam looked positively ecstatic. Dalene, however, looked entirely unhappy. "You need time to recover. If you overdo it, you could wind up worse than you were when I got here! In the entire history of the world, you are the only person we know of who has survived the ocean sickness! You must rest!"

"I'll rest, but I will also work. Since I'm the only person in the history of the world to survive the ocean sickness, I don't think a little bit of work is going to kill me."

Jorge outright smiled, while Dalene rolled her eyes in exasperation.

"Elam, how about you show me what chores you do around here. Maybe an old cripple can do enough to help pay for his breakfast today."

Colin winked at the others while Elam grinned and led the way out the door.

After lunch, the carts were loaded and the horses hitched up. Dalene took Colin by the arm, escorting him away from the others. "We must talk. Colin, I don't think you understand how serious this is. You are taking it far too lightly. I've been trying to figure out how to get you out of this. I believe you. I've watched you. Things here are so unfamiliar to you. But we must think of something or you will be worse than dead! I think the answer is that you must go away. Regain your strength, but several days before the Evaluation, you must run. Don't wait too long, because I think they will expect that, and you will be watched. I've spoken to Miran. She has agreed to provide you with food. I can't tell you where to go. No place in Aidon will be safe. But you must leave here. You must run!"

Colin smiled, grateful for her concern. "I don't think it will work."

"It will work! It's the only way! You have to try!"

"I've thought about it, but I don't think running is the answer. That's why it won't work. It won't work because I don't intend to do it."

"Then what will you do? You yourself have said that you are not the messenger of The Highest. You have no choice!"

"I don't know. There will be plenty of time to panic. For now I just want to see how it goes. I was taught a long time ago, 'Don't worry about the things that you can't change. And don't worry about the things you won't change. Save your worry and your strength for those things that you can and will change.' That's enough for now."

Dalene touched his hand lightly, "Colin, you will be careful, won't you? If you think of some way to avoid the Evaluation, you must do so. If you can think of nothing, you must run. Oh, I wish I had never come! I feel like I am somehow to blame for all this, and I can't repair it!"

"It's not your fault, so don't beat yourself up. If not for you I'd already be dead. I walked a long way to put myself in this mess. 'All will be as it should be.' I heard that somewhere. It will be OK"

She blinked back tears, and sniffed. "OK, yes. OK. You just make sure you think of something. Promise you'll try."

"I promise to try. You promise not to worry." She just shook her head, and he escorted her back to the cart, and offered her a hand up onto the box seat.

"Safe journey, Lady Dalene."

She shot him a sharp look, wondering who had revealed her title to him. The fact was, nobody had, but he had heard her addressed thus, and used the title now as a sign of respect. Marcus and Alicia occupied the box of the other cart. Veret hoisted himself up beside The Lady Dalene and took up the reins. She looked back just once, to see him still standing there looking after them.

The return to Salem was largely silent. Marcus and Alicia tried to engage The Lady Dalene in conversation, but her answers were perfunctory, and it was obvious that she was distracted, so they desisted. Officially, Marcus and Alicia were servants - employed by the house of Tregard as "expediters." Between them, they had friends and contacts in every File, every Guild and most of the families of note in Salem. Unofficially, they were as close to friends as The Lady Dalene had. The daughter of the Regent did not have friends. She was envied for the perceived advantages and power that she held, and she was feared for the same reasons. Even those who tried to use her for political advantage maintained a healthy span of social and emotional distance. She, or one like her, was the substance of prophecy, and that prophecy foretold the destruction of Aidon.

For over 4000 years, it had been thus. Each of her sister-ancestors before her had known the same loneliness, and they had borne it without complaint, as would she. Each had lived out her existence, relieved in a way, when death finally claimed them, that they had not been the instrument which had brought about the end of Aidon. Even as each had finally accepted the blessed relief which death brought to them, their hearts had grieved, and had feared, knowing that the burden now lay solely, and unshared, on the shoulders of their surviving sister-descendent.

No one knew exactly when the Councils had established rule in Aidon. The records had been lost or destroyed. There had been Kings and Queens, once. Little was known of that time. They knew that some of the kings had been good, and the people had prospered under them. But others had been evil, holding the people as little more than slaves. Before the councils, there had been confusion, turmoil, war even. It was referred to now as The Chaos. Always, there had been someone seeking to become king. The first had been Kern, but he had lived long ago – during the time of their first parents. Kern had flattered many, promising them wealth and power if they would support him. There had been a battle. Kern had been driven out, along with his supporters. But he was not the last to lust for power. Over the ensuing millennia, there had been other conflicts. Countless thousands had died, some by the sword, even more from famine. It had been the House of Tregard which had marshaled the remaining forces and led the war which finally drove the tyrants from power, but the successors of Kern had received great strength over the centuries. Aidon could no longer afford internal conflict and hope to stand against her enemies from without. To eliminate such horrific conflict, the people had agreed to do away with kings and turn the government over to the Councils. The constant vying for prominence and power was eliminated through the expedient of the Evaluation and the establishment of the Files. Each File was assigned a city along with a few satellite villages. But the Council controlled all within the File. Twelve individuals, the strongest 12 men and women who could be found in each File comprised the Council. Their rank was determined through the Evaluation. No one knew exactly when or how the Box used in the Evaluation had come into being. It was said that they dated back to the beginning. There were only 12 Boxes in all of Aidon. Fourteen if one counted the two which were built as a permanent part of certain structures. One was in the Great Hall of the Praetorium, in Salem. The other was in the Great Hall of the Temple. There had been more, before The Chaos. How many Kern and his followers had escaped with was not known, and in any event, they were out of reach and no longer of consequence in Aidon. Each File had one, which they kept and guarded. The strongest, the best suited to govern, could cause all others to yield to them in the Evaluation. The 12 strongest in each file could, as a group, persuade all others within the File as to the wisdom of their governance. Conflict was thereby eliminated. By establishing Compliance, these 12 councilors could persuade any wayward individual to see the potential harm of actions they might contemplate. From the birth of a child to clearing additional farmland, the Councils gave guidance. Individuals inclined to engage in dangerous, unknown and unpredictable experimentation were brought to see the folly of their ways. And so there was harmony. Through the expedient of determining one's appropriate station in life, and helping each citizen fulfill that station, discord was eliminated. Peace reigned, and obedience was strictly adhered to.

Thus a system of order and peace was established, except with Kernsidon. Every generation or so, Kernsidon would raise an army and attack, but lacking the harmony and organization of Aidon, they had always been defeated with little difficulty. They were too selfish, concerned only with their own survival. The troops of Aidon easily cut through them to destroy their leaders. It had been a long time since they had dared attack, but The Lady Dalene knew they would come again, and she knew her father, was worried.

For close to 4000 years, the system had flourished. The people were healthy. All were provided for. The councils ensured through the Compliance, that the necessary functions were performed. The Files of the

1st Order were predominantly farmers and laborers. The 2nd Order handled administrative details and most of the guards came from these Files, as well as metal workers and some of the more skilled weavers. The 3rd Order produced scholars, artisans and healers. Most importantly, the 3rd Order governed. It was an ideal system. The Lady Dalene intended to ensure that it endured - at least through her lifetime, as she, like her sister-ancestors before her, dreaded the thought that she might be the tool of prophecy which would undo it all.

The Regent of Aidon was the head of the High Council. This was not to be confused with the City Council of Salem. The latter was composed of the 12 strongest minds of the 12th File, for Salem was the City of the 12th File. The High Council, consisted of the heads of each of the 12 Files. On the surface, it might appear that the Council of the 12th File might hold more power than the High Council, with its lower ranking members. However, there existed a symbiosis when the 12 files were thus represented. When the head of each of the Files took their respective places inside The Ruling Box of Aidon, located in the Great Hall of the Praetorium, their combined power far exceeded that of any of the other Councils, or, for that matter, all of the other Councils combined. Thus, at the highest level of government, every File was represented equally.

For 4000 years, The Highest Councilor of Salem had always had a daughter. He might have several sons, but he only ever had one daughter, and he always had one daughter. She of whom it was prophesied:

> *And if the daughter of the most high shall yield her heart, they shall be cast out. They shall become as one and shall destroy the ruler of this people.*

In all of Aidon, there might be many ladies, but there was only one Lady - the Lady of Prophecy. Her title, her mark, and a warning to all. She, and each of her sister-ancestors before her had feared to be the destroyer - the one who would destroy her own father and bring about the downfall of the government. And so, each had dedicated herself to the lonely task of building and strengthening the government, seeking any who would harm it and ensuring that they never had opportunity to carry out their plans. For the last 2000 years, there had been little enough of that. The Councils governed carefully. The people were content. There was no insurrection. And yet, the prophecy could not be ignored. To ensure that it would not come to pass, at least not in the lifetime of each fearful daughter, each had promised that she would never yield to her heart, or yield her heart to another. In that way, the prophecy was held at bay, and her father was kept safe. It was a lonely existence, but a small price to pay for the welfare of all Aidon. While The Lady of Prophecy might survive her father, the Regent, she never survived her successor's achieving adolescence. The burden was never shared. So The Lady Dalene had no friends. Friendship. Affection. These were avenues through which prophecy might crack the armor of her heart. And like her sister-ancestors before her, she swore that would never be allowed. Only in death would that title at last be laid aside, and she could rest simply as "Dalene," having forestalled the destruction of Aidon for one more generation.

Upon arrival in Salem, The Lady Dalene proceeded immediately to The Great Hall. So much had happened. She couldn't believe that it had all occurred in just the past three days. She must report to her father immediately. He had been away when news of the stranger had arrived. To consult with her father would have taken time, so she had acted at once. He would, of course, have been apprised of the situation upon his return to Salem. Even so, he would be anxious for her report. "Alicia," she asked, "would you check my father's schedule and find out when he can meet with me?"

Alicia bowed. The protocols in Salem, and especially here, in the Great Hall, were much more rigid than they were outside the city. The Lady Dalene had a momentary pang, wishing once again to be in Tyber, where things were slower and simpler. She retired to her quarters to prepare for the audience with her father. Her rooms were located in the south wing of the Praetorium. Here were living quarters not only for the Regent and his family, but for all of the High Council. Some did not keep their families here, since their positions required them to spend almost as much time in their home cities as in Salem. However, the wing was spacious, with ample room for families and visitors when the occasion required it. While not family, as special envoys to the House of Tregard, Marcus and Alicia shared quarters adjacent to those of The Lady Dalene. She bathed and did her hair, wondering at the delay. She was, she admitted, a little nervous, and it was not a feeling to which she was accustomed. Her father might not approve of her assuming responsibility for the delegation to Tyber. She sighed. He worked so hard to maintain the peace and prosperity of Aidon. Sometimes she wished that he would give her more responsibility to ease his load. He didn't seem to understand that the more she had to do, the lighter her own burden actually became, the one she could never put down.

There was a light knock at the door. "Enter." She called out.

Alicia came in, bowing once again. "Lady Dalene," she said formally, "I offer my apologies for the delay. Councilor Tregard was in conference when we arrived. I was asked to wait until he finished. Councilor Tregard has requested that you report to him in his office immediately."

"Thank you Alicia. I know you must be tired. I don't think I'll need you this evening." With that, The Lady Dalene set out for the west wing, where many government offices were located. The Praetorium was a masterpiece of art and architecture. The Great Hall itself could accommodate almost 5000 people. Columns, sculpture and painting adorned the walls and supported the balconies overlooking the central chamber. The four wings provided housing, offices, meeting rooms, storage and armory for the city, and by extension, for all of Aidon. The stables, located out back, were clean and well-maintained, providing carts or wagons for any of the senior staff conducting government business. Her father's office was located on the third floor of the west wing. Pausing briefly at the door, she composed herself and then knocked.

"Enter!" The booming voice commanded.

As she stepped in the room, she was embraced in a bear-hug by her father, who swept her completely off her feet. "Dalene! I've been worried! So what great adventure drew you away in such haste that you couldn't wait to consult with your old father, eh?"

There were perhaps two men in all of Aidon who so carelessly abandoned her title. For a moment, she thought of another, and blushed at the memory. They both knew full well what adventure had pulled her away, but she played along, "Father! Put me down! I'm not a little girl anymore!"

He laughed, but set her down, "No, you're not a little girl anymore. So much the pity. Come, sit down. You must be tired. Are you hungry? Thirsty?" Indicating a tray with a pitcher and food.

"Later perhaps, after we've spoken." She eyed her father critically. He looked tired. Oh, he was always pleasant enough. It was a demeanor which had served him well throughout his years in office, but she knew there was a core of iron inside. He was tall. Not as tall as Colin, she thought, but few men in Aidon would be. His shoulders were broad, but he was also thickening through the middle, the result of too many formal dinners and late nights. Still, he was strong. She knew that. He was a master, no she corrected herself, he was <u>the</u> master of the Compliance. Physical strength was not his tool, but the power of his mind. His <u>will</u>. She shivered, unnoticed, knowing that her father's unmatched will would likely spell the end of Colin.

She smoothed her dress, delaying her report. Her father simply waited, looking on expectantly. Once she began, however, the words came out in a flood. "You have heard of the message we received in the evening hours four days ago. A young man from Tyber came bearing news of a stranger - strange in dress and appearance - who had collapsed on his father's farm. The stranger wore a hooded garment - a mantle - and his clothing bore no color of any file.

"Having received this word, and in the absence of the Regent - as well as several other members of the Council – I determined that a delegation should immediately be sent to Tyber to investigate. I took it upon myself to head the delegation. Haste was necessary due to the report of the stranger's ill health. It was feared that he might not live.

"We arrived before dawn. All was as had been reported. The stranger is unlike any seen or reported in Aidon. His hair is light and fine. Portions are much lighter than others. His eyes have color, as well! In some light they look almost a pale blue, while in other settings they appear almost to be green, like moss!"

Her father looked at her with raised eyebrows, head cocked to one side.

She paused, blushing, then continued. "His health was very poor. By all appearances, he was suffering from the ocean sickness. He…"

"Ocean sickness? Are you sure? None has ever survived the ocean sickness before, at least not in our records!"

The Lady Dalene nodded, "I was not certain, but the symptoms agreed with what I know of the ocean sickness. He later confirmed that he had been in the ocean, and the description of the area sounds very much like what I have been told of The Forbidden Place."

"But how could he have been cured? Was it a trick?" Her father asked.

She shook her head. "I do not believe it was a trick. I thought that he would die. I do not know how to explain his recovery. I acted as Healer."

At her father's look, she lifted her head defiantly, "I have been trained. I had Marcus bring the Healer's box. But with the ocean sickness, there was nothing to be done. At least, nothing that I had been trained with."

She hesitated, "I don't know how to explain it. I applied salt. Warm salt, to try and draw the poison, but there was no improvement and I had no hope. But then, it was like something whispered to me. It was from the old lessons - the salt, the oil and the maize - the symbols of the three Eternals."

She shook her head, "It was like something, someone, telling me what to do in order to heal him. I did it, and he was healed, but it wasn't me. It was something else."

"Dalene, that is enough. You must not speak of this. It reeks of prophecy, and you do not wear the mantle. Even I could not protect you from the Council if you spoke of this when unfriendly ears were listening. To prophesy without the mantle is no less a crime than to wear the mantle without bearing the message of prophecy. It is well that you told me, but you must not speak of this to anyone else. Are we agreed?"

She nodded, reluctantly, but did not think it wise to mention the presence of others during the healing.

"Alright, so this stranger - he was healed. Maybe it wasn't the ocean sickness, but something that looked like it. Go on. You spoke? Does he claim to be the messenger of Messias?"

The Lady Dalene hesitated, "Yes, we spoke. He was very weak at first, but he was soon up and around - sooner than I had believed possible. He is strange. Both in appearance and manner. He claims he is not from Aidon, and this I believe, because he is unlike any here. But I don't believe he could be from Kernsidon either. He is entirely ignorant of our laws and customs. When I questioned him regarding the lack of colors on his clothing, designating his File, he had no knowledge of what I was talking about. When I challenged him regarding wearing the mantle, he shrugged and offered to exchange his clothing for other! I was furious. His look. His manner. Everything was so different, I was certain that he must at least <u>claim</u> to wear the mantle by right, but he did exactly the opposite. He stated clearly, to me and in front of witnesses, that he is <u>not</u> the messenger of Messias. He has no understanding of the Evaluation. When I told him of his Evaluation before the High Council in three moons, I had to explain what that meant. Father, I do not believe him to be evil, nor do I believe that he will survive the Evaluation. It will destroy him, and I fear that we will destroy something good. Different from us, yes, but still good."

Gareth Tregard was troubled. For long minutes he considered. He knew his daughter well. He had spent most of her life preparing her for the role into which she had been cast. She was lovely and remarkably intelligent - insightful. She often saw the hidden agendas of others, and her advice had often helped to maintain peace in Aidon. He loved his daughter, but more importantly, he trusted her, for she had proven many times over to be worthy of that trust. He was at a loss as to how to proceed and yet preserve the life of this stranger while upholding their law, their custom, and ensuring the safety of Aidon. At length, he spoke. "Daughter, why did you schedule this Evaluation for three moons hence? Could you not have required his attendance at the next moon that we might conclude the matter? Much can happen in three moons time."

"I don't know why. Three moons is the maximum time permitted for the Evaluation of one suspected of a crime. I don't believe Colin will survive. It's obvious he lacks perfection. I wanted him to have life."

Gareth looked at his daughter closely. The fact that the stranger had a name did not escape him. "You don't mean to say you have feelings for this man, do you?"

"No!" she flushed, "Not like that. Colin is simply an innocent life who will be sacrificed to ensure that other innocent lives are not lost. But being with someone not from Aidon, someone whose eyes do not fill with caution when 'The Lady of Prophecy' enters a room.........He knows nothing of this - of me. Of what I may be. What I am! To him I was simply a woman. It was....nice. To just be Dalene."

Her father nodded, understanding and accepting her explanation. "It is probably as you say, but the Evaluation will be held, and he <u>will</u> attend.

That is why I dispatched The Arbor Guard to keep an eye on him. If he is indeed from Kernsidon, he will be eliminated."

"Yes, but why Halvor? Why not one of the others?"

Gareth smiled, but there was no humor. "First, because my daughter was head of the delegation. Who better than her brother to look after her? Second, because he is the best. Whether this stranger claims to wear the mantle by right or not, he is dangerous simply because he does wear the mantle. If the danger is contained, he may live until the Evaluation. If the danger begins to spread, whether intentionally or not, there will be no need for the Evaluation. We are clear?"

The Lady Dalene nodded, knowing that the interview was concluded.

Chapter 6   Education

Colin felt strangely empty, watching Dalene depart. He didn't know why. She'd saved his life, but there was more to it. Maybe it was because he had spent more time just talking to her than anyone else since he had arrived, or for that matter, since his parents had died. He knew he was going to miss her. He watched until she disappeared from sight and suddenly felt tired. His hands and head were throbbing. Not badly, but he hadn't really noticed before. The swelling was almost completely gone now, and the discoloration was fading. His strength was returning rapidly. Overall, he felt good despite having no answers to explain why or how he came to be here, but he liked this place. This non-mechanized world was amazingly quiet. The hectic pace of his modern world was totally absent, replaced by a much more measured rhythm. The air was clear. The people he had met were pleasant, hard-working sorts. The only problem was that they were likely to kill him – no, destroy him, whatever that meant - before three months were out. For some reason, the incongruity of the thought made him grin as he shook his head. "Everybody's got problems," he murmured.

He found Jorge and Elam in the field down by the hay meadow. For the next couple of hours he worked, hauling rock from the tilled area and stacking it at the edge of the woods. Colin saw numerous tracks of deer, at least he assumed they were deer, but thought of the "horses" he had seen and was uncertain. The work was hard, but it felt good. He wasn't happy being restricted to handling the smaller rocks, but his strength was still lacking, so he took it easy. He was sweating heavily, and Jorge shot him an occasional concerned glance, but said nothing. Elam was shy at first, but soon was talking happily about the farm. Colin learned a lot by listening to Elam chatter. They mostly raised wheat and maize or corn for market, but they had a large garden up by the house. The planting was done. The wheat was already up and the field where Colin had been found was their corn crop. It should sprout soon. He learned that they had chickens, a few ducks, two oxen for the heavy hauling on the farm, the two goats and two milk cows. During one of their breaks, Colin asked about their shoes. He said, "Your shoes, they seem to be made of canvas. Why is that?"

They both looked puzzled. Jorge answered, "For work in the fields and walking. We must have sturdy shoes. The soft boots are suited for indoors or perhaps the cities, but out here they would wear out quickly."

"But why canvas instead of leather?"

"What is 'leather?'" Elam asked.

"You know – the skin, the hide of animals like your ox or goats. Leather."

Jorge wrinkled his nose, "It stinks and it rots. When it's dried it's hard, like wood. Too hard for shoes. When wet it becomes soft again and begins to stink and falls apart."

Colin realized that he hadn't seen leather since he'd arrived. The harness on the horses had been canvas, as was the sheathe on the knife he'd been given. He'd seen no indication that hides or furs were used at all. Puzzled, he lapsed into silence and returned to work.

About an hour before sunset, Jorge straightened and said, "Enough. It's a fair day's work we've done. Colin, you did well. I was afraid for your health, but you did well. Elam, why don't you take Colin and show him around the farm? He'd like that, I think." Colin assured him that he would, and Elam was a willing guide. He pointed out where the crops were planted, and then took Colin through the thin band of trees that hid the stream bordering their property. In the shade of the trees, along the stream banks, Colin found dense patches of wintergreen and spearmint, or something very much like them. He plucked several leaves and rubbed them between his hands, inhaling the fragrance. Elam looked puzzled, so Colin held out his hands and said, "Smell." Elam did but was unimpressed. Colin eyed the stream and asked, "Do you fish?"

Elam looked puzzled, "Aye, there's fish. But I don't know what you mean by 'do fish.'"

Colin smiled, "Do you catch them? You know, to eat?"

Elam shook his head, "No. Waste of time. They're too fast to catch. Children try. In the shallows I mean, but you can't catch them."

"What about nets or hooks. Do you catch them that way?"

Elam shook his head, looking more puzzled, "Why? They're just fish."

"Then there are no fishermen among you – those who catch fish for their livelihood?"

Elam laughed, "You're having me on! I almost believed you! To catch fish for a living! That's good!"

Colin smiled and said, "Maybe if we have some spare time, I can show you."

They continued their explorations. Elam knew many of the trees, and pointed out hawthorne and walnut as well as thick stands of hazelnut along the creek. Colin learned that Jorge's farm was the farthest out from the town of Tyber, some two miles distant. Beyond this point was wilderness. As dusk approached, they reached the hay meadow, enclosed with a familiar snake-rail fence. The oxen were standing lazily chewing their cuds. The goats ran up to the gate bleating when they saw the men approach. Elam scratched each of them behind the ears, then grabbed two short pieces of rope off the gate post. He looped a length of rope around the neck of each of the huge oxen and handed one of the rope ends to Colin, who took it cautiously. Elam led the way with the other ox in tow and Colin followed, surprised by how easily the massive animal led. Along the edge of the field, Colin now saw several deer accompanied by spotted fawns. Other deer were scattered about, feeding singly. Colin guessed these to be bucks, but this early in spring he had no idea if they developed antlers or not. They were similar to whitetail deer, though perhaps half again as large. They lacked the white flag of a tail, but they also lacked the large ears of the mule deer. They were feeding on the new shoots, and seemed only vaguely curious at the approach of the men. Elam picked up a rock and yelled, hurling the rock at the feeding deer, which ran off a few yards and resumed their feeding. He explained, "They eat much of what we plant. I try to scare them off whenever I see them about. But it doesn't help much. Sometimes I chase them, but they just run in to the woods and soon come back."

Colin asked, "Do you hunt them?"

"Some do. At least they try. But it is difficult with a spear. They stay just out of good throwing range."

"How about with a bow and arrow?"

Elam looked at him blankly, "A bow and arrow?"

Colin was again puzzled, "Surely you know about the bow and arrow. Here let me show you," and he stooped to draw a rough stick-figure sketch in the dirt and then mimicked drawing a bow.

Elam cocked his head and looked at it, but just shrugged. Colin was intrigued. Obviously, some of the common pathways of invention familiar on his Earth had been entirely avoided here. He would have to think about this. Elam continued to talk the rest of the way home, while Colin remained silent, lost in his thoughts.

Dinner that evening was quiet. Colin wasn't sure if the reason was his presence or Dalene's absence. Halvor joined them as well, but kept himself aloof from the others. Colin thought there was tension between the family and their guest. After dinner, Colin automatically got up and began helping Miran gather the dishes from the table, to the amused surprise of Jorge and Elam. Halvor simply observed, a neutral expression on his face. Miran objected, but he just smiled and said, "My Mom taught me better than that. I'd be in trouble if I didn't help."

"What is 'Mom?'"

"Sorry. It is another word for 'Mother,' less formal in my country."

"Your mother, she still lives in Kalispell?" Miran asked.

No, she never actually lived there. She lived in a town about 150 miles away, where I grew up. Both she and my father died in an accident a couple of years ago."

"I'm sorry. You are alone then? No wife? No children?"

He shook his head, "No, my wife died suddenly about a year and a half after we were married. No children. I have an older brother and four younger sisters, but they live far from where I lived."

Miran's eyes widened, "Six children! And this was permitted?"

Colin nodded. "It was a large family, most people had fewer children, but it was left to each couple to decide."

Miran just shook her head. They carried the dishes outside to a large basin which Miran filled with water from a bucket set there for that purpose. Near the basin were two other large buckets. One was filled with sand and the other with gravel. Miran would rinse each dish in the cold water, scrubbing vigorously with a coarse cloth. Occasionally, she would grab a handful of sand or gravel to scrub a particularly difficult area on a plate or pan. The cooking pots were either cast iron or copper. Serving dishes, the plates and bowls were made of wood or baked clay. They were sturdy, but nicely finished. Eating utensils included both forks and spoons, carved from hardwood. Noticing the thin sheen of grease forming on the top of the wash bucket, he asked, "Do you have soap?"

Miran looked at him blankly, "Soap? I do not know this word."

"Soap – something to help the washing. To remove the grease from the dishes?"

Brightening she said, "Ahh! Yes! We heat the water." With that she rushed into the house and brought out the large pot of hot water and demonstrated how to rinse the dishes. "You see! The grease is much less!"

Colin had to smile and agree that yes, the grease was much less. Recalling how his earlier request for soap had been ignored when he wished to bathe, he had to conclude that this was another avenue of invention which had never been explored in this world.

Jorge extended a gruff invitation to make up a bed on the floor in the house. However, Colin found the shed to be comfortable, and didn't wish to intrude any more than he already was, so he declined. He was afraid that he was going to be sharing the shed with Halvor. It wasn't that he disliked the man – he didn't know him well enough to either like or dislike him. It was just that he felt the need for a bit of solitude. He was relieved when he learned that the tent previously occupied by Veret had been left, and that Halvor would be staying there. He laughed to himself, wondering how Halvor might take it if he knew that he preferred the company of goats. The fact was, just now he preferred no company at all. He was in what he used to refer to as "data overload." There were too many strange things that he was attempting to mentally sort out. He scraped his bed of hay together once again. He now had two blankets, and one was large enough to fold double, providing a layer both underneath as well as over top, helping to keep the hay from his skin.

Colin blew out the lantern and lay down for the night, but he couldn't sleep. He needed to think. Mentally, he began to review his situation. He accepted that he was on a planet different from his native Earth, and yet the similarities were so startling as to be beyond coincidence. First, the gravity on this planet, as well as the flora and fauna were almost, but not quite, identical to what he was used to. Through the course of the day, working and lifting the heavy stones, he had come to suspect that the gravity might be fractionally less. There was nothing definite he could put his finger on, he just felt………light. He supposed that it was entirely possible, likely even, that this planet would have a mass and diameter different from his own earth. While the animals were familiar, there were also enough differences to confirm the alien nature of his environment. But similarities, such as the reference to "hours" and "miles" were almost more disconcerting than the obviously alien observations he had made – like the moons and what they called horses. Why did their day have 24 hours, the same as on earth? Why did their week consist of 7 days? The month he could understand, since it stemmed from the phases of the moon, yet their month was awfully close to the lunar cycle on earth.

From what he had observed of the culture, it showed any number of similarities to either what he had experienced personally, or read about in Earth history. They spoke of cities, towns and villages. There was government – a representative government at that, though whether it was a democratic process or not he hadn't a clue. There appeared to be a rather rigid caste system, in the assignment to a 'File.' By what means such assignment was made, he did not know, but it was apparent that this was a key element of their society and government. Identification of a given File was to be displayed at all times, indicated by the colors one wore on their clothing. That was one of his first cultural indiscretions – he had no color. Even if he had showed up wearing the wrong color, he might have been able to bluff things through, but the lack of any color immediately marked him.

Then there was the general appearance of the local population. He still didn't have a significant sample size to draw conclusions from, but based on the……..what was it now, he had met three of the women and five of the men………based on the eight individuals he had met, all had dark hair and dark eyes. From their reaction to his hair and eyes, they would seem to be a fairly representative sample. The men all wore facial hair, though Halvor and Councilor Rabin's had been close cropped. In height, the women were shorter than the men, being about 5'4", with the men perhaps two or three inches taller. He hadn't seen anyone with a weight problem yet, but in this environment which had to be fairly labor intensive, that would be unusual.

He estimated the cultural and technological level to be more on par with medieval than colonial. He'd seen no evidence of machinery beyond the carts and wagons. The iron and copper pots, as well as the sword which Veret had carried and the dagger which he had been given showed a considerable degree of sophistication in working metals, indicating mining, smelting and casting were all known and practiced. But tanning, soap making, fishing and archery were apparently unknown, at least in this region. He was intrigued by that. As an engineer, he had to ask, "What drives invention? Why were even primitive cultures on his world familiar with the bow and arrow, while this relatively advanced society seemed totally unaware of them? Why was the art of making soap known to the ancient Greeks, but not here?"

That brought him to one of his biggest puzzles. He knew nothing of their religious beliefs, yet it was obvious that they believed in a god of some kind, and unfortunately he had arrived wearing clothing that none but a messenger of that god was authorized to wear. It seemed that their government maintained a close relationship with whatever religious beliefs were held – no separation of church and state here! And that close relationship seemed likely to result in some kind of ceremony which would eliminate his will and erase his identity. He took no comfort in Dalene's assurance that he would not be killed. From his perspective, what she had described as being "destroyed" was, if anything, worse than his concept of death.

Then he realized that he'd been completely overlooking one of the biggest puzzles of all. Language! Until this very moment, it hadn't occurred to him how totally absurd this all was – to be on an alien planet and speaking English! How could that possibly be? He remembered that first morning, waking up down by the ocean, and speaking aloud, how strange his voice had sounded! He spoke aloud: "Yes, I like apples. You have lovely hair. What kind of crops do you grow?" His brow furrowed. It sounded OK, but ……different. He tried again, "The space shuttle is being fueled with liquid hydrogen and oxygen. Plasma assisted doping of the gate structure on semiconductor devices below the 32 nanometer threshold is preferred to beam line implantation." The words were entirely familiar, but they sounded……..foreign. It was like something he knew, but it just didn't fit. He tried again. "Soap. Water. Shoe. Leather." 'Water' and 'Shoe' had flowed off his tongue. But 'Soap' and 'Leather' had felt……..strange. Breathing deeply and slowly, he closed his eyes against the darkness, and he thought about a conversation he'd had in a joking manner with some friends many years ago. He'd argued that everyone has the same favorite color, but that no two people see color precisely the same. "What I see as 'blue,' you see as 'orange.' But because you were taught to call it blue, that's what you do." It had been a nonsensical argument. The point he'd been trying to make is that with no absolutes, everything becomes relative, hence the need for absolute standards.

His head hurt, and he was trying to sort through what he was thinking. He finally had to verbalize the thought. "Am I speaking in the native language, and only when there is no word in the native language, do I then revert to my "English" in order to name what is unknown on this planet, or at least in this culture?" If he accepted that, and he wasn't sure that he did, how could such a thing happen? There was no logical explanation.

Then he had another thought. "Everything has an explanation." If science couldn't offer one, then the only logical explanation was.........God. There it was again. The same dilemma he'd faced when the two moons rose in the sky. Something had brought him here. He refused to question his sanity. And if he could be transported across, God-only-knows-how-far space to get here, it would seem pointless or arbitrary to do so without a purpose. And if God could bring him to this planet, it seemed not only reasonable but likely that God would give him the means to communicate. For God-only-knows what purpose. The thought made him grin. Of course on a historical basis, a lot of God's purposes seem to wind up making martyrs out of his various tools. The idea of dying didn't bother him <u>too</u> much, but the idea of pain bothered him a lot. Sighing, he took refuge in Occam's Razor again: In an inexplicably complex problem such as this, the simplest answer, and most likely the correct one, was that God had brought him here and allowed him to understand and speak the local language. That was nice, but for what purpose? He had 85 days before he was liable to cease to exist as a distinct intelligence.

He lay staring at the dark. 85 days. Before drifting off to sleep, he knelt to pray. Afterwards there was still no answer and no sense of comfort. His jaw clenched, and he asked himself another question: "If you knew that tomorrow would be your last day on earth......(this one or the other one?)......what would you do? What would you want to accomplish? OK, if you knew that the next 85 days would be your last days on earth, what would you want to accomplish?" In frustration, he ran his fingers through his hair. It felt oily. "I would want to leave some kind of a lasting legacy behind. I would want to make soap." The thought made him laugh.

In some ways, embracing the fact that he was soon likely to die or be destroyed was an extremely liberating experience. He had never felt more alive. He savored every moment and every experience. He found that he observed things around him far more keenly than ever before, and took the greatest pleasure in the simplest things. His intense interest in everyone and everything was disconcerting to Jorge and his family. Halvor simply observed him with curiosity. Colin was up early, and helped with the milking and feeding the livestock, noting exactly how Jorge and Elam performed each chore so he could perform them as well. He noticed the chickens. When he complimented Miran on the breakfast she had prepared, she looked half stunned, and Jorge even paused his eating, fork halfway to his mouth, before resuming his meal with single-minded determination.

Their project for the day was to cut firewood. Colin watched as Jorge and Elam hitched the oxen to the farm wagon. Miran prepared a meal for their noon rest. Elam tossed three double-bitted axes into the wagon bed and a large two-man saw. Down past the hay meadow there was a lightly-used wagon path, continuing on through the woods for perhaps a mile before coming to a small clearing. The stumps showed that this was where a lot of wood cutting had been going on. It was a large stand of oak, mixed with other hardwoods. They worked steadily through the morning. Elam and Jorge started with the saw and felled large trees, about two feet in diameter. Colin would then limb them, using one of the axes, and the saw was used to cut them into lengths suited for loading into the wagon. It was back-breaking work, but Jorge and Elam offered no complaint, and Colin did his best to keep up. By noon, the wagon was loaded and they stopped for their meal.

The three men walked down to the stream, which was about ten yards wide at this point, gurgling through pools and riffles. Colin immersed his head and then drank deeply. They rested in the shade on the stream bank and shared their meal. After lunch, they piled the limbs from the felled trees. Jorge said they would be left to dry for the summer, and then burned come winter. That suddenly brought something to Colin's recollection. "Jorge, do you mostly burn oak?"

"Aye. Mostly. Sometimes we get maple or beech. But oak provides more heat than most, and it's plentiful here."

"At home, what do you do with the ash?" Colin asked.

"We've an ash pit. I don't like scattering it about. It's a mess and Miran gets cross when it tracks into the house. So we throw it in the pit."

"Can I see your ash pit when we get back?"

Jorge looked at him strangely, and said, "If you've a wish to see the ash pit, I'll be pleased to show you." Elam snickered.

They arrived back at the house about mid-afternoon. Colin had no definite idea how the time here might compare to that on earth. He'd learned that this would be nearly the 9th hour of the day, or around 3:00 by his reckoning. After the wagon was unloaded and the wood stacked to dry, he reminded Jorge that he was going to show him the ash pit. Jorge shook his head, but obliged. The ash pit was out back of the house along a well-used path to the privy. It had obviously been used for a number of years. A large spruce hung over the pit, sheltering it from sight. At the edge of the pit was a large wooden bucket, obviously used to haul the ash from the house, and a large pile filled the pit.

Colin was delighted. The spruce would have sheltered the pit from rain and snow, assuming they had snow. That meant that the ash pile wouldn't have been leached. He asked Jorge, "Would you object if I used your bucket and some of the ash? I want to try and make something."

Jorge, by this time, was thinking that he had been stuck with a crazy man, but decided to humor him. "You're welcome to the bucket and all the ash you want."

"I'll need at least one more bucket. An old one would be preferred, but it has to still hold water."

Jorge just nodded, "One thing we have plenty of on the farm, is buckets. They're in the shed. I'll show you." Colin selected a large one, perhaps four gallons in volume.

"This one should do. By any chance have you an old piece of canvas or heavy cloth?" Curious now, Jorge just shook his head. He left the shed but returned in a few minutes with a large piece of old canvas. "From one of my old shoes," he explained.

Colin went to the spring and filled the bucket with water. At the pit, Colin retrieved the ash bucket and stepped down to scoop the bucket full, and used his foot to compress the load as tightly as possible. Satisfied, he got out of the pit and carefully poured water over the ash until it was fully immersed. "There. Now we'll let that sit overnight to leach, and we'll collect the water in the morning"

Jorge watched all of this in silence. Raising one bushy eyebrow he looked at Colin and said, "You cannot intend to drink this?"

Colin had to laugh at the look of concern on Jorge's face. Impulsively he clapped Jorge on the back and said, "No, my friend. I may be crazy, but I'm not stupid. You, however, as far as I know, are soon to be the first man on earth to wash with soap!"

Jorge just shook his head, but Colin grinned all the way back to the house. Then he cleared his throat, "Hmm, Jorge, I still need just one more thing. By chance do you keep any fat or lard – left from when you butcher one of the animals?"

Jorge was in too deep now, and his curiosity wouldn't let it rest. "We've a bit, but mostly only for cooking. If you need much, then we'd best be seeing Baylor. He has pigs, and always keeps fat on hand." Jorge glanced at the sun, "We've plenty of time before dinner. We can walk over now if you're of a mind."

Halvor had come from around the corner of the house during this exchange. He fell in behind Colin and Jorge as they took to the path leading to Baylor's farm. Colin grabbed one of the small buckets from the shed as they left. For the first time, he thought Halvor was actually showing something akin to interest.

In a few minutes, they arrived at the farm. Jorge called out, "Kath! Baylor! Are you about?"

Kath appeared almost immediately at the doorway, calling out in surprise, "Jorge! Good of you to drop by!"

But almost immediately her voice died out as she noticed the two strangers with him. She bowed deeply to Halvor, having noted the lavender fringe on his shirt. But her eyes were on Colin, and they stared with uncertainty. Colin smiled and bowed to her, holding the bow and saying, "I'm sorry for the intrusion. I am Colin Ericsson, of Kalispell. I'm afraid that I'm responsible for Jorge bringing us here."

Jorge cleared his throat and said, "May I also present Halvor, Arbor Guard of Aidon, 11th File of Salem." Halvor nodded briefly.

"Is Baylor about, then?"

Kath nodded, "Down by the pig barns. He has been slaughtering today. We'll be taking a fresh hog to Tyber market tomorrow."

"Thank you, Kath, we'll be going down to see him then."

Kath stood nervously at the doorway, watching the three men head toward the barn. Her hand rose involuntarily to her mouth as she clearly saw the hood on the back of the departing figure. "Had his eyes really been green?" She wondered.

At the barn, Jorge called out, and was greeted by a gruff response, "Jorge is it? Do you never work, man?" But as he came from the barn, his tone suddenly changed and he bowed to Halvor. Jorge made the introduction, and then dryly said, "Colin Ericsson of Kalispell, you've met."

Colin looked questioningly at Jorge, "'Twas Baylor helped haul you in from the field the night you were found. I couldn't have done it by myself."

Colin then bowed deeply to Baylor, who looked absolutely surprised, and said, "Then you are one more to whom I owe my thanks, and most probably my life."

Baylor just shrugged and said, "Not a social call, I'm guessing."

Jorge shook his head and Colin spoke, "I asked Jorge to bring me. He tells me you raise pigs, and I need some fat. I am trying to make something, and I need fat or oil of some kind to do it."

Baylor laughed, "Fat is it? Your timing is right. I've just finished skinning. We'll take this one to market on the morrow. How much do you be needing?"

Colin held up his bucket, "About half full will do. But I understand that you sell the meat, and I assume you sell the fat as well. I'd not like to take it without paying."

Halvor stepped forward and said, "I will pay. Name your price."

Baylor looked uncertain, but Colin spoke firmly, "No. This is a business transaction between Baylor and I. I can't pay you today, but if you'll trust me on this, I'll bring you a share of what I make with the fat. If you agree that it's fair value received, then we'll be even. If not, then you name your price and I'll pay what I owe. Deal?"

Baylor shrugged, "Not much market for fat anyway. Little enough is used for cooking. Aye, I'll trust you for the price of a half bucket of pig fat!" And he chuckled while he said it.

Colin stepped to the hanging carcass and picked up a large knife. The hog had been fat indeed, and it took but a couple of slices to remove a sizeable slab of fat from the hindquarters. Jorge and Baylor looked amused, while Halvor's face had returned to its mask of strict indifference.

They quickly completed the chores. Elam had already finished the milking, and the sun was down when they went in for the evening meal. Halvor didn't join them. Little was said during dinner. Colin again helped with cleaning up and doing the dishes afterwards. Miran still looked at him strangely, but accepted his help without objecting. Afterwards, rather than going out to the shed to retire, he rejoined the family in the house.

"Miran, tomorrow morning, could I borrow your large cast iron pot for the day? I need to set something by the fire while we're out." She looked puzzled, but agreed he could use the pot.

"Jorge, are you familiar with the yew tree?"

Jorge nodded and said, "Aye, there's some about. Not so much here, but up towards the foothills, they're not uncommon."

"Is it far?"

"Not so far. At a brisk pace, perhaps a couple of hours to the nearest stand I know of. There may be some nearer." By now, Jorge was getting used to the strange queries of his guest. "I reckon you'll be wanting to go." It was not a question.

Colin smiled, "I don't want to interrupt your farm work. But if we get a chance, yes, I'd like to go."

Elam spoke up, "I know where there's a stand closer. Perhaps an hour from here. I could take you. That is, when father can spare me."

Jorge waved a hand and said, "With three working instead of two, it goes well. Perhaps tomorrow. We'll see what we can accomplish in the morning. 'Tis fencing needs doing, but it shouldn't take the whole day."

"By chance do you have any birch – white birch around?" Colin asked.

Jorge rolled his eyes Such requests! "Plenty of that. And is there anything else you'd be needing?"

Colin smiled politely and nodded to his host, "Not just at this moment. But I do thank you for inquiring." They laughed.

At sunrise the next morning, Colin rolled out of bed. He was anxious to start his project, and so sleep had fled almost immediately. After getting dressed, he stopped at the spring to quickly wash and take a drink. He then returned to the ash pit and filtered the ash water through the canvas into the empty bucket and carried it to the house, where everyone was just starting to stir. The ash water was poured into the cast iron pot, and he rinsed both buckets several times at the spring. By this time, he was being called for breakfast, so he went in, carrying the pot full of ash-water. This he set at the back of the fireplace, cocking the lid so that steam could escape. Miran looked at him curiously and asked, "Is my cooking not to your liking?"

"Your cooking is absolutely wonderful. What is in the pot isn't for eating. In fact, if you did, it would probably kill you." This caused Miran and Jorge to look concerned. Colin continued, "I'm making potash. There's a chemical – a component in hardwood ash called potassium hydroxide.

That should have dissolved in the water that the ash soaked in last night. Today, the pot can just sit at the back of the fire, and as the water evaporates, it will concentrate what's in there. Then, with luck, maybe tonight it will be ready for what I want to make. It won't hurt your pot, and when I am done I'll clean it and it can be used for cooking again."

Miran seemed to accept this, and continued with serving breakfast. Halvor came in and seated himself at the table, nodding perfunctorily to those already there. His presence seemed to dampen the mood slightly, but Colin was too busy eating to be concerned. After breakfast, Jorge, Elam and Colin left to tend to the fencing that Jorge had in mind. They didn't take the wagon. Elam carried the water jug and lunch pack which Miran had put together. Jorge carried an ax and heavy sledge hammer, while Colin carried another ax. Halvor was again watching them from the doorway as they took to the trail. Colin commented, "Halvor isn't much of one for joining in, is he?"

Jorge glanced back over his shoulder and said, "Not that one. But you watch him. You can be sure he's watching you!"

"Why would he watch me?"

"Oh, no reason I supposed. Excepting maybe you're a stranger here, the like of which I've never heard of. Could be because you wear the mantle. Or maybe because you've an audience with the High Council in Salem, coming up. Make no mistake, he's here for watching you, and nothing else."

Colin tried to shrug it off. "Well, if he's here to watch me, he does a poor job of it. Letting me go off with you and Elam all day long while he hangs around the house."

"Don't you believe that for one minute! He was watching yesterday, from the woods. And the other morning when The Lady Dalene took you off for a private word, he was about then as well."

Surprised, Colin said, "I never saw him."

"Course you didn't! He's an Arbor Guard and you're always too busy admiring the trees and the birds and such. That's fine, but you best be watching that one, too. I've no idea what he has in mind, but I doubt it's looking after your well-being!"

They lapsed into silence, and continued on to the hay meadow. The rail fence was definitely in need of some repair. Colin doubted that the three of them could possibly build a fence that would restrain the massive oxen, and said as much. Jorge shrugged and said, "Aye, if they're of a mind to go, no fence is going to slow them. But they have plenty of food and water. They've no need to go pushing at the fence. Fact is, if they knew how strong they are, there'd be no holding them. That's the way it is with most things. It's thinking they can't do it that does the holding back so much more than the actual fence."

Colin thought about that and replied, "Like people."

Jorge laughed, "Aye. Like people."

Fortunately, the fence was largely in good shape, but in some places either the weather or animals had knocked rails loose, which had to be replaced. Rot and weather had taken toll on some of the rails, and the men had to go into the woods to cut replacements and then fit them into place. The gate had been knocked askew, and needed to have the posts reset. The work was hard, but went smoothly and the morning passed quickly.

As they had done the previous day, they retired to the stream to rest and eat at midday. "Elam," said Jorge, "This afternoon, why don't you take Colin to the yew stand that you spoke of last night."

Colin objected, "There's no rush. I told you I didn't want to interfere with your work. Elam and I can help this afternoon."

Jorge just waved him off and said, "I'll just be working on the pens and the garden fence up near the house. It's in better shape than this was. One man can deal with it, and Elam is itching for a walk, I think."

"Thanks, Jorge. Elam, how about it? Are you up for it this afternoon?"

"I'd be pleased," said Elam.

"Colin, you be mindful of what we spoke of this morning," said Jorge, with a quick jerk of his head.

Out of the corner of his eye, he caught a movement. Without turning his head, he kept his eye on that area, and soon saw what Jorge had indicated. Halvor was there, back in the trees. It wasn't that he was hiding, exactly. In fact, he was in plain view. He had a way of blending in with the surrounding forest that made it so you just didn't notice him. Colin was curious. Why would he be there, but not join them?

After lunch, Elam happily led off through the woods. They weren't really following a trail, but the forest was relatively open and the forest floor uncluttered. They skirted the occasional patch of brush, but the walking was pleasant. Before long, they came upon a faint trail that was heading in the general direction that Elam seemed to want to go, and so they followed the trail, which made for easier travel. Colin kept glancing about, wondering if Halvor continued to hover nearby. Reaching a clearing, Colin paused to admire the view. There were a variety of wildflowers carpeting the small meadow. Several flowering trees formed a backdrop against the darker forest canopy on the opposite side. The path cut straight across the meadow, and this made Colin remember something he had thought of the night before. "Elam," he said, "I need your help with something."

Elam had been in the lead, and he stopped and turned, "What is it?"

"Come here and lay down on the trail right here."

"Why?"

"I want to mark your height here in the dirt."

Elam shrugged. He obviously didn't understand, but he was getting used to that when dealing with Colin, and so he complied and lay down in the trail. Colin picked up a stick and marked the location of both his head and his feet, drawing a deeper line at the feet. "I want you to stand on this line right here, with both feet together. Then I want you to jump just as far as you can down the trail. I want to see how far you can jump."

Elam grinned. He was good at this sort of thing. Running and jumping were two of his favorite things. He got set, bent his knees and swung his arms a few times in preparation. Then he jumped as far as he could, a bit farther than the mark indicating his height. Colin had him repeat this a couple more times, marking his landing point each time. He estimated that Elam was about 5'4" – about as tall as his mother but not so tall as his father. So he was doing a standing long jump of approximately 6'6" by Colin's estimate.

"Alright, Elam, now I'm going to lay down, and you do the same thing for me. I want you to mark my head and feet here on the trail." Elam did so, and then Colin stood to jump.

"Mark where my heels land each time."

At the first jump, Elam practically shouted, "By heavens! You jump like a deer!" Colin looked, and saw that he was at least half again his height. Elam marked his landing point, and Colin jumped two more times, approximately the same distance as his first jump. Now Colin knew that he was 6'2. Finding a long stick, he broke it and kept checking it against the original marks Elam had made, until he could just lay the stick down twice between the two marks, indicating it was half his height. He then used the stick to measure from the point where he jumped to the point where he landed. His measuring stick fit three times, and there was still a full foot and a half, perhaps a bit more, besides, meaning that his jumps were in the range of 10' 6". Colin puzzled over this. The problem was, he didn't know how far he could broad jump on Earth. It seemed like the world record was something over 11 feet, so he wasn't breaking any records, but he was in the neighborhood. Not bad for a 28 year-old engineer, he thought. Elam had managed to jump about a foot more than his height, by Colin's approximation. That meant he had jumped his height plus about 20%, while Colin had jumped his height plus about 60%. He knew this wasn't exactly a scientific study, but he had been curious as to whether the gravity on this planet was noticeably less than on earth. Maybe. It was something to think about.

Elam asked, "Why did you want to do that?"

"I'm not sure. I haven't done that in a long time, and I wanted to see how well I could still jump - and compare to a strapping lad like yourself!"

Elam laughed, "I think I didn't compare well. Sometimes we have contests for running and jumping, and I don't think I've ever seen anyone jump so far!" Colin thought he caught some movement at the edge of the meadow, but he couldn't pinpoint it. He wondered if Halvor were shadowing them, and if so, for what reason?

They crossed several small hills, finding streams or springs running through the folds between them. Colin didn't know how long they walked. He wasn't very good at estimating the time from the sun, but at length Elam pointed and said, "There! That darker green down in the draw. Those are the yew trees you wished to find!"

The stand of yew was not large - perhaps 30 or 40 trees. Some were very large, but there were smaller trees as well. At the far edge of the stand, Colin found what he had been hoping for. A large tree was standing, but dead. It looked to have been struck by lightning, as the top was shattered and a number of branches lay scattered about. While he'd been willing to settle for green wood, finding a dry and seasoned tree was ideal for his purposes. He selected three sturdy branches, each over six inches in diameter. He used the ax to trim them and cut them to about five feet in length. "What's so special about yew?" asked Elam.

"Yew is a very springy wood. I'd heard it was one of the better varieties for making a bow. You didn't understand what I was talking about the other evening, so I'm going to show you. I'm going to make a bow and we're going to hunt deer with it."

"We? You mean I get to help?" Elam was excited.

"You bet. If I have my way, we'll make you the finest archer in the realm - at least for awhile, since you'll probably be the only archer in the realm."

Elam was too excited to worry about what being an "archer" meant. He liked this stranger who treated him as an equal, and was only too happy to be part of whatever he was planning.

There was a small spring nearby which they drank from. Colin asked, "You have your Evaluation soon, don't you?"

"At the next full moon they'll hold an Evaluation in Tyber. They always have one in Salem, but because there are several of us in Tyber who have turned 15 this past moon, they'll also have an Evaluation here," answered Elam.

"You know I'm supposed to have my own Evaluation in about three moons, right?"

Elam now seemed reluctant to answer. He looked away and said, "Yes. I have been told."

Colin was puzzled by his behavior. "So what exactly do they do in the Evaluation?"

Elam was surprised, "That's where they determine to which File you will belong!"

"I know that part of it. What I want to know is <u>how</u> do they make the determination? If you aren't allowed to talk about it, that's fine. But I'd like to know what to expect."

So Elam explained. "You must be at least 15 years of age to participate in the Evaluation. Most of us are anxious, so we have it as soon after our birthday as possible. But since the Evaluation is only held on the full moon, and my birthday fell this year right after the moon, I have to wait almost a month.

Often you must go to Salem for the Evaluation, since there are always members of every file in the city. There are Evaluations where the High Council participates, but those are never for us kids. Usually it's bad if the High Council is involved. They don't do Evaluations to determine your File, but to determine punishment."

Colin didn't understand, but listened without comment. Elam continued, "For my Evaluation, they'll bring Examiners to Tyber. At least eight Examiners – one from each File of the first two Orders. In Salem there would be twelve examiners. Each of us will be examined separately. I will be brought to the place of examination, and will be placed in the Box."

"What box?" Colin interrupted.

"Well, it isn't like a closed box. It is just a place. It's really called The Evaluation Box, but everyone just calls it 'the Box.' There are two sections, each having six sides. Elam sketched in the dirt.

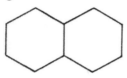

About so big." Elam held his hands about three feet apart. "I guess there are really two boxes – two halves, but since they're connected we still call it 'the Box. The examiner stands in one half, and I will stand in the other. Then we try to make the other bow to us, using the Compliance."

Colin's brow furrowed, "What's the Compliance?"

Now it was Elam's turn to look puzzled. "It is the Compliance. I don't know how to explain it. You know, it's when you reach for the other person - you reach for their center, their true-self. Then you make them - ask them..." he corrected himself, "to comply to your will. In this case you ask them to bow to you. You start with the Examiner from the 1st File. If he bows to you, you show that you have advanced beyond the 1st File. Then you must do the same to the Examiner from the 2nd File. But if you bow to the Examiner, then you are subject to him and you will belong to the 1st File. You continue to as high as you can go. When you bow, then you will know your File."

Colin was silent for a minute. "So you don't touch or anything like that? You just reach with your mind and try to force the other person to bow?"

Elam shook his head. "No. You must never use the Compulsion. The Compulsion is force. You only use the Compliance. You ask. You must persuade the other person to bow, but you must not force them."

"I'm not sure I understand. What's the difference? You're trying to get the other person to bow. You think them, will them to bow. How is the Compliance different from Compulsion?"

Elam was getting exasperated now, "It just is. It's like me asking you here, now, to bow to me. I can ask. I beg you. I can try to bribe you. That is asking you to Comply. But if I grab you and try to make you, that is to compel. It is the same thing, but with the mind. Our people do it all the time – if they touch. Mothers can get children to mind better, or help babies to not cry or be afraid. I think The Lady Dalene used the Compliance when I was in Salem and I was afraid."

"So, in my Evaluation, it will be the same? I'll stand in the Box and they'll try to reach into my mind and get me to bow?"

Elam nodded, "Yes. It's not hard. They say that it doesn't matter what File you belong to, but everyone knows that the higher Files have more choices and opportunities."

"But all of the members of a File aren't at the same level, are they? Couldn't you possibly get an Examiner to bow to you, but there would be someone else in the File whom you would not be able to best?" Asked Colin.

"Yes. So it depends on how detailed the Examination is to be. For me, it will only go until either I bow or the Examiner bows. But I'm only 15, so my File placement isn't too important. Anyone can challenge their File placement at a later time. But if you do that, the Chief Councilor of the File will select the Examiner. They usually select the hardest ones. There are Examinations conducted within a File as well, to determine who is the Regent and who will sit on the High Council in Salem. The Guilds also conduct examinations, to see who will lead the Guild. But most people don't really care about rank. For those who would lead or govern, then the Examination and their standing in the File is very important. But if there was a question regarding my File placement, they might conduct more Examinations. My parents are in the 3rd File, so if I made it to the 5th File, then I would be a member of the 2nd Order, and would not be allowed to live in any city of the 1st Order. I would be adopted, and I don't want that. But to be confirmed as really belonging to the 5th File, I would have to make the Examiner from the 4th File Comply, and would also have to make at least one person from the 5th File Comply also. There would also have to be at least one person in the 5th File who could get me to Comply, or else I would become Chief Councilor in that File. Like that would ever happen!"

Colin nodded, but said nothing. He still didn't understand how this worked. It kind of creeped him out that someone - perhaps several someones, were going to try and rummage around inside his mind, and that they were probably going to try to destroy his intellect once they found out that he didn't have whatever they thought he ought to have. He sighed, and said, "Thanks, Elam. I guess it makes it a little easier having some idea what to expect. But we had better head back home or your father will have all the chores done before we get there."

Elam nodded happily, "That wouldn't be good." But the look on his face didn't quite support his words.

Elam carried one branch, while Colin carried the other two. He called a halt when he saw a stand of white birch. They detoured to the grove, and Colin selected a couple dozen slender, straight shoots that he thought might do nicely for arrows

The sun was hanging low in the sky when they reached the boundary of the farm. Colin stopped to bathe his arms and face in the creek. When he looked up, he noticed a dense covering of low juniper on the opposite bank. This gave him an idea. "Elam, can I borrow the meal pouch?"

Elam shrugged out of the pack, and in a matter of moments Colin was busy picking juniper berries and dropping them into the pack. He didn't take the time to get as many as he wanted, but figured that he had over a pint of the fragrant berries. Elam looked puzzled, and said, "You know those aren't good to eat, don't you?"

"Not everything has to be edible to be of value. Here, pinch your thumbnail into this and smell it."

He did so and said, "It smells nice. I've done it before. It still isn't good to eat."

"No, but as you say, it smells nice, and if you rub it on your hands and arms, then you smell nice as well, instead of like a sweating ox." He smiled while he said it, so Elam didn't take offense. "And it is possible to cook the oils and fragrance from the berries and make other things smell nice. I want to try that tonight. But I think we have enough, so we had better hurry up to the house." They jogged the rest of the way, and Colin was pleased that he made it without having to stop. The sun had just set when they arrived at the house. Elam hurried to the shed to help with chores, but Jorge had already finished up. Elam was apologetic, but Jorge just waved him off, and seemed to be in an exceptionally good mood. He showed interest in the yew, but not enough to ask what they were for.

Colin asked to borrow a small pot. Miran provided one without comment, but raised an eyebrow when Colin began to fill it with the juniper berries he had picked. She echoed Elam when she said, "You know those aren't good to eat, don't you?"

Colin laughed, "So I've been told. Yes, I know, but I want to use this after dinner to make something."

He covered the hard, waxy berries with water and placed the pot on the hearth near the fire. He also checked the pot of ash-water, and found that it had evaporated nicely, and now contained an oily solution of about one-quarter the original volume. He knew that there was some way to check the concentration, "Float an egg or a potato or something," he muttered. But he couldn't remember exactly how it was done, so he shrugged and decided to skip it and hope for the best. Halvor joined the family shortly before mealtime. He was relaxed, and less intense than usual. After dinner Colin assisted Miran with the clean-up, but asked her to leave the large cooking pot for him to do later. She looked at him, curious, but simply said, "If that's what you wish."

With dinner over, Colin set to work. "Now, I'll show you what I've been wanting to make. Elam, out in the shed by the goat pen, there's a bucket with some pig fat in it. Would you get that for me?" Elam nodded and slipped out the door. Colin poured about half the ash-water, potash, he reminded himself, back into the bucket. He wasn't sure how much to use, but he didn't want the product to be too alkaline. He set the pot in the middle of the fire to bring it to a boil. Elam returned with the fat. Colin poured about an inch of water into the cooking pot and asked Elam to dump the fat in and set it on the fire as well. The fat soon melted in the hot water. Colin removed it from the fire and set it outside to cool, allowing the fat to congeal in a solid mass floating on top of the water. While it cooled, he explained. "I'm trying to make soap."

"Soap. The thing you asked for when you washed yourself and the first day when you helped clean the dishes after dinner," said Miran.

"Yes. Soap helps to clean things better. It helps to eliminate odor, and makes the task of cleaning easier. Unfortunately, I only know the basic idea of making soap. I made it once, a long time ago in a chemistry class, but that was different."

Jorge's face darkened, "Alchemy! Surely you do not practice the dark arts here!"

"No. Not alchemy. This is completely different. This is chemistry. It's like cooking. You simply add different ingredients together to make something else. Like when Miran makes bread. She adds flour, salt, lard and leaven, but she makes bread. That is chemistry as well – adding together ingredients to make something that is different from the components."

Jorge still looked uncertain, but everyone else in the room looked fascinated by this explanation – even Halvor had come to watch. Colin retrieved the cooking pot from outside. It wasn't entirely cool, but he could lift the congealed tallow which had separated from most of the impurities. He wiped the granular residue off from the underside of the tallow cake, and continued his explanation.

"To make soap, we need a base – like the ash-water that has been boiled down to concentrate it. The concentrate is called potash. It's basically potassium hydroxide we leached from the oak ash in your ash pit. We mix that with a fat or oil. Just about any kind will work, but you'll get a different result, depending on the ingredients you use. We used fat from a pig, but that will be a little different than fat from a cow or a deer. You can use olive oil or some other kind of oil. Each will be a bit different, and you can mix them if you like."

Hesitating, he shrugged and decided to add the entire cake of tallow to the potash, where it melted and poured the water from the boiled juniper berries on top. "I've added the juniper for scent. It doesn't really change the soap except to make it smell nice. You can use other things like mint or flowers as well. I'm not sure when the best time to add the scent is. Some of the smell may cook out of the soap, but some should remain."

He was now stirring the pot with an oak stick he had brought in for that purpose. "Don't use your wooden cooking implements for this. The potash will soak in and flavor your food. A little bit won't really hurt you, but it doesn't taste very good. Look! See how the mixture is changing? The ingredients are reacting, and that white, milky appearance shows the soap is being made. He removed the stick from the pot, blew on it and touched his finger to the liquid on it, then tasted it, looking guiltily at his dumbfounded audience.

"But you said it wasn't to eat!" said Elam.

"No, it isn't. Maybe I shouldn't have done that. Too much of the potash could poison you, but a little taste won't really hurt. Most of it has reacted with the fat. If the fat isn't completely reacted, the soap can turn rancid. The potash is a base, so it will have a very slippery feel and a bitter taste. I couldn't taste any 'bitter,' so I'm going to add a bit more of the potash." He did so, and continued to stir for a few minutes before once again tasting the mixture.

"See, now there is a very slight bitter taste. Here, you can try it if you like."

He offered the stick to the others, but only Miran and, surprisingly, Halvor cared to sample it. Halvor wrinkled his nose, but Miran looked thoughtful, seeming to savor it as she committed it to memory and said, "It is just a hint bitter, but not biting. I can smell the juniper in it as well."

Colin nodded as he continued to stir the thickening mixture. "Yes. It didn't all cook out. That's good. And we want that little bit of bitterness to tell us we had enough potash. That's probably as good as it will get for a first try." With that he removed the pot from the fire, but continued to stir. "It will get thicker as it cools. If we had a soap mold, we could pour the mixture into the molds now. But since we don't we'll keep stirring while it cools. Soon it will become stiff, and we'll just roll it into balls – about the size of a closed fist, I think. You'll have to be quick, because once it sets you can't work it."

When it looked to be about the right consistency, Colin scooped a handful, and promptly winced. It was still quite hot. He kept it moving in his hands to keep them from burning, molding and rolling it as it cooled. He soon had a fairly uniform ball, which he set on the edge of the table. "See how to do it? Go ahead and give it a try, if you like."

Like eager children, each of the spectators scooped up a handful of the congealing soap. "Ouch! It's hot!" said Elam.

"Keep it moving in your hands. If you don't let it sit in any one place too long, it won't burn, but you have to keep it moving." Colin told him.

Using the stick he had been stirring with, Colin scraped the remnants in the pot together, and managed to get one more ball of soap started. By now, it was cooling rapidly, and his second ball wasn't as neat as the first. Soon there were six waxy, pale white balls of soap sitting in a line along the edge of the table.

The cooking pot which had been used to melt the tallow in was still sitting by the fire. "Let me show you what soap does."

The water in the pot that dinner had been cooked in was tepid – better than cold spring water, thought Colin, and boiling the tallow in it had helped loosen the residue from dinner. Grabbing the cloth Miran used as a rag he scraped some of the remaining soap from the inside of the other pot that had been used to make it. Colin grabbed the dinner pot and said, "Look. You can still see some of the grease floating on top of the water in the pot. See what happens when I dip the soap into the water." He placed the soapy cloth into the water, and the grease immediately dispersed, moving away from the soap. "The soap helps reduce the surface tension of the water, and it helps break up the grease, so it can be rinsed away." He then scrubbed the soap vigorously on the dish cloth, raising a very mild lather. Then he scrubbed the pot, tossing the water out the front door and rinsing it with cold water from the bucket by the fire. "Feel it now. It is much cleaner, and we didn't have to scrub it with gravel and sand." Everyone felt the inside of the pot, though only Miran seemed to be impressed. Colin again poured water into the pot from the basin Miran always kept by the fire. "Here," and he handed the soap to Miran, "You take it and wash your hands. Rub the soap on them and scrub them together. Now you rinse off in the water."

Miran dried her hands on her apron, then inspected them critically, before rubbing them together softly. "They feel..........clean. Like I had just spent an hour doing clothes in the stream." She sniffed them. "I can smell juniper, too." She sniffed again, "I like this smell – from washing." She picked up the soap and handed it to Jorge, "Now you. Wash."

Jorge did so, reluctantly, but he seemed to be intrigued by the slippery feel of the soap on his hands and forearms. When he had rinsed and dried, there was an obvious band on his arm above where he had washed, showing a line of grime that hadn't been touched. But Jorge was concentrating on his hands, and was visibly impressed. "It does feel clean. It's good."

It was obvious from the way that Elam and Halvor kept edging forward, that they hoped to be invited to try the soap as well. Halvor, being a guest, was invited by Miran to go first, much to Elam's disappointment. But soon Elam was happily sliding the soap through his hands and up his arms. "It's slippery!" he called in delight as he chased the soap around the pot. Halvor kept inspecting his hands intently, sparing an occasional, puzzled glance at Colin. Finally he nodded and said, "This soap. It is good, I think. And it is just like cooking?" This last he said as if to convince himself that no alchemy was attached to its making.

Colin nodded, "It's just another recipe – but not for food. And it is good. It helps in washing clothing and hair as well. You should use soap before eating or after tending to someone who is sick. It will help to keep the sickness from spreading. The product will be better if you use rain water instead of spring water, but it will work either way."

Jorge clapped him on the back, "Soap! It is good to make soap! Thank you, Colin of Kalispell. I like this soap."

Miran smiled at her husband's exuberance, "Yes, thank you. I am anxious to wash with this. I too think it is a good thing." She took Jorge's hand and smelled it, saying softly, "And I do like this smell."

Colin thought it smelled a little gamy, in spite of the juniper, but smiled and said, "It's little enough to do, by way of thanks for your kindness to me. Come what may, I will have left something of value in this world." He was trying to be humorous, but he wished he hadn't said it, as he saw the smiles in the room fade.

Trying to lighten the mood again, he said, "Tomorrow I'd like to take two of the balls of soap over to Baylor, to see if that will satisfy my debt to him for the pig fat. I'd like to have the ball we've been using, but you're welcome to the others, and you have seen how to do it, so you can make more when you wish. I'll be happy to help if you need me to and if I'm around."

Miran said, "Baylor would be a fool to not see the value of soap. And he is no fool. But if he is," she smiled, "Kath certainly is not. I think your debt will be canceled."

The next morning Colin again awoke as the sun began to lighten the sky. He grabbed a bucket and his precious ball of soap, and went to the spring. Dipping the bucket full of water, he carried it off into the trees where he stripped down, shivering in the cool morning air. He hated being cold like this, but he really wanted to feel <u>clean</u>. Sloshing water on himself from the bucket, he then soaped liberally. It didn't lather as much as he liked, but he wasn't sure what to do about that. He scrubbed his hair vigorously with the soap, then rinsed thoroughly with the bucket. He was freezing now, but it felt good to be clean. His hair especially hadn't felt so good since………since he'd arrived in this world. He hated to put his clothes back on without washing them, but he didn't have a spare set and wasn't inclined to wear these wet. So he hurriedly put them on, grateful for the loose fit which allowed them to slip on over his wet skin. Returning to the spring, he dipped another bucket full of water and began the painful, laborious practice of shaving. He was grateful for the knife Veret had given him. It was razor sharp, but the fact was, it wasn't a razor. He again nicked himself twice before he was finished.

The sky looked to be threatening rain, and the breeze was picking up. Colin hurried back to the shed and started doing chores. He had seen to the goats and chickens, but was still leery of milking the cows. He was thinking about how to make a comb when Jorge emerged from the house, whistling. He seemed to be in a good mood. Seeing Colin with the milk pail, he came over and clapped him on the back, giving him a sly look and said, "That soap. It is good." Then he laughed, took the milk bucket and went whistling on his way, leaving Colin looking puzzled.

At breakfast, everyone was in a good mood. Halvor was polite, and even went so far as to compliment Miran on her cooking. Miran kept looking at Colin, curious. Finally she said, "Your hair. It is different today."

Colin replied, "I washed it this morning - with soap. The soap removes the oil and the hair doesn't mat down as much."

She lifted a tentative hand and touched his hair lightly, "I like this. I must try this soap on my hair also."

After breakfast, Elam volunteered to help with the dishes, much to his mother's shock. He blushed and said, "I want to see how the soap works. I like it. It's slippery." Miran smiled and gladly accepted the help.

Colin turned to Jorge and said, "What work do we have to do today?"

Jorge smiled and said, "First, we must retire your debt. We will go see Baylor and introduce him to soap!"

Colin was amazed at how taken these people were by such a simple thing. But he had to admit that he'd been pretty taken with some of the things he had seen here for the first time as well. Colin took two of the balls of soap, and he and Jorge headed towards Baylor's farm. Halvor fell in behind them. Approaching the house, he called out his usual greeting, "Baylor! Are you about?"

Immediately the door opened, and Baylor appeared, "Do you not ever work your farm?" he asked in a bantering tone.

"Aye, the farm is worked and well you know it. But a man that has a debt to pay cannot rest until the matter is settled." At that, he nudged Colin forward.

Holding out the two balls of soap, he spoke, "I've come to see if you'll accept this as payment for the pig fat you gave me the other day. It's soap."

Baylor took one of the balls, and eyed it. Jorge was like an eager child and said, "It's not for staring at! Bring a dish and we'll show you what use it is! Kath! Kath! Bring us a dirty pot, will you?"

From there, all Colin did was stand back and watch, as Jorge happily demonstrated to Baylor and Kath the wonderful workings of soap. Colin had never seen him so talkative before. It was like watching a used car salesman doing the hard-sell. While Kath was visibly impressed with her pot being cleaned, Baylor's disinterested façade didn't crack until he started playing with the soap in the warm water, rubbing it through his hands and up his hairy arms. When he was done with his playing, the water was a very dirty brown, but his arms and hands were.......clean! Kath took one dripping hand and turned it this way and that, rubbed her forefinger up his arm and inspected it critically. She turned back to Colin, wide-eyed, and said, "Your debt is paid – in full and with interest." Jorge laughed and clapped Baylor on the back.

On the way back, it began to rain, a cold, steady drizzle. The three of them made a run for it the last half of the way, but they were still fairly well soaked by the time they made it to the barn. Jorge sighed and said, "Well, there won't be much working outside today. Not a bad day for it though. The crops are in, and the rain will help. Good day for mending harness."

The barn was much larger than the shed where Colin was sleeping. It was a heavy log structure. The ground level had a dirt floor, and heavy doors swung on iron hinges. A row of six stalls lined one side of the barn, while tack, buckets, sickles, shovels and other assorted farming tools hung from wooden pegs set in the wall on the opposite side. There was a large hay mow at the back of the barn, and a ladder leading up to a half-loft overhead where additional hay could be stored. The barn provided shelter for the oxen and two milk cows. Hanging above the stalls were several harnesses. Jorge pulled down one of the harnesses and retrieved a roll of heavy canvas, a sturdy awl and what Colin thought looked like a sail-makers needle. Colin watched as Jorge carefully inspected the harness, noting where it was badly worn and frayed. Using his knife, he would cut a patch from the roll of canvas, and then stitch it in place over the worn section. It wasn't pretty, but with the coarse, heavy thread, it looked like it would hold. The problem, thought Colin, was that canvas simply wasn't all that durable. He watched Jorge work, assisting where possible. After a few minutes, Jorge pulled down another harness and tossed it to Colin. He retrieved another awl and needle. Colin sat down beside Jorge, with the roll of canvas, the knife and a roll of thread between them.

It was tedious work, but relaxing, listening to the beat of the rain on the barn roof and the steady drip from the eaves. The oxen and cows had access to their stalls from outside, and had chosen to get in out of the rain. The barn smelled of old hay and wet livestock, of dirt and manure. Colin found it pleasant. After working in silence for some time, He paused to stretch and commented to Jorge, "We need to get you some leather. It would wear a lot better. Stronger too."

Jorge shook his head, "Leather. That was the dried cowhide you spoke of the other day. I told you - weather like this, and it'll turn to mush.

You'd have to replace it every time it rained. Canvas is better. Takes some mending, mind you, but it's tough."

Colin unlaced one of his boots and tossed it to Jorge. "Feel that."

Jorge had already done that, the night Colin had first arrived, but he didn't feel like saying so. He inspected the boot again, admiring its light weight and lack of bulk. His own shoes, made of cloth and canvas, were soaked from exposure to the rain as they had run back from Baylor's. Colin explained, "The upper section of that boot is leather. It's tough, light and if you feel inside, it's still dry. It can be made fairly resistant to water."

"Aye. So it is. Fair enough then. So if I was to agree to try your leather, where would I be getting it?"

"That's the problem. If you haven't seen it before that means nobody here is making it. So we'll have to make it for you."

"Like your soap?" asked Jorge.

"Yes, kind of like that. The process is a bit more involved. It isn't hard. It just takes some time. I think we can do it." Colin replied.

"So what will you be needing?" Colin could tell that Jorge was more interested than he was letting on.

"First, we'll need a fresh hide. The process of turning a hide into leather is called tanning. I've heard that you can tan an old hide. I've only ever done fresh hides, so if we can't get a fresh hide, maybe we can try an old one, but I'd rather try what I know works first. We'll need a hide, salt, and a large tub. It has to be big enough to soak the hide in, and it'll have to soak for several days. We'll also need oak chips. We should be able to go down where you were cutting firewood and pick up all the chips we need." He paused for a moment and then continued, "I almost forgot. That's all you really need for tanning the hide, but if we want to take the hair off first, then we'll need more ash. The potash works to help loosen the hair and make it easier to remove. Do you have a draw knife?"

Jorge nodded the affirmative.

"Good. We'll use that for fleshing the hide and scraping the hair off."

By shortly after midday, the harness work was completed. Jorge said, "With the rain, there's not much to be done today. I've a need to get see old Tunsten. He's another neighbor, a bit farther than Baylor. There's no need for you to be getting wet, so you may as well stay here."

Colin nodded and asked, "Do you have any carpentry tools I can use? A small saw especially?"

Jorge led him to an alcove off the back of the barn. A large workbench filled most of it, and on the walls hung a variety of hammers, chisels, a brace and bit, a couple of hand saws, awls and other assorted tools. He said, "Just be careful with them, and place them back when you're done. Tools are dear to come by." With that, he left.

Colin took a minute to inventory what he saw hanging on the walls. It was better than he had hoped for. To a degree, the tools were crude, but considering the technology with which they had been made, he was impressed. Braving the rain, he jogged up to the shed and retrieved one of the pieces of seasoned yew that he had brought back the previous day. On his way back to the barn, he saw a grinding wheel out back. He knew he wasn't much of a carpenter, but he wasn't looking for pretty – pure functionality was all he was after. Taking a hand ax he began to rough in the shape he was after. With short chopping motions, he began to carve flat limbs on either end of the small log, and narrowed the center section, but maintained a much more rounded form in this region. It required a couple of hours to get the general shape he wanted. He then selected a hand-plane, and began smoothing the rough cuts his ax work had left on the wood. He continued to work with the plane, thinning the limbs as well as making them more narrow and rounding the waist of the bow he was shaping.

By late afternoon, he thought he had the start of a pretty good bow. Holding the wood up, he tried to estimate the length he would need. He knew he wasn't much of an archer. In fact, his experience was pretty much limited to the year he was 16. He had bought a used Bear recurve and practiced with it faithfully out in the back yard, shooting at a paper plate tacked to a stack of straw bales. He had gotten to where he could hit the plate pretty consistently at 30 yards. But despite his efforts at hunting deer with a bow, the only living thing he had ever shot at was an exceptionally unfortunate chipmunk. He thought about trying to boil the wood and make a recurve bow, but doubted his ability to get a precise curve on each end. So he opted to keep it simple and just make a long bow. Well, maybe a short long bow. He knew that the medieval English archers had been able to lob arrows into their targets at ranges in excess of 100 yards with some degree of accuracy. But Colin figured if he could propel an arrow with enough force to take down a deer at 30 yards or so, he would call that good.

As he eyed the bow now taking shape, his brow furrowed. What would be the impact of introducing such an object into this world? Would this become a "weapon of mass destruction" to these people? Apparently warfare was not unknown, but at least among the people he had met, swords and spears seemed to be the pinnacle of their military technology. How would the introduction of the bow and arrow change that? While he stared at the bow, he could see the pattern of it taking shape. It was no longer a rough-cut blank, but a completed weapon. Not really even a weapon. It was simply a tool, to be used for good or evil, as the possessor might choose. It was possible that such a tool might be used to kill – to establish dominance, to enslave. It was equally possible that it might be used to kill – but to defend, protect and ensure liberty. It was a tool. Nothing more. It is not the tool that has to be guarded against, but the application of the tool. Those applications are not hatched in inanimate objects nor in muscle and sinew, but in hearts and minds. As he stared at the crudely shaped bow, he could see the pattern of it – no longer as a crude implement, but as a well formed tool, clean and simple in design, but one that had the potential to transform a world. Not by what it was, but by what it represented. A new thing was about to be seen in this world. He smiled and thought, "Like soap."

The rain had let up, and the late afternoon sun was trying to break through the clouds before setting. Colin found a crude straw broom and swept his wood shavings together and threw them out back of the barn. He forked some hay into the stalls of the cows and the oxen. He was thinking that he was going to need some feathers for fletching, and glue to attach the fletching to the arrows. He was debating about trying to reinforce the bow with sinew as well. And he was contemplating what to use for a bowstring. Preoccupied with his thoughts, he was surprised when Elam showed up to start the evening milking

Colin was still disappointed that the milk cows didn't have some kind of "alien" appearance. In fact, he would have been hard pressed to distinguish them from the Jersey breed on Earth. They were docile, and came when Elam called them, eager to have their bulging udders relieved. Elam brought two copper pails and a one-legged milk stool. Colin had a hard time balancing on the single leg, and had to keep shifting his weight. He also wasn't very accomplished at milking. His cow kept turning to look at him as if to ask, "Do you know what you're doing back there?"

Showing her irritation with his clumsy efforts, she took to swatting him with her tail in a regular rhythm. Elam finished his cow then came to complete the job which Colin was performing poorly. Instead of being irritated, he seemed pleased that he could show this stranger a thing or two about milking a cow. Working on the second cow, Elam asked, "What have you been working on today?"

"I started on the bow I told you about. I've only used one of the yew logs we brought back, but it is roughed in."

"Can I see it?"

Colin nodded, "Sure. When you're done. It's got a ways to go."

In a few minutes, Elam was done with the milking and set the second copper pail by the door with the first, covering each with a clean linen cloth to keep anything from getting in them. Colin led him back to the shop and showed him the bow. Elam stroked the wood, "I still don't see how it works. How does this kill a deer?"

"This doesn't actually kill the deer. This is the bow. I'll have to make some arrows. That's what we shoot with the bow. The bow is just a tool to make throwing an object, like an arrow, easier. The arrow can be sent with more force and more accuracy over a greater distance than you can achieve by hand. It's just a tool."

Colin set the bow back on the work bench. But just as they were leaving the barn, Jorge strode up, carrying a heavy load which he dumped at Colin's feet. "There!" he said triumphantly. "Now we can make leather!" Colin unrolled the bundle and found three hides. Two large cowhides and a sheepskin.

"I went to see Tunsten," Jorge explained. "He raises animals for meat. Cows, sheep, pigs. I went to see if he had hides. He laughed at me, but said to take all I wanted. He only had three fresh hides, so I brought them. And I got salt."

"These are beautifully skinned. There's hardly any meat or fat left on the hide, so we don't have to do much scraping. If it's alright with you, we can salt these here and roll them up. We'll set them at an angle so the moisture will drain from them. But Jorge, this isn't quite as fast as making soap."

Jorge nodded, "Fine. We'll start and it's finished when it's finished."

"Good enough. We can get them salted now. Tomorrow we'll get them scraped and soaking."

"No." Jorge was stern. "Tomorrow is Sabbath. We do no work on Sabbath. It must wait until second day, even if the hides are ruined."

"Sorry. I didn't know. Leaving the hides over the Sabbath won't hurt anything. They'll keep." He hesitated, then asked, "Does your Sabbath begin at sundown today, or is it tomorrow."

Jorge continued to look very stern, "Tomorrow is Sabbath. Not today. But we do not work. There are some that do, but we do not. You must agree to this."

"Yes. No problem. I've always tried to honor the Sabbath, but when I was sick, I lost track of the days. I just didn't know when it was and didn't think to ask. I meant no offense."

Jorge nodded and turned to pick up one of the milk buckets, indicating for Elam to pick up the other. Colin unrolled the hides on the dirt floor of the barn, flesh side up. He sprinkled a light layer of salt, then rolled them and set them on an angled board so the moisture could drain out as it was leached from the hide. Leaving the barn, he detoured over to the poultry shed and began scrounging for duck feathers. They were heavier than the chicken feathers, and he thought they would make better fletching for his arrows.

Halvor did not make an appearance at dinner. Colin hadn't seen him all day, but didn't give it much thought. As he arose from the table to help with the dishes, Elam blurted out, "Can I help with the dishes?"

Miran looked at him in disbelief.

Blushing, Elam looked down and mumbled, "I want to use the soap."

Miran still looked surprised, while Jorge shook his head and smiled. Colin smiled as well and said, "Take advantage of him while you can. The novelty will wear off. This isn't going to last."

"I know," said Miran, "But it will be nice while it does."

Chapter 7   To Business

After dinner, Colin retrieved several of his white birch arrow blanks and began carefully scraping the bark from the slender shafts with his knife, trimming the tiny knots from the leaf buds flush and smooth with the surface. Until he had the bow finished, he wouldn't try to determine what length to cut them. Jorge was sitting at the table, repairing his shoes. His time out in the rain had taken a toll on the canvas. "Jorge, I know you told me that you don't work on the Sabbath. I mean no offense, what is permitted on the Sabbath?"

Jorge, looked at him blankly, "It is Sabbath. We do not work. We honor Sabbath."

"Yes, I understand that. But I'd like to know how you honor the Sabbath. I mean, do you go to church? Do you read scriptures, sacred books? What do you do?"

Jorge looked puzzled now. "By not working, that is honoring Sabbath. We do not need to go or do. We give honor by not going or doing."

"So you don't have a church? A place where you worship and where you're instructed in the teachings of your god?"

"I do not understand this 'church.' As for being instructed, who is there to teach?" Jorge returned to his shoes.

Colin was silent for a moment, "In my land, there are buildings built specifically to worship God. There are different organizations who perceive the teachings of God differently. The organization is also called a 'church,' like the buildings they meet in. Most of these have ministers who claim education or authority which qualifies them to teach of God and what He would want them to do. Some of their teachings are similar and others can be quite different. The Church I belong to, it taught, as you believe, that we should not work on the Sabbath. Some of the members still did, but that was their choice. Do you have someone that you believe teaches what God wants you to do – like honoring the Sabbath?"

Jorge had been getting extremely agitated while Colin spoke and when he finished he stood up and practically roared, "Why do you, who wears the mantle ask me this!?! By wearing the mantle, you claim to be the messenger! You claim to speak for Messias! Almost, I believe you. You're so different! You look different! You act different! You know things! You teach! Do you wear the mantle by right, or are you another pretender!?!"

Miran and Elam had entered during this last outburst, where they were frozen, wide-eyed and a little bit fearful. Jorge still stood, anger on his face.

Colin closed his eyes for a long moment before he spoke, "Jorge, I'm sorry to have angered you. I didn't want to give offense by violating the traditions of your Sabbath. I wanted to understand what it is you believe, so that I could try to not offend your beliefs. Dalene told me a little bit, but not enough that I really understand. What I do understand is that I'm a very long way from my home. I don't know how I came to be here, or why I'm here. I do believe that what God does not cause, He permits. I am here, so God has permitted me to be here. I am wearing what you call a mantle. I would have simply called it a shirt or jacket with a hood on it. In my land, it would have no special meaning. I don't claim to be a messenger from your Messias. I'm sorry if that makes me a pretender in your eyes. I've heard it said that we each are what we are and that we can be no more and no less. I don't agree with that. We are what we are, but I believe God wants us to become more than what we are, better than what we are, and to help others do the same. You and your family have shown me great kindness. What little I teach, I do in the hopes that it might make your lives better – allow you to do and become more. But I haven't come bearing any special message from your Messias."

It was not until then that he noticed Halvor, standing expressionless in the open doorway. He didn't know how long he'd been there, or how much of this exchange he had heard. And at the moment, he really didn't care. He just felt very tired.

Miran stepped forward and placed a calming hand on her husband's arm, urging him to sit. She said, "Colin, you have not given offense. You must understand that for many hundreds of years, there have been none who have worn the mantle by right. There have been a few who have claimed such, but when they appeared before the Council, they were not without fault, and they were destroyed. In some cases, those pretenders had already convinced many that they had the right to the mantle. Some didn't wear the mantle, but claimed authority. There was much conflict. Sometimes blood was spilled – terrible wars were fought, so our history says, before the followers of the impostors were eliminated and their writings destroyed. But there was disagreement about the prophecies and the writings as well. Because these things also caused much conflict, the Council had what writings survived collected in the Great Library at Salem, where only the High Council, and a select few scholars, mostly of the Third Order, may study them. Only when they agree as to what the writing means do they teach it to the people, and so there is peace. They agree that there should be no work done on Sabbath. My husband is sincere in following the teachings we receive, and so we do not work on Sabbath. Please understand, none in my lifetime have worn the mantle truly, so when you came, we hoped…….." And her voice trailed off, as she glanced over her shoulder at Halvor. But then she continued, passionately, "We hoped that once again, one wearing the mantle by right had come! The prophecy says, Messias will send one wearing His mantle and he will teach us! As my husband says, you are so different, we thought surely you must be the messenger, and our hearts are heavy because you tell us that you are not. Yet we cannot believe you are an impostor, because you tell us that you are not the messenger. But because we have come to truly like you, it gives us much sorrow that the Council will destroy you. Oh, can you not truly be the messenger?" She fell silent, and leaned heavily against Jorge, who sat staring at the floor.

Halvor stepped into the room, pausing to close the door firmly behind him. "That is not precisely what the prophecy says. It says, referring to the messengers of Messias,

No man shall take this honor for himself, only he shall have the mantle of authority from Messias. He shall teach this people to choose truth, which shall make them free. But the Evil One shall teach them to choose that which is pleasing to the mind, and shall bind them as slaves."

Miran looked at him, expressionless, and said, "You know prophecy."

Halvor simply nodded to her, politely, and turned again to look at Colin, as though considering an interesting problem. "Why are you really here?" Colin asked. He was not hostile, simply curious.

Halvor smiled, a tight, humorless smile and said, "As you were told. I am here to assist you, should you need it." With that, he turned and walked out the door.

The other four sat silently in the room for a few minutes. Colin gathered his things, nodded to Elam then Jorge and Miran, and walked to the door. "I'm sorry that I'm not what you want me to be." Then he left, closing the door softly behind him.

Colin woke up early, as the light began to filter into the shed. He just lay quietly for several minutes, before deciding to get up to wash and shave. He hoped that nobody else would be up too early, as he still wasn't sure exactly what was and was not allowed on the Sabbath. What did "no work" cover, exactly? Was shaving considered work? Probably, he thought, since shaving seemed to be a rarity here anyway. Washing? Maybe. He hurried to the spring, dipped a bucket of water, then went out back of the shed to wash his hair and face. Working up the limited lather that his homemade soap allowed, he shaved, and was pleased to actually not cut himself for a change. The sun was barely peeking above the distant hills. The rain of the previous day had given way to a crystal clear morning.

The Sabbath taboos, he admitted, had him spooked. He wasn't sure if they ate breakfast, or even ate at all for that matter. The fact was, the little scene with Jorge and Miran last night had upset him, and he really wasn't interested in eating this morning. Skipping meals wasn't a novelty for him anyway. In his church, they had encouraged fasting for one day each month - no food or drink for 24 hours. They donated the cost of the meals they missed to provide food for the poor. It taught you to appreciate what you had, and also to subject the body to the spirit. It had become second nature to him and he didn't want to upset Jorge and Miran anymore than he already had, so he thought he would just keep a low profile today. Jorge had indicated that he wouldn't be doing any work, so Colin wouldn't feel guilty about not being there to help. He decided to go explore the creek, up above the farm.

Cutting across the field, he dropped down through the trees and to the stream. He couldn't resist the cool water, so he stopped to drink from the stream with a cupped hand. There were an abundance of deer tracks and game trails leading from the stream up through the trees and to the fields. While the stream bed was rocky, indicating that at times there was significantly more water rushing through here, there were also an ample number of gravel bars, undercut embankments and muddy trickles from springs draining into the stream. In the mud were tracks of something like a raccoon or river otter. He didn't know tracks well enough to say for certain what. Everything here was so familiar – like Earth, he thought. He was always looking for something unique or 'alien.' He had to smile to himself, admitting that there was so much of his own planet that he didn't know that he wasn't in the best position to judge what was alien or not. The trees, for example, looked generally familiar, but some of these oaks and maples were huge! Massive trees spreading 60 feet across or more, reaching heights well in excess of 100 feet. Was this an 'alien' species, or was he simply seeing pristine forest, un-harvested by man and un-stunted by pollution and technology? All he knew was that it was truly beautiful.

As he worked his way up the stream, the channel he was following gradually became deeper and steeper. There were fewer stretches of calm water, and more frequent cascades dropping into dark pools before rushing on to the next fall. Large boulders littered the edge of the stream, and the terrain was climbing more sharply. He estimated that he had followed the stream for about four miles. He had seen fish laying in shallow pools and occasionally hitting the surface, feeding on insects skimming the water. He needed to figure out a fish hook. As the stream climbed into a narrow, rocky gorge, he was soon forced to leap from boulder to boulder in order to continue his ascent while staying out of the water. Reaching a waterfall, dropping six or eight feet, he had to cling to the rock face with fingers and toes in order to clamber up and he cautioned himself to remember that it's usually easier climbing up than down. He didn't want to strand himself. Above the waterfall was a stretch of calm water, perhaps 200 yards in length, meandering between steep rock walls and ending in another waterfall up at the head. A rough pebble beach flanked the stream, dotted by the occasional hardy shrub which somehow managed to survive the torrents that must occasionally rush through here, making do with the little sunlight that would reach the bottom of this gorge. He knew it was time to head back.

His hosts might be worried and he hadn't told anyone where he was going. It would be past midday before he could return, even if he didn't stop along the way. But he wanted to see more of this spot. Walking along the rough stone beach, he noticed streaks of color in the rock wall rising on either side of him. There were pale steaks, changing from a cream color to brown and red. The beach was made up of the same rough material. Colin paused to examine the rocks more closely. They were sharp and rough. He thought they looked like – flint? His Dad had had a collection of flint arrowheads and scrapers. The material looked similar. Picking up a large fragment, He drew his knife and struck the rock sharply with the back of the blade. It sparked! If this was flint, it would be ideal for making the arrowheads he needed. He spent several minutes selecting an assortment of pieces, roughly triangular in shape, that he thought would take a minimum amount of work to convert to arrowheads. He also picked up a couple of large pieces. They were too large to fit in his pockets, but this was such a precious find he wanted to take these even if he had to carry them by hand the whole way. He again reminded himself that he needed to acquire a pack or pouch for these excursions. Pausing for a moment to admire this peaceful gorge one last time, he turned and headed back downstream.

Carrying the two large pieces of flint wasn't as awkward as he had feared. On occasion he would toss the rocks down some particularly steep section where he needed both hands to make a descent. But he moved swiftly. He did see a pair of otters frolicking in a deep pool and startled a red fox which had come down to the stream to drink. He also found a small antler – a 3-point shed. It was not badly weathered, so it was obviously from this spring. He was delighted with this find and added it to his load, as it would be used to make the knapping tool he would need for flaking the arrowheads. By shortly after noon, he was back to the cultivated fields on the farm. His pace slowed. He wasn't sure what kind of greeting to expect after the confrontation of the previous night. He also wasn't sure if his little walk had somehow violated the observance of the Sabbath. But there was nothing to be done about it at this point. He estimated that he had covered some eight to ten miles and having skipped breakfast, was hoping that he might get lunch.

He stopped to deposit his precious collection of flint and the antler in the shed with his arrow blanks. As he stepped out into the sunshine, Miran appeared in the doorway of the house, "Oh, Colin, you're back! Halvor said you would be along shortly. Come and eat. You must be hungry."

The reference to Halvor bothered him. Had he been followed all morning, or had Halvor just seen him as he cut across the field a few minutes ago? Still he was pleased at the invitation and grateful that the unpleasantness of the night before had been forgotten, or at least was being ignored. He ducked through the doorframe into the house and saw Jorge and

Baylor sitting at the table. Jorge slid a chair toward him, saying, "Come! Sit! Eat!"

Colin sat, helping himself to some bread. Jorge poured milk from a pitcher into an earthenware mug and passed it to him. Baylor cleared his throat, glancing from Colin to Jorge and then spoke, "I've a proposal to be making to you. Well, it's Kath, really. She likes that stuff you made – the soap I mean. Well, she says it would sell at market. She was thinking maybe like a partnership. I've got plenty of fat and we're going to market every week anyway. So she was saying if maybe you was to make more of that soap, we could sell it. We'd each stand to make a bit….if you were interested, that is."

Colin had continued to eat slowly while Baylor was getting this out. It was difficult to not smile, as Baylor was so obviously uncomfortable making this business proposition. Colin thought Baylor was a man who valued his independence and didn't much care to ask anyone for anything. Much as it amused him to see this gruff, hulking figure squirm, he didn't want to prolong his discomfort. "I think we could work something out. It isn't especially difficult, but it does take some time. Jorge, are you and Miran interested in going into a partnership with Kath and Baylor?"

Jorge looked surprised to be included in this discussion. "Aye. I think Miran might give it fair consideration."

Kath and Miran, who had been out walking, appeared in the doorway. "What is it that I might be considering?" Miran asked.

Now it was Jorge's turn to look uncomfortable. "Baylor was just telling Colin here, that he thinks there might be a profit to be made selling soap at market, seeing if Colin might be interested in a bit of business. Colin was asking if you and I might be wanting to go in a partnership with the lot of 'em."

Miran nodded, "Kath was just telling me her thought on selling soap. With them as a source of the fat for making it, and Colin with the knowing how to do it though, I'd not thought of us as being partners with them."

Colin said, "Look, if you're really interested in trying this, I'll be happy to help. But as I see it, this would work best as a partnership between the five of us. With the farm work, most of the labor in making the soap is going to fall to Miran and Kath. The men can help when they have time. I can teach you what I know, but some things you will just have to experiment with and decide what works best. Since, for the present, I am living here with Jorge and Miran, this isn't going to work without them. And if Baylor provides the fat and Kath does the selling at market, it looks like a good partnership to me. I'd suggest a one-fifth stake for each – like shares. That will allow me to help pay for my room and board here and will provide cash for you. What do you say?"

Everyone nodded, with smiles of agreement. Colin continued, "Make no mistake – this will be work. It isn't especially hard, but it will take some effort. Nobody is going to walk up and hand you money you haven't earned. Baylor, I don't want to short you on selling whatever fat you have that you can sell, but we can use a lot for making soap. We'll need your ash pit as well. Kath and Miran, you'll have a better product if we add some scent to it. Think about what you might want to try – juniper berries, mint, lilacs....."

"Oh! I love lilacs!" Miran exclaimed, "Can we really make soap with a lilac scent?"

Colin nodded, "I think so. We'll just have to try some things and see what works and what sells.

And so the soap-making partnership was born. As Colin had predicted, Miran and Kath did the bulk of the labor. But rather than resenting it, they seemed pleased at the time this gave them to work together and excited by the prospect of seeing their efforts resulting in actual cash. Between helping with the chores and other farm work, Colin instructed the two women in the process of leaching ashes and making potash. Through trial and error, he was able to resurrect his hazy memory and found that the potash had been boiled to the right concentration for making soap when a raw egg would just float in the boiling liquid. He taught them how to render the fat to remove the impurities and they experimented with various additives to give scent to what was otherwise a fairly strong, harsh soap. One day Miran came in beaming, carrying a huge arm full of lilac blossoms. Colin and Elam helped her strip the flowers from the woody stalks into a pot and steam them to collect the oils. While Colin still thought the scent was weak in the resulting batch of soap, Miran was thrilled that she could capture the scent of her favorite flower, especially when Colin assured her that it would keep all year long. The next morning she appeared to absolutely glow, the faint smell of lilac wafting about her. She had also scrubbed her hair and it flowed down her back in a dazzling dark cascade. Jorge again clapped Colin on his shoulder, hard and laughed with that same sly look as he said, "That soap is good!"

The next few days were busy. Kath and Miran learned quickly and soon had a daily routine of spending a few hours making soap and leaching ashes for the next day's soap-making. Colin was also busy with his efforts of trying to tan the hides Jorge had brought back from Tunsten's the day before the Sabbath. The salted hides were unrolled on the ground out in front of the barn. Colin used an ax to cut a number of slender oak pegs and pounded these through the edge of the hide into the ground, stretching the hide as he worked his way around.

With the hide firmly pegged, He used the ax blade to scrape the salt from the hide, taking with it any sinew, meat, fat and the membrane that lined the skin. Because Tunsten had done such an expert job skinning, there was very little that had to be scraped. The sheepskin he then took and washed – with soap – in a tub of very hot water to remove as much of the lanolin from the wool as possible. This skin he would try to tan with the hair on. The two cowhides, however, he wanted to tan with the hair off.

To remove the hair, Colin decided to try two different processes. The first he soaked overnight in a weak solution of potash. The potassium hydroxide loosened the hair and the next day he was able to rinse the hide and use a draw knife to scrape the hair off. The other hide he carried down to the stream below the farm. He weighted the hide with heavy stones and left it to soak in a large riffle with the water running over the top of it. After several days, he was able to scrape the hair from this one as well.

Jorge would have Colin explain to him each day what he was doing in regards to the tanning process. Colin would carefully explain what he was doing and why. Jorge seemed to be intensely interested in every aspect, even though his farm work kept him from active participation. While the second cowhide was soaking in the creek to remove the hair, Colin decided to proceed with the other cowhide and the sheepskin. Jorge had gotten a large oak tub to soak the hides in the tanning solution. Colin cut a thin strip of skin from the cowhide all the way around, smoothing the perimeter. He set this aside to use for rawhide, which would be useful in attaching arrowheads to his arrows. The hides were placed in the tub and enough water added to just cover them and salt mixed to form a brine. Colin had been gathering up the wood chips from Jorge's firewood cutting operation and he dumped the chips into the brine until they completely covered the surface. Since oak contains tannin, Colin hoped that enough would leach from the chips to provide the tanning action necessary. He explained all this to Jorge and said, "If this doesn't work, there are still other methods to try. I've done brain tanning as well – smearing the brains of the animal into the hide and working it in. Even if the hide isn't fully tanned, we may be able to finish it by smoke curing. We wrap the hide around poles over a smoky fire for several days. The smoke helps to cure the leather and is supposed to make it more impervious to rot." At least a couple of times each day the tub was stirred and the hides checked. Colin would press his thumbnail firmly into the skin and see if the imprint stayed. When the faint mark remained, he decided that the tanning was done.

The hides were pulled from the brine and drained, then carried to the creek and rinsed. They were then laid across a pole wedged in the crotch of two trees to keep it off the ground. Here in the shade, the hides could slowly dry. Colin explained, "You can stake the hides out – stretch them and they will dry hard that way, unless you keep working them with something like a flint scraper while its drying. If we let them dry hanging loose like this, then we have to come and stretch the hide several times a day so it doesn't become hard. The color will be quite dark at first, but as it begins to dry and you pull it, the fibers break, preventing it from being hard and giving us a nice soft finish."

Jorge nodded his understanding and periodically he would take a break from the field to pull and stretch the hides. At last, Colin pronounced the tanning a success. The cowhide was heavy, so it was still fairly stiff, particularly across the hindquarters where the leather was thickest. The sheepskin leather was much thinner and so it was more soft and pliable. That evening, when they took the finished hides up to the house, Miran was enthralled by the clean, soft wool. "And you're sure it won't rot and smell?" she asked at least a half dozen times.

"No." Colin shook his head. "That is what tanning does. It cures and preserves the skin, so it is much more useful." The sheepskin is very warm and can be used to line your shoes or coats in the winter, or as a covering on your bed. He had Jorge stand on the cowhide where the leather was thickest over the haunches. Using a sharp stick, he traced an outline of Jorge's foot, then a second outline an inch and a half around the first. Miran caught on immediately, which Colin was grateful for. He knew the general idea of making moccasins, but she obviously knew the practicalities of the operation, so Colin was happy to let her take over. The second hide had finally been de-haired, after soaking in the running water of the creek and was currently in the brine solution being tanned.

On market day, Colin was down at Baylor and Kath's place early, helping them load sides of pork, buckets of lard and a box filled with balls of soap onto their wagon. He cautioned Kath against taking their entire inventory on this first day.

"Don't take too much this first trip. Nobody has seen soap before, so they aren't dying to buy it. Take maybe a dozen balls. Be a little selective even about who you try to sell it to. You want somebody with money, and somebody that the other's look up to – you know, the ones that others are a little bit envious of. If they buy it, you know they'll like it and the word will be out. You won't be able to make enough soap to keep up with the demand."

He also suggested that she take a wash basin and some fat to demonstrate the benefits of soap. Kath nodded happily, nervous, but anxious to be off to market.

That evening, Baylor and Kath stopped by. Kath was positively beaming and even Baylor was grinning through his beard. Kath brought out a small linen pouch and carefully poured 12 small silver coins on the table. "We sold every soap before midday!" she announced. All afternoon we turned people away. I should have held one back just for showing folks, but I didn't think of it until too late. Seems several of the ladies who bought them were showing others – not how it cleaned, but just letting them smell it! They kept coming, but I had to send 'em away. I told them to stop by next week and we'd have more." She divided the coins into three equal piles and pushed one to Jorge and Miran and the other to Colin.

Colin took two coins from his pile and gave one to Kath and the other to Miran, "Mine is only a one-fifth share. You two did most of the work, you get the profit. Remember? We all agreed."

Miran shook her head as she and Kath handed the coins back, "No. We've talked it over – all of us. Without you, we'd have had nothing to sell at all. We decided that a third to each of us is fair. Jorge and I are sort of one anyway and so are Kath and Baylor. This is fair, and we'll brook no argument from you!"

"I think you're too generous, especially where you've been providing me with food and a place to sleep all this time. I should at least pay you for that – now that I have something to pay with."

Jorge slapped a heavy hand on the table, "Pay? You have been paying, with your labor here. I could not afford to pay for what you do. No, it is as Miran has said. This is fair. Maybe more fair to us than to you!"

Colin learned that the small silver coins were called torals. There were copper coins of approximately the same size called subtorals and gold coins called dectorals. The monetary system was simple, as these three coins constituted the entire coinage of the realm, as it were. Each was relatively unadorned, having a crude, faint geometric pattern stamped on each side. Ten torals was the equivalent of one dectoral and ten subtorals made one toral. They told him that one toral would pay for room and board at a moderately priced inn for one day – including three full meals. He was impressed, but commented that seemed a bit steep a price for a ball of soap. Kath and Miran looked shocked, "You see how it cleans and it smells nice. The smell stays for months. No, the price is cheap. I only sold so cheaply today to get people to buy it. Next week it will be more!" said Kath. Colin shrugged. Obviously these people understood capitalism and their advantageous position in a free-market economy. And now he had money. It was a relief, in a way. While he had lacked for nothing, it hadn't set well with him, being so dependent on the kindness of these people. Now perhaps, he could be less of a burden and find some way to show his appreciation for what they had done for him.

Colin had been so busy getting the soap-making project launched and starting the tanning operation, he'd only worked on his bow sporadically. Still, it was taking shape nicely. He had left the handle section fairly thick and carved an arrow rest just above the grip, which would keep the arrow shaft in-line with the bowstring. The limbs had been shaped and smoothed, with the notches cut into the end of each limb for the string to attach. The soap-making operation had provided an additional benefit through the relationship with Kath and Baylor. This had allowed him to acquire a good supply of sinew – the heavy strands from the spinal cord of the animals which Baylor butchered. It turned out that Baylor had a working arrangement with Tunsten, so Colin was being provided with various components for his projects from two excellent sources. He had sinew and from Tunsten he also had several hooves drying down by the barn. He had chipped these and would take a number of fragments to boil down for glue. His first efforts had produced results which were not impressive, but seemed adequate to fletch his arrows. He hoped to improve the process and use the glue to toughen the bowstring and attach sinew to his bow in order to give it extra power. The hoof glue, he knew, wasn't likely to be waterproof, but he didn't plan to get the bow wet, if he could help it.

When he was tired, he worked on his arrows. He now had ten smooth, balanced shafts ready to attach the arrowheads. He had spent a long evening fletching them, muttering when the fletching broke. While the glue seemed marginal for attaching the feather to the wood, at least he hadn't had to resort to using a rawhide wrap for that operation and a thin coating of glue on the feather helped keep it from separating. He had chipped out a half-dozen arrowheads of reasonable quality. With Jorge's saw, he had sawn off one of the points of the antler he had found, leaving a length of about eight inches. This was his knapping tool. By applying the antler point to the roughed-in arrowheads, he could cause pressure flakes to slough off the surface, shaping and sharpening the arrowhead. He ruined several of his pieces and quickly learned to save his best samples for when he was more skilled. At last he had six suitable heads, but he had been delaying a critical operation. In fact, he had to admit, he had been so leery of splitting the shaft on his arrow blanks in order to insert the arrowheads, that he had gone ahead and done the fletching already. If he split the shaft too far, all that work would be for nothing. Sighing, he picked up an arrow and looked at it. With his knife positioned over the blunt end of the shaft, he cringed and gave the back of the knife a sharp rap with the smallest hammer in Jorge's collection. The wood split – just enough. Colin inserted an arrowhead into the shaft, careful not to force it and cause the wood to split more deeply. He then took a thin strand of rawhide from a cup where it had been soaking in water. He wrapped it tightly around the shaft, finishing off with a single half-hitch. The arrow was then set aside for the rawhide to dry. As it dried, the rawhide would shrink and harden, causing the wood to grip the arrowhead tightly and it would be finished. He did five more the same way and was pleased when not one of the shafts split too deeply. He then inserted blunt, unfinished pieces of flint into three more shafts. These were approximately the same size and balance as the others, but didn't have the sharpened flint. These would be his practice arrows and might find use as blunts for hunting birds or other small game. It was late, but the job was finally done. He had one last project to do. Taking several of the longest strands of dried sinew, he began to braid his bowstring. It was a clumsy effort, he admitted, but he hoped it would be adequate for a first attempt. It was well after midnight when he was done. Satisfied, he blew out the lantern and retired for the night.

The next day was the Sabbath again. Colin was tired, so he was in no hurry to get out of bed after his late night. It had been an exhausting week, but he was pleased with how much he had accomplished. Smiling to himself, he thought, "Even if they kill me after my Evaluation, this world will have changed. I will have left my mark here."

Then he frowned. Would he really have left a mark? Something of value? While the technology of these people was not advanced, neither were they the least bit backward. The rapidity with which Kath and Miran had picked up soap-making, the interest and aptitude which Jorge and Elam showed in regards to making leather indicated intelligence and a hunger for learning and innovation. Why then, had such simple arts as soap and leather making never been developed? Why had the bow and arrow never been discovered? The art of warfare, he knew, was one of the great motivators for innovation in the history of his own world. So what was keeping innovation and invention in check in this world? Would his contribution to this society last, or would whatever was limiting their technological advance erase what he had done? The thought bothered him.

Chapter 8   Corrupting Influences

The Sabbath passed quietly. Jorge and Miran had gone to visit friends in Tyber. They had invited Colin, but were relieved when he declined. He spent the day working on his bow. It was quiet and peaceful, but he decided he didn't like the Sabbath. There wasn't enough to keep him occupied. It left him feeling frustrated.

On Second day he rolled out, anxious for a day of activity to erase the melancholy that had settled over him with too much time to think on the Sabbath. Mentally, he kept thinking of it as "Monday" but they didn't seem to have names for any day except Sabbath. The rest just had numbers, two through seven.   After getting cleaned up and saying his prayers, he pitched in with the morning chores. He had been practicing striking sparks with his knife and the flint that he had found. He was getting to be fairly adept at starting a fire, assuming he had a decent nest of tinder. And that was exactly what he had found - a mouse nest made the perfect bed for the sparks he struck and he could make a fire easily. There was no shortage of those about. He had rigged a small pouch out of some badly worn canvas he found in the barn and had taken to slinging this over his shoulder whenever he went exploring, but there had been little opportunity for that this past week. Still, he kept a mouse nest in it for emergency use. He didn't need that this morning. He grabbed a mouse nest he had seen in a corner of the hay loft and made a small fire. He was boiling more of the chipped hooves this morning. He had used the fire in the house for his first batch of glue, but it had smelled terribly and polite as she was, Miran had made it clear that was the last batch of glue he would boil in her house. He'd cut the operation short, which might have explained why his first attempt at glue making had pretty marginal success.

He let this batch of glue simmer and thicken a good long time. When it looked about right, he smeared a heavy layer across the face of his bow, then quickly layered in strand after strand of the sinew he had cut for this purpose.   He had to get it laid into the glue before it cooled and hardened. One of the benefits of the hoof glue was that it retained some flexibility even when it cooled and dried. That would keep it from cracking when the bow flexed. He would let it set for the day, but hoped to try it this evening before dark.

They spent the day cutting firewood. With the three of them working, the wagon was fully loaded by midday. As before, they lunched by the stream, drinking from the cool water and washing the sweat and grime from their arms and faces. The wagon was unloaded near the house and Jorge waved Colin off regarding any further work for the day. This freed him to tend to the second cowhide which was now in the tanning bath.

By late afternoon, Colin decided to try his bow. He hadn't a quiver for his arrows, so he simply grabbed the bundle and set off to find a practice target out of sight of the house, down by the hay meadow. He wasn't anxious for an audience of this first effort. As luck would have it though, Elam was finishing chores in the barn when he spotted Colin and asked to accompany him. "If you like, "Colin replied. "But don't be expecting too much. I haven't shot a bow in years and it's going to take a lot of practice before I hit anything."

He gathered a large bundle of grass from the edge of the field, lashing it together with a short length of rope. This he set out in the field, explaining, "I really don't want to shoot at something solid, like a tree or a stump. Arrows are too difficult to make and a hard target would probably shatter the arrow if I were to hit it. I don't want to shoot in the trees, because I'll lose my arrows when I miss. So I'll just practice on a clump of grass in the field. Pretend it's a rabbit."

Elam laughed and watched with interest as Colin bent his bow to attach the string. The bow had turned out nicely. At least Colin thought so, considering it was the first bow he had ever made. It was about 45 inches in length - much shorter than an English long-bow. Probably more like a hunting bow of the American Plains Indians. Carefully, he pulled back the string, getting used to the feel of it. It felt good to him. He took one of the blunt arrows he had made and notched it on the string. Sighting along the arrow, he drew down on the clump of grass. He focused, and all he saw was the clump of grass. He saw his arrow, saw it flying through the air, piercing the clump. He saw it......... He shook his head, clearing it and slowly relaxed the tension on the string. He would have sworn he had released the arrow. He had seen it. Strange. Again, he drew back the string. He aimed, focusing on the clump, he could see the arrow and the clump. The arrow piercing the clump..........and then he released the string and saw an exact replay of what his mind had visualized just a second before!

"You hit it!" yelled Elam.

Colin picked up another of his blunt arrows. Again he drew back, aiming at the clump. He could see the arrow arcing to the target.........just before he released the string. Again, his arrow struck the clump, right next to his first arrow.

"Ha! You said it would take much practice! You're good!"

Colin smiled weakly, "I think I just got lucky. I'm going to retrieve my arrows and then move the target back a bit more. He had paced the distance at about 20 yards. Now he moved the clump another 15 yards back, 35 yards would be about the maximum range he was comfortable with for hunting. Taking a deep breath, he drew the string, sighting along the arrow and that same strange precognition occurred. He could see the arc of the arrow. Most people think that an arrow - or a bullet for that matter - flies along a straight path. But due to gravitational pull, a projectile begins to drop the instant it is released, so to hit any target down range, one has to aim above the target and lob the projectile. Most people are also surprised at how slow an arrow is in flight. The eye has no difficulty following the trajectory of even a high velocity hunting arrow, which flies at around 325 feet per second. So the arcing trajectory is very obvious. That is exactly what he saw the instant before he released the arrow - an arc terminating precisely in the clump of grass - and that is exactly what happened.

"Again! May I try? Please?" Elam begged.

Colin nodded. Too perplexed to speak. He showed Elam how to hold the bow and cautioned him to release the arrow cleanly, or the string could give him a painful welt. Elam squinted along the bow, released the arrow, which wobbled in flight and buried its head in the dirt about 15 yards away.

"You made it look easy. It's harder than I thought."

"Yes, it takes a lot of practice. You'll get the hang of it." Colin replied.

Elam tried again. This time the arrow went all of 20 yards. Elam was disgusted. "You have to adjust your point of aim. Sight along the arrow, but aim higher."

Elam nodded, grim determination on his face. His shot this time, lobbed way past the clump of grass, missing by at least 20 yards. "I didn't do very well, did I?"

Colin smiled, "I told you. It will take hours of practice, but you can do it. It becomes easier the more you practice."

"You must have practiced a lot."

"Elam, I don't know what just happened here. It shouldn't have happened. You shot about the way I expected to shoot. I just could..........see. I saw the target and I saw how the arrow would fly to the target. That never happened to me before. I don't understand it."

Elam just nodded, unconvinced. The sun was hanging low in the sky as they walked out to retrieve the arrows. Elam asked, "Are you going to shoot a deer?"

"I hadn't planned on it this evening. I thought I would just get a little practice in."

Elam snorted and said, "So now you have practiced. Now we should shoot a deer."

Colin hesitated. Shooting the bow had felt <u>weird</u>. Weird in that it was so natural - like the bow was wired to his eye and acted like an extension of his arm. It kind of freaked him out. Reluctantly he said, "I guess we could try. Let's go up the field a ways."

He led the way over to the edge of the trees, watching for game trails. There were plenty to choose from. Selecting a point where a bend in the stream channel created a natural contour, a pair of trails converged where two shallow draws came together at the edge of the field.

Colin said, "This looks like as good a spot as any. We're just going to sit here in the field about 30 yards from the trees. It's getting late, so the deer should be moving soon. As long as we sit still and don't make any noise, they probably won't pay any attention to us. But I don't want a doe. This time of year they have their fawns with them."

Elam was skeptical about sitting right out in the open, but Colin assured him it would be fine. These deer hadn't been hunted, so even the human scent wouldn't cause much alarm if they weren't moving around. They sat and waited for about 15 minutes. About 100 yards farther up the field, they could see a small bunch of deer emerge from the woods and begin feeding. Colin got to his feet, whispering at Elam to stay sitting. He didn't trust himself to shoot from a sitting position, which he had never practiced. Down the field toward the hay meadow, another group of deer was now feeding out of the timber. Elam was motioning toward them, but Colin just held up a hand to indicate patience. There! A doe and two fawns, coming along the trail just in front of them. No, two, three, four does and a total of six fawns. At the edge of the field, they paused, testing the air and looking curiously at the two motionless figures in front of them. Cautious, but unafraid, they began to feed, spreading out to either side of where they had entered the field. Elam's face was filled with excitement. A red fox emerged from the bushes about 50 yards away, sniffing the grass clumps in search of a mouse or vole. Another deer was emerging from the timber on the game trail. There were no fawns and the heavier body indicated a buck. Colin drew back the bow. He sighted, and again he could see the target, right behind the buck's shoulder. He could see the arrow embedded in the chest - just a second before he released the arrow. The instant he released, without waiting to see the impact he snatched another arrow and in one quick motion, drew, sighted and released on the fox, standing frozen at the sudden movement 40 yards distant. The fox dropped where it stood, the arrow cleanly through the chest just under the chin. The buck had leaped at the impact, running along the edge of the field for about 30 yards before slowing, then wobbling unsteadily on its feet and collapsing.

Elam jumped to his feet, "You did it! You killed the deer! And a fox! It was so fast and you hit both of them!" He was so excited he was almost incoherent.

Colin just stood there, shaken and suddenly very weak. What had just happened? There was simply no possible way that he should have been able to do what he just did! It had been almost 12 years since he shot a bow of any kind. He had never made a bow before! How could he possibly take this - and he stared at the bow in his hand - and in two seconds fire two shots that struck and killed both targets? It just wasn't possible. Not for him. Elam ran over to the downed deer. It was dead, having been hit through the lungs. Colin retrieved the fox. The fur was not prime, this time of year, but the pelt was still soft and luxurious, a deep red with a beautiful tail. It should tan nicely. He knelt by the deer in silence for a moment, eyes closed. Elam stood looking curious. When Colin opened his eyes, Elam asked, "What were you doing?"

"I was praying. Giving thanks for success in the hunt and for the meat that was provided. I was giving thanks for the animal, its life and that we have food."

Elam looked solemn, "It is your custom?"

"Yes. It is my custom."

Colin dragged the buck into the trees and rolled it on its back. The warm carcass skinned easily. There was no need to haul it back to the house, so he quickly boned it out, having done this on many occasions. In about 30 minutes, he had all of the meat wrapped neatly in the hide, ready to transport home. The fox required another 10 minutes to skin. He tubed it out, peeling the hide in a neat cylinder down across the carcass, cutting the ears from the underside, so the finished hide was complete, in one piece, including the eye holes, ears, nose and mouth. Elam was impressed, "I've never seen that done before."

Colin smiled, "But you've seen it now. It takes practice. Just like the bow."

Dusk was fading to dark when they got back to the house. Elam proudly carried the bow and arrows. Both of the arrows had been recovered. Amazingly, they hadn't been damaged and even the flint arrowheads had remained firmly in place. Colin was lugging the hide filled with meat, the fox hide thrown over his shoulder. He hoped it didn't have fleas. What meat the family would not use in the next couple of days, he would smoke and dry by the fire.

Elam was practically crowing when he raced in the door, "Colin killed a deer! And a fox! He shot two arrows so fast you couldn't even see them!"

Colin brought the hide and meat in the house, setting it on the floor near the door. He was momentarily distracted. Halvor was sitting at the table, looking at him with speculative interest while Elam continued to babble about the hunt.

"Sorry if we're late. It was my fault. I don't know if you want any of this meat for dinner tonight. What we don't use I can dry, it will keep that way."

Elam grabbed the fox skin. "Look father! He shot a fox as well. It was even farther away than the deer! And see how he skinned it? It is still all whole. It's so soft! I didn't know a fox was so soft! And he is helping me make a bow of my own, so I can hunt the deer as well and we will have more of a harvest!"

Jorge was stroking the fox, greatly interested in the hide. Miran said, "The meat is most welcome tonight. I was going to do eggs, because we are out of meat. Thank you." She hesitated, "I've never eaten deer before. Is there anything special you must do to prepare it?"

Colin nodded. "I've eaten it most of my life. I like it. Some people find the flavor a little strong for their liking, but since these have been feeding on Jorge's corn and wheat, I think it'll be good. I like it fried, but you may want to stew it to make it more moist."

Colin began to slice the loin. Jorge was still fingering the fox pelt. "You really killed a deer. I didn't think you could. I've only heard of a few times where someone actually killed a deer. I must look at your bow and arrows more closely."

Halvor was also looking at the fox pelt, but his attention was fixed on Colin when he said, "Yes, I would like to examine this more closely as well."

Elam could hardly stop talking long enough to eat. He kept telling them how Colin shot three arrows in a row into the grass clump, when he couldn't get within ten yards of it. And how Colin had stood, waiting for the deer and then shot both the deer and the fox in a heartbeat. Colin was interested in watching everyone try the venison. They all seemed to think it was wonderful, which surprised Colin, but he figured they were probably used to a bit stronger flavor in their diet of grass fed cattle, sheep, pig or whatever. Colin was beat, but he assisted Miran with the dishes as Elam was still fascinated by the deer hide and fox skin. Jorge had taken the rest of the meat out to the spring house - which served as a cooler for their perishable items.

Colin took the hides out to the shed and salted them before retiring for the night. He blew out the lantern and lay down, but sleep wouldn't come. What had happened out there this evening? He couldn't shoot a bow like that - he knew he couldn't. For that matter, the fact that he had even made a bow was rather incredible. He was a fair rough-carpenter, but that was about it. Before making the bow, his biggest carpentry achievement was a pinewood derby car when he was nine years old and his Dad had done all the cuts for that. Well, maybe that was a bit of an exaggeration, but he was certainly no craftsman. Making soap. That was another puzzle. Sure, he understood the basic idea - the history and chemical reactions. He had made glycerin soap in his high school chemistry class - once. So how was it that all these things just seemed to come together when he attempted them here? It was like all he had to do was think of it and it started happening. That wasn't to say that there wasn't a lot of work involved. He had the blisters on his hands to prove it. But the outcome was far exceeding his personal capabilities and he knew it. It was shooting the bow tonight that really made him realize it. How could this be happening? That thought kept echoing in his head as he drifted into sleep.

Even though his night had been short, Colin got up with plans running through his head. He needed time to think and it wasn't going to happen here. He needed some time on his own. He worked as he planned. The deer and fox skin were scraped. He tossed them into his tanning brine and took the cowhide down to the creek to rinse it and get it started drying.

At breakfast he abruptly asked, "Jorge, does anybody around here sell horses?"

Jorge paused in his eating, "Aye. There's some. Tunsten deals in animals. If he hasn't a horse, he'll be knowing who's looking to sell."

"How much does a horse cost? Not exact, but just an estimate."

Jorge scratched his nose, thinking, "They're dear. Don't favor 'em myself. Oxen are better. Pull more. Eat better on the table, too." He grinned. "But for buying a horse, I'd say you'd be needing two or three dectorals and maybe another five torals to boot."

Colin nodded, thinking. "Alright, that gives me a figure to work with. I want to buy some salt as well. I've been using too much of yours and there's more tanning to do. I also want to get a sewing needle. Not one of your heavy canvas stitching needles, but not too small either. And I need some heavy thread to go with it."

Miran had been listening, "I've needles and thread aplenty. You're welcome to use what you need."

Colin shook his head, "No. I appreciate your offer Miran, you've been very generous. But you won't be getting these back, so I'd like to buy them. I've got a few coins now, so I shouldn't keep using your things without payment. But I'd appreciate your help in acquiring them."

Miran nodded and said, "If you wish. Needles and thread are not costly. A packet of needles and the thread will only be a subtoral. If you need them right away, you may still use mine and we'll replace them with what you buy after market day."

"That would be great. Thank you. I think I'll accept your offer, but I may also need a little bit of lighter thread as well."

Miran nodded. Jorge just shook his head and returned to his eating. They were getting used to his strange requests by now. After breakfast, Colin borrowed the needle and thread Miran had offered. He, Elam and Jorge spent the morning with the oxen pulling stumps where they had been cutting wood. This is how the cultivated acreage would gradually increase. As trees were cut for firewood, the stumps were pulled, rock was hauled away and eventually Jorge would expand his fields or this might well be the start of Elam's farm. Pulling stumps was back-breaking labor. Even the tremendous strength of the oxen was no match for the roots of an oak tree. The men had to dig around the stump, using the axes to cut the roots, then attach the oxen to the stump and throw their might behind that of the oxen to hope to tear the stump free. The entire morning they only pulled three.

As they rested after the noon meal, Colin pulled together a small pile of tinder. He managed to strike a spark and blow it to life and soon had a small fire going. Elam and Jorge sat and watched, curious, but without comment. Colin retrieved the tongs he had borrowed from Jorge's shop that morning, along with a nail and the needle he had gotten from Miran. Holding the head of the needle with the tongs, he heated the pointed end until it was red hot. Using a flat rock as an anvil, He bent it around the nail in the shape of a U, but with the pointed end much shorter than the side with the eye. He heated the point again, until it was red hot, then tapped it flat by striking it with a stone and quenched it in the stream, after which he honed it using a long, slender stone.

Jorge finally asked, "What are you making, from what used to be a good needle?"

Colin held it up for them to see. "A fish hook." It was large, about the size of a #4 hook - a far cry from the #12 and #14 hooks he used to tie flies on and it was crude besides. But knowing that these waters hadn't been exposed to the enticements of flies and bait, he hoped it would suffice.

Jorge shook his head, "You'll do no good with that. It's too small to gaff them with and the fish are too fast besides."

"You're right. You can't take the fish with this hook, so you have to do it the other way around and get the fish to take the hook."

Intrigued now, Jorge and Elam moved closer to watch. Colin removed a few feathers and a small strip of deer hide from his pouch. He embedded the point firmly into a piece of wood to hold it while he worked. With light thread he wrapped the shank of the hook, bringing the thread back over itself to hold it securely. Using his knife, he cut a small bunch of deer hair from the hide and used the thread to tie it over the bend of the hook, forming a tail. He then took a long, slender feather, tied it on and wrapped the shank, making a crude segmented body. A tuft of deer hair formed a wing and a dark brown feather was wrapped around the eye-end of the hook for a hackle. It took several attempts before he could finish his creation with a few half-hitches just below the eye. Finished, he proudly held it up for Jorge and Elam to see.

"What's it supposed to be?" asked Elam.

Slightly deflated, Colin replied, "It's a fly - an insect for the fish to feed on."

Both Jorge and Elam stared at him for moment before bursting into laughter, "Ah, you had us both going there again, for a minute!" Jorge snorted.

"Well, it's not the best I've ever done. But without a vice or my fly-tying tools, I think it looks pretty good. I'll bet it will still catch a fish!" Colin protested.

Jorge pounced, "A bet, is it? Taken! And what will be the stakes?"

Colin smiled and said, "Loser does the evening dishes for a week."

Jorge brushed that aside, "Bah! That's no prize!"

"Well, if the stakes are too high for you………..maybe we could come up with something less costly then."

Jorge's ego was on the line now, "The dishes, then! 'Tis a fools prize but a sure bet!"

Taking his fly and thread, Colin cut a slender willow pole and notched the end. There would be no fancy playing the fish with his crude equipment, but he wanted a pole with a fair amount of give to take up the shock of the strike. The thread was probably the weakest point in his gear, but he hoped it would hold for a fish or two.

He tied the fly onto his line, leaving about eight feet of thread between the fly and the end of the pole, which was about six feet long. He wouldn't be doing any casting, really, just flipping his fly out into a pool to drift down with the current and hope for a strike. He worked his way upstream to the first pool. It looked promising. A heavy bush overhung the bank on the far side. The pool was deep and still, with a slight fall dropping into it and riffle at the end. He crouched as he approached the pool and peeked up over the top of a large rock at the side. Jorge and Elam were snickering behind him, certain that he was still just having some fun with them. He let the fly hang loose from the pole and with a little roll cast flipped it to land just below the fall at the head of the pool. This obviously wasn't going to be a dry fly - with no fly dressing and his crude materials, it promptly began to sink. He raised the tip of his pole to bring the fly up where it would drift just below the surface and swung the tip to follow the current as it dragged the fly along. There was a sudden flash of silver and a fish struck his fly! He barely twitched the end of his pole to set the hook, cringing at the strike for fear it would break his untested line. It held, and the fish was racing back and forth in the pool. Colin worked it down to the riffle at the lower end of the pool and gently dragged it into the shallows where he grabbed it, hooking the thumb of his right hand through the gill plates. It was a beautiful trout, about 3 lbs. At home, Colin would have guessed it to be a cutthroat due to the red slashed under its throat, though he had never caught a cutthroat this size. It had struck hard enough to about set the hook itself. That at least was similar to his experience with cutthroats.

Elam was whooping with delight as Colin turned to display his fish. Jorge looked dumbfounded and then his face clouded at the thought of doing dishes for a week. But his good-nature soon took over and he grinned, shaking his head. "I'd never have believed it. Why that fly of yours looks like nothing ever seen on these waters. And to think, you got the fish to take it."

Colin cut a forked stick to thread through the gills of the trout. In short order, he caught two more. Elam begged to try it. They moved up the stream to another pool. Colin stood behind Elam, coaching him on how to flip the fly and let it drift with the current. He held a gentle hand on Elam's arm. When the flash of silver came, he said, "Hit it!" His restraining hand kept Elam from breaking the line and soon Elam had the fish close to shore. Colin held the pole while Elam kept attempting to pounce on the fish.

"No. Slowly, don't try to pin it down. It's too slippery for that. Just grab him at the head and slip your thumb inside the gills - that's the only place you'll have a grip."

Elam finally got it and turned proudly to show his father, who nodded his approval. Elam's grin was contagious. When he went to slip it on the stick with the others, he bragged, "It's bigger than any that you caught!"

"So it is," Colin replied, "but I caught three." And he smiled and winked at Elam as he said it. Jorge was edging closer, a look of hope on his face. Colin took the hint, "Jorge, do you want to try for one more?"

Jorge eagerly took the pole. Again, Colin stood behind him and instructed him. Jorge was too anxious, so his cast was clumsy, but the fly landed in the pool. Colin wasn't quite ready when the sudden flash came the moment the fly hit the water, but Jorge was so keyed that he gave a mighty yank just as the fish struck the fly. The fish sailed out of the pool and over their heads. At the apex of its flight, the line snapped and the fish continued to fly, up on the bank behind them. Jorge stood looking stunned. Elam let out another whoop and bounded up the embankment to pounce on the flopping fish. Colin looked at Jorge and said, "Maybe just a little lighter next time." And they both laughed.

Colin showed Jorge and Elam how to clean the fish. Jorge continued to look skeptical. "And you're sure they're good to eat?"

Colin nodded. "I can't believe that you've never had fish. I love them. Rolled in corn meal – maize, I mean, and fried - that's my favorite way to fix them. These are even big enough to fillet."

"Maybe we ought to get a few more," Jorge suggested hopefully.

"I think this will do for today, but you've seen how it's done and you can catch more anytime you want."

Fortunately, the crude fly had remained in the mouth of Jorge's fish during its flight, so they hadn't lost the hook. Colin continued, "I like using an artificial fly, but it's probably easier and more certain if you just stick a worm or a grasshopper on the hook. You have to set the hook with the fake fly, because the fish will spit it out as soon as they taste it. But with a worm, they'll swallow the whole thing, so you just about hook them for sure every time. At home, I used to catch them and turn them loose, for that you wanted a fly so they wouldn't swallow it."

"Why would you catch fish just to turn them loose, if they're good to eat?" Jorge asked suspiciously.

"There were rules about how many fish you could keep. But I like to fish, so as long as I kept turning them loose, I could keep fishing."

Jorge shook his head. Rules for fishing! He had never imagined such a thing.

The trio worked half-heartedly at pulling another stump that afternoon, but it seemed the fishing had been too much of a distraction. "Besides," Jorge said, "we ought to get the fish back to Miran before she fixes something else for dinner." When they got in sight of the house, Elam raced ahead with their catch to tell his mother all about fishing.

Colin cooked the fish for them that evening. He filleted four of the fish, crudely. The fifth one he fried whole and demonstrated how to easily remove the bones after it was cooked, by starting at the tail and using a knife to slip the meat from the skeleton in one large piece, then flip the fish over and repeat the operation on the other side. Jorge, Miran and Halvor all sat looking suspiciously at the fish sitting on their plate. Elam poked at his a little, before putting a small piece in his mouth. His eyes lit up, "This is good! It's so tender, it just falls apart. I like this!" With that, the others were finally willing to try it and with expressions of amazed delight, agreed. It was good. After dinner, Miran began to clear away the dishes. Colin pushed back from the table and gave Jorge a meaningful look. Jorge rolled his eyes, got up and took the dishes from Miran, "I'll be doing that tonight," he said gruffly.

Miran was so startled she would have dropped the dishes if Jorge hadn't already had a hand on them. Sheepishly, Jorge explained about the bet, but with a humorous if defiant look he finished, "I still say 'tis a fool's prize!"

Miran squeezed his arm and Colin replied softly, "Sometimes, those are the best kind."

Thursday, "Fifth Day," Colin mentally corrected, was market day. Jorge, Elam and Miran were all going. Jorge had errands to take care of and Miran wanted to help Kath with selling the soap. They had been busy all week and they hadn't sold all of their inventory from the previous week either. They had made almost 100 balls of soap, experimenting with different scents. They had done batches with lilac, mint and juniper, among others. They invited Colin to come, but he really didn't feel like going and being stared at all day. He thanked them, gave them two of his torals and asked them to buy the needle, thread and salt he had requested. He also asked if they could find some short copper rod for making rivets. He didn't think they would be familiar with rivets, but Jorge knew them instantly. "What dictated which paths of invention had been followed and which had not?" Colin puzzled. The family set off to Baylor's. While town wasn't all that far, at least not by their standards, Baylor would be taking his wagon so they would all ride with him and have the chance to visit.

Halvor, as was common, had apparently disappeared. He hadn't shown up for dinner yesterday or breakfast this morning. He was an unknown factor and Colin's engineering mentality could never quite forget it. Still he didn't know that there was anything he could do about it. Since the day that Jorge had pointed out Halvor shadowing them, Colin hadn't actually seen him repeating his spying activities. A few times he thought he had caught movement out of the corner of his eye, but he never saw what made it and pretended that it was probably some small animal. Today Colin was going to relax and work on the hides he was tanning. The fox was already rinsed and drying. It was a beautiful fur, despite the season and the skin was so thin that it had tanned quickly. The deer hide would be out and rinsing by this evening. Then he hoped to shoot another deer. He wanted several hides and Miran had assured him that they would smoke and dry whatever meat they didn't eat, so nothing would be wasted. Jorge was delighted at the prospect of having fewer deer eating his crops.

Colin was sitting in the late afternoon sun knapping arrowheads. He was getting the hang of it now and had chipped out a flint scraper from one of the large pieces he had brought back from the gorge. The ax worked fairly well, but on the thin hides there was more risk of cutting the skin. The rougher edge on the flint would grab the membrane on the skin better than the smooth steel. He would have liked some obsidian to work with. The technique was the same - applying pressure along the edge and the material would flake. But obsidian was more glassy on the microscopic scale, capable of achieving an edge that not even steel could match. He heard a wagon coming along the rutted path at the edge of the field a minute or two before it came into view. Baylor and Jorge were on the seat, with everyone else piled in back. Baylor raised a hand in greeting as they approached.

Kath was beaming as she climbed down. "We sold everything and still had to turn folks away! The women we sold to last week, some of them even came back and bought the other scents. They say it was the talk of the town all week, and folks was waiting for us when we arrived." Miran stepped forward and handed him a small parcel, "Here's the things you were wanting. And your change." She placed the copper subtorals in his hand.

Jorge hoisted a heavy bag of salt down from the back of the wagon, "We got the salt as well. Should be plenty for tanning. Fellow sold it to me, was curious what I wanted so much for. Think he figured we must be saltin' a fair bit of meat. I left him with the thought,"

Kath took him by the arm and led him into the house, "Now to business. We're needing to settle accounts with our partner." Jorge and Baylor grinned and Miran smiled and took him by the other arm, escorting him to the table.

Kath took out her coin bag and dumped the contents on the table. "Three dectorals, twenty torals and ten subtorals!" she announced proudly.

While he really hadn't developed an appreciation for the value of their currency, Colin could see that the women were pleased. "That's great! You've done really well. I couldn't ask for better partners." He started to divide the coins into three separate piles.

Kath placed her hand firmly on his, shaking her head, "No. That's your share. An even third. We'd made quite a bit, you know, and the price was a little higher than the first. But we heard no complaints - fair value, it was."

Before he could speak, Jorge broke in and said, "I'm thinking you may be wanting to pay a visit to old Tunsten tomorrow. I had a word with him at market. He says he has a couple of good horses that he's willing to sell."

"And you'll be needing a cart if you're getting a horse. I'd be pleased to help you make it, if you're of a mind. Or I know a man or two what usually has one for sale," Baylor added.

Colin was overwhelmed by the eager kindness of these people. He shook his head, "Thank you Baylor. Thank each of you. But I won't be needing a cart. Kath, Miran, I think this is still too much. You two are doing all the work and in a few weeks I won't be able to help even as much as I have been. After today, it's back to a one-fifth share for me - and that is going to have to stop as well if I'm not working with you."

Baylor brushed him off, "Time enough to worry about that. Can't use water that's still in the creek. Besides, it's your knowin' that we're sellin'. To think of all the fat I've been throwin' away. Throwing away dectorals is what I was doing!"

Baylor and Kath took their leave, waving as they looked back from the wagon. Jorge shrugged off his offer to help with the chores, saying, "I've been taking my ease all day. I need a bit of work."

Colin went to the shed and retrieved his bow and arrows, heading back toward the creek as the sun hung low on the horizon. He was hunting more for a hide than for meat, this evening. But he was leery of using the bow, still slightly unnerved by his experience with it the other evening. As he had before, he made a target from a clump of grass. Selecting one of his blunt arrows, he drew back the string and took aim. Again, he could see the flight of the arrow, the impact on the target……..all in the instant before he released the string. Frowning, he selected another blunt. This time he nocked the arrow, keeping it pointed down. Swiftly, he swung the bow up and loosed the shot. The arrow flew long, landing 20 yards past the clump. He hadn't aimed. It was purely a reflex shot and the results were about what he would have predicted. So he wasn't ……….magic. He wasn't infallible. But the difference seemed to be a matter of ………focus? When he aimed, when he visualized, he made the shot. Kind of like making soap, or the tanning - even building the bow or making the fly. He still had to go through the motions, but he visualized the result and the result followed. It was an intriguing thought, but very disconcerting as well. Why should such be the case? It couldn't be him……he'd never had that happen back home. But if it was this world, why didn't he see this with Elam or Jorge? Sighing, he went and retrieved his arrows.

He found another location where several game trails converged at the edge of the field and waited for the deer to come to begin their evening feeding. He didn't have to wait long. It was a lone buck who came first this time. There was no question, as the nubs of his sprouting antlers were just visible. When the arrow struck, the deer took one great leap, then stopped, as though unsure of what had struck him. Standing there, he suddenly buckled, falling over where he kicked and then lay still. As before, Colin quickly butchered the deer, wrapping the meat in the hide to carry back to the house. He had never felt so depressed about a successful hunt before.

Chapter 9   The Horse

The next morning, Jorge suggested they go see Tunsten. Colin was anxious to acquire a horse, so he was more than agreeable. It was a good hour's walk and Jorge kept a stiff pace. Tunsten, Jorge told him, lived alone. He dealt with anything to do with animals. He bought and sold. He milked and butchered. What he didn't have he could get and what he didn't know didn't need knowing. Colin smiled at that.

Tunsten's place was functional. There was no hint of decoration anywhere. The house, barn, pens and corrals were well laid out and nicely maintained. There was no filth, at least no more than any farm or ranch operation might have. The animals were not crowded in their pens and seemed healthy enough. Jorge called out at their approach, "Tunsten! Are you about? We've come on business!"

Tunsten was a thin, reedy looking fellow, perhaps two inches taller than Jorge but a good 20 lbs. lighter, by Colin's estimate. His beard flowed down his chest like an Old Testament patriarch. He shaded his eyes from the morning sun as he exited the doorway of a dark barn, striding forward purposefully. Colin hadn't expected that from the thin old man he was facing.

"Jorge is it? You've come about the horse then?" He glanced at Colin, then riveted his gaze on him, scanning from head to toe and back. "A stranger." He said flatly.

Jorge cleared his throat nervously, "Aye. But a good man. He's been staying with us the past few weeks. Ah…..at the Council's request."

Tunsten seemed not to have heard him. He continued to study Colin, looking him up and down. "You display no File's colors." No other comment on his appearance or clothing, other than the observation regarding his lack of colors.

Colin met his stare, trying to keep his expression and voice neutral, "I belong to no File. I've been scheduled for my Evaluation two moons after this next one. In Salem."

Tunsten chewed on his lower lip, then seemed to come to a conclusion. Suddenly he nodded, "Aye, I've a horse. She's a mare, as good as any I've owned. Gentle disposition. Intelligent. Strong. Tall. She's broke to the cart. Good horse, this one. I'll show you to her."

Colin was amused by the fact that _he_ was being shown to the horse, not the other way around. He followed Tunsten around the barn to a high corral. There was just the one horse in it. Her head was delicate and equine, but set on a long, powerful neck. She was large in the body and as Tunsten had said, she was tall, her back almost even with Colin's shoulder. At their approach, she raced around the corral, skidding to a stop right in front of them, ears pricked forward. Colin stepped forward, presenting the back of his hand to her, fingers closed, letting her sniff his scent. She tossed her head, flaring her nostrils and sniffed again. Tunsten and Jorge stood quietly behind them. Finally, Tunsten walked up and reached a hand through the corral bars and said, "What do you think of him?"

It was obvious that he was not addressing Colin. The mare tossed her head and snorted. Then returned to sniff Colin's hand again. He rubbed his knuckles the length of her face, between the eyes, then let his fingers stroke her muzzle.

Tunsten spoke suddenly, "Alright. 22 torals. Bargain struck." He turned abruptly and walked away. Colin followed him back to the house where he paid the money. Tunsten fetched a length of rope from the barn, opened the coral and knotted the rope around the mare's neck, handing the other end to Colin. "Does she have a name?"

Tunsten gave him a hard look, "Are you daft? She's a horse!" With that he walked away.

As he led the mare out of the corral, Colin looked at Jorge and said, "That has got to be the strangest business transaction I've ever had."

Jorge shrugged and said, "That's Tunsten. If he hadn't liked you, it would have been stranger still."

Colin thought their visit was concluded, but as he led the mare past the barn, Tunsten came out and dumped a bundle at Jorge's feet. "Hides. They're fresh. Figured you'd want 'em." He disappeared back into the barn.

Jorge picked up the hides and tossed them on his brawny shoulder and grinned. "He likes me, too."

The mare was content to trail along behind the two men on their walk back. On the way, Jorge suggested they speak to Baylor about a cart. He said, "Baylor builds a fine cart. You'd not go wrong with him."

Colin shook his head. "No. I plan to rider her."

Jorge looked puzzled, "What do you mean 'ride her.' You ride the cart. The horse pulls the cart."

"Yes, for a cart, that's how it's done. But I plan to ride the horse. You know, sit on her back."

Jorge laughed, "Oh, aye! It's been tried before this! But the horse will have some say about that! And they always say, 'NO!'"

Colin spent the afternoon getting acquainted with his horse. Despite Tunsten's derision at the idea of giving a name to a horse, Colin was determined to do so. She was friendly enough to eat grass from his hand and permitted him to run his hands lightly over her head, neck, back, sides and legs. She was a non-descript gray, but with a dark line straight down her spine and dark ears and tail. She had no mane. Her neck was smooth and sleek, like an elk. The way she moved was graceful, almost elegant. It reminded Colin of the expression, "She moved like a gazelle." Playing off that, he called softly, "Gisele," using the soft 'g' of the French so it sounded like "Jhizel." The mare's head came up at the sound and she walked toward him tossing her head. "Gisele," he said again. She rubbed her head on his shoulder. "Alright," he said, "Gisele it is."

By Sixth day, Elam was so excited and nervous about his Evaluation the following day he was about to drive both his parents to distraction. He spilled part of a bucket of milk in the morning, broke three eggs running with them back to the house. He dumped the plate of bread on the floor at breakfast and pinched Jorge's fingers in the barn door when he was helping repair it. By noon, Jorge in good humored exasperation asked if Colin couldn't take him fishing or something. They still had only the one tattered fly, which Colin was not anxious to lose, though he now had several more needles to make additional hooks with if need be. So Elam and Colin headed down to the creek, Elam carrying the fishing pole and Colin packing a copper bucket and blanket. Colin kindled a fire and cautioned Elam not to get the hook snagged or become too aggressive setting the hook on a fish. Elam happily went to find a pool. In the meantime, Colin set the bucket of water on the fire and stripped down, wrapping himself in the blanket, like a *lava-lava* on the Pacific islands. While he had done a cold-wash job on his clothing several times, today he was going to do a thorough wash with hot water and soap. One of the reasons that he was anxious to collect some deer hides was that he didn't expect his clothing to last forever, especially not with this rough, out-of-doors life-style he had been living. In fact, he was rather surprised that he hadn't already worn a few holes, as he inspected his clothing for signs of wear. There was none. Not a hole. Not a frayed spot. Not so much as a loose thread. A phrase echoed distantly in his mind, *Your clothes are not waxen old upon you, and thy shoe is not waxen old upon thy foot.* Was that Deuteronomy? The promise made to the children of Israel when they wandered forty years in the wilderness? He remembered coming out of the ocean into that narrow death-trap. The mad escape through the tunnel that was so low he had been scrambling on his hands and knees in places. The sharp rocks had lacerated his hands and the ensuing illness had about killed him. But his knees and shins had been sore. Only sore. Not cut. No abrasion at all. Weird.

Colin got on with his washing. He scrubbed his shirt and trousers thoroughly, then put them to soak in the scalding water. After awhile, he dumped the water and took the clothes down to the creek to rinse them in the cold water and hung them over a log to dry in the sun. Then it was his turn. Warming another bucket of water, he scrubbed himself from head to toe and enjoyed the unaccustomed luxury of a warm water rinse. Wrapping himself in the blanket again, he sat down to wait for his clothes to dry. Tomorrow was Elam's Evaluation. Colin hadn't actually been invited, but he wanted to go. First, he was curious and with his own Evaluation coming up, he wanted as much information as he could get. Second, he hadn't been to town yet. While he was curious he was also very cautious, not knowing how the townspeople might react to a stranger such as he and the obvious violation of some of their customs. But he had decided that it was time to make an appearance. If he was going to go down in flames as a pretend messenger of their Messias, he at least wanted to make a good first impression and show up clean. There would be no mistake, that he wore white, with no colored fringe to declare affiliation with any File or Order. Give them something to talk about besides weaning pigs! The irrational thought made him smile. He had given up on the idea of running away, but that didn't mean he was just going to sit here for the next two months. He had always needed to see the next horizon. When he used to go backpacking he always wanted to see that next ridge. Usually all he found was another ridge, inviting him in the distance. For awhile - a couple of years - he had stopped looking for that next ridge. But Rita was dead and ever since then the ridges had been calling him again. He had a whole world here that he would never get to see. Not all of it anyway, but he was going to see part of it. He needed to get Gisele ready to ride.

His clothes were still slightly damp when he put them back on, but the day was warm enough so he wasn't uncomfortable. He had no more than finished drowning out his fire, when Elam came happily along the bank, hoisting the three fat trout he had caught. "I learned what you meant about them spitting the fly when they tasted it. I must have missed a dozen before I managed to hook these three. But I'm afraid I ruined your fly. It came apart." He held up the pole, dangling the tattered remains on the hook.

"That's alright. Even my best flies used to fall apart, and this was far from my best. We can make another one."

Elam cheered up at this and they began to walk home. "I'm still kind of scared about tomorrow. The night you showed up - when I had to go to Salem, I rode back with Marcus. He told me about his Evaluation. Did you know his parents were of the 6th File? Because he was 8th File, he wasn't in the 2nd Order anymore. They took him away. I keep thinking about that. I mean, what if I was in a different Order? I wouldn't be permitted to live with my parents." He fell silent.

"Elam, I don't know much about the Evaluation, or your customs here. You're a fine young man and I think you'll do well. I may be out of place in even saying anything, but this whole thing - getting someone to bow to you. I don't know." He shook his head and paused before continuing, "The thing is, Elam, I can't help but think that this ought to be your choice. In my country, in some of the lands I traveled in, we would bow as a sign of courtesy or respect. But we weren't forced to bow." He held up a hand to silence Elam before he could object, "I know. Everyone tells me that it isn't force, but I've never experienced it, so it still <u>feels</u> to me like there's some compulsion involved. I think you ought to just relax. But I think this is <u>your choice.</u> You choose to whom you bow, and when."

Colin wasn't surprised that Halvor had shown up during the afternoon. Elam was feeling much more cheerful when he got home and was telling his mother and father all about catching the fish. Miran had already prepared dinner, but went ahead and fried up the fish as well. Since she did no cooking on Sabbath, she always prepared extra on Seventh Day that could be eaten cold the next. Elam, of course, wouldn't be content without sampling the fish he had caught all on his own.

"What time is the Evaluation tomorrow?" Colin asked.

Jorge was doing the dishes, continuing to pay off his wager. His answer was non-committal, "Were you thinking of going, then?"

"I'd like to, unless that poses a problem. I have my own Evaluation coming up in two moons." He looked directly at Halvor as he said it. "I'd like to see how it's conducted so I have a better idea what to expect."

Unexpectedly, Halvor spoke, a thin smile on his face. "There will be no problem. I will see to that." With that, he arose and left.

Jorge and Miran exchanged a glance. Jorge nodded and Miran spoke softly, "Colin, we'd be pleased to have you. But there's some that don't know you as do we. Fact is, there's none besides us that know you at all, excepting Kath and Baylor But there've been rumors. I don't know how they got started, but there's rumors of a stranger, belonging to no File. And, they say he wears the mantle. They've heard of you already. Some have made up their minds that you're evil. But they don't <u>know</u> you, Colin!" She was rushing her words now. "There may be trouble. I don't know who'd be starting it. How could they know? We haven't told a soul! I swear it! And I know Kath and Baylor wouldn't!"

Colin shook his head. "I know you didn't, and I wouldn't care if you had. My guess is that when my arrival was announced in Salem, there was probably quite an audience and it simply spread from there. It doesn't matter. If they didn't know about me before, they certainly will after tomorrow!" He thought for a moment, "Still, I wouldn't want to cause any trouble for you. I think I'll take advantage of my 'assistant' for once and let him be my escort tomorrow."

Jorge and Miran both looked puzzled. "Your assistant?"

"Yes. After all, Halvor keeps saying that he is here to assist me, should I need it. Tomorrow, I think I'll need it." Colin waved off their weak objections and they didn't press the matter. He spent more time than usual on his knees that night before retiring. "Tomorrow," he thought, "could be an interesting day."

Chapter 10   Elam's Evaluation

In the morning Colin washed and shaved. Thankfully, he didn't cut himself. He fed and patted Gisele as she butted him playfully with her head, but he was distracted and hardly noticed. Jorge and Elam were hurrying through their chores in preparation for leaving. Colin helped himself to a bowl of what he took to be cracked wheat and packed some bread and cheese in his pouch for later. Halvor came in as he was finishing and Colin was stunned. He wore a beautifully tailored tunic and trousers. The tunic was cream colored, with a soft, velvety sheen. The trousers were a fawn color and everything was trimmed with his File's lavender fringe. A heavy belt supported a brass hilted sword and an equally ornate dagger. A lavender cape flowed off his shoulders. A heavy gold medallion hung from a chain around his neck. He looked stunning, almost regal. Colin thought that back on Earth, such an outfit would have looked ridiculous, but here in this world, it was a clear statement of station and privilege. It made him look both menacing and statesman-like. Colin said, "You look impressive."

The comment was acknowledged by a simple nod. Colin hesitated, but pressed ahead. "Halvor, you've offered to help me if I needed it. Today, I think I need it." Halvor looked at him questioningly. "Since it's going to be obvious to everyone at the Evaluation that I'm a stranger here, I'd like to avoid Jorge and Miran having to offer explanations. So I'd like to go with you and we'll just let Jorge, Miran and Elam have a nice, quiet family day."

Halvor's smile was almost mocking, but he inclined his head, saying, "I'd be pleased to escort one wearing the mantle to today's Evaluation. But there will be no trouble." His eyes were hard as he said it and held Colin's gaze for a long moment.

Miran was almost as excited as Elam. "I've something to show you before we go. Jorge! Elam! Come in now!"

Jorge and Elam came in, grinning from ear to ear. They were each wearing a new pair of <u>leather</u> boots, high-top moccasins really, that Miran had made for them from the first tanned cowhide. She had done a fine job. Where the canvas boots had been bulky, these were sleek and form-fitting. They looked very functional and much more durable than the canvas and cloth foot coverings they had been wearing. Even Halvor got down to finger the leather and have a closer look and was genuinely impressed.

"Miran! You did a fantastic job. They look great!" Colin said. Miran beamed at him.

"You don't have to do it today, but if you can get some bees wax at market and rub that into the leather really well, it will keep them waterproof. It will darken the leather and you'll have to reapply it from time to time, but it will also help to preserve it."

Jorge nodded, "Aye, we'll be sure to do it. I have to admit, I didn't believe that tanning of yours could make a hide soft like this, but still so tough! And I can't believe there's no smell either. I'm grateful to you." He winked then and said, "We may have a new business partnership in the making, you know! There'd be a ready market, of that you may be sure!"

It wasn't quite the third hour of the day when Jorge, Miran and Elam set out for Tyber. They would be early for the Evaluation, which was scheduled for the fourth hour, but the day was pleasant and Elam was anxious. Halvor and Colin waited another quarter of an hour before they left. Halvor led at a quick pace, but with Colin's greater height and longer legs, he had no difficulty keeping up. They met no one else on either the trail or the road to town. Most of the other visitors and participants would have passed by earlier.

The Evaluation was to be held in a large open patch of grass and flowers in front of the town hall. Three large oaks offered shade over a considerable portion of the field, but because the day was not overly warm, most of the crowd had congregated forward of the trees, toward a small elevated platform that had been erected. It was only about two feet above the ground, but allowed the spectators to easily see whoever was on the stage. The crowd was fairly large - Colin estimated something in excess of 500 people and they were involved in renewing acquaintances, exchanging bits of news or gossip and friendly banter. Colin stood a full head taller than most of the crowd and so was able to see Jorge, Miran and Elam up toward the front, near the platform. Kath and Baylor were off to the side talking to several people in animated conversation. There were no vendors of any kind, which Colin commented on. Halvor shrugged and said, "Today is Sabbath. No merchandising is permitted. It will be quiet compared to most Evaluations. Usually the Inns and ale houses would do brisk business and there would be peddlers and merchants working the crowd. But there will be none of that today."

Halvor and Colin took a position leaning against the trunk of the oak most near the center of the platform behind the crowd, leaving an intervening space between themselves and the throng of about twenty feet. Nobody seemed to pay them any attention, which was fine with Colin. He was here to observe, not become the center of attention. Halvor was content to relax in the background.

At the appointed hour, a distinguished looking woman dressed all in brown stood up on the platform and raised her hands for silence. She was well past middle-aged, heavy set with dark hair flowing down to her shoulders. Her face was very round, but her nose was long and sharp, giving her something of an avian appearance, rather like an owl, Colin thought. Halvor nudged him, "That's Councilor Arlena Linape. She is the High Councilor over Tyber - over all those of the 3rd File. She lives in Salem most of the time, but part of her responsibility is to oversee the Evaluations of the File she is responsible for. Do you remember Councilor Rabin?"

Colin nodded.

"Councilor Rabin is over the 4th File of the 1st Order. So he supervises Councilor Linape. The 4th File is the highest in the 1st Order, so the Councilor over the 4th File is the head of the Order. Councilor Linape was ill the night you were found, or she would have been sent here with the delegation instead of Rabin." He paused, "Or maybe not. Rabin likes to be involved in things, so he might have used rank to appoint himself to the delegation anyway. The head of the Order can do that." This was more communication than Colin had ever had from Halvor and he was surprised.

The noise gradually subsided and the people sat on the ground where they were. A few of the older folks had stools which they had brought to sit on. When everyone had sat down, Colin could see the Evaluation Box Elam had described to him when he had tried to explain about the Evaluation. It was ornate. Whether carved from wood or cast from metal, he couldn't tell from this distance. It was perhaps a foot high. Low enough for a person to step over the edge to stand in the middle and each half was in the shape of a hexagon, about three feet across. Councilor Linape had a powerful orator's voice, rather masculine, and used it to good effect. Colin thought she would have made a good revival preacher back on earth during the early 19th century.

"Folks, friends, neighbors!" she began, "We welcome you to the Evaluation of the 4th Moon for the City of Tyber!" There was general applause and some whooping from the audience. Councilor Linape raised her hands for silence again, though Colin thought that was hardly necessary, as the crowd was anxious to get on with it.

"Under authority of the High Council of Aidon, located at Salem, the following individuals have been appointed as Examiners for today's Evaluation: From the 1st File, Roger of Neims; from the 2nd File, Marion of Tremont; from the 3rd File, Jordan of Tyber." A small scattering of applause broke out, but quickly died down and Councilor Linape continued, "From the 4th File, Besalaman of Jordanon; from the 5th File, Warren of Ramah; from the 6th File, Loramine of Riverton; from the 7th File, Bauer of Troas; from the 8th File, Julaine of Sarepta."

The crowd broke into muted conversation and Linape seemed content to take a breath. Halvor explained, "In Salem, all 12 Files are represented. For the Evaluations of the First Order, only four Files above the order are present. It would be unusual, almost unheard of, for the offspring of a given File to jump more than two Files. If anyone today bests the Examiner from the 8th File, they will continue the Evaluation in Salem at the next moon."

Colin noted that the examiners were both male and female. As each had been called, they stepped forward. Each wore a plain robe, covering them from shoulder to ankle in the colors of their File with a border or hem of a brighter hue. All of the Examiners were adults, ranging, Colin guessed, from 30 to over 60. He asked Halvor, "How are the examiners selected?"

"They're assigned by the head of the File. It's something of an honor. Sometimes the cities will combine, if they have few people being Evaluated, but jealousy and the fact that Evaluations are usually good for business works against that - except on Sabbath. Some Examiners are used quite a lot, but most people are called to participate sooner or later."

Colin thought it sounded kind of like jury duty. Councilor Linape began to crank up her oration again. "Today, we have eight of our young people who will be having their first Evaluation!" Applause and whoops again halted Linape, who smiled and waved the noise down. "By lot, they will proceed in this order: Ioka, Hayden, Laraine, Colton, Jenny, Elam, Muriel and finally, Bethany!" The candidates tried to look very serious, but they kept casting anxious glances and nervous smiles at friends and family members scattered throughout the crowd.

Councilor Linape called for Ioka, the first candidate, and Roger, the first Examiner. They took their respective places in the box. Roger wore a black robe. The crowd became totally silent. Councilor Linape faced the box and then said, "The Examination for the 1st File will now commence with the blessing of the High Council and The Most High. We adjure compliance in all things! Begin!"

Ioka, a young woman, and Roger, an elderly man, faced each other and closed their eyes. Nothing happened for a long minute. But then Roger bowed deeply, from the waist, almost touching his head to Ioka when he did so. The crowd erupted in applause. Ioka looked surprised as she opened her eyes. Roger smiled, placing a hand on her arm to congratulate her.

Ioka remained in her box, while Roger left, to be replaced by a heavy-set middle aged woman in a gray robe. She smiled broadly and waved at the crowd as she took her place. Councilor Linape repeated the same introduction as he had before, except stating that the Examination was for the 2nd File. Once again, the two contestants faced each other and closed their eyes. The wait seemed longer this time, but as before, the Examiner suddenly bowed deeply at the waist to the young candidate and applause again broke out. The tension seemed higher as the Examination for the 3rd File began. People were shifting in their seats and a low murmur was silenced by Councilor Linape before she made her announcement, commencing the examination.

The contest was noticeably longer this time. Both Ioka and Jordan, wearing the brown robe of the 3rd File, swayed unsteadily on their feet, brows furrowed in concentration. Whispering in the crowd was cut off by an angry look from Councilor Linape, but it started again as soon as she looked back to the Evaluation. In the end, the result was the same and the Examiner bowed to his younger opponent. The applause was loud and prolonged. The people were thrilled that their examiner would now contest for a place in the 4th File. As before, the Examination was heralded by Councilor Linape as the Examiner in the Green robe stepped forward. The contest, however, was brief. Ioka had barely closed her eyes when she was suddenly bowing deeply to Besalaman of Jordanon. He was gracious in victory, inclining his head to young Ioka, as they turned to face the applauding crowd. Despite her loss, Ioka was beaming as Councilor Linape announced, "The 3rd File of the 1st Order of Aidon welcomes Ioka of Tyber and acknowledges her as having passed the test of Compliance and is now entitled to the privileges of the 3rd File!"

Ioka walked carefully to the edge of the platform, but upon reaching the edge, she jumped and ran to her waiting family who hugged and congratulated her.

"Does the Evaluation tire a person?" Colin asked.

Halvor nodded, "It can be very draining, especially if the two contestants are closely matched."

"Then it looks like the candidate is bucking a stacked deck."

Halvor looked questioning, not understanding the phrase.

"I mean, the candidate has to face one test right after another, while the Examiners get to rest in between."

"Yes. That is intentional. The candidate has to prove they belong to a given File in order to advance. The Examiner has nothing to prove. When there are many candidates, they sometimes will use different Examiners part way through the Evaluation. The order of the candidates is selected by lot. Some think it is better to be later in the Evaluation, when the Examiners may become more tired. But that can come back on you if they decided to change Examiners."

Councilor Linape had announced the next examination, the young man named Hayden. He didn't make it past the Examiner for the 3rd File, but was still applauded warmly.

Halvor explained, "For the present, he is accepted to the 2nd File. But it isn't uncommon in a few moons for such to request another Evaluation. The border between Files is not clear. After all, he gave Compliance to one of the 3rd File, but he might gain Compliance from someone different in the 3rd File. It is usually more exacting when the candidate attempts to move to a higher Order. The Councilor could require additional Examiners of the same File, but in that case the candidate is permitted to rest between Evaluations."

The young woman named Laraine was next. She finally bested the 3rd File Examiner. When she faced the Examiner in green, Besalaman, of the 4th File, Colin closed his eyes and tried to focus on the contestants, visualizing what it might be like standing in the Box at his own Evaluation. All he could see was black - no, two faint points of light, in the distance. Mentally, he focused on the lights, zooming in on them. It was as though he were a moth, drawn to the glimmering, flickering spheres of light, flitting around them, looking at them from all angles, brushing past them, but never quite touching them. As he flitted about the lights, he began to see that they pulsed and moved, as though they had life. Thin tendrils of light extended outward, disappearing into the darkness around, but as he traced these threads of light, he found that they connected with other points of light, a network of pulsing sources connected by thin, undulating tentacles of light. It was fascinating and beautiful. He opened his eyes and it was gone. He wasn't quite sure what he'd seen. Had it been real? Halvor was looking at him strangely, but Colin ignored him. The contest up on the platform continued. Colin didn't know how long it had been going on. He had no idea how long his eyes had been closed. It had seemed like a long time, but might have only been a few seconds. As he watched, Besalaman slowly bowed to Laraine. The applause was enthusiastic and prolonged. Laraine looked stunned, as Besalaman smiled and bowed to her again. Warren, the 5th File Examiner was dressed in a yellow robe. He was a grim looking older man. He didn't smile when he entered the box. The contest was no contest. Whether it was because she was tired from her previous four examinations, or because Warren was so much stronger, Laraine found herself bowing the moment the Examination began.

Halvor nodded, "That is common. The Examiner for the 5th and 9th File is usually selected for having great skill - power, if you will. The candidate will truly prove they belong in the higher Order before they will be advanced, and having a strong Examiner eliminates the need for further Evaluations prior to advancement."

Colin only half heard him. He was still lost in thought regarding what he'd envisioned during the Evaluation. Was that real? Was that what he was supposed to see during the Evaluation?

Colton and Jenny were next. Both bowed to the 4th File Examiner, Besalaman and were accepted into the 3rd File. Then it was Elam's turn. His contests with the 1st and 2nd File Examiners were brief and his contest with the 3rd File Examiner was scarcely longer. The applause was hearty, both welcoming and encouraging Elam. Besalaman, in his green robe came forward next. Colin watched, along with the hushed crowd as Councilor Linape made her announcement and the contest began - and suddenly ended. Besalaman had bowed, actually making contact with Elam's chest as he did so. He looked almost stunned, but recovering his composure, he again bowed to Elam and smiled, congratulating him. The applause and whoops from the crowd were long and sustained, even as Warren, the 5th File examiner entered the box. Councilor Linape made her pronouncement to begin the contest and both contestants closed their eyes. Minutes passed, with no movement on the part of either contestant. Muted whispers began to be heard throughout the crowd. As the contest dragged on, numerous comments and exclamations could be heard. Then all at once, Elam bowed stiffly, no expression on his face. Warren's eyes flew open. He looked shocked, then angry as he whirled and left the platform, causing a stir in the audience. Councilor Linape looked uncertain, but forged ahead, proclaiming, "The 4th File of the 1st Order of Aidon welcomes Elam of Tyber and acknowledges him as having passed the test of Compliance and is now entitled to the privileges of the 4th File!"

Elam walked calmly to the edge of the platform, where he jumped down and walked over to hug his beaming parents. Halvor eyed Colin uncertainly, "That was an unusual breach of protocol on the part of Warren. I've never seen him behave like that before, and I've watched him in several Evaluations."

Colin made no reply.

There were only two contestants remaining. Rather than being bored or impatient, if anything the crowd was even more excited than they had been earlier and it was getting more difficult for Councilor Linape to get them to be silent. Muriel took her place in the box and quickly forced Compliance from the 1st and 2nd File Examiners. As Marion, the 3rd File Examiner took her place, Colin again closed his eyes, trying to again see the lights he had found before. Immediately, he saw them, focused on them and was once again flitting around them, so quickly it seemed that he was simultaneously viewing them from every angle. He noticed then, the tendrils connecting the two lights - not even tendrils, but a thin, undulating ribbon rippling back and forth between them. He was fascinated. He saw it and he reached to touch it. He reached and.......

"What are you doing?" Halvor hissed.

Colin's eyes flashed open. He was still staring at the two figures on the platform. Their eyes were open staring at each other. The crowd was whispering - loudly. The Examiner shook her head and said in a low tone, "I'm sorry. I don't know what happened. I suddenly just lost you. I couldn't sense you. I'm sorry."

Councilor Linape was completely flustered, "Is everything alright? Should we continue?"

Marion, the Examiner, visibly shivered, but said, "Yes. I'm sorry. Muriel, do you wish to continue?"

Muriel had stood wide-eyed throughout this exchange, but mutely nodded her head.

Halvor was gripping Colin's arm - hard. "What did you do?" he whispered.

Colin just shook his head. "I'm sitting right here - with you. I haven't gone anywhere or done anything."

Halvor released his arm, but eyed him with angry suspicion.

The contest began again and in a very few moments Muriel bowed to Marion, establishing her place in the 2nd File. Bethany, the final contestant, entered the box. Her contests were not prolonged, but neither were they particularly quick either. She gained Compliance from the first three examiners and was soon facing Besalaman, of the 4th File. The contest began. Halvor gave Colin a wary glance, but his attention was soon focused on the participants. Colin closed his eyes, focused his concentration and immediately found himself flitting around the two bright lights. He followed the tendrils emanating from them to other lights, seeing the network of lights all connected together. He couldn't believe that he hadn't seen all this before. As he raced along the connections from light to light, he noticed very dark, thin filaments emerging from each sphere. These twined together, eventually forming a brilliant cable of light, made up of multiple strands, twisting and spinning together, joined by more strands, becoming larger, thicker, brighter but constantly moving and shifting. It formed a massive cable of individual strands, all leading off to....somewhere. He raced along the cable of light and in the distance he could see a massive, brilliant column of light extending straight up. He was torn between exploring this new sight and continuing to investigate the Evaluation. The knowledge of his own pending examination and a sense of self-preservation decided him. He returned to the glowing spheres contesting each other, an intense ribbon of light connecting them. It rippled and flowed and he had an unaccountable desire to touch it. He reached for the ribbon. He just managed to touch......and he was suddenly back in his body, eyes open, staring at the platform where Besalaman had just collapsed.

The crowd was in an uproar. The other examiners were bending over Besalaman, shaking him and stretching him out. Bethany stumbled out of the Box and was standing, staring at the inert form at her feet. Councilor Linape was shouting for everyone to be quiet. Halvor jerked Colin by the arm and slammed him backward into the trunk of the tree, the impact jarred him back from wherever he had been. Halvor was furious. "What did you do!?!"

The wind was knocked from Colin by the force of impact. His head was ringing and all he could do was stare at the angry face inches from his own. "I...I...." He stammered.

Halvor ripped the dagger free of its sheathe, pressing the point to the soft spot under Colin's chin, "_You_ did something! I want to know what and I want to know _now_! Mantle or not, prophet or impostor, I _swear_ I'll have your guts if you do not speak right now!"

"Ah, that hurts." Colin said in a choked voice.

Seeming to get a marginal grip on his anger, Halvor loosened his grip on Colin's collar and withdrew the blade a fraction of an inch. "What just happened?" he asked through gritted teeth.

"I don't know. I think I dozed off. I was sitting there with my eyes closed and suddenly you were bashing my head against this tree and shoving that knife in my throat."

"You had something to do with this. I want to know how." Halvor said flatly.

"What could I possibly have done? I was sitting right here with you. I didn't move. I didn't speak. I was just sitting."

Halvor looked doubtful, "I don't know what you did. The Box is ancient. Never has anyone outside of the Box been able to touch a person who is inside the Box. It cannot be done. But, I have never heard of anything happening like what I have seen today. It had to be you!" He insisted.

The blade had been withdrawn a full inch. Colin risked reaching up to rub his banged head. "You know more about this than me. This is my first time. I just wanted to know what to expect at my Evaluation."

Halvor suddenly put his blade away and jerked Colin back around the tree. The crowd was still in an uproar. Besalaman at least was sitting up. He looked dazed, but seemed to be functioning. Bethany was in tears, surrounded by her family. Councilor Linape finally gave up and yelled out hoarsely, "The 3rd File of the 1st Order of Aidon welcomes Bethany of Tyber and acknowledges her as having passed the test of Compliance and is now entitled to the privileges of the 3rd File..........She can try for a higher File another time. This Evaluation is concluded!!"

The audience quickly began to disperse. Halvor grabbed Colin roughly by one shoulder and propelled him around the tree, heading toward the road, but they were immediately caught in the crowd heading the same way. Suddenly, there were shouts of anger, amazement and alarm all around them. Halvor and Colin found themselves encircled by a mob, pointing, staring and jabbering, "He wears the mantle!" "Who would dare?!?" "An impostor!" "Does he wear it by right?" "Look! His hair! It's so light!" "His eyes! They're blue!" "No, green!" "He wears the colors of no File!" "Call the guards!" "The 11th File has captured him!" "He's so tall!" "He has no beard!" It was chaos.

Halvor still had hold of Colin's arm and he was circling warily, trying to watch the crowd all at once. His other hand was gripping the hilt of his sword. The babble and tumult, as well as the size of the crowd, was increasing by the minute as more people came running, attracted by the shouts and commotion.

Halvor tried to intimidate the crowd, "People of Tyber!" he yelled, "I am Halvor, Arbor Guard of Salem, 11th File of the 3rd Order! I am charged with escorting this man. You will please disperse and return to your homes immediately!"

One-on-one, he might have stood a chance, but emboldened by the relative anonymity of being part of a faceless mob, the populace ignored him. Now the questions began to fly, "Arbor Guard? What's he doing in Tyber?" "Who is he?" "Where did he come from?" "Is one wearing the mantle truly among us?" "What message does he bring?" "Is he under arrest?" "Are you taking him to Salem?"

The questions came so fast and thick, repeated over and over by others scattered in the crowd, that Halvor had no chance to answer even if he had been so inclined. Accusations of, "He's an impostor!" "He caused the trouble at the Evaluation!" now began to be heard as well. Halvor was becoming angrier as his shouts to disperse were ignored. Colin was getting slightly dizzy from the constant circling. The situation was rapidly getting out of hand.

Shaking free of Halvor's grip, Colin reached back and for the first time, drew the hood up over his head, then turned and marched straight toward the platform so recently used for the Evaluation. The crowd fell back in a mad scramble to get out of his way and Halvor ran to catch up. Besalaman had just managed to get to his feet, surrounded by several of the other Examiners and Councilor Linape, but at the sudden approach of the hooded figure, he and two of the other examiners fell backward on the platform in a tangle. Colin paused to help them up as they looked up with shocked expressions.

The crowd had closed in behind Colin and Halvor. Those at the front had fallen silent, but questions and accusations still flew from those at the back of the crowd. Turning to face them, Colin slid the hood off his head, allowing it to again hang down his back. As the clamor fell away, he spoke, "People of Tyber, I offer you my apologies for startling you just now and arriving without notice to attend the Evaluation this morning. I did not wish to become a distraction for this important event in the lives of the eight young men and women whom you came here to see today. May I introduce myself? I am Colin Ericsson, of Kalispell. I know you have not heard of it. It is far from here and as you have already recognized, I am a stranger in Aidon. The High Council of Salem has been kind enough to assign the Arbor Guard, Halvor, as an escort for me while I am here." He paused and the crowd began again to murmur and shout questions and accusations, but he held up a hand for silence. "As you have also noticed, I wear the colors of no File. The High Council of Salem has determined that I shall receive an Evaluation two moons from now. I know that my appearance is strange to you and that my attire has created concern - both here and in Salem. I apologize. I stand here before you as a man, not a messenger. I did not mean to offend or cause alarm and did not intend to disrupt your Sabbath. You will forgive me if I do not attempt to address all of your concerns, but the Council at Salem has established a prior claim on me. Now, I believe that my escort would like to leave."

With that, he nodded to Halvor who fell in beside him and they moved forward to exit the platform. Just before they reached the edge, a voice in the crowd yelled, heard clearly above the muted noise which instantly ceased, "Do you wear the mantle by right or deception?"

Colin paused, scanning the crowd, taking his time before he spoke, "The clothing is mine." He said firmly. With that, he stepped off the platform into the crowd, which parted immediately, allowing him passage - rather like Moses parting the Red Sea, and like Moses, he ignored the chaos left in his wake.

Nobody followed and in a matter of minutes they reached the edge of town, but not on the same side from which they had entered. Halvor finally spoke, "What do you think you've just accomplished?"

"I think I accomplished getting us out of town without you deciding to lop off a few heads, for a start. Right now I think that's pretty good."

Halvor stared at him and a reluctant grin slowly cracked his stern expression. "I was thinking about lopping off a few heads, as you put it." His grin faded. "Actually, I might have tried drawing a bit of blood. That usually settles a crowd quickly enough." He shook his head, "But you've kicked a hornet's nest. You were doing pretty good, but then you had to go and lay claim to the mantle! It's bad enough that you always have that thing attached to your cloak, but you had to put it on your head - and then you claimed that you're not the messenger! Are you insane?"

Colin shrugged, "I've been asking myself that more than you can imagine as of late. I don't think I am, but I'm not sure any crazy person does. The fact remains, I arrived here wearing these clothes. They're mine." He held up a restraining hand, "That doesn't make me the messenger of your Messias. I don't have a message. I'm just a man. But the clothing is mine and that includes the mantle. Package deal."

Halvor started walking, leading them into the woods to circle back towards Jorge and Miran's farm. He sighed, "Look, I'm going to level with you. I was assigned to watch you. Study you. See what kind of trouble you were stirring up and 'intervene' in a fatal sort of way if I thought it advisable."

"That's not the most shocking piece of information I've ever heard."

Halvor ignored him, "There's a healthy suspicion that you're trying to stir up insurrection prior to an attack from Kernsidon. They're due, you know?"

"If you say so."

Halvor gritted his teeth and continued, "Point is, I've been watching you. Almost every day, except when I go to Salem to report. And I report directly to the High Council. No one else." He paused, "You know what I've reported so far?"

"Haven't a clue."

"Fine, I'll tell you. I've reported that you're pretty much inept. Even the most basic skills like milking a cow or making a fire are obviously foreign to you. You've made no effort to stir up or even contact the local population - at least until today. You've not laid claim to prophecy or to be a messenger of Messias. You haven't tried to sneak away. I thought you were that Sabbath when you went and fetched the flint, but you didn't, you came right back and you met nobody. The only thing you've done is teach some farmers how to make stuff to clean themselves with better - that soap. You showed them how to make a cowhide that doesn't stink and how to eat fish. Fish! What kind of trouble-maker wastes time figuring out how to catch fish!"

Colin just grinned, but Halvor wasn't seeing the humor.

"The one thing you've done that looks remotely like trouble is making this bow and arrow. A man armed like that - what chance does a sword have against a bow and arrow? You'd pin him to a tree before he got within 30 paces. And a spear isn't going to fare much better. But the only thing you've done is shoot deer with it and you've not tried showing anyone except Elam how to use it. Let me tell you, the High Council is not happy with my reports!" He shook his head before continuing. "Everything I've seen says that you are exactly what you appear to be….some poor, lost fool who just wants to be helpful! And you stand the very likely possibility of winding up either dead or mindless at the conclusion of your Evaluation!"

They walked in silence for several minutes. Finally, Colin sighed, "Halvor, I appreciate your telling me all this. Dalene already……"

"The <u>Lady</u> Dalene." Halvor interrupted and the warning was obvious in his tone.

"She introduced herself to me as 'Dalene,' he replied coolly, "She can correct me if she wishes. As I was saying, <u>Dalene</u> already told me that my Evaluation would probably end with my being 'destroyed.' That I would no longer exist as a thinking individual. I suggested getting rid of these clothes, but she intimated that would be essentially the same as admitting that I'm an impostor and the resulting penalty would be the same - and, since I've already been seen wearing the mantle and since I do tend to stand out in a crowd, the odds of my slipping into an anonymous existence as a butcher, baker or candlestick maker seem pretty slim, so I'm stuck - right here."

The family had not arrived home by the time they reached Jorge's farm. Halvor disappeared shortly afterwards. Colin figured he had a long trip ahead of him in order to report on the events of the Evaluation to the High Council in Salem. That suited him just fine. He had things to do. First, he tended to his tanning projects, as he had two more cowhides and a couple of deer hides he was tanning with the hair on. Afterwards he spent some time with Gisele. She was pleased to see him and came to nuzzle his shoulder. He had brought one of his blankets which he folded a couple of times to form a pad. He let her smell the blanket and then he used it to give her a good rub down. She kept looking back over her shoulder at him, curious, but the feel of the blanket was pleasant. Soon he was tossing the blanket across her back and neck, even her face, all while speaking to her softly and she soon lost all concern regarding this unusual procedure. Colin progressed to tossing the blanket across her back and then laying his weight across her, getting her used to the idea of something on her back. He spent a good two hours working with the horse. Even so, she whickered her displeasure when he left. He turned back with a smile and rubbed her forehead, between her eyes, "Yes, Gisele, we're going to get along just fine. Don't worry. I'll be back." She tossed her head in agreement and then turned to her feed.

The blanket smelled a little too "horsey" for his liking, after spending so much time working Gisele. He washed it and hoped it would be dry before bedtime. He had just completed this chore when he heard the family returning. "Elam! Congratulations on your Evaluation! Are you pleased with being part of the 4th File?"

Elam grinned broadly, "Very much so! And thank you. I didn't even see you there. Where were you?"

"Halvor and I were standing by one of the trees in the back. I was afraid I might be a distraction if we were any closer."

"Aye. I heard there was a bit of a 'distraction' after the Evaluation." Jorge said dryly. Miran elbowed him in the ribs.

"Are you alright?" she asked, concern showing on her face.

"I'm fine. There really wasn't a problem. I knew that sooner or later my presence was going to be noticed, and once noticed, there would be questions. I just hope it doesn't become a problem for all of you."

"It's no problem that we can't deal with. They're good folks, most of them. They just haven't gotten to know you like we have. Don't concern yourself." Jorge said.

"Thanks. The Evaluation was certainly more exciting than I had expected."

Miran's face clouded, "Yes. I've never seen the like. Marion acted like she was completely lost when she was conducting the Evaluation for Muriel. She said she just suddenly got dizzy when she couldn't see Muriel. Poor Examiner Besalaman! He said almost the same thing. One moment he was conducting Bethany's Evaluation and suddenly he lost her. He said it was so disorienting he just kind of fell down, but he didn't think he passed out. Oh! But that 5th File Examiner! That Warren! Why he was so rude to our Elam! The way he just stormed away after Elam bowed to him! I am still just so angry!"

Elam placed a restraining hand on his mother's arm. "It's alright, mother. There was no harm done. Best of all, I am still of the 1st Order, so let him be rude. I'm right where I want to be!"

His mother smiled and Jorge clapped a hand on his shoulder. "Aye. We're right proud, son. Proud that you are of the 4th File, but pleased that you be still with us, and of the 1st Order."

It was still Sabbath, so dinner was a quiet affair, though Miran and Jorge kept up a constant review of the day's events. Apparently the town had been all astir after Colin had left. Between the near catastrophe of a most unusual Evaluation and the appearance of one wearing the mantle - whether prophet or impostor - the town had been in an uproar. Thankfully, nobody except Tunsten, Kath and Baylor had any reason to connect Jorge and Miran with the stranger. And fortunately, they weren't inclined to talk - at least not so far.

Before retiring for the night, Colin spoke to Miran, "Are you planning on going to market this week?"

"Possibly. Were you needing some things?"

"Yes. I'd like to get a couple of blankets, a small frying pan or cook pot and I need some harness rings, maybe six or eight."

Miran was concerned, "Have you been cold at night? Why didn't you say so? We've plenty of blankets. I didn't know."

"No. I've been fine, really. I just don't want to have to keep using your things - especially if I have the means to pay for acquiring some of my own."

She looked at him doubtfully, "It's no bother. We weren't using them anyway – it's not like it's winter. But if you wish your own things, either I or Kath can pick them up next market day."

"Thanks. I really appreciate it."

Colin retrieved his blanket, still slightly damp and began to make up his bed when there was a soft knock at the door of the shed. "Yes?" he called out.

The door swung open, revealing Elam standing there, hesitant.

"May I speak with you?"

"Certainly, Elam. What can I do for you?"

"Today.......at the Evaluation, you saw the 5th File Examiner?"

"Yes."

"I......well, during the Evaluation, I could see his true self. We were contesting. I think I was going to get him to Comply, but suddenly, I didn't want to. I didn't want to be taken away and have to live with the 2nd Order. I quit. I bowed to Examiner Warren." Elam hung his head with his confession.

"Elam, that was your choice. There's nothing wrong in that."

"I think Examiner Warren knew, though. He knew that he didn't get me to Comply - that I bowed on my own."

"I don't know your customs very well, but I think this was simply your choice to make. In life, there certainly are moral issues - questions of right or wrong. There are absolute standards, and you can't, you must not ever ignore those standards. Those are moral choices, and eternal law dictates right and wrong. You can try to re-label it or rationalize it, but that doesn't change the nature of the thing. Right is right and wrong is wrong. But, there are other choices which are neither right nor wrong. They are simply choices - what to have for breakfast, what clothes to wear. Some choices may be foolish, but they aren't necessarily wrong. You're entitled to choose, and then you accept the consequence of the choice. They go hand-in-hand. I think you're entitled to choose to whom you will bow, and to whom you will not. I'm proud of you, Elam. I don't think you were wrong to simply say, 'This is <u>my</u> choice.'"

Elam nodded, "That's how I felt, but I feel lots better hearing you explain it like that. Thanks. You're a good friend."

"Thanks, Elam. I hope so."

The next few days passed quickly. Colin had always been an early riser and he used that trait to good advantage. The problem he had was Halvor. The guy was just too good at being around without being noticed. Colin knew he was taking a chance, but he didn't feel like he had any options. He rolled out of bed at the first hint of the coming dawn and spent the better part of an hour working with Gisele. Colin continued to flag her with the blanket, getting her used to it flapping in her face or being tossed over her back, but since that was usually accompanied by a good rub-down, she accepted it. Colin hadn't dared to get up on her yet, but he was to the point where he could lay across her back, letting her take up his full weight and she tolerated this with curiosity, but no alarm. The problem was he really wanted to start training her for riding, but he didn't want anyone - Halvor in particular, to see him for fear they might guess what he was planning.

After breakfast he would usually spend much of the day working with Jorge and Elam in the fields. They continued to cut firewood, stack rocks, clear stumps and perform the general repairs necessary around the farm. Jorge was working on some tanning of his own now and was anxious to make a set of harness for his oxen which he hoped would prove tougher than the canvas he had been using - and tearing - while pulling stumps. Both Jorge and Elam had been developing a strong interest in fishing. They couldn't understand why Colin liked his artificial flies, when using bait was so much easier and more certain when it came to catching fish. They liked the variety in their diet, as well as the addition to their larder. Elam's bow was progressing nicely and Jorge had started one of his own. Elam had a natural gift for knapping out arrowheads, but Jorge's efforts usually wound up creating nothing but small shards of flint. Colin had several deer hides tanned now, including a hide which he had done without the hair. This meant that Miran had quite a bit of meat to smoke and dry, but rather than complaining about the work she was pleased with the additional food. Colin was laying aside a small supply of the smoked venison, stored in canvas pouches he had made. In the late evening he would get out the deer hides and work on a project he wasn't anxious for anyone to see. He had trimmed two hides and laid them hair-side to hair-side. Using leather lacing trimmed from one of the cowhides, he stitched the edges all the way around, as well as lacing the bulk together in a manner similar to tying a quilt. He was working on making a saddle-pad. He fashioned a girth and stirrup straps and attached them to the saddle. The hard part had been making the stirrup rings, but he used Jorge's saw to rough-cut the outline, then a brace and bit to hog out the center. With a rasp he smoothed both the interior and exterior contours until he had a functional, if not particularly attractive pair of stirrups. By punching a series of holes in the straps, he was able to use lacing to adjust their length.

Kath and Miran were still making soap, as much as they could, in their spare time. The demand remained high, so Kath didn't feel like she needed help getting it sold on market day. She had, however, picked up the items Colin had requested. The harness rings he was especially anxious to get, since he needed these to finish his saddle and construct a halter for Gisele. This was a new part of her education, but she accepted it willingly. Colin didn't want to force the issue of a bit and bridle, so he hoped that she wouldn't need it.

Halvor, in some ways, seemed more relaxed these days. Colin tried to keep an eye on him. About twice a week he would disappear for at least one full day. If he didn't appear for breakfast on the Sabbath, he wouldn't be seen until noon of Second Day. That set the timing for Colin to execute his plan. He'd picked Elam's brain to learn what he could about the lunar cycle on this earth. It was a 30 day cycle, resulting in a lunar year of 360 days, but Elam told him that the solar year was 370 days. Come the next Sabbath, he would have 39 days until his Evaluation was scheduled - just over 5 weeks. That was an appointment he had no intention of missing, but he didn't plan to just sit around and wait for what might well be the same as his execution either. He had five weeks to see a little bit of this world. He had no idea if Halvor would try to stop him, so he wasn't about to ask. Halvor would be tough to take in single combat, Colin figured, even with his advantage of height. Halvor didn't strike him as being the kind of guy to wear that sword and dagger for show, and the grip he had applied to Colin's arm the day of the Elam's Evaluation had definitely indicated strength. He would choose his battles, and he chose to avoid this one if he could.

Chapter 11   The Council

Halvor Tregard, Arbor Guard of Aidon, was fed up as he waited outside the Council Chambers in the Praetorium. His reports had been frustrating right from the start. He was waiting to make yet another report and they weren't going to like this one any better than they had the others. What did they expect? The man never <u>did</u> anything! Well, that wasn't quite true. He had done a lot of things- teaching these farmers how to be cleaner, how to make leather and how to fish! That last made him grin briefly, but the scowl soon returned. The Council didn't know what to think of this strange looking individual who wore the mantle but claimed no message from Messias. Thinking back to his report regarding soap, he shook his head. Councilor Viktor Samson of the 8th File had been livid, his face almost matched the deep red color of his robe. As head of the 8th File, he was also head of the 2nd Order. Much of the skilled labor of Aidon was delegated to his Order. He had been in a rage, standing and screaming, shaking his fist at Councilor Rabin of the 4th File. "This is a clear violation of the 1st Order charter!" he had accused. "You are to restrict your Files to such activities as are directly related to farming, mining and producing lumber!"

He had been backed by the angry voices of Councilors Dalba and Bret of the 6th and 7th Files, whose members produced manufactured goods primarily in metals, pottery and linen. It didn't matter that none of them had ever seen this 'soap,' or had more than a vague idea of what it was used for and no clue as to how it was produced. They smelled opportunity here and attempted to stake a claim on whatever benefit might result. Councilor Rabin became angry and defensive, "<u>I</u> never authorized this! But even if I had, I fail to see how it infringes on <u>your</u> charter. You don't make 'soap,' so why should the 1st Order not be permitted to produce it?"

Shocked at being addressed in such a manner by one of the lower Files, Councilor Samson started screaming, joined by the other members of the 2nd Order. The Councilors from the 1st Order had leapt to their feet, equally angry and equally loud in defending their 'right' to produce soap - or any other item that the 2nd Order wasn't producing for them.

It had taken the Regent several minutes and the threat of calling the guards to clear the Council chambers before things settled to a hostile silence

"Is this how it begins? The chaos that the Councils have prevented for almost 4000 years begins because each of you wishes to produce what none of you knows how to do?"

The antagonists in the room had the good graces to at least hang their heads in shame, but not without continuing to glare at their counterparts across the way.

The Regent continued, "Already, this stranger has sown discord which has reached even this Council. From your report, Arbor Guard, it seems that many of the people of Tyber are anxious to buy this 'soap,' a thing which they had never imagined, they now feel they can scarcely live without. And what will they not buy, in order to have the means to buy 'soap?' Will they no longer buy the cooking pots or the linens produced by the 2nd Order? And what of the materials they use to produce this product? Now they will no longer be available for their former uses, and once again, balance is upset."

Halvor had offered, helpfully, the observation that the materials used to make soap seemed to primarily be wood ash and hog or cow fat, for which there was little market anyway. No one on the Council seemed to appreciate this insight, so he lapsed into silence once more.

Councilor Tregard continued to review the disruption that the stranger had created. "Catching fish? Are the people of Tyber so poor that they cannot feed themselves without resorting to fish?" and he glared at Councilor Linape, who only shook her head mutely.

"The time taken from producing food and timber or mining the ores we need cannot be replaced. Fish? Can they truly be worth the trouble of catching them in order to eat them? Surely they cannot compare to that which can be grown with our own hands." The council nodded in agreement.

"If the farmers can produce this leather - and use this instead of the canvas produced in Ramah by the 5th File, then what will become of Ramah, when they can no longer exchange their canvas for food and fuel? But most troubling is the report of this bow and arrow. The archery, you call it. If a man can kill a deer at 40 paces with such instruments, then can a man not kill another man at such a distance as well? Could this not lead to conflict among the people, that they would resort to violence upon each other at a distance which they would not consider at sword's length?"

At this, Halvor had finally spoken, "There is potential for harm from these things, but Colin's motivation appears only to be a desire to show thanks to the family ordered to feed and shelter him during his recovery. It is true that these things have potential for harm, but the same must be said of all tools - whether it be a sword or a shovel. I do not believe that the tool is evil because those who use it are evil. While these things are new, I would urge your forbearance. Consider not only the potential for harm, but also the potential for good. I believe that all Aidon might benefit from these things."

Counselor Samson snorted derisively and angry scowls darkened the faces of several in the 1st and 2nd Order. The Regent nodded thoughtfully. Councilor Dean Garmon, wearing a light blue fringed robe had remained impassive. Councilor Lucinda Yearsley was a stern, humorless woman of middle age, completely covered in a dark, royal blue from head to toe, denoting her membership in the 9th File was normally one of the more volatile members of the Council. She had remained uncharacteristically calm during the discussion, which caused Councilor Tregard to watch her with greater interest. He had learned that any show of calm on the part of this impassioned woman usually hinted at behind-the-scenes bargains having already been struck. Councilor Krainik of the 11th File nodded, saying, "I believe that the Arbor Guard has spoken wisely - at least in one word. Forbearance. We need not act hastily. I suggest we continue to observe this mantle-bearer. After all, if precipitate action is required, I am certain the Arbor Guard will not hesitate to do what must be done."

While he waited, Halvor reviewed his disastrous report on the Evaluation at Tyber.

"You idiot!" Councilor Saleen had fumed, "How could you be so stupid as to allow him to go to Tyber? The whole town now knows he wears the mantle!"

"My orders were to observe the stranger and see who he contacts, or who contacts him. I was not instructed to prevent his traveling or going to town. To do so would be to arouse his suspicions and prevent him from making any contacts." Halvor replied, stone faced.

Councilor Saleen turned on Councilor Linape, of the 3rd File, "You were there! You were to oversee the Evaluation! How could you let this impostor address the entire town - and lay claim to the mantle?"

Councilor Linape flared back, "I was busy! We had an Examiner collapse right in the Box! I couldn't do everything all at once! I didn't even know he was there! All of the sudden he was being mobbed by the crowd, then he was up on the platform speaking to them. Besides, it wasn't like he was trying to stir them up. If anything he calmed the situation before it got out of hand. There was nothing I could have done!"

The bickering continued for some minutes until the Regent abruptly slammed his hand down on the table, "Enough! What's done is done! Whether we like it or not, we certainly learned more by permitting this stranger - Colin - freedom of movement than we would have by restricting him to the farm. Fighting about it doesn't help. He said that he will attend the Evaluation. He has publicly stated that he is not the messenger of Messias. That should help calm things. Unfortunately, he has also publicly laid claim to the mantle. That is going to keep things stirred up. But that isn't all that is bothering me. Arbor Guard, are you certain that he could have had nothing to do with the strange happenings during the evaluation?"

Halvor hesitated, but shook his head, "With this man, I cannot be certain. I know that he did not approach the platform until he addressed the people right before we left. He may have had his eyes closed when Examiner Marion became confused and again when Examiner Besalaman collapsed, but I can't be sure. We were at least 20 yards away from the Box, and everyone knows that only one inside the Box can affect another who is also inside the Box. So no, I don't see how he could have. But he was there, and I've never seen an Evaluation go like that one did."

Lucinda Yearsley, practically crowed, her voice shrill, "You see! He is dangerous! He must be taken into custody!"

Counselor Krainik stood, waiting for the room to quiet. "I have urged forbearance in this matter in the past. That is still my counsel. Nothing has been done that clearly shows this man to be a danger. As our wise Regent has already stated, we have learned more by permitting this man his freedom than we would if we were to restrict him." He bowed toward Councilor Tregard as he said this. "I see no reason to alter the current arrangement."

The debate had continued for some time, but as is often the case in government councils, nothing was determined, and so by default, nothing changed. The Lady Dalene had been present during the Council meeting. While not a member, her status as daughter of the Regent - making her The Lady of Prophecy - permitted her access to all aspects of government. It was accepted that the better informed The Lady was, the better her chances of preventing the fulfillment of Prophecy during her lifetime. She had spoken with Councilor Krainik after the meeting. "Thank you for advising restraint in this matter. I believe that your words carried weight with the other Council members and that this is the wisest course for the time being."

Krainik bowed, "Lady Dalene! A pleasure, as always. Yes, I believe that this man, whether impostor, spy or innocent stranger, should be allowed every freedom we can offer under our law. It is unfortunate that many of the ignorant lower Files find his presence disturbing. You have of course heard that rumors concerning him are running rampant in Tyber and the surrounding regions. Even in my own city of Hyaton word of 'one wearing the mantle' has been spread. However, I am sure that in due time all this will be settled to satisfaction, and order will be properly restored."

The Lady Dalene made as if to speak, but she simply nodded and turned to Halvor. Councilor Krainik, taking the hint, took his leave. She waited until certain that Councilor Krainik was out of earshot before asking, "Halvor, tell me, how is he doing really?"

Halvor scowled, "You heard my report, the same as everyone else. What is there to say?"

She smiled, not put off in the slightest. "You reported on what he did, whom he saw and a considerable amount of what he said. You mentioned nothing about how he is. That's what I'm asking you."

He sighed, "I know. You aren't actually interested in him, are you?"

The look she gave him would make even an Arbor Guard blanch, at least, if he weren't her brother and hadn't seen that look a thousand times growing up. But her voice still held steel. "I am The Lady of Prophecy. I will not be interested in him or any other man. If he is a spy or an impostor, I will see him destroyed." She suddenly turned away, sighing deeply and her voice became soft, "But I don't believe him to be other than what he claims to be. He is simply an unfortunate man, and it is our fear and suspicion that will cost him life."

She looked at him again, "I know something of what it is to have no life. To be connected to no one. He seemed so lonely and lost – not how he acted, it was just something I felt. I wanted him to have life. To be with others and erase that loneliness. For these few weeks, I wished that for him. I did what I could so that he might have it. Maybe I hoped that he could connect with someone, something there in Tyber. Maybe I wanted to experience that connection, if only through him. So tell me, my dear brother," and she brushed back the hair on his forehead as she said it, "How is he?"

Halvor shook his head. "I'm sorry Dalene. I'm just frustrated. Colin is well. You know he has met very few people since he got back on his feet. Your little delegation, of course. The farmers, Jorge and Miran and their son Elam like him. I can tell. They don't like me. They fear me and they fear what I might do to him, but they like him. He hit it off with the neighbor, Baylor. They're all partners in this soap making business. That got him into a few dectorals. I told you about the horse he bought. Tunsten, the old fellow he bought it from, he doesn't like anybody, but he liked him. You know how different Colin looks from anyone in Aidon, well Tunsten never said a word. Never so much as batted an eye, but he sold him one of the finest horses I've ever seen, and at a bargain price, too. I've heard Tunsten turned a man down when he offered more than twice what an animal's worth, so he liked Colin. I don't understand why he didn't buy a cart. He has money enough, and Tunsten or Baylor would sell him one." He paused, "By the twin moons, I like him. I just hope I don't have to kill him."

"Has his strength fully returned? He is no longer ill?"

Halvor laughed. "That's one thing I forgot to mention to the Council. Yes, I would say he has strength. I watched him in a clearing one afternoon. Colin was practicing jumping - he and Elam both. I watched as they marked their jumps, and looked at the marks afterwards. From a standing jump, he leaped almost twice the height of a man! He beat my mark by over two feet! I tried his bow one afternoon when he was out in the field. It takes strength to draw it. I watched him hit a target three times out of three and then kill both that fox and a deer as fast as you can blink. Yes, I think he's healthy enough."

She nodded, smiling a little now. "Thank you. I am glad for him. I hope that when he is brought to Salem for the Evaluation that he will not hate me too much."

That conversation had been almost two weeks ago. Since the uproar over the events of the Evaluation at Tyber, there had been nothing of significance to report. Colin had gone nowhere, had met no one. Thankfully, despite the rumors in Tyber - and throughout most of Aidon at this point, no one had yet connected the mantle bearer to the farm of Jorge and Miran. Tunsten could do it, but he hadn't. The harness maker in Tyber who stabled his horses and hid his cart, Faron, he could make the connection as well. If not directly to the stranger, then at least to Councilor Rabin. But he appeared to be an unimaginative individual and he'd been paid well to keep his mouth shut. But if word got out as to where the stranger was, there would be no preventing hordes of people from coming to see him. Some out of curiosity. Some to prove him an impostor and at the same time prove their own worth. Some would come out of hope and some out of fear. Whether he was a messenger or not, there would be those who made him out to be such for their own purposes and this could not be permitted.

Halvor was finally shown into the Council chambers. The Regent wasted no time in bringing the meeting to order, "Arbor Guard Halvor Tregard, please report on your assignment, the observation of the stranger wearing the mantle, known as Colin Ericsson of Kalispell."

Halvor was surprised. None of the previous meetings had been conducted in such a formal manner. On his guard now, he bowed, first to the Regent and then to the Council collectively. He took note of Dalene, sitting at the rear of the chamber, face expressionless. "Arbor Guard Halvor Tregard of Salem reporting. Honored High Council of Aidon, since my last report, the stranger bearing the mantle, known as Colin Ericsson of Kalispell, has been engaged daily in activities associated with farming. He has been stacking rocks, clearing stumps and caring for livestock. He has also been engaged in activities not associated with farming, such as assisting the two women, Miran and Kath of Tyber, in making soap. He is assisting the farmer, Jorge of Tyber in making what he calls leather. That is, the cured hides of animals such that they do not rot or smell and are useful for making articles of clothing and other things. He has continued in his activity of catching fish, which is eaten by himself and those at the farm and he uses a bow and arrow to hunt and kill deer. The meat is eaten or smoked and dried and he makes leather from the hides. Besides the individuals residing on the farms of Jorge and Baylor he has met with no one nor has he gone anywhere. That is all."

Councilor Tregard nodded to him. "Thank you, Arbor Guard. Are there any questions?"

There were no questions, but Councilor Samson of the 9th File got to his feet and spoke belligerently. "That doesn't matter. We've all discussed this at great length since our last meeting. You know it. Call for the vote. Call for the vote to see if we take this impostor, this troublemaker into custody or not!"

Councilor Tregard sighed. "The matter has been stated. Those in favor of bringing the mantle-bearer, Colin Ericsson of Kalispell, into custody, please signify by raising your hand."

All four of the 2nd Order Files raised their hand, along with Garmon and Yearsley of the 9th and 10th File. In the case of a tie vote, the Highest Councilor would decide the matter. The Lady Dalene let out a quiet sigh of relief, but just then, Councilor Krainik raised his hand as well. "I fear the time for restraint is past. Rumor of this mantle-bearer has spread throughout all Aidon. We must take him into custody and demonstrate that this Council is in control! I vote, yes."

Showing no emotion, Councilor Tregard said, "Arbor Guard Halvor Tregard, you are to return to Tyber as soon as you are ready. Fresh horses will be provided for your cart. You are to bring Colin Ericsson and all of his belongings as quickly as possible, here, to the Praetorium where he will be held until the time of his Evaluation. That is all."

The Lady Dalene sat, jaw clenched in frustration. She felt like she ought to be surprised at the outcome of the vote, but she wasn't. The subject had been hotly debated both in and out of the Council chambers ever since the debacle of the Evaluation in Tyber. She had known that the vote could go either way, but Councilor Krainik had surprised her. He had favored a policy of non-intervention in the past. To have the vote end with his recommendation to arrest Colin was bitter.

She approached her father, who was speaking with Halvor. He was saying, "Yes, I think it's a mistake to bring him in. But the Council has voted and you will carry out their orders. Are you going to take a company of men with you?"

Halvor shook his head, "I don't think there will be any problem. Colin has done nothing but express his willingness to appear for the Evaluation anyway. We don't need to make an issue of his being 'arrested.' I'll simply be bringing him to Salem a little earlier than expected. A group of soldiers just complicates things - especially for Jorge and Miran. If I show up with soldiers, everyone will know where the mantle-bearer has been staying. With emotions running high – especially if we arrest him, it could become ugly."

Councilor Tregard nodded, "I agree. But when you bring him, make sure you bring all of his things as well. The Council is interested in the bow and arrow especially. We'll determine if these things pose a risk that should be expunged with the Compliance."

Halvor looked at his sister, "I'm sorry. I didn't think this was going to happen - especially since he's been so quiet the past couple of weeks."

She nodded, "I know. You will be kind, won't you?"

He smiled, "I am always the very picture of kindness. You know that."

She had to smile at that, for it was most definitely <u>not</u> how most people would describe Halvor. It wasn't that he was unkind, he was just very focused on what needed to be done and very little under the twin moons would stop him once he got on a path.

"Yes," she said dryly, "but maybe just a <u>little</u> kinder than usual." Turning to her father she asked, "You didn't delay the vote at all. Why?"

"No. The issue had been discussed and settled before the meeting - and not to my liking. It has been quiet and with nothing to feed the rumor merchants, things were settling down. Once we bring Colin into custody, it will no longer be rumor, but confirmed fact that a mantle-bearer has appeared. People will be frantic for information and we'll have nothing to give them. Out there, he is invisible. When we arrest him, he becomes a flag that half the population will flock to - in fear or fury."

Again she nodded, "I <u>was</u> surprised by Councilor Krainik. If one of the lower Files had voted for arrest, I would have understood. But I thought he agreed with you."

"That one is ambitious. He always has been. I'm never sure if he is voting for what he believes is the best for Aidon, or if he is pursuing his own interests. In this matter.........I really wish I knew."

Councilor Krainik was pleased with his performance in the Council chambers today. Despite the fact that he was the Councilor for the 11th File, he was by far the youngest member of the Council. The next youngest member, Councilor Yearsley of the 10th File was almost 20 years his senior at age 54. He found her unpleasant and unimaginative. However, he cultivated her approval and support, as she could be a useful ally. It was a testament to his skill, that despite the fact that the two of them often voted opposite sides of a given issue, she counted him as one of her closest friends, never realizing how he groomed and coaxed her into assuming unpopular positions as a glaring public counter-point to his own reasoned deliberations and behavior. He despised her, as he despised all of his fellow Council members.

Lijah Krainik was the only son of 12th File parents. It had been a severe disappointment to them when at the conclusion of their son's Evaluation, he had been placed in the 11th File. While this did not necessitate his being taken from their home, it would perhaps have been better if such had been the case. From his 15th Birthday even to the present, they had made it clear that he had failed them. While he was acknowledged to be the most powerful mind in the 11th File, the fact was, he had never advanced. That he held one of the most important positions in Aidon meant nothing to them. He was in the 11th File, while they were of the 12th File. He didn't measure up and he would never be able to challenge Gareth Tregard in the Evaluation to become Regent of Aidon, finally delivering the revenge his father had so long hungered for. Someday, he swore, he <u>would</u>

measure up and they would see that no one in Aidon held more power than he.

Things had not gone as he had hoped the past few weeks. His position of restraint in regards to leaving the mantle-bearer free had been a calculated risk. A few more episodes like the Evaluation in Tyber and the whole country would have been in an uproar, demanding to see the messenger of Messias! Oh, how he would have loved to have seen that impostor shroud his head in that hood! It must have had those ignorant farmers shaking in their boots! He couldn't have scripted it better himself! Curse him! Why couldn't he just do that sort of thing a little bit more? It was perfect. The man had tasted the power of the thing! He had money now - a little bit at least. Why did he withdraw? Why wasn't he playing to the public? Krainik had half expected him to march on Salem and demand the seat of government. But then he had become - invisible. Not a peep, other than the rumors that were always flying about – half of which had been started by Krainik himself. He sighed. No, the best thing now would be to bring him in. Arrest him. Make it public. Violence would be good, but the chances of orchestrating that with only one man in opposition was remote. He just hadn't been public enough to gain a following. Oh, there might still be a few fanatics about who would have convinced themselves that this stranger was a messenger, but probably not enough to create a scene. He shrugged. Even so, if they could bring him in, make an issue of it, stoke the fires of speculation, he might yet create enough confusion to aid his purposes.

Then there was The Lady Dalene. She had taken an unusual interest in this mantle-bearer from the very first night - even going so far as to head the delegation to Tyber herself. Why? He knew it wasn't a romantic interest. No Lady of Prophecy had ever had a romantic interest in anyone. It was forbidden. Now there's a thought. Could he get prophecy to work <u>for</u> him? Perhaps he ought to look at cultivating her support and friendship. By the Twin Moons, it would be a more pleasant challenge than that repulsive Lucinda Yearsley! He would have to think on this.

Councilor Krainik returned to his quarters. Leaving orders with his steward that he was not to be disturbed until morning, he retired for a nap. When he arose, the sun had set. He opened the large wardrobe set at the rear of his bedroom, removed a nondescript wooden box and pulled out a simple, unadorned black cloak. After removing his own lavender trimmed robes and trousers, he donned the black garment and set a black cap in desperate need of washing on his head. Grunting with effort, he slid the heavy wardrobe to the side, revealing a section of wooden panel. A simple latch held it in place, but before removing it, he peered through a knot hole into a darkened space. Seeing nothing, he removed the panel and entered. It was cramped, filled with old buckets, mops and brooms which looked to have not been used in a very long time. Replacing the panel behind him, he peeked through another knot hole in a narrow door out into a dimly lit corridor. Seeing no one, he grabbed a bucket, opened the door and emerged, shoulders slumped, head down - the very picture of servility, just one of the hundreds of anonymous 1st File citizenry permitted to live in the capitol city to perform the dirty, mundane tasks scorned by those of the 3rd Order. Every town had need for wood-cutters, farmers, gardeners and those who cared for livestock, as foodstuffs could not be imported from the other villages all the time. Consequently, these nameless, faceless servants were common and offered the perfect disguise, since no one would ever dream of wearing the clothing of a lower File and thus demean himself.

Krainik, however, had been demeaned by others most of his life, or so he felt. And if wearing the colors of a lower File would help to earn him the respect he deserved, then so be it. He ambled down the corridor to exit at the back of the Praetorium, then crossed a large courtyard to the stables. He proceeded through the stable, nodding briefly to one other servant grooming a pair of horses tied in the aisle outside the stalls. At the back of the stables, he turned left. He made his way through darkened alleys until he found the door he was looking for. A crack of light showed underneath. He entered without knocking, addressing the black-robed figure seated facing away from the door in a low whisper, "I bid welcome to the ambassador of the 13th File."

The figure did not face him as Krainik closed the door softly. The response was harsh, female, but not feminine, "The 13th File grows impatient. What word of the impostor?"

Krainik seated himself on a low stool by the door. He never saw the face of his contact. Each time it was someone different. He cleared his throat. "There have been complications. The false mantle-bearer, Colin, has not been seen in public since the events of the Evaluation in Tyber. We had hoped that his continued appearance would stoke the fires of unrest amongst the population, but for some reason he has been content to remain out of sight."

"Then we should proceed immediately! He was never a part of the plan. Impostor or messenger, he has no bearing on the liberation of Aidon."

Krainik shook his head out of habit, ignoring the fact that his contact couldn't see him. "In confusion, there is opportunity. He will not remain out of sight much longer. The Arbor Guard was dispatched this afternoon to take him into custody. Once he is in custody, the word will spread. The ignorant fanatics will be furious that the Council would dare to arrest one who bears the mantle. Others will be equally furious that one whom they will consider to be an impostor is not destroyed or put to death immediately. Violence will ensue and the 13th File will move in, seen as the influence for peace. The 13th File has already waited over 4000 years. What harm can a few more weeks – months at most – possibly do? This is a heaven-sent opportunity."

The black-robed figure sat silently for several long minutes. Finally she nodded. "It may be best. I will convey your thoughts on this. You will report when this mantle-bearer is apprehended. It may be to our advantage if he were to die while in custody. Leave a message when he is in your hands. You will be instructed."

With that, the figure abruptly arose and exited through a dark doorway at the rear of the small room. Krainik was pleased that his advice had been taken. There was time. He would have power.

Halvor spent the afternoon making preparations for his return to Tyber. He felt no sense of urgency, only disgust at the decision which had been made. He admitted that part of his feeling stemmed from his sister - her expressed desire that Colin should be permitted freedom - life even, up until the time of his Evaluation, as she feared that he would not long survive that event. But he also admitted that the task was distasteful. Colin was a nice guy. He was polite to a fault - not that there hadn't been some missteps due to his unfamiliarity with Aidonian customs. But he had repeatedly expressed gratitude even for minor services and kindness shown to him. His speech was intriguing and the things he made - like the bow or leather were treasures of tremendous potential and Halvor was one to clearly see potential. He felt like he was betraying Colin by taking him to Salem weeks before the Evaluation. He feared that Colin was not going to take this well and he hated being the instrument of authority in this situation. Still, orders were orders.

He finished collecting his supplies - they were light, as the trip would be brief. No more than two days. There was nothing keeping him, but he was reluctant to start. Even if he set out immediately, it would be past the 3rd hour of the night and too late to start the return journey. He was not anxious for another night trip. There had been too many in recent weeks. And so he delayed. He was checking the harness when Dalene found him in the stable.

"Halvor! I've been looking for you! I thought you would come up for dinner. Why didn't you?"

He shrugged, "Getting ready to go. I probably should have left already, but to tell you the truth, I'm tired. I just don't understand the urgency in bringing Colin to Salem in order to lock him up. He isn't doing anything. I just don't want to do this."

She smiled softly, "You could always assign one of the other Guards, couldn't you?"

"No. I have to do this - whether I want to or not. If it has to happen, I guess I want it to come from……..a friend."

She looked at him, one eyebrow raised, "A friend?"

He gave her a half-smile, "Well, yeah, I guess. I mean, I like him. He's really different - can't seem to do some of the simplest things without trying three times. But other things - I mean he does things that nobody has ever imagined before! How does he do that? I always thought a mantle-bearer would show up, face etched in stone and a booming voice, shouting orders and saying, 'Thus says Messias!' Colin is about as mild as they come. He makes suggestions, but he doesn't issue orders. He keeps saying that he isn't a messenger, but he sure teaches a lot. He just doesn't fit what I've always pictured. He doesn't even wear a beard! At least he isn't bleeding all over every time he shaves it off though - like he used to." He sighed, "If he were just more of a troublemaker. Or if he just tried to stir people up, I could drag him back here and throw him in confinement with a clear conscience."

Dalene placed a hand gently on his forearm, "Halvor, are you <u>sure</u> he isn't the messenger?"

He shook his head, "No, I'm not sure. But he is. He just doesn't act like what I would expect. He's strange, but at the same time, he's just too……..normal."

She laughed, but sobered almost immediately, "And that's what's going to kill him, isn't it? He's just normal. He shows up wearing a mantle, wearing no color, looking so different, but in the end, he's just normal, and when the entire council engages in the Evaluation, they'll see all of his faults, and they'll destroy him - because he's normal, not the perfect, flawless prophet we're looking for." She paused, "Are we looking for the right thing?"

Halvor shrugged, "I don't know. I just wish I didn't have to arrest him. I think he's a good man. But I'd better get going."

"Stay the night. It will be late by the time you get there. Even if you leave in the morning, you can still be back by tomorrow night. Let him enjoy a last morning of freedom."

Halvor looked at her long, "I guess you're right. Let him have one last morning of freedom."

Chapter 12   Escape and Pursuit

The Sabbath arrived and as Colin had hoped, Halvor didn't appear for breakfast. But, he couldn't just take off without saying anything to Jorge, Miran and Elam. They had done so much for him. They had been kind, and had become, in many ways, his family here. He helped clean up the few items after their cold breakfast and then spoke. "Jorge, Miran, Elam....... I'm going away for a few weeks."

Their shocked stares immediately gave way to a chorus of objections, which he stilled with a raised hand, shaking his head.

"I'm coming back. I'll be back in time for the Evaluation in Salem. The full moon will be in 39 days. I should be back in 35."

Jorge broke in, "Are you mad? Where will you go? The greeting you received in Tyber is the very best you can expect! You show up wearing the mantle in any other town and you may not live to see your Evaluation! You can't hide! Your hair alone is like a lantern. If anything, it has become lighter since you arrived. I've never seen the like......"

He would have gone on, but Miran had gripped his arm, indicating for him to be still. "Colin, Jorge is right. There's no place for you to go. We've talked about this, late at night, trying to figure out how to save you. All we have been able to come up with is to pray that somehow you'll come through the Evaluation alright."

Colin shook his head. "I'm not running away. As for where I'm going - there's a whole world out there. When Dalene explained just how serious my situation was, I'll admit, I was pretty depressed. I'm not anxious to die - or be 'destroyed.' But I'm not going to avoid this Evaluation either. I can't. I just feel like I <u>have</u> to be there and I will. Once I faced up to my own mortality, I decided there were a few things I want to do first." He smiled. "Teaching you to make soap was one of those things. I wanted to try and leave something that would make the world a little better for my having been in it. Jorge, teaching you how to make leather was another thing I wanted to do. Has your life improved because of it?"

Jorge nodded, "It has. I scarcely ever have wet feet now, and I spend little of my time mending harness since I replaced the canvas with leather. But....." he added gruffly, "if making my life better was your goal, the leather is fine, but the fishing.....ah, there's the thing for making a man's life better."

Colin laughed aloud at this and Jorge and Elam had to join in.

He turned then to Elam, "Your bow is almost finished. The string is all done, so all you really need to do is finish smoothing it. Make the glue like I showed you, and attach the sinew like I did with my bow. You'll have to practice but you'll do well."

Elam just nodded, too choked up to speak, but too much of a proud young man to show it.

"I can never thank you enough for all you've done for me. I've come to love you like you were my own family. I hope that my having been here - and that my leaving, doesn't cause you any trouble. That's the last thing that I want. But I'm not going to sit here awaiting the Council's pleasure. There's a world out there and I'll never get to see all of it, but for a few weeks, I intend to see a small part of it."

They just stared at him blankly. "You don't mean to leave Aidon, do you?"

"Well, I'm not going to be welcome in the 12 cities, now am I? I don't know exactly where I'll go. That will depend on the terrain and whatever strikes me when I see it. But I will be back."

"You can't!" Elam exclaimed. "Nobody can survive out there! It is death!"

Colin looked at him curiously, "Elam, I was out there for several days before I came stumbling in here. Why are you all so sure that it's death to venture beyond the 12 cities?"

Miran shook her head, "That's how it is. The Arbor Guards may scout the fringes of Aidon, but no one ventures out. Those who would do so are brought before the local council. It isn't like the Evaluation, for all 12 of the Council participate. Those who would venture out will acknowledge the Compliance, and they will not go. They will no longer wish to go. It has always been so."

Colin shook his head, "That's foolish, and it can't have 'always' been that way, or you wouldn't even know about 'the forbidden place,' where I washed up from the ocean. The Council is stifling those who would venture - who would discover. Even if this were to cost me my life, it's my choice to make. What I do neither harms nor endangers anyone else. This life is mine to live. I choose to go because I want to see some of this wonderful world before I die. I don't know why I'm so determined to return for the Evaluation, but that too is my choice. Not because the Council in Salem demands it, but because I wish to do it."

Jorge looked glum and Miran was fighting back tears, so she only nodded. Colin continued, "Halvor is going to ask a bunch of questions. Answer them all. You've nothing to hide, so tell him everything."

Jorge said, "He'll be coming after you. He's an Arbor Guard, he'll find you."

Colin nodded, "He may, but I expect to have a start on him. It looks like it may rain before the day is out, and if so, tracking will be harder. Were you ever given instructions to keep me from leaving?"

Jorge shook his head, "No. We were asked to allow you stay here. We were told if there was any trouble, to let Halvor handle it."

"Good. There's your excuse then. You were never told to keep me, so you didn't try. You figured Halvor was about, keeping an eye on me, so you didn't concern yourselves. Thank you all, again, I can never repay you. Here, take this." He handed a small leather pouch to Miran. "That's most of the money I haven't spent from our partnership. You hang onto it for me. If ever I don't need it, it's yours."

She just nodded.

"I have to get going. But I have one more favor to ask of you. He retrieved a small parcel, wrapped in a tanned deer skin and handed it to her. Halvor is going to be mad when he gets back. But please give him this, and ask him to see that it gets to Dalene. It's a gift, to say 'thank you,' for these few weeks of my life."

Miran could only nod, too surprised for speech.

Colin went to the shed and retrieved his belongings - a couple of blankets, his frying pan, bow, arrows and flint. He had fashioned a crude pair of saddle bags from canvas which Kath had bought for him. He stuffed everything that would fit inside the bags. He had also made a waxed canvas case for his bow, to keep it dry in case of damp weather. It had a shoulder sling so it could hang over his back, along with a quiver of arrows. Lastly, he retrieved his saddle pad and bridle from the hiding place behind the hay mow. Gisele nickered a greeting at his approach. He hoped she would cooperate when he tried to ride her. If not, he was going to have to lead her and hope he could keep ahead of Halvor, certain that he would pursue.

He slipped through the corral bars, speaking softly to the horse. She approached, tossing her head as she came. He slipped the bridle over her muzzle and fastened it. He tossed the blanket on her, followed by the saddle and fastened the bags on behind using leather thongs. Finally, he opened the corral gate. Jorge, Miran and Elam stood watching all this with increasing curiosity. He leaned against Gisele, stroking her neck. With eyes closed, he said, "OK girl. This is what I've been getting you ready for. I really need your help now. I know this is new to you. Truth to tell, this is pretty new to me as well. I'm not much of a rider, so we're just going to have to learn together. Help me out here." Suddenly, he saw once again a glowing sphere of light, similar to what he had seen at the Evaluation, but somehow different. He <u>knew</u> that he was seeing Gisele's "true-self" - her intelligence. It was more pale than the lights he had seen before, but he knew her and as he flitted closer and closer, finally reaching and touching the light. She responded. They linked. There was no repulsion. Halvor wasn't here to interfere. There was a sense of peace and total understanding, a sense of affection and acceptance. He felt her intelligence and willed her to see what he needed her to do. She seemed to absorb it and revel in it. If he had to put words to what he felt, he would have said she was excited about what he asked of her. Reluctantly, he withdrew and found himself still standing beside the horse as she rubbed her head and neck against him. Drawing a deep breath, he placed his left foot in the stirrup and swung into the seat. Gisele turned her head to look at him as if to say, "That's different. What do we do next?" He pulled gently on the right rein, heading her toward the gate while kicking his heels lightly into her ribs, urging her forward. She immediately set off and he heard Miran gasp while Jorge muttered, "By the twin moons........."

Elam exclaimed, "He's <u>riding</u> the horse! They said you couldn't do that!"

Colin turned to grin, "Sometimes, <u>they</u> don't know as much as they think they do. Take care. I'll see you in a few weeks." And with that, he turned Gisele and booted her into a trot.

******

While Halvor was willing to spend the night in Salem, he still made an early start the following morning, departing the city shortly after dawn. The day was warm, muggy even at this early hour. It looked as if it might rain. He hoped it would hold off, as he hated traveling in the rain. His pace was not leisurely, but neither was he pushing his team of horses. The cart was light and they made good time, arriving in Tyber about the third hour. While he didn't expect any further need for secrecy, he also wished to spare Jorge and Miran unwanted attention, so he left his team in a secluded clearing and took a circuitous route to the farm. This consumed additional time, so that it was nearing midday by the time he arrived. Nobody was at the house and even more time was wasted as he looked for Jorge and Elam, finally finding them at a shady, secluded section of the creek - fishing.

"Where's Colin?" Halvor called out.

Jorge looked up from where he was drifting a fat grasshopper across the still surface of a deep pool and glared. "Shhh! You'll be scaring the fish!" he hissed.

Halvor waited impatiently. The grasshopper drifted under an overhanging limb and disappeared in a sudden swirl as the trout struck. "Set the hook! Set the hook! Don't break the line!" Elam was yelling.

"I've got it! Stay back or you'll spook him!" Jorge ordered.

In a few moments the trout was landed and added to a forked stick, already holding one other.

Halvor had been patient long enough. "Where's Colin?"

Jorge shrugged, "I've not seen him this morning."

"Didn't he come for breakfast?"

Jorge scratched his head. "Breakfast? Well, you know how he is. Sometimes he comes, but other times he doesn't. There was a couple of days I don't think we saw him until evening. But no, I don't think we saw him at breakfast."

Halvor considered this. "Well, when did you last see him?"

"Yesterday. He was here yesterday. I know that for a fact." Jorge replied.

"Fine, where at?"

"Hmm?" asked Jorge, threading another grasshopper onto the hook.

"I asked, where did you last see him?" Halvor was becoming more impatient. This wasn't like Jorge.

"Oh. Well, yes. I think it was up at the house. No, it would have been out by the barn. Yes, it was the barn."

"Do you know where he went? What he was doing?"

"Ah, him and that fool horse. You know how he's always messing with that horse. He was doing something with the horse, I think. But he left something with Miran for you."

Halvor was clearly puzzled, "For me? With Miran? What was it?"

Jorge just shrugged, loosing his line to let the grasshopper swing out over a riffle in the creek. "Package or something. You'll have to see Miran about it."

"Fine. Where's Miran?"

"I'm thinkin' she might have gone over to Kath's. Something to do with the soap, you know."

Exasperated, Halvor decided he was wasting his time trying to talk to Jorge while he was fishing. He headed up to the house to wait for Miran. A vague apprehension was starting to gnaw at him. He shrugged it off. While he was waiting, he decided, he might as well take down the tent and stow his gear. He wouldn't be coming back here.

It was past the 8th hour when he heard Miran arrive back at the house. He knocked at the door and when she came he said bluntly, "I spoke with Jorge earlier. I've been looking for Colin. Jorge didn't seem to know where he is, but said that Colin had left a package with you for me. May I have it?"

"Certainly. One second and I'll fetch it for you." She returned bearing the leather parcel. "He asked if you would deliver this to The Lady Dalene." She couldn't quite bring herself to drop the title, even if Colin had.

Halvor undid the lacing and opened the parcel. It contained a beautifully tanned fox hide and a cake of soap. He looked at Miran and asked, "This is all? Was there a message?"

"There was a message. He said it was to thank her for these few weeks of his life."

Halvor set the items down and ran to the shed. Two blankets were neatly folded and hanging on a rail near the hay where Colin had made his bed. The bow and arrow were gone, as was the cooking pot. There was nothing indicating that anyone had been living there. Haste now seemed pointless. He walked down to the barn, verifying that the horse was gone as well. Why had Colin taken the horse? He hadn't much gear and he had no cart. He would be faster alone and on foot, than leading that horse.

He walked back up to the house. Miran was busily cleaning where there was no dirt. Jorge and Elam came whistling up the trail, but fell silent when they saw Halvor. He eyed the three of them and said, "He's gone, isn't he?"

Miran looked at him defiantly and said, "He said he will be in Salem in time for the Evaluation. He said it and he'll be there, of that you may be certain. But yes, he's gone."

"I don't suppose there's any point in asking you where he's gone?"

Jorge shrugged, "You can ask, but we've not a clue. He said he was leaving and that's what he did."

No one felt like mentioning that Colin had gone out of there <u>riding</u> a horse. They figured the Arbor Guard could sort that out for himself.

As if on cue, a tremendous clap of thunder sounded and at that instant, the skies opened up and it began to pour.

******

Colin had no idea where he would go. One direction seemed about as good as another.

He didn't want to be tracked down and he was pretty sure that Halvor would try. It wasn't that he disliked his guard. In fact, he had a lot of respect for him and since their little adventure in Tyber the day of the Evaluation, a lot of the tension between them had eased. But he really wanted to see what was over the next ridge and he might never have the chance again. The problem was he really didn't know the lay of the land. He coaxed Gisele into a brisk walk, down along the cultivated fields before cutting across the creek just above the hay meadow. He paralleled the creek, heading northwest and stayed out of the heavier growth along the stream. After continuing along this heading for a few miles, he veered away from the stream, heading due north across a grassy plain dotted with groves of trees. By midday he was already more than 15 miles from Jorge's farm.

To the east, hazy in the distance, he could see mountains. The plain he was on undulated in low, rolling hills. The thick grass rippled and swirled like water in the breeze. He didn't have enough elevation to see the ocean, but he knew it couldn't be more than 50 miles to the west. The landscape reminded him of some of the prairie country he had seen around Kansas City. After resting, he walked around Gisele, stroking her neck, legs and forehead. She had been surprisingly agreeable to the whole prospect of being ridden. Tunsten had said she was trained for hauling a cart, but riding an animal trained to drive is generally a whole new proposition. The entire morning she had walked steadily, briskly even, requiring only the lightest touch of the rein to guide her. He had pretty much let her choose her own path once they had cleared the woods. Colin decided that he might as well start teaching himself, as well as Gisele, more about riding. He'd never been much of a horseman. He had done a little bit of riding growing up and he'd worked a couple of summers on his in-law's ranch down in Blackfoot, Idaho. Rita had been an accomplished horsewoman. On his best days, he was barely adequate, but he wanted to see how Gisele ran. He mounted up.

"OK, girl. This morning we took it easy. Now let's go for performance, shall we?"

Gisele eyed him over her shoulder, as if asking, "Are you sure you want to do this?"

Clucking softly and kicking her in the ribs, he coaxed Gisele into the same brisk pace she had held all morning. He loosened the reins and kicked her again and she responded by quickening her pace. She was very smooth, with none of the jolting ride of the horses he had ridden before. She seemed to glide, again reminding him more of an elk than a horse. "Alright, Gisele, let's see what you've got. HA!" He booted her in the ribs, snapped the reins against her neck and leaned forward, low across her back. Gisele took one mighty lunge forward and then she flew! She was incredibly smooth, stretching out both front legs in unison, bunching all four legs under her belly as her forefeet hit the ground then launching again, like the gazelle she was named for. There was no break in the rhythm, no jolting, just a phenomenal sensation of speed - of flying across the plain and she clearly loved it! Her neck was stretched out and the grass whipped past under her belly in an indistinct blur. Always in the past, Colin had had difficulty holding the saddle when galloping a horse, but Gisele didn't gallop, she flowed! Even on his makeshift pad, it was as though he was glued to her back as she raced across the prairie. He didn't know how long or how far they went. It was effortless. He wasn't urging Gisele on. He simply gave her free rein and let her fly, choosing her own path and when to stop. The wind whipping past his face made Colin's eyes water, tears flowed down his cheeks, blinding him, and he laughed out loud in sheer exuberance from the sensation of flying. Eventually, Gisele slowed. Reining her in, Colin dismounted. "Unbelievable! Not even a Kentucky Thoroughbred could keep up with you, Girl. Certainly not over that distance." She wasn't really even breathing hard and had hardly broken a sweat. In fact, she tossed her head, pranced and frolicked, more like an overjoyed puppy than a horse who had just run 5 miles in a matter of minutes. Colin shook his head in wonder, as Gisele walked over to him and rubbed her head up and down his chest, begging to be petted, which he willingly obliged. "Gisele, I don't think we need to worry about Halvor catching up to us until we're good and ready."

Their run had taken them to a series of low, rolling hills, the terrain climbing to the north in their direction of travel, while falling away gradually toward the west where the land would finally drop into the ocean. They continued on at a steady pace, the miles being eaten up by Gisele's untiring stride. In the late afternoon, they topped the rise of a final hill where the ground fell away into a broad, shallow valley. A large river lined with trees meandered through the middle of the valley, with several smaller streams feeding in from the hills on either side. Colin's jaw dropped as he stared in astonishment. Feeding in the lush grass not a mile distant on along the near bank of the river was a herd of elephant-like creatures. "Those can't be mammoths!" he exclaimed. But they were. He sat entranced, "I'm the first person in 2000 years to see a mammoth." Then he shook his head and corrected his frame of reference. "I guess that would be true on Earth, but maybe not here." He booted Gisele lightly, starting her down the slope toward the herd. There were 23 animals in the group, standing as high as 15 feet or more at the shoulder. Their coats were not thick, like the artist's renditions he had seen. The hair was long, but not heavy and coloring ranged from a light brown to a dark gray, with the heads and shoulders generally of a darker coloration than the body. Their tusks were long and curved, the tips almost touching on some of the adults. Their young gamboled about, playing like calves out on the ranch. They had been in a group by themselves, but as Colin and Gisele approached, they squealed and bleated, rushing to their mothers. The adults didn't appear to be overly concerned, but they moved to a blocking position between their young and this interloper. Gisele was watchful, with her ears pricked forward and a tenseness in her gait, but she didn't balk in the slightest. Colin contented himself with approaching to within about 100 yards, then sitting and admiring these huge animals, which soon returned to their feeding. He wondered what other species, extinct on his own planet, might still have viable populations here. Saber tooth tigers? He hoped not, as his puny bow and arrow offered little comfort in the face of such a formidable foe. The twin moons rising above the horizon reinforced the fact that he was along way from home.

  The day was nearly spent and Colin needed to make camp for the night. He turned Gisele and rode up river several hundred yards before he dismounted and led his horse into the trees along a faint trail. The timber was not thick and he was easily able to make his way to the edge of the river. A large clearing offered an inviting place to camp. He stripped the riding pad from Gisele and rubbed her down thoroughly with bunches of grass ripped from the meadow. He then led her down to the river to drink. The river was over 50 yards across at this point and flowed swiftly. A number of quiet pools and eddies were evident along the bank. He thought about fishing for his dinner, but was concerned about the size of the fish in the water, as he didn't want to lose one of his precious hooks. His fishing line was crude at best. Deciding to leave that as a last resort, he returned to his camp, picketing Gisele where she could feed. He then gathered a supply of firewood from the surrounding forest and after a few attempts, managed to start a fire using his knife and flint. He then strung his bow and entered the trees.

  The sun would be down in a few minutes. He didn't want to shoot a deer, as it was more meat than he could use without taking the time to dry and smoke it. He really didn't know what he was hunting, but his stomach was rumbling, so he guessed he was hunting dinner. A few squirrels chattered from the trees. He nocked an arrow, but did not draw the bow. Slipping quietly into a small clearing, he about had a heart attack when a group of turkeys exploded into flight almost underfoot. He jumped and without conscious thought pulled back the bowstring and loosed his arrow. Immediately, one of the birds folded in flight and crashed to the earth. His heart was still pounding from the scare they had given him. He never should have hit a bird on the wing – he only managed that about one shot in five when hunting pheasants with a shotgun. So how had he managed to shoot a turkey out of the air with a bow? He <u>knew</u> he didn't have that kind of skill. So why did he consistently hit what he was aiming at? No, 'aiming' wasn't right. He wasn't consciously aiming. He was focused on something, but that wasn't the same as aiming, was it? He sighed, "Questions. No answers." He brightened, "But at least there's dinner." He headed back to camp.

He lay awake for a long time. He felt……….free. While Jorge and Miran had been exceptionally kind to him, he had never gotten used to his own strangeness in that setting. It was like his trips to Taiwan. He didn't blend in. He didn't fit. Out here, he felt at peace. But he had to start answering some questions. <u>Why</u> was he here? The only power that could have brought him here was God. God didn't behave in a random, capricious manner therefore, there was a reason for his being here. What was it? How could he find out? He prayed, as he always did, but still there were no answers. When he lay back down and looked up at a sky filled with stars, he felt at peace. Whether he had five weeks or five decades of life left, he was content. All would be as it should be.

He awoke the next morning to a gray dawn. Clouds had moved in during the night. The cloud cover had helped keep the temperatures relatively warm. He hadn't slept especially well. He kept seeing mammoths and saber tooth tigers when he closed his eyes. He had awakened at one point during the night to hear coyotes yipping – distinctly different from the lonely howl of a wolf. He was stiff this morning - saddle sore. He hadn't ridden a distance like that in years, if ever, and he was feeling it. He led Gisele to the river for a drink, scratching behind her ears as she rubbed against him. Breakfast was the cold remains of the turkey from the night before. He had cooked the whole thing so it wouldn't spoil as quickly. Today, he determined, was a day to begin learning some answers.

Colin had always found talking out loud helped him concentrate on a problem. If there were other people around, he usually avoided this habit, but he figured Gisele would put up with his quirks. "OK. First thing we need is to verify our baseline." He stepped off 40 paces, tore up a large clump of grass and tied it with another swatch of grass to make his target. He extracted his three blunt arrows, sticking two of them into the soil near his feet. He then strung his bow, took a deep breath, aimed at the clump and shot the arrow. Without pausing, he immediately nocked and fired the next two as quickly as he could. He could clearly see all three had stuck in the grass clump.

As he walked out to retrieve his arrows, he continued to discuss the results with himself. "Three shots, as fast as I could fire at roughly 40 yards. All three in the target. Not one passed through the target. Verified baseline."

Retrieving the arrows, he paced his target out an additional 60 yards making 100 yards in total – well beyond what almost any archer even with the best compound bow available would normally shoot. He tried to empty his mind, wiping out any expectation as he walked back to his firing line. He was neither attempting to prove nor disprove anything. He was simply collecting data. Drawing a breath, he again aimed his first shot and had the second on the way while the first was still in flight. From this distance, he couldn't tell if he had struck the target. But when he walked out, he found three arrows sticking through the grass clump. Nodding his head he stated, "Increasing range doesn't alter the baseline, at least out to a range of 100 yards. Interesting that the arrows didn't exit the target at either 40 or 100 yards. It went just far enough to do the job and no more."

He carried his target back to the 40 yard mark. This time he sighted carefully, then moved his point of aim off target about 10 degrees, while still staying focused on the target. He tried to visualize the arrow impacting the target. He visualized the flight curvature. He could see it clearly in his mind at the moment he loosed the arrow and watched as it curved in flight to impact the target! Fighting back emotion, he slowly paced out to retrieve the arrow, attempting to study this from a coldly clinical perspective. "Point of aim appears to be non-critical. Evaluating this test when combined with the test previously run in Jorge's field, a blind shot, that is, a non-focused shot is unsuccessful, while maintaining focus on the target results in a successful hit even if the arrow is off-target when released."

He stood staring at the arrow, "That which cannot happen, does not happen. That which has happened, is possible."

He concluded that here, a different set of laws applied. Well, at least they <u>could</u> be applied. Just how far this might be stretched, he had no idea.

Riding upstream, Colin hoped to find a place to ford the river. He didn't know how Gisele would take to the water and he wasn't anxious to get his gear wet. Where the valley narrowed, the river split into a series of narrow channels, separated by small islands. While the water flowed swiftly, it didn't seem very deep. As he coaxed Gisele ahead, she sniffed suspiciously, at the rushing stream and then plunged in, almost unseating Colin, who had to lunge forward and wrap his arms around her neck to avoid falling off. The water only came up to her belly and she was soon through and onto the opposite bank. They took a leisurely pace, continuing their northward journey. The sky was becoming more threatening by the hour, so he angled Gisele more to the east, heading up into the hills where there were more trees. As the first raindrops began to fall, he found a large undercut in the face of the hill under a rock outcrop. Trees almost completely hid it from view. It wasn't a cave, really, it was too broad and shallow to be called that. Still, there was enough of an overhang that unless the storm hit directly out of the west it would provide enough shelter to keep them dry. Without even pausing to strip the gear from his horse, Colin quickly dragged together a substantial pile of fallen, dry wood for the fire. As if on cue, a tremendous clap of thunder sounded and at that instant, the skies opened up and it began to pour.

The rain came down in a deluge the entire night. Colin and Gisele remained relatively dry by hugging the back wall of the protective overhang, watching the water come down in sheets from the cliff above them. Fortunately, the slope drained the water away from their shelter. It was almost like being behind a waterfall. Colin had to content himself with the few remnants of last night's turkey, supplemented by dried meat. Gisele had snatched mouthfuls of grass during the day and did not seem to be inclined to go out in the storm to forage. Rather than stand, as a horse might do, she folded up her legs and lay down close to the fire, seemingly unafraid. Colin lay down next to her, resting his back against her warm side. He had been puzzling over his archery performance all day. Speaking aloud, he said, "The only explanation I can come up with is……..magic. In this world, I seem to have magic when it comes to archery. Elam didn't display it. But whatever I focus on, whether I aim at it or not, I can hit with an arrow. The flight of the arrow defies aerodynamics, as it will curve in flight to strike the target and it defies gravity, since firing even at a flat angle over great distance, the arrow doesn't fall - it flies straight to the target." He reached up and scratched Gisele, lying with her eyes closed, enjoying the heat of the fire. "But magic is just a label we put on what we can't explain. So am I mentally directing air currents? No, unless they were very strong, the arrow would still fall. Am I creating a channel in the air along which the arrow flies? Dense air on the sides to direct its path and less dense air in front to eliminate drag? Maybe. The velocity doesn't seem to diminish." He sat, mulling this over but without coming up with anything concrete. Sighing at last he told Gisele, "In engineering, it is often easier to describe <u>what</u> happens than to explain <u>why</u> it happens." Gisele didn't appear to be impressed. With that, he went to sleep.

******

The rain had come in a deluge. That had been over two hours ago. Halvor stood glumly in the doorway of the shed, watching water pour from the roof in a solid sheet. "There'll be no picking up his track by the time this ends." He muttered. The goats looked at him quizzically, then returned happily to their feeding. He was torn as to what he should do. Should he mount a search or notify the Council in Salem first? Where was Colin likely to go? Was he actually trying to escape? Had he known that Halvor was coming to take him into custody? How could he have possibly known? Judging by the time he had left, no one could have informed him. Colin had left even before Halvor met with the Council. It must be a coincidence. He sighed and retired for the night, opting for the shed instead of the tent which he had already taken down and stowed before the storm had struck.

The rain continued through the night, but gradually began to ease sometime before dawn. Halvor arose as the first light lit the horizon and in the breaking day could see not a cloud in the sky. He made a light breakfast of the supplies he carried with him. As soon as it was light enough to see, he set out, but he was without hope. It was now the morning of Third Day. He had spent Sabbath in Salem. That would have been the day Colin left, giving him a full 48 hours head start. Still, he had to make the effort to scan for some sign. Tracks, of course, would have been washed out, but Halvor thought it possible that Colin might not have gone far. He might just be holed up nearby – like the cleft where he had collected the flint a few weeks ago. After all, where could he go?

The search was fruitless as Halvor had feared. He covered a wide arc around the farm. The creek, up where Colin had found the flint was virtually impassable. The rain had swollen the mild stream into a raging torrent. Halvor was unable to approach the narrow canyon, let alone proceed beyond it. There was no sign of Colin. Surely Colin wouldn't have left Aidon. Nobody left Aidon – except for the occasional Arbor Guard out on patrol. There were too many dangers. No. He must remain nearby. Perhaps not near Tyber, but he would remain near one of the town or villages of the 12 Files. He had to. Where else could he stay or get supplies? The thing to do, he thought, would be to return to Salem and report to the Council.

It was past the third hour of the night by the time Halvor reached Salem. He was exhausted. He reported first to the Regent. "He's gone." He stated bluntly as soon as he was shown in to meet with the High Councilor. "He left the farm early on Sabbath. Jorge and Miran claim to have no idea where he went. I believe them. It rained heavily shortly after I arrived and found Colin was gone. Any tracks he left were wiped out."

He was surprised to see his father smiling. "My report amuses you?" he asked.

Councilor Tregard nodded, "Actually, yes. I was against taking our mantle-bearer into custody. I have no idea why he decided to leave. But yes, it amuses me that he did so – or at least it amuses me to anticipate the reactions of the rest of the Council. Come, my son!" He said, slapping an affectionate hand on Halvor's shoulder, "You must be famished! We should eat and then you must rest."

Halvor shook his head, "Aren't you going to call the Council to meet tonight? I should report."

"You shall. In the morning. There is nothing we could accomplish tonight except to cost a number of people a pleasant evening and a few hours of sleep. I will send messengers. The Council will meet first thing in the morning. First thing right after breakfast." He amended.

Halvor shrugged. He <u>was</u> tired and he saw the wisdom of his father's action. But still, he felt as if he should be <u>doing</u> something. "Is Dalene here?" he asked.

"I imagine she's in her quarters." His father replied.

"Good. At least there's one thing I can do yet tonight." He excused himself while his father called for food to be brought and went down the main hallway to Dalene's quarters and knocked.

She opened the door herself. "Oh! You're back!" Then her face fell. "Is Colin alright? Is he angry?"

Halvor stepped in, shaking his head. "He was gone when I arrived in Tyber."

Inexplicably, she felt simultaneously very happy and yet, somehow lost, like something very important was missing. "Gone? But where could he go?"

"I don't know. Jorge and Miran said he left Sabbath morning. He said he would return in time for his Evaluation. Who knows? Maybe he will. But he left this with Miran and asked that she have me deliver it to you." Halvor held out the leather wrapped parcel Miran had given him.

She took it, staring blankly, "For me? Why?"

Havlor kept his face expressionless, "The message said it was to thank you for these few weeks of his life."

She stroked the soft leather, staring at nothing, then turned abruptly and set the package down on the table, untying the string that held it closed. "Oh my!" she exclaimed as she lifted the tanned fox skin from the package. "It's beautiful!" She stroked the soft fur and brushed her cheek against it. "It's so soft. Is this what you described – tanning?"

Halvor nodded. Dalene's gaze fell on another item still in the package, "What's this?" She picked up the pale yellow ball of waxy material, holding up for Halvor to see.

"That is soap."

She smelled it. It smelled wonderful – like lilacs, her favorite flower. She smiled, but for some reason, it made a tear trickle down her cheek.

The Council was in an uproar following Halvor's brief report. Accusations and recriminations flew back and forth between the Councilors, with only two individuals holding themselves above the fray. Halvor noted that the Regent watched the scene with intense interest, but seemed disinclined to try to restore order. Councilor Krainik, on the other hand, looked ashen, as though he were ill. Everyone was startled when he suddenly came to life, slamming his hand down on the table in front of him, "Enough! This is accomplishing nothing! It is obvious that some traitor informed this impostor, this false messenger and warned him to flee! That is a matter for consideration another time. What we need to know, Arbor Guard, is what you intend to do to bring this fugitive into custody as soon as possible."

Halvor stared at him blandly, "With the Council's permission, it is my intention to acquire a patrol from the city watch and the Arbor Guards. I will station two men at each city, excepting Salem. The city watch will be notified to be on the lookout for the mantle-bearer, Colin. They will be provided with his description and have orders to apprehend him immediately when he is found. I will conduct a roving patrol of the 12 cities and the surrounding countryside with two guards. Sooner or later he'll need supplies, or we'll cut his trail. Somebody has to have seen him – or they soon will. Then we'll take him into custody and bring him to Salem."

Councilor Krainik glared at him, "See that you do so. I do not expect to see you here again to report failure."

Halvor flushed, but turned on his heel and exited the room.

Councilor Tregard eyed Krainik mildly, "I had thought this was a Council matter, not one of your private projects."

Now it was Krainik's turn to flush. He bowed slightly to the Regent, "My apologies, Councilor Tregard. I am deeply offended on behalf of the Council that this impostor should get away with flaunting our directives in such a cavalier manner."

"Why Councilor Krainik, I thought the intent of holding the Evaluation was to determine whether the mantle-bearer is an impostor or not. You seem to have determined his status without need for an Evaluation! By all indications, it does not appear that he has ignored us, since our orders were never delivered. I suggest that we be patient. I am confident that he will appear for the Evaluation, at which time the matter will be resolved."

Krainik bowed stiffly and left the Council Chambers. He was furious. What was he going to tell his contact of the 13th File? How could he turn this to his advantage? Angrily, he stormed back to his quarters, slamming the door behind him. The servants had long since learned to avoid him when he was in one of his black moods. He paced the room, restless. He had hoped to use the mantle-bearer, once in custody. He could be displayed to advantage, infuriating those who believed or hoped him to be a true mantle-bearer and inciting the righteous wrath of those who would want to see an impostor imprisoned and destroyed. But maybe he could still work this to his benefit. Perhaps if he leaked word that the mantle-bearer had fled and was sought by the Arbor Guards, might that not still incite the people? Rumors of sightings in different cities, or confrontations with the guards might serve even better than having him in custody. After all, an absent messenger would have difficulty refuting any tales of his misdeeds which might be spread. Yes, perhaps there was still opportunity in confusion. He smiled grimly, but it was erased almost immediately. He would need to convince his contact from the 13th File that further delay would work to their advantage. He <u>had</u> too.

    Halvor wasted no time after being dismissed from the Council meeting. He summoned the captain of the city guard and requisitioned twelve soldiers to search for Colin. He gathered an additional twelve from the ranks of his own Arbor Guards. One Arbor Guard was paired with one of the city guards and each pair was assigned a specific city in Aidon to watch and patrol. Colin was described in detail and they were ordered to take him into custody immediately, if he were spotted and escort him to Salem. He had the captain of the city guard assemble his entire force. They were also given instructions to watch for and apprehend the mantle-bearer. One of the soldiers asked, "If he resists, how much force do we use?"

    Halvor hesitated before replying, "As much as it takes. He is to be arrested and taken into custody."

    The soldier persisted, "Do we use our weapons?"

    "What have you been preparing for your entire life?"

    The soldier straightened, looking straight ahead, "To defend Aidon, Arbor Guard."

    "Against what?"

    Now the soldier looked confused, "Why, against Kernsidon."

    "And would you have any problem defending Aidon against Kernsidon, if we were attacked?"

    "No sir! I'd be proud to do my duty."

    "But if the Council determines that there is another enemy that Aidon must be defended against, you would have a problem halting that threat to Aidon, is that correct?"

    "But this is a mantle-bearer!"

    Halvor shrugged, "Perhaps. If so, then I don't expect he will resist. But if he does resist, he is to be taken – even if that means using your weapons, even if it means killing him. Is that clear?"

    The soldier only nodded, mute.

    "What's your name, soldier?" Halvor asked.

    The young soldier snapped to attention again, "City Guard Davie of Riverton, 7th File, Arbor Guard!"

    Halvor smiled thinly, the soldier's File was evidenced by the pink fringe on his City Guard uniform.

"You are to do whatever it takes. He is to be arrested and confined. But I don't want him injured unless it becomes necessary. Are we clear on this?"

"Yes sir!"

"Anyone else? Any questions? Any reservations about your ability to do your duty?" The line of soldiers remained rigid, at attention. Halvor continued, "Whether this man, Colin, is a mantle-bearer or an impostor is for the Council – the <u>High</u> Council to determine. The Council has decided that until such time as that determination is made, it is too dangerous to have him running around loose. For what it's worth, I've met him and I don't expect there to be any trouble bringing him in once he's spotted. You have your assignments and your orders. I expect you to carry them out. That will be all."

All except two of the soldiers filed off to begin their patrols. The other two remained with Halvor. They would form a roving patrol, focusing more on the areas between towns and villages than the towns themselves. Halvor had a suspicion that Colin would be hiding in the fringe areas – the forested regions around the settlements. He also suspected that he would stick with the lower Files. Not only did they tend to be more remote, but he would be more likely to receive assistance from the simple farmers and woodcutters than he would from the more educated Orders.

******

Councilor Krainik was both talented and ambitious. Even those who disliked him, and there were quite a number, would not deny that. But they didn't know the half of it, he thought to himself. Following the council meeting, he spent an unpleasant hour with a contact from the 13th File. While his message was being relayed, Krainik wasted no time putting things in motion. Krainik was on a tour of Aidon, so to speak. At every town, at every village, he would stop. Sometimes it was a harness that needed repairing. Other times it was his cart. In Neims he had needed a Healer and in Keefly he had purchased glass. In each location he had appeared wearing the colors of a different File. Always within the same Order, mind you, because a visit from one of a different Order was noteworthy indeed. Usually his colors were only one, occasionally two, Files removed from that of the town he visited. He always had business there – perfectly reasonable business – looking for a cow or to buy a load of apple wood. But he always had tales to tell as well. Not that he ever claimed any first-hand experience with the events he related. These were just ……..things he had heard. Maybe from his supposed home village, or maybe something from his travels along the way. Tales of a tall man, with light hair and blue eyes, or maybe green. He was dressed all in white, wearing the colors of no File. But most amazingly, he wore a mantle – the hooded cloak signifying authority from Messias - a messenger. A prophet. Sometimes, so the tales said, he had performed miraculous healings. Other times, it was claimed, he had said that the High Council was corrupt and that the Regent and Council must be overthrown or destroyed. He might claim that the High Council had no authority over him. Or he might call for the destruction of the Files themselves, taking Aidon back to chaos, the dark times.

His business never kept him in any one place for very long. Always he was gone before the authorities arrived to investigate these tales. But the tales spread. Soon, the topic of the mantle-bearer was brought up whenever people met – even at the Evaluations. The local Councils were being run ragged, trying to stem the tide of rumor. With some, the rumors created fear and a conviction that this impostor must be apprehended and punished. With others, the tales resonated, for they themselves had occasionally, quietly thought that perhaps the Files were too rigid, too restrictive and perhaps Messias had finally sent someone to sort things out. The local Councils had their hands full. On a daily basis, there was some malcontent spreading tales, who had to be brought before the Council. They would speak with him, calmly, in reasoned tones. Then they would bring out the Evaluation Box. In the Box, one of the Council would exercise the Compliance – finding his true-self – not to get the agitator to bow – not physically at least, but to bow to the demands of the Council that he cease his dangerous thoughts. This was not the Compulsion, where the will itself was attacked, forced and bent to that of the Council. This was more subtle. One could always refuse – but they never did. Once it had been explained to them and the Council had them in the Box, it was made clear. They saw how it really was and they willingly abandoned their dangerous notions. A few times, even the Compliance was found to be inadequate. Then, the Council would unite, having one of their members in the Box, with all of the others making physical contact with him from outside. The box somehow magnified their power. The one in the Box became their point of focus and their combined wills were very persuasive and thus peace was restored once again. It had been thus for thousands of years. So their peaceful lives continued, but it was becoming more difficult. The rumors kept spreading and new tales surfaced. It was even said that someone had been brought into the Box twice! That had never happened before. Surely, it couldn't be true! Could it?

******

Kath and Miran were returning from a day at Market in Tyber. The soap had sold out almost immediately, as had the few leather goods that Jorge had sent. They were giving consideration to expanding the business. Several customers had come from the 2nd and even 3rd Order communities and they had discussed revealing the secret of making soap with others – on a share basis. But right now Miran wasn't talking about that. She was incensed. All the talk at market had been about Colin. Well, they all called him the mantle-bearer. Or the impostor. Or worse. If anything, the tales in Tyber were more rampant than anyplace else, since it was here that Colin had made his one public appearance. People from every File had been here, looking for information and bringing tales to tell in exchange. It had been good for business, but that didn't make Miran any happier.

"It stinks!" She said firmly. "I don't care what they say, I don't believe it. Colin wouldn't be calling to overthrow the Councils. I don't believe he's even been to any of those places. He said he wasn't going to the 12 cities, so how could all these people claim he was there?"

Kath shrugged, "Maybe he changed his mind. After all, how could he survive outside of the cities? Out in the wilds........." She shuddered. "Besides, he knows the High Council is going to destroy him. You said The Lady Dalene as good as told him. That alone ought to be reason enough for him to change his mind."

Miran shook her head, "If he were going to run he wouldn't be running around the 12 cities! No. That just isn't like him. He wouldn't even think of running. Well, I guess he thought of it, but he won't do it. He certainly isn't going to come out in revolt against the Councils. I think the whole thing is a pack of lies."

Kath was genuinely puzzled, "Why would anyone tell lies about something like that – especially about one who wears the mantle?"

"I wish I knew. The one thing I do know is that it will go harder with Colin when he has his Evaluation. That's the last thing he needs. They have soldiers hunting him, too. That's not rumor. I saw them in Tyber just today. That Arbor Guard had just better not come back to our farm! Jorge is so angry he's fit to be tied. Oh! Why could Colin not be the messenger? Then we'd not have all this trouble!"

******

Jorge and Baylor had gone fishing. Initially, Baylor had scoffed at the idea of catching fish – much as Jorge had done. But while he hated to admit it, he had developed a particular fondness for the tender, flavorful meat. The streams and rivers were full of fish, blissfully ignorant of the dangers represented by the bait, flies and lures which were now being tossed in front of them in sporadic but growing pockets. Baylor had tried tying the fur and feathers onto the crude hooks like Jorge had showed him, but his large, clumsy fingers just couldn't seem to get the knack. He hated rooting around in the dirt looking for worms and grubs and the grasshoppers were just too fast for him. Most of the time, anyway. But he'd gotten an idea. At market, he had swapped a small sheepskin mat he had made. Jorge had shown him a thing or two about tanning and this was one of his first attempts. Most of the hide had been ruined – it was hard and stiff. Only a small section had been reasonably soft and he'd trimmed that out. At market, he'd swapped the mat for several pieces of thin copper shavings from the coppersmith. The smith had been pleased at the trade. After all, what were a few pieces of scrap in exchange for a pad to protect his hand while he handled the heated copper he was working? Baylor had been pleased as well. The copper was bright and shiny – a little like a fish, he thought. Silver would have been better, but silver was costly, too costly for what he wanted to try. The copper was thin enough that he could bend and twist it, but thick enough to hold its shape once he had it how he wanted. He sat by the stream, dangling a hook in the water and dragging it back and forth, attached to the line on the end of his willow staff. He played around, twisting the copper onto the line just above the hook, leaving an eye in the twisted metal so that it could spin freely above the hook. He found that by curving the metal, cusping it, then dragging it through the water would make it spin, shining and catching the sunlight just under the surface. He went to a deep pool and cautiously extended his willow pole out over the still water, letting his hook hang just below the surface, where he dragged it back and forth in an arc. Suddenly, there was a silver flash as a large trout darted from the shadows along the bank, hitting the coppery glint above the hook as if it were going after a minnow! The hook bit deep into the fish's mouth. Baylor hauled his catch in, grunting with satisfaction. Ha! Let the others grub about for worms. He was done with that. This was much easier.

******

Elam finished his bow and was practicing. He didn't think he was ready to go after deer yet, but he was pleased with how his accuracy had improved in just the past couple of weeks. Mostly he shot blunt tips. They were easier to make and Colin had said they were good for practice. He'd shown his friend, Tyler, the bow and arrow. Not only had Tyler been impressed, but so had his father. They were both making bows of their own. Tyler's uncle lived in Jordanon, the main city of the 4th File. His family were all of the 3rd File, but he had carved out a nice little niche cutting wood for the 4th File. He and his family had been to visit Tyler's home last Sabbath. They were fascinated by the bow and arrow they had seen being made and the tales they heard of how far and how accurately a skilled archer could shoot an arrow. They no sooner returned home than they started making bows of their own. The world, suddenly, was a changing place.

Chapter 13   The Anakims

Colin rode wherever Gisele took him. At midday and again each evening, he would unroll the piece of leather on which he was making his map. It was crude at best and gave a very narrow perspective of the immense land through which he rode, but it was a start. In the low hills he camped beside beautiful turquoise blue lakes. Falling from the high peaks he had seen waterfalls which would have shamed those of Yosemite. The broad plain they skirted had a tremendous variety of wildlife – similar to what he was familiar with on earth, but usually there was some subtle difference to set them apart. There were diminutive antelope and massive elk. There were buffalo which looked to be a cross between the African water buffalo and the American Bison, the massive horns of the former but the distinctive shaggy head and shoulder hump of the latter. Several times he saw herds of mammoths. He rarely saw carnivores of any kind. He heard the yipping of coyotes and the howl of the wolves almost every night. He saw bears – not the small black bears. They were even larger than the few Grizzly Bears he had seen on his visits to Glacier Park. These were massive – as big or bigger than any of the pictures he had seen of the Alaskan brown bear, but their coats were very light, almost blonde. Gisele didn't like them and he made no effort to coax her into proximity when they scented him and looked up from their foraging with mean little pig eyes.

In one of the streams he found several small gold nuggets when he stopped to drink. He spent a day exploring, following the stream up into an extremely narrow, rocky cleft veined with quartz. And some of that quartz was veined with gold. Sections had fallen, leaving a pile of rotten rubble from which strands of gold could be extracted – jewelry store stuff. He pocketed several of the larger pieces and he marked the find on his map. At another camp he found what he thought were sapphires. He had grown up at the foot of the Sapphire Mountains in Montana and the family of one of his friends had a sapphire mine. He'd spent several days there over Christmas vacation one year, playing in the snow during the day and then sorting through buckets of dirt and gravel from the mine each evening, sorting out tiny sapphires. But these beautiful, colorful stones were massive – one to two inches in diameter instead of the tiny gems they had found that winter. He kept several. The colors varied from a pale yellow to a deep blue. A few were red, like ruby, but were possibly garnet. He didn't know enough about them to be able to tell for certain and it concerned him not at all.

He subsisted off the smaller game, as he didn't want to take the time to cure meat and had no wish to waste it needlessly. Turkeys were fairly easy to hunt in the forest fringe during the evening hours. Some of the marmots he shot would have weighed 20 pounds and he actually preferred them to the turkeys. Twice he shot small antelope – not much larger than the marmots. Fish seemed to abound in every body of water and were readily caught. He supplemented his diet with wild onions and camas root. He hardened to the saddle and his riding skills improved. Gisele seemed almost to read his mind and he grew more fond of her with each passing day. The two times he had shot the small antelope it had been from horseback. Gisele was as fast as the antelope, but not as agile. They seemed to be able to change direction in mid-air, but even then they couldn't avoid the arrow that Colin loosed at them. That was why he didn't hunt them. This impossible – no, not impossible, he corrected himself – this incredible ability that he didn't understand just kind of freaked him out. At least when he was shooting at a sitting marmot he could pretend it was his own skill, but when he took a turkey on the wing, the illusion vanished.

The solitude was good for him. It had been over three weeks since he had said goodbye to Jorge and Miran. That meant he had less than three weeks until he was due to appear at his Evaluation in Salem. It was time to be heading back. The thought did not cheer him as he stared glumly into the small fire over which he had cooked his dinner. He was no closer to understanding what had happened to him, how he had gotten here or what he was supposed to accomplish than he had been the day he floundered out of the ocean. He about decided that his purpose in being here was to become a sacrificial lamb in the Evaluation. But it seemed like an awful lot of trouble to go to just to get him killed. "All will be as it should be." How many times had he whispered that to himself as he thought about what had happened? And how many more times had it seemed as though some small voice had whispered that in his head these past weeks? It seemed to be that same comforting voice that had whispered to him in those first months after his wife had died, telling him, "All is as it should be." Not that it was less painful, really, but knowing that this was part of the Master Architect's plan, well, that had made it bearable, even if he didn't understand the grand design. The thought made him smile wanly, as it had countless times before. Because this is where he wound up at every time. No answers, just the feeling that he just needed to keep moving forward and then all would be as it should, even if he didn't particularly like the way things were shaping up. "Tomorrow," he thought, "it's time to start back."

Colin was at peace – sort of. While he wasn't exactly anxious to get back to Aidon, he only became nervous when he allowed himself to dwell on it. There was a part of him that was actually intrigued by this whole thing with the Evaluation. Despite having been assured that they weren't going to kill him, the probable outcome was close enough that he was having difficulty drawing any real distinction. But the truth was, the idea of dying didn't disturb him. The idea of pain, now that was disturbing. But accepting death had simply made each moment of life something to be treasured all the more. One afternoon he was caught in the most spectacular thunderstorm he had ever seen. He tethered Gisele under the canopy of a stand of massive oaks and then walked alone out onto the prairie, face-on into the storm. He'd stripped off his hooded cloak and stood there, blasted by the gale and blinded by the rain. The incessant lightning flashed while the thunder practically deafened him. The sky was as black as night, even though it was mid-afternoon. He stood there in the teeth of the storm, battered, barely able to stand. He had never felt more alive than he did at that moment. His skin tingled from the electricity in the air, his nose stung by the tang of ozone from the lightning. He knew it was foolish, to stand alone on the plain during such a tremendous storm, and he didn't care. This was <u>life</u> and he was savoring it. Then, as suddenly as it started, the storm moved on. The sun broke through the cloud, sending brilliant shafts of light to dot the prairie. It was magnificent.

The days passed and Colin knew he was getting close to Aidon. Perhaps two or three days to the southeast. He was getting Gisele packed, after camping for the night by a stream in a shallow valley littered with boulders. As he tightened the saddle girth, Gisele suddenly bolted with a squeal of terror. Colin whirled around to see a section of the hill above the creek moving! He jumped backwards, falling as he did so. But it wasn't sliding down. It was moving up, growing arms, legs and finally a head! The most hideous head he had ever seen! The creature stood close to 20 feet tall, stooped at the shoulder, with arms that hung all the way to the ground. The hands were massive things, four feet across at least. The legs were stubby, but built like the gnarly trunks of oak trees. A large, bullet shaped head rested on a stump of a neck, turning slowly from side to side. The creature was bald, but the skin hung in craggy folds across the exposed expanse of flesh the same gray color as the rocks protruding from the slope on which it had been curled up. It was clothed only by a filthy girdle of what looked like moss and bark, which further aided it in blending with the natural surroundings. The face was horrid. A slack mouth hung open, exposing a sparse assortment of uneven teeth. It lacked a chin of any significance, so the head seemed to flow into the neck. The nose was little more than a pair of nostrils penetrating the face. Two large, watery eyes surveyed its surroundings and a large lump centered above the nose separated the eyes, which were located towards the side of the head. The eyes seemed to have difficulty looking directly ahead, giving the creature a cross-eyed appearance because of the lump separating them. Colin scrambled backwards on all fours before being brought up sharply by a large rock. He was unable to take his eyes off this apparition. "Dear Lord, have mercy! What <u>is</u> that thing!?!" he muttered.

Just then, the pivoting head finally brought the crossed-eyes to bear. A rumbling sound came from the slobbering mouth. "Hah! Small mans come to Anakims! Anakims eat small mans!"

The creature began to lumber forward on its stubby legs, covering the ground ape-like, swinging its arms ahead and planting the knuckles on the ground as it approached. It wasn't terribly fast, but it was so large that it could still cover ground quickly.

The threat of being eaten finally registered enough to spur Colin into motion. Quickly, he rolled over and scrambled to his feet to run. He whirled back when he heard a squeal of rage! Gisele! She bored in behind the creature, striking with her fore hooves and ripping a chunk from the back of one massive leg with her teeth! The creature let out a tremendous roar and swung one huge arm, amazingly fast, knocking the horse sprawling. Immediately its attention returned to Colin. It had hardly been fazed by the powerful blows from the horse. Colin yelled, "Wait! I'm friendly! I'm not here to hurt you!"

Even as he said it, he realized it sounded incredibly stupid. The creature wasn't the one in danger of being hurt. It appeared to see humor in this as well, its mouth distended into a hideous grin as it barked out what Colin took to be a laugh.

Colin had no idea what to do. His bow was with Gisele, who wasn't moving. He wasn't sure that an arrow would have any effect on the creature anyway. Maybe if he could blind it. It lunged and Colin dodged between two boulders, working his way up the slope. The creature howled with rage.

"Can't we talk? Why do you want to hurt me?" Colin tried again.

The creature paused, considering the question. "Small mans come to Anakims. Gath protect Anakims. Eat small mans!"

Colin had been working his way higher on the slope, trying to stay out of sight between the boulders. "Anakims? Your people are Anakims? And your name is Gath, is that right?"

The head had continued its ponderous pivoting, but keyed in on the sound of Colin's voice. The creature began its relentless approach once again, swinging over boulders, swatting the smaller ones out of its way or shattering them. "Me Gath. Me protect Anakims. Gath ugly. Anakims not let Gath stay. Let Gath guard. Gath bring small mans to eat, maybe Gath stay with Anakims."

Colin continued his retreat. He spotted Gisele, getting shakily to her feet and hoped she wasn't hurt too badly and would be able to get away even if he couldn't. The creature was ugly, no doubt about that. He could understand why the Anakims would place him out here on sentry duty, just so they wouldn't have to look at him. But what was he going to do? The problem with staying out of sight was that he also had no idea where the creature was at. Did he dare try to look? He had to. Peeking over the top of a large rock, he was staring right at a massive toe, as thick as his waist. "Hah!" The creature roared and with only a moment to throw up an arm in protective reflex, the creature struck, scooping him off the ground and flinging him 10 feet, where he rolled across the grass. Gath grinned, admiring the effect of his blow.

Colin scrambled back into the rocks as Gath started for him. He was shaken, but not badly hurt – he hoped. Just then a huge fist swung down between the two boulders scooping Colin out like a field mouse and flinging him another ten feet through the air. He smashed down, falling into a narrow cleft in a huge slab of rock, the wind completely knocked out of him. Before he could move, that hideous face was leering down right over top of him. Gath shoved his face into the cleft, "Hah! Now Gath have!"

In desperation, Colin ripped the knife from his belt. The puny blade was insignificant against this monstrous creature, but he would die fighting. He lunged upward, slashing the razor edge across the face of the giant even as it threw itself backward with a scream of rage and pain. Colin lunged out of the cleft, wanting room to move if he was to fight. He stood panting, circling quickly, looking for his enemy, but he saw nothing. He was surprised at how far up the hill he had climbed during his retreat. Gisele was on her feet, head up, nostrils flaring. Suddenly she let out a shrill whinny of warning! Too late, Colin was encircled by a massive hand and lifted clear of the ground, his arms pinned to his sides, the knife now useless.

"Hah!" Gath bellowed, as he slowly turned Colin, holding him high above his head. He was shocked to see the livid red line left by his blade had cut through the membrane covering the lump separating the two large eyes. It had barely scratched the creature, but where it had cut, the skin had separated, revealing, under the lump, a third, huge eye, now examining Colin, unblinking. "Hah!" The creature repeated. And then the mouth lifted in an atrocious caricature of a grin. "Hah! Small mans fix Gath! Now Gath not ugly! Anakims let Gath stay, maybe. Anakims let Gath stay, maybe not eat small mans. Anakims not let Gath stay, maybe Gath go with small mans! Come! Gath go Anakims. Small mans go Anakims!" And he set Colin gently down on the ground.

"Gath, you can't believe how much I hope they let you stay. But maybe it would be best if I just leave now and let you go home by yourself. I'm sure you have lots to talk about with your family and I'd just be in the way."

"NO!" Gath bellowed. "Small mans Gath friend. You come! Anakims happy see Gath. Happy see small mans."

Colin sighed. This was just too weird. The unveiling of Gath's third eye hadn't, in Colin's opinion, made him the least bit less ugly. And the blood which continued to seep from the thin, red line on either side of the eye wasn't helping either. But he really didn't want to fight Gath. The last round hadn't gone too well and he didn't think he would fare much better in a rematch. "Alright, Gath. But let me see to my horse. You hit her pretty hard. And I need to get my things."

Gath nodded agreeably and swung along behind Colin as he made his way down off the slope. Gisele had been racing back and forth, frantic during these last few minutes. "Gath, why don't you wait here for a minute. Let me go settle Gisele down before you come close. The two of you kind of got off to a bad start. Wait here."

"Hah!" Gath smiled his horrible grin and hoisted himself on his long arms, swinging his body back and forth with his knuckles planted on the rocks.

Colin went to Gisele, speaking softly. She came to him immediately, but kept tossing her head in alarm, snorting and stamping her feet while watching the giant. He stroked her neck and ran his hand along her flanks and legs, feeling her over for any serious injury. She seemed OK, but was understandably alarmed. Colin closed his eyes, continuing to murmur softly to her. He sought out the light that was Gisele's true-self. He found her and willed her to be calm, reassuring her. He didn't know how long they stood like that, but when he opened his eyes, Gisele was resting her head on his shoulder. Gath stared at them – disconcertingly with the two eyes on the sides roaming independent, while the recently uncovered eye in the center of his forehead stared unblinking at Colin and Gisele. He thought for a moment of leaping on the horse and trying to escape. He didn't know how fast Gath could move, but it would have to be awfully fast to catch Gisele. Somehow, the thought just didn't seem…….right. It wasn't honest. He'd told Gath that he would go with him and so he would. Colin smiled, "OK, Gath. Let's go meet your family."

The giant happily led the way. Colin took the reins, leading Gisele by the halter without making any attempt to ride her. Gath crossed the stream and followed a faint trail leading up through the rocks, paralleling the stream at some distance. They followed this course for over a mile. The trail approached the stream as it flowed between the narrow walls of a rocky canyon, only about 30 feet wide. This continued for another quarter of a mile or so, before it suddenly opened onto a beautiful valley of immense proportions, surrounded by steep rock walls. The stream meandered through the middle of a meadow, dotted with clumps of dense timber. The edges of the valley were heavily forested, backed by rock walls which thrust upwards from the valley floor for several hundred feet. At the head of the valley, the stream plunged down the rock face in a white ribbon of waterfall. In the distance, snow-capped peaks could be seen. The trail led off to their right. Gath quickened his pace, swinging along on his hands and arms more than he had done on their ascent. Soon they were greeted by a chorus of loud, bellowing, "Hah's!" From caves dotting the rock wall, a number of the Anakims emerged, some carrying clubs or spears. Gisele began tossing her head in alarm, emitting a shrill whistle of warning. Colin didn't like the look of the welcoming committee and began to hang further back, preparing to make a break back down the trail. Gath suddenly stopped, swinging his ponderous head around and fixing that unblinking center eye on Colin, "Small mans wait here. I go. Make sure Anakims no hurt small mans."

As Gath hurried up the trail with his swinging lope, Colin mounted Gisele, ready to flee if things should turn ugly. The thought brought a grim smile to his face. "A whole herd of Gaths – there definitely isn't <u>anything</u> pretty about that," he told Gisele. Gath reached the Anakims, about three hundred yards distant. Colin could hear lots of "Hah's!" accompanied by various hoots with spears and clubs being waved in the air. Soon a number of the Anakims surrounded Gath and were pounding him on the back. There were so many Colin couldn't tell what was happening. He was torn between his desire to flee and a sense of obligation to help Gath, as he unaccountably felt responsible for the giant's predicament. Suddenly, the mob parted and Gath came loping back, grinning broadly. The others stayed behind, continuing to hoot and shake their weapons in the air.

"Gath show Anakims! Gath not ugly! Anakims say Gath pretty! Gath stay Anakims. All Anakims want meet small mans fix Gath! You come!" Colin came.

The Anakims fell in around Gath, Colin and Gisele. Colin had his hands full for a few minutes, trying to calm the horse. Thankfully, the Anakims gave them a little bit of space, but still kept up a steady chorus of hoots. They were escorted to the caves he had seen in the distance. At their approach, a host of other Anakims came ambling out of the caves, adding to the general tumult. These, Colin surmised, were the females and young. He couldn't quite come to grips with regarding them as "women and children." If anything, they were uglier than the males. The females were adorned with scraggly locks of hair on their heads, hanging down to midway on their stocky torsos. The young ones were nearly all Colin's height or more, but he figured the smallest of them would have outweighed him by well over a hundred pounds. They were timid, hanging back behind their parent's legs and peeking at him from one of their three eyes. Reaching a fire pit in front of the caves, he swung down from the saddle, which sent the young racing away, screaming in terror. The older Anakims roared with laughter, making Gisele prance nervously. Gath grinned, "Young think small mans split, make two! Big scared! Hah!"

One of the big females approached, wrapping Gath in a bear hug, lifting him completely off the ground. A male pounded Gath on the back. Colin figured any one of those blows would cave his ribs in and eyed them warily. They were all laughing, jabbering and lumbering in a circle, the absolute picture of joy. Grabbing the couple by the hand, Gath brought them over to Colin. All three were bobbing their heads, bowing and grinning. Gath said, "Gath mother. Gath father. Small mans fix Gath."

The big female would be restrained no longer and scooped Colin up in her massive arms. Gisele lunged forward, ears laid back, neck outstretched, trying to bite. "No Gisele!" Colin yelled. She shook her head, but desisted. The female hugged Colin to her chest and in a rumbling, raspy voice croaked out. "Small mans fix Hotha baby. Hotha thank small mans." She was surprisingly gentle, both as she held him and as she set him down.

"Colin," he said, pointing to himself. "I am Colin. I'm glad I could fix Gath for you."

"K'lin." She replied. "Hotha thank K'lin. Gath not ugly. Gath stay Anakims. K'lin stay Anakims."

Colin shook his head. "No. Thank you, Hotha. Colin must leave. Soon Colin must go back Aidon."

Hoots and "Hah's!" erupted all around. "Ai-don! K'lin go Ai-don? Bad small mans Ai-don! Kill Anakims. Anakims kill, eat small mans Ai-don!" Gath's father roared. Spears had been lowered, aiming at Colin and clubs were now held low and threatening as the mob closed in around him.

"No!" Hotha yelled. "No hurt K'lin. K'lin fix Gath! Not bad small mans Ai-don!"

The mob hesitated and spears were lowered a fraction. Uncertain. Colin shook his head. "Colin not from Aidon. But I must go to Aidon. I'm sorry if men from Aidon killed Anakims. I promise, Colin will not hurt Anakims if Anakims not hurt Colin."

Gath's father glared, but suddenly gave an abrupt nod of his head. "Anak not hurt K'lin. K'lin not hurt Anakims. Anakims not hurt K'lin. Small man's Ai-don not hurt Anakims, Anakims not hurt Ai-don. Ai-don mans hurt Anakims, bring many small mans, Anakims eat!" Hoots of approval erupted all around. The crisis seemed to be past.

Anak swept Colin along, a massive hand on his back. "K'lin come. Eat. K'lin fix Gath. Anakims big eat. No eat K'lin!" He laughed at his own joke.

Leery of what the Anakims might actually be eating, Colin had little choice but to follow along. He was soon seated on the ground between Anak and Hotha. Hotha had tied what looked like a filthy wad of moss into the cavity Gisele had chomped out of Gath's leg. It hadn't slowed him down, but Hotha seemed pleased to bind up the wound. Gath sat next to his mother and kept leaning over to inspect Colin with his center eye. Each inspection ended with Gath bobbing his head, grinning hideously and emitting a satisfied, "Hah!" Soon, a number of the squat females were waddling from the caves, carrying large wooden bowls and woven baskets filled with various types of food. There were a variey of huge melons, each of which would have weighed as much as Colin. There were leafy salads, but sized in comparison to Colin that he thought it would be like trying to chew his way through canvas. The flat bread they served appeared to have been baked on stones or the hearth of a fire. There was no evidence of metal or metal working other than what Colin had brought with him. Colin estimated the gathering to consist of 60 or 70 individuals. The atmosphere was boisterous, but the Anakims were amazingly gentle and tolerant in relation to their young, who clambered over the seated figures and helped themselves to the food. When all was ready, the adults simply began to eat, without ceremony. Some used large curved platters made of some type of bark to place food on, while others nibbled from the piles of food. Colin was unsure how to proceed and Hotha seemed equally puzzled. Their smallest platter had been set before Colin, but he could barely lift it, let alone use it to collect food. Finally, Hotha grinned and motioned him to go get some food and bring it back to set on his platter. He made several trips, using his knife to hack off chunks of the coarse bread and pieces of melon, as well as other fruit which was unfamiliar to him. The food was surprisingly good and he was hungry.

After the meal, the group continued to lounge, in no apparent rush to clean things up or prepare for the night which was fast approaching. Hoping he wasn't about to commit a social *faux paus*, Colin asked Anak, "Why do the Anakims and people of Aidon try to kill each other?"

Anak shrugged, picking his teeth with a stubby finger, "Long time happen. Many long time maybe friend. Ai-don mans tell Anakims go 'way. Anakims not leave. Ai-don mans hunt Anakim. Hurt. Kill. Anakims big. Strong. Kill Ai-don mans when try kill Anakims. Small mans have metal. Metal very strong. Stronger than Anakims. Metal kill Anakims. Must leave. Come here. No small mans come here. Anakims safe. Many small mans come, Anakims fight."

He pushed Colin sharply in the chest with a massive finger, about rolling him over, "K'lin first small mans come here, live. K'lin first small mans come here, go 'way, live." Everyone thought this to be a great joke and burst into hoots of laughter. Colin didn't get the joke, but was relieved that the expectation seemed to be that he would leave here – alive. But he was puzzled. From what Anak had said, the Aidonians and Anakims must have once been friends. Well, if not friends, exactly, they at least they had coexisted peacefully. But something happened to make the Aidonians tell the Anakims to leave and when they hadn't, hostilities had broken out. Why? It was another puzzle, and, he admitted, he was only hearing one badly communicated side of the story.

"K'lin go back Ai-don? Next day?" Gath asked him.

"Soon. I will go back soon."

"Tree? K'lin go tree?" Anak asked.

Colin shook his head. "I've seen lots of trees. Aidon is not my home. I don't know what tree you mean."

Anak looked at him sternly, "Must go tree!"

Hotha shook her head, "K'lin not Ai-don. Ai-don mans kill K'lin go tree. K'lin not Ai-don home. Ai-don kill."

Anak was unrelenting. "K'lin go tree!"

"I don't know what tree you want me to see. I don't know where it is. I can't go there."

Anak glared, punching him in the chest again with his finger. This time it did knock him over. "Must go tree!"

Colin sat up, rubbing his chest. It hurt. The four of them lapsed into silence. Suddenly Hotha brightened. She jumped up and swung off, towards the caves, hooting in excitement. Gath and Anak watched her go, heads cocked to one side in curiosity. She soon returned, carrying an ornately carved wooden container. Gath and Anak's eyes widened when she appeared – at least their lidded eyes on the sides of their faces did. The unblinking center eye remained unchanged. They both let out a string of approving "Hah's!" Hotha removed the lid from the box. It was filled with some kind of dried fruit – smaller than raisins but almost blood red. Colin was amazed. How did these huge creatures collect such tiny fruit with their huge, clumsy hands and fingers?

Hotha spoke, "K'lin take. Go tree. Eat. Then go. Ai-don mans no see K'lin. No kill."

"I eat this? It makes me invisible?"

Hotha looked puzzled. "invisible" wasn't registering with her limited vocabulary. Colin tried again, covering his eyes. "I eat. Then Aidon people can't see me?"

Gath shook his head, "No. See. Not see. K'lin see Gath, see rock. Not see Gath! K'lin think rock, see rock."

Colin remembered the confrontation down by the stream, where he had battled Gath. Now that he thought about it, the Anakims didn't look all that much like rocks. The coloring and texture wasn't right. So why hadn't he seen this 20 foot giant before? He had simply seen what he had expected to see.

"Gath, you eat this and it helps you look like a rock?"

Gath grinned, nodding. Hotha and Anak looked happy as well.

"How does looking like a rock help me go to the tree and not get killed?"

The smiles faded, now Gath was exasperated. "Gath eat. Gath in rock, look rock. Gath in tree, look tree. K'lin in Ai-don. Look Ai-don."

Colin was skeptical, but he had seen too many strange things already to totally disbelieve what he thought he was being told. "This helps me blend with the surroundings? Wherever I am – like a chameleon?"

The Anakims looked puzzled. He tried again, "If I eat this, then I will look like the people of Aidon when I go to the tree?"

Grins again erupted and excited heads bobbed.

"How long does it last?" He asked.

Anak shrugged. "Long time. Gath rock years. Many years. Gath move. You see. Gath not rock."

"Years? Gath was a rock down there, guarding the Anakims for years?"

Gath grinned and nodded. But Hotha spoke, looking very serious. "Touch tree, done. No rock. No tree. No Ai-don. Touch tree, Ai-don mans see K'lin. Kill K'lin."

Colin nodded, "If I touch the tree, they'll see me. I understand. I won't touch the tree." He was confused, having no clue as to what tree he was supposed to see but not touch.

Anak punched him in the chest again, "Go tree!" It was an order, not a request.

Colin spent the night with the Anakims. At least he spent the night near them, but he politely declined to spend the night in the caves with them. He had visions of being used as a teddy bear for one of their immense young. He used Gisele as an excuse, telling them that he needed to be near her at night. They had kindly assured him that she was welcome in the caves as well and his attempts to beg off on the grounds that the horse wasn't house – or cave – trained were regarded in puzzlement. Apparently the Anakims either had no pets or simply weren't all that fastidious about such things. In either case, he and Gisele were both more comfortable out under the open skies.

In the morning, he joined the communal meal. Afterwards, Gath escorted him to the mouth of the narrow canyon which led out of their secluded valley to see him off, keeping pace with Gisele by swinging along on his feet and the knuckles of his huge hands. At the canyon, he said, "K'lin careful. Bad small mans hurt K'lin, K'lin come Anakims. Anakims protect K'lin. K'lin Anakim now. Many small mans come Anakims, Anakims fight." Then he bowed himself so low that his forehead touched the ground.

Colin was touched by this gesture. "Thanks, Gath. I'll be careful. I hope Anakims and the people of Aidon can be at peace – be friends. You be careful too. I'm glad you're back with your family."

With that, he wheeled Gisele and started her down the narrow trail. She was eager to be off. They stopped briefly at the mouth of the canyon. Colin surveyed the scene of the battle he had had with Gath. He shook his head. Broken rock and displaced boulders lay strewn about. Gath had more strength than a grizzly. How had he survived that? Broken rocks? Gath should have shattered his skull and broken every bone in his body when he flung him out of that cleft. It didn't make any sense, but he was getting used to feeling that way.

Chapter 14   Plots and Plans

The Lady Dalene was disgusted. She had gotten over being angry weeks ago, because every day was just more of the same. She endured yet another of the interminable Council meetings. They followed a very predictable routine. After unitedly condemning the absent object of their hostility they began bickering among themselves. It usually began with a heated debate as to whether the introduction of soap or leather was an inherent evil perpetrated on Aidon by the impostor. This would be brought around to a discussion as to how the manufacture and sale could best be regulated to most fairly distribute the profits, with most of the Council defining "fair" as their File having a monopoly on the commodity. More recently, the local Councils had been discussing the other new and novel ideas – such as fishing and archery. This was precisely the type of unrest the Councils had spent thousands of years suppressing! This was why they needed one who wore the mantle by right – a messenger – to give instruction to them. The Council debate was always settled by an appeal to the ancient records and of course the records said nothing about the subject of their debate and so the cycle would repeat itself the next day.

Today, if anything, was worse than usual. Halvor came in person to report. Not that he had anything to report, but he knew it was expected that he appear before the Council periodically. With no new developments, the Council took out their frustration on the unfortunate Arbor Guard, heaping scorn and recriminations on his head, which he took without expression or complaint. The Lady Dalene caught up to him in the hallway outside the Council chamber. "Halvor! Walk with me, will you?"

He hesitated for just a moment, then nodded curtly as they headed toward the residence chambers in the south wing. "Are you doing alright?" she asked.

He sighed, "Yes. I'm fine. I hate coming here with nothing to report, but it's as if he vanished. I don't believe any of the rumors we've heard about Colin being sighted. The descriptions are all the same. Too much the same. It's like everyone is reciting from the same source. Witnesses, at least so many witnesses, would have some variation. Add that to the fact that we have yet to talk to a single person who claims to actually have seen him. Not one. Everyone just heard it from somebody.. My scouts are wearing themselves ragged trying to chase these stories down, but as near as I can tell, that's all they are – stories."

"And you've been running more than any of them, haven't you?" She asked sympathetically.

"I have to. If there's even the slightest chance of finding him, I have to pursue it. That's another funny thing about the rumors we hear. He's always trying to stir things up, but we've never heard a single report of him buying supplies, spending the night or getting anything to eat. He's good with that bow. I saw that for myself. Who knows? Maybe he's hunting for his food and doesn't need to buy anything."

They reached The Lady Dalene's rooms and she said, "Do come in and eat before you go. Do you have time?"

He smiled, but without humor, "I may as well. I'm as likely to find him sitting here as I am running from one city to the next. Besides, I want to show you something."

Curious, she led the way into her room, "Alicia!" she called, "Halvor is joining me for dinner."

Alicia entered, wiping her hands and bowing to the Arbor Guard, "Greetings, Halvor. I will have food here in just a moment."

Marcus followed her in bowing as well, "Halvor! It's good to see you. I'm glad you're taking a little bit of time from your search. You must be exhausted. You've been at it for weeks."

Halvor smiled with real warmth. He and Marcus had always gotten along well. "Hello, Marcus. Good to see you as well. I expect he'll show up when he's good and ready, but I doubt if we'll see him before then. I was just going to show The Lady Dalene something."

From his pack he withdrew a bow and several arrows. "I've made these, patterned after the set Colin was helping Elam with."

Marcus hefted the bow, his hand sliding naturally into place on the grip. "This is a bow? Like what you were telling the Council?"

"Yes. Here, let me show you." He took it from Marcus and withdrew a braided string from his pocket. Bracing the bow against his right foot, he bent it and slipped the string into place. "The arrow," he demonstrated, "has a notch that fits over the string." He drew the bow, holding the feathered shaft against his cheek as he sighted down the shaft of the arrow, "You aim like so and when the arrow is released, it flies amazingly fast and can be very accurate. I've been practicing. I killed a rabbit with it last week." He gently relieved the tension from the bow, handing it back to Marcus who practiced drawing it several times. "Here." He handed The Lady Dalene a small packet.

She opened it, her eyes showing pleasure as she stroked the soft, gray fur. "Is this from the rabbit?"

He nodded, "Yes. Jorge tanned it for me. I was surprised that he did. They don't like me very much. I thought it would go well with the fox that Colin gave you."

"Halvor, I don't think it's a matter of them not liking you. They just know that you're assigned to take Colin into custody. I think they feel protective towards him."

"I know. They're really very nice. Miran still invites me to eat with them whenever I'm there. They may feel protective towards him, but I'm becoming more of a mind that it's the rest of us who may need protecting from him."

"You can't mean that! Why? What has he done?" Dalene asked.

"Nothing. I mean he hasn't even been around to do anything, so far as I can tell. But the ideas he's started. I can't make up my mind if they're a good thing or not. I mean, they seem good. Soap, for example." He looked a little sheepish as he pulled a well-used ball of soap from his pack, looking at it. "I use it myself. Can't hardly stand it anymore if I don't wash with it. I just feel kind of grimy without it. A year ago nobody had ever heard of it, now half the people in Tyber, Tremont and Jordanon act like they can't live without it. Kath and Miran have been teaching women in a few other towns how to make it. But if it's so good, why haven't we needed it before now? Faron, the harness maker out in Tyber, he's had Jorge showing him how to make leather. He thinks it will be much better than canvas for harness. That kid, Elam, he's pretty good with a bow – better than me, in fact. He's got several of his friends all using bows now as well and I've seen them showing up in a few other towns, too. My point is, there's an awful lot of change happening all at once and it can all be traced directly back to him! While I can't decide if it's good or bad, I'm betting that the Council isn't going to have any trouble at all and they're going to be out to destroy him."

Marcus handed the bow back to Halvor. Alicia had come in during their conversation, bearing a tray of food. The Lady Dalene tried to brighten the mood, "Come, Halvor, sit and eat. Marcus? Alicia? Have you eaten? Would you like to join us?" The four sat to eat, but there was little conversation until they were finished.

"So, where are you off to now?"

"I spend most of my time patrolling the 1st Order cities. They're furthest from Salem and I have a feeling that he's most likely to show up there first. I've established relay points in all the towns. If anything happens, the other patrols know to send word to each of them so I'll be notified right away. I'll probably head towards Tyber. I think Colin got pretty close to Jorge and Miran. They certainly think highly of him. Could be he'll go back there before the Evaluation."

"I'm going with you." The Lady Dalene said firmly.

Halvor and Marcus looked shocked. Alicia tried to hide her smile.

"Absolutely not! Father won't stand for it and I'm sleeping rough. You're not going." Halvor replied.

"I don't want to go with you on your patrols. Just to Tyber. I want to see Jorge and Miran."

"No. It isn't going to happen."

The Lady Dalene raised one eyebrow, "Not even if the Regent agrees?"

"If father agrees, then I'll take you. Not otherwise. But you're wasting your time. He isn't going to let you go." Halvor was comfortable with that.

A few minutes later, both Halvor and Dalene were in their father's quarters. Halvor spoke first, "I'm ready to head out again. Dalene has this crazy idea that she wants to go back to Tyber, to see Jorge and Miran. I already told her that she can't go, but she wants to hear it from you." He looked smug.

Gareth Tregard eyed his two headstrong children. "No, not children anymore," he reminded himself. He shook his head, thinking. Coming to a decision, he said, "Good. I need to speak with both of you. Let's go sit down."

Puzzled, they followed their father into another room where they sat. "I think Dalene should go with you." Gareth held up his hand, silencing Halvor before he could object. Now it was Dalene's turn to look smug. "You'll hear me out first. Aidon, I believe, is in a very dangerous position at present. This whole issue with the mantle-bearer probably couldn't have come at a worse time. I can't point to anything definite, but I believe Kernsidon is preparing to attack. I don't know how soon, but probably before the end of the year. Halvor, you and the other Arbor Guards are more aware of this than almost anyone. You've reported evidence of their scouts and possible spies." Halvor nodded and their father continued, "I don't believe half of these sighting of 'the mantle bearer.' I think someone is deliberately spreading rumors in order to stir up the people – create a division before the attack."

"So do you think that it's Kernsidon spreading the rumors about Colin?" Halvor asked.

"Maybe. I could be wrong. I hope I am. It would be easier to face Kernsidon without having to worry about internal dissent as well. But that's what it feels like to me. That's why this issue with the mantle bearer has got to be concluded as quickly as possible. We need to get this put to rest before Kernsidon attacks. I've already sent Arbor Guards out as scouts, watching for the Kernsidon army. If we can meet them on the plain south of Jordanon, we can keep them away from the cities and from our croplands. If we cut off their leaders, the attack will probably fail. But I'm worried. It's little enough we ever hear of Kernsidon, but what I have heard is bad. They got a new King several years ago. The others were bad enough, but this one is ruthless. Let's just hope he isn't smart as well. There's nothing we can do about that one way or another, but, hopefully we <u>can</u> do something about getting this business with Colin settled – quickly. That's why I want both of you out in the Files. You know him. At least you've met him. If you can bring him in and we can get these rumors halted, it should help. We just can't afford any delays."

******

As the Tregard meeting was drawing to a close, Councilor Lijah Krainik was enroute to another of his clandestine meetings with the 13th File. While he suspected that his contact was from Kernsidon, he would have been shocked to learn that this evening he would be meeting with the King of Kernsidon. Always before, King Mahon had used intermediaries – after using the Evaluation Box in his possession to strip them of much of their will and virtually any ability to think and act freely. They were the perfect couriers and they were disposable. Over the years, he had placed many such in Aidon. Men and women whom he had destroyed through the power – his power – of Compulsion. Each had been given meticulous instruction regarding how to live and how to act, so that they might continue undetected in Aidon. Mahon believed he could eventually take over the country through this quiet infiltration. But it was too slow and he was not patient. He instead used his mindless pawns to relay instructions and spread quiet discord, in preparation for the day when he would move decisively against his enemies. But this time, he had come in person to begin the long awaited overthrow of Aidon. The journey had been long – dangerous even. But he was driven to be here, to set in motion what he had waited so long for.

Mahon had ruled in Kernsidon for the past eight years, having succeeded his father, King Jacob, upon his untimely death. The fact that he had precipitated that untimely death by personally beheading his father with his own sword as he lay in a drunken stupor following his birthday celebration troubled him not at all. The man was old, inept and hadn't the courage to attack Aidon and take back the rule that was rightfully theirs. He was an obstacle and obstacles need to be removed. Mahon had lived in his father's shadow his entire life. There was no affection between the two. His father had permitted him to live only because he recognized the importance of a ruling line of succession. And he thought, mistakenly as it turned out, that he could successfully block any efforts on the part of his son to assume the throne prematurely. But Mahon had learned of the secret passage that led to the King's chambers. The two guards outside the door were no protection the night Mahon used the passage in order to visit the old king. Mahon had only absented himself from the banquet for a minute. Few remembered him being gone at all, so no taint of suspicion touched him. The grieving son had the two guards arrested immediately, their tongues torn out and put to death, as a show of his grief at the death of his father and displeasure at the failure of the guards to protect him. The ease with which he betrayed his father reinforced his own lack of trust in others. Mahon had no doubt that Councilor Krainik would betray the King of Kernsidon for whatever considerable reward the High Council at Salem would bestow on him. Whereas he was equally willing to betray the Council for the reward promised him by the anonymous representative of the 13th File. It was a delicate game Mahon played and it was very much to his liking.

Mahon had planned for the day he would be King practically from the day his father assumed the throne. His mother, Queen Jezrel, had hated his father. Oh, not to his face. She was far too smart for that. But she had seen, in Mahon, an opportunity. Not to actually seize the throne. No woman could do that. "But," she had thought, "the hand that rocks the cradle rules the world." And she intended to rule the world – through her son. Unfortunately for Queen Jezrel, Mahon, having successfully slipped one leash had no desire to submit to another and having drunk from the intoxicating well of power, decided a change of queens was called for. In short order the unknown assassin who had slain the king dispatched the queen in like manner, resulting in the death of two more of the royal guards, thus inspiring the surviving members of that elite corps to greater diligence in protecting the new king.

Being king of Kernsidon, nice though it might be, was by no means entirely satisfactory to King Mahon. While hovering in the shadows during his father's reign, he concluded that Kernsidon was in need of refurbishment. Generations of war and oppression had definitely taken a heavy toll on the populace. Anyone seen as a threat, meaning intelligent, self-motivated or ambitious, was likely to rapidly fall out of favor with the ruling monarch. Such a fall was almost always fatal. The Kings had maintained enough administrative capacity to ensure the prompt, if brutal, collection of taxes and an effective if unimaginative military force which was applied more regularly inside the kingdom than for any external expeditions. But the simple truth was that centuries of such domination had practically bled dry the intellectual and artistic reservoirs of the country. It wasn't that the kingdom was stagnant. No, that would have been far too generous. In addition to millennia of brutal reign, chronic food shortages and disease had caused a decline in the population, as well as a reduction in what limited technology they had possessed. They were no longer capable of maintaining roads and buildings at their former level of opulence. Indeed, the capitol city of Kern was little more than a shabby relic of what was once a powerful rival to Salem. Mahon intended that it should not only rival, but entirely dominate her neighbor – and soon.

King Mahon looked older than his 34 years. If his dour countenance struck fear into his subjects, his rare smile filled them with terror, for a smiling Mahon never envisaged anything pleasant. Slight of build, he was of above average height. Never having had need to perform manual labor of any kind, he was not muscular. Mahon held guards and underlings in contempt. They were cheaply bought and easily disposed of. Mahon was something rare – far more rare than those skilled warriors who guarded him. More rare even than the generations of kings who had preceded him. Mahon was a scholar.

Even from infancy, Mahon had shown an exceptional aptitude for learning. While his siblings and predecessors had generally despised learning of any sort and learning from books in particular, Mahon devoured everything he could get his hands on to read. If asked why, he would have been at a loss to explain. But he had a hunger for knowledge. It was a hunger that was never satisfied and in fact, the more he fed it, the greater it became. It wasn't a love of learning. Mahon didn't love anything. Perhaps it was best described as a lust for learning. Lust. The desire to possess, control and dominate. The hunger for more. The need to subjugate. It was this lust that led Mahon to discover the ancient architectural texts which had shown him the many forgotten passages in the palace – one of which led to the King's chambers and another to the former queen's – to his advantage and their detriment. It was the same text which taught Mahon how to engage the locking mechanism so that no one could enter the chamber through that route once he had assumed the throne. More importantly these writings led him to his greatest discovery – the library.

Buried deep in the bowels of the castle, deeper than the well-used and occupied dungeons, he had found it. The library, or so he termed it, was really little more than an average sized storage chamber. It wasn't the size or location of this chamber that made it special. It was what it contained. He called it the library. But it was unlike the library up above, up in the main palace where the sterile histories had been perused and pored over for a thousand years - and then ignored and forgotten for thousands more. They contained little of value, which to Mahon, meant power. He had devoured the texts, but they left him unfilled. He valued knowledge only as a means to dominate. They had done nothing to satiate his lust for power. Gaining the throne had served to assuage his hunger – but only temporarily. Buried in this small vault was the feast which he hoped would satisfy him once and for all. For here were the ancient records, unseen, so far as he knew, for thousands of years. And in these books he had learned the secrets that would make him ruler of Aidon. Possessed of an impressive intellect and a powerful will, even in Aidon, he undoubtedly would have qualified for the 12th File. Had he cared to reflect on this, the thought would have given him no pleasure. His goal was something higher. Something not seen in four millennia. He and he alone would be the 13th File.

The ancient texts told of the time before the founding of Kernsidon. They told of Kern and how he had been robbed of his right to rule, rejected by his inferiors who had driven him out of Aidon. All of this could be found in the other library as well. But the ancient text contained more. It contained the record of Kern himself – of how he had become the most feared man in the history of Aidon, how he had wrested half the kingdom and come within a breath of obtaining the whole of it. Well, it hadn't quite worked out for Kern the way he'd hoped. He had become King, it was true, but not King of Aidon. He and his followers had fled to establish Kern's Aidon. Mahon intended to use the same path, but to do Kern one better. This time, he would be King in Aidon as well as Kernsidon. He knew that he would need a powerful ally and the text told him how to obtain one. The dark arts – the secret oaths and rituals – had been lost for thousands of years. That was the treasure of the library vault he had uncovered. It was not military might that would subjugate Aidon. That had been tried often enough and in four thousand years had never come close to succeeding. No, success would not come through the force of arms or crushing the will of the people. Mahon had only to look at his own kingdom to see the failure of that path – governing a shell of a kingdom whose glory had fled a thousand years ago. No, Aidon must <u>want</u> him to be her king. They must demand it. With the Tempter as his ally, they would beg him to rule over them. And when they begged him, he would crush them. But tonight his attention was focused on another ally. Councilor Krainik had arrived.

The room was dingy and warm – too warm to be comfortable. But open doors and windows were an invitation to eavesdroppers. A brief breath of air entered the room with Krainik, strangled in its first gasp as he closed the door quietly behind him. As always, the black shrouded figure sat facing away from him. The moment the door closed, however, the meeting suddenly became very different. Mahon flexed his will, a little something he had learned from the ancient writings. An unseen force gripped Krainik, forcing him to his knees as the dark figure turned to face him. "Kneel when you enter the presence of the 13th File, my servant."

Too stunned to speak, Krainik remained kneeling for a long moment before he was permitted to rise.

"I am King Mahon. You have served me well, Lijah Krainik. Continue to do so and you will be rewarded. Betray me, defy me and I will crush you. Now, what news have you of the pretender called Colin?"

Krainik's heart was hammering. He cleared his throat, "It is my honor to serve you, King Mahon. I'm afraid there is no news. The only reports we've had are the tales of our own making. It's as though he has vanished. I don't understand it. The patrols have found nothing. But I'm sure, given a little more time........." He trailed off nervously, cut off by the raised hand of the figure he faced.

"It is of no matter. His absence works to our advantage. Let the people of Aidon believe that a messenger has at last come. First the messenger, then The Lawgiver! At the Solstice Observance, The Lawgiver will come!"

"The Lawgiver? At the Solstice Observance? I don't understand. That can't be! It will be the end of us!" Kranik objected.

"Your <u>understanding</u> is not required," Mahon said in a silky, dangerous tone. "Only your obedience. Did you think that Aidon would simply bow to us if we asked them nicely? Did you think that force of arms would succeed this time where it has failed a hundred times before? You are a fool, just as the Kings of Kernsidon before me were fools. Aidon waits for a Lawgiver, do they not? <u>I</u> shall be their Lawgiver! <u>I</u> shall sit upon the throne in the Temple of The Tree of Life! And when I do, they will bow and they will beg me to rule over them! And you, my noble High Councilor, will then have your reward as well - to grind your heel in the faces of those sneering, arrogant scum of the 12th File.

"This false mantle-bearer! It was almost too perfect! Half of Aidon wants to fall at his feet. The other half wish to have him torn to shreds! If he is wise and he does not return for the Evaluation, you will continue to spread rumors – the more outrageous, the better. But if he does appear, you will ensure that he is subjected to the most stringent Evaluation. It matters not what File he is assigned to, but once he is assigned, the Council will wish to try him, will they not? At the trial, they will determine to destroy him, just as they have destroyed all others who have come wearing the mantle. When I sit on the throne, I shall claim him as my own messenger and demand the lives of those who destroyed him! If he survives the Council, I shall denounce him and demand the lives of those who let him live after he falsely claimed to be my messenger. Whatever happens, he has given me the perfect excuse to destroy the Council. That, my dear Krainik, leaves the door open for you to become Regent of Aidon, under me."

"But what if he isn't a pretender? What if he really is a messenger?" Krainik asked.

"Bah! How many thousands of years has it been since any Council has supported one wearing the mantle? Legends! Superstition! If Messias ever existed, he has forgotten us. I will be Messias!" Mahon replied. "But perhaps we can use him. Whether he wears the mantle truly, or is but a pretender, he will be destroyed - unless his life might have value to us. Let us consider this, Krainik. Once he passes the Evaluation, what then?"

"He will be tried as a false messenger. Then he will be destroyed."

"Ah! But suppose he were not destroyed? Might we not persuade him to join us? To support us in exchange for his life? Many of the people already wish to believe him - believe in him. It might sway them if the mantle-bearer were to stand with us," Mahon said.

Krainik was reluctant, "I don't know. The Council is ready to destroy him the instant he's caught. The Evaluation is merely a formality. It's the trial that they're all anxious for. I don't see any possible way they would permit him to survive."

Mahon shrugged. "It matters not. But consider, if an opportunity presented itself, perhaps a Councilor, such as you, might find cause to spare his life. Do you not think that he would follow wherever you lead? Out of gratitude for his life? He could prove to be a valuable servant."

"If the council seeks to know his true-self, they will see he is but a man and they will destroy him as they have all the others. If for some reason they don't, they're still determined to destroy him. I've already set events in motion, as I thought you wished. He will not survive."

"Then we will have lost nothing. But if he is condemned, does he not have the right to appeal the punishment?" Mahon asked.

"Yes, but I don't think he understands our law well enough to claim the right. It won't work." Krainik said.

"Fool! <u>He</u> doesn't have to understand the law. <u>You</u> do! And because you are fair-minded, magnanimous even and wanting to ensure that the accused has access to every chance to mitigate the penalty, <u>you</u> could appeal on his behalf, for reconsideration of the punishment. That would place him in your custody until his appeal is considered at the next moon. We shall act before then, but you would have the opportunity to recruit him to our cause. I expect he will be willing enough – a man will do much to save his life. If he refuses, his destruction might be made more spectacular than what the Council has in mind - as a warning to any who might oppose us. You will see to it, or perhaps it will be your own death I must use as a warning to others."

Krainik had no doubt that he would do it. "It will be as you say. On my life."

"On your life." The dark figure arose and slipped silently out the back.

Chapter 15   Return to Aidon

His pace was not hurried and his path was not direct, but he knew he was now very close to Aidon. He camped that night at the edge of a large thermal spring in a secluded valley. He'd smelled sulfur in the air for several hours and had seen the thin column of vapor rising from the foothills ahead. Gisele had tossed and snorted, not liking the smell. They had ridden carefully along a watercourse, flanked by steaming pools and bubbling mud. For a time, he led Gisele along a baked mud-flat, wary of a thin crust covering a potential death trap. He hadn't seen any geysers, but the colors of many of the pools had been fantastic – yellow and red fringes surrounding pools of the deepest blue fading to turquoise and green. At the far side of the thermal valley, he found a grassy meadow surrounding the pool of a warm spring. The water was hot, but not scalding. By some quirk of geology, an ice-cold spring dribbled a trickle of water from a rocky cleft into the lower edge of the pool. The grass was lush and Gisele fell to feeding greedily. Colin waded cautiously into the warm water, testing the temperature, before stripping off his travel-grimed clothing. Using the last of his precious soap, he scrubbed both his clothing and himself. He shaved carefully – a habit he had been lax about maintaining during the course of his travels, but the warm water and the farewell to his hoarded soap gave him the opportunity to rectify the situation. Completing the job, he lay back in the warm water, only his face remaining above the surface. "Life," he thought, "is good. Why go back? Why not just stay out here? It's unlikely that anyone will come looking. Sure I'm alone, but I've been alone most my life. You get used to it. There's a whole world to explore. There was so much to see. So much to live for. Why not?" It wasn't the first time he'd thought it. He already knew he was going back. He just didn't know why.

Studying his map the next morning, he figured if he pushed it, he could be back in Tyber with one day's hard ride. The problem was, he wasn't ready to be back just yet. Tomorrow would be Seventh Day and by his calculation, the Evaluation would be Thursday – fifth Day, he corrected. He wanted to be early enough so that nobody would worry that he wasn't going to show. He figured if he arrived in Salem sometime on Third Day, he could find an inn and rest up for a full day prior to the Evaluation. While he wanted to see Jorge, Miran and Elam before he went to Salem, he didn't want to impose for too long either. What it boiled down to was that he probably had time to kill before he headed to Tyber. With no deadline pressing him, Colin decided to loop down through the south of Aidon. He well remembered the stir his presence had caused in Tyber and he wasn't anxious for a repeat performance. There would be stir enough to suit him soon enough. The risk was minimal. After all, he was on his way to Salem anyway, albeit by a roundabout path. Gisele was getting restless, anxious to be on her way. Colin stowed his gear and patted her affectionately on the neck before mounting up. "Alright girl. I guess we've got a little more territory to cover. We'll take it nice and easy. No problem." He was wrong.

By evening they had come to the bank of what Colin assumed was the Morex River. Somewhere near here there was supposed to be a bridge – an ancient stone structure which was the only span crossing the water. It was a beautiful river, flowing fast and deep, about 70 yards across at this point. He followed its course upstream to where a smaller creek emptied into the river. It was a likely looking spot to camp. Colin stripped the gear off his horse and picketed her to graze while he dug out his fishing line and cut a willow pole to attach it to. "I'd still like some better hooks to tie some decent dry-flies on," he told Gisele. She looked at him quizzically and nickered to him before resuming her feeding. In short order, Colin had four fat trout lying on the grassy bank of the stream. It was more than he would need this evening, but he would cook all of them anyway. The extra would easily see him through tomorrow.

He banked his fire and curled up in his blanket. The evening was warm and it was several minutes before he drifted off to sleep. He hadn't been asleep long when he was awakened by a warning snort from Gisele. He was instantly alert, rolling out of his blankets and crouched by the edge of the trees, straining to catch any movement or sound. He could detect nothing, but Gisele continued to pace nervously. He made it a habit to always pack his gear before retiring for the night, so it took but a moment to silently gather up his saddle and saddle bags. Quickly, he strung his bow, but was reluctant to use it unless he knew that he was being threatened. He placed one palm softly across Gisele's muzzle and whispered softly in her ear to calm her. "Come on girl. We don't know what we're up against, so we're going to retreat. Keep it quiet." He cautiously led her down river before pausing to tighten his saddle cinch. Just then he heard voices, from back the way he had come. There were at least three of them.

"There's no one here!"

"Not now, but this is the right spot. The fire still has coals in it."

"Where'd he go?"

"No idea. Do you think it was a spy from Kernsidon?"

"Had to be. Nobody else would be this far out."

"Maybe it was the mantle-bearer they've been chasing!"

"Maybe. Either way, it would mean a big reward for us if we catch him."

"Why do you think he brought a horse clear out here? He hadn't a cart. It was late when I spotted him, but the country is too rough for a cart. No roads nor any trail big enough for that."

"Don't know, but he can't have gotten far. Come daylight we'll find his trail. Nobody shakes an Arbor Guard - at least not in the woods. We'll get him."

Colin hated to attempt a river crossing at night. Thankfully, it was only a few days shy of the full moon, "Moons. Plural." He mentally corrected himself. The three-quarters crescent gave adequate light to see by. But he hadn't liked what he'd heard - especially the part about getting a big reward for capturing the mantle-bearer. That wasn't on his agenda - at least not tonight. And if these Arbor Guards were anything like Halvor, he really didn't care to cross swords with one of them, especially since he had the distinct disadvantage of not having a sword. From that perspective, the river looked positively inviting. He waded in and Gisele eagerly followed. He let the strong current sweep them several hundred yards downstream, wanting distance between him and the guards. Whether they were here looking specifically for him or were part of a regular patrol he had no idea, but from here on, he would be extra cautious.

After crossing the river, he mounted Gisele and rode hard for several miles before stopping for what was left of the night. His clothing was wet, but fortunately his blankets had remained fairly dry. He stripped off his wet things and hung them on a bush, while he rolled up in his blankets, relying on Gisele to wake him if danger approached again. He awakened at dawn and quickly dressed. His clothing was mostly dry. He wasn't wild about getting into cold, damp clothing this morning, but figured it would be more dignified than wearing a blanket, should his pursuers catch up to him. For breakfast, he wolfed down soggy fish left over from the previous night. It hadn't fared so well in the river crossing, but he didn't want to chance building a fire. Smoke, he knew, can be scented from a long distance away. He would be cautious, but for now he would continue with his plan to make a swing through the south of Aidon.

For most of the day, Colin rode along forested trails, pausing at every clearing to look for signs of either pursuit or a trap. He saw nothing and Gisele displayed no indication of alarm. By afternoon, he sat at the edge of a large clearing, falling away gently to terminate on the south bank of the river. Directly across from him lay Riverton. It was much more impressive than Tyber. Where Tyber had been little more than a quaint village, this was a walled city. Battlements were spaced the length of the wall and a heavy wooden gate marked access along the main road leading to the city. Towers and turrets were visible above the wall, the rooftops colorful with slate or clay tiles gleaming in the afternoon sun. Pennants decorated the top of the towers located in the interior regions of the city. The whole thing had a lively, medieval appearance that he found intriguing. Colin kicked Gisele lightly in the ribs, heading her up river while still clinging to the relative concealment of the trail through the trees. If his lightly sketched map was correct, a short distance from here the river should make a broad arc to the south, before climbing to its headwaters in the nearby mountains. The trail was steep as it crested a short rise, breaking out at the brow of the hill overlooking the town on the opposite bank. From here, it was a sheer drop of perhaps 30 feet down to the dark, fast flowing water. The opposite bank formed the outer edge of the river's arc. The sweeping current had carved out a broad, shallow gravel bar, covering a couple hundred yards. From his vantage point, Colin could look down on this rocky beach and see a dozen or more children at play. Their parents were relaxing in the shade of the trees, 40 yards from the boisterous children laughing and splashing in the shallows. His attention was drawn by the screams of the children down below. They were racing back and forth on the shore, pointing and screaming. One child had waded out too far and was being swept away by the current. The parents were now joining in the screaming as well, running downstream along the shore. "Come on! Come on! Somebody go in after her!" He was muttering to himself, having no idea if the thrashing child in the water was a boy or a girl. In an instant he was off the horse. "Oh, hell!" It was a habit developed by talking to cows when he'd worked on the ranch. In moments of high stress, his vocabulary tended to decay. Dropping the reins, he gave Gisele stern orders, "Gisele, stay! You hear me? Stay!" Then he jumped.

He drove himself forward in a short sprint to the edge of the cliff, legs churning the air as he fought for distance. He hit the water with a resounding splash, the force of the impact driving water up his nose and threatening to drown him. Despite that, he managed to swim swiftly toward the screaming child, just in time to see her disappear from sight. He was praying now, "Dear Lord, please help me. Please don't let her drown." Several adults were running along the shore, still shouting and pointing. As soon as he reached the spot where the child had sunk, he dove. The water was clear, but he could see nothing. It was too deep to see the bottom and he saw nothing of the small figure he was seeking either. Surfacing, he drew three deep breaths and dove once more stroking hard and fast downstream as he did so. Just as he thought his lungs would burst, a fragment of color drifted through the periphery of his vision. He changed his direction, begging for his air to last a few seconds more, as his body began to rise against his will, his fingers snagged the orange hem of a small cloak. He had her! Kicking so hard for the surface, he broached fully half the length of his body, before splashing down. Frantically, he drew the lifeless form to his chest, lying on his back and making for shore. In a moment he was floundering through the shallows, a screaming woman and sobbing man were trying to snatch the child from his grasp.

"Get back!" He roared, refusing to relinquish the small body. Others soon caught up, adding to the mayhem.

"Give me my baby! I want my baby!" The woman was screaming.

"Dear God, no! Please no! Take me instead!" The man was sobbing over and over again.

Colin was desperate. He needed room to work. He lowered his shoulders and bulled forward, knocking men and women sprawling. But they wouldn't give him room! With no conscious thought, he suddenly reached back and jerked the hood up over his head, drawing himself erect, fully a head taller than any of the others. "You WILL stand BACK!" He bellowed. They did and stood staring at him mutely.

Dropping to his knees, he lowered the small head and quickly performed three chest compressions. He was rewarded by a stream of water pouring from the little girl's nose and mouth. Laying her flat, he tilted her head back and performed mouth-to-mouth resuscitation - three breaths, then placed his ear on her chest to listen for a heartbeat. There was none. He settled into a rhythm, five firm compressions of the chest, just above the solar plexus, followed by one quick breath, his mouth covering both the child's nose and mouth. Vaguely, he recognized that the crowd was growing, but he was too preoccupied to be concerned. Just once the tearful mother moved again to take her daughter. With no time for niceties, Colin broke rhythm just long enough to snarl, "If you touch her, I swear I'll rip your arm off!" and then resumed his work. He lost track of time. It couldn't have been more than 15 or 20 minutes, perhaps not even half that, but each minute stretched into an eternity. He couldn't afford to stop, to think, to despair. There was only this little life that needed saving. Everything else was blocked from his consciousness. Suddenly, the small form gave a soft, choking whimper. Colin immediately rolled her on her side as she vomited the water she had swallowed. Her eyes clenched tightly shut and then flared open as she began to bawl. Colin thought he'd never heard a sweeter sound in his entire life, as he handed the little girl to her weeping parents. He felt totally drained and remained on his knees, offering a silent prayer of thanks.

At length, he reached up and drew the hood back from his head. Smiling to himself, he muttered, "This thing can come in handy once in awhile." The smile immediately faded as he looked up to see Halvor, staring at him impassively from a few feet away. He was flanked by two very serious looking men, both wearing swords and both looking like they would enjoy an opportunity to use them. "Welcome back, Colin. We've been looking for you."

With limited options, he decided to try and bluff it through. Forcing a smile and trying to sound delighted, he said, "Halvor! It's good to see you! Where did you come from?"

Halvor wasn't buying. Not yet anyway. "Oh, I've been traveling quite a bit lately. But I've been thinking of you - a lot. We have lots to talk about."

"Ah, yes. That we do. Do you have plans? I was going to head over towards Tremont this evening. I thought maybe I could find a nice inn.

If you'd care to join me for dinner, I'll buy. Oh, and of course your two friends are invited as well."

This elicited a tight smile from Halvor. He moved alongside, gesturing for Colin to accompany him while the two soldiers fell in a pace behind and off to the side. "I'm afraid that wouldn't be convenient this evening. We've another commitment, you see. But we'd be delighted if you would join us. In fact, I insist!"

The exchange took place with the utmost civility, but the tension in the air was tangible. All the while, the curious townspeople had been hovering in the background. The conversation was so calm and normal as to embolden some of them, who approached. One of them, addressed Colin, "You are the mantle-bearer? The one these have been searching for?"

Colin took note of the pink fringe the speaker wore on his cloak, differentiating him from the orange hem worn by most of the crowd made up of the 6th File. He smiled politely, "I am. But please, call me Colin. I carry no title."

The bold one continued, "I am Daniel Brendies, 7th File, of Troas. It was my sister's child you saved." As he gestured toward the crowd, the father and mother, still holding her daughter, no longer tearful, rushed forward, falling at his feet. "Thank you. Oh, I can never thank you enough. Truly you are the messenger of Messias! Never has any before traveled through the water like the fish! Never has any been brought back from death in the Morex! She is well! I thought she was dead. I would have taken her from you! But you brought her back from death!"

With this emotional exchange the crowd pushed forward, entirely surrounding Colin and the three guards, who were obviously feeling very uneasy. Colin squatted down beside the kneeling forms of the grateful parents. "Listen," he said, "I'm glad that I could help. But I'm not the messenger of Messias. I'm simply a stranger here and my clothing is a little different. That's all. Your daughter wasn't dead. I can't bring people back from the dead. Yes, she probably would have died, but we got the water out of her and I just helped her breathe until she could do it on her own again. You understand?"

From their confused looks, it was obvious that they didn't. Colin stood and reached down to help the parents up. The little girl smiled at him shyly from the comfort and safety of her mother's shoulder. But now the crowd was becoming animated.

"It's the messenger - the mantle bearer." The cry could be heard rippling through the crowd.

"The guards have him now!"

"What are they going to do with him?"

"Does he need help?"

"He has no right to the mantle! That's why the soldiers have him. They'll see that he's punished!"

"He saved Joyce and Scott's little girl! He's no impostor!"

The arguments were becoming heated and the guards were obviously wary now, circling, watching the crowd, hands on the hilts of their swords. The situation was rapidly building to an explosion point.

Colin leaned over to Halvor and spoke softly, "Give me a minute before you start lopping off heads, will you?"

Turning to the crowd, he yelled, "People of Riverton! Please! Be calm! I am with my good friend, Halvor, Arbor Guard of Salem. As you may have heard, I am scheduled to appear in Salem for my Evaluation five days hence. I am not the messenger of your Messias. I am simply a stranger here. Nor am I am impostor. The customs of dress in my land simply are different from those in Aidon. But please, be at ease, as the High Council in Salem has already made plans for resolving this matter. Now, please return to your homes. Let us pass, as our presence is required elsewhere!"

With that, he stepped forward boldly, having no idea which direction Halvor wanted him to go. A confused babble broke out in their wake, but they were allowed to pass. Halvor smiled with real humor this time, "You're getting better. You didn't use the hood this time."

Colin smiled back, running his fingers through his wet hair. "I hate that thing." He replied. "It messes up my hair."

The other two guards looked surprised at this exchange, but no less wary. "So where are we going?" Colin asked.

"We'll continue down river a short distance. We have our cart and supplies back in Riverton. One of the men will go back for it and then we'll head for Salem."

"Kind of early isn't it? I still have five days, don't I? Were you afraid I wasn't coming back?"

"Not me." Halvor shifted uncomfortably, "But there have been a lot of stories about you these past few weeks. The Council decided it would be best if you were in custody and in Salem. I have my orders."

"I haven't even been in Aidon these past few weeks. So whatever stories you heard, if they involved me, they were lies."

Halvor tried to reason with him, "I figured as much. But Colin, that's all the more reason for you to go to Salem now. If everyone knows where you are, it will put an end to the lies."

Colin shook his head. "Other people's lies aren't my concern. That's their choice. I'll be at the Evaluation, but there are a couple of things I'd really like to take care of first."

"That won't be possible." Halvor stopped. "We'll wait here. Laban, you go back and get our gear. Laban nodded, but the other guard shoved Colin roughly from behind, to get him to sit. Halvor whirled on the guard, but before he could reprimand him, a shrill whistle of rage split the air! Gisele! The moment Colin stumbled, she launched into battle, ears laid back, slashing hooves and snapping teeth! The guards yelled. Halvor was knocked flying by her charging shoulder. Laban fell, scrambling to get away from the enraged horse. The unfortunate guard who had shoved Colin caught both of Gisele's forehooves in the middle of his back as he turned to run. Before any of them could recover, Gisele wheeled, charging back toward Colin who threw himself into the saddle as she flashed by. He yelled back over his shoulder, "Sorry! I'll see you in Salem in four days! Promise!"

The only reply was a fading curse, he couldn't tell from whom. "Son of the Serpent! He was riding that thing! They said you can't do that!"

Colin kept Gisele at a dead run, getting distance between himself and the guards. They continued on until it was full dark. The twin moons rose, but this evening their light was cut by the scattered, high cloud cover. It was a beautiful night, but the light really was insufficient for safe travel - especially since he didn't know where he was going. Dismounting, Colin led Gisele down the trail, looking for anything that might get him off the main path. He finally found what he was looking for and followed a dim trail for several hundred yards until it led to a small clearing. He stripped the gear from the horse and turned her loose to feed. The blankets were soaked. Gisele hadn't stowed the gear very carefully before taking her swim. There was no point in exchanging his wet clothing for wet blankets, so Colin simply hung the blankets to dry and curled up in a hollow at the base of a large tree. Cold and wet, he didn't sleep well and so was up at the first hint of dawn painting the sky. Today was the Sabbath. If he was right, somewhere down river, on the opposite bank, should be the city of Sarepta, the main city of the 8th File. On his side of the river, but north of it, he should skirt Jordanon, the city of the 4th File. Due north of Jordanon, but a little to the west would be Tyber. Jorge and Miran's farm lay just west of there and that was his objective.

Colin's spirits rose with the sun which slowly dried his still damp clothing. He strung his bow and at a small clearing killed a fat woodchuck for breakfast. He was starved, having had nothing in almost 24 hours. He took the time to build a small fire and cook the woodchuck. It was large, but hungry as he was, there was nothing left by the time he was done. Fed, warm and dry, he felt immensely better and began to review the events of yesterday as he rode along. He had been angry yesterday, when he had jumped from the cliff to save the girl from drowning. Why wasn't anyone on the opposite bank doing anything? They were closer. But the woman, the girl's mother, she had practically been in awe. What had she said? Something about no one swimming - no, traveling through the water like a fish. So swimming was yet another thing virtually unknown here. Then the guards had shown up. What had happened while he was gone? What stories were being told about 'the mantle-bearer?' "That's the last thing I need right now." He told Gisele, "Somebody running around with a hood pretending to be me." Gisele flicked her ear in what Colin took to be a sympathetic manner. Whatever had happened, it was obvious that there were a number of patrols out looking for him.

The sun was beginning to set when he at last found a familiar looking stream flowing between wooded banks. He turned Gisele to follow its course upward. Soon they were back into the forest, following another dim trail. Just as it was coming on full dark, their path was blocked by a snake-rail fence. Colin recognized Jorge's hay meadow. He was back. Dismounting in order to create a lower profile in the light of the rising moons, he led Gisele the rest of the way. During the weeks he had been gone, the fields of grain had grown, now standing waist high and beginning to head out into the ear. They followed the path along the edge of the field, cutting through the thin band of timber to the barn. Gisele 'whuffed' softly, recognizing the barn and the corral that had been her home. Colin hesitated, but decided to take the chance. He stripped the gear from the horse and turned her into the corral, forking hay over the rail for her to feed on. He carried his saddle bags up to the shed where he deposited them. He was nervous. If the farm were occupied by guards, he would bring nothing but trouble. While he had every intention of going to Salem, he wanted it to be on his terms, not as some captured fugitive. He strung his bow and nocked an arrow before slipping silently from the shed. Approaching the door to the house, he turned loose of the arrow just long enough to rap softly.

The door suddenly flew open. Startled, he stood there awkwardly, feeling very foolish with a bow in hand, an arrow nocked, ready to fire. "Ah. Hi, Dalene. I wasn't expecting you."

"Colin! Oh, come in! I've been so worried about you!"

"You've been worried? About me?" He ducked through the door, slipping the arrow back into its quiver"

Dalene blushed, "Of course. We all have."

"Colin!" Elam rushed him, practically bowling him over. "You're back! I wasn't sure you'd come!"

Miran stepped forward, hugging him, "It's so good to see you again. The Lady Dalene is right. We have been worried for you."

Jorge's face split into a broad grin, "So! You survived!"

Colin felt at home here. The genuine warmth of these people made him feel almost like family. He smiled, "Yes, I managed to survive." Sobering, he asked, "Is my being here a problem? I can leave if this is going to cause you trouble."

Jorge waved a hand, "Trouble! Life is trouble. You do not bring it."

"We'll be fine. Come, sit. Are you hungry?" Miran asked.

"I'm starved," Colin admitted. "Meals have been hard to come by ever since I came back to Aidon."

Elam could hardly contain himself, "Came back? Then you did it? You really left? What's it like? Out there, I mean? Is it terrible, as they say?"

Colin smiled, shaking his head, "Elam, I saw the most beautiful country you can imagine and I didn't even scratch the surface of it. There were rivers, lakes and streams that just took your breath away. The plains roll on forever. A couple of days ago I was in a thermal valley - a place where the springs and pools coming up out of the ground are hot. Some of them are actually boiling and the colors around those hot springs were amazing - yellows, reds, blue. It was fantastic."

"Really? Hot water coming from the ground, without a fire or anything? How is that possible?"

Jorge laughed, "Elam, he's just having you on."

Colin smiled, understanding their disbelief, "No, Jorge. It really is like that. I've seen it before, back where I came from. It isn't all that far from here. I could take you there sometime if............" His voice trailed off, as his smile faded.

Miran relieved the moment, "Come, you must be tired. Sit here and I'll get you some food. We finished dinner, but there is plenty left."

The food was simple and delicious. He hadn't had the ingredients to make a decent soup in the weeks he was gone and having bread was an added treat. They waited patiently for him to finish. Well, Elam wasn't patient, but a continuous stream of warning looks from his parents caused him to wait anyway. When he was done, Colin said, "Elam, out in the shed I left my saddle bags - two bags connected together. Would you get them for me please?"

Elam dashed off and was back in a moment. Colin undid the lacing on the bags and began pulling out his treasures. "I have no idea whether these have value here in Aidon. In my land, these would be considered rare." He undid a square of leather which had been tied into a pouch to reveal his collection of sapphires and garnets. Even uncut as they were, the gemstones sparkled in the lamplight, their colors brilliant. Jorge whistled, his eyes wide. "Any one of them would purchase a farm, I'm thinking."

To Miran, Colin handed a large, dark red garnet and to Dalene, a beautiful blue sapphire.

"I know these stones, Colin and they are indeed precious. I do not think I have seen any so large. They're beautiful." Dalene said.

"They're yours." He replied.

Miran started at that, "No. It is too fine a gift, especially for me. I cannot accept it, but thank you. It is beautiful." Dalene nodded as well, both women extending their hands to return the gems.

"Elam told me once, that he was given a gift one time as well. I believe it was that knife I see on his belt. He tried to decline it, but somebody told him they were giving it to him because they wanted to – as a token of appreciation. Please accept them - as a kindness to me."

Dalene touched his hand softly, "Thank you. The value of the gift is in the thought behind it. It is kind of you to think of us."

Colin flushed at her touch. He hoped that the lamplight didn't show how red he was getting. Turning back to the saddle bags he pulled out another pouch, this one filled with the veins of gold he had cracked from the rotten quartz deposit he had found. Jorge whistled once again, his eyes wider than before. Colin handed one of the strands to Jorge and another to Elam, flakes of quartz still attached to the cracks and seams sparkled as they caught the light. "I thought you might think these are pretty. When you're done admiring them, feel free to have them melted down to make dectorals."

Elam stared, wide-eyed, before handing it back to Colin. "I have no need of such things. I am still here on the farm with my parents."

"Elam, we just went through this. Take it. Hang it on a string and admire it if you want. Melt it down and spend it. Save it. You're here now, but someday you'll want a farm of your own. Maybe this will help you get started. The gift isn't about what you need. I need to give you something - because you're my friend. You, all of you, are the closest thing to family I have here. You've all done so much for me, so please, let me do this little thing for you."

Impulsively, Elam threw his arms around him, "Then, we are brothers!"

Colin chuckled, "Well, you and I are brothers, but I don't think your mother and father are going to qualify as my parents!"

Jorge laughed. "No. We are brothers, also! But remember, I am the big brother. Well," he amended looking up at Colin standing a full head taller than he, "maybe I am the older brother."

Colin next unrolled his map, showing the features he had sketched in. Elam was fascinated by the map, especially the valley with the thermal features. Colin told of the mammoth, the huge buffalo and the great bears he had seen. He had to describe the mammoths, as they were unknown in Aidon.

"Weren't you afraid?" Elam asked.

"Of the animals? No. While I liked seeing them, I didn't really get close enough to make them afraid. They had no reason to want to harm me and I was careful, so there was no problem. The only time I was afraid was when I met the Anakims."

"Anakims!" Dalene interrupted. "But the giants are only in stories, myths!"

Colin shook his head, "They may be in your legends, but believe me, they are very much alive. In my land, Anakims are only in legend - mentioned in a book we call The Bible. In my land the mammoths disappeared a long time ago as well. But here, outside of Aidon, the Anakims and mammoths are both very real."

"It is said that the Anakims eat people. Is it true?" Asked Miran.

"That may actually be true. I don't know for sure, but the first one I met did seem to have some idea about eating me. We had a fight."

"You fought the Anakims? And won?" It was Jorge's turn to interrupt.

"I wouldn't say I won. His name was Gath and he was beating the snot out of me. I got lucky." He then proceeded to tell of his visit with the Anakims.

Dalene was dumbfounded. "I have access to the great library in Salem. There are fragments which mention these Giants, but none believe it is true. Even now, I can scarcely believe it."

"Well, it's true. But other than the Anakims, I had no trouble at all until I got back to Aidon. I ran into a patrol that was out looking for me. Then late yesterday I ran into Halvor, up by Riverton. He had two other guards with him and they were going to take me in. I just wasn't quite ready to go yet."

"Riverton! Late yesterday? But how could you get here so quickly then? It's impossible!" said Jorge.

Elam was so excited he was practically bouncing. "The horse! When you left here you were riding the horse! Do you still have it? Is it fast? Is that how you got here so quickly? You were on the horse?"

Colin laughed, "Settle down, Elam. Yes, Gisele is still with me. Yes, she is fast and yes, that's how I got here. I just need to leave before they catch up. I have an appointment in Salem."

Dalene paled noticeably when Colin mentioned Halvor. "You saw him, then. How did you escape?"

"Gisele," Colin shrugged. "I wasn't with her when they caught me. One of the guards got kind of rough and she took exception to it. Knocked all of them flying. In the confusion I managed to get on her and we ran. It should take them a day or so to catch up, even if they do come this way."

"They won't have to catch up. There are patrols in every town - or at least nearby. They all have orders to find you and take you into custody. There have been rumors of the 'mantle-bearer' practically since you left. Many of the people are becoming very excited, agitated, I guess. This is a dangerous time for Aidon and the Council decided it would be best if you were in custody, so they could put a stop to these rumors." Dalene didn't look at him at all while she spoke.

"What about you? Are you on patrol as well? To take me in?"

Now she did look at him, and the hurt in her eyes shamed him, "No. I came to see Miran. I admit that I thought you might.........." her voice trailed off.

"I don't blame you. You're right to protect your country. It's OK."

A smile flickered briefly at the corners of her mouth, "Yes. OK. You told me that before. OK."

Now he smiled, "That's right. It'll be OK. Now, we just need to decide what to do with me."

Miran interrupted. "Not tonight. You shouldn't be deciding anything right now. Tomorrow will be soon enough. Tonight, you need sleep. You look exhausted."

"I am at that. Is it alright if I sleep in the shed? I'd kind of like a roof overhead for a change."

"Of course, but we can make room in the house. You don't need to sleep out in the shed." Miran objected.

"No, the shed is fine. I kind of like it out there. It's quiet and I'm out of the way. But by chance do you have any soap? I used the last of mine a couple of days ago."

"Soap! Well of course! All you want. I'll get it for you."

Dalene looked at him seriously, "Will you be here in the morning?"

Colin smiled, "Dalene, I had to beat up an Arbor Guard and two other soldiers to get here. I'll be here. Good night."

The soft hay and warm, dry blankets felt like heaven. In a matter of minutes, he was sound asleep. He awoke sometime in the night to hear the steady beat of rain on the roof. The only thing that registered with him was that he was glad to not be out in it and immediately he fell back to sleep.

The night gave way grudgingly to a sullen, gray dawn. The rain ceased, but a light fog hugged the ground, the drifting wisps shrouding, then revealing shapes and shadows in the distance. Tired as he was, Colin still couldn't sleep once the light began to creep across the sky. He rolled out and made his way to the spring to wash and shave. He thought enviously of the hot spring where he had bathed a few days ago. It already seemed like a dream. After getting cleaned up, he went to feed Gisele. She was pleased to see him, prancing and tossing her head. He rubbed her down good, even though she really didn't need it.

By the time he finished, Elam came to call him for breakfast. Nobody seemed to be too anxious to start the chores for the day. It was as though they were all waiting for something. Colin decided that he might as well start. "Alright, so if I understand correctly, the Council at Salem wants to have me arrested - the sooner the better. Today is Second Day. That leaves three days until my Evaluation. I had planned to spend today and tonight here then go to Salem tomorrow. So, my first question……" he looked at Dalene, "Is that acceptable? Or do I need go to Salem today?"

She wrung her hands, "I don't know. I don't think that one day is going to matter. But if one of the patrols show up here, they'll certainly think it does."

"Alright. That brings me to my next question. Is my being here going to pose a danger for Jorge and Miran? Will they be punished if I'm caught here?"

Jorge snorted, "That matters not! You stay. Consequences we'll deal with as they come."

"Thanks, Jorge, but the risk is mine. I don't want you to have trouble because of me."

Dalene spoke, "I don't think so. It isn't like they've actually issued a warrant for your arrest. That would inflame those who think, or hope, that you are a true mantle-bearer. The Council would like this done quietly, I think."

Colin nodded, "Then let me ask this. Is there any advantage to any of you if you're the ones to take me into custody? The first patrol that almost caught me mentioned a reward."

Jorge was indignant, "They can take their reward and go hang! We'd not betray you!"

"Sorry, Jorge. I didn't mean it that way. I know you wouldn't, but I'm going to be turning myself in tomorrow anyway. If that can be worked to your advantage in some way, I have nothing against it."

"Advantage or not, I'd be arrested with you before I'd profit from it!"

Dalene shook her head, "No, I don't see any advantage to anyone from this. There's the reward, of course, but none of us want that. Anyone who brings you into custody will be popular with some, but there is probably an equal number who would feel animosity toward any helping to arrest the mantle-bearer."

"Alright. Dalene, I assume that you're going back to Salem. Will it harm you - hurt your station if you were seen with me?"

She straightened visibly and looked at him coolly, "I am The Lady Dalene. Neither I nor my station will be harmed by your presence."

"Last question then. May I ride with you tomorrow?"

She blushed as she glanced away. "I would like that."

With that discussion out of the way, the tension in the room dissipated greatly. Elam was anxious to show Colin the bow he had made and to demonstrate his ability as an archer. Colin said, "Sure, but could you give me a few minutes. I'd like to get your mother to cut my hair. I have an important appointment this week and I'm looking pretty ragged."

Miran responded, "Oh, I'm sorry. Today isn't so good for me. I promised Kath that I would come over. This soap business, you know."

Jorge opened his mouth as if to speak, but a warning look from his wife caused it to snap shut.

"But I'm sure," she continued, "That The Lady Dalene could take care of that for you." She handed Dalene the scissors, accompanied by a wink, as she slipped out the door.

Dalene blushed, "I really don't cut hair." She was furious at herself for blushing and at the amused look on Jorge's face. He'd caught on rather quickly. "Maybe Jorge could do it for you. I know he has sheep!" she added acidly.

Jorge could stand it no more and broke into open laughter. "Sheep! Aye, sheep I can do, but these big, clumsy fingers? Cut hair? No. No. I think you are better suited. Come, Elam. Someone must do the work today! We'll be back!" And with that he disappeared out the door.

Colin was oblivious to all this. Grabbing a chair, he sat down in front of her, "Thanks. I really appreciate it. I've been cutting it over the ears and a bit around the back with a knife. I'm afraid I've done a bit of a hack job on it. Probably looks like it was cut by beavers. It doesn't have to be perfect. Anything you do will be better than I could do myself."

Dalene hesitated, but couldn't see any graceful way out of the situation. She ran her fingers through his hair, trying to smooth it. It was so soft, very fine by comparison to hers, which was full and thick. Cautiously, she began to trim it. The top layer was so much lighter than it was underneath. Curious, she asked him, "Why is your hair like this? The end is lighter than near the root. I think it is lighter than when you left a few weeks ago. But the hair grows from the root, so how can it change color?"

He shrugged, "It just bleaches in the sun. You're probably right about it being lighter. I've been out in the sun practically every day since I left. Why? Doesn't your hair bleach?"

She shook her head, "No. We bleach cloth, to make it lighter, but I have never seen this done with hair. You have many different shades of hair. In Aidon, the hair is the same. Only when one becomes old, then sometimes there is gray as well. But many times one grows old and dies and always the hair is the same. Your hair is soft, like a child's. Not like mine at all." She was growing more bold in cutting as she talked.

"Let me see." She had worked around to the front of him as she cut. He reached up and stroked her hair. "I think you have beautiful hair. It's such a pretty color and still very soft. I like it."

She was blushing again and side-stepped away from his hand. "Thank you. But in Aidon, all of our hair is the same. If you like my hair, you would like any woman's hair as well."

"No. I don't think so. I think I would always like yours best."

She moved back around behind him, so he couldn't see how red she was. Her heart was hammering. Who did he think he was? Touching her hair like that! She tried very hard to be indignant, but a smile kept creeping at the corners of her mouth. Thankfully, he had become silent and remained so until she was finished. She looked at him critically. He did look better. "All done." She said.

"Thanks. You can leave the mess. I'll clean it up."

"No!" She was a little too abrupt. "I'll take care of it. I'm sure Jorge and Elam are waiting for you. Now go!"

He went. She carefully collected his hair, picking up a large cluster in her thumb and forefinger, holding it up to the light and admiring how it shined. Guiltily, she took a few of the clumps of cut hair and lay them on a sheet of linen which she folded over and put with her things.

Colin found Jorge and Elam down at the barn. Elam came running as soon as he saw him. "Colin! Come see my bow!"

Elam had done fine work. The finish was quite a bit better than Colin's bow. Jorge grinned sheepishly and showed Colin the bow he had just completed. "Kids shouldn't get to have all the fun." He explained. "I just finished a few days ago. Elam has been showing his bow around. Probably most of the boys and half the men in Tyber are making their own. I still can't hit a thing with it. Not sure if I could hit the barn if I was standing inside!"

"Watch me shoot, Colin!" Elam had set up target out back of the barn. He had done a good job with it, taking a dense clump of hay and tying it tightly with canvas strips. He backed off about 25 paces, and shot three blunt tipped arrows. Two struck the target, but the last one went wide, skipping across the dirt until coming to rest several yards past the target. "I always do that." Elam complained.

At Colin's prodding, Jorge fired three arrows as well. All three missed the target. "I aim, but I never seem to hit what I'm aiming at. I sight right down the shaft of the arrow. Doesn't seem to help."

"Try it again, but this time, instead of focusing so much on your aim, I want you to focus on the target. You'll line up on it naturally enough, but I want you to really focus on the target. Block everything else from your mind, from your vision. I want you to imagine. Picture it in your mind. See the arrow hitting the target before you ever turn loose of the string."

Jorge looked doubtful, but was game to try. Colin watched Jorge. He specifically didn't want to look at the target for fear of biasing the outcome. Jorge was sighting down the arrow and then Colin could visibly see him shift his attention. No longer was he looking at the arrow. Now he was looking at the target. He loosed his shot. Still, Colin didn't look, until Jorge let out a tremendous whoop and shook his bow in the air over his head. "I hit it! First time ever! I hit it! Let me try it again!" He did, twice more, with the same result.

Elam watched with growing excitement, "Let me try. It's my turn now."

Elam took hardly any time at all in aiming. Clearly, his focus was the target. Three arrows flew with scarcely more than five seconds between them. All three were clustered tightly in the center of the target. Elam was elated. "Can we go hunting tonight? Please? I think I'm ready now. Now that you showed me how to do it."

"Only if you can use the meat and only if you still need to protect your crop. As long as it's alright with your father."

Jorge was scratching his beard, "Aye, I suppose we could use the meat. But I'll check with your mother first, just to make sure." Turning to Colin he said, "Come, I've a thing more to show you."

They entered the barn. There in a neat stack were a dozen or more tanned hides. Two more were draped over a rail, drying in the cool shade of the barn's interior. Jorge grinned, "What with making leather, I've hardly time to tend the farming. I'm giving it up though."

Colin fingered one of the hides, "This is nice work, Jorge. Why are you giving it up?"

Jorge scratched his head, "Well, truth to tell, I don't much like it. I mean, it's alright sort of work, but I just prefer being outside. I may still do a bit on the side, but Baylor and Tunsten, they like it, and Faron, the harness maker in town, he's excited about it. Oh, maybe not for doing all the time, but they're better at it than me. I worked a bargain with them. I taught them what you taught me. I get a quarter share of whatever they make for the next five years. Half of that's yours. I can take it either in hides or torals. I hope that's alright with you." He looked worried.

"Fine with me. Tell you what though, you just hang onto my share for now. I probably won't need it for awhile."

Jorge nodded. "Thing is, this leather, it sure is tough. I spend hardly any time mending harness since I made it from leather. Look at my boots. I mean, the stuff is great. My feet are a lot drier, 'cause I keep 'em waxed, like you said. Not near so bulky either. I'm making a sheathe for Elam's knife – don't tell him though, I want it to be a surprise. I like using the stuff. Finding more uses for it every day. But I just don't like making it. Hope you're not mad."

"Not at all. You have something you like doing, that's great. If you can get someone else to provide the things you need to make your life easier, so much the better. You feel like you're getting a bargain, at a quarter share from both Tunsten and Baylor. They'll probably teach somebody else and work the same kind of deal. In the end, they'll make back what they're paying you and all of you will be happy. That is the essence of a perfect business arrangement. Everyone involved feels like they got good value. I'm happy for you, Jorge. I really am."

"Thanks. I've got one other thing to show you though. I think you'll like this even better." Jorge led the way over to his workbench and picked up a small wooden box. Handing to Colin he said, "Here, have a look."

Colin opened the box and found ten beautifully made, barbed fishing hooks. They were large, about a number 6 size he estimated, but with the size of the fish he'd been catching, they were just about right – at least for wet flies. "Jorge, these are perfect! Where'd you get them?"

Jorge looked extremely pleased with himself. "Traded for 'em. Tunsten had one of his lambs what died. Too bad, cute little thing. Anyway, just for practice he tanned it, like with the fur still on it. Came out pretty nice. He offered it and I took it as payment on what he owed me. Market day and that jewelry making feller from 9th File, up at Lasal? You wouldn't know him and he doesn't come here anyway, but he has a merchant what sells for him. Showed him that lamb fur and he was practically drooling over it he wanted it so bad. Figured to give it to his daughter for a present or something. Anyway, he didn't have anything I needed. Too fancy for me or Miran. But I figured that jeweler feller ought to be able to make us some hooks. Week later, next market day, sure enough he had 'em. Got 20 hooks. Figured by rights half ought to be yours."

"Thanks. I hope to try them out soon. I ate a lot of fish on my trip. Lost a few hooks as well. These are a lot better than what I had."

Jorge waved his hand, "Least I could do. I have to admit, first off I thought catching fish was crazy. I like eating 'em. But most the time it's the catching I really like. Don't know why, but it's kind of fun. Feller I got the hooks from, he ought to start selling them. Not too many catching fish yet, but Baylor and me, we showed a couple of friends. Think there might be a business there?"

Colin laughed, "It may take awhile, but yes, I think there's a business there."

Miran returned home in the late afternoon, looking very smug and pleased with herself. All she had to do was catch The Lady Dalene's eye and raise one eyebrow just a shade to have Dalene blushing. She was careful not to do it when anyone else was watching, for which Dalene was grateful. Miran had invited Kath and Baylor to dinner that evening. It was a crowded, but festive affair. Elam and his father went looking for a deer. A young buck with velvet covered antlers walked the edge of the grain field before they were even situated. Elam shot the buck, which bounded back into the trees only to collapse down by the creek. He was exceptionally proud of his achievement, but not nearly as proud as Jorge was of him. Venison, was the main course that evening.

After dinner, Kath announced, "Now, we've business to attend to. So clear off if you've no interest. Colin, you stay. The business concerns you."

Nobody left and in a moment a grinning Kath produced a small canvas bag and poured the contents out on the table. All of the coins were gold. "46 dectorals. Your share of the soap money."

Colin looked at the coins on the table, then at the smiling faces. "Thank you. But it's too much. I can't believe you made that much just from selling soap! But I really haven't earned it. I did hardly anything."

Baylor shook his head and growled in his gruff manner, "Don't be forgettin', we've made just as much and had it not been for you, we'd have made nothing."

Kath nodded in agreement, "The demand was more than what we could supply. So we've partnered with some of the women in the other cities - Rachel and Ruth over in Neims are making soap. They're in the 1st File. Rachel's sister Leah lives in Troas. That's the 7th File city. Her husband farmed over that way before he died. She just started. Sara and her sister Mara in Ramah are starting as well. They both live there, so that's two cities in the 2nd Order working with us. We made the same bargain with them as you did with us. We get one third of whatever they make. That's for five years and after that they get to keep it all. Is that alright?" She looked concerned.

"You don't need my permission. I think it's just fine. If you're happy with the arrangement and they are happy as well, who am I to complain? But this is still too much. I won't need all this in Salem. One way or another, I'm not likely to be there that long."

He wished he hadn't said it, for the moment the words were out of his mouth the mood of gaiety shifted. Everyone looked glum. Jorge tried to salvage things, "Oh, you'll be living high and fine. Salem is some city. You'll be staying at the best inns, eating the best food. You'll have a grand time."

Miran and Kath tried to smile encouragingly, but couldn't quite bring it off. Colin sighed, "Listen, I appreciate all that you've done. But I have to look at things as they are, not how I wish they would be. Maybe everything will go just fine. And if it does, I'll be back this way in a few days - a couple of weeks at most. However, the chances of things going as smoothly as we'd like are not very good. Am I right?" He looked around the room, his gaze finally settling on Dalene. She gave an almost imperceptible nod of her head.

"OK, so let's deal with reality here. From what you've told me, six dectorals should buy room and board at a decent inn for the better part of two months. That's what I'll take with me. I've still got some of what you paid me before. I'd like for you to split the rest. No, hear me out," he said, cutting off their objections. "Just hold it for me. Invest it if you like. I'll not question your judgment. So far you've shown better business sense than I ever have. If things go well, I'll be back at some point and you can return it. If not, consider it my gift to you. Will you do that for me?" They slowly nodded.

"Thanks. Now, cheer up. I want you all to know how much I appreciate everything you did for me. I owe you my life. I have had more fun - felt more alive - these past few weeks than I have in years. I wouldn't trade these weeks for anything."

Miran and Kath hugged him then. Baylor pounded him on the back with a gruff, "You'll do alright. You'll see."

"Elam, could you give me a hand out in the shed for just a minute?" Colin asked. Elam followed him out the door. Once inside the shed, Colin opened his saddle bags. "There are a couple of things I'd like you to take care of for me." He handed Elam a rolled up piece of leather and a small pouch.

"What are these?" Elam asked.

"This is the map I made - the places I went to when I left Aidon. It is a long way from complete, but it's a start. One day, I'd like to take you to the hot springs. But if for some reason I can't, you'll have the map. One way or another, you'll go there someday. The pouch contains the sapphires I brought back. I tossed the gold I found in with it. I don't want your folks to know about this for now. Put these someplace safe. Someplace where they will stay dry and protected, but not in the house. Put them someplace where you know exactly where they are at. Someplace you could go to years from now even, but not someplace that anyone else would think to search."

"But why? I don't understand," Elam said.

"Just to be safe. The gold and sapphires are valuable, of course. Anyone would want them if they knew about them. But the truth is, the map is far more valuable. The map shows where I got them and there's a lot more out there than these few I brought back. More importantly, something just doesn't feel right to me. I can't explain it. But it's like this whole society has been destroying anything that's new. Anything they don't understand just disappears. It's like there is so much emphasis on this Compliance thing that everyone just falls in line. Nobody explores. Nobody invents. The culture is stagnant. This map represents change. Exploration. I'm afraid if the wrong people knew about it, they would tear this farm apart to find it and destroy it. Maybe I'm just being paranoid. But I'd like you to keep this stuff safe for me. If for any reason I don't come back, you'll have these. <u>Having</u> doesn't do any good. If I don't come back, they're yours to <u>use</u>. Do you understand?"

Elam nodded, "But you <u>will</u> come back, won't you? We're going to the hot springs together, right? He looked like he was trying very hard not to cry.

"I'm planning on it, Elam. But whether I do or not, you remember what I said about using this stuff. I was told a long time ago, 'Things are made to use. People are made to love. Don't ever mix the two up.' You use these. One last thing." He handed Elam three dectorals. "These were left from what Kath paid me before. I want you to take this and see if you can get Tunsten or someone to sell you a horse."

"I can't do that!"

"Sure you can," Colin grinned. "How else are we going to go see those hot springs?"

It was getting late and Colin didn't feel like going back to the house. He was tired. Mentally he checked off all the things he needed to get done. He couldn't think of anything else. Just then there was a soft knock at the door. Before he could get up, Dalene slipped in, closing the door behind her.

"Are you alright?" she asked.

"Just tired. But yes, I'm OK"

She smiled at that, "OK. Good." Her smile faded. "I never did thank you for the gift - the fox fur and the soap you sent with Halvor. The fur is beautiful. I had no idea that fox is so soft. And the soap was wonderful. How did you know that lilac is my favorite flower?"

"I didn't. But I've always liked lilac myself. It just seemed to suit you."

"I like the way it makes me feel so clean. And it makes my skin smell nice, too. Smell," she commanded, holding out her hand.

He took her hand, inhaling the faint fragrance on her wrist. "It's beautiful. It does suit you."

She blushed, pulling her hand away. "That was one reason I wanted to come back here. I had almost used up the soap you sent me and I needed to get more." She hesitated before continuing, "Colin, why don't you just leave? It's not too late. You survived for weeks out there," she gestured. "You could leave here and never come back. You could live!"

He shook his head. "I know. You suggested that before, remember? I'm scared. No, that's too strong. Put it this way, I'm concerned about what may happen. But inside, I still feel calm, because I know this is where I'm supposed to be. This is what I'm supposed to do."

"How can you possibly know that? You can't! Can't you get it through your head? They're going to destroy you!"

"I think I've gotten it through my head. Once I accepted that as a very likely possibility, I was OK with it. There are worse thing in life than death. I don't know how to explain it so you'll understand. I've been thinking about this, praying about it, for weeks. This path is the only one that I can contemplate and feel at peace with. I'm still nervous. Maybe even afraid. Being afraid isn't necessarily a bad thing. But if we only do things when we aren't afraid and if we never do things that we fear, we become slaves to that fear. We never really live. All I can tell you is that underneath the fear, is this sense of calm. I just keep thinking, 'All will be as it should be.' But," he added, "That doesn't mean I'm going to like it."

She looked at him silently for a long moment before saying, "I think you are a fool."

"Good. Then you won't miss me."

A full five seconds passed as she glared at him. "I have a weakness for fools!" She snapped, then spun quickly and was gone.

Chapter 16   Evaluation

The new day dawned clear and bright. Breakfast was hurried and subdued. Nobody was in the mood for conversation. Elam and Jorge harnessed the horses to The Lady Dalene's cart. Colin packed his few belongings, pausing to look around the shed and wonder if he would ever see it again. He spent a moment at the doorway, looking out at the beautiful trees and lush fields of grain before going to fetch Gisele. She nuzzled his shoulder as he saddled her and slipped the halter over her head. He patted her affectionately and led her out of the corral and up to the house. Elam was just finishing loading The Lady Dalene's belongings onto the cart. She would leave first taking the path along the edge of the field until it connected with the road into Tyber. Colin would take the forest trails, circling the town to meet up with her on the road to Salem. Miran hugged him, tears glistening in her eyes. Jorge clapped him on the back, saying, "We'll be seeing you in a couple of days anyhow. We're coming to the Evaluation."

"No. If you want to go to an Evaluation, you go to the one in Tyber. I don't want you within ten miles of Salem," Colin said flatly.

Jorge bristled, "Now look. You're a friend and we're coming!"

"Yes, you're my friend and that's exactly why you're going to stay away. There's no good that can come of you being there. If the Council has already made up their mind, the only thing that can happen is that you get thrown in with me."

"There's worse company!" Jorge growled.

Exasperated, Colin said, "Jorge, you can't do this. I know you want to, but that is beside the point. You have to think of Miran and Elam. Your farm. I may come through this fine, but maybe not. If not, the only legacy I have to leave behind is the things I taught you. Don't throw that away. Please. As a favor to me, promise that you won't go anywhere near Salem - not until this thing is settled. Not you, not Baylor, not your families. Promise Jorge!"

Jorge was beaten and he knew it. "Aye. You've my promise. But don't you be throwing your life away to make a point! You promise me that at least!"

"No. I'll do my best on that score. But whatever happens, I don't want you being angry about it, OK? Whatever happens, it will be alright. You take care now."

With that, he swung into the saddle. He turned at the edge of the trees to look back and wave. The three of them waved back. As he disappeared, Jorge hugged his wife to him and said, "I'd never given much thought to what a messenger might be like. And I sure never imagined someone like him. But now, I can't seem to imagine a messenger who isn't like him. Curse it all! Why couldn't he be the one?" It was almost a cry of despair.

Miran said nothing, as the tears silently rolled down her cheeks.

They had agreed to meet at the second bridge east of Tyber. While the cart moved more slowly, Colin would have the more difficult route, following the trails through the forest. Still, he arrived almost a quarter of an hour before he heard the cart coming. Traffic on the road was light at anytime and at this early hour, they had seen no one. They rode along in silence, slowly covering the miles. By late morning, Dalene informed him they were about half-way to Salem. They stopped to rest the horses in a large meadow a hundred yards or so from the road, shielded from view by a thin band of trees. Dalene was petting Gisele and asked, "How did you get her to let you ride? No one has done that before. Everyone who tried was thrown off. Ages ago, the Councils decided it was too dangerous and after that nobody ever tried."

"Where I come from, people used to ride horses all the time. They used them to pull carts like yours and wagons as well. I guess there are some horses that won't let you ride, but mostly it's a matter of patience and training. Gisele was pretty good about taking to the saddle. She wasn't broken, she was trained for riding. I think she did half the training herself."

"What's it like? Riding a horse, I mean."

"Some horses are kind of rough. They bounce you around a lot - especially if they're trotting. Gisele is the smoothest thing I've ever ridden. Almost like flying."

"I would like that, I think. Flying," Dalene said.

"I can't help with flying, but if you'd like to ride, I think Gisele and I could arrange that."

"Really? Oh, I'd love that." Her eyes sparkled with excitement.

Colin mounted up and kicked his foot free of the stirrup so Dalene could use it. She was too short, so he grabbed her hand and hoisted her until she could gain purchase and swung up behind him. She giggled like a little girl as Gisele paced around the meadow. "This is wonderful!" she cried, "But it's not like flying!"

"No, we're just taxiing to the runway," Colin said, even though he knew she didn't understand. "Get ready for take-off." He pulled her arms tight around his middle to indicate that she should hang on. Then he dropped the reins and booted Gisele in the ribs, shouting, "HA!"

Gisele launched like an arrow shot from a bow. If Colin hadn't clamped a hand over Dalene's arms wrapped around his waist, he would have lost her at that first leap. Gisele stretched out, her head low and neck fully extended. She loved to run! Her rhythm was so smooth there was no difficulty keeping the saddle. Dalene squealed in delight as they flashed across the grass, the wind whipping her hair back and her skirt flipping up to reveal a shapely leg above the top of her canvas boots. Colin pulled Gisele to the left, taking them on an arcing turn around the perimeter of the field, still going flat out. Dalene laughed and buried her face in his shoulder, squeezing her arms tighter around him. Gisele looped past the startled cart horses, still wanting to run, but Colin gradually reined her in, bringing her back down to a walk. Dalene slid off and threw herself backwards into the soft grass, laughing. "That was fantastic! Oh, I just wanted for it to never stop!" She hopped up and kissed Gisele right on the forehead. "Thank you, Gisele! Thank you for taking me flying!"

"Lucky horse!" Colin muttered, just loud enough for Dalene to hear, making her blush.

She looked at him, smiling, "And thank you, Colin. That was wonderful. If I had a horse, I think I would just ride away forever! I loved it."

"It was my pleasure," he said sincerely. He slid off Gisele and they walked back to the waiting cart. They gave Gisele a few minutes to feed, while they munched on the bread and cheese Miran had packed for them.

Once on the road again, Dalene seemed more relaxed. "Sometimes you speak strangely," she said. "Like when you said that where you come from, people 'used to ride horses.' Like they don't anymore. But you ride."

"I didn't ride very much before I came here. Where I'm from, we have different transportation now. Machines. They're stronger and faster than horses, so we don't use horses much now. Mostly on some of the large ranches, but that's about it. Other than for pleasure riding."

"Machines instead of horses? I cannot imagine it. But I understand pleasure riding. Will you take me again? Sometime?"

Colin smiled, "I'd be more than happy to. But that reminds me, I'm not sure what I'm going to do with Gisele while I'm in Salem. Do you know where I could keep her?"

"There are stables attached to the Praetorium. That's where we're going. You can keep her there."

"Thanks. I don't want her ignored. She's kind of social. Would you be able to look in on her for me? Just pet her a little and maybe take her out for a ride if I'm not able to?"

The mood instantly changed and Colin was sorry he'd verbalized his concern. Dalene looked at him, understanding in her eyes. "Yes, Colin," she said softly. "I will look after Gisele for you. Until you are able to."

Before long, they began to encounter other travelers on the road. Between Colin's appearance and the fact that he was riding a horse, these encounters were always accompanied either by stunned silence or shouts of amazement. Dalene retreated behind her fortified wall. She was once again, The Lady Dalene. No expression showed on her face. She looked neither to the right nor the left. She looked regal and aloof. Colin, on the other hand, looked like a country bumpkin rubber-necking at everything he saw. Cart loads of chickens in wooden cages. A wagon filled with rolls of coarse canvas and burlap. The colors on the fringes of the clothing were varied. Some were dull and faded, while others were brilliant and vibrant. Some travelers were obviously not content to declare their File affiliation with an unobtrusive border on their garments, but were instead dressed from head to toe in black or pink, orange or lavender. As strange and fascinating as these sights were to him, he was far more astonishing to the local citizenry.

"Is that the mantle-bearer?"

"That's the impostor who wears the mantle! The one they're searching for!"

"Is that The Lady Dalene?"

"The Lady Dalene captured the impostor!"

"Why is he riding that horse? I thought you couldn't do that!"

They left a wake of confusion and dissent as they traveled.

"Do not stop," The Lady Dalene cautioned him. "They will be confused, possibly fearful or angry. Even if you stop with those who are friendly, soon, others will come. A mob will form and it could become dangerous. If not for you, then for those in the crowd. Please, Colin, you must trust me on this. Act as if you neither see nor hear them. It is best for now."

He tried, but it was all so interesting, he kept turning this way and that in the saddle, trying to take in everything. People would point and he would give them a brief nod and a quick smile as he rode by. Fortunately, Dalene was leading the way in the cart and was unaware of how much interaction he was having with the local people - he hoped.

At length, they came in sight of Salem. If Riverton had been impressive, Salem was absolutely magnificent. It looked to be the finest representation of medieval architecture that Hollywood could produce - or so he thought. It was amazingly clean. The walls were at least 30 feet high, constructed of huge stones. Pennants and flags snapped briskly in the breeze from the tops of the towers. The road had gradually widened as they got nearer to the city. It was well-graded rather than rough and rutted. Word of their approach seemed to have raced ahead of them, for here the main thoroughfare was lined with gawking people, pointing and arguing at their approach. At the city gate, their way was blocked by a dozen or more soldiers in two ranks. The front rank all bore swords, thankfully sheathed, while the rear row held menacing looking pikes. With no option, The Lady Dalene drew to a halt. Immediately, they were flanked on either side by another 20 guards.

"Not looking good," Colin thought to himself.

"I am The Lady Dalene, 12th File of Salem. We are going to the Praetorium. Remove your men and let us pass."

The captain stepped forward a half a pace in front of his men. "You may pass, Lady Dalene. We have orders to take this man into custody."

"He is in custody. My custody! Now, remove your men. You may follow us if you wish," she replied.

"Aye, we'll follow you then." As he moved to the side, he glanced to his right and gave a quick nod. Too late, Colin saw the blow coming. He never even managed to get a hand raised to blunt the impact and was too slow attempting to duck. He was hammered from the saddle by one of the pikemen. The world swam as he looked up from the dusty road. Somewhere a woman was screaming. It sounded like Dalene. He tried to speak. His mouth moved, but no sound came out. Then everything went black.

He hovered at the edge of consciousness for a long time. His head felt like it was split open. Gingerly, his fingers tried to explore his skull, but it was wrapped in some kind of bandage. He decided to leave it alone for the time being. It was dark, the only light filtered in from a dim corridor some distance from the bars of his cell. He was lying on a filthy straw mat. A bucket sat in one corner. There were no other amenities. "Kind of like that hotel outside of Allentown," he joked. The brief laugh made him catch his breath as the wave of pain slammed through his head. Very cautiously, he sat up. His vision blurred, but cleared after a moment. "No," he murmured, "Not looking good." He knelt to pray.

The Lady Dalene was struggling mightily to control her temper. Her father was out of the city and not expected to return until the following day. No one knew where Councilor Krainik was. She was facing Councilor Lucinda Yearsley of the 10th File, the highest ranking member of the Council currently available. While she was outranked, technically, by Councilor Robins and Councilor Nalin, both of the 12th File, they served on the Council of the city of Salem. Anything to do with the mantle-bearer, however, was, after all, a matter for the High Council of Aidon and so Councilor Yearsley was given more sway than her position would ordinarily warrant. The Lady Dalene considered her to be a pompous, arrogant boor, a fact which she was having difficulty hiding at the moment.

Councilor Yearsley had never liked The Lady Dalene. Not that anyone really did, she was sure. The Lady of Prophecy, after all, had the potential to destroy Aidon! It was difficult to like someone like that. Besides, she was young, slim and beautiful - all the things which Councilor Yearsley was not. And, since Councilor Yearsley held such an inflated opinion of herself, she despised anyone who shared none of her characteristics. She was extracting particular pleasure from this confrontation.

"But my dear, you well know that the High Council gave orders for this impostor to be taken into custody. Why the Regent himself supported this."

"Yes, we've covered that already. He was already in custody - my custody. We were on our way to the Praetorium when he was needlessly assaulted by the guard! My father agreed to have him taken into custody, not beaten and thrown into that filthy dungeon! I want him out of there where he can be cared for and I want it done now!"

"That's simply not possible," Councilor Yearsley replied stiffly. "Until either the Council meets or the Regent returns to clarify the orders, the impostor will remain where he is!"

The Lady Dalene's voice dropped dangerously, "The purpose of the Evaluation is to determine whether or not he is an impostor. Until that time, he is to be regarded and treated as any other citizen. That is in accordance with the laws of Aidon. If you violate that law, I will see to it that you are removed from the Council. Am I clear?"

Councilor Yearsley paled, but tried to brush it off, "Of course, my dear. Merely a slip of the tongue. There's just so much confusion about this fellow, you know."

Taking a deep breath, The Lady Dalene turned her attention to Councilor Robins and Councilor Nalin. "This man has been charged with nothing. Yet he has been injured and is being held in one of those filthy cells. Isn't there anything you can do? Keep him in custody, by all means, but he may need a healer. He shouldn't be in that place!"

Robins and Nalin were both reasonable men. Her father respected both of them, she knew. But all they could do was shake their heads sympathetically. Councilor Robins said, "I'm sorry, Lady Dalene. If he were in the city prison, we could order him released and I would do so immediately." He shot Councilor Yearsley a defiant look. "But we have no authority within the Praetorium."

Councilor Yearsley looked smug.

Just then, there was a commotion outside the door, which swung wide as Councilor Krainik rushed in. "You have him! I heard the news as soon as I got back to the city! Congratulations! Lady Dalene! So good to see you!" He bowed deeply. "I was informed that it was you who brought him in. Excellent! I'm sure your father will be most pleased."

She nodded to him, "Thank you, Councilor Krainik. Perhaps you can be of assistance in this matter. You are correct, it was I who brought in the mantle-bearer. I had assured him that he would be accorded every courtesy. Instead he was attacked by the city guard without provocation. He has been taken from my custody and imprisoned in the Praetorium dungeon. I would like to have him secured in more comfortable quarters and he should be examined by a healer. Unfortunately, Councilor Yearsley seems quite incapable of meeting these requests."

"Really? Why, Lucinda, the man is our guest, not a criminal! Surely we can accommodate him in quarters in the east wing, can we not?

With the guard barracks there, I think he can be secured quite nicely. Don't you agree?"

Councilor Yearsley was flustered. She hadn't expected this. "Why, yes, I supposed so, Lijah. I mean, if you think it's alright then I guess we could have the prisoner moved."

"Come now, Lucinda," Krainik chided, "He's not our prisoner. Our guest will think badly of us! Why don't you ask the captain to have him transferred immediately. I will see to it that my personal healer visits him within the hour! There, all settled?"

The Lady Dalene nodded to him, "Thank you Councilor Krainik. I would like to ensure that our <u>guest</u>....." and she emphasized the word, "is given every courtesy. He is to be confined, but please ensure he is made comfortable."

"Of course. Now, if you'll excuse me, I'll tend to the matter at once," he turned and left.

******

Colin was lying on the straw mat when the guards came for him. There were four of them. "On your feet. You're being moved."

He struggled to stand, weaving unsteadily on his feet. The guard unlocked the door. Two other guards entered the cell, one grabbing him by the arm on each side. Half carrying him, they hustled him down the corridor and up several flights of stairs. His eyes still wouldn't focus. The light made his head hurt even more than before. They seemed to walk a long ways. Had he not been supported by the guards, Colin would have collapsed. At length, they came to a well-lit corridor, stopping at the very end before a heavy wooden door. One of the guards pushed the door open and he was practically dragged inside. The moment he was in, they turned and left. He heard the lock snap shut after the door closed.

Looking around the room, he saw a bed over in the corner. Staggering over to it, he eased himself down gently, afraid he was about to be overpowered by yet another wave of nausea. It passed and he slowly lay down on his side. The room was fairly Spartan, but it was clean. The bed was soft. That was all that registered before he slipped into unconsciousness. The next thing he knew, gentle hands were unwrapping the bandage from around his head. His eyes flew open to see a wrinkled, elfin face smiling at him kindly. "Awake, are you boy? Nasty bump you got there. My name is Latham. I'm a healer. I'm going to see what we can do to fix you up."

Noticing Colin squinting against the light, he asked, "Does the light hurt your eyes, boy?"

Colin tried to smile. He failed. "The air hurts my eyes. My head. It just plain hurts." His voice was weak. Croaking.

"Hmmm. Busted the skull I'm guessing. Well, time will take care of that. Let's get you something for the pain." He left, but was back in a moment. "Here, can you sit up enough to drink this? That's it"

Colin struggled to sit, but only made it up onto his elbows. Latham supported his back and held a cup to his mouth. It was bitter, nasty and he shuddered involuntarily. Latham chuckled. "Pretty bad, isn't it? I made it myself, but I'm glad I don't have to drink it! Figure if the cure is bad enough, folks might be more careful about getting hurt! Come on now! Finish it up."

He finished the medicine in the cup and gratefully lay back down. Latham was fussing with his head, as he drifted into sleep. Hours later, it seemed, he thought he heard voices. He tried to see who it was, but it felt like his eyes were glued shut. He could barely make out light from a dim lamp. One of the voices sounded like Dalene, but it was little more than a low murmur and then everything was blackness again.

When he next awoke, pale light was filtering in through a high window above his bed. The chirping of the birds outside sounded like it must be early morning. He lay still, luxuriating in the comfort of a bed. He couldn't remember when he'd last lain in a bed. It felt wonderful. In fact, he felt wonderful. Suddenly, he remembered Latham. Then he remembered his fractured skull. Gingerly, he probed the back of his head. It was bandaged and it hurt when he pressed too hard with his fingers, but otherwise, he felt fine. His eyes were able to focus and the nausea was gone. He sat up. Then he stood. He couldn't believe how much better he felt. There was a cup and pitcher on a small table in the corner. The water tasted delicious as he let it trickle down his parched throat. There was a towel and basin on a stool in the other corner. He washed, wishing for a razor and cake of soap. He did the best he could to clean himself up. Unfortunately, his stint in the dungeon had wreaked havoc on his clothing. It was filthy.

Colin sat on the bed, resting his back against the wall. Some time later, he heard the door rattle as the latch was withdrawn. He recognized Latham, wearing a cream colored cloak with a light blue fringe, indicating his station in the 9th File. He was carrying a tray. "Ah, you're up. Good lad. How are you feeling this morning?"

"Much better. Thank you. You're Latham, the healer. I remember that. Thank you for fixing me up."

"Glad to do it," Latham said as he set the tray down on the table. "Are you up to having a bite to eat? Need to get your strength back. Food's the best medicine for that. Too many folks forget that."

"Thanks. I'm starved."

"Good. Good. I'd suggest you drink the medicine first. It will help with the pain, but it won't make you sleep, like what I gave you last night. It won't taste any better though!" he laughed. "But you take the medicine first, then eat. Food will help take the taste out of your mouth. Come on! Eat. I'll be back." He then slipped out the door.

Colin sat at the table. Latham was right. The medicine didn't taste any better. But the food was good. Huge strawberries, a small pitcher of cream. Some kind of fried meat, like pork, he thought, a plate of eggs and a small loaf of bread. He didn't think he could eat all of it, but he did.

The door rattled again and Latham entered. "Well, boy, nothing wrong with your appetite," he said dryly.

Embarrassed, Colin said, "Sorry. I was hungrier than I thought. And the food was very good."

Latham nodded, "Aye, they've got good food here. Now, let's have a look at you."

Latham unwrapped his bandaged head, 'hmmming' and 'tsking' as he did so. "Well, you're a good hard-headed boy. I don't think any permanent damage was done. More's the wonder. Now, what shall I call you?"

"I'm sorry. That was rude of me to not introduce myself. I think half the town calls me 'the mantle-bearer.' The other half calls me 'the impostor.' You could choose one of those, but I'd be happier if you would call me Colin. I'm Colin Ericsson, formerly of Kalispell."

Latham's eyes crinkled in humor. "Colin it is then, though I'll still call you 'boy' when the mood strikes me. One of the privileges of age, you know. And I have to confess, I was just having you on. The Lady Dalene had already told me your name, but I admit, I was curious if you'd lay claim to another. You didn't. More's the pity."

"Dalene? Is she here?"

"Aye. She's here boy. Where'd you think? This is her home, after all."

"Here? This is her home?"

"Well, not here precisely. I mean here in the Praetorium. They've got you in the east wing, near the guard barracks. You've two guards outside your room at all times. There'll be another pair outside your window as well, I'm thinking. The Regent's family has quarters in the south wing. For that matter, all of the Councilors have quarters there."

Colin looked at Latham curiously, "The Regent's family? So is Dalene related?"

"Related? Of course she's 'related.' The Lady Dalene Tregard is the first and only daughter of the Regent, you fool. Related indeed!"

"I'm sorry. I didn't know." Colin did feel the fool, flirting with the Regent's daughter. No wonder she kept looking at him as if he were something she had scraped off her shoe. She was just seeing to the affairs of the kingdom, or whatever they called it. He shook his head.

"Now, boy. It's me who should be sorry," Latham said. "It's obvious enough, even to an old man like me that you're a stranger here. Just that everyone in Aidon knows The Lady Dalene. Most fear her. Some hate her. But they all know her. I'd no call to speak to you that way."

"Hate her? But why? I think she's one of the kindest people I've ever met."

"You think what you want, but you best keep those thoughts to yourself. Not my place to tell you about her. She'll do that if she's of a mind to. But for what it's worth, I'm agreeing with your thinking. More's the pity. Now," Latham continued, "Let's see what we can do about getting you cleaned up. You're a right mess and you stink. A bath is what you're needing! You'll be wanting to put your best foot forward tomorrow, for all the good it'll do."

Colin grinned, "Latham, we really need to work on your bedside manner. But in this case, I agree with your diagnosis. So lead on to the bath!"

Latham rapped on the door and one of the guards opened it. Latham gave them an airy wave, calling to Colin as though he were a dog, "Come, boy. Let's get you cleaned up!" Colin followed and the guards fell in behind him. They were tough, capable looking men. While Colin had a good eight inches on them, he would have bet that either of the two had a good twenty pounds on him and none of it was fat. Down the corridor they turned left, descending a flight of stairs before continuing in the original direction they had started. Another left took them into an intersecting corridor, at the end of which was a bath house. A half dozen copper tubs lined each wall of the room. There was a doorway on each end. Colin could see two guards flanking the door at the opposite end and the guards who had accompanied him from his room took up position on either side of the door through which he had just entered. The room was empty except for the tubs, one of which was filled with steaming water. "Now, boy, you just dump your clothes there on the floor. Someone will be along to pick them up and get them cleaned for you. In the meantime, you get cleaned up and I'll find you a robe. Oh, and you may be wanting this. A lady said to give it to you." He reached in his pocket and held out a ball of soap.

Soaking in the tub was a complete luxury, except it was about four inches too short to sit in comfortably. But with his knees bent, Colin slid down into the steaming water, leaving just his eyes and nose above the surface. He carefully scrubbed his injured head and ducked under the water to rinse his hair. Afterwards he just sat and soaked, dozing until the cooling water roused him. Latham's timing was perfect. He came in with a large, rough towel and a soft robe and left them on a stool near the end of the tub. The robe was conspicuous for its lack of color or adornment. Colin could see where a fringe had recently been removed. He wondered what color it had been. He tried to be careful as he dried his hair, but any contact with his head still hurt. Even so, he felt much better once he was cleaned up.

Latham came back in and Colin asked, "Is there any chance I can get shaved?"

Latham nodded, "She said you'd be asking." He produced Colin's knife. "You're to be allowed a shave, but you'll have an audience. If you make the audience nervous, they'll be likely to run you through!"

Latham led the way to another room where a polished metal mirror hung on a wall over a basin of warm water. Two guards stood with swords drawn while he shaved. Latham watched him curiously. "A strange custom. And do you do this every day?"

Colin shrugged, "Not every day, but most. I just never got used to a beard. Maybe if I could grow one as nice as yours, I'd give it a shot, but mine never looked nearly so good."

Latham laughed. "To each his own. My head be good for nothing but growing hair. Yours at least is good for stopping a pike!"

After shaving, Colin surrendered the knife to Latham. They retraced their steps back to his room. Colin felt conspicuous, still wearing only the robe. But either there was very little traffic in these corridors, or they had been cleared, for he saw no one except his escorts. At the door, he was shown into the room. "Now, boy," Latham said, "Why don't you just lie down and get some rest. You're feeling pretty good now, but you still took a heavy blow. You rest and I'll be back later."

"Certainly a pleasant sort of jailer," Colin thought. He dozed for awhile, awakened some time later when he heard the door being unlocked. It was Latham and he had his clothes, nicely cleaned and dried.

"Bunch of superstitious idiots. You wouldn't believe how difficult it is to get someone to wash a cloak like this with a hood on it. You'd think I was asking them to wash the Serpent! Here. You get dressed. You'll be having a visitor and then going to dinner. Lucky boy, you!"

Colin dressed quickly. It felt good to be in his own things again, but he hoped they would let him keep the robe. It would be nice to have something to wear while he washed his clothing. He barely finished dressing when the door latch rattled again, but instead of Latham, it was Dalene who entered.

Colin jumped to his feet, "Dalene! I'm glad to see you. Are you alright?"

Momentarily, she looked perplexed at his concern, after all, it was she who was here to check on him. She smiled, "Colin! Yes, I'm fine. But you............Latham says you're doing much better. Does your head cause you much pain?"

"Not much. Latham did a good job." He paused, looking at her. She was different somehow. Here, in the Praetorium she seemed more distant. More regal. Was that it? He could sense a tension in her that he had been unaware of before. The pause became awkward.

"Well, then, if you're feeling up to it, I suggest we go to dinner." As they exited the room, two guards wheeled and led the way while two more fell in behind them. There was no conversation.

At length, they arrived in a large dining hall where a number of tables were occupied, but the room fell silent as they entered. Colin could feel himself blushing, feeling highly conspicuous. Every eye in the room was on him. Dalene led the way to a small table to one side of the hall, as the room erupted in whispered conversation and covert glances in their wake. Several people were seated at the table. They all arose at The Lady Dalene's approach. "May I present Gareth Tregard, Regent of Aidon and his wife Beatrice Tregard." Colin bowed deeply to each of them, drawing a look of interest from Beatrice. She was a striking woman, about the same height as Dalene but stockier of build. Her hair was very dark, as were her eyes. Colin would have guessed her to be in her late forties, though she might have been younger.

"I'm honored," Colin said. "Forgive me, but I don't know the proper protocol for addressing you."

The Regent smiled, "We are called many things. Even more so when we are not present, I fear. My wife is Beatrice. You may call me Gareth, Councilor Tregard or Regent, as you prefer."

The Lady Dalene continued with the introductions. "Here we have Councilor Lijah Krainik, High Councilor of the 11th File. Councilor Krainik was most helpful in getting you transferred from your cell to your present accommodations. He also arranged for his personal healer to see to your injury."

Colin bowed once again, "Thank you, Councilor Krainik. Latham has aided me greatly. And I also thank you for the change of quarters. The present ones are much more comfortable."

Krainik nodded, smiling thinly, "Let us hope the former will not be needed in the future."

"Now that was rude," Colin thought. He didn't much care for Krainik. He seemed too smooth, to the point of being oily. Something about him just didn't feel right. But as he obviously held power here, Colin smiled and nodded politely.

"Next," The Lady Dalene continued, "We have Councilor Lucinda Yearsley, High Councilor of the 10th File. It was she who first made you welcome."

Colin caught the message immediately.

Councilor Yearsley's jaw clenched, a red flush appearing at her neck. "A harmless misunderstanding. I do hope you weren't inconvenienced too much?"

Colin nodded to her, "Not at all. It was an experience which more people ought to have - at least once in their lives." He smiled in wide-eyed innocence, looking directly at her as he said this and was rewarded by seeing the anger flash in her eyes and erase almost immediately. "Another one to be careful of," he thought. She was very good at controlling her temper, but it was obviously there and easily ignited.

Continuing the introductions, The Lady Dalene said, "Finally, we have Councilor Dean Garmon, High Councilor of the 9th File. These are the Councilors representing all of the Files of the 3rd Order in Aidon." She emphasized this last and gave Colin a warning look.

Colin bowed to Councilor Garmon, who eyed him carefully. Not so much with hostility, as with a certain wariness. Colin actually found this open caution refreshing. "Here," he thought, "is a relatively honest man."

The introductions concluded, they were all seated, with Colin placed at the far end of the table, opposite the Regent and his family. Seating continued by rank, placing Councilors Yearsley and Garmon on either side of him. Servants wearing 1st Order colors served the dinner. The food was as good as it was plentiful. There was little in the way of conversation during the meal. A selection of fruit was served afterwards and Councilor Krainik asked, "Colin, is it? So tell us, where is it that you are from?"

"The city where I last resided is called Kalispell. It is a small town, much smaller than your city of Salem, but perhaps larger than Tyber. Those are the only two cities I have visited in Aidon, so that is all the reference I can give you."

"Really?" Krainik asked, "I had understood that you were recently in Riverton as well."

Colin shook his head. "I passed that way a few days ago, but I only ever saw the city from the opposite bank."

"Yet you saw fit to assault two of our Arbor Guards and one of the city guards while you were there!"

Colin smiled, "Me? There must be some mistake. While I did meet a couple of guards, I personally never touched them. Nor did I raise any weapon against them. I do recall some confusion with an animal there by the river, but since I was not under arrest or actually charged with anything, I took my leave, conducted my business and then came here to make the appointment which was set for my Evaluation."

Councilor Yearsley spoke up immediately, "Yes, I'm sure you're looking forward to that."

"Actually, I am." Colin replied. "I'm unfamiliar with this custom. I had never heard of it before. I was able to witness an Evaluation in Tyber two moons ago, but as a spectator, there was very little that I could actually learn from it. I expect that tomorrow will be far more instructive."

The Regent, Councilor Tregard, laughed at that. "I'm sure it will be, Colin. I wonder, who will receive the most instruction? But enough of this talk. Tomorrow is time enough. This evening is social. Strictly social." He gave those seated at the table a hard look. "So let us relax. Now, if you will excuse me, I have other matters to attend to." Everyone rose from the table as the Regent excused himself, followed moments later by Councilor Krainik and Councilor Yearsley.

Beatrice got up from the table. Colin immediately arose to his feet as well. She came over to him, saying, "I fear these dinners drag on too long. I am tired of sitting. Shall we walk?" She took him by the arm as she spoke. Colin caught a look of alarm on Dalene's face as her mother led him away. Councilor Garmon and Dalene fell in behind them, followed by two guards. The conversation in the room once again died, only to be resurrected in furtive whispers as they passed by. Beatrice led him onto a broad balcony overlooking a spacious courtyard, brilliant in the fading light with manicured flower beds, lawn and shrubs. She inhaled deeply, gazing out over the garden, "I love the smell of the flowers in the evening, don't you?"

"I do," he replied, inhaling the fragrance.

She turned to look at him. "My, but you are a tall one, aren't you?" Her hand reached up to finger his hair. "Forgive an old woman, but I have been wanting to touch this all evening. My, but it is amazing!"

Dalene was appalled, while Councilor Garmon looked as if he were about to laugh. "Mother!" Dalene hissed, "Stop that! Leave him alone!"

Beatrice just looked at her daughter, smiling, "Oh come, dear. Don't tell me you haven't wanted to feel his hair. Here. Feel this, unless you already have. Isn't it pretty? It's so fine and soft, almost like a little baby. Not," she added, "that anyone is likely to mistake <u>him</u> for a baby!"

Colin was blushing, but laughing at the same time, "If any old women want to feel my hair, I'll certainly forgive them, but until then, you help yourself. I really don't mind. I have to admit that since I've been here, I've seen pretty hair that I could hardly resist myself, so who am I to begrudge you?"

Between the comments of Colin and her mother, Dalene was now blushing furiously and Councilor Garmon had given up trying to hide his amusement. All in all, the ice was well and truly broken.

"Alright, now that I've gotten that out of the way - but I may come back to it," Beatrice warned, "Tell me about yourself, Colin of Kalispell."

"I'm not sure what you'd like to know."

"Well, let's start with where you're from. Kalispell. Where is that? Tell me what you do. Are you a farmer? A tradesman? And what about your family? Mother? Father? Brothers and sisters?"

Colin smiled, "So just pretend like we're old friends and you want to know what I've been up to, is that it?"

Beatrice smiled back, "That would probably be a good start."

So Colin began to tell about himself. The fact that he couldn't tell her exactly where Kalispell was seemed to bother her. She was fascinated when he told her that where he came from, variations in hair coloring was common and that women often changed the color of their hair practically at will. "Oh! I would love to be able to do something like that!" Beatrice said. Just think of what your father's reaction would be!" She laughed and elbowed Dalene who was staring at her mother as if she had never seen her before.

Beatrice was sympathetic when he told of the death of his young wife, followed by that of his parents, reaching over to touch his hand, compassion filling her eyes. She was intrigued when he told her that he was a chemical engineer, as both words were unfamiliar to her. "And what is that?" she asked.

"An engineer is a person whose job is to create things. He applies physical laws, natural principles to make a tool or a process or a machine that is useful. I specialized in chemical processes, so I was a chemical engineer. There are other types of engineers. A mechanical engineer would design or make useful mechanical systems - machines," he explained.

"So you do this work with what you call chemicals, to make new things?" she asked.

"That's right. It isn't much different than cooking - baking. You add certain things together in specific portions. You put these ingredients through a process, like cooking."

"So this is what you do when you make soap?"

"Yes. Oh, you heard about that, huh? But yes. We simply mix the correct amounts of the different components, treat them in a specific process and make something useful from it."

"And that is your trade? To make new things which are useful?"

Colin nodded, "New things, or improve existing things. More often the creative process is a series of improvements rather than some totally new invention."

It was Beatrice's turn to nod. "I think that is an admirable trade. We could use more of that around here."

She looked at him intently and seemed to come to some kind of decision, as she nodded her head once again. "Very good. Thank you, Colin of Kalispell. I enjoyed listening to you talk. We must do this again sometime, but now, you must forgive me. I am tired - the curse of old age you know - so I shall retire. I bid you goodnight."

Councilor Garmon accompanied her and the two guards who had been hovering discreetly in the background now approached to stand directly beside Colin. "I think that's a hint that it's time for me to retire as well."

Dalene led the way. She shook her head and said, "I apologize for my mother. I've never seen her like that."

Colin just smiled, "Nothing to apologize for. I certainly wasn't offended. I got a kick out of her."

Dalene was alarmed. "She kicked you? I'm so sorry! I didn't see! Were you injured?"

"No. Sorry. Wrong word again. That's just an expression. Some things don't translate very well. I just meant that she is a pleasure to talk to. I enjoyed her company."

"Ah. Like OK? You got a kick, but everything is OK? Yes?" She smiled.

He smiled in return, but then sobered. "Dalene, do you know what happened to Gisele? I'm worried about her."

"She's fine. They confiscated all of your belongings, but I was able to get Gisele placed with my Father's horses. She likes me to pet her, but I think she misses you. Hopefully she will be back with you soon."

Having reached his room, one of the guards opened the door for Colin. Dalene watched as he was locked in then returned to the south wing. But she didn't go to her quarters. Instead she went to those of the Regent and knocked firmly on the door. She was surprised when her mother opened the door instead of one of the servants. She entered the room, glaring at her mother.

"What was that all about?" she demanded.

Her mother looked at her innocently, "What was what all about, dear?"

"Don't play games with me, mother. You know exactly what I'm talking about. That. With Colin. Why the interest?"

"Why, he seems like such a nice young man. I just wanted to get to know him a little."

"There are lots of nice young men around, mother, and I've never seen you show even half that much interest in any of them. So what are you up to?"

"I'm not up to anything, dear. Maybe I just find this one to be interesting. You have to admit, his hair………." Her voice trailed off with a sigh. "Maybe I've never shown any interest in any other nice young men because my daughter had never shown any interest in them."

"Mother!" Dalene was appalled. "I'm not _interested_ in him! I can't be! You know who I am! _What_ I am! I'm simply doing my duty to help sort out the confusion over this mantle-bearer! A mantle-bearer, mother! For the first time in my life, or your life for that matter! That's _all_ I'm doing!"

Her mother simply shrugged, toying with a pillow. "I expect that if he's a messenger from Messias, then Messias will probably take care of things with minimal direction from you. And if you're _not_ interested in him, then maybe you _do_ need to spend some time playing with his hair."

Dalene closed her eyes, gaining control before speaking through clenched teeth, "Mother, for the last time, I am not interested in him. Not like that. I _am_ The Lady of Prophecy and I _will not_ yield my heart, even if I were interested! I will _not_ be the instrument which destroys my father. Destroys Aidon!"

"Lady of Prophecy!" Anger smoldered in her mother's eyes. "Scraps of parchment! Fragments of words! All we have are bits and pieces! We have no prophecy that's worth anything! For four thousand years we've turned the daughter of the Regent into a nightmare to haunt the dreams of children! In all that time the only thing that stupid prophecy has accomplished is to destroy the life of one beautiful young woman after another, and it tears my heart out to see it doing the same to my daughter! Isolated! Feared! Never given the chance to ever become truly connected with others! I hate that prophecy! I don't believe it for one minute! I came to know the Last Regent's daughter, Larissa, too late, but a kinder, lovelier woman was never born! While she lived, like everyone else, I bowed to that horrid prophecy! I avoided her. I feared her. We all whispered about her. And when she died, we all said how nice it was that it wasn't she. That she wasn't the one who fulfilled the prophecy. If that prophecy came from Messias, I think he will see to its fulfillment when he chooses. But I don't believe what those 'wise old men' pieced together has more than a vague resemblance to what the prophet said four thousand years ago. It's been lost, just as so many other things have been lost. And until Messias sees fit to send new messengers, it will remain lost and worrying about ancient words that nobody really understands isn't going to change it! And since you want to know, I am interested in this particular young man, because he is a mantle-bearer. Whether by right or as an impostor, I cannot say, but I have prayed to God night and day that He would send a messenger, because we cannot go on like this!"

Dalene was shocked. She had never heard her mother speak with so much anger and emotion. Her mother sat, her face in her hands. Dalene went over to her and wrapped an arm around her shoulders. "Mother," she said softly, "You mustn't speak like that. I am what I am. I can be no more and no less. Perhaps you're right. Maybe there is more to the prophecy than what we have. But for now, it's all we do have. We can't just throw it away. It's alright. But please, you must promise me to never speak of this again. Even as the wife of the Regent, you would be taken before the Council. They would use the Compulsion, Mother. Not the Compliance. It would be the Compulsion. A part of you would be gone. I can bear everything else, but I couldn't bear that. Promise me?"

Her mother looked at her and smiled sadly, "I have never said such things to anyone else. But I too, am what I am."

******

Colin awakened early. What he termed, 'the dawn chorus' was just warming up, the birds chirping incessantly signaling that sunrise was about a half hour off. He had watched the nearly full moons pass briefly across the high window of his cell the night before. It had taken him a long time to go to sleep. Today was his Evaluation. He wondered if he would still exist as a thinking, acting entity by the end of the day. Every moment suddenly seemed precious. The chirping of the birds, sometimes so annoying, was a performance of symphonic proportions today. As the first rays of light painted the high ceiling in his room, he marveled at how perfectly beautiful it was. A new day. A gift of opportunity. He spent a long time with his prayers this morning.

He heard the door being unlocked and expected to see Latham. He was surprised when Halvor entered, bearing a tray of food.

"Halvor! It's good to see you. Are you mad at me? Did I get you in trouble?"

Halvor regarded him coolly, setting down the tray, "I am not angry. There was some embarrassment regarding your escape, but it was not trouble."

"I am sorry about what happened. Really, I am. But I had some things that I had to do and since I wasn't exactly under arrest, well, I just felt like I needed to do them. Were either of the other guards hurt?"

Halvor was surprised at the sincerity of the apology, "The one who struck you, Dolman, was badly bruised, but no bones were broken. I apologize for him striking you. Those were not my orders. Had you resisted, I had authorized whatever force necessary. Had he not struck you, I don't think your horse would have behaved as it did and you would never have had an opportunity to escape. He has been reprimanded. So what important things did you need to take care of so badly that you felt you had to leave so abruptly?"

Colin smiled, "Just some personal stuff. In case I don't get the chance to take care of it later."

Halvor nodded, "I understand. I might have tried to do the same if I were in your place." It was quite an admission, coming as it did from the Arbor Guard. "I've brought you some food. You should eat."

"No thanks." Colin said. "I'm not really hungry. I'm fasting today, actually."

"Fasting?"

"Yes. Going without food for a period of time. It weakens the body, but strengthens the spirit. Figure I could use a little strength today. But please, if you'd like to eat, go ahead."

Halvor shook his head. "Thank you, but no. I've already eaten. I have been assigned to accompany you today. I will be both your guide as well as your guard. As you are unfamiliar with the Evaluation, I will be with you to explain things and answer any questions, if you require it."

"Thanks. I really appreciate it. I know it's not like we're exactly friends, but I do appreciate what you've done for me."

Halvor looked at him curiously, "It was my assignment. But," he added, "It was an assignment which, for the most part, I found interesting. Is there anything you need before your Evaluation?"

"Well, I'd really like to shave first," Colin replied.

Halvor looked at him, appraisingly, "Have you any other unfinished personal business you plan to attend to before your Evaluation?"

"No. I think I've done everything I need to."

"In that case," Halvor said as he flipped the dagger from its sheathe, extending it to Colin butt first, "You may shave." He smiled as he said it.

Colin completed his shaving and a few moments later the door was unlocked. Halvor looked at him and said simply, "It is time."

A company of four guards again escorted him. The hallways were cleared and they marched at a quick pace, stopping before a large wooden door. One of the guards looked back at Halvor, who nodded and the guard opened the door, standing aside. Halvor escorted Colin into a huge hall. "This is the Great Hall of the Praetorium. Ordinarily, the Evaluation would be held in the city square. In fact, the regular Evaluation will probably start there shortly. Your case," he continued, "is of special interest. It will be conducted by the High Council of Aidon. Evaluations concerning the High Council are usually held here."

People lined the balconies along the two floors above the one on which they stood. In addition, there were rows of raised seating on either side of the Great Hall, similar to stadium seats. Halvor marched Colin forward, not quite to the center of the Great Hall. Unlike dinner the previous night, there was no silence at his approach. If anything, the noise became louder as people stared and pointed. Colin tried to keep his face expressionless, his eyes straight ahead. Two seats were set in the middle of the hall. Halvor indicated that Colin should sit in one and he sat in the other. At their feet, centered in the Great Hall, a geometric design was embedded in the marble floor. It was a series of connected hexagons. A single hexagon was located in the center, with additional hexagons adjoining on each of the six sides. Four more hexagons were located at the flanks of the

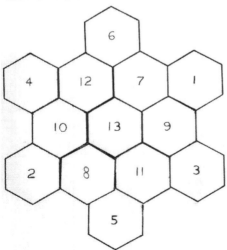

pattern, making 13 in all. Each box had a number inscribed in the center of it. All the even numbers were on the left and the odd numbers were on the right. Number 13 was in the center. On either side of this pattern were six large, plush seats. Thrones really, Colin thought.

Halvor indicated the seats, saying, "The Examiners - the High Council, in this case - will be seated there. The odd numbered Files will be on the left and the even numbered Files will be on the right."

A single row of perhaps

twenty raised, plush seats was set on the floor behind the Council seats. Set well back behind this row were several rows of raised stadium seats, already filled with spectators.

Halvor pointed to the geometric pattern in the floor at their feet. "In Tyber, you saw the Evaluation Box. Notice that the shape is similar, but instead of only two Boxes, here there are 13. Usually only two Boxes are occupied, but it is possible for all 12 of the Council to participate." He shook his head. "Usually that is not a good thing." He continued, "This Box is called The Ruling Box of Aidon. Because more individuals can be brought into play, this Box has much greater power - more capability. In the other cities, more people can be brought into play, but they must make physical contact with a person standing inside the Box. But the power is never as great as it would be if they were inside the Box. Once a person is inside the Box, they are isolated from everything on the outside. A very few people can use the Compliance over short distances, but the effect is always diminished. Outside the Box, it is usually done with physical contact. But without physical contact, no one who is outside the Box can see or reach one who is inside the Box. Even if you form a chain, reaching to one inside the Box, the further removed from the person inside the Box, the weaker is the effect. With the Ruling Box of Aidon, with twelve Boxes all focused on the one in the center, the power is very great, especially since the High Council is involved. One from each File has a more powerful effect than twelve from one File."

"How does it do that? Why would that be more powerful?" Colin asked.

Halvor shrugged, "Nobody knows how the Box works, or even who made them. They have been with us forever. In the long ago, many things were attempted. What I am telling you is everything we know. You see the pattern? Four Boxes do not touch the one in the center? It doesn't matter. Even if one person stands on the opposite side of the pattern from the other person, the effect is the same. It is just like they were in adjoining Boxes. Except for the center. When every Box is filled, all of the others focus on the center. The council can always find the true-self of the one in the center. That is the only one they can see. They cannot see each other, even though they know they are there. Like I told you, it is usually very bad if they fill all of the Boxes."

The room suddenly became hushed and Halvor touched Colin's arm, a jerk of his head indicating that he should look. The twelve High Councilors were filing in, each gowned in an ornately adorned robe in the File's assigned color. The black and gray of the 1st and 2nd file sat nearest Colin, while the lavender and purple of the 11th and 12th File were furthest away. After the Councilors, several other individuals filed in, taking their seats in the single row behind the Council on each side. Colin saw Dalene and her mother enter and sit on the end behind the Regent. Dalene was wearing a cream colored gown fringed in rich purple, with a beautiful purple scarf at her throat. A woman wearing a deep purple robe came forward to a point some distance from the geometric pattern in the center of the hall. Halvor nudged him and said, "That's Sofrina Fairfield. She's the Council's Barrister General. You watch her. I think she's fair, but she's tougher than a boiled cowhide."

She was middle aged, slender and short, but had a powerful voice. The acoustics in the hall were amazing.

"People of Aidon!" she began, "This being the 6th moon of the 4011th year of the reign of the Councils, I do hereby call this Evaluation into session! The High Council of Aidon has met this day to consider the matter of one Colin Ericsson, purportedly of Kalispell, a city unknown in Aidon. The individual in question is accused of the following:

"One: Failure to wear the colors of any File on his clothing in accordance with the laws of Aidon.

"Two: Failure to openly declare his File when questioned by a representative of the High Council of Aidon, said representative being The Lady Dalene Tregard. This also constitutes a violation of the laws of Aidon.

"Three: The wearing of forbidden clothing, namely, wearing the hooded mantle indicating position or station as a messenger of Messias, in violation of the laws of Aidon.

"Four: Using said mantle in the role of an impostor to generate unrest and insurrection among the people of Aidon, also a violation of the laws of Aidon."

She paused. The noise in the hall had grown with each of the charges she had listed. Colin's heart had sunk. Accused? He was just supposed to be here for his Evaluation.

Barrister Fairfield resumed, "I will remind the gallery, this once, you are permitted in these proceedings strictly as a matter of courtesy. You will remain silent, or I will have this Hall cleared." She glared around the room before continuing, "Because items three and four cannot be suitably addressed before items one and two are resolved, we shall commence with the Evaluation of the accused. Arbor Guard! You will escort the candidate to Box 13 in the Ruling Box of Aidon!"

Halvor took Colin by the arm, surprisingly giving him a reassuring squeeze and an almost imperceptible nod. Colin allowed himself to be led to the center hexagon, hearing the sudden chatter from the spectators which was instantly silenced by the glare of Barrister Fairfield.

"The Council of Aidon calls for Councilor Samuel Tomias of the 1st File. Please take your position, Councilor."

Councilor Tomias, in the black robe, took his place in the Box inscribed with the number 1.

Barrister Fairfield began again, using words similar to what Councilor Linape had done at Elam's evaluation. "We adjure Compliance in all things! Begin!"

Colin looked over at Councilor Tomias, who had closed his eyes. Remembering what he was supposed to be doing, Colin closed his eyes and tried to 'see' Councilor Tomias. The instant he reached out, he was stunned by the incredible ribbons of color weaving and flaring all around him. Immediately he keyed in on a single bright ball of light nearby. He simply knew that this was Tomias. As he had done at Elam's evaluation, it seemed as if he flitted all around this ball of shimmering, shifting color. But it wasn't the ball that intrigued him, it was the ribbons of light which continually shifted around the ball. Colin followed the ribbon to other balls of light nearby. "Tomias' wife." He thought. He followed two parallel ribbons, shifting and shimmering. They led to two other balls of light. Colin was certain these were Tomias' children - a boy and a girl. As quick as thought, he was back at the light which was Tomias' true-self. He made no attempt to touch it, remembering the nearly disastrous effect that had resulted when he had reached out to 'touch' Examiner Besalaman at Elam's Evaluation. He retreated back to his own self and not knowing what else to do, he opened his eyes. He had no idea how much time had elapsed. No sooner had he opened his eyes than Councilor Tomias did the same. His face was white and there were beads of perspiration dotting his brow. There was a low hum of whispering from the gallery. The Lady Dalene was looking at him very intently.

Tomias spoke, "I'm sorry, Barrister Fairfield. I cannot find the candidate's true-self."

The room exploded in an uproar. Barrister Fairfield was screaming for the gallery to be cleared. Soldiers marched in from all quarters, ushering the crowds out as quickly as they could. It took several minutes, but at last everything was quiet. Only the High Council and the dignitaries seated behind them remained. Glaring, Barrister Fairfield whirled on the unfortunate Councilor Tomias. "What do you mean you couldn't <u>find</u> him!!?!"

He was stammering, "Just that. I closed my eyes. I looked. There was nothing. I'm sorry. That's never happened to me before. He just wasn't there."

Halvor was looking at Colin speculatively. Beatrice seemed on the verge of smiling. Colin stood feeling very confused.

Barrister Fairfield turned away for several long moments. "Very well. You may be seated." She turned to address the Council. "The objective of the Evaluation is to establish Compliance. Compliance is established when the Candidate bows to the Examiner in the Evaluation Box. Under the law, if the Examiner cannot get the candidate to bow, then the candidate proceeds to the next level of the Evaluation. By tradition, we have always expected the Evaluation to conclude when either the Examiner or the candidate bows. However, that is tradition and not specified by the law. It is my recommendation that we proceed, according to law and continue until the candidate bows, at which time we will have established his File and we can move on to address the other matters."

Councilor Tregard looked at the Council and asked, "You have heard the recommendation of the Barrister. What say you? Are we agreed?"

A chorus of "aye's" echoed in the chamber, indicating unanimous consent.

Barrister Fairfield spoke, "The Council of Aidon calls for Councilor Kori Stanger of the 2nd File. Please take your place Councilor."

When she had done so, the Barrister gave her prescribed invocation, "We adjure Compliance in all things! Begin!"

Once again, Colin closed his eyes and instantly keyed in on the light which was Councilor Stanger. Following the ribbons of light which emanated from her true-self, he traced these undulating pathways, finding a husband, a grown son and a grandchild. He followed a particularly bright strand to Kori's mother. It fascinated him to see these connections and to know how they linked one individual to another. Still, he made no effort to touch Councilor Stanger's true-self. As before, he opened his eyes and almost instantly the Examiner did the same. Her lip was quivering, as she spoke softly, "I'm sorry. I cannot see him at all. He isn't there."

Low murmurs were heard around the room. Barrister Fairfield had a tight set to her jaw as she bit off her words, "Thank you Councilor Stanger. You may be seated. But this changes nothing. We will proceed and he will bow. The Council of Aidon calls for Councilor Arlena Linape of the 3rd File. Please take your place Councilor."

Councilor Linape was pale and biting her lip even as she came forward. Colin almost felt sorry for her. The Barrister announced the start of the Evaluation, as before and the result was the same. This continued on through each successive Councilor, Rabin Tyber of the 4th File, Slayton Lev of the 5th and Dalba Saleen of the 6th. Arabella Brett of the 7th File was in tears before she even left her seat and Viktor Samson of the 8th File took his place threatening to make Colin bow even if he had to use a sword to do it. But each time the result was the same. They simply couldn't see him. And each time he closed his eyes, Colin could trace the connections of each Examiner, to their spouse and family, sometimes to close friends. He learned that there existed more subtle strands of light, delicate connections that led to more distant friends or neighbors. The threads, he realized, had always been there, but he had been so focused on the brighter, shifting and undulating paths of light he had simply overlooked these more subtle, but equally beautiful gossamer filaments. And then, with Councilor Garmon, he made a new discovery. Once he saw it, he could hardly believe that he hadn't seen it before. Almost as though it were a longer wavelength, he could discern a dark but distinct tendril of light emanating from each of the true-selves he examined. But these darker strands were different. For as one dark band crossed with that from another self, the two would twine, even when Colin could discern no relationship between the globes. Every globe had this strand of dark-light or long-wave light and they all twined together, becoming thicker and brighter as more and more strands linked and twisted together and they all led off in the same direction. He suddenly realized that this was the twining tendril that had become the fascinating cable of light he had followed at Elam's Evaluation. He hadn't seen the individual strands, just the massive, growing conduit after hundreds or even thousands of these tiny filaments had twined together. No sooner did he think this, than he began to race along it, seeing it grow and become brighter, weaving and undulating into the distance and in the distance, he saw that same brilliant tower of light that he had seen before. What was it? It wasn't a 'self,' of that he was certain. It was immense and seemed to be the source, rather than the destination, of the cable of light he had followed. He raced along the cable, closer and closer to this huge glowing column, when suddenly he stopped. He could go no further. There was no barrier that he could detect. He was simply incapable of moving any closer to the source of the light. In frustration, his eyes flared open and he was back standing in the Ruling Box of Aidon. Everyone was staring at him. He got the impression that he had been gone for some time.

Barrister Fairfield announced quietly, "We will recess for 15 minutes." Halvor stepped forward to escort Colin from the box. "What are you doing?" he hissed.

"I'm having my Evaluation. How do you think it's going so far?"

"Colin, don't mess with this," Halvor whispered. That last time, Garmon must have been standing there with his eyes wide open for at least ten minutes before you. Nobody spoke, because they're not supposed to until both the Examiner and the candidate have their eyes open. But everyone was fidgeting. I thought Fairfield was going to come in there and slap you. What's going on?"

Colin shrugged, "I don't know. It's my first Evaluation. It sure isn't like what I expected. Can I have a drink of water? I'm really thirsty."

Halvor eyed him, but beckoned a guard to bring some water.

"I suppose a trip to the privy is out of the question."

"You can hold it." was Halvor's reply.

Barrister Fairfield called them back into session, having Colin resume his place in Box 13. Before they started she asked him, "None of the Examiners has thus far been able to see your true-self. What do you see? Are you able to find them?"

Colin shrugged, "So far I haven't gotten any of them to bow to me."

She looked as if she would question him more, but turned suddenly and called for Councilor Yearsley. The look she gave Colin as he took his place was pure poison. "I will find you," she whispered, so quietly that no one else could hear. "When I do, it will not be the Compliance you will feel."

At the Barrister's cry of "Begin," Colin closed his eyes. The light before him was a massive, rippling, ugly thing. It seemed to suck light from the surroundings. The only connecting trace Colin found, took him to Councilor Krainik, but he could detect no relationship there. He found this very strange. Something kept flitting at the edge of his consciousness, almost like a gnat in the dark. It was something he could almost hear, almost feel, but could never see. It was an irritant and he kept swatting it away. He cut himself loose from the ugly thing which was Lucinda Yearsley and explored other lights in the room. There was Halvor and he was amazingly, connected to Gareth Tregard and his wife Beatrice. Father and mother! That meant Dalene was his sister! For some reason, this made Colin extremely happy. He followed the strand, almost a cable really, which linked Halvor to his sister. The glow of her true-self radiated in a constant, clear, brilliant luster. It seemed larger than it actually was, because there were a thousand, no, a million filaments of light radiating out from it in all directions. He thought it was the most perfectly self-contained source of energy he had ever seen. It was so beautiful he wanted to touch it. He reached and just brushed the surface, before he caught himself, remembering what had happened to Examiner Besalaman. Instantly, he opened his eyes in fear, "What have I done!?!" his mind screamed. Desperately, he jerked his head to look at Dalene. She was sitting perfectly still, staring at him curiously. Relief coursed through him as he glanced at Councilor Yearsley whose eyes flashed open with hate, "I found him! I almost had him! Every time, he just slipped away! But I can have him! Let me try again!" She was apoplectic.

Colin could see the confidence in Councilor Krainik's eyes as he took his place. If the 10th File had almost had him, what chance did he stand against one of the 11th File? With each Examiner, however, Colin's confidence had grown with each contest as he saw more of and became more familiar with this previously unimagined plane of connected lights. It didn't make sense, he knew, but for some reason, they couldn't seem to find his true-self. As the contest began, Colin felt the same annoying attack at the fringes of his perception, but he kept pushing it back. If anything, Krainik's light was even uglier than Yearsley's had been. Instead of a clean, steady glow, his orb pulsed and shifted, dark ribbons coursed across its surface. It emanated little, but seemed to absorb much. One strand drew Colin's attention. It was dark, but incredibly intense. He followed it. It led a long distance, further, he thought, than any other connection he had followed. But at the terminus, he didn't find a light at all. It was as though he was staring into a black hole. It had color and texture, though Colin couldn't say how. It was as if he were looking at different shades of darkness - an entirely new spectrum. It felt evil and he instantly retreated back to his starting point. He didn't like being here with Krainik, so he opened his eyes to a malevolent stare as Krainik opened his.

Only one Examiner was left. The High Councilor of the 12th File, Gareth Tregard, Regent of Aidon. Colin nodded to the Regent as he took his place. Gareth regarded him calmly and returned the nod with a slight smile. As Barrister Fairfield intoned, "We adjure Compliance in all things! Begin!" Colin closed his eyes.

He faced a glowing orb of tremendous intensity. Its light shone clear and bright. Colin brushed so close to the surface it felt as if he were on fire. It was magnificent. Emanating from this glowing ball, were dozens, no hundreds, even thousands of glowing strands. As Colin looked more closely, he could see even more. Faint, but still distinct threads, radiating off in all directions. And there, there was the subtle, dark, long-wavelength cord, twining with all of the others, heading off to the source of light. He traced the connection to Beatrice, Halvor and Dalene. These were not undulating, shifting bands, but solid beams of light anchoring him to his family. The sheer strength of the man all but took Colin's breath away. He opened his eyes, glanced at The Lady Dalene and her mother, they were both staring at him intently. Dalene's mouth dropped and her mother began to smile. He quickly shifted his gaze back to Gareth Tregard and bowed slowly and deeply, from the waist, brushing the top of his head against the chest of the figure facing him. The room dissolved in a mixture of exultant cheers and cries of relief. The Regent's eyes opened and he looked at Colin curiously, a faint smile playing at the edges of his mouth, all but hidden by his beard. He gave Colin a brief nod and returned to his seat as the Barrister yelled, "The 12th File of the 3rd Order of Aidon welcomes Colin of Kalispell and acknowledges him as having passed the test of Compliance and is now entitled to the privileges of the 12th File!" She looked at him appraisingly before continuing, "The hour is late. The Council will resume tomorrow to consider the matters of the wearing of the mantle and promoting sedition in Aidon. We are adjourned!"

Chapter 17   Trial

Halvor escorted Colin back to his room without a word. A tray of food was sitting on the table when he arrived. Not until the door was closed and locked behind them did Halvor speak, "Are you alright?"

Colin was surprised. That was about the last thing he had expected. "I'm fine, I guess. I'm exhausted. I can't believe that took the entire day."

Halvor shook his head, "I think the longest examination I've ever watched took less time than the shortest one you had today." He sat down. "Seriously, do you have any idea how long you took with each of the Examiners?"

"No, I kind of lost track of time."

"Well, you kept the last three fairly short - probably only about a half hour with each of them. But poor Councilor Garmon, I think you must have been with him a full two hours! No wonder Sofrina called a recess."

Colin slumped down on the bed. "I had no idea. I closed my eyes and it only seemed like a couple of minutes, but that would explain why I'm so tired."

"So, are you going to tell me what you were doing during all that time?" Halvor asked.

"I don't know. It's kind of hard to describe. I just saw lights. And I saw connections between lights, so I followed them. I'd never seen anything like it. I'm still not sure exactly what I was seeing, or how I was seeing it."

Halvor looked worried, "You mean you saw more than one light? You should only see the one."

"Yeah. I saw the one - there in the Box. But I could see connections - leading off to other lights, so I followed them. It was pretty wild."

"That's not possible," Halvor said flatly, "No one inside the Box can see anyone outside the Box. No one outside the Box can see anyone inside. That's how it works, how we know the Evaluation is fair, because nobody outside can affect what goes on inside."

Colin wasn't inclined to push it, "Maybe you're right. I had no idea what I was doing there, or what I was seeing. Probably nothing." Playing a hunch, he asked, "You could be 12th File, couldn't you?"

Now Halvor looked uncomfortable. "Maybe. I haven't really tried."

"Why not?"

"Well, I like being an Arbor Guard. While there's really no rule against it, they kind of frown on members of the 12th File being in the guard. They push the 12th File more towards government stuff - administration and the like. That didn't interest me, so when it came to the 11th File, I kind of let up a little bit."

"I can understand that. I'm starved. Then I just want to go to bed."

"Alright," Halvor said, "I'll need your clothes anyway, so we can get a purple band put on the hem, now that you're in the 12th File."

"No," Colin responded.

"Listen, you have to. You're through the Evaluation. They put you in the 12th File. You need to wear the colors of the File. Today was hard. Tomorrow is dangerous. Don't do anything to antagonize the Council, and believe me, not wearing the proper colors is going to antagonize them."

Colin shook his head, "I'm not modifying the clothes I have. Don't ask me why. Just for now, I can't. I don't know why. But I'm not getting color put on them."

"They're going to throw you back in that filthy cell you got dragged out of a couple days ago. Is that what you want?" Halvor asked.

"No," Colin almost shuddered at the idea of going back there. "Listen, how much color do I have to wear in order to satisfy the Council?"

Halvor shrugged, "Most people go way overboard - the whole outfit, or every hem. As far as I know, the law simply requires that your File be clearly identified by displaying the appropriate color."

"Alright, then how about this. Can you get me a purple armband, about as wide as my hand? If I wear that, will it satisfy the requirements of the law?" Colin asked.

"I guess. I'll see what I can do. You'd better eat and get some rest. Tomorrow will be rough as well."

Halvor went directly to the south wing after he left Colin locked up. He knocked softly at the door, surprised when his mother opened it. "Don't you ever let the servants do their job?" he asked, hugging her affectionately.

"Of course I do, and right now, their job is getting dinner on. Come in. You're just in time," she replied.

Halvor entered and found his father and sister already seated at the table. Dalene jumped up and hugged him. "Halvor! This is a surprise! You haven't eaten yet, have you? You'll stay for dinner?"

"No and yes. I'm beat. I'm starved and I'll stay." He flopped down on a chair, resting his head on the table.

"Halvor, dear, not on the table please. We're going to be eating," his mother said patiently.

He looked up and grinned, "What a day! Have you ever seen an Evaluation like it?" Nobody returned his smile. "What's wrong?"

"We were just talking about 'what's wrong,'" Dalene said. "The whole thing was horrible! Not one Examiner could even find him! And that fit Lucinda Yearsley threw at the end! What is wrong with her?"

"What do you mean no one could find him? Father found him. He bowed."

Gareth shook his head, "Yes, he bowed, but it wasn't from the Compliance. I never had the chance. I could feel him. Sense him. He was there. But I couldn't see him. Not a glimmer. I don't even know why I opened my eyes when I did. I wasn't through searching for his true-self. I never really got started, but all of the sudden it was as if something, some contact was broken and I opened my eyes to see him bowing to me."

They all lapsed into silence while servants brought out large bowls of soup and a basket of bread. By mutual consent, the conversation remained suspended until they finished eating.

Afterwards, Halvor asked, "So, what are you going to do?"

His father shrugged, "Not much choice, really. Tomorrow he will have to answer the accusations of wearing the mantle falsely and sedition. The first is harder to defend than the second. If he's smart and keeps his mouth shut, he has a good chance of having a decision of 'not proven' returned. There's no way he'll be found not guilty, but if he can keep it to 'not proven' then he'll still be free, though the charges could be brought up again if more evidence were to surface."

Beatrice said, "You know he won't."

"What?" Halvor asked.

"He won't keep his mouth shut. I don't know what he'll do, but that's one thing I know he won't do."

"Then heaven help him," was the Regent's benediction.

"Oh, curse it!" Halvor suddenly let out.

"Dear, you know we don't approve of that kind of talk," his mother reproved.

"Sorry mother. I almost forgot though. I need to get Colin an arm band. He won't let me have a colored fringe put on his clothing. Won't let me modify it at all. But he did agree to an armband, if I can come up with one. Too late tonight. I'll have to find something in the morning. One of the seamstresses should be able to make one without too much bother."

"Maybe I can help," Dalene said. She reached up and undid the purple linen scarf from around her neck. "Here, you can wrap this around his arm. It should do nicely."

Halvor held the scarf limply in his hand, looking at his sister critically, "You're joking, right?"

"Not at all," she said defensively, a hint of color showing at her bared throat, "It's just an old scarf. You don't need to bother a poor seamstress at some beastly hour in the morning."

Her mother came up beside her, squeezing her arm tight and looking at Halvor with a glint of humor in her eye, "Why I think it will do perfectly. After all, it's just an old scarf that I gave you for your last birthday. It will be fine. Now you run along dear, it's getting late and tomorrow is another big day!"

Halvor laughed as he ducked out the door. Dalene blushed furiously as she marched to her apartment. Beatrice smiled and took her husband by the arm as he stood looking utterly confused.

Colin woke up early again the next day when the dawn chorus started. But while he had felt anxious and invigorated the previous day, this morning he just felt drained and lethargic. He lay in bed reviewing the events of the previous day and he still wasn't sure if he had done the right thing. His bowing to Gareth Tregard hadn't been a sign of subservience, no matter how others might view it. It had been a sign of respect. Seeing the man's 'true-self,' had been an incredible experience. He had tremendous power, yes, but there was something else. Integrity? Goodness? Perhaps that was the closest he could come to describing it. The man was simply good. Colin respected that. His father had been such a man. Not perfect, no, but a man of absolute integrity, who really only wished to be good. It was a thing worthy of respect.

Reluctantly, he rolled out of bed, kneeling to pray. He continued for some time and felt more at ease when he was done. The sun was well up before he heard the door being unlocked. Halvor entered, carrying a tray of bread and fruit, along with a small pitcher. "Are you going to eat this morning?" I think you should. You need your strength.

Colin shook his head. "I don't think so. The strength I need isn't going to come from food. I'll be fine. I'm kind of used to missing meals anyway and I'll have dinner tonight, or whenever this is over."

"Colin," Halvor hesitated, "If things go badly, there may not be dinner tonight. Yesterday was the Evaluation. You became a member of the 12th File. Today is basically a trial. You're accused of sedition. That includes a lot of things - failure to display the colors of your File, trying to overthrow the Councils, challenging the authority of the Councils, trying to raise an army. When you left, I had to come back here and report. I had orders to take you into custody. We had men in every city for weeks. They spent half their time responding to reports of your having been some place or other. All the things I just listed, that's what you were claimed to have been doing each time you were seen. They have the men of every patrol I sent out here today. They're here to give testimony against you. For what it's worth, I don't believe that any of those reports were true. You say you left Aidon. I believe you. But what I believe doesn't matter. It's what the Council believes that will convict you. They need nine Councilors to agree for conviction - under the law every Order must be represented in a conviction."

"I appreciate you explaining all this to me. And from where I sit, what you believe does matter. It means a lot to me. Thanks."

"Like I told you yesterday, I am both your guard and your guide, but I haven't gotten to the worst part yet. First, there is one piece of good news for you. In every trial one Councilor from the 3rd Order is assigned to speak on behalf of the accused. The Regent isn't allowed to assume that role, since he presides over the trial. Given that Lucinda Yearsley hates you, the good news is that Councilor Dean Garmon will speak on your behalf. But don't get the wrong idea. His only objective is to ensure that you're treated fairly. If he thinks you're guilty, he'll vote that way just as quickly as anyone else. I think you can at least get a decision of 'not proven' on the charges of sedition. There are lots of witnesses, but we never found anybody who actually claimed to see you or hear you. So while they aren't likely to find you innocent, 'not proven' will basically get you released until such time as further evidence is found. But the final thing they're going to bring up is your wearing the mantle. I've thought about it and I can't come up with anything to suggest. Since you're a stranger here, you could just claim ignorance and offer to get rid of it. That might work. I don't think they could get nine Councilors to find you guilty if you were to do that."

Colin sat with his head down, listening to this. After a lengthy pause he looked up and said, "I don't know if I can do that. When I first got here, I would have given up this hood in a second. I had no idea what it meant. But I'm not sure I can do it now. I just don't know."

"Alright," Halvor sighed, "We need to get going. Here, put this on." He held out the purple scarf.

Colin smiled, "A scarf? I don't look especially good in a scarf."

Halvor scowled, "Just put it around your arm. It's the best I could come up with. Actually, Dalene - I mean The Lady Dalene came up with it."

"Well, I wouldn't want to seem ungrateful to the lady." He took the scarf. It smelled faintly of lilac and something more. The scent filled him with a peculiar warmth and he wrapped the scarf above his left bicep, managing to get it tied with one hand. "I guess I'm ready."

Halvor led the way back to the Great Hall. Everything was the same as it had been the previous day. Colin was surprised to find the hall crowded with spectators once again. He thought that they would have had enough of that from yesterday. He and Halvor were seated, but had to wait about 15 minutes before the High Council filed in. Dalene and her mother were again seated behind the Regent. Barrister Sofia Fairfield stepped forward and addressed the Council.

"Honorable High Councilors of Aidon, we are met today to address charges against Colin Ericsson, member of the 12th File of Aidon. I will remind the audience in attendance, that we will not tolerate any outbursts such as we had yesterday. If need be, we will clear the Hall once again. There will be no further warning on this subject. We will first consider charges of sedition and insurrection. Councilor Garmon will represent the interests of the accused. Does the accused understand the charges against him?"

"I believe I do, Barrister Fairfield." Colin replied.

She raised one eyebrow, as if surprised he had the capacity of speech. "Councilor Garmon has been assigned to represent your interests and speak for you. Yet you have chosen to speak for yourself. Am I to assume that you do not wish the assistance of Councilor Garmon?"

Colin inclined his head to the Barrister in a brief nod of apology, "I'm sorry, Barrister Fairfield. I am unfamiliar with the customs and protocols of this Council. I meant no offense. I'm grateful for the assistance of Councilor Garmon, but I would like to speak for myself when I feel capable - as when you asked if I understood the charges. His counsel would be appreciated in helping me to not give offense in these proceedings. Would that be acceptable?"

This deviation from the usual script perplexed the Barrister. She shrugged, "We do not object if you speak in your own behalf. Please bring a chair for Councilor Garmon to be seated near the accused."

A chair was brought and Councilor Garmon gave Colin a nod and brief smile as he was seated. Colin whispered, "Thank you. Mostly I need you to help me not do something really stupid that's going to offend the Council."

Garmon simply nodded.

Barrister Fairfield spoke, "In the Council decision of the 22nd Day of the 4th Moon of this year, the accused was ordered to be brought into custody. When Arbor Guard Halvor Tregard was dispatched to carry out these orders, the accused had fled!"

"Excuse me." Colin interrupted, Councilor Garmon gripping his arm. "I don't know the correct procedure here, but when false statements are made, am I to correct them as they come up or will I be given opportunity to correct them later?"

The Regent spoke, "When a witness is giving evidence, you will have opportunity to question the witness later. However, when the Barrister is offering matters of fact, errors in those facts should be corrected as they arise. Do you wish to make a correction to some matter of fact presented by Barrister Fairfield?"

"Yes, I do, thank you. Barrister Fairfield has stated that I had fled. Since I was not charged with any crime and had not been informed that I was to be taken into custody, the fact that I had left should not be grounds for prejudice in claiming that I had fled."

The Barrister gave him a cold look, "My apologies. We will concede that the accused had left, but this should not be construed as implying flight. May I continue?"

"Please do," Colin nodded.

When the accused could not be found, the Arbor Guard returned to Salem where twelve patrols were organized to search for him. A two-man patrol was sent to each city. The Arbor Guard and the city guards were also instructed to keep an eye out for him and take him into custody if he were spotted. As evidence, we shall call the captains of each patrol to tell us what they found."

Twelve uniformed guards filed into the Great Hall, standing at the opposite side of the Council from where Colin was seated. For nearly an hour they recited tales of chasing after the mantle-bearer. It was as Halvor had predicted. The mantle-bearer was reported to have been in this city or that village. He was claimed to have called for men to march on Salem and overthrow the Council. He was said to have proclaimed himself to be the ruler of Aidon. He had claimed to be the Messenger of Messias sent to destroy the earth. Colin tired of this rapidly and interrupted, "Excuse me. May I make a request?"

Councilor Garmon leaned over and whispered, "You need to wait until they give permission. They will tell you when it is your turn!"

The Regent said, "This is not how things are normally done, but if your request is reasonable, we will consider it."

"Thank you, Councilor Tregard. In an effort to not prolong these proceedings, I am happy to concede that the patrols spent a great deal of time searching for me during my absence. But the things they are saying cannot be considered as evidence. These are simply stories which must be supported in order to be considered as evidence. My request is simply this: Can you produce one person who claims to have actually seen me or spoken to me during the time you were searching for me?"

Halvor stood, "May I address that question?"

The Regent nodded.

"I was charged with taking the mantle-bearer into custody. I organized the patrols and gave them their assignments. I personally spoke with every member of each patrol several times during the course of the search. They informed me of the leads and rumors they were following. We never found anyone who claimed to have personally seen or spoken to the mantle-bearer until five days ago in the city of Riverton. Until that time, we found no evidence, no witness that he had been in any of the locations where reports had placed him."

The Regent cocked his head and asked, "Barrister Fairfield, do you have any witnesses having personal knowledge regarding the crimes of which this man is accused?"

Her face reddened, as she replied, "I do not, Councilor Tregard."

Turning to Colin, he asked, "Do you have any further questions or statement to make before the Council considers this charge?"

Colin stood, "I have no questions. I would simply like to state that at no time have I advocated sedition or insurrection in Aidon. I was unaware of the search which was being conducted and I was not in any of the locations where I was reported to be, which would explain why the patrols were unable to find me."

Now it was Barrister Fairfield's turn to interrupt. "That isn't possible. Every city in Aidon had reports of the mantle-bearer. You had to have been in one of the cities."

Colin shook his head, "No, I wasn't in Aidon."

Whispers and muted exclamations could be heard from the audience, but the Barrister ignored it as she pounced, "Then you admit you were in Kernsidon! That's the only place outside of Aidon you could possibly have been and survived! The accused, by his own admission has been in contact with the sworn enemies of Aidon. He is guilty of treason and sedition!"

Colin waited for the whispers to die down. "I was not in Kernsidon. For almost six weeks I traveled to the north of Aidon. During that time I saw no other people. I spoke with no one from either Aidon or Kernsidon. I have never been to Kernsidon."

"Not possible!" Barrister Fairfield countered, "To survive for six weeks outside of Aidon, no food, no shelter, no other people to protect you! It cannot be done! You have been to Kernsidon! Admit it!"

"I do not know where Kernsidon is. Look at me. Do I look like the people of Aidon? I don't know what the people of Kernsidon look like but I've been told that my appearance is unknown here, so I ask you, do I look like I am from Kernsidon? No. I am 28 years old. Find one person in Aidon who had seen me before three moons ago. No one saw me, because I wasn't here. Your own eyes tell you that I am not from Kernsidon, so by my existence, standing here today, it is obvious that it is possible to survive someplace outside of Aidon or Kernsidon. Produce evidence, or submit the matter to the Council for consideration!"

The Regent said, "If neither of you have any further evidence to present, the Council will retire to consider the matter." With that, the Council filed from the room.

Colin turned to Halvor, "Thanks. For what you said. How do you think it went?"

Halvor shrugged, "I think you did fine. Unusual, but the Regent is usually willing to relax protocol in favor of one who is accused. But don't be too happy just yet. Nobody really cares about the sedition charge. Even Barrister Fairfield didn't expect to win this one, but she had to bring the charge because there were so many rumors. To ignore them would indicate that the High Council took no interest in the matter. What they're really waiting for is the other charge - wearing the mantle without authority. I doubt if they will waste too much time on this charge."

It wasn't that Colin had forgotten about that, but he was grasping for all the positive news he could get. Halvor's reply did a good job of deflating him.

Halvor was right. Within a half hour the Council was filing back into the Great Hall. The Regent said, "Councilor Arabella Brett will deliver the decision of the Council on the charge of sedition and insurrection."

Councilor Brett stood, "The decision of the High Council of Aidon regarding the charges against Colin Ericsson of the 12th File of Aidon is 'not proven!' Should additional evidence be brought forward at any time, this Council may reconvene to again consider this charge."

The Regent then nodded to Barrister Fairfield, "You may proceed, Sofia."

Barrister Fairfield addressed the Council, "We will now consider charges of a most serious nature against the accused, Colin Ericsson of the 12th File of Aidon. He is charged with the wearing of forbidden clothing, namely, wearing the mantle of authority by which he claims to be a messenger of Messias. He is charged with wearing the mantle falsely, in that he has no authority and is not a messenger." Turning to Colin she continued, "Does the accused understand the charges?"

"I understand the charges, Barrister Fairfield," Colin replied.

"We shall first call upon Councilor Arlena Linape, High Councilor of the 3rd File of the City of Tyber," the Barrister said.

Councilor Garmon jumped to his feet, "This is improper! A member of this Council cannot give evidence and then consider the charges against the accused!"

Colin placed a restraining hand on his arm, "Please. It's alright. I have no objection to her giving evidence."

Garmon was obviously unhappy, but resumed his seat. Councilor Linape stood as she was addressed by Barrister Fairfield, "Councilor Linape, you presided at the Evaluation in Tyber at the 4th Moon of this year, did you not?"

"That is correct. I did."

"It was a most unusual Evaluation, wasn't it?"

"Yes," said Counselor Linape, "There was a lot of confusion."

"But the confusion didn't end even at the conclusion of the Evaluation, did it?"

"No. One of our Examiners had collapsed. I was assisting him at the time, when I heard shouts from the crowd. The next thing I knew, the accused, the mantle-bearer, came and stood on the platform near where I was. He had the mantle - the hood up, covering his head. The Arbor Guard was with him. He spoke to the people. He told them that he was to appear before the High Council, here, in Salem in two moons. He said that he came as a man, not as a messenger and he stood with the hood over his head even when he said it!"

"Thank you," the Barrister smiled, but there was no warmth. Turning to Colin she said, "Have the facts been presented correctly? Do you have any questions or comments?"

Colin shook his head, "Except for the fact that I removed the mantle from my head just prior to making the statement related by Councilor

Linape, the event has been accurately related. I have no questions for the Councilor."

"Very well," she continued. "We will now hear from The Lady Dalene Tregard of the 12th File of Aidon, from the City of Salem!"

Dalene paled when her name was called. She stood. Halvor whispered angrily, "What is that witch Sofia doing?"

Councilor Garmon glared at him. The Barrister said, "Lady Dalene, you were assigned by the Council to investigate the initial report of a mantle-bearer having come to Aidon, were you not?"

"That is correct, Barrister Fairfield," she replied. Her voice was low, but steady.

"And when you investigated, whom did you find to be the reported mantle-bearer?"

"The accused, Colin Ericsson, recently accepted as one of the 12th File."

"Did you question him regarding his authority for wearing the mantle?"

"Yes."

"What was his response?"

The Lady Dalene looked over at him for a long moment, before looking back at Barrister Fairfield. "At first, he seemed to have no concept of the importance placed on the wearing of a hooded garment. When he understood what it signified, he offered to remove it or exchange it for other clothing. I asked him if he is a messenger of Messias. He said he was not."

Whispers could be heard throughout the hall, but were silenced by a glare from the Barrister. When it was again quiet, she turned to Colin and asked, "Now for this witness - do you have any questions? Do you challenge the evidence she has offered?"

"I have no questions. Her statements are correct." At this admission, the buzz of conversation erupted in the hall. Even a few of the Councilors could be seen leaning over to speak to their neighbor. Barrister Fairfield seemed content to let it run its course.

"Thank you, Lady Dalene. You may resume your seat." The Barrister gazed around the room, looking exceptionally smug. She continued, "This morning, we heard evidence that for a period of almost six weeks patrols were searching every city in Aidon, looking for the accused. As you heard, we have been unable to produce any witness to verify where he was in Aidon during that time. But five days ago, he was in Aidon, in Riverton! Arbor Guard Halvor Tregard, you were very persuasive this morning when you said that no evidence was found to connect the accused with the rumors which your patrols were investigating, is that correct?"

"That is correct, Barrister," he replied.

Barrister Fairfield pounced, "But he was seen in Riverton five days ago! Is this correct Arbor Guard?"

"Yes," Halvor replied. "I saw him, as well as the two guards with me. There were probably two or three dozen witnesses in Riverton who saw him as well."

Triumphant now, Barrister Fairfield proclaimed, "And we have three of those witnesses here now! Please bring in Daniel Brendies of Troas as well as Scott and Joyce Ledford of Riverton."

Colin recognized Scott and Joyce as the parents of the girl he had saved from drowning. The woman gave him a quick, frightened smile. The father wouldn't look at him. Daniel was the man who had spoken to him when Halvor had taken him into custody. Barrister Fairfield addressed them, "Please tell the Council what happened when you saw the mantle-bearer, the accused last Sabbath in Riverton."

Joyce, spoke in a very quiet, frightened voice, "We had gone down to the River Morex Sabbath afternoon. We were with a group of friends from town. My brother, Daniel Brendies is here today. He was with us. We took food to eat. The children like to play in the water. We warn them to be careful, because the river is swift near Riverton. Our daughter, Susan, she is nine. She was playing with the other children. We heard them screaming. Something had happened. She slipped or got in too deep and the current had her and she was being swept away. We ran along the shore, hoping the current would bring her back, but it was taking her away from us. We could do nothing. I heard a loud splash. I didn't see him, but my neighbor said she saw the mantle-bearer jump into the river from the top of the cliff on the other side. I was watching my daughter. She disappeared under the water and she didn't come up. Then I saw the mantle-bearer, near where she had gone under."

Barrister Fairfield interrupted, "He was near your daughter? How did he get there? What was he doing?"

"He swam. Not like a fish. His arms and legs were moving. But he moved through the water. Not drowning." She replied.

"So, the mantle-bearer, the accused, he was swimming. He was doing what is forbidden by law. He was in the element of the Serpent and yet it didn't swallow him up as it had your daughter. Is that correct?"

Joyce glanced at him, then back at her interrogator and nodded. "What happened next?"

Joyce continued, "He disappeared under the water. He was under water a long time, but then he came up. He went down again very quickly. I think he was under water even longer the second time and when he came up he had Susan. He came to shore and Susan wasn't moving. I thought she was dead. I tried to get my baby from him, but he wouldn't give her to me. He was pushing on her body, on her chest. Water came out her nose and mouth. Then he put his mouth on hers, but he kept pushing on her chest. I tried to get my baby, but he was very angry. He said he would hurt me if I touched her," her voice dropped to a whisper. "Everyone said she was dead.

They were angry that he kept pushing her chest, but they were afraid, because he wore the mantle up over his head. He kept pushing her chest and breathing in her mouth for a long time. And then Susan woke up. She spit up more water and she cried and then he gave her back to me."

The Barrister coaxed her, "You were grateful. You thanked the mantle-bearer, didn't you? And then what did he say to you?"

The frightened mother glanced at him, before looking back at the floor and in a whisper so soft that it was barely audible, she said, "He said he wasn't a messenger of Messias." Then she covered her face in her hands and sobbed.

Without a pause, Barrister Fairfield bored in, "Daniel Brendies! You were there also. You witnessed what your sister has described for us. You spoke with the mantle-bearer. You heard him speak to the crowd gathered there on the bank of the River Morex. What did he say?"

Daniel looked defiant and he spoke clearly, "He said he was not a messenger of Messias." The whispers from the gallery started up again, but Daniel continued in a booming voice, "He said he was simply a stranger here! That the customs for dress in his land are different! He said he was not an impostor and I believe him!!"

Exclamations and shouts exploded throughout the hall.

"That will be all! I will have this hall cleared!" The Barrister whirled on Daniel, "You are to keep your beliefs and opinions to yourself until such time as you stand to answer charges of your own! In this Council you will answer questions and provide evidence!" Regaining control, she turned to Colin. "Has the evidence presented been accurate? Factual?"

He nodded, smiling slightly, "Yes. The witnesses have stated the circumstances correctly. If I may be permitted to say so, they have been truthful in every regard. They have no need to feel any shame or fear for having told the truth here today."

Joyce gave him a grateful smile, while Daniel snapped him a brief nod before being led away.

"Finally," Barrister Fairfield continued, "we should like to hear from the accused. Please stand." Colin did so. "Guards!" At a signal from the Barrister, two guards stepped forward, threatening. Before he knew what they intended, one of them grabbed the hood at the back of his jacket and jerked it roughly up over his head. He shook his head to move it back from his eyes but made no attempt to remove it. The room was a buzz of whispered conversation, which the Barrister chose to ignore, raising her voice to be heard over the hum, "You see the accused stand before you wearing the mantle of authority! I ask him now, do you wear the mantle by right? Are you indeed an authorized messenger of Messias?"

The room was suddenly deathly quiet. Colin stood still and silent, his gaze seeming to touch on every person in the room. He looked at Dalene, her face was pale and she clutched the arms of her chair until her knuckles showed white. He gave her the barest of smiles. He looked at the Regent, who sat calmly, watching him intently. Finally he allowed his gaze to settle on Barrister Fairfield. He spoke in a clear, ringing tone, "I say it now and in your presence. Let there be no misunderstanding. I bear no message from your Messias."

A low hum of excited whispers could be heard. Colin paused briefly and then finished, "However, that does not alter this one fact. The mantle is mine by right!"

The room exploded in a chaos of exclamations and no amount of screaming from the Barrister would silence it. Only when the guards were summoned to clear the room did the crowd finally quiet. When it had done so, the Barrister continued, "You have heard the witnesses. You have seen the evidence. The accused wears the mantle even now! He claims to wear it by right, but we have multiple witnesses and the agreement of the accused himself, that he is no messenger of Messias! Unless anyone has anything further, this matter is delivered to the Council for consideration."

The Regent looked quietly around the room. "Does anyone have anything further to add before the Council retires to consider the charge?"

No one did. As the Councilors filed from the room, Colin stretched, slipping the hood from his head and asked Halvor, "Well, how do you think it went?"

"If your intention was to be found guilty and to have the Council determine to destroy you as a thinking individual, then it went exceptionally well. If, on the other hand, your intent was to be set free and live a long, happy and productive life, I think you have about 12 obstacles in your way. Colin, don't you understand? You can't have it both ways. If you wear the mantle by right, then that defines you as a messenger of Messias. If you are not a messenger, then you have no right to the mantle. I thought you knew that."

"I do. At least I know that's what everyone keeps telling me. What I don't know is who made up that rule."

"What do you mean?" Halvor asked.

"I understand that what you have told me is the law of Aidon. What I don't know is if that is the law of your Messias."

As it turned out, Halvor was wrong. There were, as it turned out, 11 obstacles to Colin's freedom, not 12. Councilor Lucinda Yearsley was berating Councilor Krainik.

"Are you deaf? Did you not hear the witnesses? Are you blind? He wears the mantle! He claims it by right, but makes no claim to be a messenger! The only rational determination is that he is guilty and must be destroyed!"

Krainik was red-faced, but intransigent. "I just think that the matter bears further deliberation. I move for a determination of 'not proven.' We can keep him in confinement. I myself, will accept responsibility for him. We can re-visit the matter at a later time – perhaps after the Solstice Observance."

Even Councilor Garmon opposed him, "Lijah, I don't understand. He's obviously guilty. Why are you so set on delaying the inevitable? He must be destroyed, for the good of Aidon. He's either deluded or in league with the Serpent. He must be destroyed."

Councilor Tregard said little after he initially polled each Councilor. But it was obvious that Councilor Krainik would not be moved. The discussion had dragged on longer than it should have already. It was time for it to end. "Very well," he said. Councilor Krainik is entitled to his view on this matter. While I would have preferred a unanimous verdict, it does not alter the decision of this body. Where nine are needed, we have eleven. It is the determination of this Council that the accused is guilty and the penalty is destruction. Does anyone have anything else to say? If not, we will return to the Great Hall to deliver our decision and to carry out the punishment."

Councilor Krainik was pleased. The abuse and criticism of his fellow Councilors had been humiliating – especially from Lucinda, that vile slug! But he was willing to take it – for now - knowing that soon, he would be able to grind their faces in the dirt. He would have her lick his boots – right before he killed her. Now, no one would be surprised when his compassion moved him to appeal the penalty. They would be angry, of course. Let them be angry! That alone would almost make this whole charade worthwhile. Once he appealed, he would have custody of the pretender! Of course he would also be held accountable for anything he did until the appeal was considered at the next moon, but a locked door should mitigate any danger there. Then he would find a weakness, exploit it. This pretender would be a flame to draw the simple, deluded peasants to his cause. One more tool to be wielded in the overthrow of Aidon!

The Councilors filed back into the Great Hall and Colin suddenly had a sinking feeling in the pit of his stomach. "All will be as it should be," he whispered. "But that doesn't mean you're going to like it."

Halvor glanced at him. "What did you say?" he asked.

"Nothing. Just talking to myself. I'm just nervous."

The Councilors were all seated and a hush fell over the Great Hall. Colin saw Dalene looking at him and she gave him a brief smile of encouragement. It didn't help. The Regent looked slowly around the hall, before fixing his gaze on Colin. "The accused will stand."

Colin stood, his heart hammering.

"Colin Ericsson of the 12th File, you are accused of wearing the mantle of authority falsely. The High Council of Aidon has heard the evidence and deliberated on this charge. It is our determination that you are guilty. Further, it is our determination that as punishment for wearing the mantle without authority, you are to be destroyed by this Council, united in the Ruling Box of Aidon. By your actions, you have been found to be an affront to Aidon and to Messias, whose mantle you falsely wear. You will no longer be a thinking, sentient being. By your actions, you have shown that you are not to be entrusted with the freedom to act. Henceforth, your mind will no longer be your own. You will obey every command given you by others until the end of your life. It is the determination of this Council that this punishment shall be conducted immediately. May the Creator have mercy on you. The accused will now stand in the Box inscribed number 13. You may do this as your last act of free will or the guards will bind you and place you in it. Begin!"

This was the window Councilor Krainik had been waiting for. The brief moment before the accused entered the Ruling Box of Aidon when he, or someone on his behalf could stand and claim the right to appeal consideration of the punishment. Krainik paused, savoring the moment before making his move, when he was stopped dead by two words. "I appeal!" Krainik jumped to his feet, too keyed up to stop. Who dared!?! His eyes settled on the source of the words. Beatrice Tregard was standing calmly, facing the Regent who whirled at the sound of her voice to face her. She continued calmly, serenely even, "On behalf of the accused, I claim the right to appeal for a review of the prescribed punishment. While awaiting consideration of this appeal, I assume full responsibility for his person and for his actions."

The Lady Dalene clung to her mother's hand, a horrified look on her face. Councilor Krainik sank back into his seat, having never even been noticed in the uproar that had accompanied Beatrice Tregard's appeal. The face of the Regent underwent a series of transformations. His initial stunned look gave way to one of absolute fury, which dissolved into confusion before settling on calm acceptance. He turned back to face the Council, speaking loudly enough to be heard over the uproar in the Great Hall.

"Beatrice Tregard has exercised the right to appeal consideration of the punishment which has been pronounced upon the accused. This appeal will be considered at the next full moon, 29 days hence. Until such time as the appeal is considered and a determination made by the High Council of Aidon, Beatrice Tregard will be held solely and fully accountable for the person and actions of the accused. We are adjourned!"

Colin was still standing and very confused. He turned to Halvor and asked, "What just happened?"

Halvor looked at him without expression, "I believe my mother just bought you a few more weeks of life." After a brief pause he looked pointedly at Colin and added, "I hope it will not be at the cost of her own."

Chapter 18   History Lessons

People were shouting and shoving. Some were fighting to leave, others to get onto the main floor. Loud arguments had broken out and it appeared that violence might soon erupt. Some people were calling for the impostor to be destroyed immediately, in spite of the appeal. Others were equally indignant that such punishment had been pronounced upon a mantle-bearer. Finally, Barrister Fairfield had to give orders for the guards to clear the Great Hall. Once some semblance of order had been achieved, Beatrice walked over to Colin and Halvor, linking her arms through one of theirs on either side. Smiling happily she said, "Shall we go, boys? I think dinner should be ready."

The two men escorted Beatrice back to her quarters without speaking. Once inside, Beatrice turned to her son and said, "Halvor, dear, would you tell the nice guards they can go. I don't think we'll have any further need of them this evening. Colin, please do sit down. Make yourself comfortable. Would you like something to drink while dinner is being made ready?"

"No, thank you," he replied. "I want to thank you for what you did back there, at my trial. But what exactly was it that you did?"

She snorted, "Trial! That was no trial, just a murder all dressed up pretty. As for what I did, I appealed for the Council to review the punishment which my husband pronounced on you. Are you sure you wouldn't like something to drink?"

"No, I'm fine, really. But what does that mean – the appeal?"

"What it means," Halvor broke in, "Is that the Council must meet on the next full moon to review your punishment. If they don't change their minds and there's no reason why they should, your punishment will be conducted immediately. If for some reason they do change their minds, then they will carry out whatever alternative penalty they determine – immediately. There is no second appeal of the punishment."

"Alright, but back in the Great Hall, you said something about your mother purchasing my life at the expense of her own. What did you mean?"

"What he meant," said The Lady Dalene who had just entered, "is that during this time my mother is completely responsible for you – for what you say, what you do and where you are. You are free only because of her, so anything you do wrong during the period of your appeal, will result in <u>her</u> being punished!"

Colin was shocked, "But that's not right. It isn't fair. Then lock me up. Put me back in that dungeon where I won't say or do anything to be punished for! I don't know your customs! I'm going to do something wrong. You know it and I know it."

Beatrice laughed lightly, "Colin, it's not so bad as that. It isn't like they'll punish me for your bad manners. It will be fine. You'll see. But," she continued, "I am getting to be an old woman. I can't be looking after you every minute of the day. I certainly can't be running off to that glorified cell they have you in over in the east wing. I think maybe we could get you into the guest quarters right here. That would be so much easier for me. Fortunately, I also have two wonderful children who I'm sure will help keep you out of trouble. You will help, won't you Dalene? Halvor?"

"Of course we will, mother, you know that. But I don't understand why you're doing this." Dalene replied.

Her mother smiled, "Because I can, dear. Now, go see if dinner is ready."

The Regent joined them for dinner. Colin was as nervous around him as if he were a pimply faced junior in high school there to date his daughter. The third time he addressed him as Councilor Tregard, the Regent placed a heavy hand on Colin's shoulder and said, "That really is getting cumbersome, don't you think? Here in the family quarters, why don't you just call me 'Gareth.' That should be easier on both of us." After dinner he was escorted down the corridor to his own quarters. They were spacious and comfortable, consisting of three rooms. The door from the corridor opened into an airy living area. A wooden couch and two chairs were draped with soft quilts and pillows. There was a low table in the center of the room upon which was set a vase filled with flowers, giving the room a pleasant fragrance. A smaller table held a pitcher of water and several baked clay mugs. Another door opened out the back of the room, leading to a wide balcony overlooking a central courtyard. Sleeping quarters opened off the main room and there was a smaller separate room for washing, containing a pitcher and basin of water as well as a large copper tub. It was obvious that water would have to be hauled in by the bucket, but Colin supposed that the option of private bathing facilities was considered a major luxury. After inspecting his rooms, Colin carefully cracked the door leading into the corridor. There were no guards outside the door.

A short distance down the corridor, The Regent and his wife had retired for the night. Lying in the dark next to her, Gareth finally asked softly, "Beatrice? Why did you do it? You know the danger we are in. Is the life of this one man really worth the risk?"

For a long time there was no answer. He thought perhaps she had fallen asleep, but then she squeezed his hand gently, replying in an equally soft voice, "I don't have a good answer for you. I am sorry, my love, that this makes things much more difficult for you. I know you're worried about Kernsidon. Who knows? Maybe this time they'll succeed. I just feel that if we don't value the life of this one man, perhaps we don't deserve to survive. I really don't know why I did it. Maybe just because I could."

"You know it won't change anything, don't you?" He asked. "The law must be upheld. Would it not have been kinder to have done with it today, instead of having him live under death's shadow until the next moon?"

Beatrice smiled in the dark, "Gareth, life is precious. Colin doesn't strike me as one who will live in shadow – death's or anyone else's. As for the law, sometimes I wonder if we don't have too much law. Not every decision in life is of moral importance. Perhaps there ought to be more freedom to think and choose and do, instead of being forever suffocated by the law."

Her husband was silent for a long time before replying, "I have sometimes thought much the same. But as Regent, you know that I am bound by the law. If I don't obey the law, then how can I enforce it? If it's not enforced, we collapse into chaos."

She squeezed his hand again, "I know, dear. But I still wonder sometimes, whose law are we obeying?"

The question continued to echo in Gareth's mind long after his wife's measured breathing indicated she was asleep.

The next morning there was a knock at his door. Colin had been up for some time, not sure what he was supposed to do. He opened the door to find Beatrice standing there, smiling. "Good morning," she greeted, "Are you hungry? Come along and we'll eat." She led the way back to her quarters where food was already on the table. There were only the two of them. Colin asked, "Is your husband not joining us?"

She smiled, "No, his duties as Regent often have him gone quite early. Usually he's home for the evening meal, but not always."

They ate quietly, after which Beatrice asked him, "Now, what do you have planned for today?"

Colin was surprised, "I don't have any plans. I understood that I was in your custody."

She laughed, "Well, yes, but I hope that I can make some effort to at least be a pleasant jailer! Let me try to explain how I see this working for the next few weeks. For all practical purposes, you are a free man and a member of the 12th File. That means there is very little that you are not permitted to do, or places that you are not permitted to go. I think we could almost occupy you for four weeks just showing you the Praetorium!

"But as I told you last night, I am getting to be an old woman, so I simply haven't the energy to keep up with you. As your custodian, I can ask someone else to look after you for awhile. Or I can ask no one to look after you and let you wander at will. It is simply that I am accountable for you until the next moon. Is that explanation enough?"

Colin nodded, "I don't think I ever thanked you yesterday. I don't know why you did it, but I appreciate it. I'll try to not be too much trouble."

She smiled again, "I'm not sure you can help being too much trouble. But I'm old enough that I've come to accept it."

It was Colin's turn to smile, "I think you make yourself out to be a whole lot older than you really are. And I'm not sure you've always been an innocent bystander when it comes to trouble."

She patted his arm and smiled, "We're going to get along just fine."

Beatrice took Colin on a tour of the Praetorium. It was a massive complex. The centerpiece was the Great Hall, which Colin was already familiar with. Today it was quiet. Beatrice stood at the edge of the Ruling Box of Aidon, her mouth pursed in thought before she spoke. "Twelve Files. Thirteen Boxes. We really don't know where this came from, you know. Nobody knows. There's just so much that we don't know. It's amazing that we've survived even to the extent that we have."

Colin was puzzled, "But you have history, right? I mean, this – your government, your laws – it came from your history, didn't it?"

Beatrice nodded, "Yes, but history can be lost. We lost much of ours during the dark time – before the Councils. There were wars and so much was destroyed. Much of our history prior to that was lost. Only fragments survived. There are stories and legends - several versions even. Much of it is true, I suppose, certainly not all and undoubtedly what we have is an incomplete tapestry of religion, history, superstition and tradition."

"I don't know anything about Aidon – other than what little I learned in Tyber. Do you have any books on your history that I could read to learn about it?"

She raised one eyebrow, looking at him surprised, "Books? Certainly. Some complete volumes, many fragments. Not what I suspect you're looking for."

"Well, then tell me a little about what you think is true of your history. At least that gives me some reference to try and understand your laws and culture. It might help keep me out of trouble."

"Or at least get into trouble more easily," she laughed. "Come and sit and I'll tell one version of Aidon's history."

"Our tradition says that God created the heavens and the earth. We don't use the name 'God' very often, because it is considered sacred. We refer to Him as 'the Creator' or 'the Highest' or 'the Most High.' Anyway, He created all the plants and animals, then He created man and finally He created a woman, our first parents, Aidama and Aeva." Beatrice began.

Colin felt the blood drain from his face. Beatrice noticed and paused, "Are you alright, dear? You don't look well."

Colin hesitated, but wanted to hear Beatrice's history before he said anything. "I'm fine. Just a little light-headed. I'll be fine. Please, go on."

She looked at him strangely, but continued, "The Creator made a beautiful valley for Aidama and Aeva."

Colin interrupted, "The valley of Aidon?"

Beatrice nodded, "That's right. You've heard part of the story in Tyber?"

He shook his head, "But Salem..........I mean, it's not in a valley."

"Oh no," she replied, "The valley is some distance from here, up towards the mountains."

"It still exists?"

"Of course! Why wouldn't it?" she said.

Colin could feel the pulse pounding in his forehead. Aidama and Aeva? The Valley of Aidon – Eden? His heart suddenly just seemed to melt. "Why not?" he thought. "Why wouldn't God follow the same pattern?" No wonder there were so many similarities!

Beatrice touched his arm, obviously concerned now. "Are you well? Would you like to go back to your quarters and rest? I can get a healer for you."

He shook his head, "No, really I'm fine. Please continue. I really need to hear this."

She hesitated, "If you're sure. So, Aidama and Aeva were placed in the valley. It is the most beautiful place on earth. Their every need was provided for. Water, fruit, everything. All was peaceful. There was no death. Even the animals existed in harmony. They were told that the valley was theirs, that everything in it was theirs, except for one tree."

"The Tree of Knowledge," Colin interrupted, unable to restrain himself.

"That's right. You have heard this, then?" she asked.

"I'm sorry. I shouldn't have interrupted. I've heard a similar story. I'll try to be quiet."

"That's alright. But yes, the Tree of Knowledge of Good and Evil. Aidama and Aeva were told they must not eat from that tree. They were obedient. They kept that commandment. But there was one creature in the valley who wanted them to disobey. The Serpent kept tempting them, telling them how wonderful the fruit would taste."

"And Aeva ate the fruit?" He just couldn't keep his mouth shut.

Beatrice looked at him curiously, "Of course not! I just told you they were obedient. But the Serpent kept trying to get them to eat the fruit. They continued to refuse. The Serpent was cast out, but he was very angry. No one knows how, but he returned to the Valley. He decided that if he could not get them to eat the fruit, then he would destroy them. He couldn't actually kill them. There was no death. But he could devour them. Trapped in the belly of the Serpent, they wouldn't be free. They wouldn't be able to act. They would exist, but they would have been destroyed. One day he attacked them. Aidama and Aeva fought back, but the Serpent was powerful. They tried to flee, but the Serpent was too fast. He never tired. They knew that the Serpent would win. As they were about to be destroyed, as the Serpent was about to devour Aeva, Aidama cried out in anguish, pleading for the Creator to save his wife. In answer to his cry, Messias came, leading an army of messengers. He fought the Serpent and drove it from the valley. The battle continued, the Serpent was forced to retreat. Finally, the Serpent was driven into the ocean. Tradition holds that it was where you were in the ocean. Of course we don't know for certain exactly where you came ashore, but your description sounds very much like what we call The Forbidden Place. As the Serpent fought on the sharp rocks at the edge of the ocean, it was cut in a thousand places. Its blood poisoned the rocks and to this day anyone who is cut on those rocks will have the ocean sickness. It used to be called the Serpent's sickness, but we don't like to say 'serpent.' It's a vile thing. Anyone who is cut and gets the ocean sickness, dies. They have always died. You are the first to ever survive."

"Is that why the people of Aidon avoid water? In Riverton I heard them saying something about 'the element of the Serpent,'" Colin asked.

"Yes. Because the Serpent disappeared into the ocean, all bodies of water are viewed with suspicion. We avoid lakes and rivers, even small streams." She smiled, "Your catching fish and eating them has created a lot of debate. Some say it proves you are an enemy to the Serpent, but others say that you could not be near the water to catch fish unless the Serpent were protecting you. I think I would like to try eating fish. Do you think you can catch some so I might taste it?"

Colin smiled in return, "I'm sure I can, especially if I can get my things back. I have some hooks I use for fishing – catching fish - in my gear."

Beatrice nodded, "Your things should be in your quarters by the time we return. Are you tired? Or shall I go on?"

"Please, go on. This is fascinating to me."

"Very well," Beatrice continued. "After the Serpent was driven into the ocean, Messias returned to the valley to speak with Aidama and Aeva. He told them that because they had been obedient, even when faced with destruction, that they could eat fruit from the Tree of Knowledge of Good and Evil. He picked the fruit and gave it to them and told them to eat. After they had eaten, the tree was taken away. Messias told Aidama and Aeva that they were to have children and because they had eaten the fruit, they knew good from evil. It was their responsibility to teach their children to know good from evil as well. By eating the fruit they became mortal. Death was introduced into the world.

"To help Aidama and Aeva teach their children, it is said that Messias gave them the Evaluation Boxes and the Ruling Box of Aidon, that you see here. Not all agree on this point and nobody knows for certain. If the story is true, then with these, they could help their children see the difference between good and evil, protecting them from having to have so many experiences in order to learn. It is part of what we call The Compliance – helping others to see how some things are harmful, or potentially so, while other things are good and benefit more than just the individual, but help the entire people of Aidon.

"There was another special tree in the valley as well. This was the Tree of Life. Aidama and Aeva had eaten from the fruit of The Tree of Life on many occasions, but because there was no death at that time, the fruit had no effect on them. Once they had eaten from The Tree of Knowledge, Messias caused The Tree of Life to become barren, or death would have been destroyed. That death remained is important. Death is the passage that takes us back to the presence of Messias, if we have continued obedient, as Aidama and Aeva were. The Tree has never borne fruit since. The tree blossoms, but no fruit ever appears. Some say that one day Messias will come again and when He does, the Tree will again bear fruit and we will be permitted to eat it and death again will be no more. Maybe it is not true," she shrugged, "but it is part of the legend – at least one version of the legend."

Colin was confused, "Beatrice, I don't understand. You talk about The Tree of Life as though it were here. It isn't, is it?"

"Not here," she replied, "It is in the Valley, where it has always been."

"The Tree of Life is in the Valley of Aidon?" Colin asked dumbly.

Beatrice nodded, "Yes. Are you alright? You are still very pale."

"I'll be fine. Have you ever seen the Tree?"

"Of course. At least once each year ever since I was a little girl. It is the most beautiful tree you can imagine. It isn't wide and branching. It is tall and graceful. I think it is the tallest tree in the world, as if it were reaching to heaven. It fills you with happiness just to look upon it. At its base is a large pool of clear water. It is said that this water flows through the roots of the Tree itself. It is through the water that the Tree of Life reaches every living thing on earth. We are all connected to it. It truly is the source of life."

"Can I see it? Can you take me there sometime?"

"Someday, perhaps. If the appeal of your punishment is successful, then I can take you there. But no one who is found guilty of a crime may enter the valley until their punishment is complete. I'm sorry. I wish you could see it. But perhaps after the next moon…….." her voice trailed off. They both knew he would probably be destroyed at the next moon.

"So, after Aidama and Aeva had children, they were forced to leave the valley? Is that it?" Colin asked.

Beatrice shook her head. "I don't know what strange version of this tale you have been told. There are several versions of the story. Some claim there was a second battle with the Serpent, but I have never heard any version where Aidama and Aeva were forced to leave. However, they did come out of the valley and lived here – where Salem now stands. They kept the valley as a sacred place to honor Messias. Only on special occasions do we return there. Aidama and Aeva had many children. Their children had children. They lived a long time, so the legend says. Some of their children moved to begin other cities like Riverton or Tyber, Jordanon and Hyaton. Aidama and Aeva taught their children well. They chose good. They were happy and at peace. But they had a son who was not happy. He wanted power. He wanted to rule in place of his father. Kern had learned that the Boxes had more power than just The Compliance. He discovered The Compulsion. The Compulsion is like The Compliance, but different. The Compliance just helps someone see right or wrong, or why some action might be beneficial. Like in the Evaluation, there is no force, you just try to get the other person to see bowing to you as good and desirable. The Compulsion is different. Using the Compulsion takes away a part of the other person. It doesn't matter if they see something as good or bad. They have no choice when the Compulsion is used. The part of them that doesn't want to do the thing, that part is destroyed. They are never again complete. Kern learned this and began to use it to get more people to support him. He tried to do this with one of his brothers, Aibel. Kern was very strong, but Aibel was strong also. Kern could not use the Compulsion to force Aibel to submit – at least not by himself. So Kern got eleven of those who supported him together. Somehow they got Aibel here – inside The Ruling Box of Aidon. With the force of twelve focused on Aibel, using the Compulsion, it didn't just destroy that part of him that opposed Kern. It destroyed him completely. Kern had discovered another power that the Box has. He knew that with this power, nothing could stop him. Kern tried to overthrow Aidama. He had persuaded many others to support him, promising them that they would also have power. There was a battle. Maybe even a war. We don't really know. But in the end, Kern was driven from Aidon and many of his followers with him. Kern was still determined to be a ruler – to be king. He established his own version of Aidon – Kern's Aidon. Over the years it became known simply as Kernsidon. He always hated Aidon. Many times he attacked, but he was always driven back. Sometimes people have become angry at the rulers in Aidon and they have gone to Kernsidon. A long time ago – thousands of years, perhaps – a few people from Kernsidon came to Aidon. But if the king found out they wanted to leave, they were killed or imprisoned.

"But all was not peaceful here in Aidon, either. There were others who wanted power. With so many people, it was not possible to always use The Compliance to halt discord before it became violent. Over the course of many hundreds of years, Aidon had practically been destroyed. Maybe the earth itself would have been destroyed, because many who wanted power recognized that The Tree of Life could give them what they wanted – power over every living thing. They tried to get into the valley many times, but each time they were thrown back. My husband's family, over four thousand years ago, were part of protecting the valley. Many were killed, but they fought with valor. His family name, 'Tregard' was given to honor them. My son is one of the Arbor Guards. They are charged with protecting the valley and The Tree of Life at all costs, including the cost of their own lives. Mostly they scout for an attack from Kernsidon. But my husband is worried. Kernsidon has never gone this long without attacking. He thinks that maybe they have managed to gain support here in Aidon. Your appearance here, now," she smiled, "is a complication to the current state of unrest."

"I'm sorry. I'm afraid I've caused a great deal of trouble for your family," Colin said.

"Nonsense. Trouble is simply a part of life. It is true, we have trouble enough, but you were hardly the cause of it. Unless, of course, you came here intentionally just to stir things up and turn Aidon upside down. Did you?" She asked humorously.

"I have no idea how I came to be here or why I'm here," he replied earnestly.

"Well, then don't apologize. Now where was I? Oh, yes. Wars. Aidon was all but destroyed. It may have been an attack by Kernsidon which precipitated The Chaos, but perhaps not. It was certainly fortunate that Kernsidon didn't attack during The Chaos, because Aidon was in no position for defense. That was when several of the strongest surviving families got together and created the Councils. By using the Boxes, the population could be Evaluated to determine their strength of will. By matching individuals of similar levels of will, it became less likely that anyone could usurp power, stir up unrest and create insurrection."

"The Files," Colin said.

"Yes," Beatrice replied, "The Files. You need to understand, Colin, that originally there were more of the Evaluation Boxes than what we have now. These are only the ones that survived The Chaos. Wars were fought for ownership of the Boxes. Kern managed to flee Aidon with one. At least one. We think it has survived as well, but we don't really know. When the Councils were first formed in an effort to restore peace, all of the remaining Boxes were brought here, to the Praetorium. The first Evaluation was conducted here. Individuals were assigned to their respective Files and each File was assigned a city. They were each assigned a color as well, to distinguish them, to help ensure that no one could deal falsely and gain power or advantage over those of the lower files. To not identify your File or to declare your File falsely by the wearing of colors other than your own is a crime which is punished severely. The Boxes were dispersed with the Files so that it would be very difficult for anyone to acquire more than one.

"When the cities were established, or re-established, as it were, since most had been settled previously, they also established a Council to rule the File. The first Councils were elected, but eventually it seemed to be a better plan to utilize the strongest minds in the File to govern as the Council. Everyone recognized that the wars and chaos had come about because individuals were selfish and disobedient, seeking for power and personal gain. As a result, the Councils used the Boxes to help create a harmonious climate in each city. By urging Compliance with the interests of the File, the individual is also cared for. To a degree, this ability to urge Compliance is inherent in each of us. Without the Boxes, it requires physical contact, but parents, husbands and wives, close friends even, can help support each other and the File by urging others to bow to the greater good. However, there have been times when someone continues to resist such urging by their family and friends. When such is the case, the Council can use the Box to have a greater degree of influence than they would otherwise have. If someone continues to engage in behavior or ideas that can be harmful to the community, the Council may determine that the Compulsion should be applied. The part of that person which is engaged in the dangerous behavior is excised, but that part of the person is lost forever. They are never the same afterwards. Sometimes it is hardly noticeable, but where they may have been outspoken and decisive before, they usually become very passive, almost timid even.

"For close to 4000 years now, the Councils have maintained peace and harmony in Aidon. Every few decades, Kernsidon will mount an attack to try and steal the Boxes or gain control of The Tree of Life. Since the Councils came into being, they have never come close to achieving their goals. But now, my husband is worried."

Colin sat quietly staring at The Ruling Box of Aidon for a very long time. Beatrice seemed content to bask in the quiet of the Great Hall. At length he asked, "So where does the mantle-bearer figure into all of this?"

"Of course, you would wish to know this," Beatrice replied. "Aidama spoke with Messias in order to learn what to teach his family. When Kern rebelled, this was something new. Aidama didn't know what to do, so again he sought Messias and received direction. He was the first messenger. Aidama chose certain of his descendants and gave them authority to seek direction from Messias when something new confronted the people. They became messengers from Messias as well. Do you see?"

"Yes, but I don't understand the connection to me," Colin replied.

Beatrice explained, "When Aidama gave his descendants authority to be messengers for Messias, he gave them a hooded cloak. By tradition, this came to symbolize the authority to speak for Messias. It is not too much different than the colors we use to identify the Files or the uniforms worn by the city guard. You may think of the hood as being a uniform of sorts. But during The Chaos, all of the messengers were killed. At least we think they were killed. No one really knows, but they were with the people of Aidon no longer. When the Councils eventually brought peace to Aidon once again, there were no messengers. The books, the teachings, so much had been lost and destroyed. After a time, there came some claiming to be messengers once again. But because all of those who were known to have had authority were gone – dead for hundreds of years – there was no proof. Some believed and others doubted. There was anger and fighting. It seemed that chaos and war was again about to break out in Aidon. Because there was no one that was known to have authority, the Councils determined to test any who claimed to be messengers from Messias. The test was conducted here – with The Ruling Box of Aidon. Using this box, the High Council of Aidon could evaluate anyone who claimed to be a messenger. A true messenger, one who had the right to wear the mantle, would be of perfect integrity, as is Messias. Within the box, the twelve members of the High Council can not only see the true-self, but can see inside the true-self, to know if it is without blemish. If so, then the messenger and his message are accepted. If not, he is destroyed so that the people will not be taught to be disobedient and so that there will not be fighting and war over the false message. For almost 4000 years now, there has been no true messenger. Every messenger has been flawed. Each has been false. All have been destroyed. Why does the Messias not send His messenger to us? It has been so long. We need direction. Oh, how we need direction!" Her voice trailed off in what was almost a wail and she was silent for several long moments before she continued to speak.

"When you appeared, wearing the mantle, you were the first in over 100 years. I would have to consult the records to be more exact, but it is probably closer to 200 years. Naturally, this created both a sense of excitement and alarm, especially since there are indications of an imminent attack by Kernsidon. If they could insert a false messenger at such a critical time, our forces might be divided or hesitate, allowing them to finally succeed where they have had only failure for 4000 years. Ordinarily, you would have been subjected to an Evaluation by the entire High Council – united, rather than singly as was done two days ago. But even though you wear the mantle, you made no claim to being a messenger. As a result, there was no need to perform the second Evaluation. Instead you were charged with wearing the mantle falsely, rather than being a false messenger. And that is where you have one glimmer of hope. Had you been a false messenger, you would have already been destroyed. During the second Evaluation, once the Council saw any flaw in your true-self, they would have instantly united in the Compulsion and you would no longer have been a thinking being, free to act for yourself. You would have become a mere vessel to carry out the commands of others. But because you only wear the mantle, without claiming to be a messenger, it is possible that the Council will simply apply the Compulsion to cause you to remove the mantle and reject your claim to it. Only a part of you would be destroyed. Hopefully a very small part. I don't want to raise your hopes too much, but I think that you may still live past the next moon."

Colin finally spoke. "Thank you for telling me all this. While I'm familiar with a version of your story of Aidama and Aeva, it is different in several key areas. I think I understand some things much better now. I also appreciate the great length that you've gone to in trying to save my life. But I'm more worried that you might be the one getting your hopes up too much. Please don't worry too much about me. I hope to not be killed – destroyed, as you put it. But when Aidama and Aeva ate the fruit from The Tree of Knowledge, then death simply became a part of life. It isn't really to be feared and none of us can avoid it forever. Whatever happens, I think I can accept it."

She squeezed his hand, "Thank you, Colin. It is good of you to be concerned about me. Now, unless I can bore you longer with our dusty old history, perhaps you will see me back to my quarters. I am a little tired."

That night, Colin sat on the floor of his balcony, arms crossed over his knees. The twin moons had risen in the night sky. They were waning now, the full moon just past, but they still cast a brilliant illumination on the garden below. They seemed to amplify Colin's thoughts this night. Two moons. The story of Adam and Eve, but not the same. Aidama and Aeva. Only this time, Eve didn't eat the fruit. Adam and Eve weren't cast out. The same pattern, but not the same. But they did eat the fruit. But only when they were commanded to. They were obedient. No wonder this society placed such a premium on obedience. It was practically in their DNA. But Aidama and Aeva still became mortal. Death was still brought into the world. His thoughts were a jumble of confusion. He didn't know when sleep came that night. He was still lying there when Dalene found him the next morning.

Chapter 19   The Library

Beatrice sent Halvor to call Colin for breakfast. There was no answer to his knock so Halvor entered. The moment he saw the bed he knew it hadn't been slept in. With a sense of unease, he quickly checked the three rooms. The saddle bags, bow and arrows were still sitting in the corner where Halvor had delivered them the previous day. He didn't think that Colin would leave them, but he obviously wasn't here. Halvor hurried back to his mother's quarters and announced, "He isn't there. His things are, but it doesn't look as if his bed was slept in last night."

Dalene jumped to her feet, "But where could he go? He doesn't know the city! He has to be here."

Beatrice held up a restraining hand, "I don't think there's any cause for alarm. He probably just went to the baths or out to the stables. I'm sure he'll turn up."

Dalene was not so easily calmed, "But mother, what if he doesn't? The Council...... You appealed on his behalf!"

"Yes, dear," her mother replied, "There is enough trouble in the world without going out to borrow it. He's around. Now sit. Let's eat."

Halvor was still uneasy, "You go ahead. I'll just check the baths and the stable, as you said. Maybe have a word with the guards to see if anyone has seen him."

Beatrice smiled and shrugged, "It's a rare day when your brother walks away from breakfast. Are you not eating either, Dalene?"

"Mother, if he's run off, there will be serious consequences - for you! Even as wife of the Regent......"

"Dalene!" Beatrice interrupted, "He <u>hasn't</u> run off. I spent a good part of the day with him and he's as anxious to stick around for a disaster as your brother is! He'd make a fine Arbor Guard if the Council doesn't have their way and destroy him first. Worry won't change anything, so eat."

Dalene joined her mother, but only picked half-heartedly at her food. As soon as her mother was done, she excused herself and went to Colin's quarters. All was as Halvor had described. His few belongings were there by the wall. The bed was undisturbed. What if none of the guards had seen him? Might he have left by some other route? The balcony! He may have fled from there!

Dalene hurried to the doorway leading to the balcony, half expecting to see a rope tied to the rail, dangling over the edge. But as she went to look over, she saw a still form lying over against the wall. Her heart jumped. He was dead! She rushed to his body, a mixture of remorse and relief coursing through her. At least her mother would be safe. At least Colin would not have to face the wrath of the Council. She knelt to brush back the hair on his forehead. It was not until then that she noticed the shallow rise and fall of his chest. Asleep! She was instantly furious with him! Angrily, she stormed back into the room and grabbed a cup of water. She slammed it back down. A cup? No! She grabbed the entire pitcher, marched out onto the balcony and threw its entire contents in his face. Let that teach the son of the Serpent!

As the water deluged him, Colin thrashed awake, alarmed and confused. Through blurred vision, he could make out a form standing near him, standing over him, attacking him! He lashed out at the dim form as hard as he could. It was too far! He couldn't reach! He couldn't defend himself!

Dalene laughed as Colin spluttered awake, flailing his arms, striking out blindly. But she had been careful to stand well back. Let him flail! She was too far away! Suddenly, something struck her, slamming into her chest. She was thrown backwards, sliding along the floor of the balcony. The pitcher sailed out of her grasp, over the edge to shatter on the ground below. She lay there stunned.

Desperately, Colin swiped the water from his eyes with the sleeve of his cloak. He saw the figure slide to a stop on the floor of the walkway. Instantly he was on his feet, seeking a path to escape or some weapon to defend himself with. Then it registered, "Dalene?!?" He rushed to her side. "Are you alright? What happened?"

Dalene, held one hand to her chest. It hurt, but she didn't think anything was broken. She couldn't breathe. Finally she gasped out, "You! What did you do?"

Colin was confused, "Me? I didn't do anything. I guess I fell asleep out here. Next thing I knew, I was being attacked. At least, I thought I was. Was that you?"

She slowly sat up, Colin helping with an arm behind her back. "I was looking for you. When I saw you asleep out here I thought I'd play a little joke. I threw some water on you. You looked so funny," she smiled weakly, "Fighting like that and all wet. I stood well away so you couldn't hit me or kick me when you awoke. But something hit me anyway and sent me flying back here." She struggled to sit up some more, "What did you do?"

Colin was more confused than ever. "I didn't do anything. I thought I was being attacked. I couldn't see because of the water in my eyes. I saw someone - it must have been you. I tried to hit you, but you were too far away."

Dalene got shakily to her feet. "You hit me. It was exactly when your arm flew out to strike me. Your arm didn't touch me. It was too far. But you hit me."

"I am so sorry," he apologized. "I didn't know it was you. I didn't mean to hurt you. I'm sorry. I feel terrible."

She looked at him intently, "How did you do that?"

"What?"

"Hitting me. Without touching me. How did you do that?"

"I couldn't have. I mean, that's not possible. I don't know what happened, but I couldn't have hit you. I was nowhere near you."

"Yes," she replied. "I know. And yet you did. Have you done this before? Hitting something without touching it?"

Colin thought about his archery shots, but that wasn't the same thing, was it? "No," he replied, shaking his head. "And I'm still not sure I did it this time either."

"You may not be sure," she responded, "but you should feel my chest!"

Colin raised one eyebrow and Dalene blushed. "Colin, this is serious. There are still legends – from before The Chaos. It is said that in that time, some could shape the air, to use as a tool – or a weapon. Are there any from your home which do this?"

He shook his head. "No. I don't think it's even possible. I've never heard of something like that being done."

"Do you insist on denying the evidence of your own eyes? While it may be improbable, you have shown it is possible."

Colin made no response. It couldn't have happened. Yet it had. It left him feeling very unsettled.

Colin followed Dalene. Beatrice said, "Colin! I told them not to worry. My, but you're all wet!"

"Sorry. I had some help getting up this morning," he replied while Dalene looked studiously nonchalant.

"Well, no matter. I'm sure you'll dry. I'm afraid that I've already eaten. Dalene hardly touched her breakfast. Halvor will probably be along shortly. Do sit and eat," Beatrice invited.

As if on cue, Halvor burst in the door. "He hasn't been seen anywhere!" Seeing Colin sitting at the table, he asked dumbly, "Where were you?"

"Sorry. I fell asleep out on the balcony. I was awake for a long time last night. Thinking. I hardly ever sleep once it's light out, but I guess I was just too tired. I didn't mean to worry anyone." Colin replied.

"You're all wet," Halvor observed.

"Yes," Dalene interrupted, smiling sweetly, "Colin needed a little help getting up this morning."

"Oh. I think I remember how she helps." Halvor said, a smile twitching at the corners of his mouth.

Beatrice said, "Children, if it isn't too much to ask, would you please just hush and eat. I'd like to get things cleared before it's time for dinner."

After breakfast Beatrice said, "Colin, after our conversation yesterday, I thought you might enjoy visiting the Library. If you're interested in the history of Aidon, you should see it. I think you will understand things better. Unfortunately, I won't be able to take you there today. Dalene? I was wondering, are you terribly busy today? Could you take Colin to the Library?"

Dalene glanced at Colin, "Umm, Why, yes mother, I guess I could do that."

Beatrice smiled, "Thank you, dear. Now, as his custodian, I am responsible for him, even if he's with you, of course. But I want you to take him there and show him everything. Are we clear?"

"But mother……." Dalene started to object.

"Dalene, if need be, I can rearrange my schedule to show him everything myself. Do I need to do that?"

"No, mother," she replied in surrender.

The Library was only a short walk from the Praetorium. Dalene led the way without speaking. Colin was content to be silent as well, not wishing to discuss the events that had occurred on the balcony that morning. The Library was a beautiful structure, if not so grand nor as large as the Praetorium. Granite steps led up into the building, where guards were posted at the door. Recognizing The Lady Dalene, they permitted entrance without questioning them. Once inside the massive doorway, stairs split off to both the right and left, leading to upper as well as lower levels. A huge atrium formed the center of the Library. Tables were set in three lines through the main hall and shelves lined the walls. Dalene led the way to a nearby set of shelves. "The Great Library of Salem is the repository of the history and knowledge of Aidon. Generally only those of the 3rd Order are permitted access of any kind and even then they are limited. Most of those employed in the library are of the 12th File, though there are some of the 11th File and even a few of the 10th File working here. One of these librarians would be assigned to any of the government officials who had need of finding and accessing any information here," Dalene explained.

"Why so restricted?" Colin asked.

She looked at him, clearly puzzled, "All of the information here is irreplaceable. Some of the material here is ancient – dating to before The Chaos. There are archives here where many of the texts were severely damaged before they were collected and brought here for protection. Because many of these writings are incomplete, there is some question as to their meaning. In the past, when access was less restricted, some scholars would interpret the writings to have one meaning, while others offered an alternative interpretation. What began as discussion would sometimes develop into argument. Factions would form. At best, Aidon was beset by discord. At worst, violence would break out – sometimes bordering on open warfare. The Councils determined that these things should be restricted until additional information could clarify the meaning of the texts."

Colin walked along the shelves, pausing as if he would remove a volume. He hesitated and asked Dalene, "Is this permitted? Am I allowed to look at the books?"

"My mother said you were to be shown everything," Dalene replied.

He removed a volume. Unlike his experience with the interpretation of the spoken language, the characters on the cover were unfamiliar to him. Yet he also clearly understood the meaning behind the characters. He stared at the cover, fascinated by what he was seeing. As he thought about it, he realized that he was 'seeing' the symbols. Just as when he read, he didn't necessarily see the individual letters, 'a'__'r'__'r'__'o'__'w', 'arrow'. He simply saw the collective symbol, 'arrow' and knew what it signified. In a similar manner, while he didn't recognize the individual characters on the cover of the volume he held, he immediately grasped its meaning. It was titled, *The Regents of Aidon, From the Founding of the Council, 1477 – 1977.* He flipped through the volume. Each page listed the name of the Regent, the period of his or her reign and the names of their family members. That was all. Replacing the volume, he glanced at the titles of a number of adjacent volumes. These were similar to the one he had just looked at.

Colin walked along the shelves, noting that the majority of the shelf space was empty. Reaching another section, he removed another volume. This was titled, *The Battles With Kernsidon, From the Founding of the Council, 2025 – 2483.* This volume was more detailed than the other one he had looked at. It contained the dates and location of the battles with Kernsidon, who had commanded the defending forces and the names of those who had participated as well as those who had been wounded or killed. For the most part, it was a dry, statistical accounting. He replaced the volume and turned to Dalene, "Are all of these histories?"

She nodded, "On this floor, the writings are exclusively history."

"What's on the other floors?"

"Come. I'll show you," she replied, leading him to the stairs.

They went to the floor above. The balcony overlooked the main hall. Rooms led off from the walkway. Dalene turned into the first one. It was lined with shelves, but only a few volumes occupied them. He took one down and read the title, *Mathematics*. Opening the volume, he glanced at simple mathematical formulas, nothing more complex than linear algebra. A quick glance at other volumes revealed more of the same. Dalene led him to yet another room. This one was even more sparsely populated than the previous one. He picked up a volume and read, *Unusual Astronomical Observations, From the Founding of the Council, 1950 – 2100.* Flipping through the pages, he again saw pages of raw observation – comets, unusual meteor activity, solar and lunar eclipses and then one page caught his eye. It was labeled simply, *Solar Anomaly, 4th Moon, 6th Day – 7th Day 2043.* It briefly described an event where the observer stated that the sun had been seen to set on the specified day, but the night had never become dark. The next entry was labeled, *New Star Sighting, 4th Moon, 7th Day – 7th until the 10th Moon, 7th Day, 2043.* The entry contained several pages of descriptive information regarding a previously unknown star which had been seen. It detailed the observation and its procession across the heavens, up until the day that it disappeared as suddenly as it had appeared. He flipped through a number of other pages until he read the heading, *Solar Anomaly, 4th Moon, 4th Day – 6thDay, 2076.* This gave an account of an inexplicable darkness which had enveloped Aidon. The sun had suddenly gone dark and there had been no light for the next three days. No moon. No stars. No light. The ensuing pages showed the astronomical calculations which had been performed to determine the duration of the period of darkness. There was no explanation or speculation. He shoved the volume at Dalene. "This book, it says there was a night with no darkness and then several years later, three days with no light. Do you know anything more about it?"

Dalene glanced around nervously, "This volume is history, as I told you. It contains historical fact – things which were observed and recorded. What you are asking now falls outside the province of history. This is the type of speculation which the Council has forbidden, as it leads to argument and potentially, to chaos."

"But you do know something about it? There is more to it, isn't there?"

She looked as if she would refuse to answer, but suddenly said, "We must go to the basement level." Without another word, she turned and left.

The basement appeared to be even more massive than the main floor. Perhaps it was an artifact of the dim lamplight illuminating the cavernous hall. As on the floors above, the walls were lined with shelves, but these were even more barren. The tables, however, were a different story. They were covered with texts, scraps of parchment and papers. Some were faded. Others showed burnt edges. None were complete. As he walked along the tables, pausing to inspect the materials covering the tables, it looked like a collection of impossible, incomplete jigsaw puzzles. Too many pieces were missing. None of the edges were complete. A few were mostly finished, with only occasional holes where material had been destroyed or rotted away. He shook his head and asked, "What is all this?"

Dalene bit her lip before replying softly, "This is the future of Aidon. These are the collected prophecies of our people – at least, what little survived The Chaos. Here, a select few scholars continue to try and piece things together, to give us instruction until such time as Messias again sends his messengers. But because these writings are incomplete, there is much dispute about what they say – what they mean. A few have been pieced together and ratified by the Council as fact – given the same weight as the histories you saw upstairs. You asked about the astronomical observations contained in the volume you were looking at upstairs. Those are fact. They are not in dispute. However, when you attempt to apply meaning to the observation, you cross into the province of prophecy. Even here, in the basement, such speculation is discouraged. It is not wise to discuss such things outside of here. There are those who claim that the sightings you spoke of are related to prophecies of Messias. There are legends still existing that Messias was born on one of the stars – no, not stars, but a planet near one of the stars. The Night Without Darkness is claimed to have been one of the signs of his birth, as was the new star you read about. The legends claim that he was killed on the planet of his birth and the Days Without Light signified his death. But the ancient texts that may have said this, if they ever existed, have been destroyed. Because there was much disagreement regarding this, the Council has dictated that the Compliance should be used to eliminate this subject until more information is obtained."

"So, does the Council use the Compliance to eliminate all controversial subjects? Jorge said something about this once, when I asked him about Sabbath. He said you didn't work on Sabbath – at least he doesn't - but wasn't sure about anything else. Are you waiting for more information – for a messenger to tell you what you can do on Sabbath, or find some ancient writing that says what it's alright to do?"

Dalene was defensive, "It's not like that. I mean, sort of. Colin, you must understand, Aidon exists because Aidama and Aeva were obedient! In Aidon, we value obedience, it is what Messias asks of us! He gave us instruction through Aidama and through the mantle-bearers! I don't know why he has left us alone for so long, but we must be obedient! If we don't know what we are to do, we must wait until we do know. When we had false messengers and those teaching just what they thought or believed, chaos followed. Aidon was almost destroyed!"

Colin shook his head, "I can't believe this, but it would explain so much. Dalene, there are so many things that you're missing! I mean, Aidon is missing. Soap! Your people should have invented soap or making leather 4000 years ago! You have huge holes in your knowledge base! My guess is anytime someone started doing something new – like making a bow and arrow or riding a horse, some Council decided they ought to consult the ancient texts to see if it was OK. Of course the text didn't say anything. Either it had been lost or it was something the world had never seen before! But that didn't mean it was bad, it was just new! Your people are so fixated on being obedient you're afraid to learn! No wonder your whole society is stagnating! Look at it! I left Aidon for six weeks, or close to it. I've never seen such a fantastic world as what I traveled through! There are huge forests. Those plains would grow anything! Why doesn't anyone ever leave Aidon? Why only 12 cities?"

"It is dangerous to leave Aidon. Here, it is safe. Outside, it is not known. The Councils keep us safe," she said uncertainly.

"Life is unsafe!" Colin exclaimed. "Population! There's no way you could maintain this population at this low of a level for this many thousands of years unless you had severe disease or famine or some other limiting factor. I'm guessing that the Councils use the Compliance to help people decide how many children to have, don't they?" he demanded.

She nodded, reluctantly, "But it is necessary. As you say, if there are too many people then we will have famine, or many would have to leave Aidon. The Councils help maintain the population so it is beneficial to all. Before the Councils, there was war. The records were destroyed. Now there is peace! Can you not see this?"

"No. The price is too high. A couple of hundred years ago, in my land, the people were faced with the choice of going to war or having peace, a man named Patrick Henry said, 'Is life so dear, or peace so sweet, as to be purchased at the price of chains and slavery? Forbid it, Almighty God!' Maybe I shouldn't say anything. Maybe I really don't understand, but what it looks like, what it <u>feels</u> like to me, is that your Councils use the Compliance to enslave the people and make them like it! Their intentions may be good, but the people have no choice in even the most basic of decisions – how many children to have, where to live, what occupation they will pursue! For 4000 years they haven't even been free to catch a fish or make soap! No wonder the Council wants to destroy me! You're all slaves! Slaves to tradition or slaves to your history! You're not free to dream! You're not free to <u>live</u>!" He slumped onto a bench.

"No," Dalene replied, shaking her head in return. "It's not like that at all."

Raising his head slightly, he looked at her and said, "Then you paint me a picture so I can understand what it's really like. I'm not saying that the Council doesn't have good intentions. Keeping the people safe and maintaining peace is an admirable objective, but slavery is a steep price to pay to ensure that there is never any dissent. Freedom has inherent risks, but if your people are never free to make their own choices in life, how can they ever grow?"

For a long time, Dalene just stood there, not sure what to say. At last she offered, "But Colin, surely you must agree that we ought to obey the direction we receive from Messias."

"Of course," he responded, "Every society needs to have laws – especially to ensure that no one is permitted to harm someone else. But they should make a conscious choice to obey. Maybe it would be from fear, but mostly it would be because they see the benefit of the law. Maybe I'm wrong, but this whole thing with the Compliance - people aren't told how to feel, they aren't even given that much freedom. They're given whatever feeling the Councils want them to have. There's no choice involved at all. I just can't believe that was ever the intent of the Boxes. What does your history have to say about the origin of the Boxes? About their intended purpose? Is this what it describes?"

Dalene was obviously uncomfortable now, "Well, you have to understand that so many records were destroyed, there are gaps in the teachings. But since the Councils began, the Boxes have been used thus and it has kept the peace!"

"I understand what you're telling me. I'm just not very comfortable with it." He stood and began to walk along the tables, pausing to read from some of the fragments being pieced together. At one table, which was more complete than many of the others he read,

"___*have no other gods* _____ *any graven image*_____ *not use the name of the LORD thy* _____ *Remember the Sabbath day* _____ *not do any work* _____ *Honour* _____*father* _____ *mother* _____ *days* _____ *long upon the land* _____ *not kill. Thou* _____ *commit adultery.* _____ *not steal.* _____ *bear false witness* _____ *not covet thy neighbor's house,* _____ *wife*_____"

Colin stared at this for a long time, before looking at Dalene. "The Ten Commandments," he said.

"What?" she asked.

"This is The Ten Commandments. Look, much of it is missing, but it says, 'Thou shalt have no other gods before me. Thou shalt not make unto thee any graven image. Thou shalt not take the name of the Lord thy God in vain. Remember the Sabbath day to keep it holy. The seventh day is the Sabbath day of the Lord thy God. In it thou shalt not do any work. Honor thy father and thy mother that thy days may be long upon the land the Lord thy God giveth thee. Thou shalt not kill. Thou shalt not steal. Thou shalt not bear false witness against thy neighbor. Thou shalt not covet they neighbor's house nor they neighbor's wife not anything that is thy neighbor's. The Ten Commandments."

Dalene stared at him, eyes wide,"Are you then truly the messenger of Messias? You have prophecy?"

"No," he shook his head, "but in my homeland we have these teachings – a book, several books actually, containing instruction such as this. I probably didn't quote it perfectly, but that's what this is. I recognize it. This other fragment, it says, 'be ye therefore perfect,' it looks complete."

"Yes," Dalene was excited now, "It is from this that the Council has determined to test those who claim to wear the mantle truly. If they are the messengers of Messias, they will obey his commands. They will be perfect. You see? You see how priceless the teachings are?"

"They have value," Colin admitted, "but you can't take them in isolation. What came before this statement? What came after? Why does the Council apply this only to the mantle-bearers? Why is it not applied to every man and woman in Aidon? Where is the justification to destroy those who don't live up to this fragment of command?"

Dalene looked confused again, "I don't know, but you see why we must be cautious. There must be no question, no cause for argument when the people are told what Messias requires. It is what I told you. Disagreement leads to confusion. Confusion leads to anger and anger to war. We must know before we can teach the people what to obey."

"Dalene, can't you see? By applying this fragment in the way that they have, it's probable that the Councils have been destroying every messenger sent to them for thousands of years. We're supposed to become perfect, but that may take a lifetime – beyond this life even. I think your Messias can use imperfect people to help accomplish his work and as we partner with him, he helps us to become a little more perfect – his perfection makes up for our deficiencies. You have fragments of The Ten Commandments. You have the commandment to be perfect. I'd have to look through a lot more of this, but my gut feeling is that if you have this much, you had to have received it from true messengers – those who wear the mantle by right, as you put it. And I have to believe that there were others sent as well, in order to help put this all back together for you."

Now Dalene sat, "It cannot be as you say! The messenger of Messias must be without flaw. If what you say is true, then the other messengers who have appeared before the Council……….. " her voice trailed off, her shoulders slumped.

Colin stood silent, not knowing what else to say. At length Dalene looked up, "My mother wished for you to see everything in the library. Come, there is one more room I must show you."

She led the way to a small alcove at the very back of the cavernous hall, hesitating briefly before taking a lamp from near the door and entering. Colin followed her. Inside, it was similar to the other rooms he had seen. Two large tables practically filled the room. Shelves lined the walls and as with the other rooms, they were but sparsely filled with books.

Dalene turned and faced him, her face filled with pain for a brief moment before she cleared it of all emotion. "This room is the most valuable treasure in Aidon. Here are stored the commandments and prophecies which have been confirmed by the Councils for over 4000 years as being the authentic teachings of Messias. Everything else in the library is directed toward this room. The fragments you saw on the tables outside – those are being pieced together in the hopes of having completed instruction which may then be added to these. At times we have found multiple documents, all badly preserved, but we can piece enough together to find that they all deal with the same subject. By using these multiple documents, we can discern the original teaching, so it can be studied by the Council and added here – to this collection. This room contains the law of Aidon. The law of Messias. But besides law, it also contains prophecy. The warnings against false messengers as well as the instruction for all mantle-bearers to be examined by the Council to determine if they wear the mantle truly or not and if not, to destroy them. This is part of our law, but the warnings are part of our prophecy. It was mother's intent that you read one such prophecy in particular." Dalene pulled a volume from the shelf and immediately turned to the page she sought. She set the book on the table and said, "Here. Read this."

Colin adjusted the lamp and read the brief passage – the only lines on the page,

> *"And if the daughter of the most high shall yield her heart, they shall be cast out. They shall become as one and shall destroy the ruler of this people."*

"Alright," he said, "I've read it."

"Now do you understand?" she asked.

"Understand what?"

"Who I am. <u>What</u> I am. I am the daughter of the Regent. The daughter of the most high. I am The Lady of Prophecy," she spoke through clenched teeth.

Colin shrugged, "OK. So that's why people address you as The Lady Dalene?"

She relaxed, "Yes. Now you understand."

"Understand what?"

"This prophecy is about me! Me, or one of my sister-descendents! I am destined to destroy Aidon! To destroy my father! Can't you see?" She was nearly in tears.

Colin didn't know what to say. He moved to place an arm around her shoulders as she angrily attempted to shrug him off. He persisted, pulled her close and spoke softly, "Dalene, all I see are words on a page. They have no life of their own. Your life is your own. You are free to make of it what you will. In my land we had prophecies as well. Some had multiple meanings, multiple fulfillments even. Even if this thing is completely accurate and if it came from one of those fragmented puzzles out in the other room, I doubt it is either complete or accurate, it probably doesn't have exactly the meaning you are reading into it."

"It does!" she insisted. "For 4000 years the daughter of the Regent has always been charged to ensure that this prophecy is never fulfilled! It is why we remain cold and indifferent. The people hate us! They fear us. But what we do, we do to safeguard them!" Collecting herself, she continued more calmly. "My mother wished for you to know this. To know what I am. I have been unfair to you, in not telling you of this sooner. I'm sorry. I have valued your friendship. I....I have never had a friend before. But I should not have used you falsely."

Colin released her and stood back a half a step, "So, now that you've told me this, you will no longer be my friend?"

"It is not me! It is <u>you</u>! Now that you know, you will no longer wish to be my friend, because you know what I am," she objected.

"You are the daughter of the Regent of Aidon. Lady of Prophecy. The Lady Dalene. You are Dalene. I'll call you whatever you wish, but I like the last title best. You're my friend. I hope to always be yours. You're my friend because of what you are. I've seen your true-self and I treasure the friendship of one such as you," he replied.

She was shocked, "You have seen..........then it truly happened? At the Evaluation? I thought...... I mean, I felt........... but that's impossible. Only when two are inside the Evaluation Box can one see the true-self of another. Well, sometimes if they touch. I mean, I could sense you, or I thought I could. But none inside the Box can see one outside the Box! It cannot be done!"

Colin shrugged, "It was strange. The whole evaluation was weird, though I didn't know what to expect. But seeing the lights – the true-self as you put it – that was truly amazing."

She was curious now, "Then the others, the Examiners – they couldn't see you, but you found them? You could see them?"

He nodded.

"But if I could sense you. Feel you. Why couldn't they? When you tried to make them bow – could they not feel you even then?"

He shrugged again, "I don't know. I never tried to make them bow. It just didn't feel right – trying to force them. I didn't want to touch them. I don't know why – I.......I was kind of afraid of what I might do. Yearsley said she could sense me. So did Krainik. I think they probably could. When I thought about it afterwards, there was something – like they were getting close. If it wasn't for the fact that the horses can see me, I'd wonder if I had a true-self. Anyway, when I saw your true-self, it was just so ....so pretty I guess. Like Alicia with my hair that one evening at dinner when she just couldn't resist touching it. Well, that's kind of how I felt, so I just brushed against the light. It was pretty."

She blushed, remembering her own reaction to his hair. "I thought I had just imagined it. But I know that I didn't imagine how you touched me this morning on the balcony! That hurt. How did you do that?"

Colin shook his head, "I don't know. I just kind of lashed out when I thought I was being attacked. It wasn't something I thought about or intended. It just happened."

Dalene was serious again. "I spoke of this to you this morning. There are legends of such power, from long ago. Nothing in this room – nothing the Council has decided is adequately documented. But it is said that once there were some who could mold the air. It was said they had but to think and the air itself would bend to their will. Others could work stone like it was clay. Is that what you did?"

Colin considered it carefully. "Maybe. I don't know how such a thing is possible, but there are a lot of things happening to me lately that I don't understand. If so, I certainly don't know how to make it happen or how to control it."

"You said there were other things," Dalene pursued. "What other things."

Now Colin was uncomfortable, unsure of just how much to discuss. "Well, even my being here. I don't have a clue how that happened or why. My archery – the bow and arrow – I was never very good at it, but here, it's like I almost can't miss. I told you about the giants – the Anakims, I mean. I fought Gath. When I left there, I stopped where we had fought. He had actually shattered boulders. He hit me at least once. Maybe twice. I spent most of the fight running, trying to get away. But when he hit me, he should have killed me. Instead he just threw me several yards. I don't know how I survived. Maybe it was like this morning and I used the air to shield myself. But if that's the case, why couldn't I do that the day I came to Salem? That pikeman about busted my skull."

Dalene looked at him intently, "Colin, are you certain that you are not the messenger of Messias? I mean, you don't know how you got here. What if there are other things you have forgotten as well?"

He smiled, despite her intensity, "If I am, he forgot to tell me about it and I think he forgot to give me a message as well. Besides, if the Council can ever find my true-self to have a look, they're going to find more flaws than they can catalog in a lifetime."

They sat in silence for several minutes, while Colin leafed casually through the volume he was holding. Sighing deeply, he replaced it on the shelf. "Is there anything more here you think I should see?" he asked.

Dalene shook her head, "No. There are many rooms, but most contain what you have already seen – a few volumes, but mostly remnants of different prophecies or events that we are trying to piece back together. We can look at more if you would like," she offered.

"No. I don't know what else I might learn. I just can't believe that all this," he gestured, "is the culmination of 4000 years of your society. There should be volumes on medicine, literature, science – I'm just having a hard time coming to grips with this. There's a part of me screaming, 'There ought to be more!' There's another part of me that loves this peaceful society that I've seen here. But I can't get over the idea that it's still just a very comfortable form of slavery. I'm sorry."

She nodded, hesitated before asking, "What you said.......about being my friend......It is true?"

"Dalene, you are the best friend I've had in years. Whatever happens, I am your friend."

She looked at him seriously, wondering how his words could make her so happy and at the same time make her feel like her heart was breaking. She forced a smile and grabbed the lamp, leading him out of the room so he wouldn't see the tears in her eyes.

Once outside the Library, she asked, "Is there something else you would like to see today?"

"I'd like to see Gisele. Is that possible?" he replied.

"Of course!" This time, the smile was genuine. "The stables are behind the Praetorium. My father has a small section for our animals. Gisele is with them. I'd like to see her as well."

They walked briskly, ignoring the stares they were getting along the path. Colin's height and appearance definitely drew stares. Dalene was used to the attention. She had withdrawn, erasing all emotion from her face, neither looking to the right or the left. Colin muttered, "If you can't fix it, flaunt it." He forced a smile, nodded and waved an occasional greeting at those who were staring at him. This was usually met by shocked embarrassment, except for the children. The children would stare at him wide-eyed, but when he smiled and winked at them, their faces would split into huge grins. The older ones, unaccompanied by parents, soon formed an entourage, following closely behind Colin and Dalene. He could see the color rising at her collar. When there were about twenty kids following, Colin halted and turned to face them, stooping down to be on their level. Twenty faces froze in shock as they prepared to flee. Colin smiled and it was genuine. "Hi," he said, "I'm Colin. What's your name?" He directed his gaze and question to a boy about 12 years old in the front ranks.

The boy looked at him nervously and in a timid voice said, "I am Dalran, of Salem."

Colin inclined his head to the boy, which seemed to surprise him even more, "Dalran of Salem, I am pleased to meet you. Dalran, do I look funny to you?"

Before Dalran could reply, the other children chimed in, "Your face is smooth!" "Your hair is so light!" "You wear no color!" "You're so tall!" Soon there was a commotion of shouted comments and laughter.

Colin nodded, laughing with the children, "You're right! I do look different. Do you want to touch my hair?" The kids were suddenly shy, but nodded. They pushed all around him, touching his hair, feeling his face and fingering his cloak. Colin waited patiently, giving them each a chance to touch and answering their shouted questions. Finally he said, "Now, you can all go home and tell your mothers and fathers about the strange looking man you saw today. But this nice lady and I need to be going, alright?"

Dalran blurted out, "But that's The Lady Dalene!"

"Yes, and we're friends. I looked different to you, right?"

They nodded.

"But when you felt my hair and my face – I feel just about like anyone else, is that right?"

Again they nodded.

"So I'm really not that much different. Neither is The Lady Dalene. Mostly we're pretty nice, and basically we're just people – just like you." Colin stood and started to walk away, but called back over his shoulder, "Just remember, I'm the funny looking one!"

Dalran was pontificating, using the pedestal Colin had briefly placed him on as the focus of attention, "That's right. He's just like us. And he's pretty nice. I think he's alright!"

A little girl's voice was heard to say, "I don't think he's funny looking. I think he's handsome!"

Dalene smirked, "You have an admirer."

Colin smiled in response, "Even a blind pig finds an acorn once in awhile."

"That was nice. What you did – talking to the children."

He shrugged, "Sometimes I forget that they're just people, too. But I'll bet that those kids will be sticking up for us with the others and with their parents as well."

Dalene shook her head, "For you maybe. If I had been by myself, they would have frozen or run off in terror or silently stalked me."

"Maybe," he agreed. "But if they freeze, there's your chance to talk to them. If they stalk you, do what we just did. You do that a couple of times, a few of them will get to know you, pretty soon they start saying 'Hi.' From the way Dalran was looking at you, I'm betting you picked up an admirer yourself."

When they reached the stables, Dalene led the way through rows of stalls that seemed to go on forever. Most of them were empty, but several held horses, watching them with interest as they walked by. Cows and even a few goats were also there. A number of stable hands, dressed in black, brown or green cloaks were busy working and eyed Colin and The Lady Dalene with interest. A few nodded in their direction, but none spoke to them. They passed entirely through the stable, exiting out the back into a large courtyard containing a corral, several small pens and watering troughs. Across the courtyard Dalene entered a smaller stable. This one contained only about 30 stalls. Out back of this building was another corral and a fenced pasture about an acre in size. Four horses were grazing in the pasture. Colin recognized Gisele immediately. At the sound of her name, Gisele's head jerked up as she nickered in greeting while charging toward the fence. She slid to a stop in a shower of dirt, tossing her head and whinnying, obviously pleased to see Colin. He slipped through the bars of the fence to pet her and she rubbed her head affectionately on his chest.

"How are you, girl? Did you miss me? They treating you good?" Colin spoke to her, not really caring about the words, but knowing that the horse wanted to hear his voice. He turned to Dalene, "She looks good. I think she enjoys the company as well," he indicated the other horses which were approaching.

Dalene slipped through the fence as well and was petting Gisele. "I hoped she would. She wasn't happy being in a stall all by herself. I think she needs room to run."

"People and horses," Colin agreed. "Give 'em some room to run."

Dalene looked at him curiously, but he just smiled and asked, "Is her saddle here?"

She nodded, "In the stable. Are you going to ride her?"

"Maybe for just a few minutes, if that's alright?"

"Certainly. I like to watch. It still fascinates me that anyone can actually ride a horse."

Colin slipped through the fence again and entered the stable, followed by Dalene. She showed him the tack room where the saddle was draped over a rail. Sitting next to it was another saddle, almost identical in construction, but made with a canvas shell and a layer of padding in between. Canvas straps had been stitched to the pad to form a girth. A canvas halter and reins were hanging on a hook on the wall. Colin lifted the canvas saddle and asked, "What's this?"

Dalene looked a little embarrassed, "I had our harness maker copy your saddle. He was really interested in the leather yours was made of, but of course he had to work in canvas. I was hoping to train one of my father's horses like you did Gisele – for riding. Do you think it's possible?"

"I imagine so. Here, you take your saddle. I'll grab the halters and my saddle. Let's see what we can do," he replied.

Gisele was waiting for them, her head thrust eagerly over the top of the fence. "I think she <u>wants</u> you to ride her!" Dalene exclaimed.

"Probably," Colin agreed. "Horses are pretty social animals. They like people. Gisele and I spent a lot of time together, so she's probably feeling neglected since I haven't been on her for a few days." He rubbed her down with the saddle blanket, then shook it out before folding it and saddling the horse. She was tossing her head, anxious to be off.

"Which of these did you want train?" Colin asked, indicating the other three horses standing nearby, watching with curiosity.

"This one," Dalene replied, walking over to a petite black mare. She had a white blaze and two white stockings on her forefeet. She nuzzled

Dalene affectionately as she was scratched behind her ears. "This is Kim. She isn't as big as some of my father's other horses, but she's my favorite. When she was young, she became very ill. We thought she might die. I spent a lot of time with her then, trying to get her to drink from a bottle, because she was too weak to stand. When she finally got well, she would come whenever I called and she followed me everywhere if she wasn't penned up. Kim is the one I use if I'm just taking the small cart. She's fast and I think she likes me."

"Alright. Kim it is." He walked over to the horse, letting her smell him as he rubbed her back. He took his time, talking softly while stroking her neck, passing his hands over her legs and picking up her feet. She tolerated all this with mild curiosity, getting used to his touch and the sound of his voice. "Go get the blanket and saddle," he instructed Dalene. "Let her look it over and smell it. She needs to know it's nothing to be afraid of. When she's checked it out, set it gently on her back. Don't cinch it. Just let it sit there."

Dalene did as she had been told, letting Kim become familiar with the scent and feel of the saddle.

Colin hesitated now, but finally said, "Dalene, I want to try something. With Gisele, I took several days getting her used to the saddle, the halter and my weight. To be honest, I didn't think she was ready to ride. I thought I was going to have to lead her and get her trained on the trail. But I did something with her and it seemed to work. I want to try it with Kim as well and see what happens."

"Alright," Dalene said, "Show me. Remember, you're teaching both Kim and I."

"OK, I want you to come here, beside me."

She slipped under the horse's neck to join him on the same side. "Now," he continued, "we're going to close our eyes. Just keep stroking her neck or scratching her ears, but I want you to do what you do in the Evaluation. I want you to find Kim's true-self and visualize for her, what you want her to do. What the saddle is for and how to carry you when you ride. OK?"

Dalene shook her head. "This morning you said something about horses seeing you, but animals do not have a true-self. We do not do this."

"I know you don't do this. You don't ride horses either," he answered, smiling. "But animals do have a true-self. A spirit. An intelligence. It's there. Maybe what I'm trying is foolish, but I want to try it anyway. Will you help me?"

Reluctantly, she nodded. The two of them closed their eyes, stroking Kim's head and neck. Colin reached with his mind, trying to find that glowing sphere which was Kim's true-self. He seemed to be getting nowhere, when his hand brushed Dalene's and they both froze. Instantly, he saw the beautiful soft glow. It was different than what he had seen in his

Evaluation. He knew this was Kim's intelligence, what the Aidonians called the true-self. Yes, it was different. After all, she was a horse, not a human, but she had her own innate beauty. Again he reached, mentally stroking the surface of this beautiful globe of light, visualizing what it was like to feel the saddle cinched tight around her belly, the halter on her head and the weight of a rider on her back. He tried to communicate the pull of the reins and the desired response. The intelligence that was Kim, cautious at first, seemed almost to taste this information, this sensation, becoming more eager, trying to absorb all it could. Reluctantly, Colin pulled back, releasing his mental contact with the glowing sphere before finally opening his eyes. An instant later, Dalene's dark eyes flared open, staring at Kim. Impulsively, she threw her arms around the horse's neck, "Oh, she's so beautiful! I had no idea!" She turned and looked at Colin, "How did you know? How did you do that?"

"I honestly don't know," he replied. "I mean, I've always known animals had intelligence – some more than others, of course. But as for how to see that, like this, I don't know. Before I came here, I'd never experienced it before. There's something about this place – about Aidon – this whole thing about being able to see someone's true-self. I think it's a path for a very special, very direct kind of communication. Anyway, I didn't know if it would work. I still don't know if it worked, but I did something kind of like this with Gisele and I was riding her way sooner than I would have expected. Let's see if it worked with Kim. Here, I'll show you how to cinch the saddle."

They proceeded to get the saddle and halter on Kim, who accepted them without shying. Colin said, "Keep your feet out of the stirrups at first. We'll see how she reacts when you get up on her back. If she acts up, just bail off. I don't want you having a foot caught. Are you ready to give her a try?"

Dalene nodded eagerly. Colin braced a knee for her to use as a step in order to swing a leg over Kim's rump as she settled into the saddle. Kim just looked back at her curiously. Colin still held the reins as he led Kim in a wide circle while Dalene grinned. At length, he said, "Alright. I'm going to give you the reins now. But just hold her still until I get up on Gisele. Then I want you to just follow me. Let Kim get used to the feel of the reins." He handed Dalene the reins, then mounted Gisele who had been waiting impatiently, tossing her head and stamping one of her front hooves.

Gisele wanted to run, but Colin held her back, keeping an eye on Dalene and Kim as they followed Gisele at a walk around the pasture. Colin gradually increased their pace. He was thankful that the horses of Aidon didn't share the jarring trot of their counterparts on his own earth. Gisele wanted to run, but the pasture simply wasn't big enough to turn the horses loose. They were too fast. But he did let them take the perimeter in a canter for several circuits, before he reined them in back at the stable. Dalene slid from the saddle before he could assist her. She threw her arms around Kim's neck again, "Oh Kim! That was wonderful! You are the best horse in the world!" Turning to Colin, she impulsively threw her arms around his neck as well, "Thank you! Oh, I can't thank you enough! She's wonderful!"

Suddenly remembering herself, she jerked back, blushing a deep crimson. Colin was about half stunned. Her soft feel had suddenly made him remember, feel things all but forgotten. He looked at her for a moment, her hair in disarray, eyes sparkling with excitement and the color darkening her olive skin. She was beautiful. "You're welcome," he responded softly. "That's just one of those things friends do."

They cared for the horses, giving them a good rubdown before stowing the saddles and halters back in the tack room. Dalene was so happy and excited she was practically vibrating. "Tomorrow," she declared, "we have to take them out of the city – someplace where they can run. I think Kim would like that."

"Yes, I'm sure <u>Kim</u> is most anxious to go for a run," Colin replied dryly. "Is she the only one excited about that?"

"Well, I was thinking that Gisele might want to run as well," Dalene said with a grin. Becoming serious, she continued, "I can't believe that I can ride Kim after just one day! Not even that long, really. Why has no one done this before?"

Colin shook his head. "I don't know. Keep in mind that ordinarily I would have expected training Kim to take a few weeks – several days at best. Finding Kim's true-self certainly accelerated the process, though she still isn't fully trained. The two of you will need to do a lot of riding together before that happens. But this is one of the things that keeps puzzling me – it <u>is</u> relatively easy, so why <u>hasn't</u> it been done before? What has prevented some of the most basic avenues of progress from occurring?" Immediately, he wished he had said nothing, as the mood suddenly shifted.

By dinner time that evening, Dalene had recovered her good spirits. She was chattering happily with her mother, helping prepare the meal. Halvor was not present this evening, but the Regent was. In the middle of dinner Dalene suddenly announced, "I rode Kim today!"

Her father paused, his spoon half-way to his mouth, "Who is Kim?" he asked.

"My horse. You remember. The black mare that was so sick when she was born. You helped me get her better."

He nodded, remembering, "What do you mean, you rode her?"

"Just that. I had a saddle made, so I would have something to sit on and a place for my feet to rest. Colin helped me train her and I rode her today. Tomorrow we are going someplace outside of Salem so she can run.

Gisele loves to run, but I think Kim is faster!" She gave Colin a playful look.

Her father looked at Colin, making him a little uneasy, "This is true?"

"Yes. Where I come from, it's common for horses to be trained for riding."

"I had heard the reports – that you rode on the back of a horse. But you have taught another – you have taught one of my horses for riding?"

Dalene broke in, "Kim is my horse. I will pay you for her if you wish, but she is mine."

The Regent seemed not to hear, as he continued to study Colin intently, "Yes. We spent a good part of the afternoon working with her. She's not fully trained yet, but she is learning nicely. Your daughter rides well. She and Kim make a good team."

At length Gareth nodded. "I must see this. And all this, you have done this in one day?"

"It went better than I had hoped. Kim took to it right away." Colin hoped Dalene caught his warning glance. For some reason, he really didn't want her bringing up the subject of seeing the horse's true-self. It just seemed like a potentially dangerous complication at the moment.

As if sensing his discomfort, Beatrice changed the subject, "And how did you enjoy your visit to the Library, Colin?" she asked.

The Regent, who had just begun to eat again, froze once more, his spoon half-way to his mouth. "You visited the Library?" he asked, but he was looking at his wife.

Colin suddenly wished they had talked about finding an animal's true-self. "Yes," he answered. "We spent some time there this morning."

"And what did you find there?" he asked, with his gaze riveted on Beatrice, who continued to eat, ignoring her husband completely.

Colin hesitated. Dalene appeared to be frozen. Only her mother seemed unconcerned. "I found very little," he finally said. "You're more familiar with it than I am. There are volumes of history, but very little to place that history in context."

"What do you mean?" Finally, the Regent focused his gaze on Colin.

"The history I looked at was just a collection of dry dates. A catalog of events. There was no context in which to interpret the events. There is a listing of what happened, but no explanation of why. In my land, there is a saying, 'Those who fail to study the mistakes of history are doomed to repeat them.' You have dates and events, but no discussion of the underlying causes leading up to those events. Without that, you have very little of real value."

"Conjecture." Gareth dismissed him. "You place value on nothing but the grounds for argument – the speculations of others regarding that which cannot be known. Your value rests on the seeds of discord."

"There will be disagreement, but reasonable individuals can disagree without coming to violence. The history of a man is more than a series of dates and events. The events occur because a man had thoughts and dreams. He had ideas and motivations that caused him to act. If you fail to capture that, to understand that, you have a hollow shell of a man, but you'll never understand who he really was."

"And what did you think of the lower level, Colin?" Beatrice asked.

Gareth now fixed his glare on Dalene, "You took him to the lower level?"

She nodded, timidly.

"Those writings have not been accepted by the Council!" he stated flatly. After a momentary pause he amended, "Most of them. You showed him the prophecies, didn't you?"

Again she nodded silently.

"Goodness, Gareth! The man has been condemned by our law! Surely you wouldn't begrudge showing him where we get the law by which he is condemned. I told Dalene to take him to the Library, so if you are going to be upset with anyone, it should be me," Beatrice said.

The Regent's glare suddenly faded. He sighed deeply and said, "You're right. The law is the law. He has a right to see – to understand why we do what we must do."

Turning to him again, Gareth asked, "So, what did you think?"

Colin looked at him levelly, "I think you're trying to do the impossible. The fragments of parchment I saw were so badly damaged you will never be able to gain more than a vague idea of what the text originally said. Assume you get something almost complete, but missing one piece – one word even. If that word is 'not' the writing can be given the complete opposite meaning of what was intended. Thou shalt steal. Thou shalt sometimes steal. Thou shalt not steal. Which is correct?"

Gareth snorted, "That's obvious."

"Of course," Colin agreed, "but the problem is that one word can change the whole meaning in cases that aren't so obvious. I think your laws are probably flawed for exactly this reason. Your scholars have tried to piece things together, but there are too many fragments missing for them to get it exactly right every time."

"That is why the Council must approve it before it is accepted." Gareth objected.

"And what makes the Council qualified to make that determination? Do they possess special knowledge that your scholars don't have?" Colin asked.

"Father," Dalene said, "Colin knew one of the prophecies. The one about Sabbath and stealing. You remember?"

Gareth looked at Colin interestedly, "So you <u>do</u> claim to be a messenger?"

Colin sighed, "No. We've been through this. It's just that in my home, we had at least some of these same teachings. I think your Messias corresponds to the Messiah that I was taught – Jesus Christ."

"We do not say that name!" Gareth bellowed. "It is forbidden!"

Once again Colin felt the liberating sense that comes from having already been condemned to be destroyed. "Why?" he asked simply.

Calming himself, the Regent replied, "You read the law yourself. We are not to use the name of Messias!"

"In vain." Colin corrected. "You are not to use the name of the Lord thy God <u>in vain</u>. You see? This is what we were just talking about. If you are missing even a small part of the writing, you may miss the meaning completely. How do you talk to someone if you can never use their name? How do you get to know them or develop a relationship with them? I'm not your messenger, but as long as you keep looking for this perfect, flawless individual to come and teach you, you're going to keep destroying every messenger that your Messias <u>does</u> send. And until you receive the messengers that are sent to you, instead of looking for the one you think you ought to get, I think your efforts to reconstruct the laws and prophecies are going to fail, just as they have for 4000 years."

The Regent abruptly pushed back from the table and stood, glaring down at Colin, "You will not speak of this in this house! My wife," he shot her an angry glance, "has appealed your punishment, but that will not prevent new charges being brought if you speak of this again! The law is the law and we will obey it!" With that he turned and stormed angrily from the room.

"I'm sorry," Colin apologized to Dalene and her mother. "I had no right to speak as I did, in your home. I didn't mean to anger your husband. It was a poor way for me to return the kindness you have shown me. I should probably go."

"No. Please stay," Beatrice requested. "My husband is very adamant in following the law as it has been given to us by the Council. There is great value in that. He is a good man. The weight of being Regent is sometimes difficult to bear. He may not show it right away, but he will think on the things you have said. It may take some time, but I believe he will consider what you have told him. Now, I have things that I would like to ask you. First, where did you learn the name of Messias? As you could see from my husband's reaction, we do not speak it. There are very few of the ancient writings which have this name written. Only those who study the old texts know of this. How is it that you, a stranger here, know this name?"

Colin closed his eyes and silently prayed before starting to answer. "You may not believe me when I tell you. I guess it doesn't matter too much, since I'm already supposed to be destroyed in a few weeks. I haven't told anyone here in Aidon this, because I didn't feel like it was my place to show up here and alter – contaminate, I guess is a better word – contaminate your society, your whole way of life. I really don't know why I'm here, or how I got here. Everything I've said on that subject is true. I do come from another land – a city called Kalispell. But that land, that city, is not on your earth. I am from some other world."

Dalene stared at him, eyes wide in disbelief. Beatrice stared at him, but more from curiosity than shock. She nodded her head, a hint of a smile showing, "Yes. It would explain much. Whether you are from Kalispell, here on earth, or Kalispell on another earth, your very appearance, here, in Aidon, has to completely change the way we view the world. Before your appearance, all people that we know of on earth are from Aidon. Oh, there's Kernsidon, as well, but even they will admit that they came from Aidon. Then suddenly, we have you. Obviously not from Aidon, so you cannot be from Kernsidon either. For us, the world has suddenly changed. Either there had to be people on earth not from Aidon – a thing we had never imagined before. Or, you must come from another earth. One is no more shocking than the other. So tell me, Colin, not of this earth, on your earth, you know of Messias?"

"Yes," he acknowledged, "we know of the Messiah. On my earth, there are many different lands – many millions of people. In each of these lands there are many churches – groups which teach what they believe the Messiah wants people to do. Some claim specific authority from Him. Others claim no authority is necessary. Some do not believe in Him at all, while others believe he has not yet come, but will come someday. It can be very confusing."

Dalene was obviously stunned, "Millions of people? But how do you control so many? How can you even do the Evaluation for that many?"

"It is very different from here. What you know as the Evaluation has never been heard of there. In many lands, people are simply free to follow the path in life that they wish. They will decide whom to marry, what occupation to pursue, how many children to have and where to live. In other countries, powerful men have managed to gather armies to control the people. In the past, some of these have virtually enslaved the population. In fact, there are many like that even today. But the other nations form alliances to try and prevent tyranny from spreading. It works, kind of, but my world is a very tense place. There is always the threat of conflict."

Beatrice shook her head, "I cannot imagine such a world. How can they not believe in Messias? You have writings – the prophecies? They do not believe them?"

"Some do. Some believe parts, but reject other parts. To a large degree, people are free to decide what they will <u>choose</u> to believe."

"With so many believing different things, they must have wars. Is this not so?" Beatrice asked.

"Unfortunately, yes. There have been terrible wars fought in the name of the Messiah. Men have done terrible things, and they will have to answer for those things." Colin responded.

"And what do you believe, Colin? Do you believe in Messias?" Dalene asked.

"Please forgive me for answering the way that I do, I have no wish to offend you, but I want to answer your question as completely as I can. I believe in Messias. I believe that your Messias is my Messiah and that he is Jesus Christ. I believe that he was born in Bethlehem of Judea over 2000 years ago, that he taught the people, that he healed the sick and raised the dead. I believe that prior to his coming he sent prophets – messengers – to those who would learn of him and follow his teachings. I believe that many of those prophets were rejected and killed. I believe that Jesus was killed in a city called Jerusalem about 33 years after his birth and that he was resurrected as a glorious and perfect being the third day after his death. I believe that the observations recorded in your history – the night with no darkness and the three days without light were signs shown here of his birth and of his death. I believe that Messias took upon himself the sins and pains of all those whom he created – on my earth, on this earth and on countless other earths like this – so that if we would follow his commandments, he could cleanse us, could heal all of our hurts and bring us back to our Heavenly Father. I believe that he is the Son of God and that after his death he sent prophets to teach the people what he would have them do, but just as the people generally rejected his messengers who preceded his birth, they have also largely rejected those who have testified of him after his death and resurrection. I believe that he has been sending his messengers to Aidon and the Council has been destroying them, because they aren't really looking for messengers, they are looking for the one perfect being, and that is your Messias."

Beatrice's eyes were moist as she looked at him, "Colin, are you saying that Messias was born – that he lived on <u>your</u> earth?"

"He did. We celebrate his birth in an event called Christmas and we celebrate his resurrection from death in an event called Easter. We have books of his teachings – the teachings of his messengers we call scripture. They teach of the prophecies of his coming, his life on the earth, his death and resurrection and what we must do so that his sacrifice can benefit us – can heal and cleanse us. In reality, only a small percentage of the people on my earth believe this, but <u>I</u> believe it. When he was on earth, before he died and again shortly after he was resurrected, he taught his followers. One of the things he said was, ...' other sheep I have, which are not of this fold:

them also I must bring, and they shall hear my voice; and there shall be one fold, and one shepherd.' I think you – the people of Aidon – are some of those sheep. I don't know what your teachings say, but I believe that one day he will come. He will visit Aidon."

Dalene almost, but not quite, looked angry. "Why did you not tell us this before? How could you know all this and claim to not be a messenger of Messias?"

Colin's tone was mild, "First, I am *not* a messenger – at least not the way you mean. Obviously I was sent here for some reason. What God does not cause, he permits. Therefore, God has at least permitted me to be here. But he hasn't given me any message for Aidon or for you, as far as that goes. It isn't my place to start proclaiming things to all of you that you're not ready to hear. My biggest fear is that I will contaminate your whole culture and mess up whatever plan your Messias currently has in play. There is so much here to admire – the peace and cooperation between the Files. I don't think it's perfect, but in some ways, it's a whole lot nicer than what my world has. I've heard it said that my world is the most wicked of all of God's creations. That it's the only one which would kill their God, as we did the Messiah."

"But if you would tell the Council! Make them believe you! Then they won't destroy you!" Dalene cried.

Colin shook his head, "Belief is largely a decision one makes. After the decision, either something confirms that belief to your heart, or it doesn't. That something is the Spirit of God – The Holy Spirit or Holy Ghost. I don't know your name for it. The Council wants it the other way. They want proof before they believe. That isn't my place – either to be some kind of proof to them or to try to make them believe. As far as I can tell, I'm not really part of what's going on here. I'm disconnected. Whether the Council destroys me or not really isn't important. Don't get me wrong, I'd really like to not be killed – destroyed, whatever – but if that's the price for being here, all I can say is that it has been worth it."

"But if we tell the people….." Dalene persisted before she was cut off by Colin.

"No! Absolutely not! You must not tell anyone what I've told you! You remember my telling you about the wars fought on my earth? That is exactly what would happen here! Already half the people want to have me killed and the other half think I was sent straight from Messias and ought to be king! I see how they look at me. I hear the whispers. I don't blame the Council for wanting to get rid of me. I'm not even sure that they're not right! You cannot tell anyone!"

Beatrice looked at him for a long moment and then asked, "Why did you tell us then, Colin?"

"I'm not really sure," he replied. "Maybe because of how kind you've been to me. Maybe because you asked. But I guess that's not really it. I just felt like I was supposed to. I felt like you were supposed to know. Maybe that alone is the whole reason I was brought here. I don't know." He shrugged.

Her eyes were moist, and whatever she was seeing, he was certain that it wasn't him. "Thank you," she said softly, "He lives. It is enough to know that. The testimony of two earths, it is truly remarkable." Suddenly, her eyes focused on Colin, "And to think, we have one sent from the earth where Messias was born. Where he lived. Thank you, Colin. Thank you for telling us this."

"You're welcome," he replied. "But I wasn't sent."

She nodded, but in a barely audible whisper said, "What God does not cause, he permits."

Chapter 20 Cavalry

Colin had been up less than an hour the next morning when there came a soft knock at his door. It was not yet the second hour of the day, so he was surprised when he opened the door and found Dalene standing there, smiling. "Oh, good. You're up. I was hoping we could leave early if we're going to take Kim and Gisele out. Mother has been kind enough to transfer your custody to me for the day." This last was said with a distinct smirk, as she tried to goad him just a little. "I packed some things for breakfast, if you don't mind eating on the way."

"Alright. Let me grab my things and I'll be right with you," Colin said.

Dalene led the way through the corridors. While Colin was fairly comfortable with his sense of direction out of doors, the maze of intersecting corridors inside the Praetorium still confused him. The few times he ventured out on his own, like when he attempted to find the baths, had found him backtracking and asking directions several times. He had, however, found his way to the kitchen that served the south wing. The staff was at first alarmed at his presence – not so much his physical appearance, though that was strange enough – but the fact that one of the residents would actually be in the kitchen was a major protocol gaffe. He'd been polite, actually sitting and visiting with them for a bit. Since then, he stopped by every now and again, picking up some bread or fruit to snack on. His arrival was greeted with a degree of amusement if not exactly an outright welcome. He was on a first name basis with several of the cooks and dishwashers, though they still maintained a certain distance.

Colin recognized the cross-corridor that led down to the kitchen. He was pretty sure that he spotted the way to the baths as well. While he had the bathing room in his quarters, he didn't like the idea of the servants hauling so much hot water over that kind of distance for his minor convenience. Finally they reached the stable and shortly afterwards Kim and Gisele were whistling a welcome to them. Dalene buckled the halter in place, grabbed a brush and quickly worked over Kim's back and sides before carefully placing the blanket and saddle on her back. Kim tolerated this operation, stamping her foot in apparent impatience, anxious to be going. Colin followed suit with Gisele and soon they were ready to go. Dalene hesitated for a moment before turning to him, "Do you think it's safe to ride them through the city? Or should we wait until we are outside the walls where there is more room?"

"It's early enough there shouldn't be all that many people about. You know the way, I don't. If the streets are fairly wide and not likely to be crowded, it should be OK to ride. We can always dismount if they start to act up."

Soon they were moving along briskly. Both horses were anxious to be on their way. Once they reached the main thoroughfare, they began to hear a commotion in their wake. Shouts of surprise at the sight of two horses being ridden through the streets of Salem quickly spread in front of them, with heads appearing in windows and people standing in doorways, pointing and staring. On the one hand, Colin found all this attention to be embarrassing. At the same time, it ensured a clear pathway before them. They didn't hear the whispers, but they did hear the shouts.

"It's The Lady Dalene and the mantle-bearer! They're riding horses!"

"That's not possible!"

"It's the impostor and The Lady Dalene – on horses! Is he escaping? I thought he was supposed to be locked up!"

The controversy made Colin uncomfortable, but Dalene appeared indifferent. In a few minutes they exited the city, leaving the guards standing with mouths agape. They hadn't ridden far when Dalene veered off on a road to the right, heading north. "We're not going to Tyber, then?" Colin asked.

"Very good, Colin, you're learning your way around," She approved.

"Only outside the city. I still can't seem to get my bearings in Salem. It's even worse in the Praetorium. I need a map."

They rode along in silence for awhile. Finally, Colin asked, "Where are we going?"

Dalene shrugged, "Nowhere really. This road leads to Neims and Ramah. Those are the cities of the 1st File and the 5th File. I think Ramah is about 12 miles from here. Neims would be at least another 3 miles past that. They lie at the foot of the mountains you see off to the east of us. I like this area. It isn't as good for farming as Tyber. Mostly they cut wood and mine coal and ore for smelting the metal we need. We won't be going there. It's too far to make the journey and still return to Salem in one day."

"On horses, we could do it. But it would be a long day and I guarantee that you'd be sore tomorrow. You'll probably be sore anyway," he told her.

"Why will I be sore?"

Colin laughed. "Right now it just seems like you're sitting, but you're working muscles in ways they aren't used to. Trust me, after a couple of hours your legs, bottom and back are going to be crying. If you ride every day for awhile, you'll toughen into it, but if we ride for very long today, you'll be feeling it tomorrow."

They passed few travelers headed toward Salem. Each time they did so, they were met with open-mouthed stares as people gawked. Dalene was smug, enjoying attention which was not directed at her as Lady of Prophecy. The rolling hills quickly gave way to more broken terrain. The hills were sharper, with rock outcrops looming over dense areas of forest. The road was cut by steep walled canyons with rushing streams coursing through them. Steep approaches or switchbacks had been cut, leading down to sturdy bridges upon which travelers could cross. Toward mid-morning they emerged from a section of timber into a broad valley stretching away up toward the mountain. A tree-lined stream meandered through a meadow carpeted with flowers. Dalene turned off the main road, riding toward the head of the valley where the stream dropped through a series of rocky cascades down to the meadow. She slid off Kim and unslung a pouch from her shoulder. Colin dismounted as well. He removed the bow from his shoulder and the saddle bags from Gisele. Dalene looked around, "It's beautiful here, isn't it?"

"Very beautiful," Colin agreed, looking directly at her.

Dalene blushed, but her eyes sparkled as she announced, "I want to go flying!"

Colin smiled as he watched her struggle to get a foot up into the stirrup. Finally he offered his knee for her to use as a step as she swung into the saddle. She waited while Colin mounted Gisele. With a mischievous grin she declared, "I think Kim can fly faster than Gisele!"

She wheeled Kim and kicked her into a run. Gisele didn't wait for Colin to coax her. Instantly she launched herself after the smaller mare. The meadow was all of two miles in length. They angled away from the stream to avoid the trees and bushes cluttering its banks. Both horses were in a mood to run. Gisele was the larger animal, but her load was also heavier. They skimmed over the grass, the flowers a colored blur as they ran, bunching and springing, covering yards at every leap. Colin saw Dalene glance back at him over her shoulder, laughing with delight. It was as though Gisele took her laughter as a personal affront. He felt her leaps suddenly become even faster, more powerful. In a second they pulled alongside Kim. The smaller horse took up the challenge and both animals were bounding faster than ever. As the end of the meadow rapidly approached, he began to pull Gisele up. Her competitive spirit didn't want to slow down. Reluctantly, she heeded the pull on the reins as Kim flashed away from them. Dalene gave another quick, delighted glance over her shoulder as she saw Colin and Gisele drop back. Suddenly, she realized how close they were to the trees at the end of the meadow. Immediately she pulled back on the reins – hard. Kim obeyed instantly and slid to a stop, her rump practically dragging in the grass. Dalene's momentum threw her forward and she lost her stirrups as she landed in an undignified heap on the grass in front of Kim where she lay laughing hysterically.

Colin rode up a moment later, "Are you OK?" he asked, more out of courtesy than of concern. He had watched her landing. It had been soft even if not particularly well executed.

Dalene was laughing so hard she could hardly catch her breath. When she finally managed to control her laughter, she just lay there in the grass grinning. Her hair was a mess. Tears streaked her cheeks, she had been laughing so hard. She looked beautiful. Finally she sat up, "That was wonderful!" She leaped up and threw her arms around Kim, unconcernedly cropping grass nearby. "We beat them, Kim! Oh, you were wonderful! We flew Kim! We flew!"

Gisele snorted, as if in disgust. Colin smiled and said, "You flew. Right over the head of your horse. You did great on your riding, but you might want to work on your stopping."

Dalene continued to stroke Kim's neck and spoke into her ear, making sure Colin heard, "Pay no attention to the sore losers, Kim. You are the fastest horse in Aidon!"

Gisele ignored her and fell to eating alongside Kim. Colin slid off her back. He stepped over to Dalene and brushed a little bit of dirt from her shoulder, then combed his fingers through the tangles of her hair. She stood smiling, "Thank you, Colin," she said.

"Don't mention it. I like running my fingers through the hair of beautiful women."

She blushed. Male attention was unheard of in her life, so it didn't take much to bring the color to her cheeks. "Not that. I mean for Kim. For teaching her to carry me and teaching me to ride. I love it."

Colin nodded. "Women and horses. One of the universal constants. But you're very welcome. You ride well. You look good on Kim."

They gathered the reins of their horses and led them over to the stream to drink. As they rode back to where they had left their gear, Dalene threw back her head and breathed deeply, smiling. "Sometimes I wish I could just forget Salem and live someplace like this forever. It's so beautiful and so peaceful. Did you ever feel like that?"

"Most of my life, actually. I used to love to go backpacking – hiking. Sometimes I would go by myself. Sometimes my Dad and brother and I would go together. For a couple of years my Mom would go with us. I still can't say why I love it so much. Mostly it's just a lot of work. But I love the wild country. I love taking off for a week and never seeing another person. I felt like I wanted to stay out there forever. But then reality would set in and you realize it just isn't practical, so you go back. Maybe that's why days like this are so special, because they don't last forever."

"You say 'Mom' and 'Dad.' This is your mother and father?" she asked.

"Yes, sorry. Those are common words for mother and father. More casual, but more intimate as well. I guess there is enough difference in meaning that it didn't translate quite the same," Colin replied.

She nodded, "Colin, why don't you just leave? Just ride away and never come back. You came back for the Evaluation, but they are going to destroy you. Why not just leave?"

"Even if I wanted to do that, I couldn't now. Your mother assumed responsibility for me. If I ran out now, she'd be the one they would punish. I can't do that to her."

"But they won't destroy her! They will you. Is it so important to you?" she asked.

He looked at her levelly, "Yes. It's so important to me."

They arrived back where they had left their gear. "I brought lunch," Dalene offered.

They left the horses to graze while they made their way to the edge of the stream. As they ate, Dalene asked, "The other morning, when I threw water on you and you struck me without touching me – have you thought any more about that?"

"I've thought about it," Colin admitted, "but I still don't know how I did it."

"Have you tried to do it again?"

"No," he shook his head. "I'm not sure I even know how to begin."

"But you said it was like when you shoot your bow."

"I said that shooting my bow was unusual as well. I don't know if it is like that. I've only ever done it the one time that I know of – the hitting without touching," he said.

She suddenly threw a rock at him, striking him in the chest "Hey!" he said, "That hurt!"

"Oh, sorry," disappointment was written in her face. "I thought maybe you would do the hitting thing to keep the rock from striking you."

"I gathered that already," Colin said dryly. "It was a nice thought, but apparently it doesn't happen quite so easily, or I probably wouldn't have had my brains knocked out by that pikeman."

"Show me how you shoot your bow." Dalene requested.

Dutifully, Colin retrieved his bow and quiver of arrows. "What shall I use for a target?" he asked.

Dalene looked around, "How about that large rock, there?" She pointed at a rock about 30 yards away at the edge of the stream.

"No. Rocks are awfully hard on arrows and it takes too much time to make them. You see that small tree just behind the rock?" He indicated a tree about four inches in diameter about 35 yards away. "I'll aim for where the first branch splits off from the trunk."

He selected an arrow, quickly aimed and shot. The arrow stuck, quivering where the branch met the trunk. Dalene was impressed. "Very good! You hit it!"

Colin appeared almost glum, "At home I could have tried for a week and maybe hit that target once. But that's not the impressive part. Watch. Watch where I aim this time."

Dalene watched as he lined up on the target and then very obviously shifted his aim to the left of the target about 20 degrees. He released the arrow and she watched as it arced in to impact just below the first arrow. She uttered an audible gasp, "That's impossible!"

"I know," Colin agreed, "except I just did it, which means it isn't impossible. It only should be impossible. At home it would have been. Something here is altering the laws of physics - at least the laws that I know of."

"Physics?" she asked.

"Physics. The study of natural laws. Especially those that define how bodies move and interact with each other. What I just did shouldn't happen. Well, if there were a strong enough wind blowing, then it could curve the trajectory of the arrow enough to deflect it that far. Ordinarily, it just shouldn't happen. But I've done it enough to know that it does happen so some other law that I don't know about is coming into play."

"If I hold a target, would you shoot it?"

"No. Even though it seems like I hit it every time, it would be a foolish risk. There's no reason to take the risk, so no, I won't do that," he replied.

She shoved him.

"What are you doing?" he asked.

She shoved him again, harder. "Make me stop."

"Quit. This is foolish."

She shoved him again, a grim set to her jaw. "Make me stop."

"No. I could hurt you."

Again she shoved, nearly knocking him over. It hurt this time. "Quit. I know what you want and I don't know how."

He tried to retreat, but she shoved him again, making him stumble. He was getting angry. "Will you quit!"

"Make me!" She shoved him again, anger flaring in her eyes as well.

"I'm not playing your game!" He wheeled and headed back toward the horses.

Dalene ran at him, trying to knock him over. At the last second he wheeled to grab her before she could hit him. "Stop it!"

Just before she struck him, it was as if she ran into a brick wall. There was a dull thud and she dropped to the earth, stunned. Instantly, Colin was at her side, kneeling in the grass. "Dalene! Are you alright? Don't move! Just catch your breath!"

She lay in a crumpled heap. Gently, he rolled her over. Her eyes fluttered open, "Owww! That hurt!" And she grinned.

Colin's heart finally dropped out of his throat where it felt like it had lodged. "Are you crazy? You could have been hurt!"

Dalene laughed silently, but her face wrinkled in pain. "Yes. Good thing I wasn't hurt!" she said sarcastically. She stretched her legs out from under her and her face relaxed as the pain subsided.

"Ouch. It felt like I ran into a wall!"

Colin's anger overran his concern, "And for all either of us knew, it could have been a lot worse! You don't mess with stuff like this!"

"Then how are you going to learn about it?" she asked.

The anger suddenly drained out of him. "I don't know. But please, don't do that again. That's twice I've hurt you. I really don't want to do that and one of these times it could be serious - maybe even fatal. Please don't do that."

She struggled to sit up, "Maybe," she replied. "So what did you learn?"

"I don't know if I <u>learned</u> anything. Both times this has happened, I felt threatened. I wanted it to stop - to go away. Last time I lashed out and you went flying. This time I just tried to stop you - to keep you from shoving me again and you looked like you slammed into something solid but invisible. So what does that tell us?"

"First, it's definitely you that's doing it," Dalene said. "Second, if you feel in danger, threatened anyway, somehow you respond by doing this. Maybe the amount of force you use is in relation to the degree of danger you feel. This time hurt more, but I think that was because I was running at you. Last time I was standing still, so I think this was my fault rather than yours."

"So how do I control it?" Colin asked, not really expecting an answer.

"Maybe like you did with your bow back on your world. You practice," was her reasoned response.

"How?"

"Maybe like you did with the Evaluation - when you were trying to see the true-self. You kept reaching with your mind. Seeing with your mind. Each time you went further. You saw more. It became easier and you learned to control it and where your mind went. Yes?"

"I never told you that." Colin replied.

"No," Dalene shook her head, "But Halvor reported on the Evaluation at Tyber, when you were there. Nothing like that had ever happened before, so it must have been you. And I watched you during your Evaluation. Each time, you were different. More confident. It was obvious that you were learning."

"I was," he agreed. "But I still don't know what I'm doing."

She shrugged, "Maybe you don't need to know 'what,' as long as you learn 'how.'" She made an effort to rise. Colin assisted her to her feet. She smiled her thanks. "You were right about one thing."

"What's that?'

"Tomorrow," she replied, "I am going to be sore."

Colin retrieved his arrows and joined Dalene back where he had left his things. She sat to rest on the grass. Colin began rummaging in his saddle bags. "What are you looking for?' she asked.

"My fishing gear. Your mother asked me to bring her some fish. This looks like a good place to try and catch a few."

Dalene watched with interest as Colin uncoiled his line. He had a fly already tied to it. "If I get the time, I need to make some better equipment. I can probably rig up a reel fairly easily. A decent rod will be harder."

He cut a willow pole and tied one end of his line onto it. While Dalene had eaten fish at Jorge and Miran's she had never watched them caught. Colin flipped his fly out onto a still back-eddy. It hadn't even had the chance to sink before a large trout hit it with a vengeance, bending the pole nearly to the breaking point.

"You caught one!" Dalene said excitedly.

Colin let the fish run back and forth in the deep pool, keeping tension on the line and letting it fight itself nearly to exhaustion. He worked it into the shallows. In a moment he hooked a thumb under its gill plate and hefted it out of the water, holding it up for Dalene to see.

"It's beautiful!" she said. "May I try it?"

"Sure. Come take the pole. I'll help you."

Colin strung the fish on a forked stick and weighted it in the creek before handing the pole to Dalene. Her first cast, if it could be called that, was clumsy. But there wasn't a lot of finesse involved in flipping a large fly on coarse line with a wooden pole out onto the stream. Colin wasn't concerned. The fish didn't seem to exactly be connoisseurs of proper fly presentation. The fly was drifting just below the surface. "Watch the fly," Colin instructed. "You'll probably see the fish just before it strikes the fly. The moment it hits the fly, give a short, hard jerk on the pole to set the hook."

An instant later, a fish struck. She was a fraction too slow, the fish had already spit the hook when she jerked the pole, sending the fly sailing back behind them. "Fast aren't they?" Colin commented.

Dalene was too excited to be disappointed in missing the strike. She flipped the fly out again and in almost the exact same spot the fish struck again. This time she was ready and set the hook perfectly. The fish immediately went wild. Dalene squealed with delight. "I got it! I hooked a fish!"

Colin helped her play it for several minutes, keeping it near the surface so it couldn't tangle on any obstructions on the stream bed. Finally, it was tired enough to be worked to the shore where Colin could get his thumb into its gills and land it. It was larger than the one he'd caught, a fact which did not escape Dalene. "I caught a fish! Mine is even bigger than yours! Another! Can I do it again?"

"Sure. You're an expert now. I'll let you do this one all by yourself." Colin replied.

She missed two more strikes before setting the hook on the third one. She managed to play it to shore, but when she tried to grab the fish, it thrashed wildly, tearing the hook free and escaping back into the deep water. She was outraged, "He got away! My fish got away! You could have helped!"

Colin was laughing. "At least he didn't get my fly. There are lots of fish, but I only have a few flies. Try it again."

She did, and in a few minutes had another trout at the edge of the stream.

"Hold on. Just keep your pole up. Keep the line tension on him. I'll give you a hand." Colin slipped behind her, placing his left hand over hers on the end of the pole. "Now, keep moving the tip of the pole back behind you while you squat down to where you can get a hand on him. He's slippery, so about the only place you can grab is right behind the head. Try to slip a thumb into his gills, then you'll have him. That's it." He went down with her, guiding her right hand onto the fish, helping her get it securely. The fish thrashed wildly as she lifted it from the water, splashing both of them. She barely managed to stand up when she lost her grip and the fish fell, flopping on the grass. With a cry of alarm, she threw herself on it before it could flop back into the water, scrambling madly to grab it with both hands under her belly. She finally had it and immediately threw it as far from the water as she could. Colin was laughing at her frantic efforts.

"I saved it!" She stated defensively. "No thanks to you!"

Colin shook his head, still laughing. "I don't blame you. That's a nice fish. I did almost the same thing when I caught a big fish back when I was a kid. I knew if I didn't get it nobody would ever believe me, so I jumped on it."

"Really?" she asked.

"Sure. It was the biggest fish I'd ever caught up to that point in my life. I didn't want to lose it," he told her.

They went to retrieve the fish. She eyed it critically, "It's not quite as big as my first one. But I did this one all by myself," she stated. "Well, almost all by myself," she amended with a smile. "Can I do one more?"

She wound up doing three more - all by herself, and was disappointed when Colin told her they had enough. Reluctantly, she untied the line from the pole. "That was fun. I like to catch fish." She said.

Colin accepted the fly and line back from her. "I know what you mean. Amazing what crazy things we find to be so much fun. But there's no point in catching more than you can eat, unless you want to catch them and turn them loose. I do that sometimes, but mostly I only fish when I want to eat fish. Here." Colin put away the bedraggled fly and line they had been using and handed her a new fly, also tied to a length of line. "You can have this one. You can use it for a pattern to make your own flies. That way you can go fishing even if I'm not around to go with."

She accepted the fly, studying it in her hand. "Thank you. But I don't think it would be as much fun - without my friend."

Colin placed the fish in a large canvas bag lined with grass to help keep them cool. As he tied them on behind Dalene's saddle, she asked, "Why am I carrying the fish?"

"You caught most of them," he replied. "Gisele already has the saddle bags. Besides, since you dove on that second one, you already smell like fish. I don't."

Dalene's eyes flared in mock offense, "You.......! I can fix that!" She threw her arms around him in a fierce hug. She was strong, practically squeezing the breath from him. "There!" she released him. "Now we both smell like fish."

Dalene insisted on another race before they left - this time only to the road. It was an even start and Gisele managed to edge Kim just shy of the road. Dalene was laughing, insisting on a rematch which Colin declined. The ride back to Salem went swiftly as they alternately walked and ran the horses. Nearing the city, they began to encounter more travelers and the reaction was the same as it had been that morning. Dalene was trying unobtrusively to stand in the stirrups more, giving evidence that her backside had about had enough time in the saddle. It was by now past the 10th hour of the day - late afternoon. The roads in Salem were choked with carts and pedestrians. Dalene thought they might have to get off and walk the horses, but the novelty of seeing riders on horseback caused enough commotion that a clear passage opened before them as if by magic, so rather than slackening their pace, Dalene coaxed the horses into a swift but surprisingly smooth trot and soon had them off the main thoroughfare and approaching the stables from a back road. Arriving at last, she gratefully swung down, walking stiffly with a grimace on her face. "I thought you said I'd be sore tomorrow," she complained.

"Trust me, you will be," Colin assured her.

They quickly took care of the horses before retrieving their gear and heading for the south wing of the Praetorium. He asked Dalene to identify the corridor which led to the baths and excused himself to clean-up before dinner. "Do me a favor and let the kitchen staff know that I'm cooking tonight, will you?" he requested. Dinner may be a little late, but probably not by much.

The bath felt wonderful. He regretted that he didn't have time to sit and soak. He was pleased that he still had some soap in his saddle bags. After debating briefly, he scrubbed his clothing as well to remove the smell of fish and horse as well as the sweat of the day. He had learned that whatever the material was, it absorbed water hardly at all. Even when damp, it at least looked dry and the heat of his body would quickly drive off the residual moisture. It would be uncomfortable for an hour or so, but the day was warm anyway, so the evaporation would help keep him cool.

A few minutes later, he arrived at the kitchen. He recognized the steward in charge of the kitchen this evening. He was glad, as she had been one of the more agreeable supervisors he'd met thus far. "Hello, Tiana," he greeted her, "Did The Lady Dalene ask you if I could use the kitchen a little bit this evening?"

"She did, mantle-bearer." She steadfastly refused to use his name, despite repeated requests. "Is our cooking not to your liking?" she asked gravely.

"Not at all," he assured her. "Everything has been delicious. In fact, I wish I had time for you to teach me some of your recipes. But I'm fixing something that you might find a little unusual this evening and I'll probably need your help."

She eyed the canvas sack suspiciously. Colin grabbed a large pan and started placing the trout in it. "Fish!" she exclaimed. "You are cooking fish? But where did you get them?"

"The Lady Dalene caught most of them. I'm cooking them for the Regent and his family. I'm sure there'll be enough for you to try, if you'd like," he replied.

Tiana shook her head. "Fish? Is it safe to eat? It came from the lair of the Serpent. Isn't it poisonous?"

"No, it's not poisonous. I've been eating fish since I was little. It's actually very good. Can I use a cutting board and a sharp knife? I also need a large frying pan and a baking dish. We have enough here we can prepare them a couple of different ways."

Dubiously, Tiana assisted him in getting the desired implements. Soon, the entire kitchen staff was looking over his shoulder as he filleted three of the trout. All of them were larger than what he had been catching in Tyber, but then, the stream here had been larger as well. The smallest fish he estimated at over five pounds, the largest about eight. He didn't fillet the three largest fish, simply removed the heads and placed them in a baking dish. Tiana retrieved containers of salt, some fresh chives and onion and a light oil which had some kind of a citrus infusion in it. He asked what it was, but didn't recognize the name 'laramen' so he figured it was unique to this earth. He stuffed the fish with the herbs, adding butter as well, then applied the oil liberally to the skin before covering the dish and placing it in the oven. The three filleted fish were rolled in a bread crumb and egg batter and a moment later were frying in the pan on top of the stove. As the smell of the cooking fish began to fill the kitchen, Tiana sniffed tentatively, before acknowledging that at least it didn't <u>smell</u> poisonous.

As soon as the fish was done frying, Colin tested the ones which had been baking. The pink flesh was flaking delicately from the bones and he declared it done. He slid one of the baked trout and one of the fillets onto a large platter and demonstrated how to grasp the tail and use a fork to flake the meat off the bones. He then speared a piece of meat with the fork and offered it to Tiana. She took it, eyeing it dubiously, before nibbling at it. She seemed to consider it carefully for a moment, then popped the entire piece in her mouth as the kitchen help all watched, hardly daring to breathe. She chewed slowly before declaring, "It's delicious! Not at all what I had imagined!"

Colin indicated the platter on the table, "Please, all of you, help yourselves if you'd like. I think the other four are more than enough for dinner."

They quickly retrieved utensils and soon were sampling the fish, smiling and commenting on the delicate flavor and texture. Already they were proposing other spices and ways to prepare it. Four of the staff were assigned to carry the fish and other dishes to the quarters of the Regent for dinner.

The table had been set by the time they arrived. Gareth, Beatrice, Halvor and Dalene were all there. Dalene had washed and changed as well. She excitedly greeted those who were bringing their dinner. Beatrice sampled the fish eagerly. Gareth's reaction was almost identical to what Tiana's had been down in the kitchen, sampling it tentatively before declaring it to be delicious. As Dalene and Halvor had both eaten fish while they were in Tyber, they seemed much more interested in their parent's reactions than they were in their own dinner. Dalene inquired, "What happened to the other two fish?"

"There were plenty, so I let the kitchen staff sample them. I think they'll be eager to cook them up for you the next time you bring them some fish. But these four are definitely ones that you caught."

As if she suddenly remembered, Dalene declared to her family, "Yes! That's right. <u>I</u> caught these fish! It was fun!" The Regent looked at his daughter as if he didn't quite recognize her, while her mother simply smiled.

"Thank you dear, they're wonderful. Where did you go to catch them?"

"We rode out towards Ramah. Probably about half-way. There's a large meadow with a stream flowing through it. Kim and I raced Colin and

Gisele, and we won! Well, we won the first race. We would have won the last one too, except Colin wouldn't race." She made a face at him then grinned.

Halvor was interested. "Kim is the little black mare that you liked so well, isn't she? You're riding her now? Like Colin with his horse?"

"Yes! Oh, Halvor, you have to go riding with us. When Kim runs, it's like she has wings. It's like flying! Except afterwards, my bottom doesn't feel like it was flying. I'm pretty sore," she said ruefully.

"That reminds me, we have a stable hand with a broken arm - thanks to you," Gareth said mildly.

"Me?" Dalene asked, "I don't think so. We didn't even have any of the stable hands help us."

"No, but apparently this morning one of them saw you and Colin riding away. He decided to try riding one of the other horses. He was thrown off and broke his arm. I wonder how many others will attempt the same thing, after seeing the two of you today?" he said.

Colin was equally mild in his response. "So the problem is, do you teach the people that a horse must be trained before it can be ridden, or do you simply outlaw riding horses to ensure that nobody gets hurt?"

The Regent sighed, "Yes. That is the question. The law should protect the people. We should keep them safe. Already this was brought up in the Council today."

"Perhaps your view of the law might be flawed. From another perspective, one might argue that the purpose of the law isn't to protect the people, but to protect their freedom - not allowing others to harm them or infringe upon the freedom of others, but at the same time, allowing them to make decisions for themselves, recognizing that there is a risk involved no matter what one decides. There are some horses that can never be trained to ride. And there are some people who will get hurt no matter how well the horse is trained. There are others who will get hurt even if they are sitting in a cart - a wheel comes off, they take a turn too sharply and it overturns, the horse spooks and runs away with them. Whether they get in the cart or not is their choice. Whether they get on a horse or not is their choice. I would suggest that the law should protect their right to make that choice, so long as their choice doesn't specifically cause harm to others."

Gareth seemed to consider this carefully, "There is merit in what you say. But we must be obedient to the law. We must determine if this is approved by the law or not."

Colin nodded, "Sir, not every decision is a moral choice. There is no right or wrong in deciding to eat bread and cheese or instead choosing bread and meat. Instead of trying to determine what is specifically approved by the law, maybe you ought to determine what is specifically forbidden by the law. Every time someone comes up with a new idea, the chances are that the law, written a thousand years ago, never envisioned it. Even if it did, if there's no moral ramification from the new idea the law probably would ignore it. If you're always waiting for some sign of divine approval before permitting any new thing, any new idea, you're going to wait a long time and you're going to suffocate the creative spark in your people. People need to grow - individually and as a society. They need to stretch and reach towards greatness. Don't use the law as an excuse to prevent them from reaching their potential."

"Why is it, Colin, that each time we speak I seem to either come away very angry or very intrigued by what you say?"

"Probably because we're just too different," he replied.

"Hmmm. Possibly. Or perhaps we are simply too much alike. I will consider what you have said. But it is a difficult thing to change 4000 years of our history."

"You don't change the history, sir. You change the future."

Gareth smiled at that, "Perhaps. Thank you, but you must excuse me, as I have other commitments this evening." With that he got up and left.

Halvor was still intrigued with the idea of riding horses, "Colin, you trained Kim for riding already. Is it so easy then?"

Colin glanced at Dalene, unsure of just how much to say. She answered for him, "For most people, it would be very difficult, but Colin is a very gifted trainer of horses. Why I'm sure he could even train a horse for you. The question would be how long it would take for the horse to train you to ride. I am a very gifted rider, so it took Kim only a short time to train me."

Halvor rolled his eyes at her teasing, "But seriously, you could train a horse for me? For the other Arbor Guards as well?" he demanded.

Colin nodded. "I think so. Like I told your father, there will always be some that can't be trained. It doesn't necessarily mean they're bad horses, just not suited for riding. But I'm sure we could train horses for you."

Halvor was contemplating this. "A division of mounted Arbor Guards would be much faster, more effective at being able to patrol and guard Aidon. It would be an incredible advantage. If the attack father expects were to come........if we had guards mounted, it could make all the difference. We might get the extra warning we need. I must speak to Councilor Garmon about this. You'll excuse me?"

Halvor left and Colin asked, "Why Councilor Garmon?"

"The city guards of Salem, as well as the Arbor Guards are under the command of the 10th File. Despite the fact that the guards themselves may be from various files, the 10th File coordinates and commands them. If Dean Garmon approves the idea of having guards mounted on horses, he will probably be able to generate enough support from the other Councilors to make it happen," Beatrice explained. "You may soon be busy, Colin." She was more right than she knew.

Colin was awakened early the next morning by an incessant knocking at his door. He stumbled out of bed to answer it. Halvor immediately slipped inside, closing the door softly behind him. "Sorry to wake you up. You need to get your things together. We're leaving."

"Why? What's going on?" Colin asked.

"Remember last night, I was asking you about training some horses for the Arbor Guards? After I left you, I went to speak with Councilor Garmon, he's from the 10th File and has charge of all the guards."

"I know. Your mother explained that to me after you left," Colin said.

"Well, I talked to him about getting some guards mounted on horses. Not a lot at first, but at least enough for scout duty. He spoke with the Regent - with father and they've given conditional approval. For now, they aren't going to seek the Council's approval, but we're going ahead anyway. But because we don't have the full Council behind this, we have to keep it quiet. Nobody is to know what we're doing. I'm going to sneak you out of the city. Tunsten said Gisele was trained to pull a cart, didn't he?"

Colin nodded and Halvor continued, "Good. I'll get her and one other horse to pull a cart. We'll have you in the back under some blankets and supplies. I'm afraid you'll have to stay out of sight. We don't want anyone to know you've left the city. I'd like to get ten horses and riders trained in a week. Ten as a minimum. Can you do it?"

"I don't know," Colin answered. "Normally I'd say no, it isn't nearly enough time. But.......well, things have gone pretty smoothly with Gisele and Kim. I think we can get the horses ready to ride in that amount of time. The bigger question will be the guards. Dalene was right about that. Most of their training will simply come from riding. The more time they spend in the saddle, the better."

"Great. You let me worry about that. We might be able to stretch this for ten days, but certainly no more than that." Halvor hesitated. "I have to tell you, this doesn't change anything. It isn't likely to change the outcome of your appeal - especially if most of the Council doesn't even know about it."

"Thanks for telling me. I didn't think it would, but I appreciate your honesty. It also doesn't change anything for me. I'll do what I can to help." Colin said.

The corridors were deserted as they made their way to the stables. Halvor sent Colin out to the corral to get Gisele, who snorted her displeasure when he backed her up to the cart. Halvor already had another horse in harness, ready to go. He set several wooden crates and kegs of supplies in the back of the cart, leaving enough space in between for a small bed of blankets. After Colin lay down, Halvor piled additional supplies over top of him, forming a roof over his hideaway. In short order, they were on their way. The city guard passed them with only a cursory glance. They weren't much interested in what was leaving the city, only what was coming in. When they were well away from the gate, Halvor reached back and uncovered Colin's hiding place, allowing him to sit up and breathe. "If we meet anyone, you lay back down and I'll pull the stuff back over top of you. Sorry, but we really don't want anyone knowing you're gone, especially with mother having custody of you." Halvor said.

"Does she know about all this?" Colin asked.

"Only that you'll be with me," Halvor said, "Although I'd be surprised if she hasn't guessed. She was there last night and she's pretty good at figuring things out. You wouldn't believe how hard it was to get away with anything when I was growing up!" he grinned.

"So where are we going?"

"First, we're going to see your old friend, Tunsten."

"Tunsten? Why?"

"We need horses. We could probably get that many out of the city, but sooner or later they'd be missed. We don't want to have to account for them for awhile, so we need some new stock. Since we're going to Tyber, Tunsten seemed like the best source. He already knows about you - he knew you were in Tyber anyway and he knew you were with Jorge. As far as we can tell, he never said a word about any of that to anyone. We need someone with access to horses who knows how to keep his mouth shut. Tunsten looks like a good bet," Halvor explained.

"Are we going to train them there, at Tunsten's place?"

"No," Halvor shook his head. "He's a stock dealer. Too much traffic through his place. I'm going to try and arrange with Jorge to rent his hay meadow. It's already fenced and it's remote. Makes it pretty ideal for what I want. He'll lose some hay, but with what we pay him for rent, he should be able to buy more than enough to replace it."

The journey to Tunsten's was uneventful. Several times Colin had to drop back down into his hiding place in the bed of the cart while Halvor covered him over. They stopped for one brief rest break at a small clearing along an even smaller stream - a place unlikely to attract other travelers, Halvor explained. It was approaching the 6th hour when they pulled into Tunsten's. Halvor told Colin to lie down and stay covered up while he spoke with the livestock merchant. Colin reluctantly agreed.

Tunsten came out of the large barn, drawn by the sound of the cart. "Tunsten, I'm Halvor Tregard, 11th File, of Salem. I've come to see you about buying some horses."

Tunsten eyed him carefully, then walked over and patted Gisele, who bobbed her head in recognition. "And where be the mantle-bearer?"

Halvor kept his voice neutral, "What does the mantle-bearer have with my wishing to buy horses from you?"

"Nothing, perhaps," replied Tunsten, "That's his horse. I saw him. He'd not be letting that horse go. So either they've destroyed him or he's up to sumat with you. What is it?"

Halvor smiled, "He's up to sumat with me. Colin, say hello to Tunsten, will you. I don't think we're going to get anywhere until you do."

Halvor pulled back the covering and Colin stood up. "Hello, Tunsten. I can't thank you enough for selling Gisele to me. She's a fine horse."

Tunsten nodded, his face expressionless. "You be wanting horses then? Is that it?"

"Yes," Halvor said. "I'd like at least ten. Twelve if you can get them."

"I can get them. Good stock. Not like this one," he said, patting Gisele, "but good stock. Where would you be wanting them?"

Halvor hesitated, "I'm planning on Jorge's hay meadow. Do you know the place? I haven't spoken to Jorge yet, but if the plan changes, I can get word to you."

"Aye, I know it. I've got three here, now. I'm guessing you'll not be taking them with you."

"Could you bring them out, later today perhaps?" Halvor asked.

"Aye. I'll do it. Take a few days for the rest. I'll bring them as I get them. Agreed?"

"Agreed. I'd like you to keep this quiet though. I don't want word getting around."

Tunsten turned to leave. "Your business. 35 torals a head. Bargain struck."

Halvor looked after him quizzically. Colin laughed. "He doesn't spend a lot of time dickering price, does he?"

Colin was back in his hiding place, growing more anxious the closer they approached to Jorge and Miran's. They detoured around Tyber. That was difficult and time consuming. The town was remote, so there simply weren't a lot of alternative roads to take, but Halvor knew paths and meadows that took them on a circuitous route, coming into Jorge's field below the house. Colin was ready to be out of his padded prison, but Halvor told him to stay put. "Just in case they have company," he said.

Finally, they arrived. Halvor let out a yell, "Jorge! Miran! Are you about?" They heard a "Hello!" shouted from down near the barn, but Miran and Kath appeared almost instantly at the door. "Halvor! Why this is a surprise," Miran said with a touch of coldness to her tone.

Kath eyed him with open hostility. "You'll have to excuse me, Miran. It's time I was getting home."

"No. Wait, please. For just a moment. Is there anyone else here with you?" Halvor asked, just as Jorge arrived from the barn, still panting from having run most of the way.

"Halvor is it? Why have you come? Is it done then? Has the Council destroyed him?" He demanded.

Halvor shook his head, "No. I'm sorry. I need your help." He hesitated about stating his request in front of Kath, but decided he was more likely to gain her silence if she knew of Colin's involvement. She was sure to spout bitter tales of seeing him if she left now.

"Is anyone else here?" Halvor asked again.

"Just Elam. He's about somewhere." Jorge replied.

"Alright. Colin, join us please." Halvor said as he pulled back the covering.

Colin sat up, smiling, "Hello Jorge. Kath, Miran, it's good to see you."

Kath's jaw dropped, while Miran started to cry, but she was smiling. Jorge just appeared to be dumbfounded.

"We thought....we heard......You're not destroyed?" He stammered.

"Patience Jorge. I'm living on an appeal right now, so don't be rushing me." Colin teased.

That made Jorge grin, "Get down! Come in! Elam will be thrilled. He's been moping around here for days!"

All of them went into the house where Halvor made his request. "Listen, I need your help. Colin is here to try and train some horses for the Arbor Guards to ride. Nobody can know about this. You've all been involved with Colin before and shown you can be trusted. We need some seclusion, and Jorge, we need your hay meadow. I can pay you for it. Name whatever you think is fair, I'll pay it. I think this is important."

"Does this mean that the Council has changed their mind about Colin?" Miran asked.

"I'm afraid not. His punishment has been appealed. Maybe you heard. My mother has custody of him, and for the next week, she's assigned that custody to me."

"Your mother!" Kath gasped. "Then.......the Regent is your father! The Lady Dalene, she's your sister!"

"Yes. They know where Colin is and what he's doing for us. But nobody else can know. They must think that he's still in Salem. My father.....the Regent is concerned. There may be danger - not to you - but to Colin. Some people are unhappy about the appeal. It would be best if they not know where he is for the present. Will you help?"

"I've no cause to help you." Jorge said, "But if Colin wants it this way, then that's how it will be."

"Thanks Jorge. It is what I want. But understand me on something. Regardless of what happens to me - today, tomorrow, or at the next moon, I don't want you being angry about it. Halvor was given a job to do and he did it well. Believe it or not, I count him as a friend - just as I count each of you as my friends. We don't have to necessarily like the law. You may try to change it, although I don't know enough about it to even know if that's possible. But whatever happens, please, don't be angry with Halvor, the Regent or Dalene. Whatever happens, it's alright. You're my friends and I don't want you blaming each other for things that none of you can control. Alright?"

Reluctantly, they each nodded. Just then, Elam came into the room. The moment he saw Colin he launched himself at him and wrapped him in a bear hug. "Colin! You're back! Are you here to stay? Did the Council change their mind?"

"Elam! It's good to see you. I'm just back for a few days. I still have to go back to Salem. I'm just glad I could get back here for a few days. Did you get a horse yet?"

"I did!" Elam exclaimed. "He's a beauty. Bigger than Gisele. I've got him to where I can blanket him. He takes a halter well and I can rest most of my weight on him. I'm still working on a saddle. It's almost done. Can you help me get him trained? Then maybe we can ride together!"

Colin had to smile at Elam's enthusiasm. "Slow down, Elam. I'm sure we'll get a chance to work with your horse over the next few days. I'm going to be here working with some other horses for Halvor, but I'd appreciate it if you wouldn't say anything to anyone about this for now - not about me and not about the horses. Can you keep this to yourself?"

"Sure," Elam replied. "I've never said a word to anyone. I can keep a secret."

Colin and Halvor took the cart on the path along the grain field. The wheat was tall and almost fully in the ear, the stems soon would be bending under their load as they waved in the breeze. Further down, the field was planted in corn, the dark green stalks standing tall, shining in the afternoon sun. Colin wondered if he would live to see the harvest.

They set up camp below the hay meadow in a small clearing back in the trees. Halvor explained that the other guards would be in three other camps, split into four-man teams. "I have a dozen guards who will be coming for training. The first few will show up the day after tomorrow. The rest a day or so later. Even if Tunsten can only get ten horses, I'll have a couple of reserve riders trained if I need them. We keep the camps small so there will be less chance of drawing attention, just in case anyone comes by."

They set to work, making a smaller pen inside the hay meadow. By using a corner of the existing fence, they only had to add two sides to complete it. Jorge already had a large pile of fence rails cut and stacked, so building it was easy. There would be no gate, as such. Two pairs of posts dug into the ground about five feet apart formed the entrance. Short rails were slid between the upright posts to fill the gap, so these bars would have to be removed to get horses in and out of the enclosure. It was functional, if cumbersome. They could live with it for a week. Colin didn't like the fact that there was no water supply in the hay meadow, but he decided that might work in their favor, as the riders would need to take their mounts to water at least a couple of times each day. That should help the horses bond with their riders, he reasoned.

The pen was completed. Gisele and the other horse which had hauled the cart were grazing in the hay field when they heard whistling coming from the forest path below the meadow. Halvor hissed at Colin to get out of sight while he investigated. Colin slipped into the trees, but a moment later he heard Halvor call to him, "Colin! It's clear. Just Tunsten bringing in the horses."

Indeed it was. Tunsten was walking along, following Halvor, leading the three horses he had promised. "Figured you not wanting folks knowing your business, I'd not come direct through Tyber," he explained. They turned the horses loose to graze in the meadow with the others. Halvor paid Tunsten, who gave a brief nod to each of them then turned and headed up the path without a word.

Halvor smiled, "An interesting man, that one. Did you know he's probably the wealthiest man in Tyber? Keeps to himself, but he knows his animals."

Colin had to agree with that. The horses he had brought were a fine looking bunch. "Have you selected one for yourself?" he asked Halvor.

Halvor looked at him blankly, "I thought we were going to train all of them."

"We are," Colin explained, but I think it will go more smoothly if each rider works specifically with one horse - at least to start. They get used to each other faster and develop trust. That trust is critical both in training and working with horses. So you need to choose one. You can change it later, but for now, choose one that you're going to work with."

He nodded, "The gray one we brought in with the cart. I've used him for years. We get along."

"Good. What's his name?"

Halvor looked uncomfortable, "Ah, he doesn't really have a name. People don't name livestock. They're just animals, after all."

Colin wasn't buying it. "Right. Anyone who works with an animal for any amount of time is going to name it. Even Miran's goats have names. I can't have twelve guards here all calling their horse 'horse.' So if your horse doesn't exactly have a <u>name</u>, then what do you call it when no one is listening?"

Halvor grinned sheepishly, "Smoke. His gray color always reminds me of smoke, so that's what I call him."

"Alright. We've a little time yet before we eat, let's start with Smoke," Colin said.

He caught up a brush and a halter as they walked out into the meadow. Gisele ambled over when she saw Colin and the other horses followed. Colin handed the halter to Halvor, "See if you can get this on Smoke. Just move slowly, act like you aren't all that interested. Talk softly while you do it."

Colin was patting and rubbing Gisele as he watched Halvor. Smoke stood still, grazing, but watching warily as Halvor approached. For a moment, it looked as though he might bolt, but then Halvor had an arm over Smoke's neck. He was used to the restraint of a rope and the weight of Halvor's arm made him abandon all thought of flight, so he returned to his grazing, giving Halvor the opportunity to slip the halter in place. Colin handed Halvor the brush. "Brush him all over, really good. He needs to get used to the feel of your hands all over him, so he trusts you and knows you aren't going to hurt him. Do that every time before you ride him and afterwards as well. Make sure and remove any dirt or burrs that might cause a sore, especially under the saddle. Right now you're really just working on that trust."

Halvor worked on Smoke, who occasionally would break from his grazing to eye him curiously. When Halvor was done, Colin said, "Take him over in the pen. We don't really need it, but I want him away from the other horses for a few minutes."

Following Colin's instructions, Halvor let the horse inspect and smell the blanket and saddle, after which they were rubbed along his neck, flanks, back and legs. The horse stamped nervously at first, but finding no cause for alarm continued to view the whole operation with curiosity.

"That's good enough for now," Colin said. "Now, you might think this next part is crazy, but I want you to try and bond with Smoke. Think of it like what you do in the Evaluation, when you try to bend someone through the Compliance. That's what I want you to do with Smoke. I want you to teach Smoke what it is you want him to do. Visualize the blanket and the saddle. Visualize putting them on his back and you getting up on him. Try to picture yourself riding Smoke. Running. Jumping. Give him the image of what you want him to do."

"You're right," Halvor agreed. "That's crazy."

"So I'm crazy. Humor me." Colin replied.

Halvor closed his eyes, stroking the horse's neck. His jaw was clenched in concentration. For at least ten minutes he stood, one hand or the other always in contact with Smoke, while Colin watched with intense interest. Finally, Halvor's eyes opened.

"Well?" Colin asked.

Halvor shrugged. "I tried. I don't know if it helped, but I did it."

"You didn't see anything?" Colin prodded

"No. What was I supposed to see?"

Colin was deflated. "Nothing, I guess. Just part of the bonding process. I want you to do the same thing every day from here on. Go ahead and put the blanket on him a few times - gently. Don't let it flap around and spook him. Do the same with the saddle, then give him a quick brush down and turn him loose."

Colin wandered back toward camp, puzzled. Why hadn't it worked? He had been sure that Halvor would see Smoke's intelligence - his true-self. Halvor was from the 11th File, he knew how the Evaluation worked. Why hadn't it worked with Smoke? Were animals just too different? If so, why had Dalene been able to see Kim's true-self with him? He sighed. Could nothing ever be simple?

The next day, work began in earnest. There were only two of them and five horses to be cared for. Halvor and Colin worked each of them. Initially, Gisele seemed jealous, having to share Colin's attention, but she soon became more interested in feeding and largely ignored the process. In addition to the grooming and handling, they each had to be watered and they had to be introduced to the blanket and saddle. Colin asked Halvor, "What are you going to do about saddles? We only have mine right now."

"Dalene took yours to a harness shop in Salem to use as a pattern to have hers made. She's having the same shop make up a dozen more like it. The men who're coming should have saddles with them when they arrive. Hopefully they'll have one for me as well."

While Halvor practiced "bonding" with Smoke, Colin selected a big blaze faced sorrel gelding to do the same. As before, he instantly saw the horse's true-self. There was no mistaking it for a human. Colin couldn't say quite how, but to him, it was like looking at a person and looking at a horse. The one was clearly a person - because it looked like a person. You didn't have to dissect it into different components. The glowing orb of intelligence had the same kind of distinguishing characteristics, even if he couldn't describe them. "This," he thought, "is a horse because it looks like a horse." No further explanation was necessary. Blaze, for mentally Colin had already named him, was more skittish than either Gisele or Kim had been. Colin could see the distrust and the longing for freedom, the desire to run wild in the horse's intelligence. "This one will need a strong rider," Colin thought. Mentally, he stroked and soothed the horse, willing it to trust him, teaching it the feel of the saddle and the weight of the rider, painting an image of Blaze, racing across the plain, a rider on his back, working together as a team, becoming more than what he could ever be alone. Gradually, he could sense the big horse relax, testing and tasting these new ideas, before suddenly embracing it with eagerness. "Yes," he seemed to say, "I want this bond. I want this rider." Colin continued to mentally stroke the horse even as he gradually withdrew, until at last the connection was broken and his eyes flared open. His neck was stiff and his legs were tired. He noticed Halvor staring at him.

"What?" he asked.

Halvor said, "You haven't moved in over an hour. What were you doing?"

"An hour?" Colin asked stupidly, "That can't be right. It's only been a few minutes."

"An hour. At least." Halvor insisted. "You did it, didn't you? What you're trying to get me to do with Smoke - the Compliance. You can do that with animals, can't you?"

Colin slipped the halter off from Blaze, then slapped him on the rump to get him to go join the other horses before he answered. "I don't know about animals in general, but at least with horses, yeah, it seems like I can do it. I thought you would too. Actually, I figured you'd be better at it than me, since you understand the Evaluation and the Compliance a lot better than I do."

"So is that why you can train horses and nobody else seems to be able to? Because you can do the Compliance with horses?" Halvor asked.

"No. I still say that anyone can train horses. Look, people in Aidon have been training horses to pull wagons and carts for thousands of years, right? They just gave up training them to ride after a few people got hurt. Actually, I don't think they gave it up. I think the Council decided it was dangerous, so they used the Compliance to get people to just forget about trying to ride horses. Rather than train horses to be ridden, they trained people to not ride. What I'm doing is the same thing that you're doing with Smoke. You're teaching him that he can trust you. You're teaching him what you want him to do and it works because gradually he is going to decide that is what he <u>wants</u> to do. I'm just taking a short-cut to get to the same destination. But I don't think I'm special. I think you can do this as well and I want you to keep trying. Will you do that?"

Halvor weighed what he'd just heard. "I'll try," he replied, "But I've never heard of this being done before. Are you sure you can't help me out just a little bit with Smoke?"

"If it becomes necessary, then I will. But I'd like for you to work at it awhile. I want to know if I'm right - if you can do it."

Colin was exhausted after his work with Blaze. He went back to camp and actually managed to take a nap - something he rarely did. That afternoon he worked with a black mare with four white stockings. She was lively. Frisky as a colt. He called her "Stockings." Where Blaze had been reluctant, almost mistrustful, Stockings was eager. Her true-self seemed to leap and dance all around him, intrigued by this visitor and anxious to play at whatever game he proposed. The idea of a rider seemed to delight her and she almost appeared to explode in enthusiastic anticipation. Halvor was watching and when Colin's eyes opened he commented, "Ten minutes. Why so much shorter this afternoon?"

"Different horse." Colin explained. "This one just seems to love the idea of working with a rider. Blaze was more reluctant. He needed a more detailed picture of the relationship before he would accept it. They're all different."

They ate dinner early. The days were long, as the summer solstice was less than two weeks away. Colin simply didn't feel up to tackling the third horse Tunsten had brought the day before. "I'm beat," he told Halvor. "I'm done working horses for the day. Do you want to go up and see Jorge and Miran?"

"No thanks. I'll stay here, but you go ahead. Just make sure they don't have company, alright?"

The evening was peaceful. The path left the field to pass the barn before continuing up to the house. At the barn, he saw Elam out at the corral with his horse. Colin walked over. "Good evening, Elam," he called out. "This is your horse?"

"Colin!" Elam called in delight. "Yes, this is Midnight. Isn't he a beauty?"

Colin admired the horse. He was black as coal, except for one white spot on his rump, about the size of a hand. He tossed his head and stamped his feet at the appearance of this stranger, but he was tethered to the corral bars by a length of rope. Elam had been working the horse, tossing the blanket over his back and laying his weight across its withers. "He's a good looking horse, Elam. But he's going to be a lot to handle. Do you think you can do it?"

"I think we're going to be a great team," Elam asserted. "He comes right to me when I call him. Sometimes I think he's just waiting for me to get on him, but mother made me promise to wait until you said it was alright. Do you think he's ready? Should I try to ride him?"

Colin smiled, "Well, you probably ought to finish that saddle first." On an impulse, Colin slipped through the bars and patted the horse, letting it smell him. Then he stood back. "Elam, I want you to try something for me."

"Sure," Elam replied. "What do you want me to do?"

"You remember how you did the Compliance in your Evaluation?" Colin asked, "I want you to try that with Midnight. But you don't try to force him to bow. I want you to try to visualize for him, what it would be like if you were riding him. I want you to find Midnight's true-self and show him how you put on the blanket and saddle. How you get up on him and how the two of you are going to ride. Can you try to do that?"

Elam shrugged, "I guess. I didn't know you could do the Compliance with horses, but I can try." He came around to the horse's head, talking softly and stroking his face and neck. Then he became very still.

Colin just stood and watched. Elam seemed entirely relaxed. The minutes ticked by. Colin was still a lousy judge of time using the sun, which was now hovering just above the horizon, but he guessed it must have been at least a half hour. Elam's eyes suddenly opened wide and immediately filled with tears as he threw his arms around Midnight's neck. He was too much of a man to let Colin see his tears, so he stood like that, moving his head to wipe the moisture from his eyes and cheeks on the horse's glossy coat. Finally he looked up, smiling. "I didn't know he looked like that. At first, I didn't see anything. I kept feeling for him, and then I finally realized he was right there, he just didn't look like a person, so I was missing him. Once I saw him, I couldn't believe that I didn't see him before. I did what you said. I tried to show him how we're going to ride. It was like he was pushing me back and then all of the sudden it was like he was seeing what I saw, and he wanted it just like I do. I think he's ready to ride. Is that what I was supposed to do?"

Colin nodded. "You did just right, Elam. Thank you."

"For what?" the boy asked, puzzled.

"For proving it can be done." Colin replied.

Colin waited while Elam brushed Midnight and turned him loose. Then the two of them started for the house. Unable to restrain himself any longer, Elam raced ahead the last few yards, bursting through the door, "Mother! Father! Colin is here! He's seen Midnight and thinks he's ready to ride!"

Colin ducked through the door, "Colin!" Miran greeted, "Do come in! Have you eaten? Can I fix you something?"

"No, thank you. I ate earlier. I came up to see Elam's horse and just wanted to say 'hello' while I was up," he replied.

"Come! Sit!" Jorge commanded. "You look tired. Are you well?"

Colin sat, trying to work a kink from his neck and shoulder as he did so, "I'm fine. Tired is all. The farm looks good, Jorge. Looks like a good stand of corn and wheat."

"Aye," Jorge was pleased, but tried not to show it, "Been a good year so far. If we don't get hail or too much rain and if it stays warm through harvest, we should do well."

Miran set a bowl of strawberries on the table in front of him. The smallest of them was the size of an egg. Miran cut off his objection, "You hush! Probably living on nothing but flat bread and dried meat down there in the trees when there's a perfectly good house right here. You need fruit. You just eat, and I'm sending a loaf of bread with you as well."

Colin surrendered, "Thank you." The berries were delicious.

Miran questioned him while he ate, "Are you being well treated? We heard you were injured."

Briefly, Colin reviewed the events of his arrival in Salem as well as his Evaluation and Trial. He hesitated in relating the verdict and punishment that had been decreed, but figured they'd probably already heard it anyway. When he told of Beatrice appealing on his behalf, Jorge shook his head, "We heard that there was an appeal. Thought maybe you had appealed on your own behalf. Hardly ever done. Miran had to explain it to me. I'd forgotten. But the wife of the Regent! That's something."

Miran brought him a cup of milk as well. "We were afraid they had you locked up in some dungeon. I'm glad they've at least put you in decent quarters. We've been worried for you," she said.

"I know, and I appreciate it," he replied. "I just wanted to stop and see you this evening. I think tomorrow I'm going to get awfully busy, so I may not have much chance to say hello."

"Are you in need of money?" Jorge asked. "We've been putting your share aside and you've plenty if you've need of it."

"No. I'm set for now. Maybe before I leave. I'll think about it. I probably ought to get back before Halvor comes looking for me. Thanks for the food. Elam, maybe tomorrow or the day after, we can ride. Get your saddle finished up, alright?"

Elam nodded as Colin slipped out into the dusk.

Halvor was tending a small fire when he returned to camp. He glanced up at Colin's return, "Jorge and Miran, they are well?" he inquired.

"They're fine. Thanks. You ought to take a look at the horse Elam has. He's a beauty."

Halvor grinned. "I did that yesterday. You didn't think I'd fail to scout the farm before we camped did you? But you're right, he has quite a horse there. Do you not think he's perhaps too much horse for a young boy?"

"I think if you're looking for mounted scouts and you don't recruit him, you're making a big mistake," Colin replied.

"But he's just a boy! Besides, he's a member of the 4th File. Guards are not selected from the 1st Order," Halvor objected.

"I have a suspicion that <u>young man</u> and his horse are going to out-ride you or any of your guards. He ought to be able to choose what he wants to do and what he wants to be without someone assigning him based on his File or Order." Colin said with some heat.

Halvor stared at the flames, quietly feeding sticks into the fire. "Perhaps you are right," he said, hesitating before he continued, "Yesterday when we arrived, you know that Jorge would not have helped if you had not requested it, don't you?"

Colin nodded and Halvor continued, "Did you mean what you told them? That you regard me as your friend?"

Colin was surprised, "Sure. You've always been straight with me."

"I held a knife to your throat," Halvor reminded him.

Colin shrugged, "You didn't push it in and you left no doubt as to where you stood. I probably would have done the same thing if our positions were reversed. Why let a little thing like that spoil a friendship?"

Halvor smiled slightly, "You must have interesting friends in your land. You know this changes nothing, don't you? I must still see you back to Aidon in a week's time."

"I know. I don't hold it against you. If you weren't honest and committed, I probably wouldn't want you for a friend anyway."

The next morning the routine was about the same as the previous day. After watering the horses, Colin worked with Patch, a dark chestnut gelding with a single white spot around his right eye. He seemed to have an extremely sedate personality and a desire to please. It only took Colin about 15 minutes to feel confident that the horse was anxious to have a rider. Halvor continued to focus on Smoke, but was obviously discouraged at his lack of progress in bonding with the horse. Colin wasn't sure if telling Halvor of Elam's success would encourage him or not. For the moment, he decided to keep it to himself.

It was mid-morning when the first group of Arbor Guards arrived. Colin neither saw nor heard them until they were standing at the edge of the meadow, talking to Halvor. Two of them turned and disappeared into the forest, but reappeared a short time later, escorting Tunsten who was leading a string of five more horses. The guards took the lead rope and opened the gate to let them loose in the meadow. Colin wandered over to say hello to Tunsten. "Good morning," he called out. "You must have gotten an early start. How far did you come with this bunch?"

"Jordanon. Not far. Most of it yesterday," Tunsten replied in his abrupt style. "Should have the last of them tomorrow. Troas. If I don't stand talking all day." He sent Colin a meaningful glance, turned and headed back down the trail.

Halvor caught the last of this exchange and just smiled and shook his head. He called the new arrivals over. "We're going to keep this simple," he said, "No rank. No titles. This is Colin. Whatever he says, you do. For however long he says to do it, you do it. That's all the instruction I have. Colin, this is Jeffs, Hiat, Chase and Bob." Each of the guards nodded to Colin as their names were called.

"Now," Halvor continued, "How many saddles did you bring?"

Chase spoke up, "We each brought one." He paused long enough to watch Halvor's shoulder's slump. "And one for you too, sir," he added with a grin.

A smile twitched at the corner of Halvor's mouth as he glared, "The next person who does that……………calls me 'sir,' will be running with the horses instead of riding them! And if that happens, you had better keep up!"

Colin assigned a horse to each of the guards. "This may not be a permanent arrangement. In fact, at some point I want you to trade mounts around to see if you simply get along better with one horse as compared to another."

Bob objected, "But they're just horses! Don't we make them do what we want?"

"No. Get that idea out of your heads right now. Yes, they're horses. But they have intelligence - more than some people. They think. They have personalities. This is as much about training _you_ to work with the horse as it is training the horses to let you ride. And I did say _let_ you ride. They're strong enough and fast enough, that if you don't win their trust you won't be riding them. You might win for awhile, but sooner or later they'll just run under a low branch and sweep you from the saddle or they'll buck or they'll roll on you and crush you. A horse will run itself to death for you if it trusts you, because it knows you'd never ask it do that unless you had to. If it doesn't trust you, it will never give you everything its got, and sometime your life might depend on that horse giving its all. Halvor hasn't told me all of what's going on, but you're guards - soldiers. You put yourselves at risk for Aidon. You'll be doing the same with your horse. You believe it's worth it, make sure your horse believes it as well."

He assigned Stockings to Jeffs, Blaze to Hiat and Patch to Chase. That left Bob without a mount, so Colin told him to choose one from the group of five that Tunsten had just brought in. Bob was a quiet, almost shy man. Stocky of build but standing only 5'6". He was young, probably no more than 20, but with a heavy beard that made him look older at first glance. He selected a lively leopard appaloosa mare.

"You like the leopard appy?" Colin asked.

Bob shook his head, "What is 'leopard?'" he asked.

"Sorry," Colin apologized. "Where I come from there is a large cat - like a lion - do you know lions?" Bob nodded and Colin continued. "A leopard is like a lion, except it has spots all over - kind of like this horse. We call a spotted horse an appaloosa. Usually they have spots just on the rump. If they have spots all over, we call it a leopard appaloosa. So this is the horse you want?"

Bob nodded. "You going to name her?" Colin asked.

Bob simply said, "Leopard."

"Alright, she's Leopard."

Halvor called the men together and began their instruction, teaching them how to brush the horses, speak quietly to them and get them used to the blanket and saddle. While he was doing this, Colin took Leopard aside. It was a long 40 minutes before he felt like she was ready to work with Bob. Leopard was pretty high strung and a bit mistrustful. Colin thought Bob's low-key personality might actually be a good fit for her.

Halvor's instructions to the men to practice the Compliance with the horses was met with silent but obvious skepticism. Halvor's frustration finally came boiling to the surface. "Men, Colin is the first person I've ever heard of to ride a horse! And not just ride it, but <u>train</u> it to ride. If he says you're going to get on that horse buck-naked and backwards, then by the twin moons you'll do it! If any of you knows more about training these horses to ride, then speak up now! Otherwise, go sit and meditate with your horse!"

After lunch, Colin decided it was time to ride. He asked Halvor if he could go get Elam and Midnight to join them. Halvor reluctantly agreed. Elam whooped at the invitation and as a bonus, Colin got to have lunch with Jorge and Miran, which was far better than the camp rations being shared by the guards. Colin helped Elam get Midnight saddled and they led the horse back down to the meadow where the four soldiers were saddling their mounts. Hiat asked Halvor, "Are you not coming, sir?"

Halvor jerked his head in the negative, replying gruffly "Mine's not ready yet. Been too busy getting yours ready to ride. You'll go with Colin."

Colin was nervous. He had responsibility for five untrained riders on horses that he had established some kind of mental connection with. Was he nuts? Was this going to be one huge disaster? He gave them instruction on the use of the reins and cautioned them to not hold the horse in too tightly. Then he gave the order to mount up. There was some nervous prancing. Colin checked them all and made sure they evened up their reins, but the horses all seemed more curious than alarmed. Colin mounted Gisele and led out of the gate which Halvor closed behind them. They looped along the fence as the other horses ran over, whinnying in excitement and disappointment at being left behind. They rode along the forest path. The guards were all silent despite the novelty of the experience as they devoted all their attention to their mounts. Elam, on the other hand, was ecstatic. He was directly behind Gisele and couldn't seem to stop talking - to Colin, to Midnight, or to himself. Colin glanced back and thought the boy's face must surely split if he grinned any wider. He kept them at a walk, letting both the guards and the horses adjust to each other. It was a good hour before the timber thinned and the landscape shifted to rolling plains. He had the men dismount and then said, "The reality is, I've just taught you almost everything I know. From now on, your horse is going to be your teacher. The best way to learn to ride is by riding. When you want to coax your horse to go faster, kick her in the ribs - lightly. You want her to turn, pull firmly on the reins - more on the neck than on the head so you don't jerk her around. Pay attention. They'll let you know when you are doing something wrong. If you're ready, let's ride."

As soon as they were set, Colin coaxed Gisele into a canter. The other horses, not wanting to be left behind, eagerly followed suit. With an almost vicious streak of pleasure, he suddenly slacked the reins, kicked Gisele in the ribs and let out a wild yell. Instantly she accelerated into a flat run, bounding across the prairie at incredible speed. Naturally, all of the other horses followed suit. Elam yelled with delight, as Jeffs yelled in terror. Jeffs and Hiatt fell forward across their horse's necks, clinging on for dear life. Of course this completely slackened the reins, leaving their mounts free to charge ahead with the others.

After letting Gisele run for something over a mile, he gradually reined her in and brought her into a looping arc to meet the others who were now scattered across the plains. Jeff's little mare, Stockings, had stayed right with him all the way, but as she abruptly slowed Jeffs slid forward right over her head to land in a heap in the grass. Colin rode over to him to make sure he was alright. Jeffs looked up at him, stunned and then suddenly began to laugh. He laughed until the tears came to his eyes, as he struggled to his feet. He threw his arms around Stocking's neck and declared, "She's a grand horse! She'll teach me to ride even if it kills me!"

As each of the riders caught up, their grinning faces told the story. They'd been terrified. They'd been awed. They were hooked. They loved it. They had tasted the ease and speed of riding and they were now committed to becoming riders. For an hour, Gisele and Colin led them on a game of follow the leader. They walked, cantered, galloped and ran. They did tight circles and serpentine courses. Both horses and riders were increasing in confidence, each coming to trust the other. They were just coming out of a fold in the hills at a sedate walk when Colin heard a tremendous shout behind him as a horse thundered through his line of riders. Instantly there was pandemonium, as horses and riders scattered in all directions. Gisele wheeled to face the threat and Colin was surprised to see Halvor, mounted on Smoke, wheeling to charge back through the scattering riders again. Halvor reined the horse in and cantered over to Colin. His eyes gleamed and he grinned, "I found him. Just like you said. I found him."

The next few days settled into a routine. Tunsten showed up with the final bunch of four horses. That same day, another four Arbor Guards arrived, followed by four more the day after. Halvor wasted no time in making assignments and getting the men to working with the horses. He was now a fanatic about "the horse meditation," as he called it. At least three times a day he would have the men pair off with their mounts, scattering them as far as possible if they were in the meadow, or sending them off in different directions if they were out practicing riding on the plains. Bob was the first one to really discover his horse. They were out on the plain, the 3rd day after he had gotten her. He was the last one back from the midday meditation session. He was walking, leading Leopard. Halvor rode out to meet them and Bob looked at him quizzically. "Did you know?" he asked

Halvor didn't have to ask what Bob meant. He nodded, serious.

Bob shook his head. "I'm not sure I can ride her anymore. I mean, she's like a person, isn't she?"

"Bob," Halvor said, "When you found her, her true-self, did she want you to ride her? Did she want to be your partner?"

Bob brightened, "She seemed to want it more than anything in the world."

"So are you going to let her down, or are you going to be the kind of rider she wants?" Halvor asked.

Bob looked at him for a long moment, then he turned and mounted Leopard without saying a word and cantered back to join the others.

Colin was impressed with the men and the progress they made with the horses in such a short period of time. One by one, they each experienced something similar to what Bob had, as they discovered the intelligence and personality in their horses. Halvor could usually tell when they finally found their horse's true-self. They would be late returning from a meditation session and if that wasn't clue enough, the look on their face told the story. They were all decent riders. But when they finally bonded with their horses, seeing their true-self for the first time, there was an immediate change in them – both the riders and the horses. They suddenly seemed to be different parts of the same unit, knowing almost instinctively how their other half would react. There were still mishaps. Jack still wound up sitting in the air from time to time as Lightning accelerated out from under him. Rodan did a flip over his horse's head when it decided at the last moment that the stream Rodan wanted him to jump was simply too wide. But each day, they got better, despite their sore muscles and tender backsides. They hardened into the training and even though they traded horses from time to time, each man preferred his original mount – the one in which he first saw the glowing core of intelligence.

The two brothers, Jack and Willam, were the smallest of the guards. Jack rode a small, white gelding he named Lightning. The horse wasn't big, but he had such tremendous acceleration that he completely unseated Jack the first several times he lunged into a run from a standstill. Willam was on an equally small mare named Doll. She didn't have the acceleration of Lightning, but could stay with him for mile after mile. The largest of the guards, Michael, was huge by the standards of Aidon. He was as tall as Colin, but outweighed him by at least 50 pounds. He had the biggest horse, a sorrel distinguished only by his size. He wasn't especially fast, but had massive power. Galen rode a red bay, while Dathan was mounted on a slim chestnut named Arrow. It was a toss-up as to which was faster, Arrow or Lightning, and the horses seemed to want to race at every opportunity. Steven rode a gray with a white muzzle and legs. He called her Frost. Aaron named his sorrel after his home city of Ramah. She had two white stockings on the left side, giving her a lopsided appearance, as those legs somehow looked shorter than the others. Finally, there was Rodan on a big sorrel named Thunder. Colin shrugged at that. Sooner or later, there's always a horse named Thunder, he thought.

Elam begged his parents to be allowed to ride with the guards. Jorge finally agreed to let him spend half his day with them. The group had collectively adopted him as a younger brother and he endured a considerable amount of good-natured ribbing. The one thing they didn't tease him about, however, was his riding ability. It was soon apparent that Elam was more skilled than any of them. Colin freely admitted that he had been surpassed by several of the riders, though secretly he was convinced that Gisele was by far the best horse. But Elam simply was able to coax more out of a horse than any of the others could – even on their favored mounts. Perhaps it was Elam's smaller size, or perhaps he just had the gift. He bonded with a horse almost from the moment he got on it. He didn't always win at the contests they staged. Other horses were faster than Midnight, or could jump and clear higher obstacles. But however well they performed, Elam could get them to do more.

One evening Halvor asked Colin to demonstrate the use of his bow for the guards. He'd been spending his evening hours making arrows. Elam had gathered a large number of dry, straight birch shoots, ideal for making arrows and had given Colin a couple dozen of these. Colin was still uncomfortable demonstrating the bow, as if he were presenting false credentials. He knew that he wasn't as good as his demonstration indicated, but he just couldn't seem to miss. The first evening he shot his bow, he was walking out to retrieve the arrows from the grass clump he had used as a target. He just reached the target and pulled the first arrow from it when a large turkey took flight some 20 yards away. Colin didn't even think. In a flash he simply nocked the arrow, drew and released, sending the bird tumbling to the earth in a pile of feathers. That got their attention more than any target shoot possibly could. On Sabbath, Halvor gave permission for Colin to spend a couple of hours explaining the principles behind making a bow, arrows and arrowheads. Soon, they were all making bows. Elam again became the center of attention as the men borrowed his bow to compete against each other shooting at large targets. It became their favorite pastime when they weren't working with their mounts.

The ten days were up. How had they passed so swiftly? On their last morning together, they rode as a unit out onto the prairie. Colin dismounted to address the group briefly. "Men, it has been an honor for me to be able to train with you. You have achieved more in these few days than

I ever would have believed possible. I told you in those first couple of days, that I wasn't going to train you – that your horse would do that. I know that you're being sent out as scouts to protect Aidon. I wish you well. But you're more than scouts. You're guards. You're soldiers. Being mounted gives you definite advantages over foot soldiers. You're more mobile. You have added speed to use as a weapon. You have greater height and greater reach. But you need to think about your horse as well. Sooner or later, you or your fellow-soldiers are going to ride mounted into battle. If you charge into a mass of lowered pikes, your horse will be the first to die. A smart swordsman is going to try to hamstring your horse as you charge by. I don't know the first thing about training a horse for battle. All I'm saying is they're not invincible. Don't get them killed needlessly. Take care of them. God bless you all."

As one man, the mounted guards drew their swords, pressed the hilts to their foreheads and bowed to Colin. Halvor looked at them curiously for a moment, then drew his own sword and did the same. They then sheathed their swords and Halvor addressed them simply. "You have your assignments. I expect you to carry them out. That is all." The men paired up and departed, leaving Halvor and Colin alone on the plain. "What was that about – with the sword?" he asked.

Halvor watched the last of his men depart, not looking at Colin. At length he replied, eyes fixed on the distant mountain peaks. "It is a salute – a sign of respect usually reserved for battle commanders." With that, he kicked Smoke into a gallop and headed toward Jorge and Miran's house.

The return to Salem was uncomfortable. It was past mid-morning by the time they got started, so there was considerable activity on the road. That meant Colin had to remain on his hidden bed in the back of the cart with no opportunity to emerge and stretch. The day was hot and with the blankets and covering piled over top of his hiding place, the air was stifling. His discomfort amplified every jolt of the cart and there were plenty of those. It was drawing on towards dusk when Colin heard Halvor say, "There's Salem. We should be back at the Praetorium within the hour." It was all of that and a bit more. The city guards were surly after the heat of the day. They took their time passing anyone into the city. Finally, they were through. Halvor wouldn't let Colin emerge from his hiding place until they were inside the stable and he was certain that there was no one about. The two of them quickly unloaded the cart. Colin brushed Gisele thoroughly. She was pleased to be unhitched from the cart. Halvor noted the same with Smoke, "Don't care for that cart anymore, do you Smoke?"

"Ah, he's just a cart horse. It's what he's been trained for. It's what he's good at. Leave him be with the cart. He'll be content enough." Colin said, imitating the drawling style of Tyber.

Halvor whirled on him, anger flaring in his eyes, "He's more than that, and well you know it! Smoke was as good as any of the horses we worked and better than most, why he............" His voice suddenly trailed off, seeing the humor in Colin's eyes.

Colin clapped a hand on Halvor's shoulder, "You're right. No matter how well he was trained as a cart horse, it seems he had more ability just waiting for someone like you to bring it out. You did well, Arbor Guard."

It was getting late, but Colin was not to be denied a hot bath. It felt good to get the grime of ten days camping off him, as well as the sweat and dust of the road today. He had replenished his supply of soap while in Tyber and he used it liberally this evening. He wanted to just sit and soak, but was afraid that if he did, he'd fall asleep in the tub. Reluctantly he toweled dry and slipped on his clothing, still damp from having been washed. At least he could change into his dry robe once he got to his quarters.

He managed to find his room after only three wrong turns. He was begrudging the fact that none of the wrong turns had taken him to the kitchen either, as he was feeling half starved. He was pleased to find a meal tray in his room There were the usual bread and meat, along with fruit and cheese and a small pitcher of cool milk which he drank, not bothering with the cup. He stripped off his damp clothing and slipped on the robe he'd been given the day of his Evaluation. How long ago was that now? It seemed like years. Exhausted, but clean and fed, he flopped onto the bed and thought he had never felt such luxury. Almost immediately, he was asleep.

Chapter 21　　　Invitations

The next morning Colin slept late and awoke feeling groggy. He usually felt lousy when he slept in, like he'd lost half the day. He stumbled out of bed, making his way to the wash basin where he dumped the entire contents of the pitcher over his head. He dried his hair and shaved. Afterwards he felt about half alive – and starved. He thought about trying to find the kitchen, but didn't know what excuse to offer if they asked why they hadn't seen him around. He wished he hadn't been so hungry the night before. He'd eaten everything on the tray. He really hated imposing on Dalene and her family all the time. He felt like a lap dog. Unfortunately, right now he was a hungry lap dog and there was only one place he was likely to be fed. Colin sat and went through a mental assessment. The bottom line, he was feeling trapped and a little nervous. He knew much of this stemmed from being overly tired. The stifling journey back from Tyber the day before had been a stark contrast to the daily freedom of riding the forest trails and racing across the plains. He had felt accepted by the Arbor Guards and enjoyed their congenial camaraderie. The return to his cell – even if it was a pleasant cell – had brought him up short mentally and emotionally. His brave counsel to his friends in Tyber had been honest and heartfelt. He didn't want them to be angry and he knew that everything would be alright, but he also knew that "alright" in the eternal sense could be unpleasant in the here and now. He was thoroughly depressed.

An abrupt knock at the door brought him out of his self-absorption. He opened the door, hopeful that if might be Dalene. He was disappointed to see Councilor Krainik. "Good morning, Colin. I was sorry to hear that you were not feeling well. I'm glad to see you up. May I come in?"

Colin was too surprised to speak. He simply stood back and swung the door wide as Krainik swept into the room. He paused, briefly, making an obvious show of scanning the apartment. "My, they certainly didn't want to spoil a guest of your stature with comfort, now did they?"

Colin finally found his voice, "They've treated me well. I've no cause to complain. What can I do for you, Councilor? Is that the appropriate way to address you?"

Krainik smiled, but there was no warmth in his eyes, just a cautious assessment. He continued to inspect the room, as if studying it for a trap. His eyes finally rested on the meal tray from the previous evening. "'Councilor' is appropriate. However, you may call me Lijah, if you wish. There's no need for formality here. Have you eaten? I had some business to attend to this morning, so I was unable to have breakfast. I hate to eat alone. Would you care to join me?"

"That is kind of you," Colin replied. "But I should probably check with the Regent's wife first, since she has custody of me."

"Nonsense," Krainik waved his hand in dismissal, "If she hasn't stopped to check on you before now then she's undoubtedly busy. For the moment, you will be in <u>my</u> custody. That will be sufficient. Come."

Colin <u>was</u> hungry. He saw no harm in having breakfast with the man, even though there was something about him that made him uncomfortable. He remembered his aversion during the Evaluation. Maybe it was just his air of authority, a hint of conceit and arrogance that seemed to emanate from him. Well, he was probably entitled, as High Councilor over the 11th File. Colin made his decision, "Thank you. I guess I'll join you."

Councilor Krainik led the way. They passed along several corridors, through the Great Hall and out the front steps of the Praetorium. The street was crowded, but as he followed Krainik the crowds made way for them. Colin realized that they were parting for Krainik, Lijah, he reminded himself, before they ever saw him. Councilor Krainik was an imposing figure in his solid lavender robes with designs embroidered in gold on both the front and the back. Colin supposed it was probably real gold at that. For some reason, Colin felt shabby and out of place. The single purple scarf wrapped around his left arm looked tattered. He felt conspicuous in his hooded cloak. He watched Councilor Krainik. The man didn't walk so much as he flowed, sweeping everything out of his path without effort. "This," thought Colin, "is a man who enjoys power." The thought was tinged with a hint of envy. In a moment of brutal self-assessment, Colin admitted to himself that he was afraid. A few months ago he hadn't cared much about anything. But something had happened to him in the short time he'd been here. He finally <u>felt</u> alive for the first time in years and he desperately didn't want to lose that. The depression and grief that had threatened to crush him for so long hadn't made the transition with him to this world, but with the sudden sense of confinement and abandonment, he felt himself withdrawing from life once more, becoming cold and detached and he <u>hated</u> that feeling.

The Councilor turned into an inn, ignoring those lined up at the door. Nor did he pause once inside, but continued to the rear of the establishment where a large table sat, secluded and vacant, ignoring the bows and stares of the patrons and waitresses as he did so. Krainik indicated where Colin should sit and then seated himself at an adjacent corner of the table so they would be close together. Immediately a procession of waitresses appeared, placing plates, cups, eating utensils and platters of food on the table before them. Colin was impressed. "The service here is certainly very good," he commented.

Lijah smiled, "Yes. I come here on occasion. They know what to do if they wish to keep my business. Actually, I retain tables at several of the Inns around here. One of the privileges of rank, you know."

"I didn't know," Colin replied flatly.

"Of course not! And how could you? Despite the fact that you are a mantle-bearer, you have hardly been accorded the rights that are due you!"

"I wouldn't make too much of my being a mantle-bearer. After all, the Council did determine that I don't wear it by right."

"Yes, well," Lijah replied, "You know that Council decisions are not necessarily unanimous, don't you?"

"No, I didn't know that either. Are you saying that you didn't vote to condemn me?"

"I was in the very act of rising to appeal your punishment, but Beatrice was a fraction faster than I. If not for that, I would have been your custodian during your appeal. I assure you that your quarters would have been far better suited to you, and dining in places such as this..........well, this would have been the least of pleasures you would have enjoyed. Now please, eat. If it gets cold, I'll have fresh dishes brought."

For some reason, Colin wasn't as hungry as he'd thought. The food was good, there was no question about that, but he was uncomfortable with the way Lijah kept eyeing him - studying him as if to determine how he should be dissected. Kranik managed to maintain a steady stream of small talk through much of the meal. He continually waved to and pointed out various government functionaries, a few of whom approached the table and made a show of bowing to the Councilor. To Colin, it seemed as if he were watching an elaborate performance. When they were done eating, the dishes were immediately cleared away. Lijah studied Colin openly before asking, "What is it you would really like, Colin?"

Intentionally being obtuse, he replied, "Nothing more, thank you. The food was excellent but I couldn't eat another bite."

Lijah smiled, but there was a cold glint in his eye. He didn't like being misunderstood. "No, not food. I mean what would you like from life? Here, in Salem? Money? Power? Women? What?"

Colin was surprised at how open Lijah was being, but puzzled as well. "Right now, I'd settle for life and freedom," he responded. "But as you know, neither of those is exactly being planned as part of my future."

Lijah leaned forward, "What if I could arrange that? Not only life and freedom, but all the rest as well. You are the mantle bearer. Certain privileges should be yours, you know."

"Are you saying that you believe I wear the mantle by right?" Colin asked.

Lijah waved his hand dismissively, it was a gesture he performed very well. Almost artistically. "What I believe is of no importance. It is what they believe," and he waved his hand expansively to take in the whole of the room, implying, somehow, much more, "That is what really matters. Many of them believe you to wear the mantle truly. Others could be persuaded. Colin, you are a stranger here, so you are unaware of the dangers that Aidon faces. There are certain elements in the government who wish to maintain power. They continue to oppress the people and create unrest. I am engaged in an effort to unite the people and ensure peace. You <u>could</u> be a key part of this effort. Those who believe you to be a true mantle-bearer could add great strength to our cause - of peace. It would be a great service to Aidon, and Aidon would of course wish to show her gratitude. You wish for life? For freedom? Granted! And much more besides!"

"The Regent and his family, where do they stand in all of this?"

"Those who hold power, of course, wish to keep it." Lijah explained. "Why do you think Beatrice was so quick to appeal your punishment? She had to know that <u>someone</u> would. By doing so herself, she has managed to keep you out of sight, a virtual prisoner. Those who would rally to your plight have been lost, with no standard to gather to. You see, she has all but made you disappear. Who will mourn the destruction of a mantle-bearer no one ever saw? The Arbor Guard? Their son? He of course supports them completely. He craves power just as they do. The Lady Dalene.......ahh, there <u>is</u> a question! Of all the Regent's family, she, more than any other knows the injustice and oppression of the present system of rule! Such a lovely young woman! And to be so feared, hated even. Why, it must break her heart. You could help her, you know. End the fear and scorn which she's subjected to. Elevate her to a position of honor, even reverence, as The Lady of Prophecy who dared free the oppressed of Aidon!"

Colin eyed his host appraisingly, "And what would I have to do, to accomplish all this? After all, as you said, I am still basically a prisoner. How do I gain my life and my freedom?"

Lijah leaned forward, a smile of satisfaction on his face, "Only support us. When the time comes, you support us – support me, and everything we've talked about will be yours. You know that next week is the Solstice Observance, don't you?"

Colin nodded.

"The Solstice Observance is the most sacred celebration in Aidon. You should attend." Lijah told him.

"I was told that I'm not permitted to attend, because my punishment is under appeal," he replied.

"Unfortunately, that is true. It is the law. Of course," Lijah added, "The law is one of the things we'd like to change - for freedom. I can't help you. But if you ever get to The Valley, you really should see The Tree of Life. It's beautiful. If you can't get there, it probably doesn't matter. But if you <u>did</u>, The Tree of Life is worth seeing. It could well be <u>your</u> life. Do you understand?"

"Not really, no."

The hard glint reappeared in Krainik's eyes, "Change is coming to Aidon. If it comes in time, I may be able to spare your life. If things remain as they are, you will be destroyed, Mantle Bearer. So decide what you want.

Now, you must excuse me. I have business to attend to. The responsibility of government, you know. You can find your way back to the Praetorium, I trust? Very well. Good day." With that, Lijah Kranik arose, leaving Colin sitting, wondering what he had just heard.

Colin was so preoccupied with thoughts of his conversation with Councilor Krainik, that he afterwards had no recollection of making his way back to the Praetorium. He found himself sitting on a stone bench in the Great Hall, staring at The Ruling Boxes of Aidon embedded in the floor. "What did he really know of these people?" he asked himself. Did he have any business choosing sides? That there were differences of opinion in the operation of the government was no surprise to him. Such was normal in any system. It wasn't as if Krainik had threatened revolution or war. In fact, when he considered it, Krainik had actually said very little, only requested Colin's support. That was hardly unusual in politics. Was the Regent truly oppressing the people of Aidon? It certainly seemed as though he wanted to keep things as they were, which was completely understandable since he held the highest position in government. Colin didn't agree with this segregation by Files and the limitations it placed on the people, but what did he know about it really? It was true that he was effectively held as a prisoner - even if the jailers were pleasant. It was also true that he was generally kept out of sight. Why? Why had Beatrice really appealed his punishment? Was it to save him, or to isolate him until his destruction could be carried out? Colin couldn't say that he was honestly tempted by whatever Krainik had been offering – assuming he was offering anything at all. In the first place, he still didn't like the man, though he wasn't naïve enough to go through life expecting to like everyone. Far more importantly, he didn't trust Krainik. He just couldn't say why. He sighed deeply. No, he admitted, the real problem was that he was depressed and suddenly having nothing to occupy himself with gave him too much time to think about things that had no answers. The depression was threatening to consume him, drawing him back into what he referred to as his "dark place." He wanted very much to not go there, but the likelihood of his pending destruction had him chained and he didn't know how to break free.

The afternoon sun had dropped below the high windows of the Great Hall when Dalene finally found him. "Colin! Here you are! I've been looking all over! We were worried when you weren't in your room."

"Sorry," he replied. "I guess I should have stayed in my cell."

"Cell? Are you alright? Is there something wrong with your quarters?"

Suddenly feeling guilty, Colin apologized, "No. I'm sorry. Everything is fine. I just needed to be out. I guess I was feeling a little cramped after camping out in Tyber this past week."

She still looked concerned, but accepted his explanation. "How was everything? Did you see Jorge and Miran?"

"I didn't get to see them much. Too busy with other things, but they were doing fine. Elam is the one who's changed. He's growing. He also trained his own horse and he can really ride."

"Halvor told me," she said. "He also said you did a great job working with the Arbor Guards. Thank you - for all your work. I mean, after the Council condemned you and everything. You were still willing to help. Thank you."

Colin shrugged. "I needed something to do anyway. I'd go crazy if I just sat in my room all the time. Not that there's anything wrong with the room," he assured her.

"You must be hungry. You haven't eaten all day. Come, mother would like you to have dinner with us," she invited.

"Thank you, but tonight I'm really tired. I think I'd rather turn in. I'm just not up to being social tonight."

Dalene looked at him, then reached up and felt his forehead. "You do look tired. I'll tell mother, and I'll have something sent to your room for later. In case you get hungry. Do you want me to call a healer for you?"

He shook his head. "No. Thank you. I think I just need to rest."

He didn't rest. While he felt physically and emotionally exhausted, he simply couldn't go to sleep. He just felt so alone. "Where, in all this world, is there anyone who has the slightest clue as to just how lost I am? Does anyone care what I'm feeling?" He knew he was just feeling sorry for himself and he knew it was foolish, but he couldn't help it. It was well past midnight when he finally knelt and poured out his heart in prayer. All of his fears, all of his questions, they all came out in a rush. He knelt there for a long time, feeling drained, but no better. He had to drag himself off the floor and into bed, where he dropped into a dreamless slumber.

Awakening the next morning, he lay in bed watching as the first hint of dawn began to paint the walls of his room. He still felt drained and empty. But there was something else as well. Resignation wasn't the right word, for that was far too fatalistic. Nor was it hope, for he had no particular confidence or optimism. It was a simple acceptance of his circumstances and an impression that he was not entirely alone. Whatever the path, he would walk it. While he was still concerned, at his very core he felt calm. He realized that he had come untethered from his anchor of faith. But he had found it again - regained his spiritual and emotional equilibrium, as it were and he could face whatever came. That still left the question: Which of the factions currently working for control of Aidon were acting on moral principle? Were any of them? He knew that he couldn't change the world, but he was determined not to let the world change him. For now, it was enough.

For what seemed a long time, Colin lay still, basking in the sense of peace that was gradually building within him. It was such a relief from the darkness that had been clouding his mind and choking his heart, that he almost felt as if he were floating. He closed his eyes and everything was white, calm and peaceful. At that moment, he wished for nothing so much as to just remain there - floating and at peace. He drew a final deep breath, exhaling it slowly before he opened his eyes. "Not yet," he thought. "Perhaps soon, but not yet." With that, he rolled out of bed to wash and shave. He was still drying his face when he heard a knock at the door. He opened it and found Beatrice standing there, looking very concerned. "Are you alright?" she asked.

He smiled, "Much better, this morning, thank you. I need to apologize to Dalene. I really wasn't doing well yesterday."

"Are you sure there's nothing we can do to help? I don't think we've really considered how difficult this must be for you."

"No, really. I'm much better. I'm sorry. I just let things get to me," he assured her.

"Well, do you feel up to eating this morning? We'd like for you to join us," she invited.

"Yes, thank you. I'd like that." He took the arm she offered and escorted her back to her quarters where they found Halvor, Dalene and the Regent waiting. Dalene looked exceptionally worried. Even Halvor and Gareth looked concerned and Colin felt suddenly very self-conscious and ashamed for having been the cause of it.

"Good morning," he greeted.

"Are you well?" Dalene asked.

"Yes. I'm sorry I behaved rudely yesterday. I shouldn't have gone off without letting anyone know where I was. And I apologize for not joining you last night. I'm afraid I wasn't good company at all - even for myself. I'm doing much better this morning."

Everyone looked relieved, as they invited him to sit and eat.

"Halvor tells me that the training of the horses went well." Gareth said. "That should be a tremendous benefit to the patrols, out on the borders of Aidon."

Colin smiled, "I think training the horses was the easy part. Training the men is what took more time. But they're all skilled riders - most of them are better than me, in fact."

"Well, for a time at least, you were the best rider in Aidon - until you taught me," Dalene said, smiling.

Her humor helped make him feel more at ease. "And then for a time, I was the second best rider in Aidon. But now, I think I'm far down in the rankings." Becoming more serious, he asked, "Why was there such urgency? Are you expecting trouble?"

Gareth and Halvor exchanged glances. Gareth spoke. "I'm afraid so. Kernsidon has rarely left us in peace for so long. There are some who hope that they may have done with us once and for all. I don't agree. The problem is, we don't know what they're up to. The only contact between the two lands has been war, and in my lifetime, we haven't even had that. Once in a great while someone manages to escape. A few of those survive long enough to make it here. That's about our only source of information. Rumor really, for we have no means of checking the accuracy of what we hear"

"Do you ever send out spies to try and scout Kernsidon?" Colin asked.

"We used to." Gareth replied. "Ages ago. None of them ever came back. Ever. To show how blind we are, we don't exactly know where Kernsidon lies. We know in the past, they've always attacked from the south. We try to get our forces into place before they reach Aidon. Many a battle has been fought on the plain to our south and west. Rarely have they ever entered Aidon. But I don't know. Something just doesn't feel right. I keep wondering if they haven't come up with something new this time. That's why I wanted the horses - to keep our scouts out further and give us more warning if they prepare an attack. Thanks to you, they're out there now. It could prove to be a critical margin. You never know."

"Come now!" Beatrice moved to change the subject. "All this talk of war is not fitting for Sabbath. We should discuss more pleasant topics, especially as the Solstice Observance is only three days from now. Gareth, when shall we be leaving?" she asked.

"Hmm. Day after tomorrow I should imagine. Same as always. I like to be there a day early. Not so crowded on the roads," he replied.

Beatrice turned to Colin, "We shall be gone for perhaps three days. I'm sorry that you won't be accompanying us. Will you be alright here, by yourself?"

"By myself? Does everyone go?"

She laughed, "I'm sorry. No. I didn't mean you would be all alone in the Praetorium. Attendance each year is by lot. Only about one fifth of the people will be there, but that is still a large number. What I meant is that we will not be here. The Regent, and his family of course, are expected to attend each year. Not," she added, "That it is a hardship. It is perhaps the thing I look forward to the most each year. I just wanted to know if I should ask someone to check on you or make sure you had a guide if you wished to explore the city."

He shook his head, "No. I'm sure I'll be fine. I can usually find the kitchen and there's not much else I need."

"Good," Gareth said, "If you'll excuse me, Sabbath or no, there are things I must attend to." Halvor also made his excuses and left.

Beatrice turned to Dalene and asked, "Have you taken Colin to see the rooftop gardens? It should be lovely there today."

Dalene shook her head, "I haven't. But I'm afraid I can't today either. I promised to help check supplies for the Observance. I'm sorry."

"That's quite alright dear. You run along. I think Colin can take care of one old woman, don't you?"

Dalene rolled her eyes and smiled, kissing her mother on the cheek. She glanced at Colin and asked, "I'll see you this evening, won't I?"

"My schedule is pretty open. I think I'm available."

She smiled at him and left.

Beatrice offered her arm to Colin. He escorted her through the corridors as she pointed out various works of art and architecture in the Praetorium. They took so many different passages, that Colin was quite certain he could never find his way back without assistance. At last they came to a long, curving staircase which led up onto the roof. It took him a moment to orient himself and realized they were on top of the south wing, so it must have been a circuitous route indeed that Beatrice had taken to arrive back here above the family quarters.

The rooftop garden was beautiful. The pathway meandered among flower beds, potted shrubs and small trees. Colin couldn't imagine how much labor was required to maintain it. He wondered if they had to haul water or if there was adequate rainfall to provide moisture for the growing plants. Beatrice led him along the path, pointing out the various flowers and telling him the names of many of the trees, few of which he recognized. They arrived finally, at the east railing. From their vantage point, the city stretched out beneath them. None of the other buildings on this side were higher than they, so their view was unobstructed. But it was not the city which drew Colin's gaze. Away to the east, no more than a few miles, stood the most magnificent mountains he had ever seen. He'd noted them before, but often they'd been obscured and never had he seen them from this vantage. There was no transition of gentle foothills and lesser peaks. These mountains simply lunged out of the valley floor, snowcapped peaks dominating the horizon.

Beatrice hugged his arm to her and said, "Aren't they beautiful? I have always loved these mountains. Some people fear them, but how can one possibly fear something of such beauty?"

Colin nodded in agreement, "I've always loved mountains as well, but I don't think I've ever seen anything to compare to these. What are they called?"

Beatrice shrugged, "They are simply called the Mountains of Aidon - the whole range. The two peaks there, directly in front, on the right is South Cherubim and on the left, North Cherubim. In between, that deep cleft, do you see? That is the entrance to The Valley of Aidon. That is where we will be going for the Solstice Observance. That is where The Tree of Life is."

Colin stood silently, trying to etch the view into his mind. Finally he asked, "What is so special about the Solstice Observance? In my land, the only ones who make a big deal out of the Solstice are those who worship the sun. I know you don't do that."

She smiled, "No, not the sun, but the Son of the Highest. To us, this day, the day of greatest light, represents the Light of the World - Messias. It is the day we remember the prophecies of his coming, and remind our children to look forward to the day when he will come. It is a day of celebration and a time to spend as families. It is the happiest day of the year in Aidon."

"That is much like the celebration we call Christmas, in my land. When we commemorate the birth of Messias and try a little harder to live his teachings of peace and goodwill to all men. Our celebration is very near the winter solstice. Do you have a celebration then as well?" he asked.

"No. There is no celebration then. It is just another day. We recognize it, but that's all. Only the longest day is a cause for joy and The Tree of Life is the symbol of that joy. I think you should see it. You cannot understand the joy without seeing it."

"I would like to," Colin responded. "If things go well, then maybe next year I will be permitted to attend. My whole life, I have read scripture - ancient texts if you will - which speak of The Tree of Life. I would like to see it. I would like to see The Valley of Aidon. In my land, we have the story of a garden - The Garden of Eden. I think it is the same as your Valley of Aidon. If it is half as beautiful as the stories I've read, I think it would almost be worth dying for, to see the Valley and the Tree."

Beatrice looked at him. Colin's gaze was fixed on the cleft between the two peaks. A sense of longing tugging at his heart. "I think you're right," she said. "I think you should go. I think it would be worth dying for."

Her words shook Colin from his contemplation, "No. If it were just me, then perhaps. But I'm in your custody and they would punish you as well. That would _not_ be worth it. Even if I were willing to risk it, I kind of stand out. I wouldn't make it halfway there, let alone past the Cherubims there."

She smiled at his humor, "You know the story then? How the cherubims were placed to guard the Tree?"

"I know _a_ story, but it's probably not the same as yours. But yes, the cherubim was placed to guard the Tree. My story is not as happy as yours, however."

Beatrice nodded, "Sometime, I would like to hear your stories. I think there is much to be learned - even from unhappy stories. But I still say you should go." She held up a hand to cut off his response, "I am an old woman and the wife of the Regent. He would be displeased at what I say. But I think my punishment would be light, if they did anything at all. I would not be dying and we both agreed it would be worth dying for. I think you should go."

"Listen, I appreciate what you're suggesting. But I don't think it's worth the risk - to you. Besides, I can't get in there anyway. It isn't worth discussing. Alright?" Colin really wanted this line of conversation to end.

She still smiled, "Just foolish talk. Still, if you could find a way, I would do it. If I were going to be destroyed, I think I would want to see The Tree of Life before I was no longer a person. The wife of the Regent has certain privileges. I don't think they would touch me. It's foolish talk, but if you could find a way, you should go. You should see the Tree of Life."

For the rest of the day, Colin was distracted. He wasn't very good company at dinner. Even Dalene was unable to hold his attention for any length of time. She kept looking at him strangely, worried. He would pull himself back into the conversation, but within a few minutes, his mind would wander. Beatrice's words kept echoing in his head, "I think you should go. You should see The Tree of Life." But he couldn't go. Even if he tried, they would stop him. And if he was caught, what would they do to Beatrice? If he caused her mother to be punished, then Dalene would surely hate him. But it didn't matter. He couldn't go anyway. Finally, he excused himself. He thought the others were relieved when he finally left to return to his quarters. He wandered out onto the balcony. The light was fading from the sky, but he found that if he leaned out as far as he possibly could, he could just see the outline of North Cherubim silhouetted against the sky. The image burned in his mind even as he went to sleep that night.

The next day was hectic. Not for Colin. If anything, he was utterly bored with the lack of anything to do. The others, however, were fully occupied with preparations to leave the following day for the Valley of Aidon. Colin found that he was only underfoot, so he made himself scarce, wandering the halls of the Praetorium and the gardens outside. He found himself in the kitchen, quite by accident. Tiana was on duty and she wrapped him in an enthusiastic hug when she saw him. "The fish were wonderful!" she exclaimed. She pestered him until he promised to bring her more so she could experiment with different methods of preparation. Extracting his promise, she then proceeded to enthrone him in the kitchen and ordered all of the cooks to bring him samples of whatever they were preparing. Soon he was laughing and joking with all of the kitchen staff and even allowed himself to be recruited for dish duty. It was a pleasant distraction for a few hours and he left feeling very full from all the samples he had consumed and happy at the friends he had made. Late into the night, he continued to strain in order to see North Cherubim. Disgusted with himself, he finally prepared for bed. Remembering that he had promised Tiana that he would give her a ball of soap to try, he opened his saddle bags to retrieve one. As he rummaged to find it, he spilled the contents of one of the bags on the floor. His pouch with a few gems he hadn't left with Elam fell open, scattering the precious stones across the floor. He knelt to collect them, muttering at his clumsiness. As he returned the pouch to the saddle bag, he saw an unfamiliar packet. "Where did that come from?" he wondered. He carefully unfolded it. Small, shriveled, red seeds. He remembered. The seeds that Hotha had given him when he visited the Anakims. The dried fruit that was supposed to make him look like the Aidonians.

Colin sat back and contemplated. This was ridiculous. Even if the seeds made him look like an Aidonian, what about his clothing? What about the hood he wore that had gotten him into this mess in the first place? Even if he ate this stuff and it worked, was it worth the risk? What would they do to him? More importantly, what would they do to Beatrice if he were caught? But this was all crazy. How could it possibly work? But then, how had a 20 foot tall giant manage to look like a boulder lying on a hillside? How come he never missed when he shot his bow? And how could he possibly train a horse to ride in a matter of minutes, when it ought to take days or weeks? He couldn't totally discount the possibility that it might work and if it did work, who was to know? He could be back before they even knew he had been gone! If it worked. But how did he change back, assuming the seeds did something? He shrugged, it seemed like Gath had changed back when he wanted to. If it worked, probably you just had to focus on it, want it badly enough and then you changed. Crazy. Not possible. But maybe. He hesitated, then scooped up a half dozen of the dried seeds in his palm, considering them. "So, how are you supposed to take them?" He wondered. "How many are you supposed to take?" "How fast did they work?" "What if it poisons me?" The last thought made him reckless. They were planning to destroy him anyway, so what difference did it make? He popped the handful of seeds into his mouth and began to chew. He would have preferred to just swallow them, but if this was going to work, he wanted to extract whatever component was needed to make it succeed. They were terribly bitter. He almost spit them out. But he chewed, washing the residue down with a large cup of water. His stomach seemed about to rebel, but he forced everything to stay down. Other than a nasty taste in his mouth, he didn't feel any different. There was a dull metal mirror he used for shaving. He grabbed it and looked at his reflection. Nothing. It had been a crazy idea anyway. Would have been nice though. He stripped off his clothing, put on his robe and went to bed, feeling foolish.

Chapter 22   The Serpent

It was Sabbath. Specifically, the Sabbath before the summer solstice. It was one of the two days of the year in which the Serpent could be called forth. Mahon didn't plan to wait for the winter solstice. Deep under the castle foundation which his ancestor, Kern of Aidon had laid, was a dark, still pool. Mahon's treasury, his library of the ancient texts, had revealed its existence. It had taken much additional searching to uncover the tunnel which led to this spot, unused and unknown for centuries, since his ancestor had failed to conquer Aidon and his successors had lacked the courage to repeat the attempt using <u>all</u> the tools at their disposal.

A single lamp offered illumination in this chamber, but it failed. The black walls seemed to devour the light even before it reached them. The walls were smooth, polished even. There was no crack or seam. There were no corners either, the walls curving into the floor and the floor sloping to the circular pool at Mahon's feet. The tunnel leading here had been similar, a flattened circle roughly six feet high. Even after all these centuries, it was as smooth and seamless as the day it had been formed. Mahon knew how it had been formed. He had learned the secrets of commanding the air. His focused will could send a wall of air to flatten a man. While he could not yet create a shaft of air to pierce his heart, he knew that would come. There had been a time when others were able to master stone. They had been able to form it like soft butter, or penetrate it like water, as it flowed around them. The ancient writings had taught him this much, but they hadn't taught him <u>how</u> it was done. The Serpent had been the master of stone. It had formed this chamber and the tunnel leading to it. And it had formed this pool, where one who executed the dark ritual, spilling the blood of 13 sacrificial victims, could call it forth. Once here, it was bound to the one who had summoned it. Kern had summoned it, but Kern, still shaken by his failure in the attempt to take Aidon, had used it as a servent, never an ally. He had harnessed the power of the Serpent, using him to build his castle. Kern had not used his own blood as the 13th sacrifice, but that of another hapless victim. Thus the Serpent had not been his brother. When Kern died, the Serpent vanished once more, disappearing down the dark pool from whence it had emerged. Kern had lacked courage and vision. Mahon lacked neither.

Mahon was well along in the rite. The twelve corpses surrounding the pool bore mute testament to that. Their blood still drained down the black stone to disappear into the dark water. But it required the blood of 13 to complete the ritual. He would be the 13th sacrifice. With his blood, the Serpent would be bonded to him. Thus would begin the fall of Aidon.

Mahon clenched the knife, dripping still with the blood of the twelve lying scattered around the pool. He raised his left hand and drew the blade slowly across the palm. He cut deep, and the blood flowed freely as he clenched his hand around the blade, mixing his blood with that of the others before it dripped into the pool. As the blood struck the surface, the water boiled, becoming more violent until it splashed and swirled around Mahon's feet. His heart was hammering as one by one the twelve corpses were washed into the pool and vanished. For a time he thought that he too must surely be swept in. The rock was slick and his footing was not secure. Suddenly the boiling ceased and the water receded. It was as calm and still as before. He wondered if he had failed. But then something broke the surface of the black water without a sound and without a ripple. He was staring at the flat, triangular head of the Serpent. Its yellow eyes drew him in. The mouth did not move, yet he heard it speak, *"Brother, we are bound, you and I. My life to yours and yours to mine. What is it you seek?"*

Mahon was terrified, but a lifetime of hate gave him strength, "I seek The Throne of The Lawgiver. I seek to restore the Serpent to Aidon!"

The Serpent's mouth gaped open as the head rose from the water until it was even with his face. The tongue flicked about his head and body, tasting him. *"Brother, you are a King. You have mastered air. You would master stone. Will you master Aidon? Shall you sit on The Throne of The Lawgiver, to destroy the law?"*

"I shall <u>be</u> The Lawgiver! I will rule Aidon!" Mahon shouted, his voice echoing in the chamber.

"It shall be as you say, Brother. We shall rule Aidon!"

The Serpent slithered out of the pool. Its head was all of three feet across. It was difficult to see the outline, for it was as dark as the stone of the chamber. It led the way, entering the tunnel through which Mahon had come, its bulk almost filling it, for it had formed the tunnel millennia ago. Mahon was shaking as he followed it through the tunnel. He was glad that he had sent his troops on the invasion of Aidon already. The sight of the Serpent might well have caused his soldiers to scatter, despite knowing what he would do to them if they did.

Mahon had no illusion that his forces would conquer Aidon. In 4000 years of war, they had never achieved that objective, despite having nearly accomplished it a time or two. But he needed them as a threat. As they massed along the border, panic would ensue. It would take time for Aidon to marshal her forces to meet this threat. His soldiers would spread death, terror and destruction while Aidon gathered an army to meet them. In the meantime, Mahon would come as The Lawgiver - Messias - on the very day they would most expect him, the Solstice Observance. He would offer peace, achieved without paying the price of war. The sheep would flock to his call. Krainik would be agitating on his behalf within the government. They would capitulate in a matter of days, embracing him as their ruler. He would bring in his forces - peacefully of course - to secure his hold on Aidon. At worst, there would be a few weeks of fighting, but he would already hold The Throne of The Lawgiver. Not even the Regent could offset that advantage. Civil war would ensue and his forces would rage through the heart of Aidon, uniting with the faction that would flock to The Lawgiver. Either way, Aidon would fall - to him. Executions would follow, unfortunate, but examples would have to be made. Nothing like terror to keep the sheep in line. Then he would have a kingdom fit to rule. There would be peace. The kingdom would flourish, from art to agriculture. He would achieve what Kern had attempted. Mahon would not fail.

They passed the library chamber which held the secrets that had made this all possible. The Serpent still led the way, up the dark stairway to the upper levels. Mahon heard a commotion up ahead, the Serpent's tail thrashed wildly and there were screams. He smiled. It was unfortunate he hadn't been able to prepare his servants for what he was about to bring. Some brave but foolish guard had apparently tried to defend his post. Mahon emerged into the great hall of the castle. The Serpent lay coiled at its center. Shouts and screams rang out all around, as people ran frantically, some to get away and others in preparation for defense. Mahon smiled again. There was no defense. "Silence!" he bellowed.

Even in their panic, his voice registered. The unknown threat of the Serpent was drowned in the certain knowledge of what awaited them if they disobeyed that voice. It was deadly silent.

"Today," he continued, "I begin the liberation of Aidon. The Serpent, unjustly driven out, is about to return! Kern failed! King Mahon, King of Kernsidon and King of Aidon WILL NOT FAIL! Sheathe your weapons! The Serpent is no enemy to Kernsidon. He is our ally and my brother! Now, assemble the King's Guard!"

With nervous glances, the people scattered while the Guard assembled in the outer courtyard. Mahon would be accompanied by 100 of his guards. He wouldn't need more than that. Their line of march was one which none expected. They would return to Aidon through The Serpent's Tunnel.

When Aidama and Aeva had rejected the invitation of the Serpent to eat from The Tree of Knowledge, Messias had banished the Serpent from the Valley. The twin peaks flanking the entrance to the Valley, North and South Cherubim, had once been guarded by the cherubim, to prevent the Serpent from returning. The Serpent, however, was master of stone, able to shape it like metal, mold it so it could pass through impenetrable rock. It had been banished, but had not given up. If Aidama and Aeva would not unite with the Serpent, it would destroy them. The Serpent bored through the mountain, from near where Kernsidon presently stood, to emerge near The Tree of Life. It almost succeeded, but the cherubims and forces led by Messias attacked before it could devour Aidama and Aeva. It had fought fiercely as it retreated. Wounded, it at last was driven into the ocean depths at the Forbidden Place. Its blood had poisoned the rocks as a parting gift, but its physical presence was banished from this world. As the Serpent had attacked before, so Mahon would attack again - through The Serpent's Tunnel. He would emerge to claim The Throne of The Lawgiver.

They marched west, Mahon and the Serpent, followed by a contingent of the King's Guard. If they were frightened by the Serpent, they were terrified when they saw the dark hole into which they would go. They had been led into a sheltered valley at the base of the great mountains. At the head of the valley, a quiet pool, perhaps 30 feet in diameter bubbled up from the solid rock. The valley was lovely, its floor covered with grass and dense thickets of trees. Flowers blossomed and a stream, fed by the water from the pool babbled pleasantly as it rippled along to exit a half mile distant down a cascade, flowing toward Kernsidon. Above the pool, the rocky face of the mountain was dotted with caves. One cave, off to the left of the pool, looked different than the others. It was more uniform, a flattened circle about six feet in diameter. It seemed, somehow, to be darker than the others. Into this cave, the Serpent led the way. The soldiers lit their lanterns and nervously followed. Mahon brought up the rear. The journey through the mountain would take two days. It must take no longer, for in two days was the Solstice Observance.

Chapter 23   The Tree of Life

Colin awoke feeling ill. He had a horrible taste in his mouth and his eyes didn't want to focus. He stumbled over to the wash basin and rinsed his mouth directly from the pitcher set there. Getting the foul taste out of his mouth immediately helped him feel better. He washed his hair and face, but didn't feel like shaving this morning. He slipped out of his robe and tossed it on the bed before reaching for his pants and cloak hanging on a hook. He slipped into his pants and froze. They were black. Solid black. They hadn't been that way a moment ago, had they? He looked at his cloak, now lying on the bed where he had thrown it. It was the same as always. The pants felt the same, but even the styling was different, a much coarser cut. What had happened to his pants? Immediately he was worried. If he went out wearing these, he was sure to get in trouble, But he didn't have any other clothing. He had no choice. Still worried, he pulled the cloak on over his head and froze again. It was black, just like his pants. That was impossible! He pulled it off again and examined it. Sure enough - it was solid black and the hood was missing. He tossed it back on the bed and sat down to think, but when he looked at it again, there it lay, the same as always - a white, hooded cloak with a purple scarf tied around the left sleeve. A slow grin spread across his face. "It works! I have no idea how, but it works!"

Colin grabbed his boots. They still looked brand new, not so much as a scuff mark. He slipped the right one on his foot. He no sooner did so, than it changed, so fast he couldn't really say how. It was now a nondescript dirty, gray canvas boot. When he touched it, even his fingers had a difficult time convincing his eyes that wasn't what they were feeling. When he closed his eyes, he felt the smooth, supple texture of the leather. When he opened his eyes, only by the most stringent concentration could he determine that what he was feeling was <u>not</u> dirty canvas.

Not even taking time to slip on the other boot, Colin rushed back to the wash basin and grabbed up the mirror he used for shaving. He looked and started to laugh. "I'm a kid!" Well, not exactly a kid, but he was certainly younger than his 28 years, at least according to the image he saw in the mirror. The reflection was poor, but grinning back at him through a peach-fuzz beard was a dark-eyed dark-haired youth of perhaps 17 or 18. Probably closer to 17, he thought. He spent a minute making faces at himself, seeing this stranger mimic his every expression perfectly. He quickly finished dressing and used the mirror to inspect himself as best he could. He was dressed all in black, except for boots dirty enough to almost look black. His hair was coarse, dark and curly. He liked that. He'd never had curly hair before. His eyebrows were dark and thick, almost bushy. The mouth was straight and thin, the nose undistinguished. By all accounts, it was a totally unremarkable face. Certainly no one would give him a second glance. Black. That meant he was of the 1st File. Good. The 1st File laborers worked everyplace so he could go wherever he wished – at least anywhere a menial laborer might be found. It was almost as good as being invisible. He paused, concern reflected on his face. He couldn't be found in these quarters. He glanced out the window. The sun was up, but it was still early. Even so, he had to get out of here before he was discovered. Quickly he strapped on his belt and dagger, grabbed the money pouch from his saddle bags and snatched up his bow and arrows. He hesitated a moment, then took the packet of seeds he had obtained from the Anakims. He rolled it tightly and placed it in the bottom of his quiver - just in case his disguise wore off sooner than he wanted. He opened the door a crack and peered out into the deserted hallway. It wouldn't do to be seen coming from his room, not looking like this. He raced down the corridor, slowing suddenly as he heard footsteps approaching. At that moment, Halvor stepped in front of him from a side passage. He looked at him curiously and asked, "What are you doing here, lad?"

Colin stammered, trying to come up with an excuse to explain his presence, "Ummm. I…..ah……a horse. Master…..I mean, Councilor Tomas, I mean Tomias is wanting a cart and horse for today. For the Observance. I just be gettin' his orders, sir."

Halvor's brow furrowed, as though he wanted to pursue the matter, but he shrugged and said, "Good enough. Is your business concluded then? You'd best be back to the stables before trouble finds you."

Colin bobbed his head and scurried down the corridor, risking a quick glance back over his shoulder to see Halvor still looking after him.

He found his way to the stable. Now he was in a quandary. If he hung around here, he ran the risk of someone asking why he was there and what he was doing. At best, they would put him to work. At worst, they might run him off. The problem was he didn't know how to get from here to The Valley of Aidon. He knew the general direction and was sure he could eventually find it, but here in the city, it was too easy for him to get turned around. His sense of direction got messed up too easily. He thought it would be best if he could just follow someone whom he knew was going there - someone like Dalene and her family. But he didn't know exactly when they were leaving. They would be taking carts, so this seemed like the best place to wait, but there was too much activity here to stand around if he was in the 1st File, doing nothing. Colin stashed his bow and quiver in a corner of an unused stall. Positioning himself where he could watch the main courtyard, he grabbed a pitchfork and began mucking empty stalls into the center passageway. Periodically, he would fetch a wheelbarrow and haul the used straw and manure out to the large pile on the other side of the courtyard, near the exit. Later this would be loaded into a wagon and hauled away. Everyone ignored him. They wore black, brown or green, the colors of the 1st, 2nd and 3rd Files, but they took no notice of a stable hand mucking stalls. He'd been at it for over an hour when he saw two carts brought to the courtyard. Marcus and Alicia were overseeing the loading. A few minutes later he saw the Regent escorting Beatrice and The Lady Dalene. Dalene was speaking, "But mother, where could he be? It just isn't like him to be gone so early, and without telling us. He knew we were leaving today. Don't you think he would have wanted to say good-bye?"

Her mother replied, "He's a grown man, dear. I'm sure he has things to do. My, the way you moon after him! What is a mother to think?"

"I am not mooning after him! It's just strange. He hasn't been himself since he got back with Halvor. I'm a bit concerned."

Dalene suddenly stopped and glared at him. Colin realized that he had stopped dead, standing there holding the handles of the wheelbarrow. He felt like an idiot. "Uh, 'scuse me. Uh, do you know where I'm supposed to take this?" It was the best he could come up with. He knew he was blushing and tried not to cringe. He sounded like an idiot too.

Beatrice smiled kindly at him, "I think you're supposed to dump it on that pile over there," she said, pointing.

He bobbed his head in thanks and set off with his wheelbarrow. By the time he dumped it and returned to the stable, the carts had departed. Quickly, he grabbed his bow and quiver from where he had left them and raced across the courtyard. Someone yelled after him, but he ignored them. In a moment, he lost himself in the crowded street beyond the alleyway to the stables. Fortunately, his height advantage let him see the carts, moving at a slow pace down the road, off to his right. Relief flooded through him and he trailed after them.

The trip through the city was uneventful. Due to the crowds, the carts had to move slowly. This gave Colin time to approach a vendor selling bread on the street. He purchased a half dozen hard rolls, slipping them inside his cloak. His mistake occurred when he attempted to pay for his purchase and handed the woman in brown a dectoral. "Are you daft?" she exclaimed. "How would I be making change for this? And where would the likes of you come by this much money? Is it a thief you are?"

Colin snatched the coin back, handing her a copper subtoral instead. She continued to berate him, her voice shrill, calling after him, "It's no good end you're coming to! I'll have the guards after you!"

Several people looked at him, curious, but not enough to involve themselves. He quickly lost himself in the crowd and hurried to close the gap between himself and the carts, munching on the bread as he did so.

There was no exit from the city on the east side. The walls extended all the way to the sheer face of the cliffs which formed an impenetrable barricade against attack. However, as they came closer to the mountain, the buildings gradually thinned, as did the crowds. They crossed over a number of small streams, fed by springs and bridged for easy passage. Here in the shadow of the mountain, there were few residences. Mostly there were orchards and small farms, giving this section of the city a very rural feel while still within the safety of the walls. They were climbing now, but the carts were able to move faster in the absence of the crowds. There were still a lot of people, but now almost all of them were heading in the same direction. They were all going toward the Valley for the Solstice Observance. The crowd was taking on a festive air. People called greetings to each other. The class distinction of the Files even seemed to relax, as individuals from different Files joked and exchanged bits of news from their various cities. The only note of discord seemed to be a number of heated discussions Colin overheard regarding the fate of the mantle-bearer. The conversations were strident in condemning the Council for their rush to judgment and the penalty they had pronounced, or in condemning the Council for having not over-ruled Beatrice and carried out the destruction of the impostor immediately in spite of the appeal. It wasn't that he was the topic of every conversation, but in Colin's mind, he was the topic of far too many of them and it made him feel guilty.

The procession gradually ground to a crawl. People were standing idly, visiting with their neighbors, eating food which they had brought or purchasing supplies from the numerous vendors who now lined the road. The line was moving, but very slowly. Colin was unsure of what was going on, but as nobody else seemed concerned and he still had the carts ahead in view, he relaxed. It took almost an hour before he realized that the way ahead led through a narrow, heavily fortified gate. Guards were stationed there, checking passes. He saw several of his fellow travelers anxiously inspecting their passes, which appeared to be made of stiff, starched canvas. There was writing on both sides and a large, official looking stamp over top of the writing. His heart sank. He hadn't known he would need a pass. He should have known. Beatrice had told him that only about one-fifth of the population would be permitted to attend. He just hadn't thought about it. Now what? Briefly, he toyed with the idea of trying to steal a pass and immediately felt guilty. That would rob someone else of their opportunity to attend, or worse, might land them in prison. He considered trying to buy a pass from someone. After all, he had a few dectorals, but he suspected that such an attempt might draw unwanted attention. He was getting closer to the gate now and he could see it was well patrolled. Stern faced guards wearing swords or carrying pikes eyed the crowd warily. Several in the crowd tried to joke with them, but were met with stony silence. These men were professionals. They were serious and not about to be distracted. Colin was about to panic. The only thing he could think of was to try and bribe a guard to let him through. When it was his turn, he desperately grabbed all the coins he had in his pocket. He held them out, hoping nobody else would notice what he was doing. A guard with red-fringed clothing, marking him as being from Sarepta and of the 8th File eyed his extended hand without touching it. "Your pass says you've come all the way from Neims? Is that right?"

Colin was too stunned to answer, he just nodded his head. The guard was simply seeing what he expected to see.

"Surely you didn't make the trip all today, did you?" the guard asked.

"Ah.......no. I spent last night in Salem," Colin stammered.

"In Salem? I'm surprised they let you in! With the Observance, they don't usually let your lot into the city. Inns are all full, you know."

"Ah......yes. I know. My brother works at the stables. At the Praetorium. They let me sleep there last night. Because of my brother." Lying is hard work, Colin thought.

"Hmm. Your brother must be well thought of then. Alright. Move along. Others are coming, so keep moving." With a jerk of his head, the guard urged him on and Colin staggered through the gate, weak in the knees.

"Thanks, Hotha," he whispered. He was through.

The cleft between North and South Cherubim was darker and deeper than it had appeared from his view back at the Praetorium. Colin lost sight of the Regent's carts again, but he wasn't concerned. Everybody was heading in the same direction and there was now no chance that he would become lost. The sharp rock walls rose above him to incredible heights. It made him dizzy when he craned his neck to look up at the narrow band of sky above him. These first cliffs alone must reach to well over 2000 feet, he thought. The passage between the walls was no more than a couple hundred feet in width. While that was ample for passage, it still felt extremely confined with those rock walls towering over top. The road hugged the left side of the canyon. It was broad and well graded, though they were still climbing. The procession of travelers spread out forming a moving front filling almost half the width of the canyon floor. They were flanked on the left by the rock face and on the right by a stream coursing over the polished rock where it formed numerous pools and small cascades. Children were playing in the water, keeping pace with their parents, either afoot or on carts, moving in the crowd. They continued this way for almost an hour. Colin estimated that the canyon must extend for close to two miles. Up ahead he could see it opening up into a broad expanse. They topped a small rise. The creek had fallen away below them and from the rise Colin viewed the most beautiful sight he had ever seen.

The valley was a large oval, several miles in length and nearly two in width. It was entirely walled by sheer cliffs, similar to what they had just passed through. More distant peaks, snow capped and majestic surrounded them. It was an island of paradise protected by a sea of stone. In a hundred locations, small waterfalls cascaded down from incredible heights to splash into small pools at the base of the cliffs. The cliffs themselves were painted with moss, growing in every imaginable shade of green, but also yellows, purples and reds, making it look as though every cliff had a rainbow embedded in its face. The stream alongside which they had been traveling was the only outlet he could see. The water from the various sources flowed together, forming a small lake at the tail end of the valley. Small stands of trees dotted the valley floor. But it was the color of the place that was most amazing. The valley floor may have been carpeted with grass, but he couldn't tell for the preponderance of flowers covering it. It rippled and flowed with color as the flowers swayed in the breeze. There were occasional islands of stone, pushing up through the ocean of flowers. He could see children running through the meadow and climbing on the rocks.

Without conscious thought, he moved forward with the crowd. As they reached the valley floor, they dispersed in all directions. A few tents had been erected. Carts were scattered about the valley. Catching sight of Dalene far ahead, Colin continued to follow the Regent and his group. As they passed near a stand of trees, Colin saw every imaginable kind of fruit hanging. It was incredible. There were apples and pears, peaches, oranges and limes. He recognized fruit which he had seen in the markets of Taiwan and Singapore, but didn't know the names of. For every one he recognized, there were a dozen more he had never seen before. All seemed to be ripe and seeing others pluck fruit from the trees in passing, he did the same. It was delicious. He had never tasted anything so sweet and so wonderful. Tears filled his eyes as he thought, "Eden. Never have I imagined it would be so truly beautiful." He noticed children pulling plants along the edge of a small stream. He walked over and did the same. The root was similar to a small onion. He tasted it. It was strong, pungent and very pleasant. Even as he watched, the soil he had disturbed settled and leveled. Already there was a new shoot growing. In a moment, the plant he had plucked had been replaced. It was as though nothing had disturbed it. He saw the children toss the tops of the plants they had been eating to the ground. In seconds, they shriveled, decomposed and returned to the soil. He shook his head, disbelieving his eyes. It was a place of magic.

Half in a daze, but somehow infused with the sheer joy of this place, Colin followed the meandering stream. He lost track of Dalene and her family, but for the moment at least, that didn't concern him at all. On occasion, he stopped to sample whatever he saw others eating, pulling tubers and plucking fruit. Children dashed past him, splashing in the shallow water, then racing on. He was nearing the head of the valley now. He thought that nothing more could surprise him, but he was wrong.

He had been eyeing something in the distance for sometime. At first he thought it was an especially colorful cliff, but as he drew nearer he realized it was something growing in front of the cliff. It was a tree. The most incredible tree he had ever seen. There was no question in his mind that he was looking at The Tree of Life. There was also no question regarding the origin of the column of light he had seen, both at Elam's Evaluation and his own. He recognized the pattern of it. He knew that every living thing in Aidon - on this planet, for that matter, was connected to this Tree.

From his first observation at a distance, he realized that it must be hundreds of feet tall. Its crown stood almost exactly even with the balustrade of the cliff immediately behind it. The Tree itself actually brushed against the cliff face. It appeared that there were windows or doorways carved into the rock face. The Tree touched, and in some places, extended through the openings, so close to the cliff did it grow. It didn't have spreading branches. It stood alone. Tall, slender and graceful. Its branches swept out from the trunk only about twenty yards, making them look almost stubby in relation to the girth of the tree. Colin doubted that 50 men standing fingertip to fingertip could girdle its massive trunk. To the right of the tree, extending practically under its branches, was a clear pool of water, about 50 feet in diameter. It seemed to be fed from some subterranean source, as there was no inlet. But the inrush of the water caused the surface at the center of the pool to boil, rising almost a foot above the rest of the pond. The floor of the pool sloped so abruptly that he couldn't see the bottom more than three feet from shore. Behind the pool, a series of steps had been carved into the face of the cliff itself. At the top of the steps, a huge set of doors stood closed. He recognized the uniforms of the Arbor Guards lining the steps and standing in front of the door. As his eyes traveled up the face of the cliff, he took in the ornately carved windows opening into some kind of structure within the mountain itself. He would have studied it more, but the Tree drew his attention.

The Tree of Life was absolutely alive with color. When he finally drew near enough, Colin could see the branches covered with blossoms. They were of every imaginable size, shape and color, from smaller than a thimble to larger than his hand with fingers outspread. As he watched, a bud would form and in a matter of a minute, perhaps two, it would grow, rupture and blossom, spreading its color and releasing a heavenly, delicate scent. A few seconds later, it would drop its petals, creating a constant cascade of color falling from the limbs, but no petal ever quite touched the ground or the surface of the pool. They seemed to shrink as they fell, disappearing just as they would have brushed the tops of the grass and flowers growing below. It was like standing in the middle of a mass of butterflies, whirling all around, but never touching. The colors ranged from delicate pastels to explosively bold reds and yellows. Some of the petals were iridescent, like the wings of some incredibly colored beetle, while others were all but transparent. Unlike the other trees he had seen in the valley, this one bore no fruit, just an unending profusion of flowers. Colin stood mesmerized, totally losing track of time. He became aware of someone standing near him. He glanced over and was jolted to see The Lady Dalene smiling at him. He glanced nervously at his cloak, to make certain it was still black.

"You like to watch the petals fall, also?" she asked.

He nodded, "Yes. I've never seen anything like it before."

She looked at him curiously, "Never? But surely you have been here before this! You're too old for this to be your first visit."

Catching his mistake, Colin said, "Of course. I meant, I've never seen anything to compare to it. Here. Or outside the valley."

Dalene nodded, "Of course. I'm sorry. It is beautiful, isn't it?"

"It is," he agreed. "It suits you."

Surprised, she turned to face him, "What did you say? Do you know who I am?"

Colin bobbed his head, refusing to meet her gaze. "Yes. I'm sorry. You're The Lady Dalene. I meant no disrespect. I just meant that this tree………I meant you being part of the Regent's family and all………that you're like royalty and so's this tree……" his words trailed off as he mentally kicked himself.

Recognition flared in Dalene's eyes. "I know you! You're that boy! From the stables this morning!"

Relief flooded through Colin, "Ah……yes, Lady Dalene. I'm sorry. I don't speak very well. I'm sorry. I……ah……I'll be going now." With that, he turned and quickly walked away, promising himself that he would avoid her until he was safely back in Salem and rid of this disguise. A momentary fear washed over him. How <u>did</u> he get rid of this thing? Oh well, no point worrying about it just yet. He glanced back to see Dalene still staring after him and he quickened his pace.

The day was far spent. The sun was on the verge of dipping into the cleft between North and South Cherubim. Even so, the temperature was absolutely perfect. Colin shook his head. "No wonder Adam and Eve didn't mind running around in their birthday suits," he thought. Reluctant to leave the Tree of Life, he hurried away from Dalene, but only as far as the first suitable clump of trees. Here he was well fed from the variety of fruit growing on the heavily laden branches. The thought of having to leave this place caused him an almost physical sensation of pain. Could he not just stay here forever? He lay down amongst the flowers. The sound of the stream running close by was soothing. In an instant, he was sound asleep.

Colin awakened slowly. He had been dreaming again. He was someplace peaceful. Calm. White. He had been floating. Someone else was there. They told him…….why couldn't he ever remember? He lay in the grass, amongst the flowers, feeling perfectly rested. He hadn't a single ache or pain. His eyes opened and the first thing he saw was The Tree of Life. It brought a smile to his face. The mountain peaks above it were just now being painted by the sun's first rays. Today, he thought, is the solstice. He rolled over, trying to soak in the beauty of the scene. Rising, he went to the stream and washed his hands and face, checking to make sure that his clothing showed black, indicating that the Anakim's magic still kept him concealed. He again had that uneasy thought, wondering how he would finally shed this disguise, but he brushed it away. Nothing could be done about it right now.

All over the valley, there were sounds of life. The birds had been chirping for some time, but now he heard the sound of children laughing and greetings being called between friends. For a moment, a sense of loneliness and isolation overcame him. He belonged nowhere. Not any longer. The feeling threatened to overwhelm him, but when he looked up at the Tree, it faded into the background. He ate from the trees under which he had slept before returning to drink from the stream. The sun was just beginning to touch the valley floor, when he saw the Regent, Beatrice and Dalene being escorted by Halvor and several other Arbor Guards up the stone steps in the cliff behind The Tree of Life. Other people were gathering as well. Colin drifted that direction. He saw Gareth exchange words with the guard. The massive doors at the top of the steps were opened. The Regent's family went inside, with several others following behind. Colin watched for a moment and noted that those entering were of no particular File, nor did the guards appear to be checking passes or doing anything other than standing impassively alongside the doorway. Colin tagged along behind family group heading up the stairs, trying to be less conspicuous. They wore the yellow of the 5th File, but seemed to tolerate his presence, so he followed them.

What had seemed like a doorway from the outside, was more like a massive hallway on the inside. It extended into the cliff for at least 15 feet. Once past the entryway it was like entering a massive cathedral. To his left, in the center of the hall, Colin noticed a curious design carved into the stone floor. No, carving wasn't right. There was no seam. It almost looked like a stone inlay, because the color was different, but if it were an inlay, it was the finest possible work. It was the same as that he had seen in the Great Hall of the Praetorium. He was looking at the pattern of The Ruling Box of Aidon.

Hearing the family in yellow talking to their children, he tried to unobtrusively hover closer so he could listen in. He heard the mother explain to her young son, about 6 years of age, "Look, Timon, this is the Great Hall of The Temple of Life. This was made over 4000 years ago - even before the Councils. You see how smooth the walls are? They say it was made without tools, that men could form the rock like your father does with clay, to make the bowls and pitchers we sell. Can you imagine doing that with rock?"

Timon made some reply which Colin couldn't make out. His mother laughed and then continued, "Yes. They had to carve all this out. Over there," she pointed, "Is the doorway to the upper levels. Only the Arbor Guards and the High Council of Aidon and their families go through there, to the second level. They say that as you go up, the carving of the stone becomes more beautiful. Beyond that is the highest level, the third level. That is where The Throne of The Lawgiver is at. No one except The

Lawgiver himself can go there. One day, he will come. It will be on a Solstice Observance, just like today. He will sit on the throne and everyone in the valley will hear his voice and he will become our ruler. Do you know who The Lawgiver is, Timon?"

This time Colin heard Timon's reply clearly as he shouted, "Messias!"

Chapter 24   Attack

General Boris was a frightened man. He should have encountered the first villages of Aidon two days ago. He had marched his men hard, but they were still behind schedule. King Mahon was not one to deal lightly with those who upset his plans. General Boris knew that the only hope he had of saving his skin, was to smash any defense that Aidon could mount and push forward rapidly. His orders were to press the attack as hard as possible until he received word from King Mahon that Aidon had surrendered. The problem was he had no idea exactly where Aidon lay. It had been over 75 years since Kernsidon had last attacked. Keeping records had never been one of the strong points of the army. It had been six days since he had sent his scouts out. They had left their signal flags posted on the tops of distant hills to mark the line of march for the army, but still they had seen nothing of Aidon. Surely they should have turned east by now! They had marched south from Kernsidon before turning west to cross the mountain pass. Once through the pass, they had continued westward, their march dictated by the impassable mountains which flanked the south bank of the Morex River. Where the mountains ended, the river dropped through a narrow chasm which they were able to bridge with huge trees cut from the forest. Once across the river, they swept north. Three days ago they had briefly turned east. General Boris thought that would take him straight to the heart of Aidon. But inexplicably, the scouts had shifted their march to the north again. Curse them! By the Serpent's blood, if they had fouled this, he would have their hearts! He would make them beg for death! Of course, he would have to make sure it was done before King Mahon did the same thing for his general. He needed to talk to his scouts, but they were staying out in front, only leaving flags to urge the army onward. General Boris knew that he would have to push the men even harder. They had to make up the schedule! He had to attack soon, for tomorrow was the solstice.

Had he been able to meet with his scouts, General Boris would have been even more frightened as they were now three days dead. The Arbor Guard, Chase, had surprised two of them while riding patrol on his horse, Patch. The shock of seeing an apparition of death bearing down on horseback had so unnerved them that they tried to flee rather than fight. They were too close to the army to take any chances on their getting away, so Chase cut them down and loaded the bodies on his horse. He hauled them out of the line of march, leaving them undiscovered by the army. Bob had encountered another pair of scouts. He was afoot at the time, having tethered Leopard near a stream so she could get water while she fed. The Kernsidon scouts felt the odds to be well in their favor at two to one, and so had charged, yelling ferociously. Quiet, unassuming Bob hadn't even drawn his sword. He was just setting up to practice shooting his bow, but instead of unleashing on his target, he placed an arrow in the throat of one attacker and in the chest of the other. He too had hidden the bodies well, after removing the signal flags from their packs.

The last pair of scouts which General Boris sent out had the misfortune of meeting up with Aaron and Michael. Michael had ridden his big horse, Giant, right over the top of both of them. They lived long enough to disclose the signal codes the Arbor Guards would need in order to lead the army further north and away from Aidon. Jack, on Lightning and Dathan, on Arrow were dispatched to carry word to Salem that Aidon was under attack. The Arbor Guards doubted that they could continue to pull the army north much longer. Soon, the enemy must surely recognize the deception and turn east. When they did, there would be no stopping them.

******

The Arbor Guards were right. General Boris didn't have a detailed map and the writings from the more recent attacks on Aidon were sketchy at best, but he knew they had come too far north. He sent a large patrol out to find his scouts, but they returned with nothing. Furious, he called a halt for the night in a boulder strewn valley near a small stream. They would rest for now. In the morning, he would double-time the men all the way to Aidon – wherever it was. He figured if they swung east, they would turn back south when they hit the mountains. It might not be the fastest route, but he knew Aidon lay at the base of the mountains. They'd find it, and then Aidon would pay! He had been told to restrain the men, since they intended to conquer, not just pillage. By the Serpent! There would be no restraint! He knew he'd been tricked even if he didn't understand how. Aidon would suffer! Before he faced King Mahon, he would level every town and kill every living thing he encountered! He had the word spread. No quarter. No prisoners. No questions.

******

Jack and Dathan rode together as far as Tyber. They decided that Dathan should take Arrow and ride for Salem. The capitol must be warned of the approaching army. The Arbor Guards and city guards had to be called out and organized as quickly as possible. Jack would ride Lightning to warn the outlying cities. But they were scattered. It would take time. Then he remembered Elam. Immediately, he turned back and raced for Jorge and Miran's farm. He was back-tracking, he knew, but if he could recruit Elam to help spread the word, they would halve the time it would take to warn the cities and call up the army. He raced into the farm late in the afternoon - tomorrow would be the Solstice Observance. That was a problem. Most of the Arbor Guards would be in the Valley. It would take time to get word to them and more time for them to get here. But it couldn't be helped. Miran heard the horse galloping up the path and slide to a stop. She ran out the door to see an exhausted white horse, head down and legs splayed, gasping for breath. The strange rider was almost as breathless. "Are you Miran?" he demanded.

Too surprised for words, she could only nod.

"Your son, Elam? Is he here? I must find him immediately!" Jack said.

Before Miran could answer, Jorge and Elam came running up from the barn, alerted when they heard the commotion up by the house.

"Jack!" Elam yelled. "What's wrong? Where are the others?"

Quickly, Jack explained, "Kernsidon's army is on the way. We found them a couple of days ago. The others are trying to cut off the scouts and fool the army into following them further north. It won't work for long, but it might buy time. Dathan is riding for Salem, but it will be a mess up there with the Solstice Observance. If things go well, the enemy will have to backtrack. That means they'll attack from the north this time. Probably better for us. Rougher country there, easier to defend. Elam, I hate to ask this, but you're the only one who rides a horse. I need you to take Midnight and warn the cities to the south and east of here - Jordanon, Sarepta, Tremont and Riverton. Tell them to assemble whatever forces they can and have them meet at Troas. That's likely to be near where we'll meet Kernsidon. Will you do it?"

"Sure," Elam replied. "Midnight is fast. We should be in Jordanon before nightfall."

Jorge stood by, grim faced, "Then war has come. If you don't mind a bit of advice from an old farmer, I have a suggestion for you."

Jack nodded, "Anything that will help."

"Good. First, rest your horse. You kill or cripple that animal now, it will cost Aidon dearly. And do the same for yourself. You're riding toward the enemy. You need to let our army catch up to you, unless you plan to fight them all by yourself, so slow down."

In spite of himself, Jack had to smile. "Thank you Jorge. I see why Colin speaks so highly of you."

"There's one more thing," Jorge continued, "I see you have a bow. Seems like half the folks around here have been playing with them. You're going to need every man you can get. While you ride, you might call for any man with a bow to hurry to Troas as fast as they can. They aren't going to replace your Guards, but they may be of help."

******

Colin spent over an hour admiring the interior of The Great Hall of the Temple. He could see some of the branches of The Tree of Life extend inside the mountain through the windows above him. The more he looked, the more he was amazed. Stone benches, couches and tables had been carved from the solid rock. Apparently, they had been formed in-place, as there were no seams. The workmanship of some of the creations was exquisite. There were bas-relief carvings on walls and furnishings depicting what Colin supposed were historical events. There were scenes showing a man and a woman by two trees. The one was obviously The Tree of Life and Colin guessed the other was The Tree of Knowledge of Good and Evil. They showed the Serpent, first offering the fruit to the man and woman and then attacking them. As the Serpent was about to devour the woman, a heavenly figure with a drawn sword descended to do battle with the Serpent. Another scene showed the Serpent disappearing beneath the waves of the ocean. The carving was so detailed that Colin could recognize the point where he had come ashore. Obviously the carvers had visited the spot and reproduced it beautifully. The craftsmanship was superb. There were designs so finely carved that Colin doubted a razor could be inserted into the spaces. High above, in the arched dome, were intricately carved windows – not only to the outside, but extending inward, from this huge atrium to convey light to rooms and passages further in the mountain than where they presently were.

As beautiful as the interior was, Colin was drawn once more back outside, where he could view the Tree. In the field nearby, a number of games and contests had been set up. Mothers and children were playing ball, the children running and laughing as they chased the ball through the flowers. A group of older children were using a smaller ball and a series of small metal rings mounted on spikes. It appeared that the object of the game was to get the ball through the opposing team's ring. A group of the Arbor Guards were having a contest with sheathed swords. They practiced thrusting and parrying, cheered on by good-natured on-lookers. Nearer the tree, a group of young men, several wearing colors of the 1st Order were practicing with bows. Colin was surprised to see so many – there had to be twenty or more. "How had this spread so rapidly?" he wondered. Colin wandered over in their direction, interested in seeing the designs of their bows as well as their skill.

The archers were shooting at a large target constructed by wrapping some badly worn canvas around a large clump of grass they had collected. They were shooting at a distance of about 25 yards and the target was large, so they were hitting it every time, though some of the archers were grouping their arrows surprisingly close together. Colin had an idea to make the contest more interesting. He interrupted the group playing the ball game and asked if he might borrow the extra rings they had lying there. They happily told him to help himself. Colin carried them over to the archers.

"Would you like to make the contest more of a challenge," he called out as he approached.

A husky young man, wearing the green of the 4th File responded, "A challenge is it? Well you'll be challenging me, as I've already bested this lot!" He had a broad, cheerful face. The others offered up catcalls and teased him about his boasting, but he shrugged them off.

Colin laughed and said, "Fair enough. I'll challenge the champion, and if that's you, we'll see how you shoot."

He approached the target, but instead of using it as a target, he intended it for a backstop. The rings would be the target. One of the young men had a heavy walking staff of about six feet in length. He borrowed this to align the rings. The first ring was offset about one half diameter to the right. The third ring was offset a half diameter to the left, in relation to the center ring. The other archers immediately grasped the objective. An archer would have to be pretty good to fire through the first ring. He'd have to be a lot better to fire through two of them. It would require extreme precision to shoot through all three, as there was almost no overlap.

The cocky young man in green was impressed by the novelty of the contest. "You'd have to be able to split a feather to shoot all three," he said. "But being as I'm the champion, I claim the first three arrows."

"You shoot all you like, then I'll show you how it's done," Colin replied. The other youths hooted their skepticism.

The archer in green fired his first shot cleanly through the first ring, but it dropped in flight and deflected off the bottom of the second. "One ring!" The cry went up from the gathering audience. His second shot missed the first ring altogether, but skimmed through inside the second. "One ring again!" The other boys yelled. "Does that count?" One questioned. "He missed the first ring!"

Colin was feeling generous, "We'll count it. Fire your last one."

The archer fired his last shot. It flew cleanly through the first two rings, hitting the backstop without ever nearing the third. "Two rings! That's four total," the self-appointed scorekeepers yelled.

The archer smiled, "It's a good challenge, alright. Now, you show me how it's done."

Colin stepped to the firing line. He didn't notice that the group of Arbor Guards gravitating over to watch the archery contest. Just as he was about to loose his first arrow, a voice behind him asked, "Are you trying to shoot through one of those rings?" It was Halvor, flanked by a half dozen of his fellow guards.

Colin looked at him for a brief moment and then replied with a grin, "No, all of them."

Instantly he loosed his shot and it sailed cleanly through all three rings, burying half its shaft in the backstop beyond. "Three rings!" the spectators yelled. "He only needs one more to tie Cardon!" Immediately Colin regretted his rash act. He didn't want Halvor becoming suspicious. He was already looking at him all too intently. Colin quickly shot his next two arrows, but was careful to make sure that each shot only cleared two rings. "Seven rings! Well done!" Cardon was the first to congratulate him. Colin smiled and accepted his congratulations. Right now, all he really wanted was to retrieve his arrows and slip anonymously away. As he turned to leave, he halted as Halvor held his bow out in front of him, blocking his path.

"Didn't I see you yesterday in the Praetorium? Up in the south wing?" he asked.

"Ah…..yes, perhaps you did. I was up there arranging for a cart…….for Councilor Tomias. I think you did see me, sir."

Halvor nodded, not fully satisfied. "You shoot well. But as the new champion, certainly you'll accept a challenge, won't you?"

"Um. OK. Yes, certainly, sir." Halvor looked at him even more intently and Colin cursed himself for the slip.

Halvor stepped to the line and drew his first arrow. It sailed cleanly through the first and second rings, missing the third. "Two rings for the Arbor Guard!" The crowd had grown.

Halvor smiled, glancing at Colin. "Five rings to tie and six to win, eh?"

His second shot sailed cleanly through all three rings. "Three rings! Five now for the Guard!"

With hardly a pause, Halvor drew and fired his final shot. Instantly Colin knew it would clear all three rings. Childishly and without thought, Colin slammed a thought at the arrow, willing it to strike the third ring. The arrow deflected, striking the top of the third ring and sailed high into the air. The thought which had deflected it, seemed somehow to also have accelerated it as it soared away. Immediately he regretted his petulant act. It had been one thing to choose to do less than his best, but it was an entirely different matter to interfere with someone else. The crowd yelled, "A tie! Seven rings to the Arbor Guard and seven to the 1st File!"

Before the crowd even finished yelling the score, Colin, who had never taken his eye off the errant shot, sprinted away, yelling back, "I'll get it!" The arrow was still in flight even as he raced off. But a moment later, he was horrified to see it impact high up on the trunk of The Tree of Life.

Colin heard the yells behind him, but he ignored them. He felt rotten for deflecting Halvor's shot and even worse that the arrow had stuck in The Tree of Life. All he could think of was that he had to get the arrow. Maybe there wouldn't be too much trouble if he did. He knew it wouldn't really hurt the tree, but it was obvious that The Tree of Life was sacred to these people and he was seriously afraid that Halvor might be held to account when it wasn't his fault at all. He <u>had</u> to retrieve that arrow from the tree! The branches swept practically to the ground. The moment he reached the tree, he climbed. His earth-trained muscles swung him upwards easily. Coupled with the invigorating environment of this valley, he practically flew up the tree. Higher and higher he went. The branches were large and so closely spaced, he progressed rapidly. He could hear the shouts below him, but he was already high up. Finally he could see the arrow. It was lodged in a fork off the main trunk, about 200 feet from the top of the tree. He reached it and pulled it free when a voice froze him. "Curse you, you young fool! By the twin moons, what do you think you're doing? You're not permitted up here! No one is permitted to touch the Tree! You know that!" Halvor had run up the stairway inside the mountain and was climbing out onto the branches about ten feet below Colin. Halvor looked up and froze. "Oh, Colin! What have you done?" It was a cry of purest despair. Colin glanced at his cloak. It was white. He suddenly remembered Hotha's warning, "Touch tree, Ai-don mans see K'lin. Kill K'lin." He had touched the tree. They were going to kill him.

Halvor was now fully out on the tree, moving very carefully. "Colin, you didn't touch the sap did you?" Colin looked at the clear, oily substance coating the arrow. He hadn't noticed it before. It was slick to his touch. "I'm sorry, Halvor. It was my fault your arrow flew up here. I deflected it. I just wasn't thinking."

Halvor shook his head, his face grim. "You're not even allowed in the Valley! Mother is responsible for you! By the Serpent's blood, what a mess! At least tell me you didn't get any of the sap on you."

Mutely, Colin held out his hand to show it covered in the clear, oily sap. Halvor's face went white, and then the world exploded.

******

Mahon had driven his guards mercilessly through the bowels of the mountain. There were no landmarks. The dim lantern light by which they traveled seemed to soak into the rock. They stumbled often, because they couldn't even distinguish the floor. They had no idea how long they had been underground or how far they traveled. The darkness was disorienting. Even so, it seemed the tunnel did not follow a straight line. The only sounds they heard was the slither of the huge serpent in front of them, the uneven echo of their steps, the heaving panting of their labored breathing and the ceaseless cursing of King Mahon coming along behind them. A few times, the solid wall was broken by the form of a doorway, distinguished only by a darker outline in the rock. They had no idea how long they stopped to rest. It might have been five minutes, or it might have been five hours. Three of the guards, driven mad by fear and exhaustion, attempted to bolt past Mahon to run screaming into the dark, without a torch. Two of them made it. The first did not, as Mahon's sword buried itself in his bowels. That alone prevented the sword from reaching the other two as they tripped over their dying companion before regaining their feet and racing away into the dark. It seemed the journey through blackness would never end. Totally exhausted and half mad, the survivors suddenly plowed into the tail of the huge Serpent. Recoiling in terror, they ran into Mahon, who froze them with his glare. Then, most chilling of all, they heard a voice echoing inside their skulls, *"Brother, we are here."* Two more of the King's Guard went mad in that instant.

Mahon commanded, "Take us in. Hurry!"

The Serpent voice came again, *"The stone has changed. The entrance is sealed. It cannot be done here."*

"It <u>must</u> be done!" Mahon screamed. "You must do it!"

"Not here," the Serpent replied. *"We must go back. Only a short distance. Past the seal. We will make a new entrance. We will not fail, Brother."*

Mahon led the way back down the tunnel. He retreated several hundred yards, becoming angrier with each step when the voice stopped him. *"Here, Brother. Here, there is no seal. Here I will make a new tunnel. Soon. It will be soon."*

They couldn't see the head of the Serpent, but they could feel the rock vibrating all around them. Suddenly, the tail before them disappeared and Mahon was immediately on the soldiers again, cursing them and urging them onward. The new tunnel took off to the right, leading upward, but still angling forward in their original direction of travel. The angle was steep, almost 45 degrees and the men had trouble maintaining their footing on the slick rock, almost as smooth as glass. They again lost all sense of time. It seemed that they climbed for an eternity. At last! There was light! A flood of light illuminated the dark tunnel. After so long in the darkness, the men were blinded, tears blurring their vision as hands jerked swords free from their sheathes. They stumbled out of the tunnel into a large chamber, beautifully decorated and ornately carved. It was not the Great Hall of the Temple. They had climbed far beyond that, to emerge into The Lawgiver's Hall on the third level. Here, they were past where the Councilors were permitted to go. There were stairs leading upward at the far end of the hall. Mahon ordered the men to guard the great doors leading into the hall. He took the lead, the Serpent following and headed toward the stairs. The men he left behind watched until he disappeared, then dropped to the floor in exhausted relief.

Mahon climbed upward, but he hadn't far to go before the stairs ended. He stepped out onto an ornate patio carved from the top of the cliff. The top of The Tree of Life was exactly even with where he stood. There at the edge, sat a massive, carved throne. The Lawgiver's Throne. To the right several entryways led off the patio and back into the mountain. A polished trough carried a small stream of water from one of the entrances where it made a gentle curve leading to The Lawgiver's Throne. Under the throne was a small crevice, whether carved or natural was uncertain. Here the water disappeared, swallowed up by the mountain. Mahon went directly to the stream, following it into the mountain through the largest of the arched doorways. The chamber they entered was neither large nor ornate. In fact, it looked quite unfinished. Unlike the other halls within the temple, this one was rough, more like a cavern. The floor sloped gently upward, away from the entrance. While there were a number of passages to be explored, Mahon ignored them, following the stream toward the sound of splashing water. At the rear of the chamber, carved from the mountain itself was a small basin with a simple inscription in the stone above it. *Living Water.* Mahon smiled in satisfaction. The legend was true. Water flowed from an opening at the edge of basin where it protruded from the rock, forming a pool, perhaps six inches deep and a foot in diameter. The water overflowed at the leading edge of the basin in a thin sheet which fell a short distance, splashing into a small pool, before flowing away through the water-polished trough he had been following.

Mahon stared at the basin for a long moment. *Living Water.* From here flowed the source of life for Aidon - for all the earth. The *Living Water* disappeared into the mountain. Deep in the earth, the roots of The Tree of Life drew it forth. It circulated through the branches and leaves where some of it was expired, evaporating to mix with the clouds and be returned back to the earth in the form of rain. Some of it was returned to the soil through the great Tree's root system, filtering into the pool at its base. The legends claimed that The Lawgiver was life, but when The Lawgiver did not occupy the Throne, this water, flowing as it were from the Throne of The Lawgiver, nourished the Tree, and from the Tree, all life on earth. This was why Mahon had come here. This is why he had no need for armies. There was about to be a Lawgiver in Aidon once more. There was no further need for *Living Water.* Without looking, he spoke to the Serpent. "Destroy it."

The Serpent hissed, then whipped its mighty tail, shearing the basin cleanly from the wall. In its place, there was ……….nothing. The granite was unmarred, left coarse as though by the blade of some stonecutter, but there was no hole, no crack from which the water could emerge. The flow of water had been cut off.

Mahon nodded in satisfaction, then turned and marched back to The Lawgiver's Throne. In a few minutes, the water would cease to flow into the crevice beneath the Throne. The legends said that from this seat, the law had been delivered to Aidama and Aeva. That from this seat, every person in the Valley of Aidon fell under the sound of The Lawgiver's voice. On either side of the massive throne, hanging out over top of the Tree itself, was a huge carving of Cherubim, the heavenly guardian placed to guard The Tree of Life. Perhaps there once really had been a cherubim, but now, there was only a huge carved angel, standing with drawn sword, watching over The Tree. It stood 60 feet high. Its sword was fully 40 feet in length. It had to have weighed hundreds of tons. Mahon stood, smiling in satisfaction. All was going according to plan. Aidon would be his! The Serpent coiled at the side of the throne. By now, his troops should have massed along the western border of Aidon, laying waste to her cities and enslaving her people. He had won. Aidon might not know it yet, but her fall was certain.

The Serpent interrupted his thoughts of victory, *"Brother, look!"* He walked to the edge and looked. A huge crowd of people was gathered near the base of the Tree. Had they seen him? How could they know he was here? And then he saw two figures, in the branches of the tree far below him. An Arbor Guard! And a figure in white. The mantle-bearer? It had to be! What were they doing? Were they trying to attack him by climbing the tree? Were they such fools? He would show them <u>power!</u> "Kill them!" he ordered.

The Serpent hissed. Again the tail lashed out, cutting through the base of the great stone cherubim like a razor slicing through flesh. The statue sheared cleanly from the side of the mountain and it toppled through the branches of The Tree of Life.

Instantly, Mahon leapt to the throne and seated himself. "People of Aidon!" he bellowed, "Your Lawgiver is come!" His voice roared and echoed through the whole of the valley. Everywhere, people froze. The voice was accompanied by a horrendous rumbling and a series of splintering "CRACKs!!" as the stone Cherubim shattered and tore branches from The Tree of Life. Those close to the Tree saw branches explode. Far away, people saw the tree sway, slamming into the cliff and rebounding as though it would be ripped out by the roots. Halvor was looking up and saw the statue start to topple. He threw himself at the trunk with a shouted warning and hung on for dear life. The sword of the statue cleaved several large branches just above him before spiraling out into space. It missed Colin by mere inches. The impact threw him hard against the trunk where he hung on, dazed.

As Halvor and Colin clung to the Tree, they heard a voice declaring something about The Lawgiver. The Tree rocked with repeated impacts as the statue shattered branches all the way down, before burying itself in the soft meadow at the base of the tree. The voice bellowed once again, but this time they heard it clearly. "I am The Lawgiver. I am Mahon, King of Kernsidon and sent by Messias to rule over you! Even now, my people from Kernsidon are marching to unite with the people of Aidon! No longer will there be two lands, two rulers. I am come to be the ruler of this people! The ruler over all the earth! You will accept me, or you will die! Your Council has failed you! They have kept you in bondage! They have embraced a false messenger – the mantle-bearer whom they should have destroyed! See! Even now he tries to destroy Aidon! He has destroyed The Tree of Life! He sought to climb The Tree, to gain The Throne of The Lawgiver! MY Throne! He will be destroyed! All who acknowledge him will be destroyed! Save yourselves, my people! Come to me! Accept me! Follow me and you shall have peace! In a softer tone, he continued, "For over 4000 years, you have rejected the efforts of Messias to unite this people. Many times he sent the Kings of Kernsidon as his messengers to free you. But your Councils rejected them! This last time, he calls to you. He has been patient, but he will be patient no more! This last time, he will show mercy. He has established me to be your King, to be the head of the

13th File! But, if you would have mercy, then the High Council of Aidon must come to me, bow before me, acknowledge me as their ruler - as your ruler! If so, then will I bring the army of Kernsidon in peace and we shall be one people. Reject me at your peril! There will be peace, even if I must bring it at the point of the sword! Remember the ancient promise. The Lawgiver has come to sit upon the throne, that peace may fill the earth. I await the answer of the High Council of Aidon, but until that answer is given, the army of Kernsidon will not be restrained!"

Colin was frozen. "Halvor?" he called out. "Are you OK? What's going on?"

A tired voice came back, "OK. I should have known it was you when you said that. I should have clubbed you on the spot. Are you alright? Can you move?"

"I'm alright," he replied. "Hold on, I'm coming to you."

"NO! Don't come near me. You can't help me. Can you get down? Can you move without touching any of the sap?"

Colin ignored him and quickly scrambled down though the broken branches to rest beside Halvor. "Come on," he said. I think we can make it over to that window you climbed out of."

Halvor slowly shook his head. "I can't. I'm covered with sap. All life on Aidon is bonded to The Tree of Life. It's in the water. It's in our blood. I wanted to keep you from touching the sap. I'm sorry, I was too late. Once you touch it, it bonds to you. I can't move. I can't believe you haven't been stuck yet."

The shattered branches had indeed covered Halvor with sap, which continued to flow over him. Everything was covered with it. It immobilized him like an insect caught on fly-paper.

"Are you crazy?" Colin asked. "I've had this stuff on me since I pulled the arrow from the tree. It isn't sticky. If anything, it's slippery. It feels almost like oil. Come on. I can help get you out of here."

Halvor looked at him in disbelief. "That can't be. All life in Aidon, all life on earth, is connected to the tree. Bonded. You cannot touch the sap without becoming entrapped by it."

Colin attempted a grin, "Maybe it's lucky I'm not from Aidon – or your earth either. Come on, we have to get out of here." He dropped lower. Sap was now pouring from several broken branches, coating him more by the minute.

Halvor managed to barely shake his head. "There is nothing you can do. Don't worry. I won't die. The Tree won't let me die. It will continue to pump life through my body, but the Tree will grow around me, through me, until I am part of it. We are all part of The Tree anyway. Go, my friend. Quickly."

Colin shook his head, "Not without you. I can help." He tried to hold onto a branch, but by now he was so completely coated, he couldn't grip anything. It was too slick. If he moved, he would fall. He was not from Aidon. The Tree of Life held no bond for him. Even as he stood, he felt his feet slip, "Like an air hockey puck," he thought. "I have no connection here. The tree is rejecting me." He had to try. He reached for Halvor to try and free him. But the instant he moved, he began to slide. And then he fell, right past the anguished eyes of his friend.

Once he started to fall, there was no stopping. Colin slid and bounced, through the branches. Faster he fell and when he struck branches, the impact was severe, knocking the breath from him. A particularly brutal jolt sent him spinning out away from the trunk. There was no hope now. Down he fell. He closed his eyes and curled up tightly into a ball. With a tremendous impact, his body shattered the surface of the pool at the base of The Tree of Life. Down, down, he went. It seemed he would never stop sinking. At last, he felt his body start to rise. Feebly, he tried to kick toward the surface. His legs didn't seem to work right. Still he rose. He thrust his hand up above him, trying to stroke. His hand impacted on a hard surface. He was inside an underground tunnel, being swept along by a powerful current. There was no air pocket. Everything was black. He could only tell he was moving by his fingers scraping along on the roof of the tunnel and the occasional impact his legs made with the walls. His lungs were empty, all the breath having been pounded from him when he struck the water. He had to breathe. He had to draw air. He was drowning....... ......and then he wasn't.

******

Colin's eyes fluttered open to familiar surroundings. He'd been here before. Memory returned in a flood and he jerked up into a sitting position. Everything was white, beautiful, pervaded by a sense of complete peace, yet somehow, he was not at peace. He saw a familiar figure approaching from between the columns across the way and he stood. Despite his surroundings, he was filled with a feeling of sadness. The figure stopped in front of him and spoke, "Welcome back, son. Are you alright?"

"I guess so. I'm sorry I failed, Dad. Is it over then? Am I dead now?"

His Dad smiled, but shook his head. "You're far too anxious, Colin. Now is a time for life. The transition you think of as death will come, but not yet."

"Then why am I here? I failed. I destroyed The Tree of Life."

"That wasn't your doing. The damage done to the Tree was due to the choices of others and it's not destroyed. At least, not yet."

"But why am I back here?" Colin asked.

"I thought you might want the chance to catch your breath,"

Colin caught his meaning. "Yeah, I could use one. But I still don't understand. You told me before that I wasn't being sent there - to Aidon - to be a prophet. But that's what they expect me to be - because of the clothes I was wearing when I showed up there. Half the people think I'm supposed to have some message for them. The other half want to kill me!"

"Colin, you've been around people who wanted to kill you for most of your life. Remember David, in junior high? Jeanne, your first year at college? People wanting to kill you is really nothing new."

"Yeah," Colin continued to argue, "but these people have the means to do it!"

"Perhaps," he agreed. "But so far they haven't, so don't be too concerned."

"But I failed! I flunked out back on earth! I couldn't connect with anyone anymore and now I'm failing here! I can't do this!"

"Son, you didn't fail back on earth. You had to become disconnected from there in order to be able to make the transition to Aidon. You haven't failed there either, not unless you quit."

Colin hesitated before asking, "So I'm not done yet? I have to go back?"

"Yes, there's more for you to accomplish. You need to go back."

Colin was silent for a long moment, before finally looking up with pain filled eyes, "Will it hurt? Like last time?"

"No. Not like last time. This time, the pain will be different."

Colin made a sound that was half laughter and half sob, "I don't want to do this. I just feel so isolated. There's no one really like me. No one I can talk to. I don't think I can do this by myself."

With a look of infinite compassion came the response, "That's why you have to go back."

******

Everything was black. Colin's mind focused on one desperate thought, "I must breathe!" it screamed. He blew the last air from his lungs, having wrung every last molecule of oxygen from it. His body would no longer be denied, he sucked in, knowing that the lungful of water would spell his death, but he couldn't help it, he gasped and was shocked to not feel the icy burn of the water filling his chest, but cool, sweet air. In the blackness of the tunnel, he still could feel nothing. He knew he was still in the water. He continued to use his right hand to fend his head off the rock wall above. There was no break at the surface. He blew out again, rapidly exchanging the air in his lungs, but before he could draw a third breath, he was swept out of the tunnel, seeing light somewhere above. Madly, he kicked and clawed upwards toward the light. Just as his hand broke the surface, it was trapped in a powerful grasp that jerked him halfway out of the water and flung him to the bank where he lay panting, his face buried in the cool grass. He was finally able to roll over and stare upward at his benefactor. The sun was in his eyes. All he could make out was a burly silhouette. A gravelly voice spoke, "Welcome, mantle-bearer. Welcome to Kernsidon."

Chapter 25   The Messenger

Colin was stunned. He struggled to sit up. "Kernsidon? Then, am I a prisoner?"

The figure towering over him squatted down. Immediately Colin could see he was not so tall as he'd first appeared, but he was every bit as burly as he'd seemed. His shoulders were massive and he had an unruly tangle of dark hair and a tremendous bushy beard hanging halfway down his chest. The face was lined and creased, yet somehow serene. He studied Colin for a moment, before replying, "Well, I suppose that could be arranged, if that's your wish. It's entirely up to you."

"Well, no." Colin said, "But I thought Aidon and Kernsidon were enemies. At least that's what I was told."

The figure nodded, "Partly true. Kernsidon is certainly an enemy to Aidon. Aidon isn't really an enemy to Kernsidon. They just want to be left alone."

"Who are you?" Colin asked.

If Colin was surprised before, he was in complete shock at the reply. "I'm Elias, the prophet."

"You're the prophet!?!"

"Well," Elias responded, "I'm a prophet. Or the prophet Elias, or Elias the prophet. Not sure that I'm the prophet. Could be more, I suppose. But if so, I've not been told about 'em. Maybe just not my place to know, so I can't say for sure."

"But this is great!" Colin exclaimed. "Half the people in Aidon keep thinking that I'm the prophet! But I'm not. I keep telling them that. But if you're the prophet, you can go there and sort this whole thing out!"

"Sure, I could do that." Elias said, "And the moment the Council got their hands on me, they'd be destroying me just like they have all the others. They're not ready yet, I'm thinking. Soon maybe. But not yet."

"But you're the prophet! You have to! You don't understand. Somebody just took over The Lawgiver's Throne. They destroyed The Tree of Life! They're going to enslave Aidon! You have to do something!"

Elias just looked at him blandly. "I'm a prophet. A messenger. It would do no good for me to go running in there and spouting off only to be destroyed. And from what you're saying, I'm guessing that whoever is taking the Throne of The Lawgiver isn't going to stop at destroying. They'll be killing - prophets, Councilors and anyone else they think might be a threat."

"Then what are you going to do?" Colin asked.

"Me? I'm waiting for you to straighten things out so I can be about delivering my message," he replied.

"Me?!? Are you crazy? How am I supposed to fix this?"

Elias shrugged, "Don't know. All I was told was to be here and pull you out of this pool then get you on your way to finish what you started. You do that, then I can do my job." He started to walk away.

"Elias! Please! You've got to help me out! At least tell me what you know!"

Elias looked back at him and grinned. "Come along. You look like you could use something to eat. We'll talk."

Elias led the way along a dim path toward the face of the cliff. They passed by a large cave, almost perfectly round and roughly six feet in diameter. It was so smooth it looked to have been polished. Elias continued on, up into the rocks and into a narrow cleft. Here there was a shallow cave, hidden from view and protected from above by a large overhang. Colin could see a wooden bed, a small chest and various cooking utensils neatly arranged along the wall of the cave. A small fire smoldered at the entrance, underneath the overhang. Elias uncovered a pot sitting on the dying embers of the fire and ladled soup of some kind from it. He handed the bowl and a carved wooden spoon to Colin before serving himself. They both sat on the ground as there were no furnishings in the cave besides the bed. Elias said nothing while he ate. When they were done, he took the bowl from Colin and said, "I can't tell you what I know. But I'll tell you what I can. Don't argue with me. You just think about it and it will make sense to you."

Colin slowly nodded. "Alright. I'll listen."

"Good. You're probably wondering why a prophet is here in Kernsidon. I'll start there. I was born in Kernsidon. My parents were good people. Not a lot of value is placed on 'good' here, but they were good. King Mahon, and before him, his father King Jacob have been pretty thorough in destroying anyone or anything they think might hint of opposition. You know how the Compliance works?"

"Not really. They tried to explain it, before my Evaluation, but I'm not sure I really understood," Colin replied

"You don't have to <u>understand</u> it, exactly, just know what it does. You don't <u>understand</u> what you're doing when you shape the air, do you? But you've managed to do it, haven't you? So listen. You've been through the Evaluation, so you understand the Compliance, right? 12th File, eh? Not showing much color for a 12th File. Usually they dress up like peacocks."

Colin was a bit self-conscious on this topic. "I did go through the Evaluation, but I didn't really understand that either. I never made anyone bow to me. They couldn't see me - my true-self, I mean. I bowed to the Regent. I felt like I wanted to."

Elias nodded. "That's right. I forgot. You're not from here, are you? No matter. Probably good that you did bow to the Regent. No telling what might have happened if you hadn't. Most likely they'd have either tried to make <u>you</u> Regent or they'd have killed you. I'm betting it would have been the latter. But you went through the Evaluation, eh? What did you think?"

Colin paused, "At first, I couldn't see anything. But each time I closed my eyes and searched for the other person's true-self, it was like I saw more every time. It was amazing. You know, the lights connecting them to others in their family and the way everyone connected to The Tree of Life. It was the most beautiful thing I'd ever seen."

Elias' eyes widened in surprise, "You were able to see all that? When you were in the Ruling Box of Aidon?"

"Yes, both then and earlier. I attended the Evaluation of a friend of mine - in Tyber. I could see it at his Evaluation as well, but not as well as I could later, at my own Evaluation."

"Amazing!" Elias shook his head. "You could see the connections - between people and the connection to The Tree of Life itself? And you weren't even in the Evaluation Box? That is a rare gift indeed. Look at me, mantle-bearer and I shall look at you. See my true-self, as I shall see yours. What connections do you see?"

"Alright, but my name is Colin. Colin Ericsson. I'm still not very comfortable with this 'mantle-bearer' stuff."

He closed his eyes and focused on Elias. Almost instantly he could see the glowing orb which was Elias' true-self. It gave a strong, clear, steady light. The intensity was brilliant. Colin felt like he ought to have to look away, it was so bright, but he wasn't using his eyes, so there was no need. He studied the glowing sphere. He saw a single, delicate strand. He raced along it and found - a sister. An older sister. Her light was very dim. Colin thought that she probably had little time to live. He returned to Elias' true-self. As he looked closer, he could see thousands, tens of thousands minute threads, extending outward in every direction. It was similar to what he had seen of Dalene, at his Evaluation. He concentrated harder and then, he saw the dark strand which he knew would lead back to The Tree of Life. But this was strange. The strand dove into the pool from which Colin had emerged. The strand did go back to the Tree, but it went through the waters of the pool. Why? At last, Colin opened his eyes to find the questioning gaze of Elias on him. Elias slowly nodded, "A strange one, you are, mantle-bearer."

Colin was excited, "Then you could see me? You found my true-self?"

Elias shook his head, "No. I could sense much, but saw little. It was like looking at a hole in the dark. Knowing that you were there, but unable to see you. Only by looking away from you, faintly, perhaps, I saw something of what you might be. It is as if your true-self is meant to be seen by different eyes. You form the air. I could feel the power of it in you. You do things from believing, not from knowing. You seek for answers and when no answer exists, you create answers. Yours is the power of the ancient ones – the makers of things. You are of those who had no fear of that which is not known. You hunger to know and understand but you act even without the understanding. You wish to shape the world rather than be shaped by it. You choose to act rather than allow your surroundings to act upon you. You have the gift of air and stone – to form these and use them as tools, yet you are ignorant of how to use the gift. I cannot teach you. There have been none in thousands of years who use this power. But you must master this. It's in you. It is much of what defines who and what you are. You must embrace this part of yourself if you are to succeed or Aidon and Kernsidon will be lost."

Colin's head was swimming. He didn't even begin to comprehend what Elias was talking about. Sure, he sought for answers. That's what engineers did, right? Was trying to make the world a little bit better what Elias referred to as trying to shape the world? But this stuff about shaping air and stone, that made him distinctly uncomfortable. He felt like a fraud every time he shot his bow, but shaping stone? He'd never done anything like that. Before he could ask anything further, Elias interrupted his thoughts. "What did you see?" he asked softly.

"I saw your true-self," Colin replied. You glow with a brilliant, steady light. Your connection to The Tree of Life is very strong, but it goes through the pool - through the water, back to the tree."

"Naturally," Elias replied. The waters of life. From The Tree of Life. Its roots extend deep in the earth. I don't know if it's the Tree which gives power to the waters, or the water which gives power to the Tree. In either case, from here, it's the most direct connection and the conduit is very strong - almost as strong as being right beside the Tree itself. What else did you see?"

"I saw thousands and thousands of faint connections - to a great many people, both here and in Aidon. But I saw only one family connection. An older sister, I believe. Her light is very dim. I'm sorry, but I don't think she has long to live."

Elias nodded, "My sister, Mary. You are correct, Colin, in that she is older than I, but only by a few years. You are wrong, however, in thinking that she has little time to live. Unless she meets with violence or accident, she could live a long time, probably longer than me. What you saw is the effect of the Compulsion."

"I don't understand."

"Of course you don't. But what you saw is the real difference between the Compliance and the Compulsion. The Compliance is an exercise of force as well, but it leaves both parties whole, complete. At some point, one or the other will choose to comply with the wishes or demands of the other. It was never intended for the purpose for which they use it in Aidon. It was nothing more than a tool to assist in teaching. The Boxes of Aidon are like a lens to focus the intellect, they make the teaching more efficient. Through the Compliance - or what it originally was, parents could teach their children. A craftsman could teach an apprentice. Not only skills, but knowledge could also be taught in this manner - spiritual truths as well as physical laws. In what they call The Chaos, this was changed. No longer was it enough to simply teach. Behavior and even beliefs were distorted and changed. Like all tools, this one also may be used constructively or destructively. You already know that they can and do destroy individuals, don't you? Especially, those who wear the mantle?"

Colin nodded.

"The Compulsion," Elias continued, "is nothing more or less than partial destruction of the will - the intelligence underlying the ability to choose and to act. The Compulsion destroys a part of the true-self, leaving it less than complete. That is what you saw with my sister. Not a diminishing of her life, but of her self. As I told you, my parents were good people. I was raised questioning much of what I saw in Kernsidon. Messias called me to be a messenger. Don't ask me why. I don't know. There must be many others better suited than me, especially in Aidon. I still don't understand all of this - a prophet from Kernsidon?" He shook his head and was silent for a moment before continuing. "My sister believed me to be a messenger. When King Jacob suspected this, I had to flee. I've been hiding here for several years - waiting for you. My sister was caught. Mahon used the Compulsion to eradicate her faith in me as warning to others. But that belief was deeply rooted. The damage was extensive. This is the power the Serpent has sought from the very beginning - to become The Lawgiver, in place of Messias, not to build, but to destroy the law, to destroy the right and ability to choose. He would have us become mere pawns to be used for his purposes. He failed before. Now Mahon has brought him back to make it all possible."

"But you can stop him, right?" Colin asked.

"Not me. You. Who do you think I've been waiting for?" was the reply.

"That can't be right! I'm not even from here! I don't know anything about Mahon or how to stop the Serpent. You're the prophet. Surely there's something you can do!"

Elias shook his head. "Almost, I wish I could trade places with you. I teach when I can but rarely does anyone listen. Of course lately I haven't even had anyone to teach. Colin, why do you think I was sitting down there at the pool when you popped up? Fishing? Like you do? No. I know a little about you, but only a little. I had no need to know more, so I've not been told more. Oh, how I'd love to have you teach me! Some of those things you know from wherever you are from! But it's not my place to know! If it ever is, we'll be told. Right now it isn't your place to teach either. So you see, I have things to do. Yes, I'm a messenger, and I'd dearly love to be about delivering the message I've been given. Problem is, if I'd done that here, Mahon would have killed me long ago. If I were to try it in Aidon, they'd have me destroyed inside of a moon - as you well know. That's where you come in. You need to fix it so I can deliver my message. Don't ask me how you're supposed to do it. I just know I've been waiting a long time for you to come and get it done. You've already noticed that things here aren't exactly like what you're used to from wherever you call home. I have a message just for you on that, so pay attention. Here it is. 'That which has happened, is possible. It is often easier to say what happens than to explain why.' You got that, or do I need to repeat it for you? Don't ask me to explain it. I was just told that you needed to hear it."

Colin sat silently for a long time, staring at the dead fire. At last he looked up. "Then I have to go back. Right away."

Elias nodded. "Of course you have to go back. No way to stop Mahon from here."

"Are you coming with me?"

"I'm coming behind you, so don't be too long about taking care of Mahon and that Serpent. Mahon summoned the Serpent. The only way he could have done that is through a blood-bond. You mustn't forget that. If he used his own blood, and I expect he did, that means he's linked to the Serpent. You have to understand, the Serpent isn't real. It exists, but it isn't really a Serpent. It is a physical manifestation of evil. If Mahon called it into this world with his own blood, then he's no longer bonded to The Tree of Life. Evil is now his life and he is the anchor which allows evil in that physical form to exist in this world. They are now parts of the same whole and you have to get rid of the whole or we have no hope. Do you understand?"

Colin didn't, but he nodded anyway and Elias continued.

"Good. You don't have time to go around the mountains, so you'll be going the same way that Mahon did - through The Serpent's Tunnel. You'll have to move quickly. There're a couple things I need to tell you that might help. First thing is this: you get near the end of the tunnel, there will be a split. Don't take the tunnel that goes up. You do that, and you'll be dying before you get around to doing anything else. I've been told that for sure. Second thing, whatever you think you're going to do, you can't do it by yourself. You're going to need help. Don't ask me where you're going to get help, because I don't know. I'll be coming right along, but I'll be slower than you, and you can't wait. I've got to bring some of the records."

"Records?" Colin asked dumbly.

"Sure. Records. I guess Aidon went and lost or destroyed most of theirs. At least the ones they knew about. But back before The Chaos, a whole bunch of their records were hidden away. There are whole libraries full of records inside the Serpent's tunnel. Last place anyone would look, especially since the entrance was sealed at the other end inside The Temple of The Tree of Life. Nobody's been able to open it in 4000 years. But here, look, this is part of what I have to take back."

Elias got up and retrieved a thick leather-bound book from his bed. "See here," he said, "All kinds of stuff the people in Aidon need. Here - see? A whole chapter on the use of the *Teaching* Boxes of Aidon. Nothing at all about that *Evaluation* they've been doing. At least they got the name right on The Ruling Boxes of Aidon. Problem is they're supposed to use them to be taught how to rule the people. That's not what they're doing. Look at this! Must be a couple hundred pages here just of prophecies they probably have all messed up."

Colin accepted the volume from Elias and gently turned the pages. There were no frayed edges. No missing sections or words. It was whole. Complete. He thought of what this could mean to the people of Aidon. As he turned a few more pages, suddenly, the words seemed to jump off the page at him.

> **To save her people from oppression** *the daughter of the most high* **must yield to her heart**. *He shall be* **an** *Outcast. They shall become as one and shall destroy the* **false** *ruler of this people.*

It went through his mind, through his heart, like a bolt of lightning. Dalene had it all wrong. He handed the book back to Elias and said, "Show me the Serpent's tunnel. I'm going back. Now."

Elias shook his head. "First things first. Have you examined yourself?"

"I don't know what you mean," Colin replied.

"It's simple enough," Elias said. "A few minutes ago you examined me. You saw my true-self. Have you looked at your own true-self?"

"I don't know how to do that. I mean, I'd need some kind of special mirror or something, wouldn't I? How can I see myself?" Colin asked.

Elias smiled, "Maybe you can't. Nobody else seems to be able to, but if anyone can, it's you. Your true-self doesn't reside on this plane. When you looked at me, it wasn't your physical, or natural eyes doing the examining. You've already discovered that you can trace connecting lines between individuals and between individuals and the Tree. You simply need to turn your attention inward. Examine yourself. What do you see?"

Colin closed his eyes. Almost immediately he could see Elias – his true-self. But he couldn't seem to get oriented for self-examination. He traced the connection between Elias and his sister, then back again. Pausing at the edge of the glowing sphere which was Elias, he tried to turn and look back at where he thought he'd come from. It felt like trying to look at his face without using a mirror. As hard as he tried, he couldn't quite seem to see his "self." Then suddenly, he could. He couldn't even say <u>how</u> he knew that he was looking at himself, but he did. Colin realized that he could shift his perspective. One moment he was looking at the dull, mildly pulsating sphere of light which was his "true-self," and the next moment he was looking at the tiny tendril of light which connected his true-self to the tiny orb of light – his probe, as he thought of it - at the edge of the presence he knew was Elias. He shifted his perspective back and forth, very quickly and found that it left him feeling slightly nauseous. He wondered if he could actually view both this tiny probe and his true-self from yet another perspective. He had no sooner thought this than he did it. He could see his true-self and the probe, connected to his true-self by a tendril of light. The experience was so disorienting that he lost the contact and found his perspective shifted back to that of his true-self. When he regained his equilibrium, he again shifted his view to the probe he positioned near the glowing sphere which he knew was Elias. From this vantage point, he inspected his true-self. There was no intensity and it showed more pulsation than others he had seen. It was a pale yellow, but with shifting regions of red and green flowing across the surface. He was fascinated by this representation of himself, but he was struck by the realization that he saw no connections. There was no connection to The Tree of Life. There was no thread connecting him to anything. No, that wasn't quite correct. Very, very faintly he could see a few threads, but they didn't connect him to The Tree of Life. They went up. Straight up. He tried to follow them, but for some reason, he was unable to. He tried to see any of the faint connections that he had seen when he had examined Elias, but they were absent. Suddenly, he didn't want to see any more. He opened his eyes.

Elias was looking at him expectantly, "Well?"

Colin shook his head. "I don't belong here. I'm not connected to anyone."

"Not just anyone. You're not connected to any <u>thing</u> either. This I could sense even when I couldn't see. You're not connected to The Tree of Life. Whatever you're connected to, it's too far away to sustain life. You're dying." Elias said flatly.

For some reason, Colin was unsurprised. He simply nodded, "How much time do I have?"

Elias shrugged, "How long have you been here? A few weeks? It can't have been much more than that without a connection to The Tree of Life. You have time – a little at least. Who can say if it's enough or not? But I wanted you to see what <u>is</u>, not what you hope or think. You must deal with reality. Colin, I am sorry. I knew you had no connections here. Even if I can't see <u>you</u> I should be able to see a connection to someone or something, but you are not part of this earth. It is important for you to understand this. How I'd love to talk to you about where your connections <u>do</u> lie, but it isn't my place to know. I wish I could help you, but there's no time, and even if there were, I don't know what to do. I felt you should know. Will you still help?"

Colin smiled, a little sadly, "Of course. I guess I shouldn't be surprised. Even on my own world I think I'd lost my connections. In some ways, maybe this is better. I may not be connected here, but there are a number of people here that I care about – very much. So now I have very little to lose and everything to gain – for them. I don't know what to do, but I'll do what I can. Now, take me to the Serpent's Tunnel."

Chapter 26   Repercussions

The Valley of Aidon was quiet now. There had been pandemonium following the shattering of The Tree of Life. The great Tree still stood, but even from a distance, the damage was obvious. On the side nearest the cliff, fully a third of the branches had been shorn from the huge trunk. Fathers and mothers had been frantic to find their children. Even those too young to fully understand what had taken place sensed the terror of their parents and added their cries to the mayhem as they fled the Valley in panic. Terrified at the news of the approaching army of Kernsidon, many were too afraid to return to their homes in the outlying cities and sought refuge in Salem. The news spread rapidly. A Lawgiver had come. He had denounced the false mantle-bearer who had attempted to destroy The Tree of Life. He had denounced the Council as well. From Salem, word of the disaster spread like wildfire. Every city, every village heard - The Lawgiver had come - and in that coming, many heard the death knell of Aidon.

Not all who were in the Valley fled. Some stayed to welcome The Lawgiver so long foretold. Many of the Arbor Guards stayed - ordered to remain as long as there were any others in the Valley. Their job had always been to protect The Tree of Life. This day they had failed and they felt that failure keenly. Somehow, the impostor had managed to access the Valley. Worse, he had touched the Tree - climbed it even! Many had seen him. There was no question it was he, for he had been seen often enough in the Praetorium these recent weeks. Worst of all, he had destroyed the Tree. Well, if not destroyed, he had certainly been the cause of severe damage. None could explain how he had toppled the great statue of the Cherubim, but The Lawgiver himself had pointed it out - had identified the culprit clinging to the tree just before he had fallen to his death. The Serpent take his soul! Their anger was intensified by grief. Not grief for the damage done to the Tree alone, though that was severe enough. But one of their own had fallen in his attempt to stop the false mantle-bearer. He wasn't dead. They knew that, for they had climbed the stairs inside The Temple of the Tree of Life. They had seen him, trapped by the coating of sap which bound him inexorably to the shattered branches. He could no longer speak. The sap which so completely bonded him to the Tree had sealed his mouth. They could see his pleading eyes and had they not known the futility of the attempt, they might have tried to end his life.

Their grief, however, was as nothing compared to that of The Lady Dalene and her mother. The guards tried to stop them, but they would not be denied. They climbed the steps and looked out at their entrapped son and brother. No longer was there access to the Tree through that window. The few branches which had not been shattered were so coated with sap that to touch them would have meant the same eternal living-death for any would-be rescuer. Silent tears trickled down the cheeks of the grieving mother, while the quiet sobbing of The Lady Dalene fanned the hatred the Arbor Guards felt for the impostor, but there was nothing on which they could vent their rage.

The loss of their commander had, for a time, thrown the Arbor Guards into turmoil. However, the command structure held. Praxis Landaur assumed command and led most of the forces to meet the threat they soon expected on their western border. Whether the Council decided to acknowledge The Lawgiver or not had yet to be determined. But if the decision was to fight, they would be in position to offer battle to Kernsidon. They redoubled their preparations after Dathan arrived in the night, half dead from exhaustion. Arrow had fared worse and Dathan was afraid she might not survive the effects of her desperate race to bring word of the impending invasion. While Mahon had told them of this, they had hoped it wasn't true. But the message from one of their own caused that hope to vanish. Even now, the outlying towns might be facing the wrath of the enemy.

The Council was embroiled in their own bitter debate, as they had been throughout the night. They met in a small alcove off the great hall of the Temple, the door secured by two of the City Guards of Salem. No spectators were permitted to remain in the chamber while the Council met. The faction supporting capitulation to The Lawgiver was led by Councilor Krainik, strongly backed by Councilor Yearsley. Slayton Lev and Dalba Saleen of the 5th and 6th Files had united with them. Councilor Saleen was most adamant. He considered himself to be an accomplished student of the law and repeatedly proclaimed, "The prophecies in this matter are clear! He who sits upon The Lawgiver's Throne is The Lawgiver! If he were not, then he couldn't gain the throne! The commandment is equally clear. 'Him shall you hear and obey in all things!' We must give him our obedience if we are to have any hope of survival!"

The Regent reluctantly agreed. That was how the prophecy and the law read. If he had been challenged on the subject the previous week - even the previous day, he would have agreed with Councilor Saleen. But today………he couldn't do it. It just didn't feel right. Up until now, everyone had thought that The Lawgiver referred specifically to Messias. He didn't know who this Mahon was, or how he had accessed the Throne, but he certainly wasn't Messias. The rest of the Council seemed to be waiting to follow his lead, but he didn't know what to do. They had been at this now for almost 24 hours. He was exhausted, unsure. He just wanted to rest. But there was no time for rest. He wasn't sure that they had time for anything. In the hours before darkness had fallen after the attack on the Tree, it became readily apparent that The Valley of Aidon had changed. Petals continued to fall from The Tree of Life, but for the first time in mortal memory, the petals reached the ground where they carpeted the earth in a wilting mass. The trees throughout the valley had dropped all their fruit and none had begun to grow and replace that which had fallen. When anyone pulled the edible tubers, the soil remained disturbed, a stark blemish on the valley floor and no new plant sprung forth from the earth. The valley, or its magic, appeared to be dying.

Councilor Krainik was frightened and the more frightened he became, the more furious he got. He had spent months preparing for this day! He had thought it would be easier to sway the Council, especially once the 13th File had taken The Throne of The Lawgiver. Curse the obstinacy of the Regent! If he would just give in, the others would all follow suit. But if he delayed much longer, Krainik feared what Mahon might do - to him. His role in all this was to sway the Council, but they wouldn't budge without the Regent. This was taking too long. If only he could get Gareth Tregard out of the way!

And then, Krainik had an idea. It well could solve all of his problems. "Councilor Tregard, I believe we could all use a recess. I move that we break for an hour. We need to eat, rest and take some time to decide what would be best for Aidon. Perhaps when we reconvene, we can approach this a little bit differently."

Without waiting for a consensus, several members of the Council immediately stood. The tension was getting to all of them. Krainik grabbed Councilor Yearsley by the arm and in a quiet voice said, "Find me one of the City Guards - now! Keep it quiet, I don't want you yelling for them. Bring him to me - outside."

Councilor Yearsley was surprised at Krainik's intensity. She knew he was onto something - something important. She set off immediately. There was no shortage of guards about. Most of the Arbor Guards had been sent to meet the threat gathering at the border, but there were still quite a number stationed near the tree. A large contingent of the City Guards were always present during the Solstice Observance. As the threat to Salem was still somewhat remote, they had not yet been dispersed and were congregating near the Temple, awaiting instructions. Lucinda soon found one of the guards and was pleased to see it was someone she recognized - Veret Lev, the son of the 5th File Councilor, Slayton Lev, in company with three other guards whom she ignored. In a moment she managed to insinuate herself into the group, successfully isolating the object of her attention.

"Guardsman Lev! I'm so glad you're here. The Council has an urgent matter requiring your attention. Will you please come?" It was phrased as a request but her tone implied a command.

Veret Lev was young and relatively ambitious. He knew that times of crisis provided opportunity for distinction. Like many of the guards, the unprecedented events of the past 24 hours appalled him while at the same time drawing him like a moth to the flame. His comrades were of a similar mind. Once the initial mad panic subsided, with no further developments, they had been forced to settle into the boredom of waiting. Guardsman Lev was more familiar than most with political maneuvering, having watched much of it first-hand due to his father's position on the Council. Lucinda's mention of the Council instantly gained his attention and he willingly followed her. His bored companions trailed along.

Councilor Krainik was waiting for them off to the side of the main entrance to the Temple. He recognized Veret Lev at once. Behind the pleasant expression he affected, he was calculating how to gain the young guard's cooperation. "Ah, guardsman Lev! I'm so relieved that Councilor Yearsley found you! In times such as these, it's difficult to know whom to trust, but with your father being on the Council....... Well, there's no question we can rely on you! The Council will be pleased."

Young Lev bowed to Councilor Krainik. He was pleased as well. The Council had confidence in him! And why shouldn't they? He prided himself in being a good soldier and carrying out his assignments precisely and superbly. "How may I serve you - and the Council, Councilor Krainik?" he asked.

"Please. Call me Lijah. The situation is far too grave to deal so much with formalities. You know, I'm sure, of the grave danger we face?"

"Of course.........Lijah. I am ready to do whatever is necessary to defend Aidon!" Veret replied.

"Good. These are troubling times, are they not? But times of greatness, also! To think, my friend, that such as we should live to see The Lawgiver! To have a King unite Aidon and Kernsidon - in peace! The Council is ready to acknowledge our rightful ruler! Wonderful, is it not?" Lijah asked.

Now Veret was suddenly unsure of himself. Had the Council already decided? Had they acknowledged Mahon as their King? Hesitantly, he asked, "Then, there is to be no war? The Council will accept Mahon's terms?"

"War? Against The Lawgiver? Oh, no! That must not be. Messias has sent him to bring peace. You are a soldier, but I know you understand that warfare is not your objective, but to ensure peace. The Council recognizes this as well. We are working very hard to make sure that we do not have war. Of course, there are those who hold power and would do anything to retain it - even if it meant plunging Aidon into war and causing the deaths of tens of thousands of our citizens. They would do anything to retain their grasp on power! They are dangerous! Unstable! That is why we, why the Council needs your help - guards who can be trusted. Commander Lev, this is vitally important!"

"Um, yes sir," he responded, "But sir, Lijah, I'm not the commander. I'm just a guard. But if you need the commander, I'll find him for you!"

Lijah shook his head, sadly, "Ah, Veret, but that is the problem. The present commander is one of those who has power, is he not? Can he be trusted? The Council, I assure you, has absolute confidence in you. Others, we cannot be so sure of. It may well be that when we have joined with Kernsidon under King Mahon, opportunities for those who have helped bring about……..peace, may become available. Do you understand?"

Veret's head was spinning. The Council didn't trust his commander? What had he done? What did they know that he did not? With grim determination he squared his shoulders. "Yes sir! You can trust me! And my men," he said, indicating the three who had followed him. In reality, they were not exactly 'his men,' but the implied promise of command was already having an effect on Veret. "I'll vouch for them as well. They're all trustworthy. What are your orders?"

Lijah allowed his shoulders to slump, an expression of relief on his face. "Thank you, my friend. I knew I could count on you. The Council is engaged in a very delicate stage of negotiation right now. It is imperative that the wife of the Regent be brought quietly to aide in the deliberations. The Council would be most grateful if you would find Beatrice Tregard and bring her to our chambers. Immediately."

Veret snapped a salute to the two Councilors and then marched smartly away to issue orders to his companions.

Lucinda made sure the guards were out of earshot and then commented, "My, but the Council has certainly been busy with a number of things that I missed out on. What are you planning to do with the Regent's wife?" she asked.

Lijah smiled. "I plan to remove an obstacle."

******

The Council reconvened. It was immediately evident that neither side had altered their position. Krainik didn't even bother to listen to the repeated arguments. He was listening for something else.

******

It was easy. Guardsman Veret Lev had but to ask around and he was soon directed to the carts and tent of the Regent's family only a short distance from the Temple. Beatrice Tregard was there, along with Marcus and Alicia Verlach. The Lady Dalene was nowhere to be seen. That suited Veret just fine. He would never admit it, but she made him nervous. The Lady of Prophecy had been a source of terror in too many of his childhood dreams - dreams of the destruction of Aidon, heralded by The Lady of Prophecy. In his dreams, he had been a guard. Sometimes he was killed. At other times, he had managed to kill The Lady and had saved Aidon. As he approached the Regent's camp he felt as though he might be living that very dream.

******

Beatrice Tregard looked wan and haggard. She had spent much of the night high in the temple, watching her son being slowly incorporated into The Tree of Life. He was imprisoned in a cell that would never permit him to die, but he would never again truly live either. Her mother's heart felt that she could not bear this. When the guards came, telling her they were to escort her to the Council's deliberations, woodenly she arose and went with them. Marcus and Alicia would have accompanied her, but they were told to remain. They were accustomed to not being included in many of the dealings of the Regent and his family, so they stayed. On a day of so many unusual happenings, nothing seemed out of the ordinary to them.

******

The moment he heard the door, Councilor Krainik hurriedly arose and met the guards. He gave orders for two of them to secure the heavy door and remain there, while the other two escorted the Regent's wife. The moment he saw her, Councilor Tregard rose, puzzlement etched on his face. "Beatrice, are you alright? What are you doing here?"

Before she could answer, Councilor Krainik spoke, "It is evident that we shall need more time to conduct our deliberations. Rather than waste that time in delay, I felt we should address one of the other important matters before the Council. After all, we face this dire situation only because of the actions of Beatrice Tregard, who has failed to maintain custody of the false mantle-bearer!" His accusation rang out in the still chamber.

The Regent was furious, "That's enough!! That is a matter for another time! You will not speak of my wife in this manner!"

"Another time?" Krainik asked smoothly, "There may not be another time! You continue to refuse our chance for peace! While you wait, our people are undoubtedly being slaughtered in Tyber and Jordanon! What we must ask is how did the impostor get here, into the Valley, in the first place? In your carts? Did you bring him here to destroy The Tree of Life? To destroy Aidon? And while you stall, you destroy our one chance for peace!"

"You lie!" Gareth bellowed. "My family had nothing to do with Colin being here! We left him at the Praetorium!"

Before Krainik could reply, Beatrice spoke in a quiet but clear voice. "I told him to come here."

There was dead silence, except for a single agonized cry from the Regent, "No! You don't know what you're saying!"

Beatrice looked at her husband as he slumped into his seat, "I'm sorry, Gareth. I believe he _is_ a messenger from Messias. He needed to come here." Addressing the rest of the Council in the same calm voice, she continued, "My husband did not bring him here. Nor did I. I don't know how he came, but it was not with us. But I did tell him that he should come. I believed then and I believe now that he is a messenger."

Several voices were raised in angry objection:

"He can't be!"

"He, himself denied he was a messenger!"

"He attacked the Tree!"

"He destroyed the Tree!"

"He is responsible for the death of your son!"

Beatrice waited calmly for the objections to cease and then responded, "I know that Colin said he was not a messenger, but not all messages are spoken. His very existence is a message if you have sense enough to understand it. I don't believe he attacked the Tree of Life." She raised her hand to silence their objections, "I know he climbed The Tree of Life. By the account of the witnesses, he had gone to retrieve my son's arrow. He was wrong to do that but it was not an act of attack. The damage done to the Tree was caused by the statue of the Cherubim falling. It fell from above, effectively killing my son and Colin as well. It is impossible to determine that Colin caused it to fall."

Councilor Saleen replied angrily, "The Lawgiver himself identified him! He showed us the impostor in the very act of attacking the Tree and denounced him as false! You cannot deny it!"

She shook her head, "I do not deny that is what the one who desires The Throne of The Lawgiver said. I simply tell you that I do not believe he spoke the truth."

The room again erupted in an uproar. Councilor Krainik finally silenced them, raising his voice to a tremendous roar, "Enough! You may wish to debate these matters, but that is not our purpose! Do you deny that you failed to keep custody of one who had been found guilty and was sentenced to be destroyed?"

She looked at him calmly and directly, "I do not deny it."

"Do you admit to encouraging him to violate the terms of his custody by entering The Valley of Aidon?"

"I admit it. He was wrongly found guilty. As a citizen of Aidon and a member of the 12th File, he had the right to be here," she replied.

"You are not on the Council. That verdict was not yours to give," Krainik sneered. "And do you persist in your belief that this impostor is a messenger of Messias."

"I do."

Councilor Krainik whirled to address the rest of the Council. "You have heard her testimony. She has admitted her guilt. The law is clear. By show of hands, shall the penalty be carried out? How say you?"

Eleven hands, some reluctant, others with great vigor, rose skyward. The Regent sat, head hanging down on his chest, arms limp at his sides.

Councilor Krainik gave a satisfied smile, "Very well. Beatrice Tregard, it is our determination that you are guilty. The law is clear in regards to the punishment as well. You were negligent in maintaining custody of the false mantle-bearer. You admit that you encouraged him to disobey the law while in your custody. You encouraged him to enter The Valley of Aidon during the Solstice Observance. But your greatest crime is that you maintain that one who has been determined to wear the mantle of authority falsely is held by you to be a messenger of Messias. The law demands that you be subjected to the same punishment as was decreed for the one for whom you assumed custody. You are to be destroyed by this Council, united in the Ruling Box of Aidon. You will no longer be a thinking, sentient being. By your actions, you have shown that you are not to be entrusted with the freedom to act. Henceforth, your mind will no longer be your own. You will obey every command given you by others until the end of your life. I decree that this punishment shall be carried out immediately."

"No!" Gareth cried out desperately, "On behalf of the accused, I claim the right to appeal! I'll assume responsibility for her!"

"You know there is no right to appeal for one who has violated the trust of custody!" Councilor Saleen retorted. He had never liked the Tregards. It gave him great satisfacton to crush the Regent like this. "The sentence must be carried out immediately!"

"Not true!" shouted Councilor Garmon. It pained him to convict the wife of the Regent, but her guilt was obvious. To have voted not to convict her would have been to make a mockery of all they stood for. "While the guilt of the accused is obvious, the law does *not* require immediate punishment."

"Councilor Garmon is correct," a quiet voice stated. Councilor Kori Stanger of the 2nd File rarely spoke. In truth, she was quite uncomfortable with her position on the Council. To make up for her sense of inadequacy, she had devoted much of her life to studying the law. She didn't make a pretense of it the way Councilor Saleen did, but she probably knew more about their law than any on the Council and perhaps in all of Aidon. "The precedent was established by the Council under Andrew Solmais. Any individual convicted of a crime with destruction specified as the punishment is entitled to a stay for a period of one day, so long as they are in custody and of no threat to any other person. This was decreed as a show of mercy so as to allow them to settle their affairs and to permit loved ones to say their farewells. No Council since that time has seen fit to overrule that decree."

"The delay is unimportant," Councilor Krainik sneered. He had achieved what he wished. "We will accede to our esteemed Councilor

Stanger's knowledge of the law. The punishment will be carried out tomorrow at the 6th hour. But at that time, the punishment will be executed!"

Gareth glared at the other members of the Council. He knew that they were correct. According to the law, he had no options left. His wife would be destroyed in the Ruling Box of Aidon. The law required that he participate. His entire life he had subjected himself to that law. He had obeyed every rule with meticulous care – not from fear. Not from pride. If one were to attempt to draw comparisons, one would have to conclude that Gareth was one of the finest Pharisees of Aidon. Like the Biblical Saul of Tarsus, Gareth simply believed. He didn't necessarily understand, but his life had been built around a belief in the law and he had done his very best to obey it. Gareth was fighting a fierce internal battle. He was obedient. He had always been obedient and he had demanded obedience from others as well. His gaze softened. His internal conflict resolved. He spoke calmly, "So be it, but I will not be party to it."

Beatrice looked at him with concern, "Gareth, it's alright. This won't change anything. I love you and I know you love me. It's alright for you to do this."

He shook his head, "No. This is wrong and I will not do it. I do love you, but this is more than that. I know what the law demands, but I cannot obey. I will not obey. Not this time."

Scarcely able to keep the smile from his lips, Krainik feigned surprise, though this was working out precisely as he had hoped. "Councilor Tregard, you do know that if you refuse to perform your duty in this matter, you will be removed from office – both as Regent and as Councilor for the 12th File?" He turned to look at Councilor Stanger, naked hostility in his gaze, "That is correct, is it not Kori?"

Reluctantly she nodded.

Gareth smiled at his wife then turned to Councilor Krainik, "I am well aware of that. You will do as you choose, as will I and we will each be held to account." For some reason, he was perfectly calm.

Krainik now smiled broadly, "And so I shall, Gareth." He then turned to Veret Lev, standing stunned at what he had involved himself in. "Guardsman Lev, you will order two of your men to secure Beatrice Tregard in quarters here in the Temple. Find a room, but she is to be guarded at all times. No one but family members are to be given access. You will dispatch a messenger immediately to Salem. Find Councilor Nalin of the 12th File. Inform him that he is to arrange to have either himself or another representative of the 12th File here at the Temple by tomorrow at the 6th hour to participate in the destruction of Beatrice Tregard. You may inform him that Gareth Tregard has refused to fulfill his obligation. If his refusal continues he will be removed as Regent and Councilor Nalin will then make arrangements to hold an Evaluation to determine the new High Councilor for the 12th File once the present crisis is past. If Councilor Tregard fails to do his duty, in accordance with the law, I shall fulfill my responsibility by acting as Regent until the new 12th File High Councilor is selected."

The other members of the Council nodded. Krainik was immensely pleased. Everything had worked out perfectly. By this time tomorrow, he would be acting Regent. Opposition to acknowledging Mahon as King would be entirely eliminated and he would personally handle the capitulation of Aidon and take his place at the head of the 12th File. Mahon would reward him by making him Regent permanently. He would rule under King Mahon. Let the 12th File choke on that!

Chapter 27   Retribution

Beatrice had been gone for over an hour by the time The Lady Dalene returned. "Where is mother?" she asked Marcus and Alicia.

"Your father sent for her. He wanted her at the Council meeting," Marcus replied.

For some reason, this made Dalene uneasy. Why would her father want her mother at a Council meeting? Especially at a time like this? She busied herself with minor chores, packing her things and helping to straighten the camp in case they needed to depart quickly. She had gone to see Halvor, but as far as she could tell, he was unaware of her presence. He was encased in a hard, opaque layer of translucent sap now, like some huge insect trapped in amber. She couldn't stand to see him like that and had quickly left. Restless, she had taken a long walk. The petals from The Tree of Life lay thick and still under the tree, surrounding the pool at its base. The meadow and trees, so beautiful and full of life only a couple of days before looked tattered and wilted. Colin was gone – dead. How she hated him! He had done this! Why had he come? What had possessed him to attempt to climb The Tree of Life? Still, she couldn't quite manage to convince herself that he was solely responsible. True, he had been climbing the Tree. Halvor had raced to stop him. There were too many witnesses to refute. But destroy the Tree? The Tree _had_ been nearly destroyed. Perhaps it was destroyed. It seemed to be dying. But had Colin done that? The damage had been done by the falling statue of the cherubim. It had very nearly killed both Halvor and Colin. She had arrived in time to see that for herself. How could Colin have possibly made that statue fall? It seemed more likely that Mahon could have done that. He had claimed the Throne of The Lawgiver and had been closest to the statue. She felt physically ill. How could Colin have betrayed their trust, _her_ trust, like this? What would happen to her mother?

As Dalene thought of her mother, a sudden pang of terror lanced her heart. The Council! Her mother had been summoned to the Council! She rushed out of her tent and called out, "Marcus, Alicia! Who came to get mother? Was it father?"

"No," Marcus replied. It was a group of the City Guards – from Salem. Actually it was Veret Lev. At least he was the one who seemed to be in charge. We would have gone with them, but he said that only your mother was permitted." Dalene stared at him, feeling the blood drain from her face. She began to run.

Arriving at the Temple, she raced up the broad stairway to the entrance. The two Arbor Guards standing there started, as if they would attempt to stop her, but they hesitated when they recognized her, knowing she was the sister of their companion trapped by the Tree they were sworn to protect. Dalene suddenly slid to a stop and whirled on the guards, "My mother! Did you see her? Is she here?"

They both nodded and one of the guards replied, "Yes, Lady Dalene. She came through here about two hours ago. Four of the City Guards were with her. They went there," he said, pointing, "in that room just past The Ruling Box of Aidon. That's where the Council is meeting."

The Lady Dalene thanked him, then composed herself and walked quickly to the room the guard had indicated. The entry was barred by two of the City Guards. She addressed them, "I need to speak with my father, the Regent." They looked uncomfortable, but one of them replied, "I'm sorry, Lady Dalene, but Councilor Krainik gave orders that no one is to enter. Wouldn't do you any good anyway. Your father isn't in there," he added helpfully.

Momentarily distracted, she said, "Councilor Krainik? Since when do the City Guards of the 12th File take orders from the 11th File Councilor?"

"Ahh, well, Lady Dalene, Councilor Krainik is sort of acting as Regent for the time being."

Councilor Krainik acting as Regent? What was going on? Dalene felt the panic beginning to rise. "Do you know where I can find my father, then?" she asked.

The guards looked even more uncomfortable than before, but the talkative one replied, "Maybe. Last I saw they were taking him and your mother up that way, towards the upper levels. I think they might have gone to the second level."

Dalene nodded her thanks and headed toward the second level. The doors were bracketed by two of the Arbor Guards, "Did the Regent and my mother pass through here recently," she asked.

"Aye, Lady Dalene. Perhaps an hour ago," one of them replied.

She seemed to remember his name, "It's Arbor Guard Lowell, isn't it?" she asked.

He nodded, pleased to have been recognized, though he couldn't have said why. This woman had always intimidated him, frightened him even.

"Do you know where they went?"

"I do. Go through and up the stairs to the second landing. The third corridor on that level, you go down about half way. You'll see the City Guards there. Can't miss 'em." He almost snarled this last.

"City Guards? In the second level?" she asked. "Lowell, what's going on?"

For a moment he looked as if he would refuse to answer, but the words suddenly came in an angry rush, "I'm supposed to know? Councilor Krainik is giving orders letting the City Guards in here. They march your mother and the Regent in like they were prisoners! That madman mantle-bearer, he all but destroys the Tree and your brother winds up good as dead when he tried to stop him! Kernsidon is on the attack and their King says he's to be our Lawgiver! I don't know what's going on!"

"I'm sorry, Lowell. I don't understand it either. But right now, I need to find my mother."

Dalene followed the guard's directions. The corridor was a long one. It was dark, but a single torch burned, clearly showing the door secured by the two city guards. She drew a deep breath as she approached and asked, "Is my mother being held here?"

Both guards looked distinctly embarrassed. Without a word, one of them opened the door. Dalene entered. "Mother! Are you alright? Father, what's going on?"

The room was comfortably appointed. Two lamps provided adequate lighting. Beatrice was curled up, her husband's arms wrapped protectively around her. Beatrice looked up at the sound of her daughter's voice. Her eyes were moist, but she was smiling. "Dalene! Oh, my dear, I'm so sorry. We tried to send word, but none of the guards would carry a message. I had hoped to ask you not to come."

"Why? Mother, what's wrong? What's going on?"

Gareth looked exhausted. He patted the couch beside him and said, "Come. Sit by us, Dalene."

Mutely, she did so.

"I'm afraid things are very bad," he said. "If you've managed to come here, you've probably already heard that Krainik is acting as Regent. I've quit. Tomorrow it will be official and he will be named acting Regent – until a new High Councilor for the 12th File can be found. But I'm done. I just couldn't do it."

Fear was continuing to build, "Do what?" Dalene asked.

"Destroy me," was her mother's reply.

"Destroy you! No! Mother, they can't! Father, you can stop them! You have to do something! You must!" She was almost hysterical. Her father wrapped a comforting arm around her, while her mother reached over to pat her hand tenderly.

"It's alright, Dalene. I've made my choice. This isn't your father's fault."

"But they can't! Mother, they can't. It wasn't your fault! It was Colin! He did it! He's dead! Can't they be satisfied with that?"

"Dalene!" her mother spoke sharply, "It wasn't Colin! This was my choice. I asked him to come here. I wanted him to see The Tree of Life. Don't ask me why, I just felt it was important. It didn't work out like I thought it would. I don't know what I expected, but not this. Not your brother….." her voice faltered, but then she continued. "Dear, it's alright. I don't understand it, but I can't say that I'm sorry for what I've done. That's why the Council is going to destroy me. Perhaps they're right. But I believe that Colin was a messenger, even if he didn't know what message he was supposed to bring. And I don't believe he destroyed or even attacked the Tree and that's why they are going to destroy me."

Gareth snorted, "That's not why! They're destroying you because they wanted to get rid of me! Sure, they're mad enough at you, but Krainik wants the Council to accept Mahon as King – as Lawgiver! I wouldn't do it. By getting rid of me, he becomes acting Regent. Tomorrow, he'll surrender Aidon to Mahon."

Beatrice stared at him aghast, "But Gareth, if that's true, you have to stop him! You <u>must</u> participate with the Council tomorrow! I know you don't want to, but if you don't, Aidon will be lost and it will change nothing for me! Please! You have to do this!"

"NO!" He roared. "All my life I have done whatever the law required of me! But this time, the law is wrong! If the survival of Aidon demands that you be sacrificed, then Aidon isn't worth saving! If the law will not protect the individual then it cannot protect the society! Today I <u>choose</u>. This is wrong and I will not do it!"

The three of them sat huddled together for some time, taking comfort in each other's presence. Finally, Dalene spoke, "Mother, can I get you anything? Is there anything you need?"

Her mother smiled her thanks, but indicated a tray with food, "No dear, they've been very kind. I don't need anything, really. I'd just like to sit with the two of you, while I can remember………." Her voice trailed off. "I would liked to have held Halvor once more. I don't want you to grieve for me. I have been truly blessed throughout my life. While I would wish for more time with each of you, I have no regrets. My life has been full. I guess if I were to do one last thing – other than just sit here with you, I would like to have eaten fruit from the Valley once more. I'm glad it's going to happen here – in the Valley. In some ways, I'm glad that I won't be here when Krainik surrenders Aidon to Mahon. This is an evil thing he is doing. How can Messias let this happen?" She paused a moment, then continued. "In some ways, I think I am more fortunate than you. You must face whatever happens with courage. I don't want you being angry. Please don't be angry at me. I don't think I could bear that. And you mustn't be angry with Colin either. I know he didn't intend for this to happen. I wish he were alive so that I could tell him that I forgive him, that it wasn't his fault. I just want you both to remember that I love you. I will always love you. This is so very hard – for all of us, but I keep trying to believe that in the end, Messias will make it alright. I don't understand how. If I were dying, it would be easier. But if they destroy my true-self………….I don't know if even Messias can restore me to you after this life. I hope so. I want you both to live for that day. Promise me that you will. Promise?"

They both nodded, too emotional to speak. Dalene finally arose. "I have to go out for a little while, but I'll be back. I have some matters to attend to. Marcus and Alicia must be told. They must be worried by now. I love you." She kissed her mother on the forehead and left. She felt as if her heart must surely break. Colin. Then Halvor. Her father stripped of the Regency. And finally, her mother. If not for her anger, she would have collapsed in tears.

The Lady Dalene was in full fury, but also fully in control of herself. The title she had always hated, she now recited to herself over and over to feed her anger and give her strength. "I am The Lady of Prophecy. While I live, Aidon will not fall!" She marched directly to the chamber where the Council was meeting. The same two city guards were stationed at the door. They expected her to stop and talk, perhaps request permission to enter the chamber. Instead, she did what neither anticipated. She never so much as broke stride as she stormed straight past them, throwing the doors so wide they struck the guards, sending them staggering off balance. Before they could react, she stood before the Council and in a loud voice demanded, "On whose authority has the sanctity of the Temple been violated?"

The guards rushed in behind her, but hesitated to seize her despite their orders that no one be permitted to disturb the Council. Councilor Krainik and several of the Councilors glared at her. Lucinda Yearsley jumped to her feet and shouted, "You have no right to be here! Guards! Throw her out and if she attempts to enter again, lock her up with her mother!"

At the mention of her mother, an icy calm settled over The Lady Dalene. She spoke in a low and threatening voice, "You stand now in defiance of the law - the same law that you have used to strip my father of his office. I am The Lady of Prophecy! I am authorized by <u>law</u> to be present at <u>every</u> meeting of this Council. Each one of you," and she let her gaze rest on each of them, "is here by the grace of your respective Files and Messias. If you ever again attempt to restrict me from this meeting, I will call for a new Evaluation in each of your Files, and then we'll see who has the right to be here!"

Councilor Yearsley blanched. Several of the other Councilors looked ill. They knew the respect accorded their offices paled in comparison to the fear the people felt of The Lady of Prophecy. While each of them liked to believe it was their incomparable will within their respective Files that had won them their office, they each knew that in reality, there were perhaps dozens who could unseat them. Those others simply lacked interest in the office of the High Council. But the wrath of The Lady Dalene could undoubtedly inspire others, perhaps many others, to seek office should she call for a new Evaluation to determine who would fill their seats.

Satisfied with their silence, The Lady Dalene continued in the same dangerous tone, "I asked, who authorized the desecration of the Temple?"

Councilor Saleen began to bluster, "You don't know what you're talking about! Who has desecrated the Temple? Ridiculous. You know nothing of the law! Who are you to question *us*?"

She fixed him with an icy glare, "For your incompetence and apparent lack of knowledge regarding the law - especially as it pertains to The Temple of The Tree of Life, Councilor Saleen, the 6th File shall be the first to hold an Evaluation to verify how unsuited you are for the seat you presently hold. Now, who authorized the City Guard of Salem to enter the second level?"

Councilor Krainik tried to smooth things over, "Lady Dalene, I know you are distraught. You have no idea how it pained us to take the actions we were required to this morning. Your poor mother…… And of course, your father's reaction was quite understandable, but as you have already noted, the law does have specific requirements and we must be obedient. However, you must admit that we are faced with extraordinary circumstances and we felt it would be best to…….supplement the Arbor Guards by allowing the City Guards to assist them."

The Lady Dalene inspected him as though he were a previously undetected insect in their midst, "So you, Councilor Krainik, took it upon yourself to overrule the laws of Aidon? You authorized the City Guard to enter the second level?"

His face flushed scarlet as he tried to hold his anger in check. How dare she! Well, tomorrow *he* would be Regent and this vile woman would feel his wrath. "It was the decision of this Council! As I explained, we felt it best to increase the guard strength after your mother failed to maintain proper custody of the false mantle-bearer!"

"What my mother did or did not do is no excuse for your violation of the law, Councilor Krainik. If you wish to use the City Guard, do so - but use them on the first level only. You will remove them from the second level at once. This Council will instruct the guards - all of them - to see to it that the law is respected. No one except Arbor Guards, this Council and their families are permitted to enter the second level. I want the doors to the third level secured as well. I would like to know how this pretender to The Lawgiver's throne gained entrance."

"He *is* The Lawgiver!" Krainik raged. "Now it is *you* who oversteps! You would do well to remember that this Council will determine to give obedience to King Mahon!"

She was not intimidated. "*If* the Council makes that determination, then I will consider it. Now, don't you have some orders that you'd like to issue, or shall I begin issuing some of my own?"

Krainik was furious at having to back down, but he knew he had no choice. If he refused, he could be removed as readily as had the Regent. He couldn't afford that. Not now. He forced himself to smile, "Of course, Lady

Dalene. It was a mere misunderstanding caused by our anxiety to protect the Tree. I will give the orders at once."

She took a moment to let her gaze rest on each member of the Council. Without another word, she turned and left, not even glancing at the wide-eyed guards who stared after her.

Leaving the Temple, Dalene made her way back to the camp. Marcus and Alicia were there. She wasted no words in explaining the events which had occurred that morning. They were both in shock. "Isn't there anything we can do?" Alicia asked tearfully.

Dalene shook her head. "I've not been able to think of anything. But I need your help. I want to go back and spend as much time with mother as I can. I don't trust Krainik. I need the two of you to stay in the Temple. Keep an eye on things as much as you can. I know you can't go into the second level, but if anything happens it is probably going to start there at the first level anyway. If you do see anything suspicious, you'll have to get word to me. I think we can trust Councilor Garmon as well as Councilor Tomias and Councilor Stanger. Find out if they have family here and if so, where they are at. If you need me, get one of them to come find me. Stay away from Krainik and Yearsley. I don't trust Councilor Saleen either, and I'm not sure about Lev."

Marcus snorted, "Lev! It was his son that came and got your mother! And I sat here like an idiot and let her go!"

"It wasn't your fault and there's nothing you could have done anyway," Dalene told him. "Now, I'm going to go back. Mother wanted some fruit from the Valley. I'll see if I can find any that hasn't fallen or spoiled. I can't believe this. I never thought I would see the Valley like this. I think the whole world is ending."

"We gathered some just a little while ago," Alicia offered. "You're right. It isn't as nice as what it should be, but it's the best we could find today. Please. Take it to your mother. Tell her we love her. Tell her we're praying for her."

Dalene smiled wanly, "I will. Thank you. Thank you for being kind to mother and for………..for being my friends. I'm sorry I haven't been more kind to you."

Marcus shrugged, "You've never been less than kind to us. But you are The Lady of Prophecy. Your load has been heavy. I'm sorry we haven't been able to make it easier for you."

Dalene was surprised, "But you have. You do. I really don't know what I would have done without you. Except for my family, you were the ones whom I was most comfortable with. Until Colin……." She stopped.

Alicia touched her hand, "He didn't mean to. I don't think he was a bad person."

Dalene shook her head, the grief threatening to overwhelm her anger. She couldn't let it. She couldn't afford it. She needed the strength. "Does it matter? Whatever he intended, it has brought us to this."

******

General Boris was not a man who frightened easily. While he wasn't frightened right now, he had to admit he was badly shaken. What were those <u>things</u>? By the Serpent's blood! They'd been hideous. Where had they come from? The previous night he had called his captains together to issue his orders. In the morning they were to head south by south east, angling towards the mountains. He was certain they had passed by Aidon. Something had happened to his scouts. He didn't know what, but he was taking no further chances. They would follow the mountains back south. Eventually they would lead him to Aidon. In a way, this might even work in his favor, since they would be attacking from the north instead of from the south as had always been done in the past. Everything had been fine as they had retired for the night.

He was up at first light. The men were busy preparing their meal before beginning the day's march. He went down to the stream to wash. There didn't seem to be anything amiss. Then the entire hillside had come to life. Well, not the hill really, but the boulders. One moment they had just been lying there and suddenly they were lunging to their feet! Feet! The boulders had feet! Except they weren't boulders. They were the most horrid looking creatures he had ever seen. And they were huge! At least 20 feet tall! His men were so terrified they hadn't even attempted to fight. It had been total chaos. They had run screaming back over the hill the way they had come the night before. He still didn't know how many men he had lost, but he'd seen those creatures swinging their clubs, dashing out the brains of his men or snapping their spines like dry twigs. The spears they'd hurled were as thick as his arm! He'd seen one of those creatures throw a spear and skewer three of his men like they'd been so many fat sausages. The screams of terror, the shrieks of pain from the wounded, accompanied by the ferocious roars of the giants and their barking laugh, "Ha! Ha!" as though the mayhem was some kind of sport! It had been chaos. The recollection made him shudder anew. Many had been killed. He had at least a couple of hundred wounded with him and a good portion of his troops were scattered. They were probably still running from those creatures.

He reassembled as much of his force as he could, but there was no question, his ranks had been depleted. Curse this place! And curse his scouts! Well, no matter, he still had more than enough for the job. Aidon would fall. General Boris knew that was his only hope for saving his own skin. He reiterated his orders to his men: Destroy at will. Nothing was to be spared.

******

The scouts from the Arbor Guards watched the battle, if it could be called that, from a distant hilltop. They were as shocked as General Boris had been, but as long as those creatures were attacking the Kernsidon forces, the Arbor Guards were cheering for them, albeit quietly. As the army fled, the guards hoped that they might be panicked enough to abandon their invasion and return home. However, it soon became evident that they were reassembling and taking their march toward the south. General Boris was setting a brisk pace. If they followed the course they were now setting and maintained their rate of march, by tomorrow morning they would be threatening Troas. Chase and Michael were grim faced. There was nothing more to be done here. They had delayed the enemy as long as they could. Now they needed to join the defenders of Aidon. They mounted their horses and set out at a brisk trot. Troas was going to need all the help it could get.

******

Colin had no means of determining time in the darkness of the Serpent's Tunnel. He simply ran. The tunnel was too low. He had to keep his neck or his knees bent all the time and even then, if he ever got off-center his head would strike the ceiling. Fortunately, it was smooth, otherwise he'd have probably knocked himself unconscious a number of times. He ran as long as he could then walked while he caught his breath. He knew he was pushing too hard. He knew he had to conserve his strength. What he didn't know was what he was going to do once he arrived back in Aidon, but whatever it was, he would be useless if he arrived too exhausted to even stand up. So he forced himself to rest, but with no means of telling the time, he feared to stop too long. Once he fell asleep, jerking awake from a terrifying dream of the Serpent about to devour Dalene. It was like that carving back in the Temple, when the Serpent was about to devour Aeva, but then the heavenly host had come and saved her. This time there would be no heavenly host. Just him, and he didn't know what to do. So he ran.

Several times he had the impression of having passed doorways as he ran through the dark tunnel, darker holes in a world where everything was blackness. The light from his lantern seemed to strike the surface only to be absorbed by the black stone. Once, he pushed himself too hard. He ran too long and finally fell to the floor of the tunnel gasping for breath. He retched and heaved there on the floor - a warning that he had to pull back. He was past the limits of his endurance. When he recovered, he found he had fallen right by a doorway similar to what he had glimpsed as he was running. Physically weak, he staggered to his feet, feeling drawn to the room. There was no door, just a black opening. He only spent a couple of minutes there, but he was astonished when he entered. It was a library. Not like the supposed Great Library of Salem. This one was full of volumes of all kinds.

He read some of the titles and flipped open a few of the books. One had been called, *Prophecies of Zoran and Lemhi on the Coming of Messias.* Another was titled *The Founding of Aidon and the Fall of Kern.* Beside it was *Communicating with the Beasts of Aidon.* One was called simply, *Laws and Commandments.* He flipped it open - somewhere near the front, and there they were, the Ten Commandments. Complete. Unambiguous. He closed his eyes, praying. Somehow, the people of Aidon had to get access to these things. Even if he died, he had to clear the way for Elias. He slipped the volume into his pack and re-entering the tunnel, began to jog once again, into the darkness.

Elias had given him the pack. It held bread and several small flasks of water. He was on his last flask when Elias' final warning seemed to echo in his ears. "You'll have no friends there, you know. Mahon has already tried to kill you. Everyone in the Valley thinks you tried to destroy the Tree of Life. They'll want to kill you as well. If you ever had any friends there, you don't anymore. I can't help you, just know that as soon as you're recognized, they'll want your blood." He remembered the seeds. Frantically, he stripped the quiver from his shoulder and turned it upside down, shaking it. The arrows scattered all over. He shook it again, and a small, tightly wrapped packet fell out. Quickly he unwrapped it. It was damp inside, but hopefully not too damp. He didn't know if it mattered anyway. He stared at the remaining seeds he had received from Hotha. They had helped get him into this mess. Maybe they could help get him out of it. He sprinkled several in his palm and tossed them into his mouth. He didn't want to chew them, but he was afraid they wouldn't work if he didn't, so he chewed. They were just as bitter as they'd been before, but he didn't care. He washed them down with the last of his water, fighting back the urge to vomit. He couldn't afford that. He gathered the spilled arrows as his stomach settled, and then he began to run once more.

Chapter 28   Resistance

Councilor Nalin arrived before dawn. He was a frightened, unhappy man. The last place he wanted to be at the moment, was here, in The Temple of The Tree of Life. But he was also a man accustomed to comfort and the trappings of power. Councilor Krainik had made it clear that the Regent had, for all intents, been removed from office and that if Councilor Nalin refused to support the destruction of the Regent's wife, then he would be as easily removed. It would mean the end of all the privileges he enjoyed and, he rationalized, it would not affect the outcome of events in regards to either Beatrice or Gareth Tregard. He made his decision. He would participate.

At the appointed hour, Beatrice was escorted from the chamber where she was being held. She walked calmly, holding the hands of her husband and daughter, both of whom wore expressions of grim determination. They would be strong for her sake, but it was taking every ounce of the iron control they had developed during their lifetime of public scrutiny. Yet they were no more stone-faced than the Arbor Guards who escorted them. They felt trapped by their duty and for the first time in their lives were beginning to question it. At the doorway descending to the first level of the Temple, they were relieved by a contingent of City Guards. Krainik suspected that the Arbor Guards held reservations about the destruction of Beatrice and the removal of the Regent from office, so he was taking no chances. While the City Guards could still be a problem, they were bound more tightly to the Council than were the Arbor Guards. After all, it had been a Tregard who had founded the Arbor Guards millennia ago and there were deep traditions of loyalty between them and the family.

The City Guards took over escort duty. Veret Lev was in charge, yet unable to completely mask his internal turmoil. He was wondering how he had ever gotten involved with this mess. The hall was cleared except for the guards and the Council. Krainik was giving the populace no chance to interfere, remote though it might be, since most had already left the Valley. The party stopped in front of The Ruling Boxes of Aidon, the pattern incorporated in the solid floor carved from the mountain. Councilor Krainik spoke, "Gareth Tregard, Regent of Aidon, High Councilor of the 12th File, will you perform your duty in executing the punishment of Beatrice Tregard as specified by law and in accordance with the will of this Council, or do you choose to relinquish your position and be stripped of your title?"

Gareth stood defiantly, "What you do this day is an affront to the law and to justice. I refuse to be part of it. I will accept the consequences of my choice, just as surely as you will be held accountable for that which you do here."

Krainik smiled and continued, "So be it. Gareth Tregard, you are hereby stripped of both title and position. Councilor Nalin will assume temporary standing as the High Councilor representing the 12th File until a permanent replacement is named. As the ranking member of the Council, I will assume the office of Regent for the duration of the present crisis. Beatrice Tregard, for your crimes against Aidon, you are to be destroyed by this Council. You will take your place in the box labeled 13. You may do this as your last act of free will or I will have the guards bind you and place you there."

Beatrice looked at him coldly and replied, "That will hardly be necessary, Lijah. You really must learn to reserve your threats until they carry weight." With that she calmly took her place and smiled at Gareth and Dalene. "Remember. I love you."

Gareth's jaw quivered and silent tears trickled down Dalene's cheeks. The members of the Council, accompanied by Councilor Nalin took their positions. There was no sound as they closed their eyes, seeking the light that was the true-self of Beatrice Tregard. She stiffened as her eyes flared and she remained frozen in that posture. She made no attempt to see the dozen lights whirling and circling about her true-self. The combined minds of the twelve Files held her captive in the darkness. They found her core, but there was no gentle persuasion involved here. The lights lanced into her true self, attacking and retreating. Each time they retreated, they took with them some fragment of her, releasing it to drift into the void. Unable to respond in any way, Beatrice first felt as if she were being torn apart and was certain she was going insane, unable to distinguish herself from her surroundings. Dalene started as if she would run to her mother, but the guards blocked her. Gradually, Beatrice became less and less - of anything. The circling scavengers of light continued to dip and snap at her, diminishing her. At length, the brilliant, glowing intellect which had been Beatrice Tregrad, was reduced to a dull, indistinct orb. This was her life-force, which they would not touch. While there was some tiny spark of "self" remaining, Beatrice no longer had any particular awareness of who she was. She would act, when commanded, but no longer had even the most basic instinct of self-preservation. Though her self remained, she was neither truly aware of it nor placed any value on it. The intellect remained only to the extent that it could understand and obey, but it lacked even the most fundamental self-direction. Beatrice Tregard had been destroyed. The members of the Council opened their eyes. To those watching, it had seemed to take an eternity, but in reality this brilliant, wonderful woman had been destroyed in less than a quarter of an hour. In a bored tone, Councilor Krainik said, "Beatrice Tregard, you may leave The Ruling Box of Aidon. Guards, you will take custody of Gareth Tregard and hold him on the second level until Councilor Nalin has held the Evaluation to determine his replacement."

"Umm. What about the Regent's wife?" asked Guardsman Lev.

"Gareth Tregard is no longer Regent!" Krainik snarled. "As for his wife, she is of no concern to me. Let her remain with him, if he wishes. Perhaps she will remind him of what awaits those who defy King Mahon."

Beatrice walked to the edge of the box as ordered. The moment she exited, she stopped and looked around as if slightly confused yet uninterested. She simply existed, waiting for the next command by whomever cared to issue it. Dalene stepped forward, the tears flowing freely now. "Come with me, mother. I'll take care of you."

Her mother appeared frail, her vibrancy extinguished, but she obediently took her daughter by the hand and allowed herself to be led away. Gareth followed, his back straight and head erect as he followed his wife and daughter, tears wetting his cheeks before disappearing into his beard. He accompanied them back to the second level room they had vacated less than an hour ago.

When they were gone, Councilor Saleen was the first to speak. "What are we going to do about her?" he demanded.

Everyone present knew that he referred to The Lady Dalene.

Councilor Krainik smiled in a satisfied manner, "Oh, I don't think she will trouble us much longer. It is an interesting question for the law, is it not, Councilor Stanger?"

"She is still The Lady of Prophecy," Kori replied. "You dare not touch her."

"Hmm. Perhaps. But if we acknowledge Mahon as King of Aidon, then he becomes "The Most High." In that case, Dalene," and he emphasized her name, "is not The Lady of Prophecy. Just another overbearing wench who needs to be taught her place!"

Kori refused to back down, "I......I don't think prophecy can be so readily nullified."

"No matter. I'm sure such details will work themselves out. Now, we have business to attend to. Councilor Nalin, you are dismissed. Thank you for your participation. You will return to Salem and make arrangements for a new Evaluation for your File. Schedule it as soon as possible." He ordered. "The rest of you, follow me."

He led them back to the room they had used previously for their deliberations. When everyone was seated, he said, "It is most unfortunate that Gareth Tregard refused to see the wisdom in recognizing that The Lawgiver has come to claim his throne. This delay has undoubtedly cost the lives of many of our citizens to the liberating army of Kernsidon. We must act swiftly to end the slaughter and bring peace to Aidon. As the High Council of Aidon, we must go to King Mahon and acknowledge him as our King. As acting Regent, I call for an immediate vote. Declare yourselves now, by a show of hands. Will you bow to our King?"

Seven hands were raised. Councilors Tomias, Stanger, Brett and Garmon remained passive.

Krainik's eyes narrowed. He was running out of time and he knew it. "Well, then, it seems we have a clear majority. The only question remaining is - do you four support the decision of this Council, or shall we reconvene at The Ruling Box of Aidon?"

His meaning was clear. If they did not agree to support the decision, they would be destroyed. Grim faced, each of the four nodded in turn. They would bow to Mahon. The Council had decided and they would submit to that decision.

"Very well," Councilor Krainik soothed. "We must delay no longer. Come. We will go to the third level and pledge our obedience to The Lawgiver, King Mahon."

Escorted by the City Guards, the eleven Councilors were taken to the second level where the Arbor Guards barred the way. At a nod from their commander, the doors were opened and the Council proceeded through the great hall to the stairs that led upward. On occasion, they had climbed these stairs to view the Tree and the Valley from the vantage points of the windows high in the cliffs behind the Tree. They stopped to rest several times, panting with the exertion. Impatient now, Krainik drove them on. Finally, they came to the great doors at the entrance to the third level. None of them had ever proceeded past this point. Here, Krainik finally permitted enough time for them to fully catch their breath, his eyes glowing with excitement. Even those who had been reluctant to support him couldn't help but feel a thrill of anticipation. They were about to enter in where no one had gone for many centuries. Councilor Krainik at last ordered the doors to be opened. The two Arbor Guards who had accompanied them on their climb unlatched the massive doors and swung them outward. Eagerly, the Councilors rushed forward to enter, but were shocked into immobility, confronted by a bristling wall of swords. A fierce looking soldier stepped forward. "Councilor Krainik?" he asked. "Come. King Mahon is expecting you." The Council was drawn in, surrounded by soldiers and the doors were pulled shut in the faces of the two stunned Arbor Guards.

******

General Boris pushed his men hard. Through the course of their march, stragglers caught up and they overtook small groups whose flight had outpaced the rest of the army. He discarded most of the wounded. Those who were unable to keep up were killed or left behind. He estimated that he had lost fully a quarter of his troops, but those remaining should be more than adequate for the job at hand. They had encountered the first farms over an hour ago. They were deserted, but his men burned the buildings and tore down the fences. It served to whet their appetite. They wanted nothing more to do with those monstrous giants they had run from in the rocky valley the previous morning. What they wanted was flesh and blood from which to extract their revenge. Troas. It had to be Troas. The army was sweeping in from the northwest. They left the plains and made their way through rolling hills, becoming more steep as they approached the mountains. Isolated clumps of trees gave way to dense stands of timber separated by rushing streams in narrow canyons. The army swept forward, inexorable, irresistible. The General was mildly disturbed that he couldn't maintain contact with his commanders very well. He had more than twenty couriers racing back and forth to convey orders and maintain an even advance, but the terrain kept working against him. Either the men were being bunched together too much in the rocky defiles or they were being spread too much as the hills and forest forced them to adjust their march. No matter. It would be soon now. Each small clearing they encountered held a farm. Sometimes two. The columns of smoke now were all that remained to mark their passage. Soon.

Commander Lodi was hoarse from yelling. Curse this terrain! He raged. It was impossible to keep his men in a battle line when they were constantly being split by rocky outcrops and dense stands of timber! They should have gone back and swung in from the south - sticking to the plains. This was no place to fight! He had 500 men under his command and at the moment he couldn't see more than 50 of them, scattered as they were. The occasional farms held no plunder and he was worried about being ambushed.

Suddenly he heard distant shouts of alarm, pierced by shrieks of pain. "What's going on?" He yelled. "Get me a courier! Converge! Everyone converge! Is it an attack?" He led his men, charging toward the screams and confusion. A steep, rocky cliff barred their way and they were forced to detour, giving up the high ground as they skirted the timber at its base. The screams and yells were louder now. "Report! Curse you! I'll feed you to the Serpent if I don't get a report! What's going on?" he bellowed. Suddenly he choked. He couldn't seem to speak. He looked down to see a feathered shaft protruding from his throat. "What...........?" he thought, as he dropped to his knees and then thought nothing at all.

******

When alarm of the pending attack by Kernsidon went out, the initial reaction was, of course, panic. The first elements of the Arbor Guards were already arriving. Runners were sent to warn the outlying farmers who promptly gathered their livestock, hid what few valuables they had and evacuated to the city. They had been raised on tales of invasion, so while they had never endured one themselves, the response was practically ingrained, so the degree of panic was surprisingly limited. However, certain aspects of this attack were very different from any which had occurred previously. For one thing, the mobility of the mounted Arbor Guards had allowed them to range much further afield and so they had detected the invading army much further from Aidon than would normally be expected. The Arbor Guards had gambled on being able to mislead the Kernsidonian forces by cutting off their scouts and appropriating their signal codes. This gamble had paid off handsomely, buying them a few days of additional preparation time. The horses had again proved their worth in spreading the warning to all of the cities in Aidon. What normally would have required two or three days was accomplished in less than half the time. Finally, the defenders introduced a new element into the deadly game of war. In all previous encounters, the battle had largely been decided through the test of arms – with the arms being restricted, for all practical purposes, to swords and spears. To be sure, there were any number of farmers enlisted in the ranks of defenders, but they were primarily armed with axes, scythes and even sharpened sticks and clubs. While they were certainly skilled in wielding their farming implements, they were untrained in applying their strength at cutting down men and so were rarely decisive in the engagement. Following Jorge's advice, however, the plea had gone out for archers to head to Troas as quickly as possible. The face of war was about to change.

The Arbor Guards were both highly skilled and highly disciplined. The latter was their true advantage. They had been outnumbered in almost every engagement, yet they had been able to marshal a determined wedge to counter-attack and drive into the heart of the invading host in order to cut down their commanders and leave them unable to operate as a coherent unit. With their leaders dead, the invasion stalled and the soldiers would soon desert in the confusion, heading for home as quickly as they could.

The mounted Arbor Guards tried to approximate the numbers of the approaching enemy. Galen and Steve turned their horses over to Aaron and secreted themselves in small stands of trees – shrubs really – directly in the path of the oncoming army. The small copse offered little in the way of concealment, so the Kernsidon forces paid it scant attention. It required almost two hours for the army to pass by. The two scouts were grim as they rejoined their companion. The odds were not at all favorable.

General Boris was an adept student of the military history of his country – such as it was. But like many histories, Kernsidon had tended to emphasize the positive while neglecting the negatives. One of the negatives which had been neglected was any mention of the numerous attempts which had been made to subdue Aidon by attacking from the north. The rough terrain made this a difficult task at best. While the terrain was suitable to mask the movement of the army, it also offered countless opportunity for the defenders to stage an ambush. The General knew that the Aidonians had a nasty habit of focusing their attacks in a manner to kill the commanders. As a result, he had partitioned his army to ensure that it would be nearly impossible for the defenders to cripple his command structure. Before being depleted in the battle with those creatures yesterday, he had almost 40,000 men under his command, nearly double that of the previous invasion. At the moment, he had eighty separate groups pushing towards Troas. With 500 men in each battalion, they were a force to be reckoned with. The combined might of eighty such groups would be irresistible. While he maintained overall command through a system of couriers, each commander would execute their own tactical plan in support of the General's overall strategic objective. General Boris was highly pleased with this innovation. He promised rich rewards for the successful execution of this invasion and he promised painful execution for its failure. The troops, he felt, were properly motivated by the prospect of plunder and the threat of torture. The General was confident as the first muted sounds of conflict reached him.

This confidence began to turn to puzzlement. There was no clash of armor. There was no roar of battle cries, only scattered cries of pain and alarm. The first couriers began to trickle in with news of the enemy having been engaged, but there were no details as to their numbers or disposition. The couriers were coming from too many of his commanders all at once. Was the enemy everywhere? What was going on?

******

Elam was feeling queasy – somewhere between scared and terrified. He and the Arbor Guard, Hiat, were high in the branches of a large oak, just back from the edge of a small clearing. Hiat showed Elam how to smear his hands and face with mud and attach foliage to his cloak and trousers to blend in with the leaves and bark of the tree in which they hid. Hiat climbed out on the limbs and broke off several smaller branches, carefully smearing the stubs with dirt lest the whiteness of the freshly exposed wood should reveal their position. In this manner, he had improved several shooting lanes directed toward the nearby clearing. Elam had to look very carefully in order to detect those hidden in other trees, also waiting in ambush. From his vantage point, he was able to see the steady stream of enemy soldiers approaching as they crossed distant ridges and forest clearings. He knew he was seeing only a small portion of the attackers and yet it seemed they would never stop coming. Elam had completed his desperate ride the day before, having warned all of the southern cities of the pending attack. The ride on Midnight had been fun. There was just enough of the element of fear to make it an adventure, but he never felt personally threatened at all. In fact, it had appealed to his boyish ego to race into the various towns and villages on his horse with news of the Kernsidonian invasion. The people had almost been in awe of him. They'd treated him like a hero and loaded him with food and drink before he set off for the next town. But he had gotten the word out, both of the attack and the call for defenders. Instead of the usual ranks of farmers, loggers and townsmen, there had also been a specific request for every archer twelve years of age and up to gather at

Troas. A number of women – wives and mothers – accompanied them and were even now hurriedly assembling arrows as fast as they possibly could. Many of them would be crude, but their desperation made quick studies of the women. The Arbor Guards grimly stated that they would need a lot of arrows.

It was now just past midday. Arbor Guards and City Guards had been gathering in and around Troas for the two days since the Solstice. Elam's voice cracked as he asked, How many men have we got?" His heart sank at the reply.

"Not nearly enough. Perhaps 5000. Given a few more days, they might gather three, even four times that number, but for a day or two, that's all we are going to get."

That morning, Chase had attached the various City Guards to the Arbor Guards. They would attempt to fight a delaying action in order to give their forces more time to arrive. Surprisingly, there had been over 300 archers. Elam was amazed and a little jealous. He hadn't thought there to be nearly so many, but his heart fell when he realized they weren't nearly enough. Chase divided the archers into three groups and sent them with the advance units to take station along the most likely avenues of travel. Some would position themselves in the trees while others would take up hidden positions on the ground. Their instructions had been simple. Make no noise – none at all. Not before, during or after the attack. Stay out of sight. Shoot only when reasonably certain that they would not be spotted. Fear of the unknown was to be their primary weapon. They were too few to do much damage, but what damage they did would be amplified a hundred fold in the imagination of an enemy unable to determine the source of the attack. Lastly, they were to kill. They were instructed what to watch for in order to identify the commanders – the plumed helmets or the medallion on the left shoulder. These were to be their primary targets, but ordinary soldiers were fair game as well, although these were to be wounded rather than killed, if possible, so long as the wound was incapacitating. There was no mercy in this order. The Arbor Guards wanted the screams of pain and fear. They wanted wounds inflicted by an invisible enemy to demoralize the attackers, but the archers were instructed to take no chances. When in doubt – kill.

Elam's mouth was dry and his palms sweaty. He didn't know if he would be able to hold his bow properly, the grip made slick with sweat. He didn't know if he could kill a man, but then he thought of his mother, busy packing their belongings back in Tyber and preparing to flee. He thought of Laraine. It wasn't like she was his sweetheart or anything. He hadn't even talked to her. Well, at least not since they had been kids. She was one of the young women who'd had her Evaluation the same day as his. Elam had grown up with her, seeing her on the occasional trip to town at various festivals and social events. He liked her, but the last few years she made him kind of nervous, so he hadn't spoken to her much, but he was thinking about her quite a bit. Clinging to the branches high in the tree, he thought about her now and what was likely to happen to her if the enemy were not halted. The anger pushed back his fear. He didn't want to fight. He didn't want to die and he didn't want to kill. He wanted to be left alone, to farm with his father and ride Midnight and maybe talk to Laraine. The invaders were going to destroy all chance of that. The anger burned more fiercely. He fed it, letting it fill his mind, his heart. Then he banked it, pushing it back to form a hard, white-hot knot in his core. He had fed the anger and now it would feed him. He would do whatever was necessary to stop the enemy. He could function now and he would kill.

A sharp hiss from Hiat called Elam's attention to the clearing. Enemy soldiers were filtering in. They looked to be a dirty, ragged lot. For a brief instant, Elam imagined Laraine and her terror, her pain, if these should reach her. He pushed the image from his mind and swore they would never get the chance. Carefully, Elam slipped three arrows from his quiver. He nocked the first one, holding the other two in his bow hand. Hiat nodded and whispered one word, "Wait."

Elam nodded. Chase was leading this section. They would have to watch sharp, for there would be no battle cry. No command to attack. No order to fire. Silence, surprise, terror. Those were their most important weapons. He might not even see the first arrow fired by Chase. No matter. Others would.

Elam was concentrating on the clearing. There were at least 20 men in it now. They were advancing rapidly. Then he saw it. One of the soldiers wearing a plumed helmet suddenly stumbled, dropping to his knees without a sound. He looked up and Elam would have sworn the wounded man looked directly at him. Then he fell, sightless eyes staring up at the sky, a feathered shaft protruding from his throat. Instantly, Elam selected a target and loosed his arrow. He watched it all the way. It buried itself in the man's chest, just above the solar plexus. Only the fletching was visible through the thick beard. It might kill him. It probably would, but not immediately. The man looked down, seemingly puzzled. Awareness dawned on his face and he let out a shriek of pain. Elam suddenly realized that there were a lot of shrieks of pain. Why hadn't he noticed them before? He shook his head and instantly selected another target. He loosed his next arrow and watched it embed in the side of huge, burly soldier, just below the rib cage, eliciting a choking scream.

It was not that there was a hail of arrows. The defenders were far too few for that and the attackers too scattered. But every few seconds, Elam would see another arrow flash across his vision. The archers were selecting targets carefully. While there was a lot of movement in the clearing below, none of the enemy was standing. Several lay still, while others writhed on the ground in pain, screaming and cursing or crying and calling for help. Other soldiers rushed to their aid. In a matter of minutes, the clearing was carpeted with bodies. Elam saw another soldier. He had either made it through the clearing or had bypassed it altogether. He was past the tree where Hiat and Elam were hidden. Elam had just a momentary glimpse of the soldier through the foliage and he loosed an arrow, striking the man hard, high up, near the spine. He sprawled on the ground screaming. From there, Elam's memory was never clear. It was a blurred, indistinct, impression. A glimpse of an enemy through the branches of the tree. An arrow being loosed. Screams. Cursing. Another enemy. He didn't know how long he had been firing. He was surprised to realize that he had only a half-dozen arrows remaining. He had started with almost 50, but he could only distinctly remember firing the first three. Where had all the others gone? He felt like he was awakening from a dream and was almost surprised to see the number of bodies lying scattered in the clearing and on the forest floor below. A few were thrashing feebly, but most lay still. There were none left worth wasting an arrow on.

Now they heard the clash of swords, accompanying the screams of the dying and wounded. A troop of City Guards from Jordanon had been placed to block those who made it past the ambush. The steep terrain and dense timber tended to force the attackers into a few narrow lanes of approach. The moment they saw the guards, the Kernsidonian soldiers bellowed with rage, charging ahead. They had suffered the gauntlet of arrows and now they would have their revenge on the previously unseen enemy! A few of them made it to the waiting guards, but while they launched their attack at the enemy in front, archers, hidden in the heavy underbrush began to fire into their flanks and rear. Mostly these were the younger boys. They lacked the strength to pierce the heavy canvas and metal armor the soldiers wore, but the backs and legs of the enemy were largely unprotected and the boys fired into thighs and buttocks with considerable effect. Even those who were not crippled found themselves at great disadvantage in attempting to face the grim City Guards and they were quickly hewn down.

The soldiers soon learned to avoid the clearings. They were death-traps. They were furious, but almost helpless in the face of the invisible enemy. A few finally discerned the archers hiding in the trees. The foolish ones sheathed their swords and tried to climb up to their tormentors. They were usually picked off by archers in other trees, hiding nearby. If they did manage to climb up, they wound up swallowing an arrow before they were near enough to do any damage, or even pose a serious threat with their swords. The spearmen fared no better. The dense branches made it impossible for them to throw their spears at the hidden archers with any effect. Their spears weren't really made for throwing anyway, for no spearman marching to battle would willingly part with his primary weapon unless his situation was desperate. These heavy spears were intended for thrusting, or clubbing a swordsman from a safe distance. But against the archers, they stood no chance and they were quickly dispatched. Through all of this, the defenders made no sound. No yells of triumph. No attempts to goad and harass the enemy. With grim determination, they carried out their deadly work. Their mud-smeared faces became all the more terrifying to the enemy for their silence.

When there were no more of the enemy left to kill, the archers finally climbed down from the trees. The younger boys moved in amongst the dead and wounded, accompanied by a number of the City Guards. The boys were busily recovering what arrows they could, whether wrenching them from flesh or shoving them all the way through. It made no difference if the victims were still alive or not. The arrows had value. The lives of their enemies had none. Perhaps if there had been time they might have offered assistance, but they had already been informed of the odds they were facing. Any who attempted resistance were held at bay by the guards. If they resisted further, they were dispatched and the arrows recovered. Weapons were gathered and what they had no immediate use for, they cached for later recovery. The wounded were permitted to care for themselves and their comrades, but the defenders had neither the time nor the resources to spare. Throughout this operation they uttered not a word, despite the pleas and cursing of their enemies.

The recovered arrows were distributed amongst the archers in a small clearing littered with the dead and dying. Two of the Arbor Guards from Salem joined them. They nodded in satisfaction. Elam recognized one of them. Oerlik had been in Tremont when he arrived on Midnight to spread the alarm. He was older than many of the Guards and reminded Elam of his father. The thought made a lump rise in his throat and his eyes suddenly sting. He swiped his sleeve across them and fought back the lump. Oerlik was speaking, "You've done well. Far better than I had hoped, but we've no time to rest. I'm sorry, but we missed one column of attackers. There were just too many and we didn't have the forces to cut them off." He knelt in the dirt and with his finger drew a rough sketch. "They're already past us. There's a deep cleft to our south about a mile. It arcs around this hill and then it will break into the plain just above Troas. If we hurry, we might be able to catch them before they make it into the open. If they do, they outnumber us and we'll have a fight. But the cleft they're in is pretty deep. It should slow them down. If we can get ahead of them, circling through here, then we might be able to keep them bottled up. We think this may be their command column. One of the wounded said they're led by a General Boris. That's about where we would expect him to be, but if this *is* the command column, it will be a strong force. I'm sorry we haven't time to let you rest, but we'll be lucky to cut them off as it is, if we run. Can you do it?"

Grim men and boys nodded. Oerlik's grin showed briefly through his beard. "Didn't figure I had to ask. I know you can do it. But it's important that you know it as well. If we're lucky, one or two of the other groups may converge on the mouth of the cleft about the same time we get there. I've sent runners to Troas to get as many arrows as they have ready. The good news is that they'll be heading towards us at the same time we're heading for them. That'll shorten the supply line. Any questions?"

An older man, Elam didn't know his name, but the colors he wore indicated he was from Troas, leaned over and spat. "Can we kill 'em all ourselves? Or are you gonna make us share with the others?"

Oerlik smiled grimly, "We're not saving any. If the others want a share, they'll have to hurry it up. Let's get moving."

******

The tunnel suddenly ended. Colin had no idea how long he had been running. He had read about runner's insomnia once. It had described how distance runners sometimes drop into an almost trance-like state, the mind retreating from the pain and tedium of running. Brain wave activity would sometimes become similar to what is typical during REM sleep, the result being that the brain itself was relatively rested, to such a degree that it refused to shutdown during a normal sleep period. He felt like he was emerging from such a state and he had only come out of his stupor just in time to avoid smashing headlong into the tunnel wall. He had no idea why or how he managed to stop when he did. Panting heavily, he dropped his pack and set down the lantern. He ran his hands over the smooth surface. It wasn't as smooth as he had first thought. It had some texture to it, rather like coarse sandpaper, which helped to explain why it soaked up the light the way it did. But there was no seam, no irregularity in the surface. The tunnel didn't taper at all. It simply ended in an abrupt wall. There was no way through.

Had he missed something? Some turn? He picked up his gear and quickly retraced his steps, looking for a doorway or some other way out. In a moment, he found it, looking like a hole in the darkness. It was another tunnel, almost identical to this one. It angled up, but still headed in the same general direction. Colin immediately started up it, but Elias' words flooded into his mind, "Don't take the tunnel that goes up. You do that, and you'll be dying before you get around to doing anything else." How had he forgotten that? He slammed his fist into the wall, but turned and headed back the way he'd come, walking slowly, belying the panic he was beginning to feel. He was looking for something - anything - a doorway, some irregularity in the tunnel wall. But there was nothing. Soon, he was back at the dead-end. With a sense of failure, he dropped to his knees in desperate prayer. When he finished, he remained on his knees but nothing came to him. He wanted to scream, to cry. He was finished. In sheer exhaustion, his head dropped forward slumping against the wall. He felt it give. Just a fraction, but he was sure it had yielded to his touch. Excitedly, he pressed his hands against it. Solid. He pressed his face to the hard surface. It was warm. That was strange. He expected the stone to be cold. Standing, he retraced his steps back down the tunnel several yards. When he placed his hand against the unyielding stone, it was definitely cool to his touch. Going back to the end of the tunnel, he felt it. Warm. Whatever sealed the tunnel, it was different from the wall just a few yards back.

Intrigued, Colin felt carefully all around the edge. The blockage was abrupt, like someone had dropped a wall right across the tunnel. There was no tapering of the bore. The wall intersected the tunnel at a perfect 90 degree angle. He pressed against it, but it remained solid. He closed his eyes and rested his fingers lightly on its surface. He pressed harder and then he saw something. Through closed eyes, it was as if he could see the dark imprint of his hand against a faint web of light. The light radiated from his touch with thin strands of dark blue and purple, so dark as to be almost invisible against the blackness of the wall. He pressed again and the intensity of the light increased, as though resisting his touch. He slammed both hands against the wall and then his entire body, seeing the threads of light vibrate, radiating outward as though they were stress lines in the surface, resisting the pressure he was bringing to bear, but it didn't yield. He pressed harder, beads of sweat were forming at his forehead, the muscles of his arms began to ache, but the wall didn't budge. For some unknown reason, Colin suddenly closed his left hand, trying to grasp one of the strands of light between his thumb and forefinger. As he pulled his hand back from the wall, the strand of light followed. He held it carefully, fascinated by what he saw. He reached out with his right hand to grab the strand, pulling it toward him and the other strands bulged outward, gathering like a spider web with the strand that he held. Quickly now, he began to ravel the light. He paid no attention to where it was going, he just pulled it toward him as rapidly as he could, as if he were drawing in a net or a rope. Surprised, he realized that the strands were disappearing into his hands. Faster and faster he pulled them. They glowed more brightly the faster he pulled them. He could see strands not only defining the end of the tunnel, but beyond, they laced the entire tunnel in a dim web of light. The strands were being pulled toward him, stretching before stripping from the stone. He had no idea how long he reeled in the light, or how it kept disappearing into his hands. He half expected to see a pile of the glowing threads gather at his feet. The light now grew even more faint, the threads less numerous. In a few moments, the last of it disappeared. He opened his eyes. His lamp illuminated the tunnel beyond. It looked no different than where he stood. He shook his head, picked up his pack and his lamp and jogged once more into the darkened tunnel. But this time he went only a short distance when his way was blocked by a massive wood door. He raised the heavy latch and stepped through into a dusty room. No, not a room exactly. More of a closet. There were brooms and mops, several buckets and old rags. Colin blew out the lantern and set it down. He had but to reach out in order to unlatch another door. The hinges creaked when it swung open and he was looking down a short hallway. A few steps brought him to the intersection with another hallway. To his right, the passage dimmed, but to his left it joined a bright area. He headed quickly toward the light and found himself standing in the Great Hall of The Temple of The Tree of Life. He was back.

Chapter 29   Reckoning

Councilor Krainik confidently led the way through The Lawgiver's Hall. The carving here was exceptionally ornate. Water features lined the Hall, with fountains seemingly carved from the stone of the mountain itself. From some, the water burst forth in a celebration of sparkling cascades. Others were fed by the barest of trickles emerging from apparent crevices in the rock. Several overflowed to form streams gurgling along the edge of the hall, only to disappear into other cracks or carved features in the floor. Moss grew on the damp, water-polished stone, giving a splash of color and a sense of life to this level which was absent below. At the far end of the hall, another stairway led upward. The Council followed after Krainik, gawking as they gazed about. It had been many generations since any from Aidon had walked through this hall. And yet, despite the grandeur which surrounded them, they kept glancing back nervously at the soldiers who guarded the door and surrounded a gaping black hole adjacent to it. What were soldiers from Kernsidon doing in here, of all places? How had they gained entrance? The answer seemed to be the dark tunnel near the door, but if so, where did it lead?

The presence of the soldiers was disconcerting, but they appeared to offer no threat to the members of the Council. Krainik strode forward, the others following in his wake through the Hall and up the stairs. They climbed a long way, the stairway narrowing as they ascended, becoming almost claustrophobic with such a large group. The ornate carvings of the 3rd Level disappeared as soon as they began the final ascent. The stairs were drab, stark by comparison to the hall below. It was with considerable relief that they could at last see a shaft of light penetrating the gloom up ahead. While they didn't speak, each of them hoped that this was the termination of the stairs and not just a well-lit landing. As they neared the top, indeed they could see the open sky above. Unconsciously, they began to hurry their steps. Finally, they emerged onto a large patio carved into the top of a shoulder of the mountain. To their right they could see a series of entryways carved, leading back into the mountain. To their left, a simple stone railing defined the edge and just past the railing they could see the topmost branches of The Tree of Life. It looked different - almost sickly, rather than the majestic thing of beauty they had expected. They stood in the afternoon sun, blinking after emerging from the gloom of the last stairway. Startled by a sudden, harsh shriek, they whirled to face the source of the sound. Lucinda Yearsley was shaking and pointing, "That thing! Dear Heavens! What is that horrid thing doing here?!?"

Their heads jerked round to face where she pointed. There lay an enormous snake. While they stared in horror, it rose, lifting almost a third of its great length off the floor, towering over them. Its mouth gaped and they heard it, inside their heads, *"Welcome, my children. Come, and bow at the feet of your Ruler."*

The snake dropped its head, swinging it in a short arc to point toward The Throne of The Lawgiver. Seated there, was a glaring visage almost more terrifying than the Serpent. King Mahon growled in a low, threatening voice, "You should listen to my brother. His advice is generally worth following."

Councilor Krainik separated himself from the others, taking a position about halfway to the throne. He smiled, "I have brought them to you, my master, just as I promised. The Council of Aidon is here to give obeisance to you."

"Are you insane?" Councilor Stanger yelled. "The Serpent is the enemy to all Aidon! How did it get into the Temple? It was banished thousands of years ago!"

Dean Garmon ripped a small dagger free from his belt. He held it in front of him in a futile demonstration of defiance. "Never! We will never bow to that thing or to any piece of filth associated with it!"

Instantly, all eleven of the Council were slammed to the hard stone floor. Councilor Krainik screamed, "I'm not with them! I brought them to you! I did what you wanted! You OWE me!"

"I owe you nothing!" Mahon snarled. The Serpent raised its head once again, now it oscillated in a slow, threatening pattern over the top of the prostrate figures sprawled on the stone. "I am your KING! You will obey me, or you will be destroyed! I can crush your minds in an instant and then you will be my slaves for as long as I permit you to live! You may choose this as an act of will, or I will shred your souls! You think you can resist my power? Behold!"

Councilor Saleen got to his feet. He didn't want to. More than anything in the world, he wanted to lie there with the others, but he couldn't help it. He got up. The others struggled as hard as they could. They thrashed around a little but they were unable to rise. Councilor Saleen walked forward, stopping several yards in front of the throne. He stood rigid, unable to move except for his uncontrolled shaking. Tears flowed freely down his cheeks. He was terrified as he looked up and saw the huge, triangular head of the Serpent descending, the jaws gaping wide. He wanted to run, scream, but he could only stand. The mouth enveloped him, over his head, his shoulders, down to his waist and then it paused. The others lay still, too horrified now to even attempt to struggle.

Mahon arose, a cruel, vicious smile parting his thin lips. "Shall he live? Or die? At my thought, my brother can swallow him alive, where he will experience the pains of ten thousand deaths. It can take days, weeks even, to die in the belly of the Serpent, or if I choose, he can be dead before the jaws even close! His life, your lives. The lives of every living thing in Aidon belong to me! Your Tree is destroyed, because you hadn't the courage to destroy the false messenger. The Tree of Life? The Lawgiver is Life! When I took this throne, I became The Lawgiver! I am death! Or I can be life. Your Tree is nothing! Just a shadow of what it was. In a few more days, it will be dead and when it dies, every man, woman and child in Aidon who has not sworn loyalty to me will die with it! Once you are sworn to me, if you ever attempt to break that oath, you will cut the bond which ties you to me and you will die. Enough!"

At his word, the Serpent withdrew, leaving Dalba Saleen untouched. He still trembled uncontrollably, but he was unharmed. Except he was forever changed. The hair of his head, his beard, even his skin, was now a pale, translucent white. The Serpent had marked him. As of yet, he didn't know what had been done to him, but the others in the Council did. They saw, and the sight filled them with terror.

Councilor Krainik found himself free to move. Cautiously, he rose to his feet. Mahon looked at him, an amused expression on his face. "I owe you nothing. It is you who owe me. If you ever forget, the Serpent will remind you in a much more permanent manner than he has just demonstrated on your esteemed fellow-Council member. However, you have served me well. For that, you shall be rewarded. You shall be the first to pledge your loyalty, and you shall be the Regent of Aidon. You will see to it that my commands are obeyed. Come!"

Mahon walked to the edge of the court, seating himself once again on The Lawgiver's Throne, overlooking the dying Tree and the dying Valley. He spoke and when he spoke, those few who remained in the Valley heard. "People of Aidon! Your High Council has come to a wise decision. They have come to bow before me as their King! As your King! I did all I could to protect you, but your former Regent had embraced the false mantle-bearer! I was too late to stop him. He has destroyed The Tree of Life! I could not save it, though I have tried these past two days. But in my mercy, I can still save you! I will be your tree of life! Your Council has come to bow to me, to beg me to be your King so that I might save you. If you will bow to me, swear loyalty to me, bind yourselves to me, then I will become your new source of life. I and my brother!"

At that, the Serpent reared up, towering over Mahon and Krainik. Even though the distance was great, those on the ground could still see this dread apparition. The members of the Council could hear the distant shouts and screams.

"Do not be afraid, my people! My children! The Serpent is not your enemy! He is my brother! Your rulers in the past have kept you enslaved to tradition and superstitions. They have kept you bound to a tree! A piece of wood! I have come to free you! You will be bound to me, your Lawgiver! There will be peace, and you shall live as my people! See! Even now your High Council has come freely, to honor your King! All of you shall honor me! I shall save you. Aidon and Kernsidon shall be one people!

Councilor Krainik, shall be the first, and because he shall be first to honor me, I shall honor him! He shall be the Regent of Aidon. He shall rule the 12th File, and you will obey him as if his voice were my own! Councilor Krainik, come!"

Krainik moved forward to kneel before Mahon, the Serpent hovered menacingly overhead. He spoke in a loud voice and the magic of the Valley carried it to every corner. "I am Lijah Krainik, formerly High Councilor over the 11th File of Aidon, now High Councilor over the 12th File of Aidon and Regent of Aidon. I swear on my breath, on my soul and by the Throne of The Lawgiver, to honor and obey King Mahon, King of Aidon, King of Kernsidon and ruler over all the earth! May he reign forever!"

Krainik prostrated himself on the ground in front of the King, his arms extended past his head, with his palms and forehead touching the stone.

"Rise, Regent Lijah Krainik! Your oath is accepted, and you are truly mine! Now, Councilor Garmon, come!"

******

Colin's knees almost buckled with relief. A small fountain near the entrance drew his attention, reminding him of his thirst. Trying to remain unobtrusive, he slipped along the edge of the hall over to the fountain and dipped water using a cupped hand. Surprised, he froze. The sleeve of his cloak was pink, indicating membership in the 7th File. He leaned over to view his reflection in the small pool below the fountain. A haggard face he didn't recognize looked back at him. It was well past middle age. Lines showed around the eyes above a very thick beard. He reached up to stroke it, but of course, it wasn't really there, just the light stubble of perhaps two or three days growth. The hair was also dark and thick, coming down heavily to blend into bushy eyebrows. The cloak, thankfully, was a nondescript tan, except for the pink sleeves. The trousers were slightly more conservative, with only a thin band of pink material at the cuff. Suddenly a voice spoke near him, "Are you alright, sir?"

Colin turned. Two Arbor Guards were looking at him with curiosity. "Ah, yes. Thank you. I'm fine. Just felt a little dizzy for a moment, but I'm fine," he replied.

The guard eyed his bow and reached out a finger to touch it. "Nice bow," he said, "A friend of mine, Halvor, he had one of those. Showed me how to shoot it a couple of times. I had hoped he would teach me."

Colin's heart was hammering, "What happened to him?" he asked.

The guard's eyes became hard. "He's the one who was trapped by the Pretender – the false mantle bearer. Trapped in the Tree of Life and left for dead, only death would be better! I thought everyone knew that. Where've you been?"

"Oh. Ah, well, I just got here. I didn't know." Colin stammered.

"Just got here? Everyone else is leaving! So why did you just get here?" Both guards were resting their hands on their swords.

"I mean I just got here. To the Temple. I've been here in the Valley. I couldn't leave. Councilor......umm....Councilor Brett? Of the 7th File? Umm...she needed me to stay. Just for a few days. I just didn't know that the Halvor you were talking about was the Arbor Guard. I thought maybe you were talking about another Halvor."

The guard glared at him, but finally nodded and turned away. Colin waited for a minute until they left. He wasn't sure if drinking from the fountains in the temple was permitted or not, but he was thirsty. He tried to be inconspicuous as he snatched several handfuls of water and drank greedily. He had no idea how long it had taken to go through the tunnel, or how long it had been since he had used the last of his water, but it tasted good and helped to calm him. Glancing at the high windows in the Hall, he estimated that it must be afternoon. The sun was high yet, but during these longest days of the year it would remain so until late evening. His heart just wouldn't seem to settle down. It was still racing like crazy. Finally he sighed. He had no idea what he was supposed to do, but he figured he had better start doing something.

Colin hitched his pack and quiver more comfortably on his shoulder. Now that he knew the disguise created by the Anakim's magic worked, he didn't feel the need to hug the wall so closely. He walked directly down the center of The Great Hall, pausing at The Ruling Box of Aidon. For some reason he stopped there – standing directly in the center of the 13th Box, as he had done during his Evaluation. For just a moment, he closed his eyes and instantly he could see dozens, even hundreds of glowing spheres representing the people in the vicinity of the Temple. Immediately he was alarmed. He could see the connections between the individuals and The Tree of Life. This time he didn't have to look for them. Always before they had been very faint but vibrant ribbons of deep blue and purple. They had been distinct, radiating strength. Now, however, the ribbons were obvious. They glowed with more color, regions of yellow and orange, even red seemed to ripple through the darker colors. They looked unhealthy. "Cancerous" was the word that came to mind. Something was attacking the connection. "Either that," he thought, "or something is wrong with the Tree." The moment he thought this, he mentally focused on the Tree. Instead of the powerful, radiating tower of light he had always seen before, it appeared weak and shriveled by comparison. There was no strength or intensity to the light. His fear was realized. The Tree was dying.

Colin withdrew, back to his true-self. For a moment, he examined it. His light continued to pulse and flow, but once again, he looked for any connections and could find none. Not to this world. The sense of loneliness threatened to overwhelm him once again. Mentally, he regrouped, then expanded suddenly, allowing his mind to race from one light to the next, and then he stopped. He had found her. Dalene. She was near. He recognized the characteristic powerful glow of the Regent as well. But with them was something, no, someone unfamiliar. It had no presence. It simply was, but it lacked distinction. A sudden fear gripped him. It was like Elias' sister, only more faint. "Dear Heaven, no," he prayed. "Please, don't let this be Beatrice." But even as he thought this, he knew it was true, and he knew it was his fault. He withdrew again, and then impulsively, he reached out and touched Dalene. Instantly he felt her warmth and for a moment, her image was all he could see. Reluctantly, he pulled back. He had work to attend to. The Tree of Life was dying and he had to stop it.

He opened his eyes, taking a moment to reorient himself. He was more calm now. He still didn't know what to do, but he knew that he was fighting for more than Dalene, for more than Aidon. He was fighting for the power of life itself. The only problem was, he had no clue what he should do. "Stop Mahon." That's what Elias had told him. Alright, the last he'd seen of Mahon, he was on the courtyard or patio - whatever it was, up at the top of The Tree of Life. Fair enough. Then that's where he needed to go. Colin walked quickly through the hall and halted at the short flight of stairs leading to the huge doors. At least a dozen City Guards were stationed there, flanking the doors. He had been here before, the day of the Solstice Observance. How long ago had that been? He shook his head. There had been a woman. She had told her little boy that this led to the upper levels, up to The Throne of The Lawgiver. He had to get past the guards. Lacking any ideas, he simply walked up the stairs and spoke to the captain.

"Excuse me. I need to get through." He winced. It sounded pretty stupid even to himself. A snort of derision from one of the guards behind him confirmed that his opinion was shared.

The captain raised one eyebrow. He replied, not unkindly, "Listen, old man, you're not an Arbor Guard and I don't think you're a member of the High Council, since they've already gone through. That means you aren't coming through. The Lady Dalene about had us skinned for being in there, so trust me, you don't want to go in there. Why don't you just be on your way? Go rest up and head for wherever you call home."

Colin's heart leaped, "The Lady Dalene? Is she in there?"

The captain nodded, "Aye, but she's not to be disturbed. Been a pretty hard day for her. I feel sorry for her at that."

"But could she give permission for me to enter?" Colin asked.

"Old man, after the way she chewed up me and my men and the way she handled the Council, The Lady Dalene can do whatever she wants! I'd not buck her, that's certain!" Several of the men laughed, then the captain added, "But you're not getting in to see her. Now move along or I'll have to lock you up!"

Colin slipped the pack off his shoulder, noting that several hands immediately went to sword hilts, but he didn't care. "Can you give her something for me? And a message? I can pay!" He pulled out the book he had carried from the tunnel below, the book titled *Laws and Commandments*. "Just this. Will you give her this?"

The captain stroked his beard. "You said you'd pay. What did you have in mind?"

Colin quickly rummaged through his pack. It wasn't there! Then he remembered. He carefully shook the arrows from his quiver. There in the bottom was his money pouch. He tossed it to the captain. "There! All of that. Just take the book to her and tell her this. Say, 'It's more complete than the one you showed me last week. But I have to come in <u>now</u>, or it will be lost again.' Will you do that?"

The captain was hefting the money pouch in his hand, "And if I do that, I'll have no more trouble from you? On your word?"

Colin chose his words with care. "You deliver the message, and I'll leave if she doesn't let me in. Alright?"

The captain still looked undecided, "And if I do, who shall I say this message is from?"

"Just tell her, Miran's friend from Tyber. Will you do it?"

The captain suddenly smiled and relaxed. "No harm. With this," he hefted the money pouch once more, "My men and I will have a fine time when we get back to Salem! I'll have this sent, and I'll ask for a response. You can wait if you like, but if you cause any trouble while we wait," he looked at his lieutenant. "then you kill him." He gave Colin a hard look, "Are we clear on that?"

Colin nodded.

Colin hadn't even noticed a small door off to the side of the large double doors he stood in front of. The captain went to this small door and knocked. It was immediately opened by one of the Arbor Guards. Beyond it, Colin could see a passageway leading off into the mountain. The captain spoke briefly with the Arbor Guard who nodded and accepted the book before closing the door. The captain returned and stated simply, "Now we wait."

The Arbor Guard immediately took the book to where the Tregards were being held. Two guards were stationed at the door of their quarters, they had no orders to prevent anyone from coming to see them. Councilor Krainik considered this particular threat to have been thoroughly neutralized and was content to ignore them completely. The guard knocked at the doorway. A tired voice called out, "Enter."

He entered, nodding deferentially to the Regent. He couldn't help it. He still thought of him that way. He saw The Lady Dalene, sitting quietly with her mother, holding her hands. Beatrice simply stared blankly into the room. He cleared his throat and spoke, "Lady Dalene, Captain Sykes is stationed at the doors to the second level. He said there's a man there, wearing the colors of the 7th File, who sent this." He handed her the book.

She took it, curious. A spark of interest lit her eyes as she read the title. She gently opened the pages. She knew it was old. Very old. But it was in perfect condition. She read from the page, "The Ten Commandments." It was exactly what Colin had said that day, in the library when he had looked at the fragments scattered across the table. She looked at the guard, "Who brought this?"

"He said to tell you he was Miran's friend, from Tyber. He said that this one is more complete than what you showed him last week, but that he has to come in now or it will be lost again. The captain says he wants to come into the second level. What shall I tell him?"

The Lady Dalene's jaw clenched, and she gave the guard a look that made him take a step back. "You tell him that Miran's friend is dead, and if he were not, I would kill him myself. Thank him for the book. Tell him I will examine it. That is all."

The guard nodded and turned swiftly to leave. Just as he was closing the door, The Lady Dalene called out, "Wait!" A faint gnawing of doubt stirred in her. She went to her shoulder pouch and removed a small package. "In exchange for the book, give him this. If he can tell me by what means these were used to heal Miran's friend, in Tyber, then I will see him. Otherwise, he is to be removed from the temple."

The guard nodded again and quickly left.

Gareth looked at his daughter. "What was that all about?" he asked.

She shook her head. "I don't know. Probably something Krainik has dreamed up. I don't know why. But this," she touched the book, "makes no sense. Not from Krainik. Colin is dead. He caused all of this! And he's dead! I should have let him die in Tyber! None of this would have happened! I'm such a fool!"

Gareth smiled faintly, "Perhaps. I think all of us are fools at one time or another. The question, daughter, is, were you a fool then? Or are you a fool now?"

"I was a fool then! I trusted him. No matter what he said, I just felt like there was something good there - something worth saving. If I had just been more obedient. If we would have just destroyed him at his trial........." her voice trailed off.

"Your mother thought he was worth saving, and your mother was never a fool." He shook his head, "Well, perhaps once, when she married me. Dalene, I don't understand this either. I fear that we are seeing the end of Aidon. Perhaps your mother is the fortunate one. She is at peace. But your mother saw something in Colin. Even today, she still saw it. I know she had no regret regarding her decision. She felt the price was worth it. I don't know. Maybe she was right."

Dalene could make no reply. She just sat, staring at the book in her lap, but seeing nothing through tear-dimmed eyes.

It seemed to take forever. Colin was becoming more anxious by the moment. At last! The small door swung open and a grim faced Arbor Guard exited. The captain looked at him expectantly, but he addressed Colin directly, "The Lady Dalene thanks you for the book, but she says that Miran's friend from Tyber is dead and if he were not she would kill him herself. She asked me to give you this." He handed Colin the package he had received from The Lady Dalene. "She said if you can tell her by what means this was used to heal Miran's friend in Tyber, then she will see you. Otherwise, you are to be escorted from the Temple. Immediately."

Colin untied the package. In it were two smaller packets and a tiny flask. He removed the stopper from the flask and sniffed it. The odor was faint. He inverted it, capturing a few drops on his finger. It was slick. Oil. He untied the smaller packets. A coarse yellow powder in one, coarse white granules in the other. He tasted it. Salt. The other was familiar, but he was uncertain, was it cornmeal? He had no idea what he was supposed to say. A rising sense of desperation enveloped him. "I don't know! I was unconscious! I know she packed my arms in salt, but I don't know what she did! Please, just tell her that."

The Arbor Guard's face remained expressionless. He turned to Captain Sykes. "You are to escort this man from the Temple immediately. Assign two men to conduct him out of the Valley. If he resists, kill him."

The captain nodded, "Aye. We'll see to it. You two," he indicated the two guards near the foot of the stairs, "See him on his way. You heard the orders. If you can hand him off to any of the other guards, fair enough, otherwise, see him on the road to Salem."

Colin's shoulders slumped in defeat. They took him to the foot of the stairs. He had failed. Everything was lost. There was no more time! Sudden anger flared in him, a white hot rage at Mahon and what he was attempting to do. Some things were worse than death. He halted, his escorts looked at him curiously, fearing nothing from this tired, old man. Colin glanced back. The captain and the Arbor Guard were still looking after him. He let the package Dalene had sent him fall open in his hands, cradling the oil, salt and corn meal. It began to glow. Jaws dropped and the guards were too stunned to react. It glowed brighter and brighter, an intense light of incredible energy. The guards shielded their eyes, but Colin continued to stare at it. Suddenly, the light retracted, absorbing directly into his hands. They were empty. The sleeve of his cloak, he noted, was white. He had no idea what had just happened, but whatever it was, it had burned away his disguise. He stared at his hands, a residual glow still emanating from them. He saw the faint, ragged scar marking the webbing between the second and third fingers on his right hand glowing even more brightly, his hands pale by comparison. Back in high school he had lacerated it badly when a piece of glass tubing had shattered while he was working in the chemistry lab. He'd had to get a dozen stitches - right at the start of the tennis season. To stay on the team, the coach made him play and he had to win. He wore a light leather glove over the wounded hand, so his opponent had no clue regarding his injury. After losing the first set, he tore out the stitches which allowed him to play better and he squeaked out a win in the second set, but he needed something more. Shock value. At the start of the final set, he walked up to the net, keeping all expression from his face. Staring impassively at his opponent and without saying a word, he peeled the glove from his hand, held it across the net and poured blood all over the court before pulling the glove back on, never taking his eyes from his stunned opponent. He won the set 6-0 and with it the match. With the memory, the scar seemed to shine with an added intensity. He needed shock value. Elias had said he had the power to form air and stone. He'd said he could use these as tools – that he must use these if he was to succeed, and now he was on the verge of failure. There was no time left. He called out to the stunned guards, "Deliver one more message for me, will you, please?"

He focused and very deliberately plunged his hand into the wall of stone at the base of the stair. The pain was intense and it took tremendous concentration, but the stone parted, flowing around his hand like soft clay. The guard's jaws dropped in amazement as he made two quick, slashing motions, carving the image of a heart into the stone, a beautiful, polished wound in the smooth wall. He clenched his fist. Withdrew it from the cavity he had just created. He opened his hand. There in his palm rested another heart, smaller than what he had formed in the wall, but shimmering white, almost translucent. He tossed it to the Arbor Guard, who caught it purely by reflex. "Tell Dalene, it was the same power by which her gift was used to mold this heart of stone."

Before the guards could react, Colin turned to the opposite wall and without hesitating, stepped into the solid rock, disappearing like a pebble dropped into molten lava, without so much as a ripple.

Captain Sykes couldn't tear his eyes from the spot where Colin had disappeared. "But that's impossible!"

The Arbor Guard looked grim, "Accept it captain. The impostor is back, and he's here in the Temple."

The captain finally managed to look at him, "What are we going to do?"

"You find every guard you can. City guards are to seal off the Temple. Nobody goes out. Find one of the Arbor Guards. Have them round up whatever forces they can and have them report to the second level - immediately!"

"What are you going to do?" Sykes asked.

He looked at the heart, glowing in the palm of his hand. "I guess I have a message to deliver."

The Arbor Guard made no pretense of restraint. He ran as fast as he could to where the Tregards were held. He didn't bother to knock. He simply burst through the door, breathless. "Lady Dalene! Regent! We have trouble! I'm sorry, but it was the impostor! The false mantle-bearer. I didn't recognize him, but it was he who sent the message to you. He was disguised. He was being hauled out of the Temple, as you ordered, but he escaped. He left a message though. He said, 'Tell Dalene it was the power by which her gift was used to mold this heart of stone.' And he sent you this." He handed her the translucent stone heart and panted, breathless, suddenly realizing that not much of what he'd said made any sense.

Gareth looked at him calmly, "What's your name, Arbor Guard?"

He snapped to attention, "Regent, sir, this Arbor Guard's name is Kyle Malof, 9th File, from the city of Lasal, sir!"

"Very good, Kyle. Now. Relax and tell us exactly what happened," Gareth ordered.

Kyle drew a deep breath and as quickly as he could, described what had occurred. Dalene sat silently, a grim set to her jaw. "It's him. It really is him. How could he have survived that fall? I know they never found his body, but even so......."

Her father nodded. "It's him. The question is, what are we going to do about it?"

Dalene looked at him in surprise, "He has to be stopped! Whatever he's doing, it can't be permitted! Kyle, send for all the guards you can! Quickly. Have them assemble at the doors to the third level."

"Are you so certain then?" her father asked mildly.

"Of course! Look at everything that's happened since he came here! He's all but destroyed Aidon! He's back to finish the job and we have to stop him!"

Gareth nodded, "Aidon is all but destroyed. I fear The Tree of Life is dying. I feel it. But think for a moment. Tell me, what specifically has Colin done to cause all of this?"

"Father! There's no time! He came here! He attacked the Tree!"

"Your mother didn't think so," he replied. "Think. Yes, he was in the Tree, but so was your brother. One could as easily claim that Halvor attacked the tree as Colin. After all, they were both there together."

"You know that's not true! Halvor was there to stop him! He failed!"

"Calm yourself. May I see that?" he asked, indicating the heart she still held. He accepted it from her and studied it. "Amazing. I don't know if I've ever seen anything more beautiful." As if remembering their former conversation, he continued, "Yes, I know it's not true. Halvor didn't attack the Tree. But your mother was correct. The statue fell from above - from where Mahon was, at the Throne of The Lawgiver. He is the one who said that Colin attacked the Tree. The Tree was certainly damaged. Colin was there. We all thought he was dead. But who are we really fighting? Is it Colin? Or is it Mahon? Who is Colin fighting? Is it us? Or do we have a common enemy? You're right. We have no time, but we had better be sure we aren't attacking an ally instead of an enemy. Come. There is work to be done."

At the door, Gareth gave orders to the two guards. "You are to remain at this post. Protect my wife at all costs. No one is to countermand my orders until the Temple is secure. Do you understand?"

The guards snapped to attention and nodded. It never occurred to them to point out that Gareth Tregard was no longer Regent and therefore in no position to give them orders. The man had presence. Dalene trailed after her father. She was confused by what her father had said, yet it made sense. Her mother had flatly stated that she didn't believe Colin had attacked the Tree. What was he doing here? How had he disappeared into the rock of the mountain like that? Where was he? Was he their enemy? She just couldn't accept that last. He had been too kind - not just to her, but she had seen how he had acted with Miran and Elam, how considerate and appreciative he had been even towards the servants in the Praetorium. But it was so hard to turn loose of her anger! She was furious with him, blaming him for what had happened to Halvor and to her mother! But was he her enemy? Every time she came back to that, she rejected the thought. He might be to blame for many things, but he was not their enemy. The enemy was Mahon - and Councilor Krainik. She would not forget him.

Gareth seemed almost to grow larger as he marched through the dimly lit corridor. He somehow became more menacing. This was not the gentle Regent of Aidon. This was the battle commander of Aidon. Though he may have been stripped of his title, his heart had long ago been given to his people. It would remain so until it beat its last. He paused for only a brief moment in the great hall of the second level, just long enough to strip a sword from an ornamental hanging on the wall. He ripped the cape from his formal dress and dropped it on the floor as he walked. It would only be in the way when it came time to fight. Since yesterday, he had carefully banked and hidden his anger. Now, he was unleashing it. Aidon was threatened. Heart and soul, he had given his life to her protection. The rage was barely contained as he stormed through the hall. Dalene followed her father's example and stopped briefly to grab a light sword from another of the wall displays. Her father had trained her in the use of weapons, but she had never had cause to wield them in anger. Somehow though, the sword felt natural in her hand and a fierce pride coursed through her as she watched her father's back, strong and straight, broad shoulders and head erect. Come what may, she would follow him. She was The Lady Dalene, and Aidon would not fall while breath remained in her body.

At the far end of the hall, perhaps three dozen Arbor Guards were congregated. Most of the guards had previously been dispatched to confront the threat on their borders. They were so few. For a moment, despair gripped Dalene's heart. Was it enough? Kyle Malof was there. She recognized several others - friends and acquaintances of Halvor's. The thought of her brother sent a momentary surge of grief through her, but she knew he would approve of what they were doing and pushed him from her thoughts. The Guards drew back from the door. As if on a signal, every sword was drawn from its scabbard.

Gareth spoke, "Guards, you all know that by the laws of Aidon, I am no longer your Regent. Councilor Lijah Krainik now holds that position. You are under no obligation to follow me or obey me. In fact, by our laws, you are supposed to prevent what I am about to do. The Council has gone to yield to King Mahon. I believe this is wrong. I don't know how he got here, but I believe he is a creature of evil. He must be stopped. Whether I succeed or fail, it may well be that Aidon will not survive. But there are things more important than survival. I have lived my life, obeying blindly every dictate of the law as I understood it. What I do now violates much of what I have spent my life upholding, but I will no longer obey blindly. Today I choose. I choose to listen to my heart, and my heart says that the Council is wrong and that any law which upholds them in this affair is wrong. Therefore, I will not obey. Today I fight! I will fight you, if you seek to stop me, and I will fight those who seek to destroy Aidon. Now, you must choose. But if you oppose me, the battle begins here!"

As one man, they raised the hilts of their swords to their foreheads, blades held high, glinting in the late sun coursing through the high windows, and they bowed, acknowledging their Regent.

There was no hesitation, Kyle Malof stepped forward, "We follow the only true Regent of Aidon! The battle doesn't begin here! The enemy is through those doors!"

Word of the Kernsidon soldiers on the third level of the Temple had, of course, spread like wildfire. The Arbor Guards had been furious at this further desecration of their stewardship. Between the damage to the Tree, the loss of one of their most respected comrades and their traditional enemy holding the most sacred level of the Temple, their urge for some object on which to vent their rage and frustration was all but overpowering. The third level doors opened outward, and the door was barred from within. Despite their massive size and thickness, fully eight inches of heavy timber, the doors were never designed for defensive fortification. True, their location at the top of the stairs would make it extremely difficult to bring a battering ram into play. The fact that the doors opened outward would mean that the heavy planks would have to be splintered, rather than managing to burst the doors inward on their hinges. They were so expertly fitted that there was insufficient gap to insert any tool to lift the heavy bar which held the door shut. However, the fact that the doors swung outward also meant that the hinges had to be located on the outside of the great doors. Eagerly, the guards hauled one of the massive tables up the stairs, setting it at an angle, leaving a sharp corner raised well above the top step, forming a sharp edge to be used as a fulcrum. Other guards raced back through the hall, calling for axes and mallets to be brought. The City Guards who protected the lower level quickly brought the requested materials. It took only a matter of minutes for another of the huge tables to be split. The heavy table top was separated into a half-dozen boards, each of which was all of fifteen feet long. The ax was applied to one end of each board, cutting a sharp bevel. Any work done near the doors was conducted in silence. They would need the element of surprise on their side. The boards were inserted underneath the edge of the huge doors, resting across the fulcrum formed by the table on the stairs. At the signal, 30 men threw their weight onto the levers. The doors lifted cleanly off their hinges, and with a loud crash, fell outward, clearing the way to the third level. With a roar, Gareth charged in, followed closely by the yelling, screaming guards. They saw the shocked faces of the soldiers from Kernsidon, but they weren't too shocked to react. Above the sound of their battle cries, Gareth heard a thundering voice. It said, "People of Aidon! Your High Council has come to a wise decision. They have come before me to bow to me as their King........" The battle was joined, and he heard no more.

******

Elam was exhausted. They raced madly through the broken terrain, trying to get ahead of the approaching enemy. They managed it, but barely. Scouts had been keeping track of the advance. There was some good news. Elam's group had not been the only one to engage in battle earlier. There had been dozens of groups such as his which managed to ambush the advancing columns in the steep canyons and dense timber. Hundreds of the Kernsidon soldiers had been killed and wounded while the defenders had suffered minimal casualties. Many of these smaller parties had moved on to try and blunt the attack of other columns. The group Elam was with was joined by others, converging from the south to take position between the attacking army and the city of Troas, now visible in the distance. The rest of the news was bad. The Aidonian army still had not arrived. At least three separate columns of the enemy had linked up, meaning the enemy they would soon face was much larger than what they had fought this morning. Worst of all, the terrain was not so favorable. A number of the younger boys had gone to harass the rear and flanks of the enemy forces. It slowed their advance, but not by much. The canyon ended abruptly at this high plain on which they now stood. When the enemy cleared the mouth of the canyon, they would immediately be able to spread out. The occasional rolling hills and pockets of timber could be easily avoided, and in any case, they provided inadequate cover to mount an effective ambush. Chase, Hiat and Oerlik had been meeting with several of the other guards. The meeting soon broke and Chase came back to address them.

"I'll not lie to you. Our situation doesn't look good. We were lucky last time. We had cover and terrain on our side. This time, we'll be fighting without much benefit from either one. Our best chance is to try and keep the enemy bottled up. We need to hold them in the canyon as long as we can. Runners have been sent to find out if we can expect to be reinforced by the army any time soon. I'm sure they're coming as fast as they can, but it might help if we know how long we have to hold. Willam and Jack have assembled all the archers they could find. They were in battle this morning as well, but they've swung north to join up with us. Best guess is we've got better than 2000 men coming at us, and with everything we can muster, we might have 500 men to meet them - less than half of those are archers, but we're the best hope for slowing them down. Once they break out and can match us sword for sword, they'll chew their way through and be in Troas in less than an hour. They're evacuating the town. I'm trying to get whatever arrows they have ready brought down to us at once. But if we can't hold them until our army gets here, there'll be a lot of folk dying before nightfall."

Elam looked around at the grim faces. He was ashamed of the fear he felt. He hoped it didn't show on his face. The others all looked so determined. He wondered if he was a coward.

"You know what you have to do," Chase continued. If we don't hold, nobody in Troas stands a chance. Go with the Arbor Guards. They'll help get you positioned. There's too many to hold back indefinitely. Don't go getting killed for no good reason. Give ground when you have to, just make sure you make them fight for every inch. Good luck."

Elam turned to go, but Chase called out, "Elam, I need you for a moment."

He turned back and Chase explained, "I've had your horse, Midnight brought up. What do you think? Can you ride him and fight? I think it may confuse the enemy. Give them something to worry about anyway. It will be dangerous. You'll be right out there in the thick of things. I'll be with you of course. Patch is with Midnight and we should be joined by Jeffs and Steven before the battle starts, maybe even a couple of others. If things go badly, I want the horses massed, backed by whatever Arbor Guards we can muster and try to cut through to their General. Reports are he's in this column. In the past, when we've been able to take out their commander, the attack has kind of fallen apart. Are you up to it?"

Elam nodded, not trusting his voice enough to speak. He thought again about his mother and Laraine. He wondered if he would ever get to tell her how much he liked her. Following Chase, he trudged back to where the horses were being held. He wondered where his father was. He hoped he was safe.

Elam and Chase were mounted up. Midnight frisked about, glad to see him. Elam checked his quiver, adjusting it over his shoulder and making sure it was full. As promised, Jeffs and Steve came riding up on Stockings and Frost. They grinned and lifted a hand in greeting, "Elam!" Steve called out, "We heard you had quite a ride! So after this, are you going to join us for good, or is Tyber looking better to you all the time?"

In spite of himself, Elam had to smile, "Right now, I'd rather be back on the farm building a fence with my father more than just about anything."

Jeffs grinned, "And I'd like to be there with you. Well, not to worry, all we have to do is take care of this little problem and we'll be at that fence before you know it!"

They turned their horses and trotted toward the canyon mouth. They hadn't positioned archers up in the trees. Chase feared that the massed enemy would cut them off and there would be no chance of retreat if that were to happen, so he dispersed his forces into the timber. They would have at least one good chance for a surprise attack and then they would resort to a fighting retreat, trying to keep ahead of the enemy swords and spears while inflicting as much damage with their arrows as possible. The horses were held back, past the timber where they could be most effective. They wouldn't have long to wait.

******

General Boris was pushing his men hard. They had to get out of this cursed canyon! The silent enemy continued to flit around his flanks. Their advance was marked by the continuous screams and cursing of the wounded. Many of the wounds weren't serious, but they kept slowing their march as men would fall out to help their comrades. That wasn't as much of a problem as it had been. The men soon learned that stopping to help another was an open invitation to become a target. For the most part, they kept moving. One of his scouts had just reported in. They were nearly at the top. Soon they would break out of this draw onto the plain. From there they could see Troas. The sight of the city would be like the scent of raw meat to a pack of wolves. His men would storm through the defenders and then they would extract the first payment on the debt of revenge they were owed.

******

They heard the screams first. A few minutes later, they could see their men ghosting through the timber, pausing momentarily to fire one or two arrows before retreating once again. Tree by tree, the defenders were being pushed back. The screams and cursing now came in a steady stream. Elam wiped his hands on his tunic. He had one arrow nocked, two others held in reserve in his bow hand. He reached out and patted Midnight on his neck. "Come on boy," he whispered, "Don't let me be a coward today." The horse tossed his neck as if he understood. The defenders gave ground grudgingly. Finally, they were among the swordsmen. The enemy was now breaking from the timber. Arrows continued to rain down on them and almost every shot found its mark, but there were just too many. A few of the soldiers, driven almost insane by anger and frustration, ran screaming at the enemy they had been unable to touch. They were almost always cut down by a flight of arrows, but a few would make it into the ranks of the defenders where they were immediately engaged by the waiting swordsmen. But they kept coming. Elam was startled when Hiat spoke. "It's time, Elam. Are you ready?"

Elam nodded and immediately kicked Midnight into a run, but everything seemed to move so slowly. He could distinctly hear every hoof beat. But he couldn't hear the men's voices. He saw faces contorted in rage as he fired at target after target. He saw his arrows strike home as men folded up in agony. He saw arrows zip past his face, mere inches away as he raced between the opposing forces. There was no room for fear. No room for thought even. He simply acted and suddenly, he was out of arrows. Time sped up. He heard the din of battle and his own labored breathing. Above the racket, he heard Chase yelling, "Arrows! If you're out, get stocked up. They've brought up arrows!" He saw young boys running madly, carrying bundles of arrows in their arms. Immediately he raced toward one of the nearest and took his entire load, cramming them haphazardly into his quiver, then wheeled to re-engage the enemy. He was shocked at how far from the mouth of the canyon they were, and yet the enemy continued to pour out. He had no sense of time, just a rising sense of fury and frustration. They had no right to be here! All he wanted was to be left alone, in peace! These men had come bringing war! They had come to kill. So be it! He would bring them death.

Again Elam charged. He was suddenly aware of another horseman keeping pace with him. Bob caught his eye and grinned, "I'll watch your flank, Elam! A finer day for battle we'll never live to see!"

They were in the thick of it again. Elam fired arrow after arrow. He was selecting his targets more carefully now. He knew he hit a number of commanders, but they still kept coming! Almost at the point of despair, his rage flared hot, swallowing it up as he wheeled to charge once more. And suddenly, he was lying stunned, flat on his back. One of the spearmen had lashed out and swept him from the saddle, knocking the breath from him. He looked up to see a giant of a man charging down on him, screaming, a sword held high over his head in both hands, and still Elam couldn't move. The soldier skidded to a stop. Elam could see the sword descending. His attacker froze, staring down in horror at the length of steel protruding from his belly. Elam heard an angry bellow, "NEVER TOUCH MY SON, YOU SCUM!"

His father jerked the blade free and stood facing the charging enemy. Jorge slammed the sword back into its sheathe and calmly unslung the bow from his shoulder, nocking an arrow. He stood there, back-to-back with Baylor. Baylor had no bow, or even a sword, but he was wielding a huge double-bitted axe with terrible effect. All was confusion now, attackers and defenders so completely mingled it was impossible to define the line of battle.

"You alright, Elam?" His father yelled while loosing an arrow. Baylor practically cleaved a swordsman in two.

Elam clawed to his feet, nodding, "How'd you get here?" he asked.

"The army," his father replied, dodging a blow and releasing his next arrow at point-blank range. "You didn't think we were going to leave the whole battle to you, did you?"

Midnight came charging up, knocking soldiers out of the way or trampling them under his hooves.

"Now, I'm kind of busy here," Jorge said, "and I think your horse would like to get back to the war!"

Suddenly, Elam felt good. His father had just saved his life and there was a battle to be won. He leaped to the saddle and saw the mounted Arbor Guards assembling a hundred yards distant. Several other defenders joined his father and they were making a good stand of it. Elam kicked Midnight and they charged towards the other horsemen. Chase grinned in greeting as he arrived. He had seen Elam knocked from the saddle, "Good to see you. Thought maybe they had you. The army has come up, but we can't hold them here. They're spreading out. Soon they'll flank us and either cut us to ribbons or keep us pinned while part of their force rips through Troas. But we've still got a chance. There's the general." He pointed with his sword.

Elam saw the commander, perhaps 150 yards away. Certainly not more than 200 yards. But between them lay the massed forces of two armies, with hundreds of individual battles being fought. "Surely," Elam thought, "he can't mean for us to charge through all that?"

As if reading his thoughts, Chase continued, "Troas has one chance. We've got to take out their commander. It may not work. They may keep coming. But even if it takes some of the heart from them, it will give our forces more time to come up. What do you say?"

Hiat swiped blood from his eyes. He had a nasty gash across his forehead. "Talking won't get the job done. Best be after it then."

Steve and Jeffs nodded. Just then Willam and Jack came thundering up. "Is it time then?" Willam asked.

Chase nodded. "Guess so." We'll have about forty men on foot with us. They'll try to protect our flanks. Don't get distracted. That command group is what we want. Nothing fancy. Kill every one of them you can. You all set for arrows?" They all nodded. "Luck to you then."

They wheeled enmasse, charging into the battling host. Once again, time suddenly slowed down. For the first time in the battle, they charged, screaming their rage. Straight into the heart of the fray they went. Swords flashed all around. The Arbor Guards on foot kept pace with the horses, their attack slowed by the men surrounding them. Yet still they forged forward. Elam fired arrow after arrow. Each time he watched it strike. They made no attempt to wound. As Chase had admonished, just plain killing. Amazingly, their hail of arrows protected the foot soldiers to a considerable degree. Still, they lost several. Others were limping, but they still engaged the enemy. Elam was surprised to see how far they had come. They were less than 50 yards from the General and his commanders now. He could see their eyes, but he still couldn't hear anything, so focused was he on the objective. They charged, the sea of men boiling around them, the course of their advance obliterated in the wash of bodies in their wake. Midnight reared up, lashing out with his hooves, clearing screaming men from their path. Elam saw Jeffs cut from the saddle. He saw a red line of blood traced across Stockings flank as the horse went berserk, bucking and pitching through the mass of men. And then he saw the General. Suddenly, that was the only thing he could see. As if in a dream, he reached up over his left shoulder and slipped an arrow from his quiver. He felt as if each arm weighed a ton, so slowly did he move. He nocked the arrow and drew back. He could see the General plainly. Could see his eyes. At just that moment, the General's eyes locked on his. They flared wide in alarm and he opened his mouth to yell. Elam released the string. He watched the arrow. He <u>willed</u> it. He saw its trajectory clearly, and watched it as it cleanly drove home, right between the wide eyes of General Boris. And then something slammed into him. He was lying on his back, looking up at the clear, blue sky. He thought he had never seen anything so pretty. But it was growing dark. He was puzzled. Why should it be dark? A bolt of pain lanced through him then, and everything was blackness.

******

Colin had no time to think about what he was doing. The pain was so intense he thought he would pass out. He knew if that happened, he would die here, inside the rock. And if he died, what chance did Aidon stand then? He forged ahead, not knowing how. All he knew was that the rock flowed around him, but it was slow, like swimming in lava, he thought. All at once, he broke free. Instantly, the pain was gone. There was no residual effect, just a searing memory of what it had been like. He was standing in a narrow passage. At that moment he heard a thundering voice. It said, "………you are truly mine! Now, Councilor Garmon, come!" Stairs led upward and he raced forward.

The passage emerged unexpectedly into a plain, darkened alcove which opened into a larger cave. It appeared to have been carved in the rock, but it lacked the refinement of the halls and passages he had seen below. Cautious now, he still advanced swiftly. The cavern opened through a number of doorways onto a large patio. Through a stone railing, he could just see the topmost branches of The Tree of Life. He had made it then! But now what?

He ran quickly to the entryway and peered out. He recognized the members of the High Council of Aidon, either lying still or writhing futilely on the ground. Councilor Garmon was getting to his feet. He was moving slowly toward the throne, as if being dragged by an invisible chain. He could see the back of Mahon's head, seated on the throne. Next to him, Councilor Krainik stood. But what drew his attention was the most enormous snake he had ever imagined. "That thing can't be real!" he thought in a panic.

As if to confirm his worst fears, the huge head swung around to face him, as if it somehow sensed him. Colin didn't even think. He snatched an arrow from his quiver and loosed a shot directly at the Serpent's head. His attention never wavered. He had no idea how heavy the bone and scales might be at his point of aim, but his focus, his target was a good foot and a half deep in the creature's skull. The arrow flew true and he saw it embed itself, only a small amount of fletching still protruded. The Serpent's head whipped back and forth in pain, emitting a squeal accompanied by a horrendous hissing noise. Colin swore he heard it speak, *"Brother! An enemy attacks us!"*

Instantly Colin fired another arrow at Mahon, but with a slashing movement of his hand, Mahon blocked its flight. It fell to the floor as if it had struck an invisible wall. Mahon made another movement, lashing out at Colin. Colin felt something strike him, knocking him flat as he was sent skidding across the floor. Quickly, he rolled over and scrambled to another archway, glancing cautiously around the edge. Mahon spotted him and made another striking movement. Unconsciously, Colin moved as if to block the blow. He felt it as he was knocked sideways, but he had somehow blunted its force and kept from being smashed flat as he had been before. Concentrating, Colin unleashed a pair of blows of his own, calling upon the air, mentally shaping it, focusing it, compressing it before releasing it. The first blow flattened the Serpent, but it was up again instantly, hissing its fury. The second blow merely staggered Mahon, who threw up a hand to block it.

Mahon threw back his head and laughed. "Very good, mantle-bearer! Where did you learn that? What hidden library have you uncovered? But why fight me? You must see that you can't harm me. Yield to me. With our combined power, there will be none who can stand against us! Wealth? Comfort? Women? What would you like? It can all be yours. You and I, we will rule the earth!"

Colin scrambled back, trying to stay out of view. He didn't see any point in talking, unless he could somehow distract Mahon. "How about Krainik?" he called out. "Isn't that the offer you made him?"

Colin closed his eyes, trying to find Mahon's true-self, hoping to find some weakness to attack. He saw him immediately. Colin shook his head. Compared to the others, this was no light. If anything, it was a black hole, its presence distinguished more by a lack of light than by any illumination it offered. This was a shrunken, mottled orb. Orange, green and brown splotches moved angrily across its surface. Colin could see the connections as well. Two were obvious. A powerful bond to the Serpent and an intriguing thread to Krainik. There seemed to be some kind of bi-directional flow. The deep violet bond he had seen between the Tree and everyone else connected Mahon to Krainik. Flowing from Mahon to Krainik. Overlaying this was another kind of connection, like veins on the first. Colin's impression was that it was the sense of will, and it flowed from Krainik to Mahon. There was no connection from either of them to The Tree of Life.

Mahon was puzzled. He could not find the true-self of this interloper. "Where are you mantle-bearer? Why can I not see you? I know you're there. Join me. Rule with me."

Mahon could clearly see the other eleven forms scattered across the plaza. Twelve if he counted the Serpent. That presence was so unique as to be unmistakable. But where was his enemy? He had seen him with his natural eyes, why was his true-self hidden? There he was! At the doorway! Mahon made a sweeping gesture. The wall of air caught Colin full in the back, sending him flying out of the cavern to sprawl headlong into the mouth of the stairway up which the Council had come a few minutes ago. Mahon was irritated. That blow should have crushed his enemy, not sent him sprawling.

Colin tried again. He sent his mind lancing into the malignant sphere of Mahon's true self, but he couldn't penetrate. The surface just slid away from him, almost like the sap of The Tree of Life. However hard he tried, his attempts were just shunted to the side, yet Mahon still seemed to be completely unaware of his presence. This was getting him nowhere.

The Serpent was advancing now, the arrow protruding in an almost comical manner from between its eyes, giving it a cross-eyed look. Colin saw this, but without humor. Too late, he saw that sweeping gesture of Mahon's arm and again found himself knocked forward to land amongst the prostrate forms of the Council. He landed heavily across Lucinda Yearsley, grateful to her bulk for breaking his fall. He rolled off her. She looked at him, horrified.

"The impostor!" She squeaked, "You're the cause of all this!"

Colin looked at her, disgusted, "Don't be an idiot your whole life. Take the rest of the day off."

He lunged to the side, catching the movement from Mahon in time. Councilor Yearsley and two others were knocked forward, landing at the very feet of Mahon. He snarled in anger.

The stairway suddenly belched forth a stream of armed men. Colin was shocked to see the Regent in the lead. He barely had time to yell, "NO! Go back!"

He saw Mahon's fist pound downward in a crushing movement. Colin threw out an arm as if he would block it. The Regent and Arbor Guards were hurled sprawling in all directions. None of them was moving. Colin launched himself at Gareth, dragging him back out of sight in the mouth of the stairs. He was unconscious.

"You!"

He whirled. Dalene stood there, two steps below him. A ribbon of blood darkened the left shoulder of her gown, but the sword she held menacingly never wavered, ready to thrust it into Colin.

"Four thousand years my sisters prevented this! Then you! I trusted you! My mother trusted you! I was a fool! I ignored the prophecy. I yielded my heart! To you! And you made me part of this! You've destroyed my father! You've destroyed Aidon! I should have let you die. I should have killed you!"

She jerked the sword back as if preparing to thrust.

"If you really believe all that, then get on with it! Kill me! I won't stop you! Use your head! Stop being a slave to that stupid prophecy! They got it all wrong. It was corrupted. I've seen the real prophecy. Your whole life you thought you'd cut yourself off from ever bonding with anyone for fear of that prophecy! The reality is you've given yourself so totally to serving Aidon that you're bonded to every person here! I know. I've seen it. Seen your true-self! You were never going to cause the destruction of Aidon, you're the only hope they have! Forget the prophecy, listen to your heart! Either kill me or help me, but we're out of time!"

The blade might have dropped - just a fraction, but she steadied it, "What have you done to my father?" she accused.

"Not me," he objected with a jerk of his head. "Him. Them."

Dalene craned her neck to see past him, across the top of the stairs. She paled at the sight of the huge Serpent, weaving forward slowly.

"Do something!" she squeaked.

"There's a thought," he mumbled. Somehow he had retained his grip on the bow. He hadn't had much success getting at Mahon, but maybe he could take the Serpent out of the game. In a flash, he released two arrows.

"NO!" came the roar from Mahon, accompanied by a shriek of pain from the Serpent and a renewal of angry hissing. It thrashed blindly, knocking several of the Councilors across the floor and nearly crushing Rabin. The three arrows now formed a straight line - one through each eye and one in the center of the forehead.

"Can it not be killed?" Dalene asked.

Colin shook his head. "Don't think so. Elias said it was bonded to Mahon. Got to kill 'em both, and I can't get at Mahon."

"Who's Elias?"

"Long story. Have to wait."

Desperately, Colin thought. When he had gone after Mahon, tried to attack his true-self, he had seemed like the sap from the Tree. He could get near him - maybe even a molecule away, but he could never quite touch him. He just slipped away - like trying to grab the Tree covered with sap. He just slid right off. But Halvor had been able to touch the tree. He grimaced. That had ended rather badly, but he was running out of time and ideas.

"I need your help. I don't think we can hurt Mahon. Not here. If we have any chance at all of defeating him, it will have to be by going after his true-self."

Dalene was confused, "But, that means we have to either get hold of him or lure him down to The Ruling Box of Aidon. It won't work."

Colin saw Mahon make that smashing motion again. He reacted, thrusting back hard. The counter-blow staggered Mahon, even sending the Serpent back several yards. They remained safe for the moment.

"No. We can do it from here. I think. I can find him, but he's blind to me. You have to link with me. For some reason I can't touch him, but I think you can. I can hide you - get you inside his defenses before he knows you're attacking. I can get you to him, but you'll have to kill him. You're going to have to thrust with everything you've got. You're going to have to want to shred him. Destroy him completely. Can you do it?"

"I think so. I'll try. Are you sure about this?"

He grinned, "Not at all. But I never wanted to live forever anyway. I'm going to try and hit him once more, knock him off balance. Maybe it will buy us some time, then we go. OK?"

She tried to smile, "OK, yes. Alright. It will be OK. Promise?"

He flashed her a quick smile, then lunged to his feet, lashing out with both hands, mustering all the power he could. The Serpent flew backwards, sprawling into Mahon. At the last moment, Mahon attempted to block the blow, the result being that the Serpent was buffeted from both sides. Immediately Colin dropped.

"Ready?" he asked.

She nodded and he grabbed both her hands. They closed their eyes, and Colin saw her true-self. "Man, she's beautiful." He thought. He could see the tentative probe she sent out. Immediately he embraced it, wrapping his light-form protectively around her, shielding her. She was blind, enveloped in a velvety shroud of blackness. She trusted him, allowed herself to be carried, and he raced toward that malignant thing which seemed to glow with even greater power and venom than it had before. He shepherded her to the very edge of the orb, feeling unclean in its proximity. He kept himself wrapped tightly around the form that was Dalene. Mentally, he caressed her, hugged her, and then.......released her.

There was no hesitation. She launched herself at Mahon's true-self, lancing through this undulating shell, striking at his very core. Somewhere, they heard him scream, but she was not distracted. She found herself immersed in a maelstrom of filth. The vileness of it repulsed her, but rather than retreat, she burrowed deeper, lashing out at everything she could see, everything she could touch. She felt him shred, pieces of his self flying into oblivion. She channeled her hatred of all that he stood for, and her love of all that she held dear into this paroxysm of destruction, unleashing everything she was and felt in destroying this nightmare.

And suddenly, it was gone. Colin's eyes flared open just in time to see Mahon, standing rigid and erect on the throne, stiffen spasmodicaly and topple over the edge. The three fatal wounds in its head, and its link to life now cut, the Serpent thrashed wildly, and then lay still. Colin slumped to the floor, exhaustion and relief causing him to collapse.

A movement caught his attention and he desperately tried to roll over, to protect Dalene, but from his awkward angle lying on the stairs, he knew he would be too late. An expression of pure malevolence on his face, Lijah Krainik stood with raised sword. It was already descending in the fatal arc that would kill both of them, but the blade suddenly fell off to the side and Krainik stared down in horror at the steel protruding from his abdomen, his spine cleanly separated. Gareth Tregard grabbed him by the hair and jerked the blade free, throwing the paralyzed form down the stair behind him. "Never touch my daughter, you scum!" he growled and then collapsed on the floor beside her.

Chapter 30   Life and Death

They were still lying there when the Arbor Guards came up from below. The soldiers from Kernsidon had put up fierce resistance. The Regent and a few men had fought through, managing to gain the stairs, but the rest, badly outnumbered, had battled furiously, unwilling to have an active enemy to their rear when they ascended. The arrival of the sprawling corpse of Councilor Krainik caused them to redouble their efforts and the last of the enemy had been dispatched, freeing them to charge up the stairs. At first they thought the three still forms were dead. Several of the Council up on the patio were staggering to their feet, staring about, dazed. Kyle Malof was one of the last to climb up, clutching a shallow wound in his side. A deeper cut in his left thigh slowed him considerably. Still, he was the first to kneel by the Regent, cradling his head gently. "Sir," he coaxed. "Are you alright?"

Gareth, slowly opened his eyes, squinting now against the evening sun, low against the western cliffs. He smiled, "You made it, eh? Good man, Kyle. The others? How did we fare?"

"We lost some, sir. I haven't had time to get a full tally."

"You have time now, son. See to the men. I'll be fine." He sat up and reached for his daughter.

Kyle eyed the third form on the stairs and prodded it with his boot. "How about this one, sir? Do we take him prisoner?"

"Prisoner! By the twin moons, man, if not for him we'd all be dead by now! Just leave him. See to the men."

Colin struggled to sit up. He immediately reached for Dalene as well, concern etched on his face. "Is she OK? Alright, I mean. She was the one who did it. I couldn't reach him, but she could. She destroyed Mahon. Is she alright?"

Dalene moaned, her brow furrowed in pain, but her eyes crept open.

Colin smiled, "For a moment there, I thought you were dead."

She smiled weakly, "I think I was, and I liked it there. Except the scenery here is better."

Colin smiled. "Welcome back then. You did it. He's gone."

"Then it's really over?" she asked.

He shrugged, "Is anything ever really over? That threat is gone, I think. But there's more to do. We need to hurry."

The three of them struggled to their feet, assisted by the guards. Weak though he was, the Regent didn't hesitate to issue commands. "Throw that thing," he indicated the inert corpse of the Serpent, "over the edge. Whatever's left when it hits the bottom, have it hauled away and buried deep. I want it out of the Valley."

He limped over to The Lawgiver's Throne and hesitated, but resigned himself. This once, he would have to sit there. He had to speak to the people of Aidon and this was the fastest way. "People of Aidon!" His voice thundered through the Valley. "We have faced a grave crisis. King Mahon was evil, bent on destroying all that we love. He has been vanquished through the valiant efforts of my daughter, The Lady Dalene and the true mantle-bearer, Colin Ericsson. Mahon was in league with the Serpent. Traitors among us helped him, bringing us to the very brink of destruction."

The assembled guards managed to drag the Serpent's corpse to the far edge of the court and heave it over the rail. They could hear the shouts of alarm as it rebounded down the face of the cliff, landing with a sodden thud at its base.

The Regent continued, "Our victory was not without cost. Several of our Arbor Guards have been wounded. Some have been killed. Nor is our struggle over. Even now, our people on the western border are fighting the invading army of Kernsidon. We would have peace, if they would let us alone, but if they bring war, we will give them death. Our people must have reinforcements. I call upon all able men to go to their aid at once. I shall lead a party myself, on the morrow."

"Now is a time for unity. We must draw together. We must support each other. This entire matter will be investigated once our borders are again secure. A general Evaluation will be held and each File will determine whether or not they wish to select a new Councilor. For now, I shall act as Regent, until a replacement is chosen. Councilor Krainik has been killed. He was cohort with Mahon and the Serpent. The immediate threat has passed, but we have others looming. My people, return to your homes. Prepare our defenses. Support our armies in any way that you can, so that peace and freedom can be restored to Aidon. For now, I bid you farewell."

He stepped down from the Throne, pausing for a moment to rest a hand on its arm. "I never thought to sit there," he said. "I hope to never do so again, but perhaps one day, I might be fortunate enough to see The One whose right it is to occupy this seat, and then will my heart be glad."

Colin walked to the edge where he could look down at the Tree of Life. It seemed stark and barren. So many leaves had been lost. He closed his eyes and could see how little life remained in it. He remembered something he'd seen. It was right after he had emerged from the rock, back in the barren cavern. He whirled and headed that direction. There, against the back wall, he saw it, the inscription. *Living Water*. But there was no water, only a smooth, bare wall. Off to the side more of the story was revealed. A basin. A fountain of sorts, sheared cleanly from where it had been mounted. Dalene and her father, trailed by several of the Council and a few of the guards followed him into the alcove where they stared about, curious.

"Help me," Colin said as he struggled to lift the stone basin.

The guards offered eager hands as they took the weight from him.

"Over here," he commanded, "under the inscription. Hold it tight against the wall."

They did so. Colin stared at the spot, then without hesitating, he rammed his fingers into the solid stone, anticipating the searing pain, but ignoring it. He heard the others gasp, but he ignored that as well. His eyes closed now as he concentrated, feeling for something inside the granite, trying to see. Ah! There. He found it. He reached for it, a ribbon of incredible intensity. Light beyond anything imaginable. He grasped it, wrapping it around his fingers and pulling it, opening a channel for it within the mountain, drawing it through the rock, until it burst forth, sparkling and tinkling into the stone basin. He released the thread of *Living Water* he had brought forth and stroked the shorn edge of the basin, blending and welding it seamlessly back onto the stone face from whence it had been torn. The water overflowed, filling the trough and flowing toward the Throne.

At last, Colin broke the contact. He was so tired, but there was no time to waste. He turned back, facing the wide-eyed stares of those who witnessed what he had just done. Gareth shook his head, "How is such a thing possible?"

Colin could only shrug. "I'm not sure. Elias said there used to be those who could carve air and stone." He looked at Dalene, "Do you have that heart I sent you?"

She nodded, reached in her pocket and withdrew the shimmering, white heart, holding it out to him in her open palm.

He didn't take it, just looked at it for a moment. "It was your gift, you know. The corn, salt and oil. Or at least, what they represented. It wasn't your power that healed me, any more than it's my power that carves rock or pulls the water from it. There's a higher power, but love is the conduit through which it flows. Your love of life. Compassion for someone you didn't even know. My love for freedom and for a people who had made me feel like I belonged, even when I didn't. Somehow, here, in this place, the impossible is simply difficult, but not impossible. The love of your Messias - our Messiah - and of a Father who loves us enough to allow us to choose, even when we choose to reject him, that's what has saved us all."

"But not all of us," Dalene said softly.

"All of us who choose to follow Him," Colin replied. "On this earth, or another. In this life or the next. In the eternal scheme, it doesn't matter. All of us."

"I hope you're right, Colin. Oh, how I hope you're right."

Colin couldn't seem to rebound from the exhaustion that was dragging him down. He shook it off as much as he could. There just was no time! "Now, I need your help. Gareth, sir? Could you ask the Arbor Guards to help me? I need all the helmets you can gather up. I know they're tired, but I need all of them - even from the floors below. I want them filled with water from this fountain, then follow me."

The guards heard the request. They shrugged, but hurried to comply. Several went down the stairs to gather the helmets from their fallen comrades as well as the enemy soldiers.

"Everyone," Colin urged, "Grab a helmet, two if you can manage. Fill them up and come with me." Even the Councilors were pressed into service, some eagerly and some with a great show of reluctance. But soon there was a procession hurrying down the stairs. They passed through the third level, through the broken doors and into the second level. There! He saw what he was looking for. Colin dashed over to the window. He was certain this was the spot, but Halvor was so thoroughly encased in sap he was hardly discernible. If there was anything to be grateful for, the flow of sap had practically stopped as the tree began to die. It was dried now, minimizing the risk to himself or others. He carefully set the two helmets full of water that he had been carrying on the floor against the wall.

He climbed into the window, but Dalene called out, "You can't! The branches are broken! It's too far to jump. You'll be killed!" She had spent many hours sitting at this window, and she knew.

Colin glanced back at her, grateful for her concern, "It's a small risk. I can jump pretty far, and right now my life isn't as valuable as it might be. I'll be alright."

He leaped, catching the broken branch stub and pulling himself into the tree. He shuddered. He hated heights. "Alright, now find something to use as a pole. Drape the chin-strap of the helmet over it and start passing them out to me. As soon as we empty a couple, I want relays running back up to the top level to refill them until I tell you to stop. If you can find some buckets, that would even be better. You got it?"

The guards didn't understand, but they "got it." They managed to find two poles, so while Colin was pouring water from one helmet, another was already being replaced and extended to him. The Arbor Guards were eager. They had no idea what he was up to, but they knew whatever it was, it was for their fallen comrade, so they raced up and down the stairs with a will. Dalene thought she knew what he was trying to do. She was afraid to hope, for it was truly hopeless. Still, she busied herself loading and unloading helmets onto the poles.

Colin's arms, neck and shoulders ached. His thighs were screaming from squatting on his precarious perch. Still he worked. There was no time! Sap still seeped from some of the wounds on the Tree. There was no one else who could do this, not without risking becoming trapped, just as Halvor had been. Helmet after helmet was trickled out and with each sluicing, a fraction of the hardened sap was being washed away. Colin could see Halvor's face clearly now. His eyes were closed, his brow furrowed. By all appearances, he was dead. Colin refused to believe that and continued his ministrations. The face was clear now, the water soaking in and softening the sap more efficiently. Halvor's forehead moved. His nose twitched and the eyes struggled to open, still glued shut by the sap. Colin released a huge breath. He was alive! He continued to pour water and the eyes finally opened, then the mouth.

"GAAHH!! That itches something fierce!" he growled.

"Halvor!" Dalene shrieked. "You're alive! Oh, praise Messias! I never thought it possible!"

The news that Halvor was alive and speaking injected new vigor into the water carriers. Even Councilor Yearsley quickened her pace. The *Living Water*, applied so liberally to Halvor's head, had been flowing down across his body, softening the sap there as well. Once his head was clear, the rest went more quickly. In another half hour he was free and had been pulled to a more secure perch on the broken limbs.

"No other way," Colin told him. "You've got to jump. Wait. Hold onto the pole. When I count to three, you jump. The guards on the other end will pull. They should be able to heave you across the gap. Ready? One. Two. Three!"

Eager hands pulled strongly on the pole, jerking him so hard he flew clear through the window, softening his landing by piling on top of his fellow guards, who rolled around laughing and cheering. Gareth wrapped his son in a tremendous hug. Dalene joined in. She whispered, "I never believed it possible. I thought to never see you again."

Tears flowed down all of their faces. Colin was quite forgotten for the moment. He was tired. So very tired. Still, he thought he could make it. He launched himself out over space, smashing into the wall just below the window. The guards heard the impact and his grunt of pain and leaped to help haul him in, grabbing the hands and wrist before he slipped. He landed in an undignified heap on the floor.

Dalene rushed to him as he struggled to his feet. "Thank you. For bringing him back to us. We wouldn't have even tried. How did you know?"

Colin brushed himself off, wincing at his new bruises. "I didn't. But I think the Tree draws its strength from the *Living Water*. It seemed that if anything could cut through that sap and free your brother, that was the one thing that stood a chance."

Gareth embraced Colin. "Thank you. You've restored my son back to me."

Dalene said, "If only we had mother." She regretted it the moment the words were out. She couldn't help it.

Halvor was immediately alarmed. "What's happened to mother? Where is she?"

Dalene bit her lip. She was trying so hard not to cry. Her father wrapped an arm comfortingly around her, "The Council. Councilor Krainik. They destroyed her."

The mood instantly changed from jubilation to gloom. Halvor whirled on the Councilors who had been busily hauling water to help free him, "You! You destroyed my mother?!? She was better than all of you put together! By what right………" his voice trailed off as his father squeezed his arm.

"It's alright, son. They were deceived. They followed the law with precision. Following blindly can paint some of the most terrible deeds in shades of righteousness, and make some of the noblest actions appear black. I've been guilty myself. So have you. Your mother, I'm afraid, was one of the casualties of this war."

Colin had been listening in silence. He knew that his actions had been the cause for much of what had befallen Beatrice. "Take me to her," he said simply.

******

Elam drifted in and out of consciousness. The sound of battle seemed so distant, but he kept being kicked and trampled. The searing pain in his head made him want to scream, but his face was pressed in the dirt. He tried to rise, at least to roll over. Something smashed him flat and he felt bones snap. He did scream then, for a brief instant before the blackness swept him away once more.

The next time he awoke, he was cold. He was shivering uncontrollably, sending spasms of pain shooting through his body, especially his arm and head. He felt he must surely suffocate if he couldn't get his face out of the mud. The stench was overpowering and he had to fight the waves of nausea. He was certain that if he threw up now, it would rip his body apart. Gasping with the effort, he finally managed to roll over. A moan of pain escaped his lips as he sucked in the fresh air. It was night. Darker shadows hovered over him. "Here's one," a voice said.

"Take him then," was the reply.

Elam tried to speak, but rough hands grabbed him. He felt the bones grind in his left arm. He started to scream, but it was cut off by the blackness.

Elam was floating and he had no idea how it was possible. He liked this place. There was no blackness. Everything was white. It was so peaceful here, and he didn't hurt. He just wanted to rest. Here, everything was alright. But the pain began to gnaw at the edges of his consciousness. He tried to ignore it. Tried to push it away, but it persisted. Suddenly a great wave of pain lifted him, propelling him out of his white refuge and launched him once more into the place where darkness and pain dwelt. His eyes opened and he was staring at a small window. He head felt like it was coming apart. He tried to sit up but he was too weak. The effort made him gasp. The darker shadow was back. A soft, woman's voice spoke, "You're awake then? Here. Drink some of this. It will help with the pain."

He drank. It was terribly bitter and he tried to push it away. A soft laugh, "Awful, isn't it? Finish it. I'll give you some water to wash it down with."

The water tasted good and helped to clear his head almost immediately.

"Where am I?" he asked.

"In Troas, of course. You were wounded in the battle. They've been half the night bringing in the injured. You were one of the last. They thought you were dead."

"Then the city didn't fall? Have we won?"

The voice sighed deeply, "I don't know. Troas didn't fall, but the enemy didn't quit either. They were fighting their way south, toward Tyber. We haven't heard anything more."

At the mention of Tyber, Elam lurched as if to rise. Firm hands pressed him back. "Lie still. You must rest."

"Sorry," he said. "My mother..........she's in Tyber. That's where I'm from."

"I'm sorry. The army held here. Maybe they can push them back from Tyber as well. I'm sure your mother has already evacuated, but you must rest."

Elam didn't want to rest. His mother.......father.......where were they? Were they alright? He fought the darkness which tried to envelop him, but in the end, the blackness won. Elam slept.

The next time he awoke, it was daylight. He looked around. He was in a barn. It was neatly kept but he saw no livestock. Gingerly, he rolled over, gathering his knees under him. Nausea threatened to defeat him, but he fought it back. He managed to rise unsteadily to his feet. His vision was blurred but he held his balance. Slowly, he made it to the doorway. He was so startled by the voice he almost fell, "You shouldn't be up," it scolded. "If you fall I'm not strong enough to drag you back to bed."

Elam caught himself on the edge of the door. An elderly lady stood at the corner of the barn, an orange fringe decorating her skirt and a basket of eggs hanging over one arm. She glared at him disapprovingly. "I.......I'm sorry. I had to get up. I need the privy," he explained.

"Hmmph," she huffed. "I'd have done for you, but since you're up, I guess it'll save me the trouble. Come along then."

She set down her basket and offered an arm for him to lean on. His left arm was in a splint and his head was heavily bandaged. Using his right arm, he brushed a hanging corner of the bandage back from his face and was relieved to see it did a remarkable job of clearing his vision. She escorted him slowly to the privy and to the wash basin afterwards.

"Use the soap," she ordered. "Helps a lot with the cleaning."

He picked it up and stared at it. "My mother makes soap," he said, feeling foolish as he did so.

"That's right. You said you were from Tyber, didn't you? Then you must be Miran's boy. Unless you're Kath's boy, but I don't recall she said she had any youngsters."

"You know my mother?" he asked.

"Miran, I'm guessing. Oh, sure. Set me up in business, she did. Making soap. Made my life a lot easier. My man's been dead now better than two years. Been tough running the farm. Been easier since I started making soap. Now I can hire some of the heavy work to be done."

"You farm? But you're of the 7th File," he said, indicating her orange border.

"Yep. Folks in the File kind of looked down on my man for it. But he liked farming. Came from farming stock. His folks were from Tyber. Why we settled here. Couldn't live in Tyber, him being 7th File, but this was close. You're up kind of late for breakfast, but you ought to eat. Come in, I'll fix you something."

She escorted him to the house. It was a tidy home. She told him her name was Leah. After the battle, the older men from Troas who hadn't been fighting scoured the battlefield looking for any who had been wounded. They had spent much of the night getting them to Troas and securing aid and shelter for them. Elam had been the last one brought in. Troas was full of wounded so they had brought Elam here, to Leah.

"I don't think they figured you to live," she told him.

Elam felt better after eating. Leah gave him some more of the bitter drink, which helped to keep the pain at bay. After he ate she brought a basin of warm water and gently soaked the blood encrusted bandages from his head. She tsk'd in a disapproving manner as she examined the wound. "Came close. A little deeper and I'd have gotten more sleep last night. Didn't trust my old eyes to do the stitching last night, but this one needs it. What do you think, boy, you tough enough?"

Leah stitched Elam's head, clucking like an old hen the entire time. Sweat was pouring down his face by the time she was done. He felt feverish. It didn't take any effort on Leah's part to get him back to bed.

Something kept butting him. Elam tried to ignore it. He wanted to sleep, but it persisted. Until he was jerked awake by Leah's shrill scream, "Get away from him you filthy beast! Get out! Get back!"

Alarmed, Elam tried to shove himself backward, away from the danger. In the dim light of the barn, it took a moment for his eyes to focus. "Midnight!" he yelled.

Ignoring the pain, he scrambled to his knees and threw his good arm around the horse's neck. "It's alright, Leah! It's Midnight! He's my friend. My horse."

Just then Elam heard the pound of hooves outside the barn. His eyes snapped over to the door in time to see Hiat and Steve burst through the door.

"Told you!" Hiat crowed. "The way Midnight was acting, I knew he was alive. Led us straight here!"

Steve snorted, "Straight here! We spent half the day following that horse!"

Leah bristled, "If that creature belongs to you, get it away from my patient! He's a sick boy!"

Hiat grinned. "Not ours. It belongs to him, and that's no boy. Your patient is the man who probably changed the course of the whole war when he killed General Boris, who just happened to be the commander of this particular invasion!"

Hiat walked over and acted as if he was about to pound Elam on the back to congratulate him, but Elam cringed so badly, he laid a gentle hand on his shoulder instead.

"We've been worried about you. Right after you shot, you took a spear right in the head. Everyone thought sure you were dead. Bob caught Midnight and we kept fighting. We started looking for you as soon as it was over, but it was Midnight that found you."

"Over?" Elam asked stupidly. "Did we win?"

"Sure we won!" Steve said. "After you killed the general, things were pretty confused. We hoped it would end there, but a second column broke through from the south flank and connected up. About the same time another column linked up from the rear. We thought we were really going to have a rough time of it then. It was a mess, but it seemed like they kind of forgot about Troas. The whole mass started rolling towards Tyber," he shook his head. "But things actually turned out to work in our favor. Dathan was leading reinforcements from Salem. Jack had ridden ahead of the troops he got moving from Jordanon and Sarepta. They had just come through Tyber when they ran head-on into the Kernsidon army. With their general dead, the commanders spent as much time fighting each other as they did planning any strategy to attack us. Our forces from the south had them pinned and we were chewing their flank to shreds. They had a choice - surrender or be killed. They surrendered."

"Did you see my father? Is he alright?"

Hiat shook his head, "Haven't seen him since the battle yesterday. He was fine then. I don't want you to worry, Elam, he's probably alright, but we lost some good men. Willam didn't make it. Bob and Jeffs, too. Victory is rarely cheap, and it's never free. You have to be prepared for that."

The mood in the barn sobered considerably. Leah huffed around for a minute, still not liking the way Midnight kept nuzzling her patient. But she soon warmed enough to insist on feeding "the boy," as she persisted in calling Elam and made a show of grudgingly inviting Hiat and Steve in to be fed as well. The twinkle in her eye belied her gruff manner.

First thing in the morning, Hiat and Steve rode off. They had been assigned to check on the wounded in Troas and then make a sweep of the northern border to ensure that no other enemy columns remained a threat. After the excitement of their visit, Elam felt an oppressing sense of loneliness. His physical reserves were very low, forcing inactivity which gave his mind too much time to feed his fears. He became drowsy sitting in the morning sun and drifted off to sleep. He was floating, but again something was gnawing at the edge of his conscious. This time it wasn't pain. It was soft and warm, almost as peaceful as the white region in which he had been drifting. His eyes opened slowly to see a familiar silhouette outlined against the sun. "Mother?"

"Hello, son. I was starting to think you were going to sleep forever," she said softly.

He sat up, pressing his face against her shoulder as the tears came. "What are you doing here?"

She stroked the back of his neck gently, "I've been in Troas since the start of the battle - making arrows. I knew you and your father were here, and I figured I had seen more arrows made than just about anyone here. If you were fighting for Aidon, I didn't want you running out of arrows because I wasn't doing my part, so I came."

His voice was muffled because he didn't want to take his head from her shoulder. "What about father? Have you heard anything?"

She smiled, "Well, you could ask him."

Elam's head jerked up to look into the face of his father, kneeling a few feet away. A jagged cut angled down across his forehead, creasing the bridge of his nose before ending on the opposite cheekbone. It had been stitched shut and the area around the left eye was swollen and terribly discolored, but he was smiling.

"So, what will it be? Farming or soldiering?" Jorge asked.

Elam struggled to free his good arm and throw it around his father's neck. His answer was almost a sob, "I just want to go home!"

******

Gareth was grateful to see the two Arbor Guards still on watch outside the room where his wife remained. He knew it had to have been hard for them to stay, guarding this woman while their comrades raced into battle. It was a tribute to their character that they had remained, placing value on a life that no longer had value. Halvor's fury momentarily abated, swallowed up by a sense of infinite loss and sadness as he hugged his unresponsive and uncomprehending mother. Colin thought his own heart must surely break. There were many things which had happened for which he felt no responsibility. Others had made choices. Many blamed him for everything. But of all that had occurred, this alone rested solely on his shoulders and the burden was crushing him. It did no good that Gareth had assured him repeatedly that this was done by his enemies in an effort to strike at him. Colin knew that was true, but he also knew that if it were not for his own choices, his own actions, that avenue of attack would never have been opened for Krainik to exploit. He almost wished that Dalene or Halvor would lash out at him, give voice to the guilt which consumed him. It was almost worse that they instead hugged him and tried to whisper words of comfort to him. The tears slowly fell as he knelt beside what remained of this kind, generous woman. "I am so sorry. If I could take it all back, if I could do it over again, I would spare you this."

Dalene squeezed his shoulder, "No, you couldn't. Mother was right. You had to be here." She shuddered, "I can't imagine what would have happened if you hadn't been. If Mahon had succeeded.........."

Gareth placed a heavy hand on his back, "She's right. We all could have chosen differently, but there's no telling what the outcome would have been. My wife would have chosen this even had she known. She would have said the price was worth it."

Colin couldn't accept it. He gently took Beatrice's hands in his, closed his eyes, silently begging her forgiveness. Unbidden, he was suddenly viewing her true-self, or what remained of it. It had no glory, none of its former brilliance. It was a wounded, dying thing. A life, but without direction. He reached out to touch it, trying to offer some measure of comfort, but she simply slipped away at his approach. He could do nothing. He became aware of the other three lights, the glowing power of Gareth and his two children. He saw the powerful bonds that tied them together and realized that even now, they held onto that vital connection to their wife and mother. Beatrice was no longer able to feed that connection, but the strength of these three maintained it. For a brief second, Colin felt an incredible sense of loneliness. He was connected to no one, nothing, in this manner. He simply didn't belong here. He yearned for that connection. He reached. He couldn't make the contact for himself, but perhaps he could wrap himself, just for a moment, in the bond that connected these four. It closed around him like a fluid. It flowed around and through him. He was too grateful to be amazed. While he could not seem to make contact with the individuals, he found comfort in being able to immerse himself in the twining of the connections they had with each other. For an instant, he felt a part of it, and then he was swept along the common thread into the core of

Beatrice. It was not the lifeless sphere he had thought it to be. It was a tortured, violent place. A soul in search of itself and unable to find it. It screamed its defiance of the waiting void, refusing to surrender, but lacking direction to fight back. He saw the broken pattern of what once was. She could no longer fight, but Colin could. He pulled the delicate connection more tightly around him. Just as he had protected Dalene, hidden her as she attacked Mahon, so now did he hide himself in the power and illumination of Halvor, Gareth and Dalene. He launched himself into space. He shielded himself, flowing within the strands which led to The Tree of Life. Already he could see the change, the Waters of Life nourishing and restoring the Tree. Here, where all life on earth connected, he found fragments of light. Flashing, unconnected bits of energy, scattered and unorganized, photons of intelligence seeking a home. At the speed of light, he touched and tasted fragments, seeking those which fit the damaged form to which he was still linked. Like cells rushing to repair a wound, he channeled these bits through the connection, back to Beatrice, to her true-self, fitting them into the ruptured pattern. As he built, the pattern became more defined, the incorporation of the missing pieces accelerated. Her energy flowed, her intellect directed him. He had no sense of time, just an urgent need to complete the pattern. To re-build what had been destroyed.

At last, it was done. He paused now. The vibrancy of what he saw took his breath away. It was finished. He opened his eyes, staring full into the brilliant eyes of Beatrice, wet with tears and shining with intelligence. "Thank you, son, for bringing me back."

Colin slumped against her knees. He was enveloped once again. Not in patterns of light, but in arms of flesh and blood. All of them were sobbing now. Dalene was whispering in a choked voice, "How did you do it? It has never been done. It's not even possible."

Exhaustion threatened to collapse him. He couldn't even lift his head. "That which has happened, is possible. Not me. You. All of you. Your love made it possible. I see patterns, but you molded a heart from stone."

A new voice spoke gently, "Was there enough time, mantle-bearer?"

It took a moment, but Colin finally managed to raise his head, a tired smile at his lips, he spoke slowly, but with warmth, "Elias! You really were right behind me, weren't you? Wish you'd have been in front. Elias, may I introduce Gareth Tregard, Regent of Aidon, his wife, Beatrice, son, Halvor and The Lady of Prophecy, his daughter, The Lady Dalene. Beatrice, this is who you've really been waiting for. This is Elias, the Prophet from Kernsidon. The true mantle-bearer and messenger of Messias. If I ever had a message for you, this is it: Listen to Elias."

Elias came over to him, resting a hand lightly on his head. "It's enough, Colin. Rest now. You've completed your task. Rest."

Colin shook his head, "Not yet. No time. Please. Just a little more. One last thing."

He gripped Elias tightly by the hand, closing his eyes. They remained like that for a very long time. The others in the room hardly dared to breathe. More than an hour passed. As Colin slumped to the floor, Dalene and Halvor were instantly at his side. His eyes slowly opened and in a weak voice said, "Elias, you were right. There was time. Just enough time."

Elias dropped to his knees beside him, tears brimming his eyes, "Mary. Thank you, mantle-bearer, for giving me back my sister."

Colin's voice was no more than a whisper now, "Teach them, Elias. They've been waiting a long time." He turned his head, slowly, to look at Dalene. He wasn't in pain, but he was so tired. "Thank you, for these few weeks of life. I wouldn't trade them for anything."

And then his eyes closed one last time.

Epilogue

The day was cold. Rob stood with his arm wrapped around his wife, staring down at the blue-green ribbon of the Flathead River, some hundred feet below. It was late fall. The water was low. The river appeared almost sluggish. He had looked at it many times over these past months. It didn't seem possible that such a beautiful river could have claimed the life of his brother. This would be his last trip. With all the witnesses and the extensive search, the court had declared Colin dead without dragging it out. Rob had been the executor of the estate. There wasn't a lot. The house had been sold along with Colin's truck and motorcycle. A few personal belongings Rob kept. His sisters had a few keepsakes as well, but much of it had simply been given away. There had been a quiet memorial service – mostly family. It was over, but Rob wanted to come here one last time, though he couldn't explain why.

"It still doesn't seem right." Lisa insisted. "It's just not that big of a river. They should have been able to find his body."

Rob shrugged, "You would think so. But the flood of 1964 washed half the railroad into the river. There are still places where he could have gotten hung up on twisted metal, or washed under an overhang and pinned by the current. If it was his time to go, he would have approved of the setting. He always claimed he wanted his body dropped in the Great Slave Lake wilderness up in Canada. He would have settled for this."

"I know. But it still doesn't feel right," she replied.

"No. It doesn't. But maybe he's happy now. You know, after Rita died, Colin was kind of a wreck. Oh, he functioned OK, but emotionally, he was devastated. I thought he was healing, but when Mom and Dad were killed so soon after, it was like something just broke. He couldn't seem to connect with any of the family – not like before. I kept hoping he'd get better. It wasn't like he didn't love us – the family – but he'd be sitting right there beside us, and you could tell he was still alone. There was a gulf there that none of us could bridge. He knew it. I could tell. But he didn't know how to get across it either."

They stood silently for a few minutes. Lisa said, "I was packing some of his books this week – the ones you wanted to save. I was putting them in a box when an old sheet of paper fell out of one. It was a story. I'd read it a long time ago, but I always kind of liked it. You probably remember it, too. It was about a little boy who used to call 'Information,' whenever he had a problem. The information lady sort of became like a grandmother to him. When his pet bird died, he called, and she told him that there were other worlds to sing in. It helped him feel better to think of death that way. He grew up and moved away, but years later he made contact with her again. When he called one day, she had died, but the message she had left for him was the same thing. She told him, 'I still say, there are other worlds to sing in.'"

Rob nodded, accepting the message. "Maybe so. I hope Colin found some other world to sing in."

******

Gareth, Beatrice and Halvor sat and basked in the warm glow that seemed to emanate from The Tree of Life. The statue of the cherubim had been replaced. The original, of course, had been completely shattered, so a new one had been lovingly carved. It was different. This one depicted a female cherubim and bore an unmistakable resemblance to Dalene. The Tree had rapidly recovered. After Colin restored the flow of *Living Water*, within a matter of days the broken limbs regenerated and the Tree had exploded in its celebration of life and color. The Valley had been rejuvenated as well. The scars had evaporated almost overnight. That had been over two years ago and today they would start the second of their annual pilgrimages to Tyber. They would always start here, at The Tree of Life. It seemed fitting. Of course they came here more than just once a year, just as they visited Tyber more than once a year. After all, the Regent had responsibility throughout Aidon. But this trip they made together. This year, Marcus and Alicia would join them as well. They had been almost like family to Dalene for so many years that Beatrice thought it appropriate to include them.

There had been a remarkable number of changes in Aidon. Except for this Valley and The Tree of Life, it seemed as if almost everything had changed. The High Council of Aidon was quite different. The Evaluation was now the stuff of history. There were still contests using the Boxes of Aidon, but for the first time, each of the Councilors had been elected by the residents of their respective cities. Everyone had a voice and everyone had a vote. Gareth Tregard had been elected Regent. He tried to decline, but his wife and Elias, the prophet from Kernsidon, persuaded him to stay on and help with the transition from the old ways.

Elias had expected resistance, having come from the traditional enemies of Aidon. There had been reluctance, to be sure, but it had been surprisingly mild. With the death of Mahon, Aidon had sent emissaries to Kernsidon. A reconciliation of sorts was underway. A few entrepreneurs hoped it would lead to new trade. Not everyone had been pleased. There had been a few demagogues in Kernsidon who dissented and moved farther east. Some day they might have to be dealt with, but for now, there was peace. The scholars who had expressed opposition to Elias had quickly become some of his most ardent supporters once they'd had the opportunity to examine the book of *Laws and Commandments* which Colin had given to Dalene, not to mention the perfectly preserved libraries in the Serpent's Tunnel. While hooded cloaks weren't exactly in fashion, no one was in danger of destruction for wearing one either. Many of the scholars had soon become teachers. Under the direction of Elias, the people now waited in eager anticipation of a day said to be not far distant, when the true Lawgiver would reign in Aidon. Until then, they were now more concerned with helping their fellowman than in demonstrating superiority over their neighbors.

Jorge and Miran now made a comfortable income from the proceeds of their partners in the soap and leather trades. They really didn't need to work the farm so much, but Jorge loved his farm and Miran admitted that she did as well. They wouldn't have known what to do without it to keep them occupied. With the elected Councils, suspicion of any and all things new had pretty much disappeared. There was a renaissance of sorts going on. Advances in artistry, industry and farming seemed to appear on a regular basis. A few ideas went rather badly, but people were free to experiment and the occasional mishap was little enough to pay for the privilege of being allowed to try. There had already been a small population explosion. Alicia was expecting. Kath had twins and Baylor happily made a fool of himself playing with them every chance he got. New communities were popping up and there was talk of expanding the borders of Aidon out into the plains. The idea made some nervous, but others were excited by the prospect of creating something new and building a future for themselves and their children. It wouldn't all happen overnight, but change was definitely in the air.

Emissaries had been sent to the Anakims as well. Negotiations were underway to allow them access to the Valley as they had once had. The Arbor Guards had related the role that the Anakims had played in the battle against Kernsidon. While the Anakims had neither known nor cared who they were attacking – all they'd known was that an invading army had entered their territory – the fact that they had assisted Aidon turned the tide of public opinion in their favor quite nicely.

Elam had recovered from his injuries. For several months, he'd been content to slip into a quiet routine, farming with his father. His status as a war-hero made him something of a local celebrity. Laraine had stopped by several times while he was recuperating. They weren't exactly courting. They were both too young for that, but there was a definite friendship which offered potential for the future. As Elam recovered, a restlessness had taken him. He'd had a taste of something. It wasn't adventure, exactly. His father told him that adventure was hearing about someone else in danger, but when it was you, it was just plain scary. Still, he had a yearning in him to see the places Colin had talked about. He was too young to settle down but his parents thought he was too young for the explorations he had his heart set on.

Change had even touched old Tunsten. Elias' sister, Mary, had joined her brother in Aidon. She and Tunsten had struck up an acquaintance which blossomed into romance. They'd been married this past spring. Where Tunsten had formerly been exceptionally sparing with words, he was now one of the most jovial conversationalists around. Jorge still claimed that was the most miraculous thing he'd seen.

The Lady of Prophecy had ceased to exist. Colin had been right about Dalene, she just never realized it. She had devoted her entire life to the service of Aidon, sacrificing all of her personal hopes and ambitions in defense of her people, isolating herself for their protection and in so doing, had created an unbreakable bond of love to those whom she served. But she no longer wore the hated title. She was simply Dalene, and few things made her happier. Colin had been right about something else as well. The children had been the first to embrace her. She could never walk down the streets of Salem alone. In a matter of minutes she would be holding hands, forming a chain with dozens of small children, eager to laugh with her and talk to her. She loved it, and she loved them.

Gareth and Beatrice, like Jorge and Miran, still preferred their carts to traveling by horseback. They were content to leave that to the younger generation. However, the invention of spring suspensions had added greatly to their traveling comfort. While they were greeted warmly everywhere, the people in the various towns granted them their privacy, knowing this was a special time for this very special family. They spent the night at the farm, before continuing on their journey to the hot springs. Elam still had the map Colin had given him. He didn't need it to get to the springs anymore. He'd been there several times now. But he liked to unroll it and look at the markings, imagining when he might see the sights it depicted and perhaps add his own discoveries to it. It was a long day, but they moved steadily. The sun was low in the sky when they finally came in sight of the large pool, steam rising from the calm surface into the cool fall air. They had decided that this would be the best time of year for their pilgrimage. The harvest was in, so there wasn't as much to be done on the farm, but the days were warm and pleasant. Even when the weather wasn't so nice, they were comfortable, immersed in the warm water bubbling up from the hidden springs. Last year they had erected two cabins at the edge of the large pool. This year they would add at least one more. It was good to work together as well as play and relax. Gareth in particular relished the physical labor as he had few opportunities with his responsibility as Regent.

Alicia suddenly stood up in the cart, pointing. "Look!"

All eyes turned where she directed. "By the twin moons!" Gareth exclaimed.

"Those must be mammoths!" Beatrice said. "Colin told us about them, but I've never seen them here before! Oh, they're wonderful! So huge!"

The mammoths were still a great distance off. Their presence added to the air of magic that accompanied this trip. In a few minutes, they arrived at the cabins. They busied themselves unpacking and setting up tents. Their group had grown, so the two cabins wouldn't accommodate all of them. In very little time, they had the camp organized and soon were basking in the warm water of the large pool. This one was the perfect temperature for swimming and lounging. Some of the smaller pools were much warmer. The cliffs along the eastern shore lunged sharply from the water to a height of about 30 feet. They gradually tapered on the side to disappear in the tall meadow grass surrounding the cabins. A spring of cool water emerged at the base of the cliff, providing drinking water and a much cooler zone in the pool which they found invigorating if they had been soaking too long. While the older couples hadn't taken to riding, they were all now adept at swimming. They loved coming to this secluded oasis to relax and enjoy each other's company. Tired after their journey, they were soon dozing, lulled to sleep by the gentle motion of the water. Elam knew they shouldn't. He knew that someone should remain on guard, but it was just so nice. He slept.

A bellowing battle-cry jerked them awake. Instantly they were thrashing for shore. Out of the corner of his eye, Elam saw a figure hurtling toward them from the top of the cliff! A tremendous splash sent a surge of water up his nose, causing a spasm of coughing. Before he could recover, strong hands grabbed his head and shoved him under. He surged to the surface, spitting water, shaking his head to clear the water from his eyes, ready to fight. Colin grinned innocently, treading water away from his irate victims, "Hi guys! Did I wake you up?"

Jorge gave him a baleful look, the scar across his eye and nose making him look especially sinister, "You don't fight fair. That's your problem. You always know where we're at, but we can't sense you!"

"You cheated!" Elam accused. "You formed the air! There's no way you could make a splash big enough to drown us if you hadn't cheated!"

Miran shook her head and laughed, "Now boys, play nice or I'll send the lot of you to the cabin. Then maybe Dalene and I can enjoy some peace."

Dalene appeared, walking slowly, holding the finger of her little toddler who was pointing at the water and cooing in excitement. "Hello! Sorry I'm a little slow today. Rita is insisting on walking everywhere. Did I miss the first battle already?"

"First round to the good guy!" Colin called out.

Jorge and Elam exchanged a glance and with yells of pretended fury lunged after Colin. The "good guy" was going to be swallowing a lot of water in a few minutes.

The water-fight was terminated by a temporary truce. It would never be truly over. Colin tried to take over watching Rita, while Dalene swam off with Miran to visit and exchange news but he didn't stand a chance of holding onto his daughter with her grandparents nearby. Dalene and Colin had built their own cabin here at the springs, higher up at one of the more secluded pools. Gath had placed the boulders and Colin had used his gift to mold them into a seamless shelter of stone. They had a small garden and the start of an orchard. They spent more time here than the others did. Colin could have happily lived here, but Dalene still had responsibilities – Lady of Prophecy or not, and Rita would need other people – just as he did, he admitted.

Colin closed his eyes and again took in the view he never tired of seeing -the light-web connections between these people whom he loved. He had died that day in the temple, he knew. He had no connection to The Tree of Life. He still didn't. But when he died, or perhaps an instant before, these people had forged a bond of love to him – with him. That bond of love was his bridge to life. He wasn't connected to the Tree – not directly, but he was connected to each of them, and through them to every person in Aidon. He could still view his original bond, extending straight up into space. He still thought of his family on that other earth which seemed so much like a dream. He hoped they were as happy as he was. He wished he could tell them he was OK, but he still couldn't trace that connection. It caused him a brief pang, but he smiled as he whispered, "All is as it should be."

Maybe he had died that day. Perhaps Aidon had as well. But if so, the resurrection of each was far better than what had been sacrificed. With that thought, he swam to reclaim his little blue-eyed, blonde-haired daughter. With her birth, Aidon had been forever changed.

The End

About the Author

Eric Bergman presently resides in Kalispell, Montana where he enjoys a number of activities, including writing, reading, hiking, fishing, backpacking, cooking......the list goes on. He earned a degree in Chemical Engineering from Brigham Young University, after which he accepted employment in the semiconductor industry as a process engineer. His employment has taken him throughout much of the U.S., Europe and Asia. His professional accomplishments include 49 U.S. patents as well as the publication of a number of technical papers, but, nobody outside the semiconductor industry cares. He is the author of ***The Burrowing Terror,*** a seminal book on gopher hunting specifically for those on a "low fact diet." He has also authored ***Old Indian Tricks and Hunting Lore: The Legend of The Mighty Hunter***, presently in limited distribution. He is working on a sequel to ***Destroying Eden*** and has even written a few poems, though he avoids limericks. Eric is still amazed that his lovely wife, Anita, ever agreed to marry him. He is not alone in this, as on more than one occasion one of his acquaintances, upon meeting Anita for the first time, has commented, "But............you seem so nice!" He is the loving if barely tolerated father of two vivacious daughters, Rachel and Jessica, as well as three strapping young Arbor Guards, Ryan, Kyle and Grant. He may be contacted at H2O4_engineer@hotmail.com

erinrecht@gmail.com

Made in the USA
San Bernardino, CA
28 January 2014